I0662039

WULF'S DEN

MARISA CHENERY

Copyright © 2018 Marisa Chenery

All rights reserved.

ISBN-13: 978-1-98865-928-2

CONTENTS

BEOWULF AND ROXIE

When Roxie and her friend, Candice, decided on a girls' night out she didn't realize Wulf's Den would be more than she had anticipated. Roxie soon learned to expect anything. The presence of a super-abundance of super good-looking men surprised her, and when the best of the bunch stared at her as if he wanted to devour her, surprise turned to amazement.

Beowulf recognized her as his mate the instant she crossed his path and her scent filled his lungs, but he must overcome one hurdle. She was not one of his kind—a werewolf. He had waited for years to find his mate, and he would claim her even if she was a mortal. He would soon teach her all about werewolves.

Roxie is caught up in strange events. Archaic markings appear on her wrist, and strong forces threaten to tear her away from her love as two other male werewolves try to claim her as their own. Would Roxie and Beowulf be able to keep the bond love had forged or would they lose each other forever?

DEDICATION

For my daughter, Roxanne, who made it so I wasn't alone in a house full of males.

Thanks go to my father, Ray Chenery, who wrote the spell I used in this book.

CHAPTER ONE

Roxie Stone had second thoughts about what she'd agreed to do that evening. She sighed as the cab slowed and pulled up in front of the club. She didn't normally do the club scene. Even in her twenties, she hadn't done the club scene. Now, at thirty-one, she had no ambition to break a world record in bar hopping.

Roxie glanced at the evil being who sat next to her, the one who'd used her evil powers to make this evening happen—Candice Taylor, alleged best friend.

"What?" Innocence oozed from Candice's voice.

"I have no idea why I let you talk me into this. I feel like a fool." Self-consciously, Roxie ran her hands down her skirt, trying to smooth away nonexistent wrinkles.

Candice turned so she could look Roxie up and down. "You look hot, hon. You have nothing to be ashamed of, so no more second thoughts. Besides, you promised, and I'm holding you to it."

Knowing there would be no budging her, Roxie reluctantly climbed out of the cab. She immediately tugged on the hem of her short skirt. Candice came around the back of the taxi and slapped Roxie's hand as it twitched toward it once more. She arched a finely shaped brow. "Roxie."

Roxie sighed and dropped her hand to her side. "Okay, maybe

3

I do look kind of good, but to say I'm hot is taking it a bit too far."

The outfit Candice had picked for her had been chosen with meticulous care. The hoped-for result of this evening was Roxie going home with a man. So there Roxie stood in a lightweight black skirt that hugged her curves—what few she had—falling just slightly above her midthigh. A matching short-sleeved blouse, on the tight side, veed in a low-cut neckline. The shoes on her none-too-petite feet matched the color of her outfit and were high, strappy affairs.

Candice ignored her and dragged her to the entrance. Roxie glanced at the bright neon sign above the door. WULF'S DEN. A shudder of apprehension ran down her spine.

"I'm not so sure about this, Candy." Wulf's Den didn't seem all that different from any other nightclub in San Francisco. Why Roxie suddenly felt chills, even though it was a balmy July evening, she couldn't explain.

"Nonsense, Rox." Candice gave the bald, muscle-bound bouncer her patent I-wanna-do-the-nasty-with-you look, and he waved them to the front of the line and into the club.

Thank God. If they'd had to wait to get inside, Roxie would have lost her nerve and beat a hasty retreat to her home.

It took a moment for Roxie's eyes to adjust to the dimness. She barely had enough time to get her bearings before Candice grabbed her by the arm and led her to one of the empty tables at the back of the club.

The damn skirt Candice had been so insistent on made Roxie take quick, mincing steps in her high heels to keep up with her friend. It was by no means graceful, but it was either that or fall flat on her face. High heels and Roxie did not mix.

Candice reached the table first and sat, immediately scanning the room for her next hunk *du jour*. Even sitting, she moved in time to the music blaring out of the club's sound system.

Roxie made it to the table without killing herself and plopped down in the chair next to Candice. Maybe if she were lucky, she wouldn't have to move her butt off it until it was time to leave.

Candice craned her neck for the millionth time while she bopped away in her chair. Roxie had to ask, "What the hell are you doing? We haven't even had a drink yet. You're starting to freak me out."

Candice gave Roxie a winning smile, then said, "I'm man hunting, of course."

Roxie stifled a groan. She pitied the poor sod Candice set her sights on. He wouldn't stand a chance. Her friend was a beauty. With long, wavy blonde hair, flashing blue eyes, and the face of a beauty queen, Candice stood out in a crowd. This always surprised Roxie, considering Candice's full height was five feet three. She, on the other hand, could not claim to share any of her friend's charms. She stood at five feet six, had straight brown hair — dyed a golden-brown — that fell to the middle of her back, and hazel eyes, and was so average-looking she could easily disappear in a crowd.

Roxie resigned herself to being stuck at the nightclub, then decided to check out the other people around her. The club was full but not a huge crush. Most of the tables were filled with people talking as they sipped on drinks while others were moving to the music on the dance floor. She scanned the large open space and couldn't help noticing there was more than one gorgeous guy present. Not just good-looking, but make-you-drool, want-to-jump-their-bones gorgeous.

The sound of Candice laughing drew Roxie's attention back to her friend. "Are my eyes playing tricks on me, or are there sinful amounts of hunks here?"

Candice laughed once more. "Isn't it great? Gail at work told me about this place. I didn't believe her at first, but after I came here last Friday and found she told the truth, I knew you had to come check it out."

A perky little waitress stopped by their table. Roxie ordered a glass of white wine. When the girl moved to take Candice's order, Roxie glanced at the bar. Immediately, all the air rushed out of her lungs. She'd thought the other guys she'd seen were gorgeous, but the one standing behind the bar outshone them all.

He had to be no less than six feet seven. His straight soot-black hair brushed the tops of his shoulders, accentuating the sharp angles of his face. His shoulders were broad and padded with muscle, the same with his chest. He wore a tight black T-shirt. Roxie couldn't help but notice how the muscles in his arms bunched as he poured drinks. She wouldn't be able to see what color his eyes were, even if he had been looking at her, which he wasn't. Drop-dead gorgeous guys didn't usually notice her.

Roxie sighed with longing, then dragged her gaze off the bartender and looked at Candice, who had a wide smile plastered on her face. It took Roxie only a few seconds to figure out who her friend had seduced with her smile. A guy, not as good-looking as the hunks but not shabby in the looks department by any means, sauntered to their table. He smiled at Candice and asked her to dance. Candice looked at Roxie, who waved her friend to go. At least one of them should be enjoying themselves.

Alone, Roxie glanced back at the bar to see if the waitress had picked up their drinks yet. Her breath caught in her throat. The bartender looked straight at her, or at least she hoped he was. She turned her head to make sure there wasn't anyone standing behind her. She couldn't believe he stared at her. And it wasn't that he was merely staring; he seemed to be devouring her with his eyes. Finding no one standing at the rear of her, she gulped and looked back.

She couldn't tear her gaze away from him. The way his moved over her, it almost felt as if he caressed her. The world seemed to fall away. She no longer heard the loud music or perceived the other people around her. Her whole being centered on the man behind the bar. It'd been so long since someone had looked at her in that way. Her sex-starved body thrilled at his touch, even if it was only with his gaze.

She squirmed in her chair. Unable to take her gaze off him, Roxie watched his drop from her face to her chest. Her breasts swelled, and her nipples hardened into tight buds. They begged for his touch, for the feel of his hot mouth sucking her. Not wanting to be left out, her pussy demanded her attention too. A throbbing ache built in her core, and wetness pooled. She squeezed her legs together, trying to alleviate some of it, but that only made the throbbing increase. Never had she been brought to full arousal merely by being stared at.

If he can do that with his gaze, what would happen if he touched me?

The waitress returned and placed the drinks on the table. Roxie wrenched her gaze off the bartender and tried to calm her body down. She picked up the glass of wine and took a big swig. It immediately went down the wrong way, causing her to gasp for breath while she coughed to clear her lungs. By the time she got over her choking fit, her eyes were streaming, and she had the feeling her face was an unbecoming shade of red.

Unable to look at the bar to see if the bartender had been watching her try to cough up one of her lungs, Roxie slid out of her chair. She quickly made a beeline for the restroom. She splashed cool water on her face and gave her hair a quick fluffing, then prepared to face the world once more.

Roxie stepped back into the club, squared her shoulders, and headed to her table. Her luck ran out. One moment she was walking, and the next her klutzy side reared its ugly head. She didn't just stumble, not anything as simple as that, no. With her right foot, she stepped down and twisted her ankle over. When the side of it hit the floor, she knew she was in trouble. She threw her hands out and prepared to meet the tile as she started to fall.

Expecting to land in an undignified heap, Roxie was shocked when strong arms grabbed her around the waist, effectively breaking her fall. Her hands came to rest on a rock-hard chest. She blinked in surprise as she looked up into the bluest eyes she'd ever seen. She groaned in embarrassment. Her rescuer was none other than the hunky bartender.

CHAPTER TWO

Roxie ducked her head. Her body had burst into flames at seeing who her rescuer was. She was so turned-on she had to fight herself not to act out the images filling her mind. She had an overpowering urge to wrap her hands in his silky hair, drag his mouth down to hers, and kiss him until he begged for mercy. When he spoke in his deep voice, her bones melted. With her hands still pressed against him, she felt each word rumble inside his chest.

"Are you okay?"

Roxie nodded. The feel and smell of him made it hard to think straight, let alone answer him in a coherent manner. The heat from his body seeped into hers. His scent—a mixture of the cologne he wore and musky maleness—brought hot, sweaty sex to mind. He smelled sinfully good.

"If you're sure, I'll put you down."

Roxie realized her feet were no longer touching the floor. He held her tightly against his wide chest. At her nod, he slowly lowered her so she could stand on her own. The instant her twisted ankle held her full weight, it gave out on her. This time her face ended up pressed to his solar plexus. Without thinking, she shoved her nose closer and took a deep breath. Realizing what she'd done, she froze, shocked by her behavior. *You're losing it, Roxie. You just took a good whiff of a total stranger.* Slowly, Roxie lifted her head to look at her rescuer. He smiled. Before she could protest, he scooped her up into his arms. As he walked in the opposite direction of the table where she'd been sitting, she found her voice.

"Ah, where are you taking me?"

"Obviously, you've injured yourself. I'm going to look at your ankle."

"That isn't necessary. I just twisted it. I should return to my friend. She'll be missing me. Besides, I don't even know you."

"I have a feeling your friend won't be too worried about where you are. Last I looked she was busy on the dance floor. My name is Beowulf, and I own this nightclub."

*

Beowulf smiled at the lush bundle he held cradled in his arms. He'd noticed her when she'd walked through the door of the club. While her friend had garnered most of the attention from the other males with her stunning good looks, this one's beauty was subtler. When she'd walked past the bar, trying to keep up with her friend, her scent had washed over him. Hers was a heady mix of spices and woman. To his kind, scent was more alluring than looks alone. The smell of her brought a part of him roaring to life. And she seemed just as affected, considering how she'd filled her lungs with his scent. He liked her more for doing that very thing.

Beowulf easily held the woman as he took the stairs to his second-floor office two at a time. He pushed open his door before he kicked it shut behind him. He crossed the room in two long strides, then gently placed her on the leather couch. She scooted away when he sat beside her. He gave her no quarter. He took hold of her injured ankle and worked on the straps of her shoe. She squawked in protest and slapped at his hands. With little heed, he worked the slim bands from around her foot and let the shoe drop to the floor. Gently, he ran his hand over her ankle, checking for swelling.

*

Roxie forgot to breathe as he touched her bare skin. With each brush of his fingers, awareness surged through her. With the thought to distance herself from his touch, she fell back on what she normally did in situations in which she wasn't comfortable — she rambled like an idiot.

"Since you've introduced yourself, I should at least tell you my name. I'm Roxie Stone. So you're Beowulf. What kind of name is Beowulf anyway? Isn't it a bit archaic? The only Beowulf I've heard of is the one in that really old tale called *Beowulf and Grendel* where Beowulf is the hero and Grendel is the monster he kills."

Feeling as if she'd made enough of an ass of herself, Roxie clamped her mouth shut. Beowulf had stopped rubbing her ankle and now stared at her. He was probably wondering what insane asylum she'd escaped from. She needed some space between them and tried to pull her foot free. Instead of releasing her, he tugged on her leg, pulling her even closer. He didn't stop until he had it settled across his lap. He draped his heavy arm on top of her legs, holding her to him.

"Nice to meet you, Roxie. So, you know the story of *Beowulf and Grendel*? It's not as well-known as it once was. You can say that tale strikes close to home for me."

"What do you mean by that? You fight monsters as well as own a nightclub?"

"Don't we all have our own monsters to fight?"

"I guess. Look, I should go back downstairs. My ankle doesn't feel all that bad now, and I really should see where my friend is. I think I'll just call it a night."

"I won't hear of it. Your ankle is a little swollen. At least let me put some ice on it for you."

"I wouldn't want to put you out. I can take care of this when I get home."

Roxie grabbed Beowulf by the wrist and tried to shove his arm off her legs. He didn't move so much as an inch. She attempted to pull herself out from under it. This only made her skirt ride up even higher. Something large and hard pressed against the backs of her thighs. Much to her shock, she realized her legs were draped across the crotch of his pants. Slowly, she tried to pull one out from under his arm. The bulge jerked in response.

Roxie lifted her gaze to his face and found Beowulf intently watching her. His dazzling blue eyes were heavy-lidded and darkened with desire. His sensual lips slowly formed a smile. Her breath left her lungs in a rush when he wrapped his other hand around the nape and leaned in.

"Why are you surprised by how my body reacts to you?"

Beowulf's deep voice was a mere whisper, his breath gently feathering across Roxie's face. Her body melted, going soft and pliant. At the first brush of his lips, she knew she was in over her head. She clutched his shoulders as a firestorm of desire rushed through her.

He kissed the corners of her mouth and then gently swept his tongue across her lips. When she opened, giving him better access, Beowulf sucked hers inside. He moaned and acted as if he couldn't get enough. Slowly, he lowered her onto the sofa, stretching full-length on top of her with his hips cradled between her legs. He deepened the kiss, then brought his hands down to her hips, anchoring her body to his. He rubbed himself against her hot core as though his body demanded he take her, claim her as his. It was raw, primal, and predatory, an almost animalistic urge.

A momentary shiver of fear ran through Roxie as Beowulf pushed her down, but it quickly disappeared when he settled on top of her. She relished the feel of his hard body pressed tightly to her softer one. Shamelessly, she ground herself against him, fanning the flames of desire licking at her. Moaning, she let go of his shoulders and ran her fingers down his broad back. She tugged the hem of his T-shirt out of his black jeans before she thrust her hands under it. She traced the muscles there with her fingertips. Heated skin quivered as she caressed him. His kisses drove her wild. He licked and sucked at her mouth, feeding off her, demanding more.

Roxie moaned in protest when Beowulf's mouth left hers, but she soon gasped as he trailed his lips down her chin to the side of her neck. He nipped the sensitive skin with his sharp teeth only to lick the spot, giving her pain followed by pleasure. As he moved down the column of her throat, his hands released her hips and cupped her breast. Through the material of her blouse, he took one of her pebbled nipples between his teeth and tugged. Roxie arched up off the sofa as moisture pooled between her legs. She was drowning in heat, her body desperately craving more. This was new for her. She'd been with a few other men in her past, but none of them had been able to bring her to such heights of wild longing. And with that thought, she suddenly realized what she was doing. She'd acted like an animal in heat with a man she didn't know.

Before he could weaken her defenses any more, Roxie grabbed a fistful of Beowulf's silky hair and yanked hard. "I can't do this."

He lifted his head, making her gasp. His eyes appeared to be glowing. Roxie pushed at Beowulf's shoulders, trying to free herself. He snapped his teeth at her and snarled. Panic rose to clench at her gut. Uncaring whether she hurt him or not, she struck out at his neck and head until she was able to slip out from under him. She snatched her purse before she ran out of the room, then slammed the door behind her.

CHAPTER THREE

She took the stairs down to the club at a run. At the bottom, Roxie stopped, not wanting to draw attention to herself. With her first hobbling steps, she remembered her other shoe was still in Beowulf's office, lying discarded on the floor. She wasn't going back for it. She yanked off her remaining one and took only enough time to glance around the club in search of Candice. She wasn't at their table, of course.

Not wanting to take the chance that Beowulf would come after her, Roxie decided Candice was able to find her own way home. With her gaze glued to the club's doors, Roxie quickly walked to them, expecting to be jumped on before she could reach them. No one stopped her. When she reached them with no interference, she let out the breath she'd been holding. Once outside, she headed for the curb and hailed one of the unoccupied taxis.

* * * *

Beowulf groaned as he fought to bring himself back under control. She was the one. After all this time, after he'd concluded there wouldn't be one for him, he'd found his mate. The instant he'd touched her, smelled her scent, he'd known. The mating urge rode him hard. The beast within had urged him to claim her as his. To let nothing stop him from taking her body, to possess her so he couldn't tell where he ended and she began. All that had scared the hell out of Roxie.

Beowulf used his powerful senses to see if Roxie was still inside the club. She wasn't. He couldn't feel her presence or smell her scent. He'd messed up. As he called himself three times a fool for letting things get out of control, he spied the high-heeled shoe on the floor. He smiled as he snatched it up. She had run out of there so fast she'd forgotten it. It gave him an idea. He wrenched the office door open, then quickly walked down to the club. He searched the crowd, his gaze easily latching on to the one person who could help him find Roxie.

* * * *

The sound of the phone ringing brought Roxie out of a fitful slumber. Sleep had eluded her for most of the night. She'd managed to fall into a dreamless rest just before dawn. Groaning, she rolled over and reached for the phone on the bedside table. "Hello?" Roxie was tempted to hang up when she heard the voice on the other end. It was Candice.

"So you're alive, and don't you dare hang up that phone on me."

"I would never do that to you, Candice."

"Of course you would. I know all your nasty little habits. You aren't running away from me so easily like you did last night."

"Who said I ran away? I decided to go home is all, and you'd found a new boy toy to play with. I was only the third wheel."

"Nice try, Roxie. You were running, and you know it. Why you ran from a hunk like that I will never know."

"What hunk would that be?"

"Did you leave your brain behind along with your shoe when you hightailed it out of the club? Come on, Roxie. That man was to die for, and he seemed really into you."

"You talked to Beowulf?" That was so not what Roxie had wanted to hear. Candice would never understand. Christ, even she didn't. It wasn't as if she'd met other men who snarled like an animal and had glowing eyes.

"Aha, you're so busted. You know exactly which hunk I'm talking about. And yes, I did talk to Beowulf last night after you bailed on me. He said he helped you after you twisted your ankle. And that you'd gotten spooked and left your shoe behind. He asked where you lived so he could return it."

Roxie closed her eyes and silently prayed, Please don't say you gave him my address. Please don't say you gave him my address. "And?"

Candice fell silent for a few seconds. "Well, I kind of gave him your address."

"Candice! How could you?"

"I'm sorry, Roxie. It seemed like an all right thing to do last night, but now that I'm talking to you about it, I'm getting the impression I might have made a mistake."

"You can say that again."

"I thought it was sweet that he wanted to personally return your shoe. It's almost like Cinderella and her glass slipper."

"Well, I hate to tell you this, but Beowulf is no prince, and I'm sure as hell no Cinderella."

"I can see you're in a fine mood this morning, Rox. I'm sorry. I just think you're making a mistake letting that one go. At least I gave you warning. If I were you, I would get out of bed. He'll probably show up in the next couple of hours."

Roxie rubbed her throbbing temple. She now had a monster of a headache. "I'm going to hang up on you now, Candice. And to give you fair warning, I'm going to get you back for this."

Candice laughed. "I wouldn't expect anything less. Cheer up, hon. You never know. He could be the one. Call me and tell me what happens."

"Yeah, right." Roxie hung up the phone.

Roxie swore under her breath as she looked at her bedroom clock. It was barely ten in the morning, and after the sleepless night she'd had, she wanted nothing more than to burrow deeper into her blankets and sleep until noon. Now that Mr. Freaky was coming to call, that was no longer an option.

Roxie threw back the covers, then dragged herself out of bed. She muttered to herself as she showered and then dressed. Not wanting to give Beowulf any ideas, she dressed comfortably and not to impress. She wore cut-off jean shorts and a tank top. Not one to fuss with her hair even on a good day, she left it down, letting it air dry.

Downstairs she headed for the living room. Roxie picked up her laptop where it sat on the coffee table, then crossed the room to the smaller one just off it. It was the perfect size for her office, and one of the main reasons she'd bought the house. Having her own small web-design business allowed her to work out of her home.

She left the laptop on her desk, then switched on her desktop computer. Roxie waited for it to boot up as she mentally went over the projects she was currently working on. Even though it was a Sunday, she wanted to work for a couple hours. She enjoyed what she did and never felt as if it was work. Computers and the Internet were her life. Because of that, Candice called her a computer geek, as well as a hermit. Unlike her friend, Roxie was quite happy to sit at home, working on the computer all day and watching television in the evenings. She didn't need to be out at the clubs. She had only agreed to go out the night before because Candice had finally worn her down with her constant nagging. And look where that had gotten her.

Roxie pulled up the files she needed, then lost herself in her work. Thoughts of Beowulf and his supposed visit were pushed aside, forgotten. When the doorbell rang an hour later, she decided to ignore whoever was calling and continued to work.

* * * *

Beowulf put his black Mercedes-Benz Cabriolet into park as he stared at Roxie's modest two-story house. Like the woman who owned it, it was pleasing to the eye in a subtle way. It was no showpiece home.

Before getting out of the car, Beowulf glanced at his reflection in the rearview mirror. Even though he had the top up on the car, he wanted to make sure he looked presentable. For some reason, he was nervous about seeing Roxie again. Maybe it was because of what she was to him, or it could be from the erotic dreams he'd had of her during the night. All he knew was he couldn't mess up a second time. If she rejected him once again, he didn't know what he would do. Until he claimed her as his own, he was a walking time bomb, waiting to go off, something the males of his race suffered through when finding their mates. With Roxie for his mate, it made matters that much worse. She wasn't a female from his race and wouldn't know what was expected of her.

Beowulf walked up to the front door and rang the doorbell. In one hand he carried Roxie's shoe. Not hearing anyone moving inside, he rang the bell a second time. Candice had assured him Roxie would be home, that she was always at home. Still not hearing any sounds coming from the other side, he pounded on the door. That seemed to work. Footsteps heading toward it soon reached his ears.

She yanked open the door and, much to his surprise, glared at him. "What do you want?"

Beowulf smiled. She looked pissed as hell at him, something he was better equipped to handle than the fear he'd seen in her eyes the night before. "Nice to see you again, Roxie. Your friend was nice enough to tell me where you lived so I could return your shoe. Can I come in?"

Not taking any chances, Beowulf crowded her until she took a few steps back, allowing him to walk into the house. He shut the door behind him. Roxie scowled, then turned on her heel and walked away.

Without turning around, she said, "Just put the shoe down anywhere, then you can leave."

Beowulf became flustered as Roxie disappeared into the other room. She was not acting like a chosen mate should. He put her shoe on the coffee table in the living room before he stepped through the doorway where she had gone. He found her sitting behind a desk, typing away on her computer.

Unable to see another chair in the room, Beowulf sat on the edge of the desk across from where Roxie worked. One glance at the computer screen was enough for him to know he had no idea what she was doing. It looked like a bunch of nonsense to him. "What are you working on?"

Roxie stopped typing and slowly turned her head to look at him. She seemed surprised to see him there. "Not that it's any of your business, I'm working. I thought I told you to leave."

"What kind of work do you do?" Beowulf chose to ignore the last part. He had no intention of leaving, and she would have to accept that.

"I'm a web designer." She turned back around and typed away

once more.

Beowulf bristled with irritation. He clenched his hand against his thigh and concentrated on keeping the scowl off his face. Usually when potential mates found each other, they had a hard time keeping their distance. He was feeling it. Being close to Roxie, able to smell her scent, to be near enough to touch her, caused his body to go rock hard. He fought the urge to yank her out of her chair and put her on the desk so he could bury himself inside her. It was a blow to his male ego that she didn't seem as affected as he was.

*

Roxie forced herself to keep her gaze glued to the computer screen. Beowulf sitting on the edge of her desk, watching her work, was doing wicked things to her body. On the outside she appeared not to be noticing him, but on the inside, it was the total opposite. He took up so much space her office seemed too small with him in it. The room was filled with his scent. Each breath she took was laced with it. It made her think of how it had felt having his hard body pressed to hers, his mouth devouring her. She could still taste him. *Why wouldn't he leave?* Everything about him screamed sex. She couldn't shake the feeling that if she acted on her impulses, he would want not just her body but her soul as well. She didn't do well with letting other people that close to her. If she did, she was usually found lacking in some way.

Without any warning, Beowulf moved off her desk and yanked her chair back before he pounced on her. He slung her over one shoulder so her head hung down his back. He walked out of her office.

All her blood rushing to her head, Roxie asked, "What do you think you're doing? Where are you taking me?"

Having found the stairs to the upper level, Beowulf moved in their direction. "To bed. It's what we both want, and I'm not going to have you push me away." He reached the upstairs level, then calmly asked, "Which one is your bedroom?"

Roxie reared up on his shoulder and tried to break Beowulf's hold. "I never said anything about going to bed with you. Put me down."

"Be still." Beowulf turned his head and bit her on her bottom.

Roxie yelped. "Ouch! Put me down right this minute."

When Beowulf only chuckled, she figured two could play at his game. She hung down his back once more, then pinched his ass — hard, digging her nails into it for good measure. She didn't let go until the hold he had on her slipped enough for her to squirm out of his arms. Roxie sprinted down the hall to her room, hoping to buy enough time to close the door before he followed her inside. His hand blocked it before she could slam it shut. She backed away, trying to put some distance between them.

Beowulf rubbed his butt as he stalked Roxie around the room. "That wasn't very nice. I should make you kiss it better."

She continued to walk backward until her back came up against the wall. He quickly caged her in, placing his hands on either side of her head. Beowulf could move fast. One minute he was across the room from her and the next he'd trapped her. Roxie gulped and kept her gaze on his broad chest. If she looked into his eyes, she would be lost.

Beowulf took a step closer and brought their bodies together. She felt every inch of him against her. Already fully aroused, he pressed his erection into her stomach, showing her how much he wanted her. "Don't you want me, Roxie? I know I want you. I've done nothing but think about having you since last night."

Roxie closed her eyes as liquid heat pooled between her legs. Oh, she wanted him all right, but not like this. They were going way too fast. "I will admit I'm attracted to you, Beowulf." When he lowered his head to claim her lips, she gently pushed it away. "Wait. Hear me out. You can't expect me to jump into bed with you just because we have the hots for each other. I don't know what the other women you've been with are like, but I'm not like that. I barely know you, and I sure as hell don't hop into the sack with just anyone."

"Is that what you think, Roxie? That I have the hots for you and only want to bed you?" Beowulf shook his head. "I can honestly tell you, it's much more than that to me."

"How can that be? We only met last night. I'm not sure how I feel about you. You come on way too strong for me, Beowulf. Quite frankly, you scare the crap out of me."

Beowulf stiffened at Roxie's confession. "I'm not trying to.

Look, let's start over. Okay? Let me take you out for dinner tonight. I promise to take things slower."

She looked Beowulf in his gorgeous blue eyes and saw he was sincere. Roxie bit her lower lip and nodded. "Okay. I'll have dinner with you tonight."

Before Roxie could protest, Beowulf captured her lips and kissed her soundly. He seemed to be savoring the taste of her, almost as if he had to make it last until he saw her again.

He released her, then rested his forehead against hers and groaned. "You're killing me, Roxie. I'll pick you up around six."

Roxie was only able to nod again. After Beowulf left the room, and she heard the front door shut behind him, she slid down the wall to sit on the floor. He'd turned her legs to jelly. If he kissed her like that again, he would turn her brain into mush.

She picked herself up, then headed downstairs to her office. There were too many hours between now and when Beowulf was to pick her up. She needed to get back to work or she would end up spending the rest of the day having sexual fantasies about him. And that wouldn't do at all.

CHAPTER FOUR

Beowulf drove up the winding drive that led to his home. In contrast to Roxie's small house, his was quite large. The sprawling mansion had been in his family for several years. After his parents' passing, it had become his. It was too large for him, but he couldn't bear to part with it.

He opened the front door, then scanned the large entranceway. Immediately, his gaze fell on the man who stood leaning negligently against the wall where he had a perfect view of the front door. Beowulf had hoped he could avoid his brother, but obviously that was not to be.

"I take it all didn't go as you expected. If it had, you would not be back here so quickly unless you had your mate in tow."

"Shut up, Wade. I'm not in the mood to deal with you right now."

Wade pushed away from the wall, then followed Beowulf into the spacious living room. Beowulf went to the bar and poured himself a shot of scotch.

"Went that badly, did it?" Wade asked.

Beowulf finished the scotch in one swallow. "You could say that. Roxie is not one of us. She's resisting me."

"Are you sure she's your mate? I can't recall a human ever being a mate to one of our kind before."

"It has happened in the past. A very long time ago. You

21

weren't even born yet. That's why you don't remember it."

There were a lot of years between him and his younger brother—a great many years. Their parents had thought there would be no other children born to them after Beowulf. Wade had been their miracle child.

"If she's resisting you, what are you going to do about it?"

Beowulf poured himself another shot of scotch. "I have to woo her." When his brother howled with laughter, Beowulf tilted the scotch down his throat. He placed the empty glass on the bar, then turned to Wade. "You can stop laughing anytime. I don't particularly find anything about this amusing."

Slowly bringing himself back under control, Wade shook his head. "Woo her? Beowulf, you aren't the wooing type. I've never known you to romance a woman. The tactic you use to get one into bed is to overwhelm her with your massive sex appeal, then batter her down until she can't resist any longer. You wouldn't know how to romance a woman to save your life."

"Well, brother of mine, this is when I get to pick your brain. You're the romancer of the family." Beowulf threw an arm across Wade's shoulders and grinned. "You're going to help me. I have a date with Roxie this evening, and I need everything to be perfect."

Wade groaned. "What did I do to earn this punishment?" He headed to the bar so he could pour himself a drink. "I think I'm up to the challenge, but we have to get started now. You've a lot to learn, and not enough hours to do it. All I can say is your mate had better be worth it."

"She is. And if this doesn't work, I'll just tie her to my bed and keep her there until she accepts me."

* * * *

Roxie looked at the mound of clothes piled on her bed. She couldn't make up her mind what to wear for her date with Beowulf. She was having mixed emotions about this evening. On one hand she was drawn to him, and on the other she wanted to get far, far away from him. The part of her that wanted to be with him was winning the battle. After he had left, she'd spent the rest of the day remembering how it'd felt to be in his arms, to have his lips claiming hers. Her traitorous body ached for him.

After going through every article of clothing she owned, Roxie had found something wrong with each one. She hated being so indecisive. It was so unlike her. When the doorbell rang, she nearly jumped out of her skin. It couldn't be Beowulf already. It just couldn't be. Looking at the clock, she was shocked to see how late it was. She'd been deciding on what to wear for the last hour and a half and had found nothing suitable. She had to cancel their date.

Roxie marched down the stairs, determined not to let Beowulf sway her, then yanked open the front door. He arched a brow in her direction as he seemed to take in the tank top and shorts she still wore.

She squared her shoulders and tried to put what she hoped was a serious look on her face. "I think I made a mistake. I don't think I should go out with you tonight."

"Why?" Beowulf drawled. He wrapped his fingers around her wrist, holding her in place.

Unable to stay firm with Beowulf touching her, Roxie ducked her head and said sheepishly, "I don't have anything to wear."

Using his other hand to tip her head back so she looked at him, Beowulf smiled. "Is that all? It doesn't matter to me what you wear. If I had my way, you wouldn't be wearing anything at all."

Roxie's breath caught in her throat. The man was pure sin. "You might have no problem with me walking around naked, but I do. I'm not like the other women you date. I'm not into the hair, clothes, and makeup thing. I don't normally dress how I was last night. That was Candice's doing. I prefer to be in shorts rather than a skirt."

"Then I have to say you're already dressed."

Before Roxie could react, Beowulf picked her up and flung her over his shoulder. He stepped into the house, then snagged her keys from the key rack on the wall next to the door. He locked the front door before taking her to his car.

"This is starting to become a habit with you, Beowulf. You have to stop acting like a caveman, hauling me over your shoulder every time I don't do what you want."

"If you would stop being so unreasonable, then I wouldn't find it necessary to do it. There are perks having you in this position." To emphasize his words, he fondled her backside, then briefly dipped his hand between her legs. She jerked.

Beowulf opened the passenger door of the car before he gently placed Roxie onto the seat. Once she was belted in, he slid into the driver's side. She tried to ignore him as he pulled out of the driveway, but it was impossible. Her face was flushed, heating with every stroke of the glances he cast her way.

She was lost. Roxie didn't want to accept it, but it was the truth. That simple brush of his hand against her most intimate spot had proved it. Even now, sitting beside him, not even touching him, she could think of nothing else but having him. She ached for his touch, craved him. She didn't think she could make it through the evening without jumping him. It was as if she were in heat. If she didn't have him, she would go crazy. Each time he touched her, the feeling grew stronger.

As the car slowed and Beowulf pulled into a parking lot, Roxie realized he'd taken her to Wulf's Den. She could only hope he didn't plan on staying there all evening. Her clothes wouldn't exactly stand up to the dress code, and being barefoot only made matters worse. Before she could question him, he got out of the car and came around to her side to help her out. He linked his fingers through hers as he led her to the back door. It took only a few seconds for him to unlock it and usher her inside.

Beowulf pulled Roxie into the main part of the nightclub. It was too early for it to be open. The room was empty, except for a man who stood behind the bar with his back toward them. As if sensing he was no longer alone, he turned and smiled at them. She couldn't take her gaze off him. *Was everyone who worked at the nightclub drop-dead gorgeous?* This guy stood as tall as Beowulf and had the same muscular build. Even his eyes were the exact shade of blue. The only difference was his hair, which was a rich chestnut while Beowulf's was black as night. Their looks were so similar she could only assume the man was related to Beowulf in some way. Beowulf's next words proved her correct in her thinking.

"Roxie, this is my brother, Wade, and you can stop staring at him. You're with me this evening, and I don't share."

Embarrassed at being caught staring, Roxie felt herself blush. "Nice to meet you, Wade." He was incredibly good-looking, but Beowulf's looks appealed to her more. Turning to Beowulf, she apologized. "Sorry. I didn't mean to stare. It's only, well, do you hire only good-looking men? I couldn't help noticing that last night."

*

Beowulf smiled to himself. His people were known for their good looks. A great number of his employees were either from his pack or were connected to it in some way. "It wasn't intentional." Turning to his brother, Beowulf asked, "Is everything ready?"

Wade nodded while giving Roxie a knowing smile. "Yes. I'll make sure no one disturbs you."

"Good."

Assured they would have no uninvited guests, Beowulf led Roxie up to his office. He opened the door and quickly scanned the room. He was going to owe his brother big-time for this. It was perfect. He stood aside, then waved her in. He could tell from the look on her face that his brother had thought of everything. While she took her time looking around, he quietly closed and then locked the door.

Roxie audibly gulped. Candles were set up on almost every available space, and the soft glow of candlelight filled the room. Soft music played in the background. The couch had been pushed out of the way. In the center of the space, one of the tables from the club was set up, draped with a white tablecloth and holding two place settings and a vase filled with a dozen red roses. A bottle of white wine sat chilling in an ice bucket.

Beowulf pulled out one of the chairs, then seated Roxie. He poured her a glass of wine before he served food from the hot trays set up on his desk. Not knowing what type of food she liked, he'd had the chef at the club prepare something simple. The aroma of beef tenderloin, roasted potatoes, and grilled vegetables filled the room, making his mouth water. He sat across from her before he popped a piece of meat into his mouth. It was done to perfection—juicy and pink. He sighed in contentment.

Beowulf looked across the table to see how Roxie was enjoying her meal and found her staring intently at his mouth. All the blood in his veins surged to his cock, giving him an instant rock-hard erection.

"Roxie, if you don't stop looking at me like that, the food will go to waste."

Roxie took a sip of wine before she carefully placed the glass back down on the table. "I'm not sure I'll be able to eat. I can't believe I'm going to say this, it's so not like me, but I would rather taste you."

Beowulf sent his chair flying and dragged Roxie to him. He wrapped an arm around her waist and held her pinned to his body. He threaded his fingers through her hair, holding her head where he wanted it. "All you had to do was ask. I'm happy to oblige." With a growl, he lowered his mouth to hers.

Roxie seemed to give herself up to the sensations surging through her body as she wound her arms around his neck. She no longer resisted him. He wanted her to feel things no other man could make her feel. She could either fight how she felt for him, putting them both through hell, or she could accept what he offered. She surrendered herself into his keeping and greedily returned his kiss.

All the promises he'd made to himself about taking it slow with Roxie flew out the window. Beowulf molded her body to his, devouring her sweet mouth. He couldn't get enough of her. As she went soft in his arms, he released her hair and trailed hot, wet kisses down the slim column of her throat. He pressed his lips against the artery in her neck and felt her blood racing through her veins.

Beowulf made a rumbling sound in the back of his throat, then moved lower. He intended to lick every inch of Roxie's body before the night was through. To know it as well as he knew his own. To fill his lungs with her scent so it would be forever imprinted inside his mind, never forgotten.

Beowulf pushed Roxie up against the wall, pinning her with his body. He lifted her leg and wrapped it around his waist. He stepped into the space between their bodies, then shoved the hard ridge of his cock against her sex. She pushed back on him and moaned. He bent his head and laved the tops of her breasts with his tongue.

Roxie's knees seemed to give out on her. If not for him holding her, he was pretty sure she would have slid down the wall. He pressed against her core, thrusting. Panting, she held him to her as he tugged at the neckline of her top with his teeth. When it didn't go low enough, Beowulf grabbed the bottom of her shirt and pulled it over her head. Cupping her full breasts, he suckled her through the lacy material of her bra. She arched her back, giving him better access.

Beowulf unhooked Roxie's bra before dropping it to the floor. He feasted his eyes on her full breasts. He placed his hands under them and flicked his tongue across each taunt nipple. "So beautiful. I have to see more of you."

He slipped open her shorts, then tugged them down her body until they pooled at her ankles. Beowulf went on his knees, pulled her shorts free, and dragged his tongue across Roxie's flat stomach. At her belly button, he swirled his tongue inside, making her stomach muscles quiver. He encountered the top of her panties when he moved lower. Taking them in his teeth, he slowly pulled them down her body before he tossed them aside.

Beowulf ran his hands up the inside of her legs, spreading her open before him. He dipped his head and flicked his tongue across her clit. Roxie closed her eyes as his tongue stroked her. He opened her even more. He pushed one finger inside her, then sucked and licked her clit until she panted. Her legs shook as he used two fingers to stroke inside her. He moved them in and out, rubbing and stretching her. He replaced his fingers with his tongue, and she moaned.

*

Roxie held his head to her, rocking her hips against his mouth. The pressure built inside her. She was so close. Her release was almost upon her when Beowulf alternated between jabbing his tongue into her hot opening and laving her clit with the flat of it. Her climax hit her hard, making her hips jerk. Gasping and moaning, she pushed against him harder. He licked and sucked until her body stopped convulsing.

Lost in the aftereffects of her release, the low growl that left Beowulf's throat hardly registered. She wanted more of him. She needed his cock inside her, riding her hard. Roxie grabbed his shirt, pulled him up, and locked her mouth to his. She could taste herself on him. She reached for his pants, then quickly pushed them open. She pulled them down past his hips, freeing the part of him that she wanted.

She wrapped her fingers around his thick cock, then slid her hand down the length of him. Beowulf groaned. He lifted one of her legs around his waist before he brushed her hand aside and pushed the head of his penis into her. Before he could slide home, the sound of someone pounding on his office door brought them back to awareness. Cursing under his breath, he released Roxie, then cracked open the door.

CHAPTER FIVE

"I thought I wasn't going to be disturbed." Beowulf growled at his brother.

"Sorry, bro." Looking down, Wade grimaced. He had to know he'd interrupted at the wrong time. "We have a slight problem."

"I'm sure you can handle it." Beowulf moved to shut the door, but Wade pushed it back open.

"This problem is not something I can handle on my own. If you don't come down and fix it, we could have a fight on our hands."

Beowulf focused his acute hearing on the sounds drifting up from the club. Underneath the pounding music, he heard grumblings of anger. *What complaints could the man have this time?* "Fine. Give me a few minutes; then I'll be down."

He shut the door and took a deep breath before turning to face Roxie. Seeing her standing against the wall, naked, he had to resist the urge to sweep her back into his arms. Instead, he adjusted himself before he zipped up his jeans. She wrapped her arms across her chest and looked at her feet.

"Something has come up down in the club, something only I can take care of. Stay here. When I come back, I'm going to finish what we started." He took a deep breath, pulling her scent into his lungs before stepping out of the room.

29

* * * *

Beowulf approached the small group congregated near the bar and mentally prepared himself to confront his nemesis. The man had a great sense of timing to have picked tonight of all nights to stir up crap. "Hello, Gren. Have you come to drink or have your ass thrown out as usual?"

"As if I would touch anything you had to offer."

Beowulf's hackles rose. Gren was spoiling for a fight. If Roxie hadn't been waiting upstairs for him, he would have gladly obliged. "I'm not in the mood for your bullshit."

The other man curled his lip and went to stand nose to nose with Beowulf. Being of equal height and body mass, when they crossed paths, it usually ended in a draw. And they had butted heads numerous times.

"I wouldn't provoke me if I were you, Beowulf. One of these times I may get the upper hand and your days of playing the high and mighty leader will be finished."

"I'd like to see you try. If you're done antagonizing me, either say what you have on your mind or get the hell out of my club."

Gren took a step back and gave a sly smile. "I hear you have a new woman friend. A mortal human woman, to be exact."

Beowulf grabbed the front of his shirt, then slammed Gren against the bar. He growled in warning. "You will stay the fuck away from her. You come within a foot of her, I'll rip out your throat."

"I do believe this woman means a great deal to you. Has the great Beowulf lost his heart to a mortal? Has she set off your mating urge? She must be extraordinary if that's the case. When do I get to meet her?"

Realizing they drew the attention of the non-pack patrons in the club, Beowulf relaxed his hold on the other man. "Outside. Now." Knowing Gren would follow, he headed for the door to the back alley.

* * * *

Her body still throbbing from release, Roxie gathered her

scattered clothes, then quickly dressed. There was no way she was going to stand there naked, waiting for Beowulf to return. And that had been one hell of an orgasm. The man had a magical tongue, and he sure knew how to use it. Oral sex usually wasn't a big deal to her. She didn't mind going down on a guy — in fact, she found it a turn-on — but having one do it to her never did anything for her. She never reached an orgasm that way. She had thought she was defective in that area, but she hadn't been today. That fact alone made her want to keep him around. If oral sex was that great with him, lovemaking should be mind-blowing.

Roxie heard raised voices coming from the direction of the back alley where Beowulf had parked. She walked to the room's only window and opened the curtains. It had a bird's-eye view of the alley, and what she saw was a disturbing sight. Beowulf stood at the end of it, confronting what looked like a huge dog. She peered closer and realized that was no dog. The thing had to be a wolf, but it was the largest wolf she had ever seen. *What would a wolf be doing in the middle of downtown San Francisco?*

As she watched, the wolf took a menacing step toward Beowulf. It growled, and its rusty-brown fur bristled around its large neck. When Beowulf made no move to escape, a chill went down Roxie's spine. She turned back to the room and searched for something she could use as a weapon. Her gaze landed on the half-empty bottle of wine sitting in the ice bucket. She snatched it, then walked out of the room.

Not wanting to be seen because of the way she was dressed, Roxie stealthily headed downstairs and then out the back door of the club. After quietly shutting it behind her, she froze. There were now two large wolves. A coal-black wolf had joined the first one.

The wolves seemed to ignore her as their deep-throated growls echoed in the alley. Looking around, Roxie couldn't see Beowulf anywhere. As she searched the shadows for him, she slowly inched forward. The man seemed to have disappeared. Then it hit her. She was alone in a dark alley with two extremely large wolves with only a bottle of wine to defend herself. Not the smartest thing she'd ever done.

When the growling ceased, Roxie knew she had been spotted. The first wolf with the rusty-brown fur had turned and appeared to be slowly stalking her. The black wolf snarled and snapped his teeth at the first. The brown wolf ignored the threat and continued to step forward.

Not wanting to make any sudden movements, Roxie slowly backed up. The wolf matched her steps, keeping what little distance there was between them. Remembering the bottle she held, she threw what was left of the wine into the wolf's face. It yelped as the alcohol splashed into its eyes. Shaking its head, it left the alley at a run.

That's one down and one to go. The black wolf hadn't moved from the spot at the back of the alley. It was no longer growling and seemed to be staring at her. Cautiously, it walked toward her. Mesmerized by its blue eyes, Roxie froze. Before it reached her, she shook her head, breaking the spell.

Roxie raised the bottle above her head. "Nice wolfy. You can just run along and play with your friend. You don't want to bite me." The wolf cocked its head at her as if listening to her, but that didn't stop it from coming nearer.

She took aim, then sent the bottle flying. She had intended to hit the wolf in the head or an equally damaging body part, but of course her aim had to be off. It hit the pavement inches in front of the wolf and smashed, sending shards of glass into its chest. The wolf yelped and jumped into the air. Landing on all fours, it ran past Roxie, brushing against her leg before leaving her alone in the dark alley.

Roxie's legs shook. She hoped she hadn't hurt the wolf too badly. It really was a beautiful animal, and its fur had felt quite soft as it had brushed against her bare leg. She was just glad it hadn't decided to take a chunk out of her before running away.

Now all she had to do was find Beowulf. Roxie wondered if he had somehow managed to make it back to his office without her seeing him. She walked through the back door. She couldn't see how that was possible. *I would have seen him, wouldn't I?*

* * * *

The office was empty, and it didn't look as if Beowulf had been back at all. The food still sat on the table where they'd left it. Roxie sat on the couch and decided it was best to stay put. He'd told her not to leave his office in the first place, so it should be there he would come looking for her.

Minutes ticked by, and Beowulf still didn't return. When her stomach growled loudly, Roxie decided the food was too good to waste. After taking a seat at the table, she filled a plate. It was now cold but tasted delicious. Once she'd eaten everything she'd taken, she slowly sipped what wine was left in her glass. Considering she'd chucked the rest of it at one of the wolves, she wouldn't be getting a second glass anytime soon.

She'd now been back in the office for an hour with no sign of Beowulf. She went from being worried about him to being completely ticked off. *What the hell is keeping him? Did he forget he has me stashed away in his office?* Having reached the limit of her patience and feeling as if she had been stood up, Roxie picked up the office phone. She pushed buttons until she got an outside line, then dialed Candice's number. Luckily, her friend was at home.

"Roxie, what are you doing calling me? I thought you had a hot date with Beowulf this evening."

"I did, but now I don't."

"Okay, I'm confused."

"Never mind. Come pick me up and I'll explain it to you during the ride home."

"Aren't you at home?"

"Of course I'm not. If I was, do you think I would be calling you for a lift? I'm at Wulf's Den. Oh, and can you bring my spare set of house keys?"

"What happened to yours?"

Starting to lose her cool, Roxie snapped. "Just get into your damn car and come pick me up, Candice. I need to get out of here — now."

"All right, all right. No need to be rude about it. I'll pick you up at the front of the club in fifteen minutes."

"Sorry for snapping at you, Candy. It's just been one of those nights where I don't know whether I'm coming or going. I'll be waiting for you."

Roxie hung up the phone and decided to see if she could find her keys before she left. After searching the top of Beowulf's desk and any unlocked drawers, she figured he must still have them in his pants pocket. Just terrific. Now she would have to get her locks changed.

She managed to walk out the front door of the club without drawing too much attention. When the bouncer gave her a strange look, she pulled her shoulders back and, with as much dignity as she could muster in bare feet, walked to the curb where Candice sat waiting in her car. Before shutting the car door, she looked at the bouncer and found him laughing. She hunched down in her seat. She looked away and stared out the windshield. *Can I be any more embarrassed?*

Candice wove her way into traffic and shook her head. "Now are you going to tell me what's going on? And why are you dressed like that to go out on a date? I'm almost embarrassed enough to disown you as a friend."

Roxie blew a breath out in a huff. "I so don't need you to start in on my clothes right now. It wasn't my choice of what to wear. Believe me, I wasn't given any. That man is a Neanderthal. He just slung me over his shoulder, snatched up my keys, and hauled me away."

Candice appeared to bite the inside of her cheek to stop from laughing. If her friend so much as laughed at her, it would only make her madder.

"I assume *that man* is Beowulf. So let me get this straight. He just showed up at your house and took you away? You didn't do anything that may have made him feel as if he had no other choice?"

"Well, not exactly."

"What did you do this time, Rox?"

"Nothing! Why is it you always think I did something wrong?"

"Because you usually do."

Knowing Candice wouldn't let it go until she was proved right or wrong, Roxie sighed. "Fine. Maybe it had a little bit to do with me. I couldn't find anything to wear so when Beowulf arrived, I told him I'd changed my mind about going out with him."

"Roxie. What am I going to do with you?"

Candice pulled into the driveway, then passed Roxie her spare set of keys before following her inside. She threw herself onto the couch and waited for Roxie to continue her story. When Roxie took the extra time to make sure the front door was securely locked, Candice loudly cleared her throat. "Well?"

Roxie sat on the couch and turned to face Candice. "I don't know, Candy. Beowulf is great-looking and all, but there's something not right with him. I can't put my finger on it."

"*Hmph.* Don't talk to me about weird men."

Relieved to be able to get the subject off herself, Roxie asked, "The new guy didn't work out?"

"No. The guy was eye candy, but he was a few bricks short of a load. When we went back to my place for a couple drinks, he made a move on me." Candice shuddered. "The man was all teeth. After he bit me twice and growled like some kind of animal, I told him to leave. Then the idiot had the audacity to say he thought I would want him to bite me. That he thought I was one of the others who came to the club, and that it was all an act. I made him leave anyway."

Roxie bit her lip. *Was Beowulf's growling all an act too?* She didn't think so. Candice hadn't said anything about glowing eyes. "Sorry it didn't work out, Candice."

"Enough about me. What happened to you tonight?"

"Things seemed to be going all right, even though Beowulf acted like a caveman in the beginning. He took me to Wulf's Den where he had his office all set for a romantic dinner. The room was lit with dozens of candles, and he had roses."

"So…"

"So we got interrupted by Beowulf's brother. Something was going on down at the club, and apparently, Beowulf was the only one who could fix it, whatever that was. The man left and never came back. I wasn't going to wait around for hours."

"Beowulf has a brother? And what exactly did he interrupt?" Candice smiled knowingly.

Roxie shook her head and absently scratched an itchy spot on her left wrist. "Is that all you ever think of? Men and sex?"

"Of course. Without them, life would be boring. I agree with you that it wasn't right for Beowulf to leave you waiting like that. Are you sure he'd forgotten about you?"

"I'm pretty sure. When he wasn't in the back alley with the wolf, I figured he would be back."

"Whoa there. Back up. What wolf? Roxie, there aren't any wild wolves in San Francisco."

"That's what I thought. After Beowulf left, I heard loud voices coming from the alley. When I looked out the window, I saw he was down there. The largest wolf I've ever seen had him cornered. So I went to see if I could help."

"Are you crazy? The thing could have turned on you. What did Beowulf do when you showed up?"

"That's the strangest part. When I got down to the alley, Beowulf had vanished. Instead of one wolf as I had seen earlier, there were two."

"Two wolves? And you were alone in the alley with them? You must be insane."

"Well, obviously, I survived the ordeal." Her left wrist was itchy now. Could she be having an allergic reaction from the food she'd eaten for dinner?

Roxie continued clawing at her wrist until Candice brushed her hand aside. "Stop scratching that. You'll only make it worse."

"I can't help it. It's itchy. I wonder if I'm allergic to something." The skin around her wrist was not only itchy but red and bumpy, almost as if she had hives.

"If you don't stop clawing, you'll end up with an infection. Go put something on it." Candice stood and headed for the door. "I'm going to run. Unlike some other people, I have to get up early for work tomorrow. Try not to let tonight make you think the worst of Beowulf. There's probably a logical explanation for all this. Give him a chance. You don't want to pass up a good thing."

Roxie closed the door behind Candice and thought about what she'd said. Maybe Candice was right. Maybe she had acted a little hasty in her decision that Beowulf had stood her up. Still scratching her wrist, she went upstairs to the bathroom. She pulled gauze and some cortisone cream out of the medicine chest. If she didn't get some relief from this rash, she would never get to sleep.

CHAPTER SIX

"How did this happen again?"

Beowulf glared at Wade. His brother couldn't quite wipe the smile off his face. "I told you already. The wine bottle shattered when Roxie threw it at me."

Even though Beowulf scowled fiercely, Wade didn't hold back his laughter. "That's priceless. Our valiant leader is brought low by a woman wielding a bottle of wine."

Beowulf winced as Wade pulled another sliver of glass out of his chest. They were in the club's cellar. There was a hidden entrance to it that only members of his pack knew about. The room was set up for just such emergencies. Being wounded and stuck out in the open with mortals about was never a good thing. They tended to overreact when seeing one of his people in wolf form.

"At least she got rid of Gren for me."

"She saw both of you?"

"Yes. She threw the wine in Gren's face. Me, she threw the bottle at."

Wade howled with laughter. "Two male werewolves in their prime, and one mortal sends them both running with their tails between their legs."

"My tail was not between my legs. Now hurry up and finish so I can get back to Roxie. Lord knows what's going through her mind."

The door leading up to the club cracked open, and Carl, the club bouncer, stuck his head into the room. "Hey, boss. I thought you'd like to know your woman left about five minutes ago."

Beowulf cursed under his breath. *When will Roxie ever stop running from me?* "Thanks, Carl. Did you happen to see where she went?"

"Yeah. The looker who was here with her the other night picked her up. Now that one I would like to get a piece of."

"I'll see what I can do about introducing you."

Beowulf shook his head after Carl shut the door. The big man had a soft spot for petite, beautiful women. And the surprising thing was the women didn't seem to mind having the bald-headed, hulking bouncer showing interest in them.

"What are you going to do about Roxie?"

He hissed as his brother pulled out a particularly large piece of glass. "For now, nothing. I have to heal first. Roxie isn't stupid. She'll be able to put one and one together and figure out it was me in the alley. I don't want her finding out that way. I want to slowly ease her into it."

"You know, she might be upset with you. For all she knows, you forgot about her. Why else would she have called for her friend to pick her up?"

Beowulf grinned as he fished the set of keys out of his jeans pocket and held them up. "As long as I have her keys, I have the upper hand. I never said I was going to play fair."

* * * *

She felt free as she ran through the trees. This was where she belonged. All her worries fell away, leaving nothing but a sense of peace. She looked behind her, trying to see if he followed. She laughed to herself as she hid behind the largest tree she could find. Whenever they came to the deepest part of the forest, they played this game. They enjoyed the hunt — him as the hunter, and her as the hunted. The roles never changed. He would find her eventually, she counted on it. For being caught was the best part of the whole game. Once he found her, he would pull her down to the forest floor and make love to her. Her body already throbbed in anticipation.

She peered around the tree and spied the large wolf a few yards away. His nose was down, sniffing, trying to pick up her scent. She quickly ducked back behind her hiding spot. She placed a hand over her mouth, to stifle her laughter. She dared to look again and found the wolf almost upon her. She shrieked with laughter as she picked up her skirt and took off at a run. The large wolf easily kept up with her, running at her side. When she could no longer run anymore, she stopped, and the wolf licked her hand, then moved a little away. She reached for the fastenings of her gown and waited.

The wolf's shape blurred, then slowly changed until a man stood in its place. Her lover smiled and took her into his arms. Already naked, she felt how aroused their game had made him. She looked lovingly into his glowing eyes and smiled as he took off her gown. With a growl, her wolf lover pulled her down.

* * * *

Roxie gasped as she bolted upright in bed. The dream had seemed so real. She could almost feel strong arms wrapped around her. As a child, she'd dreamed of wolves, but they'd stopped once she'd hit her teenage years. And they had never been as erotic as the one she'd just had. It must have been seeing the wolves at the club that had set it off.

Knowing she wouldn't be able to go back to sleep, Roxie stretched and got out of bed. Before getting into the shower, she decided to see what her rash looked like. She pulled off the gauze and found it still a mess. A red lumpy rash about an inch in width now circled her whole left wrist. It didn't itch anymore, but it was tender to the touch, as she found out when she poked it. *Now that's disgusting.* Hoping the shower would help get rid of the rash, she left the gauze off but rewrapped it after she was dressed.

Roxie slipped into her typical work-day routine and soon left the real world behind, but when she took a break for lunch, she remembered Beowulf still had a set of her house keys. After her chat last night with Candice, she didn't know if she should get the locks changed or not. It would be so much easier for her not to have to call a locksmith. Beowulf hadn't shown up at her place during the night, which was something she'd thought he would do. Maybe he would be a gentleman and return the keys. Then again, he didn't seem to be the gentlemanly type, given his habit of throwing her over his shoulder when she didn't cooperate.

In the end, she decided the best course of action was to call Beowulf and see if he would return the keys to her. It was then she realized two things. One, she had no idea what his last name was, and two, she didn't know his address so it would be impossible to look up his home phone number. That left only one way of contacting him—she would have to wait until Wulf's Den opened in the evening and hope he was there.

The rest of the day flew by. Roxie was pleased with the amount of work she'd done. She went to the kitchen, then searched the cupboards to see what she could make for dinner. They and the fridge were decidedly empty. She made a mental note to go grocery shopping. She settled for something quick and snagged a can of soup. That and a sandwich would have to do for tonight.

She placed the pot on the stovetop and looked out the kitchen window. She had an unobstructed view of her backyard. Another thing to add to her to-do list—cut the grass. Out of the corner of her eye, she caught movement outside. Roxie peered into the lengthening shadows. There was something out there. She walked toward the window, then watched as a figure emerged from the shadows. She blinked. *It couldn't be.* Unless her eyes were playing tricks on her, the wolf with the rusty-brown fur stood in her backyard. It looked right at her.

The sound of the phone ringing caused her to jump. She turned and picked up the cordless phone hanging on the wall. When she turned back around, the wolf was gone. "Hello?"

Beowulf's deep baritone answered. "Hi, Roxie. Will you talk to me or are you still upset?"

"What happened to you last night? You were gone for so long I thought you weren't coming back."

"The situation at the club turned out to take a lot longer to settle than I'd anticipated. Sorry. I should've sent someone up to the office to tell you."

"I guess I should have waited a little longer for you." Roxie snapped off the burner before the soup boiled over and was about to pour it when she heard a wolf howling.

"What was that?"

"You aren't going to believe this, but I've been seeing wolves lately. I saw two behind your club last night, and just a few minutes ago, I saw one in my backyard. I think that was it howling, but I can't see it anymore."

Beowulf's voice grew sharp. "What color fur did it have?"

"A rusty-brown. I think it's one of the wolves I saw last night." Roxie was a little surprised Beowulf took it as a given fact that she'd seen wolves. It was stranger still that he would want to know what color fur the wolf had.

"I want you to listen to me, Roxie. And for once do what I ask. Lock all your windows and doors. No matter what happens, don't open the door. I'm coming to pick you up."

"That's really not necessary. It's a wild wolf. It's probably more afraid of me than I am of it. And I don't have any intention of going outside with it."

"No," Beowulf said gruffly. He paused for a second, then continued in a softer tone. "No, Roxie. I don't want you there alone. Grab what things you need for an overnight stay, and I'll be there in a few minutes."

"Beowulf, I really appreciate you looking out for me, but I think you're overreacting a little. It's only a wolf. I'll be safe in the house. Besides, I just made some soup for my dinner, and I would like to eat it before it gets cold. Oh, and one other thing. I want my house keys back."

"Roxie, you don't understand. I'm responsible for you now. As your ma—" Beowulf stopped talking midsentence.

"As my what?" When Beowulf remained silent, Roxie shook her head, even though he couldn't see her. "Whatever, but you can answer me this first before I decide if I should listen to you or not. If I don't do this, are you going to throw me over your shoulder again?"

Beowulf chuckled. "What do you think?"

"Why did I even bother asking? Fine. You win. I'll be ready when you get here. And where exactly am I going to be staying?"

"My place, of course."

"Of course. You better have Internet or I'm going to be one pissed-off houseguest."

"I do. I think you'll like my house. Maybe you'll like it enough to stay for a long visit."

"Don't push it. I'm going to hang up so I can pack. See you

when you get here."

Roxie hung up the phone and grumbled to herself. She went upstairs, then stuffed pajamas and a change of clothes into a backpack before jamming in a brush, toothpaste, and toothbrush. Back downstairs, she went to her office to collect her laptop. With more care, she slipped it into the carrying bag she used when taking it out of the house. She returned to the kitchen, then poured the now cooled soup down the kitchen sink. She filled the pot with water, leaving it there to be washed later. She sat in the living room to wait for Beowulf to arrive.

* * * *

Beowulf couldn't get to Roxie's house fast enough. Even though she thought nothing of a wolf being in her backyard, he knew better. It was no run-of-the-mill type of wolf. Far from it. As her keen mind had remembered, it was indeed one she had seen last night. The bastard, Gren, must have followed her home somehow. Beowulf didn't think Gren would do anything harmful to her, but he still wasn't going to take any chances. Gren liked to make Beowulf's life hell, had for years, and used every means available to do so. Right now, Roxie was his greatest weakness, and Gren knew it.

Turning onto Roxie's street, some of the tension left his body. Lights shone in her windows, and, through the half-open curtains, he saw her sitting in the living room. He walked to the front door. He didn't bother knocking. He unlocked it and walked in.

Roxie stood in the entranceway with her hand held out. "I'll take those back, if you don't mind."

Beowulf slipped the keys onto her outstretched hand. Unbeknownst to her, he'd had an extra set made that afternoon. "Are you ready to go?"

She nodded. She slung her backpack over one shoulder, then picked up her laptop and purse. The keys she stuck inside the latter. "As ready as I'll ever be."

"Good."

He pulled her up against his hard body and took her lips in a searing kiss. He'd been so close last night. She could have been completely his if not for Gren, but once he had her under his roof, she would be. All day he could think of nothing else. He'd spent half of it with a raging erection. Images of how Roxie had looked as she'd climaxed haunted him. The urge to bury his cock deep inside her pussy beat at him.

Roxie's whimper of need brought him out of his haze of lust. With Gren lurking about, it wasn't a good idea to be thinking about sex. Beowulf broke the kiss, then looked at her. Her lips were puffy from his kisses, and her cheeks were slightly flushed. Her pupils were dilated, and she looked to be in a daze. He smiled to himself.

"That was to say sorry for last night. Here, give me your bags. I'll take them out to the car for you."

Roxie blinked a couple of times. "I'll carry them. This is my laptop, and I don't let anyone touch that."

He nodded in understanding before he led the way outside.

*

Roxie turned out the lights and then closed and locked the front door behind them. She followed Beowulf to his car. She couldn't shake the feeling that she wouldn't be back at her house anytime soon, which was ridiculous since she was only going to be away for one night.

She climbed into his black Mercedes, then looked at Beowulf. She still had a hard time thinking a man like him could want her. He was every woman's dream come true. With his gorgeous face and tanned and muscular body, a woman would be crazy not to want him in her bed. She felt like a bitch in heat whenever she was near him. She couldn't help herself.

She watched the streets go by, soon realizing they were now in the upper-class section of the city. *Figures, good-looking and rich.* She had guessed Beowulf would have money since he owned his own nightclub and drove a Mercedes, but she hadn't thought about how much of it he had. Being stinking rich she hadn't counted on. The bloody man lived in a mansion.

Privacy gates swung open as they approached and then closed automatically behind them. As Beowulf drove up the long, circular drive, Roxie couldn't help but feel intimidated. He was so out of her league in every way. And with that thought in mind, she panicked. There was no way things could work out between them. With his lifestyle, he needed one of those tall, shaped-like-a-model-type women who reeked of elegance and grace. One who'd complement him in the looks department.

Beowulf opened the car door for her, then stood waiting for Roxie to get out. Having convinced herself that she wasn't good enough for him, she made no move to take his outstretched hand. She kept her gaze glued to the car's dashboard. She couldn't look at him.

"Roxie, are you going to get out of the car, or are you going to sleep out here tonight?" When she didn't so much as turn her head, he leaned inside. "Do I have to drag you out of the car? Now that I think about it, I could just make love to you out here. I don't have close neighbors. The only one who would see us would be my brother."

Roxie flinched at his words. "I think I'm making a terrible mistake. This will never work."

Beowulf groaned. "Are we back to that again? Roxie, Roxie. When will you ever learn?"

He reached into the car and scooped her up into his arms, bags and all, before he headed for the front door. He didn't put her down until after he had it safely shut behind them. Roxie stood in the entranceway, holding her bags in a death grip. Beowulf pried her fingers free, then took them from her and placed them on the floor close to the stairs.

He stared at Roxie as he shook his head. She could tell he was getting a little exasperated with her.

"Roxie, what's wrong?"

Roxie swallowed loudly and kept her gaze away from Beowulf's face. "This isn't going to work. We don't match."

"What do you mean 'we don't match'? Believe me, we are a perfect match."

Roxie bit her bottom lip, then forged on. "No, we're not. Far from it. Look at where you live. How can I possibly compete with that? I'm not from your world."

He took her chin in his hand and forced her to look up at him. "Do you think I care whether or not you have money? And why would you think you have to compete? You're unlike any woman I've ever met. You're perfect just the way you are. Enough of this." He threw an arm around her shoulders, then walked her to the stairs. He collected her bags on the way before he led her up them.

She couldn't think. The feel of Beowulf rubbing against her side as they walked upstairs halted all her mental processes. Being this close to him, all she wanted was to finish what they had started. Her body was aware of every inch of him. His scent, so familiar to her now, wrapped around her. The panic she'd been feeling slowly drained away.

A bit more relaxed, Roxie let Beowulf walk her through one of the open doors in front of them. Thinking he was showing her the room where she would be staying, she stumbled when she realized this was no guestroom. The furniture was masculine in style. The fabrics and carpet were dark. The colors varied from a rich chocolate-brown to a burnished gold. A large king-size bed dominated the room. She couldn't take her gaze off it. This could only be Beowulf's bedroom.

"Is this your room?"

Beowulf placed her bags on the bed. He turned to face her, and all the air left her lungs in a whoosh. He looked at her as he had that first night at the club, as if he wanted to devour her. Just as it had then, her body responded. Her breasts swelled, and her nipples tightened into buds. Her heart sped up so it madly thumped against her ribs. The man standing before her became the center of her world. Nothing else mattered. Before he could pull her into his arms, her stomach growled—loudly. The spell of desire he'd woven around her broke.

Beowulf smiled. "To answer your question, yes, this is my bedroom."

"Am I going to be sleeping here?"

"Yes." Beowulf stepped to Roxie, then brushed his body against hers. "Yes, you are sleeping here. Do you know how many dreams I've had of you lying in my bed? Tonight, I finally get to make them a reality."

She shivered. Her voice came out a mere whisper. "Oh my." Images of what she wanted to do to him, in his bed, played through her mind, but once again her stomach rumbled loudly. She smiled sheepishly. "Sorry. I didn't get a chance to eat dinner."

"I guess I'd better feed you, then. For what I have in mind for tonight, you're going to need all the energy you can get."

Roxie felt herself flush. The man overwhelmed her senses. She wouldn't kid herself. There would be no happily ever after for them. They were just too different. Beowulf would eventually grow tired of her or get fed up with her hermit ways. Just as had happened with the other men she'd let into her life. The others did not compare to Beowulf, though. Would she be able to get over him the way she had the rest? She seriously doubted it, but he was already in too deep for her to walk away now. Her body wanted him and wouldn't take no for an answer.

*

Beowulf took Roxie by the hand, then led her downstairs before he could act on all the sexual fantasies he had swirling around inside his mind. She was obviously hungry, and he hadn't been kidding when he'd said she would need all her energy. He intended to make love to her until they both could no longer move. His body recognized her as his mate, and he was finding it hard to ignore its demands. As it was, he ended up walking around with a constant hard-on whenever he was around her.

He led her to the kitchen. He plunked her down onto one of the chairs at the kitchen table before he opened the stainless-steel fridge and pulled out ingredients to make burgers. He switched on the grill next to the gas range as he glanced at Roxie. She seemed to watch his every move. "I hope you like burgers."

"That's fine. You know how to cook?"

"Yes. I see that surprises you."

"Yeah, well, I thought since you live in a house like this you would have a full-time chef to cook for you."

Beowulf flashed a grin. "I do, but sometimes I like to cook for myself, and today is the day off for the woman who usually makes my meals for me."

"What about your brother? I don't see him around."

"The club is closed tonight, so he must be out enjoying his night off." Beowulf had kicked Wade out of the house after he'd gotten off the phone with Roxie. He wanted no interruptions. Not tonight.

The patties sizzled when he placed them on the grill. The

kitchen soon filled with the scent of cooking meat. The wolf in him rose to the surface, something he usually embraced. Meat was a large part of his diet, as it was for all his kind. He forced back the wolf and concentrated on finishing the burgers.

Beowulf placed a plate of food before Roxie, then slipped into the chair beside her. He picked up the burger and took a large bite. It was juicy and still pink on the inside. Roxie took a bite of hers. She held it in her mouth for a few seconds before she chewed. When she noticed him looking at her, she turned and smiled.

He finished his burger, then went to the wine fridge and took out a bottle of white wine. He snagged two wineglasses from the cupboard before he poured them each a drink. Roxie picked up her glass and took a large swallow. She took another bite of her burger, then quickly chewed and chased it down with another drink of wine.

He cringed inside. She had to be washing the food down with the wine. He'd forgotten she wasn't like him. He'd cooked the burgers to his taste—practically raw. Watching her force down another mouthful, he took pity on her and pulled the plate away.

"You don't have to finish that. I have a feeling you aren't enjoying it as much as I did mine."

Roxie pulled the plate back toward her and shook her head. "No, I'll finish it."

He pulled it away again. "Roxie, I know you're washing it down with the wine. No need to play the polite guest."

"You made it for me, so I'll eat it."

Using more force than was necessary, Roxie grabbed the edge of the plate and yanked. It slid across the table, fell into her lap, then crashed to the floor. She appeared to take in the mess she'd created before she closed her eyes. The pained expression on her face said, *Why do things like this always happen to me?* Bits of burger were on her lap, the juices slowly soaking into her jeans. What was left of it was on the floor along with the now broken plate.

"Sorry, Beowulf. I'll clean that up." Standing, she brushed the meat off her lap and then proceeded to pick up the mess.

"Don't worry about the plate. It could happen to anyone. Sit down and finish your wine. I'll take care of this."

In a matter of minutes, Beowulf had the floor clean. He took

Roxie by the arm, then brought her to her feet. He saw she was embarrassed, but that only endeared her more to him. He traced her lips with the tip of his finger. They softened beneath his touch. Unable to resist tasting them, he bent his head toward her. Before his mouth touched hers, she reached up and pushed him away.

"Wait. I don't even know your last name."

"That can easily be remedied. It's Thorsson."

Before she could think of something else to delay their mating, Beowulf wrapped a hand around the back of her neck, holding her in place. He brushed his lips along hers. Roxie sighed. He licked the plump sweetness of her mouth. She clutched the front of his shirt. Snaking his other arm around her waist, he pulled her against him, but it wasn't enough for him. He needed to taste her. He swept his tongue inside her mouth. He loved the taste of her.

Beowulf kept their mouths fused as he crowded Roxie out the kitchen door. At the bottom of the stairs, he wrapped one of her legs around his waist. "Put your other leg around me," he said gruffly.

Roxie did as he'd said. He cradled her against his chest, taking the stairs two at a time. He didn't let her down until they'd reached his bedroom. He released her so she slowly slid down the length of his body. He sucked her lower lip into his mouth, then tugged at the plump flesh. He pushed up her shirt until the undersides of her breasts rested on top of his hands. He left her mouth, then nipped her chin with his sharp teeth. He moved lower, making a trail of wet kisses down the side of her throat to the tops of her breasts. He took hold of her shirt and pulled it over her head. After unhooking her bra, he let it fall to the floor. Beowulf groaned as he lowered his head and sucked a nipple deep inside his mouth. She laced her fingers through his hair, holding him to her.

With an arm around her waist, he bent her over. He released her nipple, then moved to the other, sucking and swirling his tongue around the tight peak. Roxie made small mewing sounds as she pressed closer. Beowulf shoved her jeans off her hips and down. Wanting rid of the offending garment, she kicked it away.

With a boldness she hadn't shown earlier, Roxie took a step away. Beowulf tried to pull her back. She smiled and shook her head. He'd seen all of her, and now it seemed she wanted to see him. Without saying a word, she pulled off his shirt. She sucked in her breath. She trailed her fingers over his defined pecs, outlining them before running them through the small amount of dark hair across his chest. She encountered his flat nipples and circled each one with her fingertip until they hardened into little nubs. She ran her hands across his abs.

Her lips and mouth joined in her exploration of his body. She followed the same path her hands had taken and licked a path across his wide chest. With the flat of her tongue, she laved each of his nipples. He took a quick intake of breath at her licking him in such a sensitive place. She tugged on one of the tight buds with her teeth. Beowulf groaned, making her do it once again. Going down on her knees, she pressed her lips to his stomach. She skimmed her hands up and down his taut thighs before she found the muscles of his ass. She took a firm hold as she pulled him closer.

She followed the fine line of hair that disappeared below the waistband of his pants, and rubbed her cheek against the hard bulge that begged for attention. Beowulf inched his hands toward her, and she shoved them aside. She obviously wasn't ready to relinquish control. She undid his jeans and freed his erection. His cock was large and thick. He couldn't wait to have it inside her, but first she appeared to want to see how far she could push him before he reached his limit of control.

She took hold of his shaft and licked the very tip. She moaned, and his cock jumped. Roxie held him firmly, licking from base to tip. Beowulf fisted his hands at his sides. She seemed to like the power she had over him. She took the very tip of him into her mouth. He hardened as she circled it with her tongue. She applied suction, taking in as much of his hard length as she could.

No longer able to keep his hands off her, Beowulf pushed her long hair to the side, giving him a better view of Roxie's face. His cock swelled even more. Drowning in the feel of her hot, wet mouth surrounding him, he jerked his hips. He had to stop her soon but not just yet. Her wicked tongue stroked him as she sucked, and it felt too good. Lost in the urge to claim his mate, he let the wolf inside loose. A low growl of need rose.

Beowulf rode the instinct to dominate his mate. He pulled away from Roxie and brought her to her feet. He quickly shed his pants before wrapping her into his arms. He slanted his mouth against hers, picked her up, and carried her to the bed. With the mating urge fully upon him, he put her down in the center of the mattress and climbed between her legs. Able to smell the musky scent of her arousal, he knew she was ready for him. He took hold of his engorged cock and pushed the head into her wet opening. He forced her legs wider apart before he shoved forward, stretching her, until she took all of him inside. He groaned as her inner walls clamped around him.

With hands under her hips, he angled himself so each stroke rubbed her clit. Roxie wrapped her legs around his waist. Keeping the pace steady, Beowulf pumped in and out of her wet sheath. She felt so good, too good. He was close to his climax, but he wanted her to come first so he could watch her face as her body flew apart. It would be the first of many he would push her to have. Unlike mortal males, his kind didn't lose their erections after release. He could stay hard for hours.

Beowulf rose onto his elbows and looked down at Roxie. Her eyes were closed. He increased his pace, thrusting into her, pushing her ever higher. As she climaxed, her inner walls squeezed the whole length of his cock, milking him. She clamped her legs around him and moaned. It was almost enough to send him into his own release, but he wanted her looking at him when he did. So she would see how much pleasure she gave him.

"Open your eyes, Roxie. I want you to look at me."

With small spasms rocking her body, she looked up at him. Beowulf still rode her hard, drawing out her climax. Her breath seemed to catch in her lungs when she stared into his eyes. He knew what she would see. They would be glowing, like two pieces of glacial ice. He pushed her into another intense climax. She seemed unable to pull her gaze from his face. His cock swelled even more before he threw back his head and erupted, filling her with his cum.

Beowulf was still hard. He pulled out of her and turned her so she lay on her stomach. With a leg on either side of her body, he lifted her hair aside and licked the back of her neck, causing her to shiver. He bit into the soft flesh there. He moved downward, leaving a wet trail as he followed the line of her spine with his tongue. At the twin globes of her bottom, he nipped. He knelt between her spread thighs and urged her up onto her hands and knees. He gripped her hips as he sheathed himself in one stroke. Roxie gasped as his cock hit her cervix. He withdrew until only the very tip of him was still inside her before he thrust back into her again. In this position, she could take more of him.

Not letting go of her hips, he pumped into her, holding her in position for his invasion. She tried to push back on him, but Beowulf wouldn't allow it. He dug his fingers into her hips and rocked into her, hitting her cervix with each stroke. She whimpered as her inner muscles clenched around his hard shaft. Her climax tore through her. Beowulf's strokes grew faster and harder before he howled his release.

*

Roxie could barely move. She felt as if her body had been turned to mush. Little aftershocks of pleasure still rocked her. She closed her eyes, vaguely feeling Beowulf pull her up against his chest and covered the two of them with the blankets. The man was going to kill her. She lay next to him, and his still-hard cock was pressed against her hip. *How could he still have an erection?* With that last thought, Roxie let sleep claim her.

CHAPTER SEVEN

H er body ached in the most delicious of places. Roxie had never felt this satiated after spending the night with a man. Nor had she made love as many times as she had with Beowulf during the long night. The man's stamina was amazing. No matter how many times he climaxed, he never went soft. He was a woman's fantasy come to life.

She reached out and found the spot next to her empty. Roxie cracked open her eyes before looking around the room. Beowulf was already awake and gone. She sat up and stretched. Her muscles screamed in protest. He had taken her in so many different positions muscles she didn't even know she had ached.

The bedroom door swung open, and Beowulf entered, carrying a tray of food. Roxie pulled the sheet up to her chest. She couldn't help but notice he was naked. Smiling, he walked to the bed and placed the tray on the mattress beside her.

"You finally woke up. I thought you were going to sleep the whole day away."

"I have a good excuse to." Dawn had begun to lighten the sky when they'd last made love.

"Very true."

He leaned across the bed and took her lips in a searing kiss. When he pulled away, Roxie groaned in disappointment. Even after hours of lovemaking, she still wanted him. Hoping to distract herself, she looked down at the tray of food. There were two plates with eggs, scrambled and fried, crisp bacon, and hot buttered toast. Roxie's mouth watered. The undercooked burger Beowulf had served her the night before had not appeased her stomach, but this morning he'd more than made up for not feeding her edible food.

Beowulf placed a plate on her lap. Roxie dug into what was on it with gusto.

"I hope you like everything. I wasn't sure how you liked your eggs, so I did them scrambled and fried."

Roxie swallowed a mouthful of toast. "It's delicious." She looked his hard body up and down. She couldn't help but ask, "Do you always cook breakfast naked?"

"No." Beowulf gave her a sultry look. "I decided clothes would only get in the way. I find myself hungry for something other than food this morning."

Roxie licked her bottom lip. "And what did your brother think, seeing you walking around the house without a stitch of clothes on?"

"Wade didn't come home last night. We have the house to ourselves." Beowulf reached for her left hand. He started to lead it to his fully engorged cock, but when his fingers encountered the gauze wrapped around Roxie's wrist, he held it up for his inspection instead. "What happened?"

Roxie snatched her hand back. "I didn't hurt myself. I have a rash. A disgusting-looking rash. I must have gotten into something I'm allergic to."

"Has this happened before?"

She shook her head. "Not that I can recall."

"Maybe I should look at it."

"No. I put some cream on it that should make it go away."

Beowulf picked up her wrist and peeled away the gauze. Roxie tried to pull away. He snarled and snapped his teeth. She froze, then mumbled about having to use the washroom. He released her as she wrapped the bedsheet around herself and then disappeared into the bathroom. She heard him swear under his breath before she closed the door behind her.

Still wrapped in the sheet, Roxie stepped back into the room after giving herself a few minutes and picked up her backpack.

"Ah, I just remembered I was supposed to go see my parents today. My mom hates it when I don't show up after we've made plans. So if you don't mind, could you give me a ride back to my place so I can get my car?"

Not giving Beowulf a chance to answer, she went back into the bathroom and shut the door.

*

Beowulf hit the mattress with his fist. After last night, he had thought for sure Roxie would no longer want to run from him. They were mated now. He had claimed her. Making love to her had only made him want her more. As mates, they should want to be close to each other; they needed to be close to each other. There should be an invisible link between them. During the first time they'd made love, he'd felt his soul reach out to hers, but obviously Roxie hadn't felt it the same way he had. Thinking the separation would be good for her, he pulled on some clothes. Maybe a few hours away from him would push her into accepting their mating. Then again, maybe humans never felt the same pull with their mates as his kind did. This was new territory for him.

* * * *

After dressing in the bathroom, Roxie felt more on an even keel. She didn't know why she'd panicked like that. Instead of outright asking Beowulf about all the strange things he seemed able to do, she ran. It wasn't as if she was afraid of him exactly, though any normal person would have freaked out by now. It was just the growling he did seemed familiar to her on some basic level. She'd never met anyone who made those sounds before, so that sense of familiarity confused her.

Roxie took a big cleansing breath, then walked back into the bedroom. Beowulf stood waiting for her, fully dressed. His expression was stern. She felt as if he held himself from her, unsure of how she would react. Strangely enough, she felt the loss. Sometime during the night, a connection had grown between them. The urge to throw herself into his arms, knowing he would make everything better, was almost too strong to ignore. She wasn't ready to need him that much, but she couldn't let things stay the way they now stood.

She crossed the room, then stood on tiptoes and lightly brushed her mouth against his. "I'm not running away. Not this time. I really do need to see my parents."

Beowulf tucked her hair behind her ear. "Are you sure?"

"Yes. I'll come back after my visit. And to prove it, I'll leave my laptop here."

"Well, that sets my mind to rest." Gently pulling her into his arms, Beowulf rested his forehead against hers. "Don't give up on me yet, Roxie. I know you don't understand what's happening between us. Give it some time."

Roxie nodded. "I'm usually not the running type. The urge to do so only seems to happen with you."

"That does wonders for my ego." Beowulf kissed her forehead before he took her backpack. "You're going to need a change of clothes and something to wear to the club tonight."

"Can't I stay here and wait for you to come home?"

"Absolutely not. The days, or should I say nights, are over where you're going to stay in the house trapped behind your keyboard. It's time to start living, Roxie."

She rolled her eyes. "Just great. Now I'm going to have you *and* Candice harassing me." Seeing Beowulf's determined look, she held her hands up in defeat. "Fine, I'll go to the club with you, but don't expect me to serve drinks or anything. I'm liable to dump them on some poor sod's head."

Beowulf draped an arm around her shoulders. He chuckled and walked her out of the room. "You have a deal. Now let's get you to your place. I want you back here well before the club opens. I intend to show you how much I missed not being with you."

Roxie's knees grew weak. She knew exactly how Beowulf was going to show her that he missed her. Damn, now she wasn't going to be able to think of anything else but hurrying back to him for hot, sweaty sex. Increasing their pace, she practically ran to his car. In her mind, she calculated how many hours it would take to see her parents. If she played her cards right, she would be back in three hours tops. She could wait that long, hopefully. Maybe. Who was she kidding? It was going to be a long three hours.

* * * *

After seeing Beowulf off, Roxie called her parents. She'd told him a little white lie about having to see them. She was supposed to visit them this week but not for another couple of days. She dialed her parents' number, hoping they were at home. She really did have to talk to her mother, and she didn't want to do it over the phone.

Her father picked up after the third ring. "Hi, Dad. Are you and Mom going to be home for a few hours?"

"I don't think your mother has anything planned for today. I thought you weren't coming over until Thursday?"

"Yeah, well, I decided to drop by today instead."

"What's happened now?"

Roxie groaned. "Why do you assume something has happened?" Her father's silence said it all. "Okay, okay. I admit things tend to happen around me, and not always good. This time I promise it isn't anything bad. I just need some advice."

"Then I guess we'll see you in a few minutes. And plan to stay for lunch. You know how your mother worries you aren't eating properly."

"Fine, but lunch only. I have plans for the rest of the day."

"What kind of plans would that be?"

"Ones that don't include you or Mom. Now hang up so I can leave already."

After hanging up, Roxie raced to her room. She emptied out her backpack and decided it really wasn't big enough. She picked one of her smaller suitcases, then packed it with a few days' worth of clothes. She still thought most of them weren't good enough, or stylish enough, to wear to Wulf's Den. If she was going to be with Beowulf for a while, she would have to go shopping. For tonight the only outfit she would be comfortable wearing, knowing she wouldn't embarrass him, was the one Candice had picked out. Hopefully, Beowulf wouldn't mind seeing her wear it a second time.

Throwing the suitcase into the trunk of her car, which was not as classy as Beowulf's, she made the twenty-minute drive to her parents' house where Roxie had grown up. It was a typical two-story middle-class home. She being an only child, her family hadn't needed anything bigger. Her father waited for her on the front porch. A man in his late fifties, he didn't look it. Unlike most men his age, he took care of his body. His dark brown hair was just graying at his temples. He stood straight and tall, all six feet of him. Sharp gray eyes followed her as she walked to where he stood.

"Hello, Dad."

Lucas Stone hugged her to him, squeezing until she grunted. Something he'd done since she was a child and had refused to stop doing now that she was an adult. "Hi, baby girl. Your mother has lunch almost ready. When she found out you were coming, she started cooking up a storm."

"I didn't expect her to go to a lot of trouble."

"Try to tell her that. Let's go in and see if she needs any help. Since it's such a nice day, your mother decided we're going to eat out back."

The aromas filling the kitchen smelled delicious. Roxie closed her eyes and took a big breath. A pot of her mother's homemade soup sat warming on the stove. Her mother stood at a counter, slicing freshly baked bread. She turned to face them and smiled at Roxie. Belinda Stone was everything Roxie was not. Her mother always looked perfect. Her classic beauty didn't fade. If anything, age seemed to enhance her looks. Unlike her klutzy daughter, she was all poise and grace. The only thing Roxie shared with her mother was her looks, something she was eternally grateful for. When she was fifty-six, she hoped she looked as good as her mother did.

"Can you take this out back, dear?" Belinda shoved a plate of sliced bread into Roxie's hands.

"No problem. Do you want me to come back in and help you with the soup?"

"It's all right. Your father can do that. Go sit down and make yourself comfortable."

After walking out onto the back deck, Roxie placed the bread on the patio table. Her mother had already set out cutlery, and the large umbrella was up to keep the sun off them while they ate. Her parents joined her, and they sat for a few minutes without talking, enjoying their food. She used that time to organize her thoughts. Her mother would not stay silent for much longer.

Belinda placed her spoon down and looked at Roxie. "Your father said you needed some advice."

Her mother could be so predictable at times. "Yes. Well, it's two things, really. First of all, I've met someone, and second, I want to ask you about the dreams I used to have as a child."

Of course her mother would latch on to her meeting someone new. Once Roxie had hit thirty, her parents had given up any hopes they had of being grandparents.

"When do we get to meet him, dear?"

"I'm not sure. I'd rather talk about the dreams first."

"Why the sudden interest? I thought you left those behind with your childhood."

"So did I, but the other night I dreamed about a wolf. Only this one was different from the others."

Her mother sat straighter. "In what way?"

"I'm running through the forest, this time as a woman and not a child, and there is a wolf stalking me. Not to hurt me. It's more like a game. Now the strange thing is I want the wolf to catch me, because I know he'll change, then..."

"Then what?"

"We will do...you know."

"No, I don't know."

Roxie rolled her eyes. "You're going to make me spell it out, aren't you? I mean we will have s-e-x."

"Roxie dear, you're a grown woman, and you can say the word 'sex' around me. It's not as if I've never had it, you know."

"Way too much information, Mom."

"Fine, we'll move on. Now, are you saying you have sex with a wolf in your dream?"

"No, he definitely isn't a wolf. He's a wolf to start with, but after he catches me, he turns into a man." When her mother stared at her with a concerned expression, Roxie thought maybe she should have kept that part to herself. "It was only a dream. Not like it actually happened." Feeling self-conscious, she rubbed her rash.

"Of course it was only a dream, dear. Why are you scratching at your wrist like that?"

"I have a rash, and it's really itchy."

Belinda slipped into nurturing mode and motioned for Roxie to let her see her wrist. Knowing there would be no getting out of it, she placed it on the table. Her mother slowly pulled away the gauze. Roxie took a bite of the still-warm bread, savoring the taste. Her mother bent over her wrist, staring intently at it.

"I know it's revolting. I have no idea how I got it."

"Could it have been when you got this tattoo?"

Roxie pushed her mother's hand aside and looked at her wrist. The rash had scabbed over and lifted in large sections. Underneath were black markings. She used one finger and quickly rubbed the area where the rash had been. More of the black markings appeared. Stunned, she held up her hand to her face, turning it to look at it from all angles. Circling her entire wrist, and about an inch in width, was what looked like a Celtic knot. The black design was intricate and really did look as if it were tattooed onto her skin.

Roxie shook her head in denial as she jumped up and ran to the kitchen. She stuck her arm under the running tap, frantically scrubbing at the mark. No matter how much she rubbed, it never faded. And lathering it with dish detergent did nothing at all.

After turning off the water, her mother calmly dried her arm. "Obviously, you didn't get a tattoo."

"No, I didn't. If I ever did get one, I would never get it where it couldn't be hidden. I don't know how this happened."

Taking her by her shoulders, her dad got her to sit at the kitchen table. He sat in the chair next to hers and asked, "You said you met someone."

"Yes. His name is Beowulf Thorsson. I met him at this nightclub called Wulf's Den. He owns it."

"How do you feel about him?"

"I'm a little confused about how I feel for him. He seems like the perfect man, and I'm drawn to him. He makes me feel things no man has ever made me feel."

"But?"

"I don't know if I'm imagining it or not, but sometimes I swear he growls, and a couple of times, his eyes looked as if they glowed."

The look her parents gave each other was one that only they

understood.

"I know it sounds crazy. Maybe I'm losing my mind."

"I'm sure you were mistaken, dear," Belinda reassured her.

"That's all you have to say?"

"Roxie, we know you aren't crazy. Maybe it's just your subconscious playing tricks on you because of the dream you had. Try not to let it upset you."

"You're right. That's the most logical explanation, but what about my wrist? I think I would remember getting a tattoo."

"That's not so easy to explain away. To be honest, I don't know what to tell you."

Roxie looked at the clock on the wall and saw how much time had gone by. For some unknown reason, all she could think about was getting back to Beowulf. She missed him. It was almost a tangible ache inside her. *How could I be missing him by only being away for two hours?*

Knowing she wouldn't get any more answers than the ones she'd already gotten, Roxie kissed her parents. She needed to see Beowulf, but first she had to do something to hide the mark around her wrist from him.

CHAPTER EIGHT

On the way to Beowulf's place, Roxie stopped off at a drugstore to pick up gauze and tape. After making her purchases, she sat in the parking lot and wrapped her wrist. She wanted to keep the tattoo-like markings hidden, especially from Beowulf. She didn't want him asking questions to which she didn't have the answers.

Roxie pulled up to the closed gates, then buzzed the house. Within seconds, they silently swung open. Continuing along the sweeping drive, her body went into intense arousal. Her pulse raced as she thought about being in Beowulf's arms again. Having him kiss and caress her, bringing her to the very edge of release. By the time she reached the front door, her heart raced and her pussy dripped.

Before she could turn the doorknob, the door was thrown open, and she was yanked to a hard chest. Beowulf's lips took hers in a searing kiss. He stepped back with her firmly in his arms, then kicked the door shut and pushed her against it. Roxie moaned as she threaded her fingers through his thick dark hair. Hungry for him, she swept her tongue along the crease of his mouth, then pushed her way in. He sucked her tongue farther inside. He lifted her off her feet and urged her to wrap her legs around his waist. With her back still pressed against the door, he rocked his hips into her, his hard cock meeting her pussy with each stroke.

Wade stepped into the entranceway. He cleared his throat, then growled low. Beowulf's head instantly came up as he growled back. Beowulf released her so she could stand on her feet before he gathered her close, shielding her from his brother.

"Was there something you wanted, Wade?"

"Yes, I wish the two of you would go find a room. Please take pity on the single male and keep such displays behind closed doors, if you don't mind."

Roxie stiffened at the sound of Wade's voice. Beowulf must have known his brother was in the house, and still he'd been unable to restrain himself. If his brother had waited a few minutes more, she was sure Wade would have caught Beowulf with his pants open and hips pumping as he plunged his cock inside her. That would have been a disaster.

"Sorry, Wade. Are you heading out?"

Wade flashed a crooked grin at his brother. "Yes, I think that would be best for all concerned. I'll be at the club."

"Roxie and I'll be there in time to open."

"I can handle it if you get...delayed." Before leaving, Wade kissed the top of Roxie's head. Beowulf snapped his teeth at him. Wade shook his head and chuckled. "You have it bad, bro."

After locking the door behind his brother, Beowulf tilted Roxie's chin so he could look her in the face. "I apologize for that. It would seem I don't have much control around you."

Roxie placed a finger against his lips. "Don't apologize. You weren't the only one with no control."

She soon lost all train of thought. Beowulf opened his mouth and sucked her finger inside. A burning need to have him rose inside her. She couldn't ignore it. After pulling her finger free, she worked on the button and zipper of his jeans. She parted the material before she wrapped her hand around the hard, thick length of him. Squeezing tightly, she worked her grip up and down his cock. He felt like velvet-wrapped steel. With her other, she yanked his head down and kissed him.

Roxie dragged her lips away from his, then put a hand on Beowulf's chest and pushed, making him walk backward. She didn't stop pushing until his heels hit the bottom stair and he sat. "Please tell me we have the house to ourselves."

Roxie continued to stroke him, knowing exactly what kind of effect it had on him. Beowulf nodded. "It's just us."

"Good." Roxie grabbed the bottom of his shirt and pulled it off. "I need you now, and having to wait until we're in bed is not an option." She quickly tore off her clothes.

She slammed her mouth down onto his and frantically pushed at his jeans until they were past his hips. She sat on Beowulf's lap, straddling him. When she shifted her hips, the head of his cock brushed against her opening. Rocking, she let the tip slide in and out of her, coating him with her wetness before taking him all the way inside. The sensation of having him stretch her, filling her with his hard cock, sent waves of pleasure shooting through her body. She held on to his shoulders as she slowly rode him. With each downward stroke, he hit her cervix.

Arching her back to take even more of him put her breasts within easy reach of Beowulf's mouth. He cupped them in both hands and swirled his tongue around each nipple, making them tighten even more. Roxie's breath caught as she pushed against his hands. When his hot mouth closed over a nipple, sucking her, her inner muscles clamped down around his shaft. He moaned, and the sound vibrated against her breast. She squeezed him again, riding him faster, angling her hips so his cock rubbed against her clit with each downward stroke.

Panting, Roxie's climax started as her inner walls spasmed. She pushed Beowulf away from her breast, then leaned forward. Using her teeth, she clamped down on the flesh where his shoulder and neck met—hard. She didn't know how she knew the movement would instantly send him into an intense orgasm, but she just did. As her climax tore through her, his cock pulsed inside her, filling her. He held her head to him as he bucked his hips up into her.

Roxie collapsed onto Beowulf's chest. She tasted the coppery tang of blood on her tongue. Horrified, she lifted her head to look at his neck. She'd bitten him hard enough to draw blood and leave teeth marks.

"I don't know what came over me, Beowulf."

He pulled her head back down and kissed the top of it. "I'm not complaining, my love. You were just making sure everyone would know I'm yours."

When Roxie tried to get up, he held her down. His cock, still hard, was buried deep inside her and he made no move to leave her body.

"I shouldn't have done that. We have to clean that up before you get an infection."

"Relax, Roxie. It's nothing."

"How can you say it's nothing? You're bleeding."

Beowulf held her face between his hands and intently looked at Roxie. "I liked that you bit me." He leaned into her, kissing her passionately before pulling away again. "I want you to do it."

"I'm not going to bite you again."

Ashamed of herself, Roxie pulled away from Beowulf, separating their bodies. Standing, she set about collecting her clothes. He stood on the stairs, watching her. Feeling his gaze on her, she looked up. His cock was wet with her juices and stood out straight from his body. Her pussy ached at the sight of him.

"We need to get ready to go to the club."

"I know." Beowulf held out his hand, then pulled her onto the stair beside him. "I can wait until later. We still have the whole night ahead of us, and I plan to make good use of it. You can have the shower first, and I promise not to join you."

As they started up the stairs, Roxie remembered her suitcase outside in the trunk of her car. "I brought more clothes, but I left them in the car."

"I'll get them while you shower. That way I won't be tempted to break my word about joining you. You'll find fresh towels in the bathroom and anything else you may need."

*

Watching Roxie's bare bottom as she walked up the stairs, Beowulf bit back a groan. She had the perfect body. Her legs were long and shapely. Her hips weren't too narrow and her breasts were more than a handful. Once she was out of sight, he pushed back thoughts of her being naked in the shower, lathering her body with soap. He would need a cold shower to bring his raging body back under control. He touched the bite marks on his neck and smiled. She may not be like him, but she acted like a female who had chosen her mate. The mark was a clear warning to other females that he was a mated male. Maybe when it came time for him to tell Roxie the truth, she would accept him for what he was.

* * * *

For a Monday evening, Wulf's Den seemed to fill up quickly. When Beowulf and Roxie had arrived at the club, there had already been a line waiting to get in. Beowulf was working behind the bar and expected to be there most of the night. Roxie managed not to kill herself in the dreaded high heels. She plunked herself onto one of the barstools. She didn't mind that he would be busy pouring drinks; she was just happy to sit near him and watch him as he worked. She took great pride in thinking the hunk was her boyfriend. The other good thing about sitting there was she could make sure the other women left him alone. He was hers, and they could hit on one of the other hunky men in the club.

Beowulf set a glass of white wine in front of Roxie. "You don't mind that I'm stuck behind the bar, do you?"

"Not at all."

"If you want to dance, let me know, and I'll try to get Wade to cover for me."

Snorting, Roxie shook her head. "No way. I have a hard enough time just walking in these shoes. Trying to dance in them would be way beyond my capabilities."

"Fine. I thought I would ask just in case."

When a waitress came up to the bar and ordered drinks, Roxie turned around to watch the other people in the club. There were quite a few on the dance floor, moving to the music blaring out of the speakers. The fast tempo had some dancers gyrating around the room. She never danced fast, only slow ones that didn't involve complicated steps.

During one of her sweeps of the club, Roxie couldn't help but notice the guy sitting alone at a table not too far from the bar. He was extremely good-looking, like most of the other men present, but there was something vaguely familiar about him. She didn't know why since she was pretty sure they hadn't met before. Still, she couldn't get over the feeling that she knew him. Lost in thought, she didn't realize she stared until he got up and walked toward her.

Quickly turning to face the bar, she looked for Beowulf, but he was no longer there. She remembered him telling her a shipment of wine had come in and that he had to take care of it. She looked down the length of the bar and saw Wade pouring drinks. He wasn't going to be any help. She picked up her glass of wine and took a sip, keeping her eyes down.

Roxie tried to act as if she hadn't noticed when the guy came and sat on the stool next to hers. She hoped if she didn't look at him, he would take the hint and leave her alone. Fate was not on her side tonight.

"You look like you could use some company, sitting here alone at the bar."

"No, I'm fine. I don't mind being alone, though I'm not really. My boyfriend is here."

"I've been watching you, and I haven't seen you with anyone else."

"He's working behind the bar tonight. There was a delivery, but he'll be back shortly."

"Well, then, I'd better ask you to dance before he gets back."

Roxie plastered on a smile and turned to look at him. "Look, I have a boyfriend, and I'm not interested. I'm sure you can find someone else to dance with."

"No. I only want to dance with you."

Before Roxie could protest, he plucked her off the stool and then pulled her away. Not wanting to make a huge scene, she tried to yank her arm free, but he didn't loosen the hold he had on her wrist. Once on the dance floor, he swung her into his arms and moved to the slow song that played. She opened her mouth to blast him, but his words stopped her.

He leaned toward her and spoke into her ear. "Relax. I only want to dance. I couldn't think of any other way to get you away from the bar. I know you're with Beowulf."

Roxie pulled back and looked at him. His hazel eyes held a smile. He was handsome. There was still something about his looks that drew her. The golden-brown hair that fell just past his broad shoulders was familiar, almost as if she'd run her fingers through its length before. She knew his chiseled lips, square jaw, and straight nose. It didn't make any sense.

"Who are you?"

He smiled. "My name is Royce Larrsson."

"Have we met before?"

Royce shook his head. "No, I don't believe so. Why?"

"I feel as if I know you."

"Maybe we met in your dreams." Royce brought his head up and looked across the dance floor. "We've been spotted, and Beowulf is not pleased. I'll leave you for now, but we'll meet again."

Before Roxie could stop Royce and ask him what he meant about meeting in her dreams, Beowulf pulled her into the protection of his arms. "Are you okay? He didn't do anything to upset you, did he?"

"No."

Beowulf held himself stiffly, almost as if he were ready for an attack.

"He only danced with me."

"If you wanted to, you only had to ask me."

"I didn't ask him to dance, if that's what you think. He dragged me out here."

Beowulf searched her face. "You would tell me if he did something to you?"

"Of course I would. What's the big deal? Royce seemed to know you."

"So it was Royce. I haven't seen him in years. I wonder why he decided to come here." Beowulf looked in the direction Royce had gone.

"If you know him, why are you worried he would do something to me?"

"I don't know him as well as I once did. Things happened in the past. Royce usually keeps to himself nowadays."

Roxie let Beowulf lead her to the bar. She couldn't help looking back to where Royce had disappeared.

*

Beowulf made sure he spent the rest of the evening at the bar so he could keep an eye on Roxie. Seeing her dance with Royce had made his hackles rise. He didn't like her being in the arms of another man, but Royce particularly made his protective instincts go into overdrive. Roxie was his mate, and as such, he needed to think of her wellbeing. Being a mortal and unaware of what his people truly were, she could find herself in a precarious position. Single males sometimes tried to take other males' mates from them, and it was usually the female who put the aggressor in his place. Roxie wouldn't have a clue how to do that.

Lost in his thoughts, he didn't at first hear Roxie talking to him. "Sorry. What did you say?"

"I asked when we were leaving."

"In another hour or so. I have to stay to close up. Is that okay with you?"

Roxie nodded. "No problem. Would you mind if I sit in your office for a while? No offense, but this whole club thing is not my cup of tea."

Beowulf flashed a smile. "I can tell."

"That obvious, is it?"

"Just a little. Let me grab you a bottle of wine; then I'll take you up. The computer in the office has Internet. I'm sure you can find something to do on it to help pass the time."

"Wine and Internet. Sure to make me putty in your hands."

Beowulf walked around to the other side of the bar with a wine bottle and glass in hand, then brushed his lips against hers. "And here I thought it was what I do to you in bed that made you putty in my hands."

"Oh, you do that and more."

"I'm glad to hear it." Beowulf ran his tongue along the outside of Roxie's ear. She shivered, and he took her earlobe between his teeth and gave it a small tug.

Beowulf helped her off the stool, then led her up to his office. After placing the items he carried on his desk, he pulled out the chair for Roxie. She brushed her bottom against the front of his pants as she moved past him to sit. He bit back a groan. Seeing the heated look she sent his way, he shook his head.

"You're too tempting by far, Roxie, but I really do have work to do."

"Are you sure?"

"Positive. Let me put it this way — the longer I stay up here, the longer it will be before we can leave. Think about how much time we'll be missing out on tonight. In bed."

Roxie stood and pushed Beowulf out the door. "Don't let me hold you up, then. I'll be fine here."

* * * *

Wade met Beowulf at the bar when he returned downstairs. "If you and Roxie want to leave, you can. I don't mind closing on my own."

Beowulf shook his head. "No, not tonight. I prefer to be here."

"Because of the guy Roxie was dancing with? I know he's one of us, but I don't recall ever seeing him here before."

"Yes, he is. His name is Royce, and he has never come to the club until tonight. He left the pack a long time ago."

Wade whistled. "A lone wolf. I can see why you were concerned about Roxie being near him. Do you think he'll end up being a threat?"

"I hope the hell not. We were friends at one time."

"What caused him to leave?"

"It's a long story, one I don't want to get into right now. Suffice it to say, Royce made a choice to take a different route in life. Not everyone agreed with his decision."

"Must have been pretty drastic to make him go lone wolf."

"You could say that, but he never really did say exactly why he left. I have to wonder why he's back now, though."

"I'll keep my eye out for him. I only saw him with Roxie that one time, and I haven't seen him since. Maybe he won't be back."

Beowulf spent the remainder of the evening watching for Royce, but it turned out Wade was correct in his assumption. Royce didn't make another appearance and he wasn't in the crowd that filed out at closing time.

Beowulf pushed thoughts of Royce aside and went up to his office. He opened the door, then gazed at his desk. Roxie was no longer there. He started to panic, thinking something had happened to her until he walked farther into the room and found her asleep on the couch. He cursed himself for overreacting as he knelt beside her and gently shook her. She slowly opened her eyes and looked sleepily up at him.

"Sorry. I couldn't keep my eyes open anymore. I think drinking that whole bottle of wine was a bit too much for me. I don't usually drink that much."

"Well, then I'd better get you home and tuck you into bed." Beowulf scooped Roxie up into his arms and then started downstairs.

"I can walk, you know. I didn't have that much to drink. People are going to start thinking I'm an invalid or something."

"You're fine just where you are."

Roxie rested her head against his shoulder. Beowulf smiled when she relaxed against him. He hadn't been thinking about how much she'd had to drink before taking her up to the office. Alcohol didn't affect him as it did mortals. He had to drink more than one bottle of wine to even feel its effects. Gently, he placed Roxie into the car. Sliding into the driver's seat, he saw she'd fallen back to sleep. He shook his head. So much for how he'd wanted to spend the night.

CHAPTER NINE

Running, she raced past the tree line and into the open meadow. She looked behind her and laughed. He always gave her a head start, but she could see he was catching up. She lifted her skirts higher and tried for another burst of speed. He soon ran beside her, easily keeping pace. His wolf's body was made for running. It was times like this that she wished she could be like him.

Gradually, she slowed to a walk. She reached down and threaded her fingers through his soft golden-brown fur. Hazel eyes stared back at her. She could read the love he felt for her in them. He leaned against her leg, pushing her in the direction of the small creek.

She took a seat on the large boulder next to the water's edge as he stuck his muzzle into the water and took a drink. Once he was finished, he threw back his head and howled, letting the others know where he was and to stay away. A shimmering light engulfed him as he made the change.

He stood with his back to her. She skimmed her gaze over his wide shoulders and muscled back. His long hair, the same color as the wolf's fur, fell just past the tops of his shoulders. She moved lower. She couldn't help but look at his hard, muscled bottom.

Without turning around he asked, "Are you staring at my buttocks again?"

"I can't help myself. You do make a fine figure of a man standing there naked."

"Maybe I should give you something more interesting to look at."

He turned and smiled. He held his arms open wide, and she walked into his embrace.

* * * *

Roxie came awake with a gasp. In the first dream, she really hadn't seen the face of her wolf lover, but the one she'd just had was more vivid, more real. She could almost smell the wildflowers growing in the meadow and hear the burbling sound of the slow-moving water in the creek. It was seeing the face of the man that had brought her awake. When he'd turned, she'd found herself looking at Royce. It disturbed her that he walked in her dreams.

She looked at the clock and saw it was still early in the morning. She rolled to her side, then snuggled against Beowulf's back. She could tell from the even rise and fall of his chest that he still slept. She closed her eyes, trying to go back to sleep. They popped open when she remembered what Royce had said before leaving her on the dance floor. He'd said they would meet again. Not if she could help it. Somehow, she would have to convince Beowulf to go to the club without her tonight. She didn't want to take the chance of Royce showing up.

* * * *

Roxie slowly awoke to the feel of Beowulf nuzzling her neck. Sensing she was awake, he lifted his head and smiled. "Good morning, sleepyhead."

Stretching, she felt the hard length of his cock pressed against her side. "I see all of you is awake."

Beowulf bent his head and ran his tongue between her breasts. "Very much awake. And since you fell asleep last night, we didn't get to enjoy what was left of it."

"I'm sorry. I promise to make it up to you." She reached down, took him in her hand, and squeezed.

"Well then, you can start making it up to me now." He slid out of her grip before he got off the bed and pulled her with him. "First, let's take a shower."

Roxie followed Beowulf into the adjoining bathroom. She loved his shower. It was large enough that the two of them could fit into it with room to spare. The walls and floor were tiled in slate, and it was enclosed with a clear glass surround.

She shut the shower door behind her, watching Beowulf turn the brass knobs of the faucet. Warm water fell from the large showerhead in the center of the ceiling and sprayed from the smaller heads set into the one wall. She tipped back her head and soaked her hair.

Having adjusted the water to his liking, Beowulf came to stand in front of her. He held a bar of soap. He rubbed it between his hands until he built up enough lather, then passed it to her.

"I want you to wash me." He ran his soapy hands across her breasts.

She loved the way he touched her, just as much as she loved touching his hard body. After quickly making lather, she ran her hands down his chest. Once she finished washing that part of him, she moved around to his back. She relished the feel of his wet skin beneath her palms. She rubbed and stroked her way down to his hard ass. She cupped each mound of flesh and gave them a squeeze before moving downward to his muscular legs.

Finished with the back of him, Roxie moved around to Beowulf's front. His eyes were heavy with desire. She soaped up her hands again as she looked down at him. He was fully erect, his cock standing straight out from his body. Taking hold of him, she ran her soapy hand up and down his full length. He pumped his hips in time with her movements and moaned.

He allowed her to play with him for a few minutes before he pulled her hand away. "My turn now."

He took the soap from her and ran it down her chest, circling each breast. Her nipples pebbled, begging for his touch. With a thumb and forefinger, he plucked at them until she arched into him. He pulled her back into the stream of water, then rinsed away the soap before he bent his head and sucked one of her nipples deep inside his mouth. Roxie groaned as waves of pleasure shot down from her breast to her pussy. She clutched Beowulf's shoulders as he moved to the other tight peak. He backed her against the glass surround before he licked his way down to her bellybutton. His tongue swirled inside before he continued lower. He knelt at her feet, gently pushing her thighs apart.

"I want the smell of you all over me, Roxie. But I like the taste of you even more."

He spread her nether lips with his fingers and licked her pussy with the tip of his tongue. Roxie took her lower lip between her teeth and closed her eyes at the feel of his hot tongue on her. He licked at her opening, lapping up the wetness. At her clit, he licked, then sucked on the small nubbin of flesh. She went on her toes as he pushed first one finger, then a second deep inside her. She squeezed her inner walls around his fingers and rocked her hips.

Having to know she was close to shattering, Beowulf came to his feet. He lifted her to him, took his cock in one hand, and slowly pushed it into her hot channel. Roxie wrapped her legs around his waist. Thrusting her hips, she matched his strokes. She loved the feel of him deep inside her. Sex had never been this good. She had a feeling he'd spoiled her for other men. No other would ever take his place.

Her climax building ever higher, Roxie clamped her inner muscles around Beowulf's shaft. He groaned in response, pushing her closer to her release. He reached between their joined bodies and rubbed her clit. She moaned as her release slammed into her. He increased his pace, holding her still as he pumped his hips. He threw back his head and groaned as he climaxed inside her.

Once their hearts had slowed to a steadier beat, Beowulf pulled out of her and let her down onto her none-too-steady feet. He was still hard. She smiled. He was ruining her. At this rate, she would expect every man she slept with to be able to keep an erection after climaxing.

"I see I'll have my work cut out for me in making it up to you."

Beowulf reached over to the taps and shut off the water. "I'm sure you won't find it a chore. Now that we've had our shower, I want you again. This time in the bed."

Beowulf picked Roxie up, then carried her to bed. He didn't

seem to care that their still-wet hair soaked the bedsheets, so neither did she. They spent the rest of the morning exploring each other's bodies, finding what spots increased their pleasure when touched or stroked. By noon she was sated and in need of a nap. Curled up against his side, she drifted off into a dreamless sleep.

* * * *

"What do you mean you don't want to go to the club tonight?"

Roxie had been holding back all day, unsure how Beowulf would react to her decision to stay home. She finally broached the subject during supper, knowing Wade would be joining them. She was taking the chicken way out, but she had her reasons. She hoped Wade would back her up if Beowulf decided to push.

"Look, it's not that I don't like spending time with you at the club, because I do. It's just I have work to do. I'm falling behind."

"You have your laptop. Why not bring it to the club with you? You can work in my office."

"That's the other thing. The laptop is all right for doing some of the work, but what I really need is my desktop at my place. So I figured while you were at the club tonight, I would go home and work." Roxie could almost see the wheels turning in Beowulf's mind as he thought of another reason for her to go with him. She continued before he could say anything more. "And don't even suggest that I move my desktop to your house. No offense, but I'm not quite ready to talk about moving in with you."

Seeming to take pity on his brother, Wade interrupted. "You know, Beowulf, things have been pretty quiet since the other night. I don't think you have to worry about anything coming from that direction. And the other doesn't know where Roxie lives."

Even though she really didn't know exactly what Wade alluded to, Roxie still wanted to hug him for taking her side. "See. Even Wade thinks I should go home. I don't know why this is such a big issue with you, but I'll make you a deal. I'll go home, and you come and stay over at my place tonight. I feel as if I've mooched enough off you. In the morning I'll make you a big breakfast."

"Okay, you win. I'll take you up on your offer of breakfast, but

I get to follow you to your place; then I'll go on to the club."

"Beowulf, I'm perfectly able to get home by myself."

Beowulf gave Roxie a hard stare. "Take it or leave it. The choice is yours."

Roxie threw up her hands. "Fine. You can follow me home. I still think it's a waste of time."

"It's always better to be safe than sorry. You never know what could be lurking about in the dark."

* * * *

Beowulf not only followed her home but had to come inside the house to make sure all the windows and doors were still locked. Before he left, he pulled her into his arms and kissed her until her knees gave out. He also made her promise not to open the door to anyone but him.

She turned on her computer, then settled in for a night of work. She really was behind. Unlike Beowulf, who didn't need to worry about money, she needed all her clients to keep her business going. She had a reputation for doing quality work and for always finishing a project on time. She wasn't about to start backsliding. It'd taken her over two years to get where she was now.

The doorbell rang. Roxie looked at the clock on the bottom of her computer screen and saw only a half hour had passed since Beowulf had left. Thinking it had to be him wanting to check up on her, she opened the door, prepared to tell him to go back to the club. Much to her surprise, it wasn't Beowulf standing at her door. It was Royce.

Roxie tried to act as if his dropping by her house was a normal occurrence and smiled. "Royce, what brings you by?"

"I told you we would meet again."

"Yes, you did. How did you find out where I live?"

Royce flashed her brilliant smile. "I have my ways. May I come in? I just want to talk. About Beowulf."

Roxie was nuts for doing it, but she opened the door wider and stepped aside so Royce could come in. There was something about the man, something she found familiar, comforting, as if he would never do anything to hurt her and would defend her at all costs. And then there was the dream she'd had of him. She shook her head over her foolish thoughts as she closed the door and followed him into the living room.

Taking a seat on the couch, Roxie asked, "What about Beowulf?"

Royce sat next to Roxie, then stared at her, his gaze roaming her face. When she cleared her throat to get his attention, he shook his head. "Sorry. You look very much like a woman I once knew."

Roxie didn't miss the sadness in Royce's voice. "What happened to her?"

"She died many years ago. I still miss her."

"You must have loved her very much."

"I did. I still do, but I didn't come here to talk about her. I'm sure Beowulf told you we were indeed friends at one time."

"Yes, and that it'd been years since you'd seen each other. He was surprised you were at the club last night."

Royce laughed. "I bet he was more than surprised. After my ma...my wife died, I pushed everyone away. Her death hit me hard, and I didn't feel comfortable being around people, especially my friends. So I packed up my things and moved away. In doing so, I left Beowulf in a tricky situation."

When Royce didn't explain what that situation was, she had the feeling that would be all he was going to say about it. "Just to set the record straight here, I've only known Beowulf for all of four days. I'm not sure I'm the best person you should be talking to about this."

"Maybe not, but you're the closest person to him now. I would like to resume our friendship. He acts differently around you. Maybe you could put in a good word for me."

Roxie bit her lip. "I don't think that's such a good idea right now. Having me pass messages to him from you would more than likely upset him, to say the least. He's a tad protective of me. I mentioned seeing a wolf in my backyard a couple days ago and he rushed over here as if it were a life-or-death situation. He wouldn't even let me stay in the house alone."

Roxie jumped as Royce shot to his feet and headed to the back of the house. Going to the kitchen, he peered out the window, searching her backyard. Obviously finding nothing, he checked to make sure all the windows were securely locked. She followed him as he finished with the lower level and started up the stairs.

"Have all the men I know gone crazy or something? First Beowulf, now you. Don't you think you're overreacting just a little here? What harm could a wild wolf do to my house? It's not as if he could break in or anything."

"You never know."

When Royce brushed past her and headed for her bedroom, Roxie grabbed hold of his arm to stop him. "Oh no, you don't. That's my bedroom." He ignored her as he pulled her behind him. Slapping his arm didn't even cause him to flinch. Once inside the room, she let go before he checked the lock on her window. "Am I allowed no privacy?"

Having finished what he'd wanted to do, Royce went to stand in front of her. "Everything seems to be secure. Promise me you'll do what Beowulf says. I have to leave now. I have to go do some hunting, it would seem. I still want to finish our conversation, but it'll have to be another time."

Royce moved quickly, brushing his lips across Roxie's before she could voice her protest. He turned on his heel, then walked out of the room. Finally coming to her senses, she ran down the stairs only to find him no longer there. She opened the front door but couldn't see him anywhere. The man could really move when he wanted to. After closing and then locking the door, she headed to her office. Before she sat in front of her computer, she decided it would make things easier not to tell Beowulf about Royce's visit. Some things were better left unsaid.

*

In wolf form, Royce put his nose to the ground, trying to pick up the scent of the other wolf that had been in Roxie's backyard. He'd managed to do the change just as Roxie had opened her front door. He kept to the shadows, his dark fur helping to hide his presence from her. It'd been easy enough to slip into her backyard once she'd gone back inside. He needed to know whether it'd been merely a wolf or a werewolf.

After a few minutes of snuffling around, he managed to pick up the scent. Even though it was days old, he recognized it. He curled his lip at the smell. Beowulf had done right, whisking Roxie away. It'd been another werewolf, and one who would love to strike against Beowulf using any means possible.

Royce hid deeper inside the shadows, having decided to stay and stand guard. He wouldn't let anything happen to Roxie. Now that he'd spent more time with her, he couldn't help but see all the similarities. He didn't want to get his hopes up. For now, he was content to sit back and watch.

Two uneventful hours passed. About ready to leave and go in hunt of the other werewolf, Royce saw a light switch on inside the house. Roxie walked into the kitchen. She opened a cupboard and took out two wineglasses. Out of the corner of his eye, Royce watched Beowulf enter the room. He came up behind Roxie and wrapped his arms around her waist. She leaned back into Beowulf's embrace and laid her head against his chest. Beowulf took the glasses from her, then placed them on the counter. He turned Roxie's head toward him and lowered his lips to hers. Royce looked away as the kiss became more passionate.

Heading to the side of the house, Royce changed into a man, willing clothes onto his body after the change. He walked to where he'd parked his car a few houses away from Roxie's, trying to swallow past the ache in his throat. Seeing Roxie and Beowulf together had brought up too many memories of times spent with his mate. There was some happiness that Beowulf had at last found his mate, but in a way, Royce couldn't help but feel his friend had taken something that belonged to him.

* * * *

After three nights of work, Roxie felt caught up enough on work to feel she was back on schedule. Unlike the first night, Beowulf picked her up after closing Wulf's Den and took her to his place. She didn't bother arguing with him about it. She had to admit his house was a lot nicer than hers, and she was starting to become attached to it, as well as its owner.

She and Beowulf were closer than ever. To be near him, to touch him, was something she found unable to fight. Being separated from him for a few hours seemed too much for her at times. She knew it was crazy, but it didn't make the urge any less powerful. It also seemed to affect Beowulf. Every night after work, he would sweep her up into his arms and kiss her like a man dying of thirst. He couldn't get enough of her. Not that she was complaining.

Knowing she would have to go to the club that night, Roxie called Candice and suggested they do some shopping. She desperately needed new clothes. Candice, of course, jumped at the chance to go. Beowulf had tried to give Roxie money, saying it was because of him she needed to buy the clothes in the first place, but she adamantly refused.

She did, however, approve of Beowulf's idea that the three of them should meet up at the club before it opened and have supper there. Candice was more than happy to join them. Roxie was glad her friend had also agreed to stay with her while Beowulf worked behind the bar. She hoped that as long as she wasn't alone, Royce wouldn't approach her if he came to the club.

They'd just finished eating when the bouncer arrived. He glanced to where they sat and nodded in Beowulf's direction as he headed for the kitchen. When his gaze happened to land on Candice, he did a quick about-face and came to the table. Roxie caught sight of Beowulf's smile before he lifted his napkin to wipe his mouth. She cocked a brow in his direction, but he shook his head.

"What's up, Carl?" Beowulf stood to greet the large man.

"Not much, boss. Just thought I would come over and introduce myself to the ladies."

Carl kept his gaze glued onto Candice. Now she understood Beowulf's smile. Carl was just another victim of Candice's good looks. She peered at her friend and was surprised to find Candice equally returning the bouncer's stare.

Hoping to draw some of his attention away from Candice, Roxie stuck out her hand for Carl to shake. "Nice to meet you, Carl. I'm Roxie, and this is my friend, Candice."

Carl shook her hand but only spared her a glance before focusing all his attention back onto Candice. Roxie gave up trying after that and let them talk to each other without her interference. The conversation was soon cut short, though, when Beowulf motioned to Carl and asked him to help get the club ready for the night.

When they were alone, Roxie turned to Candice and put her hand on her friend's forehead. "Are you sick? It doesn't feel as if you have a fever."

Candice pushed her hand away. "Of course I'm not sick. Why would I be?"

"Let's see. Maybe because you were actually nice to a guy who seems to be half decent."

"I'm not that shallow when it comes to men, Rox."

Roxie snorted. "I beg to differ. You are that shallow. Let's face it. Carl isn't exactly the type of guy you usually hunt down."

"Well, maybe I'm ready for a change. I'll admit I've been with too many losers lately. Now that I've seen you with Beowulf, I would like to find someone who'll stick around for the long haul. I'm not getting any younger, you know."

"Shall I get your cane, Grandma? Give me a break, Candy. It's nice to hear you want more than a boy toy in your life, but Carl?"

"What's wrong with him? He's just as good-looking as any of the other guys who work here."

"Yes, he's good-looking, I agree with you on that, but did you look at the size of that man? You barely come up to his chest, standing on your tiptoes, that is. He has to be at least Beowulf's height. The man is just plain scary-looking with all those muscles and his bald head. I'm sure he could pick you up in one arm and carry you around as he would a doll."

Candice winked and smiled. "He can carry me wherever he wants. I wouldn't mind that at all, especially if it meant I got to fondle every inch of him."

Roxie laughed and shook her head. "You're incorrigible, you know that? Just remember you agreed to keep me company tonight. So no sneaking off too many times to visit Carl outside while he mans the doors."

"I promise. There's always time after the club closes for me to get to know Carl better. I'll only go out once or twice to make sure he's still on my hook."

"So in other words, you're going to tease the poor man."

Candice blew on her fingernails, then rubbed them on her shirt. "I do have my ways."

"Well, the opportunity to work your wiles on Carl has arrived. He's coming this way. Promise not to go too hard on the guy."

"I promise. Now scat. Three's a crowd and all that."

Thinking Candice would never change, Roxie headed over to

the bar. Her friend would join her as soon as she'd had a chance to set her hooks into Carl. The poor man wouldn't know what hit him.

CHAPTER TEN

Roxie spent the rest of the evening catching up with Candice. They decided not to sit at the bar, but instead sat at a table nearer the dance floor and not too far away from where Beowulf worked.

"So, when are you going to take Beowulf to meet your parents?"

Roxie yanked her gaze to Candice after looking toward the bar. Just as the first night she'd come to Wulf's Den, Beowulf watched her as if he wanted to devour her. And he damn well knew what he was doing to her from the cocky grin he wore.

"Soon. They know about him. I'm not sure if Beowulf's ready for the meet-the-parents kind of thing yet. It's been barely a week since I started seeing him. I don't want to get too pushy and scare him away."

"You really are starting to have strong feelings for him, aren't you?"

Roxie nodded. "You could say that. I've never felt this way about another guy before. I can't stop thinking about him. Even being away from him for a few hours seems too long. I sound like a nutcase."

Candice patted her hand. "No, you don't. You sound like a woman who is falling in love, and falling hard." Seeming to take note of the gauze still wrapped around Roxie's wrist, she asked,

"What's up with the rash, Rox? You shouldn't still have it. Have you seen a doctor about it?"

Roxie placed her hands on her lap and gave Candice a pained expression. "It's nothing. The rash is almost gone. I just don't want people staring at it." She made a mental note to find something besides the gauze to hide the markings circling her wrist.

"No need to get touchy about it. I just asked. Now if you'll excuse me, I have to check on Carl and make sure he still wants to meet up after closing."

Roxie waved Candice off and watched her walk to the club entrance. Before stepping outside, Candice pulled the neckline of her top down a fraction lower than it had been. Roxie shook her head. Carl was as good as caught.

Hoping to distract herself until Candice returned, Roxie turned to look at the bar. Beowulf blew her a kiss before he walked out from behind it and headed in the direction of his office. She seriously considered following him up there but thought better of it. Candice would think she'd run out on her again. Deciding to behave herself, she turned to watch the people on the dance floor.

Thinking Candice had returned when the chair next to hers scraped across the floor, Roxie opened her mouth to ask how things had gone with Carl. She quickly shut it again as a man slipped into the vacant chair beside her.

"I see you need another drink. Shall I order you one?"

"That's nice to offer, but no, I'm fine."

"Come now. What better way to get to know someone than to have a drink with them? I want us to be very close, Roxie."

A chill ran down Roxie's spine. There was something about this man that made her shudder. He was good-looking, but there was a cruelness to his eyes. That he knew he frightened her. Desperately, she looked for either Beowulf or his brother, but neither of them were in sight. She pushed back her chair, then tried to stand. The stranger wrapped his hand around her right wrist and roughly pulled her back down. He leaned forward as he painfully squeezed.

"Oh no. You aren't getting away that easily. I'm not done with you yet. I haven't had my chance to play, and you owe me for the other night."

"I don't understand. I don't know who you are. You must have me mistaken with someone else."

His laugh was anything but pleasant. "It would seem Beowulf has been keeping secrets from you. Maybe I should do him a favor and tell you what he's been hiding."

"And maybe you should remove your paw from the lady before I rip your arm off, Gren."

Roxie had never been happier to see Royce than she was then. He grabbed Gren by the shoulder and hauled him away from her. He held the man in front of him and gave him a hard shake. Fury was written all over his face. His lip curled back in a snarl, and he made a grumbling sound in the back of his throat.

Gren shoved him away. "Watch yourself, lone wolf. It's obvious you've been by yourself for far too long. You forget your place."

"As you seem to have forgotten yours. You know what Beowulf will do to you when he finds out you've touched what belongs to him."

"Then he shouldn't have allowed his mate to sit alone. He may have part of his pack working here, but it doesn't mean others outside it won't try to take what's his."

Mate? What did he mean by that, Roxie wondered.

"It seems to me you're the only one trying to do that."

Gren laughed. "That's interesting. Isn't that why you're here? Why else would you stand up for Beowulf's mate if you didn't intend to steal her from him?"

Royce growled before he grabbed Gren by the front of his shirt and hurled him into the table behind him. Roxie had a hard time believing what she was seeing. Royce had picked Gren up and thrown him as if he weighed no more than a rag doll. She slowly backed away when he growled once more.

He turned to look at her. Roxie stifled a gasp as she looked into his eyes. They were glowing. This time she couldn't trick herself into believing what she saw wasn't real, as she'd been able to do with Beowulf. Royce did nothing to hide it from her but gave her the full force of his stare.

Realizing how quiet the club had become, Roxie noted the crowd gathering around them. If she wasn't mistaken, a few of the men had glowing eyes as well. She wondered what she'd gotten herself into. Out of the corner of her eye, she saw Gren launch himself at Royce. Caught off guard, Royce went down hard as the other man hit him in the back.

Slowly backing away, Roxie watched as the two men swung at each other. The animalistic sounds of growling and snarling were unmistakable. Backing up even farther, she couldn't help the scream that slipped past her lips as she came up against a hard body. Reacting without seeing who stood behind her, she struck with her elbow, hoping to get away. Two arms wrapped around her, hindering her movement.

"Stop it, Roxie. It's okay." Beowulf's voice sounded in her ear.

She waited until Beowulf had relaxed his hold before she pushed him away. When he moved to pull her to him again, she held up her arms as she walked out of reach. "Stay away from me."

Beowulf's features grew grim as he looked between her and the two men still locked in combat. Moving faster then she expected, he grabbed her by the arm and pulled her away from the crowd. She tried to wrench out of his grasp, but he only squeezed harder as he forced her up the stairs to his office. After throwing open the door, he shoved her inside. Roxie stepped away as he closed and then locked it.

*

Beowulf blew out a breath. He had to have been an idiot to think bringing Roxie to the club would keep her safe. He'd realized his mistake the moment he'd seen her standing alone as Royce and Gren pounded on each other. He'd thought everything would be fine tonight, that she would have an enjoyable evening with Candice. She was close enough he could keep an eye on her while allowing her to be alone with her friend. He'd only intended to be up in the office for a few minutes while he looked for an invoice. She had been fine. How could he have known Gren and Royce would decide to make an appearance at that exact moment, let alone zero in on Roxie?

"What did they say to you, Roxie?"

She jumped at the sound of his voice. "I don't want to talk about it."

He bit back a growl, seeing the fear in her eyes. "We have to. I have to make you understand."

Roxie wrapped her arms across her chest as she stared warily at him. "Make me understand what? That you're a freak of nature? I almost had myself convinced I imagined your eyes glowing, and that the sounds you made were not as animal-like as I'd first thought, but not anymore. Not after seeing what I saw."

"I've wanted to explain it to you. I held back because I was afraid of your reaction. This isn't something most people are willing to accept."

"You think?" Roxie asked sarcastically. "Just what the hell are you, Beowulf? And why did Gren and Royce call me your mate?"

The anger in her voice built as she questioned him. Anger was good, better than fear. He decided to answer her second question before tackling the first. "It's true. You are my mate."

"Like bloody hell I am. I don't remember you ever asking me to marry you, if that's what they meant by me being your mate."

"We are mates. You can't deny what you feel, that you need to be near me, that you can't stop thinking about me. Being away from me, not able to touch me, makes you feel very uncomfortable. We're connected, you and I. It's the way of my kind. We don't marry like yours does."

Roxie pinned him with a hard stare. "What do you mean by your kind? You sound like you aren't totally human."

"I'm not, Roxie."

"Then what exactly are you?"

"I'm a werewolf."

She laughed. When her humorless laugh sounded this side of hysterical, Beowulf moved to console her, but she lurched away. "Don't touch me. If you're a werewolf, then prove it. Change. Or can you only do it by the light of a full moon?"

Beowulf fisted his hands at his sides to stop himself for reaching out to Roxie again. The fear grew in her eyes once more. "It doesn't work that way. I can change whenever I wish."

"Then change. Now."

"I don't think that would be wise. Give it some time to sink in."

"Change!" Roxie bellowed.

Beowulf went to the middle of the room as he willed the change upon himself. He knew what she would see. His eyes would glow, then gradually his body would shimmer, blurring as it took on his wolf form. Being able to shape-shift was more of a magical gift than a physical ability. Unlike most movie werewolves, he didn't need to be naked to change, and his body didn't go through it in easy-to-see stages. One minute he would be a man, and the next a wolf. And there was no pain involved either.

Once the change was complete, he waited to see how Roxie would react. Her eyes widened as she must have recognized him as the black wolf she'd encountered before. He looked into her face and silently willed her to accept this part of him. He could no more cope with being separated from her than she would be able to while separated from him.

"It was you. You were the black wolf in the alley. Who was the other?" Roxie fell silent, appearing to think; then she answered her own question. "I know who it was. It was Gren. Now I understand what he meant when he said I owed him one."

Thinking she was more open to his being a werewolf, Beowulf padded over to Roxie and pushed against her leg. She jumped away almost as if he'd tried to attack her. He was about to change back but stopped when she sank her hand into the fur running along his back.

"I can't do this right now, Beowulf. Sorry. It's too much. I need to be alone to think. I'm taking your keys so I can collect my things at your house; then I'm going home. If you follow me there, I'll phone the police and tell them you're stalking me. And please, stay as a wolf at least until I've had enough time to get back to my place."

Beowulf felt a tingling under his skin where Roxie held on to him. It wasn't painful, but he found the sensation odd, especially when it radiated from his back to the rest of his body. At the sound of her pulling open his desk drawer to take his house keys, he decided enough was enough. He wasn't going to allow her to leave him. Not like this. He willed himself to change. Nothing happened. He tried again and again. Still he remained as a wolf. For the first time in his long life, his shape-shifting ability failed him.

Unable to change, he couldn't say the words he wanted to say to Roxie. Silently he watched her walk to the door and unlock it.

He quietly whimpered as she pulled it open. She gave him one last look before she closed it, trapping him inside. Hoping to draw attention to his plight, Beowulf clawed at it. His large paws gouged marks into the wood. It soon became obvious no one could hear the racket he made. Defeated, he went and sat in the center of the room. Sooner or later Wade would come looking for him. Hopefully, it would be sooner.

*

Roxie fought back tears that threatened to fall. She didn't know what was wrong with her. She should be running screaming from the club, afraid of what Beowulf had revealed to her, but it wasn't fear she felt. She was more afraid of her easy acceptance of it all. Seeing him change, it'd been exactly like when Royce had done it in her dreams. And because of the dream, she was a bit shell-shocked seeing Beowulf as a wolf.

Lost in thought, Roxie walked out of the club and headed for the curb, hoping to hail a taxi. It wasn't until Candice had called her name three times that she forced herself back to reality. She turned to face the club and waited for Candice to meet up with her on the sidewalk. Carl hung back, keeping his gaze on them as they spoke.

"What's the rush, Roxie?" Candice stared at her with a concerned look. "Something's wrong. What happened?" When Roxie just shook her head, Candice gave her a little shake. "Snap out of it, Rox. I can tell you're upset about something. Maybe I can help."

Carl came to stand beside Candice. "What's up?"

Candice shook her head. "I don't know. She won't tell me. Come on, Roxie. You don't have to tell me everything. Just tell me what has you so upset."

Knowing there would be no escaping Candice until she at least gave her something, Roxie took a deep breath, hoping to calm herself down. "There was a fight. Inside the club. I can't stay in there anymore."

Carl gently pushed Candice aside as he took hold of Roxie's ice-cold hands. She flinched, but when he refused to let go, she looked to find him staring at her. "Who was the fight between?"

"Royce and Gren."

Carl swore, then quickly dropped her hands before he took off running inside the club. Seeing an empty taxi across the street, Roxie raised her hand to draw the driver's attention. Candice followed her as she walked to the waiting cab.

"Go back to the club, Candice. I'll be fine. I just need to be alone for a while. You have plans with Carl. Don't disappoint him."

Candice held on to the taxi's door before Roxie could shut it. "I'll do what you say, only because I have the feeling that if I don't let you go, it would just upset you more. Promise me one thing. You'll tell me what's going on. I mean it."

"I promise. It may take a few days, but I promise." Roxie pulled the door closed, then gave the taxi driver the address to her house.

* * * *

Beowulf threw himself at the door. Roxie had been gone five minutes, and he'd had enough of sitting doing nothing. He backed up, then took another run. This time he heard a satisfying *crack* as the frame started to give way. He was just about to take a third try at it when his brother pushed it open. Seeing Beowulf in wolf form brought him up short.

"What are you doing going wolf now? And where's Roxie?" Beowulf shook his head. "This is no time to be stubborn. Royce and Gren made a hell of a mess. I had to do a lot of sweet-talking to get the mortals watching the fight to believe it was just a show. That was a chore and a half, considering more than one member of our pack almost went wolf. So could you hurry up and change."

Once again Beowulf shook his head. It was frustrating not being able to tell his brother that something was wrong, that he couldn't shift to human form. All he could think was the longer he stayed wolf, the more time Roxie had to get away. He wanted to throw back his head and howl in desperation, but it would only draw unwanted attention his way.

Carl burst into the room. Seeing Beowulf, he looked from one brother to the other. "Is everything okay here?"

Wade, finally seeming able to see the frustration in Beowulf's eyes, shook his head. "I don't think so. I think we have a problem. I'm guessing Beowulf can't make the change." Beowulf bobbed his wolf's head up and down, and Wade sucked in a breath. "You can't make the change. That's not possible."

"Maybe not," Carl said, "but if Beowulf can't, then it must be possible. Right now we have bigger fish to fry. Royce and Gren are gone, to where I have no idea. I also saw Roxie outside. She was upset. I think she was leaving as well."

Wade scrubbed his face with his hand. "Can things get any worse? Roxie ended up being in the middle of the fight. From what I was able to find out, Gren accosted her, and Royce tried to drive him off. Things were said. Things Beowulf hadn't managed to explain to her yet." Turning to look at Beowulf, he said, "Real brilliant changing in front of her after she went through all that. No wonder she got the hell out of here. What were you thinking?" Beowulf bared his teeth at him in answer.

Always the practical one, Carl went to stand between the two of them. "This really isn't helping. It's almost closing time, so I don't think it'll be too hard to kick everyone out a little early. Once all the mortals are gone, we can sneak Beowulf out to the car and you, Wade, can drive him home. Hopefully, his not being able to change is temporary, because I don't have a clue what can be done to fix it." Once Wade left the room, Carl looked down at Beowulf. "Don't worry, boss. We'll figure something out." The big man left as well.

Alone again, Beowulf hunkered down to wait for Wade to get him once the club was empty. He *was* going to change back. Being stuck as a wolf was not an option. He had a runaway mate to chase down, and being unable to make the change was not part of the solution.

CHAPTER ELEVEN

Royce took a deep breath before he buzzed up to Beowulf's house. He hadn't wanted to come there, but considering what had happened the night before, he felt it was the least he could do. He needed to see how affected Roxie was by the things he and Gren had said. Mostly, he wanted to prove to himself that his intentions toward her were not what Gren had accused him of doing. He'd spent the remainder of the night searching inside himself, asking if he was really capable of trying to steal Roxie away from Beowulf. He'd been disgusted to find how appealing he'd found it.

Royce tamped down his wayward thoughts as he drove up the drive and the gates swung open. He had to get himself back under control before he came face to face with Roxie. If Beowulf sensed anything of what was going through his mind, he would have another fight on his hands. One of the biggest faults of a werewolf male was how territorial they were when it came to their mates. He being a lone wolf would only cause Beowulf to act more violently toward him.

Before he could reach the door, Wade pulled it open. "You have a lot of nerve showing up here after last night."

"I've come to see Roxie and to apologize for my part in what happened."

Wade crossed his arms in front of his chest. "It's a little too late for that, I think. And to be honest, right now, I have a lot more to worry about than you trying to smooth things over with Roxie."

"What do you mean?"

"Follow me."

Wade turned on his heel and headed back inside the house. Royce followed him and shut the door behind him. Wade waited for him just inside the large living room. Royce crossed the distance. He was surprised to find Beowulf in wolf form, glaring at him. Roxie was nowhere to be seen.

"Where's Roxie?"

Wade curled his lip. "Not here, as you can see. She took off last night. I assume she's back at her place. I'm more concerned about Beowulf."

Royce searched Beowulf for injuries, but couldn't see any. "He looks all right to me."

"He may look all right, but he isn't. He can't make the change."

"What?"

"He's stuck in wolf form. The fool decided to show Roxie exactly what he was last night and hasn't been able to change back since."

Royce stiffened. It couldn't be. He'd only known one other individual who could inhibit a werewolf's ability to change, but she was long gone, much to his everlasting sorrow. *Could Roxie have done it?* He couldn't totally discount the possibility. She'd supposedly been the last person to be with Beowulf before he'd gone wolf. If it'd been her... He didn't want to finish that train of thought. He gave himself a mental shake and found Wade watching him intently.

"You know what happened to him. I can see it in your eyes. You know what's wrong with Beowulf."

"Not exactly. If I'm correct in my thinking, you can stop worrying. He should be back to himself by tonight. It usually takes about twenty-four hours to wear off." With Roxie alone at her house, Royce couldn't shake the feeling that he needed to check on her, and the sooner the better. He turned around and headed for the front door.

Wade followed him. "Where are you going? And what do you mean it takes almost twenty-four hours to wear off? What are you talking about?"

Royce looked at him before he stepped through the door. "I can't tell you any more than that. Beowulf will be fine."

After closing the door behind him, Royce rushed to his car. He couldn't get the notion out of his mind that if he didn't get to Roxie soon something terrible was going to happen. He wasn't going to fail her by not being around to protect her. He'd failed once before to protect someone he cared about and had paid the ultimate price. He couldn't live through another such failure.

* * * *

Roxie immersed herself in her work. She didn't want to think about the night before. If she did, she would just drive herself crazy. There were too many things she didn't understand, and she wasn't sure she wanted the answers. She didn't know if what was happening to her—the dreams and the strange markings on her wrist—had anything to do with her supposedly being Beowulf's mate. And she didn't want to go down that road. Being a mate to a werewolf had never been high on her "Things to Accomplish in Life" list.

The only thing she regretted about last night was leaving her things at Beowulf's place. She'd chickened out, not having the nerve to go there in case he showed up before she'd had a chance to leave. The clothes were no big deal. It was her laptop she missed the most, but going over and getting it was not an option now. She wasn't ready to face Beowulf yet. She needed time to sort out her feelings. She felt deeply for him, and the whole werewolf thing wasn't much of a detriment. It just put things on an entirely different level. One she hadn't expected to be facing at this early stage in their relationship.

Her day proved uneventful with no one phoning or coming to the house to see her. When her eyes started to feel gritty from sitting too long in front of a computer screen, she decided to call it quits. She looked out the window and was surprised to see the sun slowly setting below the horizon.

She really didn't feel like eating. Instead, Roxie decided to take a bath. A good long soak in hot-as-she-could-stand water, with bubble bath added, was what she needed more than food. Before going upstairs, she checked to make sure all the windows and doors were locked. It'd become a habit now. After having Beowulf, and then Royce, drum it into her head that she wouldn't be safe otherwise, she didn't want to take any chances.

Slowly climbing the stairs, she walked to the bathroom and then filled the tub. After adding a good amount of her favorite scented bubble bath, she left it to fill and went to her bedroom. Once she stripped out of her clothes, she gathered her long hair up into a bun, securing it with a large clip. The bath was just about ready when she returned to the bathroom. Roxie stepped into it, groaning with pleasure as the warm water settled around her. She turned off the taps, then laid her head on the back of the tub and closed her eyes.

"I think I'll join you in there, if you don't mind."

Roxie's eyes snapped open at the sound of Beowulf's voice. Water sloshed almost out of the bathtub as she quickly sat up. "How did you get in? I know the door was locked." Suddenly realizing Beowulf was pulling off his clothes, fully intending to join her, she shook her head. "Oh no, you don't. This tub isn't big enough for the both of us."

Beowulf ignored her protests as he kicked off his pants and then stepped in with her. Sitting, he positioned Roxie's legs so they were on either side of his hips. The water rose precariously high, threatening to spill over the top.

He ran his hands up and down her thighs. "I missed you too."

Roxie scowled. "Don't try to change the subject. How did you get into my house?"

"With a key."

He was being deliberately obtuse, trying to rile her up. "And where did you get this key?"

"I had it made when you left your keys with me. I had a feeling it would come in handy one day."

Roxie kicked her leg, splashing sudsy water into Beowulf's face. He only smiled as he wiped it away. "You had an extra key cut for my house? How dare you? You had no right to do that."

Beowulf grabbed her ankles and gave her a hard yank until she sat on his lap, facing him. "Calm down. I only did what I thought was necessary to protect my mate."

"I wasn't your mate then, and I'm not too sure if I am now."

"You are my mate, Roxie. I knew it the moment I first smelled your scent. I've waited a very long time for you. You are mine."

"What if I don't want to be your mate? This isn't the dark ages, you know. Women aren't forced into marriages anymore."

"You may find my motives primitive, but they worked then, and I can't see any point in changing what works."

"As if you would know from firsthand experience," Roxie scoffed.

"Actually yes, I do."

She didn't know whether to burst out laughing or smack Beowulf for saying such a ridiculous thing. "Come on. You can't expect me to believe that. Next you'll be telling me you're *the* Beowulf in *Beowulf and Grendel*."

"I am."

"That's not possible." Roxie looked into his eyes and saw he was serious. She shook her head in disbelief. "That's not possible," she said again.

"It is." Beowulf pulled her closer. Roxie pushed at his chest, but he didn't relax his hold.

"How can that be? *Beowulf and Grendel* was written over twelve hundred years ago. It's the oldest Old English tale ever written."

"It was written down that long ago, but it's much older than that. It's more like fourteen hundred years ago when it started being told in mead halls."

Roxie's mouth opened and closed like a fish out of water before she could continue. "That would make you over a thousand years old."

"Yes, well over a thousand, actually. I'd already reached my twentieth year when that tale was written." Roxie opened her mouth to speak, but Beowulf placed a finger across her lips. "I know this is a lot for you to take in, but believe me, it's true. Werewolves live very long lives."

Roxie pulled his finger away from her mouth. "Are you telling me you're immortal?"

"No, we're not exactly immortal, nor are we exactly mortal. We do eventually die, but not for many, many years. The oldest of our kind lives for around three thousand years. Both my parents lived to be well over two thousand."

"So where does that leave us? If I'm your mate—and that is a big if since I'm still not convinced—are you telling me you'll outlive me? I'm mortal and will always be mortal, unless there's a way to turn me into a werewolf as well."

Beowulf shook his head. "You have to be born one. A mortal has never been turned into one of my kind."

"I see. So let's get this straight. You're pretty darn close to being an immortal so you'll live practically forever, whereas I will stay a mortal and will eventually grow old and die, while you'll stay young and probably live for at least another thousand years."

"It sounds a bit morbid the way you've described it, but yes."

Roxie shoved away from Beowulf, then stood and stepped out of the tub. She picked up a fresh towel from the counter before she vigorously dried herself off. "If that's the case, you're way too old for me."

Also stepping out of the water, Beowulf grabbed Roxie's hands, stilling her movements. "It'll be okay." He took the towel from her and dried the rest of her body. Taking her left arm in his hand, he froze as he seemed to stare at her wrist. "When did you get this mark, Roxie?"

Roxie looked down at it, remembering she'd decided not to cover it since she hadn't expected to be seeing anyone that day. Cursing herself, she figured a little white lie was in order. "You mean my tattoo? I got that before we met."

Beowulf cocked a brow at her. "A bit of a coincidence, wouldn't you say, that the rash you claimed to have had is in the very exact spot where you now have a tattoo?"

"I lied, okay. I thought you wouldn't like it, so I decided to cover it up. The whole rash thing helped explain the gauze."

"I think you're still lying. I don't recall seeing a tattoo on your wrist the first night we met."

"Are you telling me you memorized everything about me that night? I find that doubtful. We weren't even together for an hour before we parted company."

Beowulf took hold of Roxie's chin and forced her to look him in the face. His ice-blue eyes glowed mutedly. "I want the truth. When did you get this?"

Unable to look away, she swallowed hard. "After the first night we met. Honestly, it did start out as a rash. It wasn't until after a couple of days had passed that it scabbed over and fell away. Underneath were these Celtic markings. I have no idea how I got this. Is it bad?" Roxie asked quietly.

He turned her wrist over to see the markings on the underside of it, then sucked in a breath. "Keep this hidden, do you understand me? Especially from anyone who you think is a werewolf."

A shiver of fear ran down her spine. "What aren't you telling me?"

"I need to get more information before I start jumping to conclusions. For now, keep it out of sight."

"You're scaring me."

"I don't mean to. Come here."

Without a second thought, Roxie stepped into Beowulf's open arms. She sighed with contentment as he pulled her close. She had been fooling herself, thinking she could live without him in her life. For the first time that day she felt complete. No longer did she feel as if she were walking around with a big, gaping hole in her middle. She lifted her face, then nuzzled her lips against Beowulf's throat. Only with him did she feel whole.

*

The feel of Roxie's lips against his skin sent blood rushing to his cock. He'd pulled her to him to comfort her, but now all he could think about was burying himself inside her sweet body. Being separated from her all day, and not being able to change, had nearly driven him crazy. The only thing that had saved him was Royce's reassurance that whatever had affected him was only temporary. How Royce knew that, Beowulf could only guess, but he'd silently thanked the man the instant he'd changed into human form just before the sun began to set. Now he had something else to worry about—the markings around Roxie's wrist. He was pretty sure he recognized the design. If he was correct in his thinking, it was tied in with a very old prophecy, one he hadn't looked at in years. The only thing about it that made him think he could be wrong was the fact Roxie wasn't a werewolf. The prophecy had been quite clear on that fact. The one bearing those markings would be one of his kind.

Beowulf pushed those thoughts aside, then reached down to cup Roxie's bottom and pulled her tighter against his fully engorged cock. Her lips tickled his flesh as they moved over the throbbing vein in his neck. He stiffened in anticipation as her tongue flicked against his skin. He held the back of her head and urged her closer. Her teeth scraped the side of his throat before she opened her mouth and bit him. He groaned and pumped his hips into hers as the feel of her marking him as hers sent his senses reeling. Even though she didn't break the skin, the bite mark would be visible for all to see.

He threaded his fingers through her hair, then kissed her. He slanted his mouth against Roxie's, pushing his way inside. Tasting her, smelling her scent with each breath he took, filled his senses. The thought of how close he'd come to losing her made Beowulf want to bury himself deep within her until he couldn't tell where he ended and she began. Needing her more than anything else in his life, he picked her up off her feet and took her to her bedroom.

With their mouths fused, he gently placed her on the bed. The instant he lay on top of her, Roxie squirmed beneath him. Beowulf took hold of her hips and held her still.

He lifted his head and stared down at her. "Sorry, I can't hold back anymore. I need to be inside you. Now."

"Then what are you waiting for?"

Roxie took hold of his cock and led it into her already wet opening. Beowulf moaned at how good she felt as he sheathed himself to the hilt. Her body fit his like a glove, as if it'd been made just for his. After pulling back, he moved on her, keeping the pace steady as he pumped in and out. She wrapped her legs around his waist, taking more of him. He bent his head, then sucked one of her nipples deep inside. She arched her back, holding his head to her breast. Her inner walls gripped his cock with each pull of his mouth.

He wouldn't last much longer without spilling. He reached between their joined bodies and stroked Roxie's clit. As he played with that sensitive nubbin of flesh, he increased his pace, pushing her ever closer to her climax. When her body spasmed around his, he lifted himself onto his elbows and surged inside as he emptied himself deep within her body. Out of breath, he collapsed on top of her.

Mindful of his heavier weight, Beowulf remained on his elbows while keeping their bodies joined. Roxie's eyes fluttered open. "Sorry I didn't last very long. I promise to take things slower the next time."

Roxie reached up and caressed his cheek. "I can already tell there will be a next time. How can you still be hard? Don't you ever have to rest in between?"

Beowulf grinned. "No, I don't have to. Unlike mortal men, werewolf males can keep an erection for hours, climaxing many times before losing it."

"I think you've wrecked me for other men."

Beowulf pulled back until he was almost out of her body, and said, "That's good, because there will be no other men. Ever." He slowly pushed his full length back inside so Roxie felt how hard he was.

"And there will be no other women for you."

Roxie flipped Beowulf over onto his back, then straddled his hips. His cock still buried deep, she rode him, taking even more of him. She placed her hands on his chest and slowly lifted onto her knees, then lowered herself on his hard shaft. The head of his cock hit her cervix with each thrust in. She couldn't look any more beautiful than she did now. With her hair streaming down her back and her face flushed with passion as she rode him, she was a sight he would never get enough of seeing.

He held on to her hips, lay still, and let her set the pace for her own pleasure. Her eyes were closed as she centered her being on what she felt. He could tell the moment she started to climax before her inner walls gripped him, milking him. Roxie whimpered. Once her orgasm ended, he flipped her onto her back and rode her hard. His climax was intense, seeming to go on forever. Afterward, he rolled onto his side and pulled her against his body. Beowulf tugged the covers over them both, then closed his eyes, feeling as if this was where he belonged. He wouldn't let anything come between them. Ever.

CHAPTER TWELVE

O nce again Royce found himself hiding in the shadows of
Roxie's backyard. Beowulf was inside the house with her,
but he couldn't shake the feeling that if he left, something
would happen to her.

Unlike the other time he'd staked out her place to watch over
her, he stayed in his human form. It was risky. If Roxie or even
Beowulf should see him, it would spell trouble for him. She was
liable to call the police on him.

Seeing the lights go out in the upper part of the house, Royce
decided Roxie would be safe enough. Beowulf would be there to
protect her. He was sure the pack leader wouldn't let her get too
far out of his sight, especially after the scare he'd had being unable
to make the change. Royce was pulled in two different directions
on how he felt about that whole thing. He was glad he'd been
correct in his assumption that Beowulf's inability to change was
only temporary, but it held a greater meaning for him.

Sighing, he turned to head out of the backyard, only to be
brought up short when he smelled the scent of another. That he
could smell it on the slight breeze meant this trespasser was
deliberately letting him know he was nearby. He stood with his
legs slightly spread apart for better balance and readied himself
for the possibility of an attack. Using his keen senses, he easily
pinpointed where the scent came from. He didn't have long to

wait before Gren stepped out of the shadows to confront him.

"Still playing the part of the noble protector, Royce?"

"If you were a smart man, Gren, you would leave. I'm not the only one here who wants to keep you away from Roxie."

Gren shook his head. "Royce, Royce. What do you think Beowulf will do to you if he finds out you've been stalking his mate? I think he would be just as likely to go after you as he would me, rather than fighting at your side."

"I have every right to be here. I've a greater claim over Roxie than Beowulf does."

"I would love to hear how you came up with that one. I think you're making excuses for yourself, lone wolf." Gren stepped closer until they stood toe to toe. "I wonder what your fearless leader would have to say about that."

Royce growled low in his throat, warning Gren to back off. The other man turned his attention to a spot just behind Royce. Too late, Royce realized Gren was not alone. Gren had deliberately lured him out as the rest of his men had worked their way behind Royce. They were downwind from him, so he couldn't smell their scent. Pain exploded inside his head as something slammed into the back of it. He fell to his knees and shook it, trying to clear it. Before he could come back to his senses, they hit him again. He lost the fight to stay conscious and collapsed in a heap at Gren's feet.

* * * *

Knowing she wouldn't be able to hold off Candice indefinitely, Roxie finally broke down and called her the very next day. She'd hoped Candice would be satisfied with only a phone call, but she quickly dispelled that notion. Candice cut her off before she could start any explanations about the other night and said she would be over shortly.

After Candice hung up on her, Roxie stared at the phone for a few minutes, then returned it to its base. Seeing Beowulf eyeing her strangely from where he sat reading the newspaper at the kitchen table, she shook her head. "I guess we're going to have some company. Candice is coming over."

"Do you want me to stay, or would you rather I leave so you

can have your girls' talk in private?" Beowulf closed the newspaper with a snap.

"No, you can stay. This shouldn't take too long. It's not as if I can tell her exactly what happened the other night. For one thing, I don't think she would believe me, and for another, she would probably say I was nuts."

"You never know. Candice may be more accepting of the whole thing than you think."

"I doubt that. She tends be the type of person who has to have it shoved into her face before she believes what she's seeing. Short of you changing in front of her, I won't hold my breath that she'll take my word for it that you're a werewolf."

"I think I'll pass on that. I've already had one hysterical female to deal with and I don't need a second."

Roxie was about to say something further when she caught on to what Beowulf had implied. "Hey, I resent that. I was by no means hysterical when you changed in front of me."

"Okay, maybe you weren't that bad, but you weren't exactly taking it well either."

"I took it better than most would. I wasn't raised like you, knowing werewolves were real. It takes a little getting used to."

Before Beowulf could comment, the doorbell rang. Roxie went and answered it. Out of the corner of her eye, she saw he had followed her. She mentally rolled her eyes. After Royce's confrontation with Gren at the club, Beowulf had doubled his watchfulness over her. To be honest, she didn't know how much longer she could stand being supervised as if she were a child whose every move had to be monitored.

She pulled open the door and was shocked to see Candice was not alone. Carl stood beside her with his arm draped around Candice's shoulders. "You didn't tell me you were bringing Carl with you, Candice."

"I thought I would surprise you. You haven't exactly been returning my phone calls, so I thought I would do this in person. I'm now seeing Carl." When Roxie only stood there with her mouth hanging open, Candice added, "Are you going to invite us in, or do we have to stand out here on the porch all day?"

"Sorry, come in."

Roxie stepped aside so the couple could walk past her. Beowulf shook Carl's hand. Seeing the two men together made her wonder if there was more to their relationship than Carl being the bouncer at the club.

Turning to Candice, she said, "Would you excuse Beowulf and me for a few minutes? There's something I need him to do in the kitchen." Roxie took hold of his arm on the way by and pulled him into that room out of earshot of the other couple.

Beowulf leaned against the counter with his arms crossed over his chest. "Okay, Roxie. What's bothering you?"

"I can assume Carl is like you, a werewolf. Is it safe for Candice to be around him?"

Beowulf chuckled. "Not all werewolves are like Gren, Roxie. Yes, Carl is one of my kind, and he would never do anything to harm Candice in any way."

"How can you be so sure?"

"Carl is a member of my pack. I've known him since he was very young. If you don't believe me, why don't you ask him? He's standing right behind you."

Roxie turned on her heel and saw Beowulf was correct. Carl stood just inside the kitchen. Luckily, Candice was nowhere in sight to overhear what was being said. "No offense, Carl. I had to make sure."

The big man grinned at her. "None taken. It's something I would expect from my pack leader's mate."

"Pack leader?" Looking back at Beowulf, Roxie asked, "You're pack leader? You never told me you were the head honcho."

"I am. I just hadn't gotten around to mentioning it to you yet. We were a little busy making up for lost time last night. It kind of slipped my mind."

Feeling her face turn beet red as Carl chuckled knowingly, Roxie scowled at Beowulf. "Anything else you may have overlooked?"

"Nothing comes to mind now."

Just then Candice walked into the kitchen. Roxie desperately tried to think of something to say that would make her go back into the living room.

Her friend rolled her eyes. "What's this? Is it let's-keep-Candice-out-of-the-loop day? If all this secret whispering has anything to do with me knowing Carl is a werewolf, you can relax. He already told me, and I'm cool with it."

Roxie's jaw dropped open for the second time since Candice had come to call. "You know what Carl is?"

"It was kind of hard not to miss the whole glowing eyes and growling thing. Roxie, you can't tell me you missed seeing or hearing it when you were with Beowulf."

"Well, no, not exactly. I did try to talk myself into thinking my eyes and ears were playing tricks on me. That's beside the point. I thought you would be the last person on Earth who would accept what they are without running away screaming at the top of your lungs."

"Are you kidding me?" Candice went to Carl's side and allowed him to pull her against him. "The whole not losing an erection for hours on end is something I'm not willing to give up. Once you go werewolf, you never go back."

Roxie gasped. She looked at Candice, sure there was a stunned expression on her face, unable to think of what to say in regard to her friend's last comment.

After a few minutes, she was able to pull her thoughts back together. "Okay, that was way too much information."

"Oh, don't be such a prude, Roxie."

Beowulf wrapped an arm around Roxie's waist. "Roxie is no prude, Candice. Believe me. I have firsthand experience to know she's quite the opposite."

Roxie elbowed Beowulf in the ribs, feeling well-compensated for his last remark as he grunted when she made contact. "Now that we have thoroughly discussed each other's sex lives, I don't think we need to say anything more about it." Turning to Carl, she asked, "Just how old are you?"

"I'm six hundred." He gave her a crooked smile.

"I see. So you're a baby compared to Beowulf's thousand-plus years."

"Actually, the baby of the pack would be Wade. He's only three hundred years old."

"Okaaay." Roxie turned back to Candice. "So you don't mind dating a man who has over five hundred years on you?"

Candice winked at Carl before she answered Roxie's question. "Not at all. If anything, it turns me on knowing he's that old. He's had a lot of years of practice making love to a woman. Now I get to benefit from all that experience. Don't you agree, Rox? All the years Beowulf has been alive, he must know how to turn a woman into a pile of mush with just a touch. He's positively ancient compared to Carl."

"Let's keep our minds out of the gutter, if you don't mind. Considering he's *the* Beowulf from *Beowulf and Grendel*, I guess you could say he's a tad on the ancient side."

"You can say the same about Gren, considering he's the other half of the tale," Carl added.

Roxie's gaze flitted between the two men. They each gave her a questioning look, as if to say she should have known that bit of information. After pulling out a chair, she sat at the kitchen table. "I need to sit down. This is starting to go way beyond my normal realm of understanding. Are you telling me Gren is actually Grendel?"

The others joined her at the table. Beowulf sat next to her. "I thought you would have figured that out by now, Roxie. You seemed to know the tale very well."

She gave him a pointed stare. "Yes, I do, but just because Gren's name is similar-sounding to Grendel doesn't mean I would in any way think it was him. If you go by the story, he died near the end of the tale. And he was described as a monster, a creature that lived in a cave."

"Like any old tale of that age, there is more myth than truth in it. At the time, Gren was considered more beast than man. To be perfectly frank, he still is. He's a killer, pure and simple. He lives for the hunt. He preyed on those weaker than himself, taking pleasure in the fear he caused."

"As pack leader, don't you have some sort of control over him?"

Beowulf shook his head. "No. Gren is not a member of my pack. He's part of a rival one. His pack's numbers have declined dramatically over the years so there's no leader. It's now just Gren and the few men he's been able to keep at his side."

"It explains why he hates you so much, but you would think some of the animosity he feels for you would wear off a bit over the years."

"I can't ever see that happening. He feels he has every right to hate me. One part of the tale is true — I did kill his mother."

"What happened? If you go by the tale again, it says Grendel bled to death after having his arm cut off and that his mother attacked, wanting revenge for her son. The last time I saw Gren he had two arms, unless being a werewolf gives you the ability to grow back limbs."

"No, we can't do that. Gren's mother was literally insane. She's partly responsible for Gren being the way he is. As for her attacking me, she retaliated after I beat Gren to a pulp. I didn't set out to kill her. She forced my hand when she decided she couldn't defeat me and went after innocent villagers. I couldn't let her kill them in cold blood."

"Does Gren know what she did?"

"He wasn't there to witness the attack so he thinks I lied to him. He also thinks I murdered his mother."

"Lovely. Okay, I now understand why he hates you, but I don't get why he would deliberately set out to antagonize Royce like he did the other night. He did everything in his power to piss Royce off."

Carl and Beowulf exchanged a look that said Royce was something else entirely. Beowulf sat back in his chair and nodded to the other man. Carl took a moment to get his thoughts in order before he spoke. "Royce, his story is a little more complicated than Gren's. At one time, Royce was a member of our pack until he decided to go lone wolf. Most werewolves keep to their packs. Very rarely does one of us choose to go it alone, not wanting any contact with other pack members. We call that going lone wolf. Once a werewolf has done so, especially if it happens to be a male, and he should return, it tends to make the other males uneasy. The lone wolf is usually no longer trusted. In Royce's case, that's doubly so. Before he left the pack, he was pack leader. He chose Beowulf to take his place."

"Do you think he's back to take up his old position in the pack?" Roxie couldn't see Royce doing anything of the kind, but she felt she had to ask.

"We really don't know. He hasn't stuck around long enough for us to find out, but we can't discount it as a possibility."

"He told me he lost his wife. Was it after her death that he went lone wolf?"

Beowulf sat straighter. "He told you about his mate?"

"Yes." Roxie couldn't see what the big deal was. "Does that mean something?"

"Did he tell you how she died?"

"No, only that she had and that he still loved her."

"No one really knows how his mate died. He kept her away from the pack. We only knew he'd found one and nothing more. It wasn't until after her death did we learn she was a mortal woman."

That explained a lot about why Royce was so protective of her. She was Beowulf's mate and a mortal, he didn't want to see what had happened to him happen to the present pack leader. Even though it seemed as if Royce was only trying to help, there was still something about him she couldn't put her finger on.

* * * *

Beowulf returned to his house before the club opened and headed for his study. There was still the small matter of the Celtic markings around Roxie's wrist to investigate. Since she had refused to go to the club with him, for which he couldn't blame her, he'd decided to use the time apart to look into ancient werewolf lore. There was one story in particular he wanted to read. He pulled a large leather-bound book off the bookshelf and then went and sat in an overstuffed armchair. He flipped through the pages and came to the one he looked for. He quickly skimmed it until he found what he sought—a drawing of what the Celtic markings were supposed to look like. He felt the blood drain from his face. The markings in the book were an exact copy of the ones around Roxie's wrist. He shook his head in disbelief.

His people had always considered this story more myth than actual fact. Long before his birth, a female werewolf who had been gifted with second sight had a premonition. She foretold the coming of a werewolf who would tie all the packs together. This individual was to be born after their numbers had declined by half. There was no mention of whether this werewolf would be male or female, only that he or she would be gifted with abilities no other of their kind had ever possessed. He or she would hold the ultimate power over all the packs.

The rest Beowulf wasn't too sure whether to believe or not.

Some of it sounded like pure fantasy. What he couldn't understand was why Roxie would suddenly have those marks appear on her skin when she wasn't a werewolf. There was no way to change a mortal into one. He closed the book, then placed it on the bookshelf. It was impossible that she was the one who was foretold, but the markings said otherwise.

They also put her in a very precarious position. Most, if not all, werewolves knew the story of the foretold one. Regardless of whether Roxie was a werewolf or not, some would try to tie her to them, using her to have the ultimate sway over the rest. Beowulf was glad she'd had the foresight to keep the marks hidden. The fewer people who knew about them the better.

* * * *

Since she was going to be spending most of the evening alone, Roxie decided she was caught up enough with her work to take the night off. Instead of working, she figured she would enjoy a couple glasses of wine while she watched one of her DVDs. She thought the movie she picked to watch was very appropriate, all things considered.

Turning on *Beowulf and Grendel*, she settled in to watch hunky Gerard Butler strut his stuff dressed in chain mail. Roxie had read the original story when she was a teenager, but it was from watching this movie that she remembered what she'd read years before. Gerard Butler, who portrayed Beowulf, wasn't really a match for the real man, but with his sexy Scottish accent and killer body, she wasn't going to complain. As for the movie's interpretation of Grendel, they were way off base. When she'd watched it the first time, she'd thought it made sense that he was a man and more like the missing link than monster. Having met the real Grendel up close and personal, she had to rethink that whole monster thing.

Absorbed in watching the movie unfold, Roxie at first didn't hear the howls coming from her backyard. She put the movie on pause and waited, listening for the sound again. When the howling started back up, she slowly walked to the sliding glass doors. Her heart raced as she picked up not just one but three different howls.

She pulled back the curtain that covered the glass doors, then let out a shriek as the animal on the other side threw itself against it. From its size it had to be a werewolf in wolf form. The beast snarled and bared his teeth. Roxie had to remind herself he couldn't get in, all the windows and doors were locked, and there was no way in hell she was going to open them for any reason. When a second werewolf joined the first, she slowly backed away from the window. *Where was the third?*

"Hello, Roxie."

She spun around and her heart jumped into her throat as she caught sight of Gren standing in her living room. She didn't know how he'd gotten in, but she now realized the other two werewolves had been distracting her, giving Gren the time he needed to make his way inside. Slowly backing away, Roxie wondered if she could somehow manage to grab the phone from the kitchen and call Beowulf for help. Gren didn't give her the chance to try. He crossed the room with the speed only a werewolf was capable of, grabbed a fistful of her hair, and hauled her to his side. "Now, Roxie, this can go either of two ways. You can cooperate, and I won't have to harm a hair on your pretty little head, or you can fight me. Either way, I'll win."

Keeping a good hold on her hair, Gren walked her back over to the sliding glass doors. He unlocked them and stepped back as his two men, changed into human form, walked into the room. Gren threw Roxie onto the couch.

"Beowulf is going to rip you apart when he finds out about this. If I were you, I would leave now before he arrives."

Gren shook his head and chuckled. "Beowulf will be at his stinking piece of trash club for another hour. That'll give us just enough time to have a bit of fun with you."

Roxie tried to get off the couch, but Gren was on her before she could get very far. His mouth slammed down onto hers, cruelly crushing her lips against her teeth. With a free hand, she raked her nails down his cheek. He lifted his head, and she saw the bloody tracks she had made in his flesh. Snarling, he backhanded her, causing her to see stars for a couple of seconds.

"You bitch." He looked at his men and ordered, "Come and hold her arms down. It would seem this cat has claws."

Doing as Gren had commanded, each man took hold of one of

Roxie's arms and pinned them down onto the couch cushions. Even though she fought with everything she was worth, she couldn't break free. In the ensuing struggle the wristband she wore around her left wrist shifted, exposing the markings underneath. The werewolf holding her there stiffened. She looked to where he stood at the back of the couch and found him staring at her wrist.

"Ah, Gren, you'd better look at this." The werewolf lifted her arm and moved it so Gren could clearly see the marks on her skin.

Gren slid off Roxie and pulled her to her feet. Keeping her wrist in a viselike grip, he turned it, looking at it from all angles. "Well, well, what do we have here? This is unexpected indeed. Now I have to rethink what I'm going to do with you. It would seem you'll be more useful to me in one piece, so that rules out having some playtime with you."

The werewolf who hadn't found the markings snarled at Gren. "You said we could each have a turn at her."

"These marks change everything. It would seem Beowulf's little bitch here is something special, after all."

"She isn't a werewolf. If she is who you think, she would have to be one of us. I'm not letting you take away the piece of ass you promised me I would get just because you think she's something she isn't."

"I'll give you only one warning, Thomas. Back off and do what you're told. You know you can't defeat me in a fight." To give his words more emphasis, Gren growled menacingly at Thomas. The other werewolf backed up a step. "A very smart move. I think it's time we give that spell another try. Roxie is a perfect candidate."

"It didn't work the first time you tried it; why do you think it will work with her?"

"Such a pessimist, Thomas. Those marks on her wrist were what we were missing the first time." Gren trapped Roxie's wrists in one of his hands before he pulled her to him. "I'm afraid you are coming with us. I can't leave something as precious as you in Beowulf's keeping."

Roxie didn't see Gren's fist coming until it was too late. When it connected with her jaw, her world went black.

CHAPTER THIRTEEN

Beowulf stopped his car in Roxie's drive, and an overwhelming sense of wrongness took hold of him. He slammed the car door, then ran to the house. He tried the front door and found it locked, but the uneasiness didn't leave him. With his set of keys, he unlocked it and then stepped inside.

"Roxie?"

His call was met with silence. He called out a second time and still had no response from Roxie. Beowulf took a deep breath. He growled as three werewolf scents filled his nostrils.

He changed into wolf form and bounded upstairs, following the trail where one of them had been. At Roxie's bedroom he saw the shattered glass that had fallen onto the floor when the window had been smashed. Nose down, he sniffed around the debris. He bared his teeth at the recognizable scent.

Beowulf returned to the lower floor and followed Gren's scent to the living room. The sliding glass doors were open wide, the curtains flapping in the breeze. Here he could easily pick up the scent of the other two werewolves. He continued to follow the scent trail, which led to the couch. His fur bristled as he caught the smell of the three werewolves and Roxie on it. He threw back his head and howled with rage.

Knowing what had to be done, Beowulf changed back to human form. He closed the sliding door, then returned to his car.

Before driving away, he used his cell phone to make the one call that would rally the men he would need. Confronting Gren while he had Roxie to use as leverage was not something Beowulf wanted to do alone.

* * * *

Roxie groaned softly as she slowly regained consciousness. She had no idea how much time had passed. The only thing she knew was she was in a car being driven to who knew where. She cracked open her eyes just long enough to see who was with her. The werewolf named Thomas drove the car. The second werewolf, the one who had found the marks around her wrist, sat in the front passenger seat. Even though she tried not to make any sound, she must have, because he turned to look at her where she lay on the backseat.

"Finally awake, are you? Just in time too."

The car slowed before coming to a stop. Thomas leered back at her. "What do you say, Kurt, about having a little fun with her before we take her to Gren?"

Kurt shook his head. "No way, man. Gren would kill us both if he ever found out."

"How's he going to find out? I'm sure she won't say anything. There wouldn't be any point." Thomas sneered.

"You may have a death wish, but I don't." Kurt got out of the car, opened the door, and pulled Roxie out of the back. "Let's just get this over with, and then you can find someone else to get your rocks off."

Not to be put off, Thomas went to stand in front of Kurt so he blocked his path. "I like this one. Gren shouldn't have gone back on his word. So what if she has those marks on her? I still think they're meaningless."

Thomas took hold of her arm and tried to pull Roxie to him. Kurt, who already held the other, pulled her back. Caught between the two, she gritted her teeth as each man yanked on her as if she were a rope in a game of tug-of-war. Their voices grew louder, but there wasn't anyone around to hear them.

Once Kurt had pulled her out of the car, she was able to get a better view of where they had taken her. They were at Muir

Woods National Park. She had come there many times while growing up with her parents to see the giant, majestic redwood trees. The park wasn't a long drive from San Francisco. She loved coming there and standing next to trees that stood more than two hundred and fifty feet tall. Some even reached an astounding height of more than three hundred and seventy-five feet. Not only were they the tallest of all living things, they were long-lived as well. The average age of the redwoods was six hundred to eight hundred years, but they could live up to twenty-two hundred years of age. Roxie couldn't help but think these trees would give Beowulf a run for his money when it came to longevity.

"What the hell are you two doing? I told you to bring the girl to me."

While they'd been bickering over her, Thomas and Kurt had failed to notice Gren's arrival until the moment he'd spoken harshly to them. They each fell silent as their leader approached. Roxie stayed trapped between them.

"Answer me."

When neither man spoke up, Roxie decided to use it to her advantage. "Thomas here decided not to follow your orders and wanted to play with me, after all. Kurt, on the other hand, tried to get me away from Thomas. Basically, you could say they fought over me. In a different situation, I would find that flattering with all the attention they're paying me. Right now, I feel that whoever wins, I'm not going to be too happy with the outcome either way."

Gren glowered at her before he slammed his fist into Thomas's face. If Kurt hadn't still been holding her, Roxie would have hit the ground just as Thomas had.

Giving Thomas a kick in the ribs for good measure, Gren snarled down at him. "Don't ever disobey an order I've given you. Next time you pull a stunt like that, it'll be your last. Literally."

Motioning for Kurt to follow him, Gren led them into the woods. Thomas held his ribs and painfully pulled himself to his feet before he fell in behind Kurt. It soon became obvious Gren had a certain destination in mind. He walked off the main trail and into the woods at a brisk pace with no hesitation.

Having only stuck to the marked trails when she'd come to the park in the past, Roxie soon lost her bearings. As the vegetation grew thicker, the darkness pressed in all around them. With excellent night vision, the three werewolves seemed not to notice. She could barely see her hand when she held it in front of her face. Feeling practically blind, she stumbled over fallen branches and large rocks, much to the disgust of the men.

After what seemed like hours of hiking through the thick trees, Gren led them to a small clearing. In the center of it sat a large flat rock. It looked too much like an ancient altar for Roxie's liking, the kind that could be used to offer up a sacrificial victim to some equally ancient god. As Kurt dragged her to it, she realized there was someone else already in the clearing. The man appeared to be unconscious. At least she hoped he was unconscious and not dead, and he was bound hand and foot. He lay on his side on the ground with his back facing her.

Gren crossed to where the man lay, grabbed a handful of his hair and lifted his head. "Time to wake up, lone wolf. You don't want to miss the show."

A shiver of fear ran down her spine when she saw it was Royce who lay on the ground.

Gren dragged him to his feet and turned him to face Roxie. "Since no introductions are necessary, you can keep each other amused while I get things started." He shoved Royce, pushing him onto his knees. Roxie rushed to his side.

Thomas stepped to watch over them, standing a few feet away as Gren turned his attention to a pack sitting next to the rock. With the help of Roxie, Royce managed to awkwardly get up onto his feet.

He searched her face. "Are you all right?"

"So far. I'm only a little bruised." Roxie reached up and touched her swollen jaw where Gren had struck her. "Given the situation, it could be worse."

Royce's eyes glowed mutedly. "The bastard hit you. I'll rip his throat out for that."

Keeping her voice low, Roxie spoke. "Don't do anything stupid, Royce. I need you. So don't let your anger get the best of you. We have to keep our wits about us or we'll never get away from Gren. Can't you change and get out of those ropes?"

"You're right. And changing won't help free me. There are silver threads mixed in with the rope. It won't harm me, but silver hampers my ability to change into wolf form and keep it. Where's Beowulf?"

"He was still at the club when Gren and his men broke into my house. I'm sure he knows by now something has happened."

"Gren didn't try to..." Royce left the sentence unfinished.

"No, but that was his original intention." She held up her left arm and continued. "Finding these made him change his plans."

Royce stared at the markings around her wrist before he looked back at her. "Has Beowulf seen this?"

Roxie nodded. "Yes. He said I should keep them hidden. He never did tell me why, though."

"He had a very good reason to want you to keep those markings out of sight. It has to do with a bit of ancient werewolf lore."

"And what does that have to do with these marks on my wrist?"

"Yes, Royce, do tell the girl what those particular marks mean." Gren had focused his attention on them once again.

Royce shot him a dirty look before he answered Roxie. "The story goes that a werewolf bearing those marks would be the one destined to rule over all the werewolf packs and would have abilities no other had."

"I'm not a werewolf. And I sure as hell don't have any special abilities. It has to be a mistake."

"Oh, you may not be a werewolf now, but before this night is through, I hope to change that." Gren took hold of Roxie and forced her down onto the large rock.

Roxie fought him, but in the end he was just too strong. With her on her back, he held her down as Kurt took hold of her wrists and Thomas grabbed her ankles. Once she was properly subdued, Gren moved back to Royce, who lunged at him. Gren stepped aside and let the other man fall at his feet.

"It turns out, lone wolf, you're more useful than I originally thought." Gen grabbed a handful of Royce's hair, pulling his head back, exposing the side of his neck. "The spell doesn't say how the blood has to be extracted, but I like to think I'm more civilized than I once was. So we'll do this with less muss and fuss."

With his other hand, Gren jabbed the end of a syringe into the vein at the side of Royce's neck. Royce swore. Once the syringe was full, Gren released him and went to where Roxie lay on the rock. "Now it's your turn." He pushed Roxie's head to the side, then pushed the needle into her neck, shoving down the plunger, injecting it into her bloodstream. Stepping back, Gren threw the syringe to the ground with a smile. "Now for the last step – the spell."

"The magic of the wolf's blood is now in thee.
A wolf you become to run wild and free.
Where once there were two, now only one we see."

The words of the spell resonated inside Roxie. The spot on her neck where Gren had injected her with Royce's blood burned. Like quicksilver, it shot through her body until she felt as if she were burning up. Gasping, she tried to pull free of her captors. Having them touch her became almost too much for her now sensitive skin. When Gren motioned for Thomas and Kurt to release her, she rolled to her side and curled up into a ball, panting.

The burning slowly abated. Once it had receded to a manageable level, Roxie took stock of herself. Blinking, she found herself able to see more clearly in the dark. She heard the insects buzzing on the forest floor. She could not only smell the rotting vegetation around them, but each individual scent of the other four men with her.

With a look of extreme satisfaction, Gren reached for Roxie. Acting on instinct, she growled low in her throat and slipped off the rock to stand next to Royce. Moving quickly and with a strength she hadn't had before, she yanked off the ropes binding Royce's hands and feet. Once he was free, she turned back to face Gren, who moved closer.

"Now that wasn't very nice, releasing Royce like that, but since it was his blood that sired you, I'll let the lone wolf go. You, on the other hand, are another matter. You're the one in the tale, and with you, I can rule all the packs. Be a good girl and step away from Royce."

As Roxie stood her ground, Gren lunged for her. A surge of power rose through her, engulfing her whole body. Throwing back her head, she howled as the change took hold of her. She looked down and saw a pair of paws covered with fur the color of golden wheat. She bunched her hind legs beneath her, then threw herself at Gren, knocking him over. Without slowing her momentum, she leaped over him and ran into the thick trees.

* * * *

Before Gren or his goons had a chance to react, Royce changed on the fly and went after Roxie. He picked up her scent and followed her at a discreet distance. He had to make sure neither Gren nor his two men found her.

He was still finding it hard to believe Gren's spell had worked. If he hadn't been there to see Roxie change into the she-wolf himself, he would never have believed it. It all made sense now. The spell was meant for one human and one human only — Roxie. He was a hundred percent sure it had indeed been her who'd caused Beowulf's inability to change. The magic had already been in her, just sitting, waiting since her birth for the right time to surface.

Lost in his thoughts, Royce didn't realize he'd almost caught up with Roxie until he spotted her a few feet in front of him. She waited for him. He crossed the distance between them before he brushed his larger wolf's body against her smaller one. She shook. He bent his head and rubbed his muzzle across hers, trying to let her know it would be all right. He stiffened as a wolf's howl reached his ears. It could only be Gren and his men. They must have picked up their scent.

He nudged Roxie and pushed her to run. He kept pace with her, circling back the way they'd come. If they were lucky enough, they would be able to reach the parking area before their adversaries did. He had no qualms about hotwiring one of their cars.

* * * *

Beowulf roared across the Golden Gate Bridge and floored the gas of his Mercedes as he sped down Highway 101. Though Muir Woods was only twelve miles north of the Golden Gate Bridge, it seemed a lot farther away. The thought of Roxie being alone in the woods with Gren made his skin crawl.

After calling for backup from his pack, he'd gone in search of Gren. Having made it a point to keep a watchful eye on him over the years, Beowulf had investigated all his known haunts. Since Gren couldn't be found at any of them, Beowulf had decided to go with the next best thing—he'd beaten the information out of one of Gren's men.

Once he'd passed on that information to his men, Beowulf couldn't wait for them. He told them to meet him at Muir Woods, jumped into his car, and sped away, leaving the scent of burning rubber behind him.

Finally reaching the parking area, Beowulf got out of his car and walked to the two others parked there. One, he knew for sure, was Gren's. He stepped onto the main trail and searched the tree line for any sign of Gren or Roxie. He stopped walking when his keen hearing picked up the sound of something moving fast in the woods just ahead of him. He prepared for an attack and stood silently waiting, not wanting to give his presence away too soon. Seeing the two werewolves burst out of the trees and onto the trail, he relaxed his guard. The bigger of the two, the werewolf with the golden-brown fur, he knew was Royce. The second, a female whose fur was more golden than brown, he didn't recognize. As they bounded toward him, Royce changed into human form.

"Gren and his men aren't too far behind. We have to get Roxie out of here."

Beowulf turned a shocked expression to the she-wolf. She looked back up at him with fear in eyes he knew so well. He took a step closer and went to pick her up in his arms. Roxie skittered away out of reach. Much to his disappointment, she went and leaned against Royce's leg.

"We have to go now, Beowulf. Roxie's too scared and isn't skilled enough to make the change under these conditions."

Howls came from the woods. They were too close for Beowulf's liking. He nodded and bit back a snarl as Royce changed into wolf form and urged Roxie into a run. Following, Beowulf was pleased to see another car come racing up. Carl, Wade, and three other males of his pack stepped out of it once it had stopped. Before he could reach them, three werewolves burst out of the trees. Beowulf turned and held his ground.

Gren changed into human form to confront him. "She belongs to me now, Beowulf. It was my magic that changed her into one of us."

Beowulf heard his men step up behind him. "You're outnumbered, Gren. Roxie is not yours and never will be. I claimed her as my mate, and nothing has changed. If you still want a fight, then let's have at it. You've gone too far this time." Baring his teeth, he growled loud and long.

Gren slowly backed away. "I'd watch your back if I were you. This isn't over yet. I'll be coming to collect what's mine."

Showing Gren his threats had no effect on him, Beowulf turned his back on the other man. He walked to his car, then opened the back door so Royce and Roxie could get in. After slamming it shut, he turned to find his brother standing behind him. "Thank Carl and the others for coming so quickly. Also tell him I'll talk to him later."

Wade looked around Beowulf at the two werewolves in the backseat. "What happened out there? And what is Royce doing with Roxie?"

"That's what I intend to get to the bottom of very soon," Beowulf answered dryly. "Go with the others, Wade. Roxie and I'll meet you at home later."

Beowulf hung on to his anger by a mere thread. Wade nodded and got into the other car. Beowulf waited until they'd pulled away to give Gren one last menacing look before getting into his own car.

Once he hit the highway, he looked into the review mirror at Royce. "Change so we can talk. You better have a good reason you were able to come to Roxie's rescue before anyone else. Because right now, I'm more than ready to rip your throat out for just being near my mate, lone wolf."

*

Roxie felt the tension building between the two men. She wanted to change, but she didn't have the slightest idea how to go about it. She wasn't even sure how she'd managed to get into wolf form in the first place. She looked between Beowulf and Royce and saw they weren't in the mood to give her any instructions on how to live as a werewolf right at that moment. They seemed more interested in biting each other's heads off, figuratively speaking.

"Just what are you insinuating with that remark, Beowulf?"

"Only that it seems a little fishy that you would happen to be with Roxie in her time of need. How did you know Gren had taken her?"

"I didn't, at least not until he brought her here. How *I* got here is Gren and his men ambushed me the other night, and I couldn't escape until now. Roxie was the one who freed me."

Cursing, Beowulf pulled the car to the shoulder of the road. He kept it idling, then turned in the seat to confront Royce. "Where were you when Gren took you captive? I know he was watching Roxie's house so I'll ask you again. Where were you?"

Through clenched teeth, Royce bit out his reply. "I was in Roxie's backyard."

Beowulf grabbed Royce by his shirt and yanked him against the back of the front seat. "You had no reason to be there. Roxie is my responsibility."

Fearing they would come to blows, Roxie whimpered and inched farther back in the seat, hoping to stay out of their way. She was now glad she'd never told Beowulf that Royce had been inside her house as well. There was no telling how he would react to that bit of information.

"Back off, Beowulf. You're frightening Roxie." Once Beowulf had released him, Royce sat back and placed a hand on her neck. He seemed to ignore Beowulf's look of warning, and he continued. "Roxie is as much my responsibility as she's yours. It may have been Gren who performed the spell, but it was my blood he used to sire Roxie."

"Not good enough. That still doesn't change how I feel about you taking things into your own hands."

Royce stroked Roxie's fur and sighed. "There is more going on here than you know. There's an even greater connection between Roxie and I."

"What the hell are you talking about?"

"You'll just have to take my word for it. I can't say anything more about it right now." Royce's face grew hard. "When I can, you'll understand, and there'll be nothing you can do about it."

"The only reason I haven't hauled your ass out of this car and beaten the crap out of you is that you were once my pack leader and I consider you a friend. Don't count on that lasting forever."

Beowulf turned back around, slammed the car once more into drive, and took off, sending rocks flying. Royce's words echoed inside Roxie's mind. She wasn't sure she wanted to know what he'd meant by a "greater connection." Her life was spinning out of control, and there was nothing she could do to stop it.

CHAPTER FOURTEEN

Once they'd reached Beowulf's house, Roxie gratefully walked past Wade, who held the door open for her. She padded to the living room, then waited for the others to join her. She heard Beowulf's and Royce's raised voices even before they reached the room. She sat on her haunches and sighed inwardly. She hoped they would calm down soon. She needed one of them to tell her how to change back, but that didn't seem as if it was going to happen that quickly. As Beowulf yelled at Royce to get out of his house, Roxie decided to take matters into her own hands.

She went to where Wade stood, watching the theatrics, and bumped his leg with her head. He looked down at her as she stared beseechingly back up at him, hoping he would understand what she wanted.

Wade squatted to her level, then said, "You don't know how to change back, do you?" He looked over his shoulder at his brother and shook his head. "Beowulf's in one of his moods, and he hates to back down. So it would seem you're stuck with me. The thing you have to remember about the change is that it's pure magic. The power is inside you. You just have to learn how to tap into it to use it." He gave Roxie a second to try finding it, but when she shook her head, he made another suggestion. "Okay. You may not find it as easily as I can since you weren't born a werewolf. Close your eyes and concentrate. Try to think of what it felt like when you made the change to wolf. Try to focus on where you first felt the power building, then will yourself into human form. Go on and give it a try."

Roxie closed her eyes as she tried to concentrate. It was kind of hard to do with Beowulf and Royce yelling obscenities at each other, but by slow degrees, their voices fell away. She focused her attention on the inside of her body and thought of the power that had risen and engulfed her just before the change.

Buried deep inside her, she found a small spark of the magic Wade had talked about. When her mind touched it, it quickly grew in power until she felt it in every pore of her body. Surrounded with bright light, her form changed from that of a she-wolf to that of a woman. She held out her hand and smiled to see she had fingers again. She looked at Wade, laughed, and hugged him.

Flustered, Wade gently pried her off him. He kept his gaze away as he removed his shirt and then handed it to Roxie. "Your next lesson will be how to will clothes onto yourself after the change is complete. For now, you'll have to make do with my T-shirt."

Roxie felt her cheeks turn a bright shade of red. She thankfully took the shirt from Wade and slipped it over her head. It just barely reached her midthigh.

"Uh, thanks." She realized all the shouting had stopped. Beowulf and Royce stared at her and Wade. Seeing Beowulf's scowling visage, Roxie rolled her eyes at him. "Oh, come on. You can't be thinking your brother now has designs on me. Look, you two idiots were so intent on beating your chests, trying to prove you're each manlier than the other, I gave up on you helping me with the change. Listening to you guys arguing over me and not being able to put my two cents in was starting to tick me off. Wade thoughtfully volunteered his services."

"I'm sorry, Roxie." Beowulf walked to where she stood staring at him with her hands on her hips. "I wasn't thinking."

Royce, who'd also come to stand in front of her, spoke next. "I think, Roxie, you would be better off coming with me instead of staying with Beowulf. I can do a better job than he in showing you what you'll need to learn about your new life."

Snarling, Beowulf pushed Royce back. "Roxie stays here with me. How many times do I have to tell you—she's my mate, not yours."

"And how many times do I have to tell you that I have more right to her than you do." Royce emphasized his last remark with an equally hard push to Beowulf's chest.

Before the shoving match could turn into an all-out war, Roxie put two fingers into her mouth and let loose with a shrill, high-pitched whistle. The combatants instantly stopped fighting and put their hands over their ears. Now that she had their undivided attention, she gave them a piece of her mind, something she'd been aching to do for the last twenty minutes.

"I've had enough of this crap. I am in the room, you know, and very capable of making my own decisions, I might add. It would be nice if, instead of fighting over me, you could at least think of how I may be feeling. I was turned into a werewolf, for Christ's sake. Not once have either one of you asked if I'm handling this well or not. All the two of you can think about is ripping each other's head off." When both men started to interrupt at the same time, Roxie narrowed her eyes at them. "Don't you dare say a word. I've heard enough. It's your turn to listen to me. Royce, thanks for the offer, but since Beowulf is my mate, I'll be staying with him. If he starts acting like a chest-beating Neanderthal, I'll be sure to accept your help. Beowulf, no more displays of jealousy. I find it really annoying. It's late, and I need to sleep. That's all I wanted to say. Now if you still want to kill each other, go ahead, but please wait until I'm upstairs."

With as much dignity as she could muster while wearing nothing but an oversize T-shirt, Roxie swept past Beowulf and Royce and then walked up the stairs to Beowulf's bedroom.

* * * *

Beowulf sat on the back patio and watched the sun rise. He hadn't been able to sleep. He'd gone upstairs to check on Roxie during the early-morning hours, but hadn't gotten into bed with her. What Gren had done to her, changing her into a werewolf, haunted him. Along with the marks on her wrist, it was a glaring reminder of what her destiny had become. He didn't know if he could protect her from it. If it were simply a matter of locking her away from the rest of his kind, he would feel more comfortable having done so, but Roxie would never stand for that. And if he was to try, he would lose her. With his thoughts running rampant inside his mind, he'd quietly left the room and come outside to think.

He not only had to worry about Roxie's position in werewolf society, he also had the added problem of what Royce was going to do. Now that he wasn't so blinded with jealousy, Beowulf knew Royce would only push his suit if he really had a claim over Roxie. Royce never acted on impulse. While pack leader, his ability to stay calm and think clearly had saved the pack many times. So Beowulf couldn't totally discount what Royce had said as desperate imaginings. There had to be some truth to his words.

Beowulf rubbed his face with his hands as he slumped back in the patio chair. When had his life become so complicated? Who would have thought that finding his mate would be so life-altering? He closed his eyes, no longer able to fight the demands of his overtired body. He drifted off into a fitful sleep.

A short while later, he came awake to the sensation of Roxie gently stroking his face. She smiled. "You didn't sleep out here all night, I hope?"

He sat straighter and rubbed his gritty eyes. "No. I came out to watch the sunrise."

Roxie pulled out the chair next to his and arched a brow. "And why don't I believe that was the only reason you're sitting out here? I missed having you in bed next to me."

"I only would have disturbed your sleep, and after what happened last night, you needed your rest. How are you feeling?"

Roxie shrugged. "Fine. Except for being able to hear, see, and smell like never before, I don't feel all that much different. I was able to follow your scent through the house and out to here. Amazing, really, when you think about it."

"You might find your senses will become a tad overloaded, especially in a crowd, but you can use them to your advantage."

"What's going on inside that mind of yours, Beowulf?" Roxie reached out a finger and rubbed the frown lines away that had to be showing on his forehead.

Beowulf removed her finger, then kissed the tip of it. "I won't lie to you. I'm worried about what will happen next. I not only have Gren, but Royce as well, trying to take you away from me. And now that you've been changed into a werewolf—something that has been literally unheard of before—that tale can't be totally discounted. I'm not sure how the other packs will react."

Roxie got up from her chair and sat on Beowulf's lap. "As for Gren and Royce, we'll figure something out. And for the other, it's just a story. Nothing more. So Gren was able to turn me into a werewolf. There has to be another reason it worked on me, and not because I'm part of this werewolf prophecy. Can you see me ruling over all the packs? I'm a hermit, remember? I'm not a take-charge type of woman."

"I wish I could feel as you do. Say you're right, that it's all just a tall tale. As long as those marks are on your wrist, every werewolf who sees it will believe you're the one in the prophecy, regardless. We tend to be a superstitious lot. I think it stems from having magic inside us."

"Well, I'm not superstitious and never will be. I don't want this to change the way I have to live my life. I'll have to be more careful until Gren and Royce are put in their places, but after that, I don't intend to do anything different from what I've been doing."

"I stayed up all night thinking about this. I have to insist for your own safety that you stay here, and that you don't leave the house alone—ever."

"I don't know if I can handle being basically kept in a gilded cage. I understand that as my mate you instinctively feel it's your right to protect me, but I'm perfectly capable of looking after myself."

"Judging from what happened last night, I beg to differ."

Roxie slid off Beowulf's lap. "That wasn't very nice, throwing that at me."

"You need to face reality. Your life is going to change, no matter how much you fight it. I'm afraid you're going to have to do what I ask and without question. I know what needs to be done to keep you safe." Beowulf could easily see by Roxie's expression that he'd gone too far with that one.

"Oh, really now? So, I'm supposed to just let you tell me what to do and meekly accept it? Not in this lifetime, mister. I need to get out of here."

As Roxie headed for the patio door, Beowulf moved to follow her. "Where are you going?"

"I have to see my parents. I have to somehow explain to them what has happened to me. They're more likely to take me to see a shrink than anything else after I tell them, but I can't hide this from them. I was going to ask you to go with me. Now I've changed my mind."

"I told you. You can't leave the house alone."

"Enough, Beowulf. This time I'm putting my foot down. I'm going alone to my parents'. Please don't make this any worse by trying to stop me. I'll be back in a couple of hours."

Roxie placed her palm on the center of his chest. A jolt of power surged through it and passed into him. Once she'd turned and headed inside the house, he found himself unable to move. Helplessly, he heard her open the front door. A few seconds later, the sound of her car starting reached his ears.

Once she was gone, he tried moving again. Nothing. He briefly closed his eyes. This was the second time she'd inadvertently done something to keep him from following her when she didn't want him to. He could no longer deny it. Even though Roxie had no idea what she'd done, she carried great power within her. This was all the proof he needed to accept that the prophecy was real and it could no longer be considered a myth.

* * * *

Still fuming over Beowulf's high-handedness, Roxie pushed open the front door to her parents' house. Closing it behind her, she called, "Mom? Dad? Anybody home?"

Her father's answering call came from the direction of the kitchen. She headed there. She stepped into the room, then instantly froze. Unable to stop herself, Roxie growled menacingly at the unwanted visitor.

Royce quickly stood from where he'd been sitting at the kitchen table with her parents and walked to her. "Now, Roxie. Pull it back a bit. You're going to scare your parents acting like that. They may have a hard time seeing their daughter's eyes glowing with anger."

She shoved him away, then snarled. "Get the hell away from them. You have no right coming to my parents' house."

"Actually, he does, Roxie."

She found her mother looking at her sadly.

"What exactly are you saying, Mom?"

"Sit down. It's time we had the talk I'd been hoping to avoid."

Royce tried to take her by the elbow to help her into a chair. Roxie quickly snatched her arm away and sat without his assistance. "All right, start talking. I can see you're already acquainted with Royce in some way. What have you been keeping from me?"

Belinda took a deep breath. "Yes, your father and I know Royce." She looked Roxie in the eye. "I've known him all my life. He's our grandfather, Roxie."

Roxie resisted the urge to grab her mother and shake her for saying such a thing. "'Our grandfather'? So, what you're saying is you've known all about werewolves your entire life and that we're descended from one of them? You never once thought it was something I should know?" She was flabbergasted, and a little ticked off, that her mom could have kept something that important from her. She had the right to know.

"I've come to regret that decision. Honestly, I thought it wouldn't be necessary. With each generation, we've been born with some knowledge of where we'd come from. We all dream of running with the wolves. I still dream about them. With you, the dreams stopped when you were so young. I figured maybe it'd finally skipped a generation. When you came here and said they had started again, and that they'd changed in nature, I realized I'd made a terrible mistake."

Unable to sit there watching her mother's eyes fill with tears, Roxie turned to glare at Royce, who sat across from her. "So, is this what you meant when you said your claim over me was greater than Beowulf's? Because I'm your granddaughter?"

"Before you get started on that subject, you need to hear the full story. Remember when I first met you, I told you my mate had been mortal? She was your grandmother. I kept Alicia away from the rest of my pack, knowing most of them would not approve of their leader taking a mortal as a mate. I only wanted to keep her safe. She had great power of her own. She was able to wield magic without really thinking about it. It was a gift she was born with.

"Of course it caused her to be ostracized by the rest of the people in her village. So she lived alone in a small cottage a little away from them inside the woods. I figured she would be safe there. And when our daughter was born, and she showed no signs of inheriting my werewolf genes, I knew there would be no harm in letting them live there. I'd not counted on one of the village boys spying on us. He saw me change to wolf form and ran back to the village to tell them that the witch lady who lived in the forest had taken a demon for a lover."

Royce's hands curled into fists where they sat on the table. "That evening they gathered and, in their superstitious fear, killed Alicia. She managed to hide our daughter from them before they pulled her out of the cottage. When I arrived, I was already too late. They'd burned her. I would have killed them all if I hadn't heard my baby daughter's cries. That's why I went lone wolf. I gave it all up and went to Europe to raise my daughter. And I've watched over each generation since then."

Now a lot of what Royce had told Beowulf made sense. As her grandfather, though many, many times removed, by blood his claim was the greater. Then it suddenly hit her. "That's why Gren's spell was able to turn me into a werewolf. Your blood was the key. On a genetic level, I already carried your werewolf DNA. Having more of it introduced into my system was all it needed for it to surface. Gren thought it had something to do with these marks on my wrist."

"I think Gren wasn't too far off on thinking that. It wasn't just because we're related by blood. You inherited Alicia's magic as well as her looks."

"There's nothing magical about me. At least there wasn't until last night."

"You've already used your powers once."

"When?"

"The night Beowulf showed you he was a werewolf by changing at the club. You used a spell Alicia once used on me. He was unable to change out of wolf form until the next evening."

"I only told him to stay in that form until..." Roxie's words trailed off. Had she put a spell on Beowulf without knowing she had? "I'm having a hard time believing that."

"Believe it. You did something to stop me from following you when you left to come here." Beowulf stepped into the kitchen.

"What is this? Has my parents' home become werewolf Grand Central Station?"

Beowulf came to stand next to her chair. "I made it my business to find out where your parents lived."

"I don't know if I can stand all this male werewolf protectiveness. I'm beginning to feel as if my life is no longer my own."

Her mom gave Roxie a pained look. "Get used to it, dear. After my parents died in that plane crash, Royce was the one who raised me. I know exactly how you feel."

Noticing how Beowulf stiffened at her mother's comment, Roxie filled him in on her family history. He looked at Royce with new understanding showing in his eyes. "You didn't have to go lone wolf, Royce. My family, along with other families in our pack, would have welcomed your daughter and helped protect her. You didn't have to do it alone."

"Maybe not, but at the time I feared that if I stayed, my daughter's fate would end up being the same as my mate's. Nina was all I had left of Alicia."

"I understand. Now that I know about the tie you have with Roxie and her family, I will acknowledge you as grandsire to my mate."

"That isn't the only reason I'm making a claim for Roxie."

Beowulf's visage became icy, and his light blue eyes turned hard. "Roxie is my mate. We've bonded."

Turning to Roxie, Royce said, "Tell me about your dreams. Your mother said you dreamed about a man who could change into a wolf, and that the dreams were on the intimate side."

"Mother!" Roxie exclaimed. "How could you tell him about my dreams?"

"After you told me about them, I knew I had to get in touch with my father. And don't look at me like that. My parents died when I was three. Royce is the only father I know. I knew he would understand what was happening to you."

"Belinda made the right decision. I need to know what happened in those dreams and who you saw in them before I say anything more."

At her mother's look of concern, Roxie relented. "All right. You both win. I know it's me in the dreams, but they take place in the past. The first one I had, I was hiding in a forest. It's a game I'd played often with my lover. I see the wolf, and the hunt is on. He catches me, then changes into a man. In the second dream, I'm racing with the wolf, wishing I could run like he can. There's a creek. Once again, the wolf changes into a man. This time I'm sitting on a rock, admiring him in all his naked glory." Embarrassed, Roxie shook her head. "Look, I'm not going to give you all the intimate details. All I'm going to say is in this one I can see his face more clearly, and he speaks to me."

"He asks whether you're looking at his buttocks again." Royce spoke in a hushed tone, almost as if he'd said the words to himself.

"Yes. How did you know?"

Royce looked at her with such longing in his eyes, and she shook her head in denial. "No way. It can't be."

"Who was the werewolf? You saw me in your dream, didn't you?"

The floor suddenly dropped out from under her. Roxie stared at Beowulf. He stood with his jaw clenched and refused to look at her. "Yes, it was you I saw." As soon as the words left her mouth, she knew everything was about to take a drastic change, and not necessarily the way she wanted it to.

Royce stood to confront Beowulf. "Roxie is my mate reborn. What she just described are memories, of events that happened between Alicia and I. Roxie not only looks almost exactly like Alicia, she is her. The powers, all of it, are the same. By rights, Roxie is my mate and not yours."

Without saying a word, Beowulf bobbed his head in acknowledgement, then walked out of the kitchen. Roxie ran after him. "Beowulf, stop. Where are you going? Are you just going to leave and walk out of my life just because Royce claims I'm his long-dead mate reincarnated? I'm not Alicia. I don't have the same feelings for him as I do for you. You're my mate, not Royce."

"That's exactly what I'm doing."

"You've got to be kidding me. Don't I have a say in this?" Roxie took hold of his arm and pulled Beowulf around to face her. "Damn it. You just can't walk out on me like this. I love you."

"Royce's claim over you is one I can't ignore. This isn't the first time a mate has been given a new life and found their other half from their first life. By werewolf law, I must give you to Royce."

"That's bullshit. You're pack leader. Change the damn law."

"Because I am pack leader, I must abide by the laws. If I were to do what you ask, I could lose my standing with my pack."

"So, you're telling me you won't give up being pack leader to keep me and will hand me over to another man without a fight because he feels, not me, that I once was his mate?"

"Correct."

Feeling as if she had just been slapped in the face, Roxie released her hold on Beowulf. Through a fine mist of tears, she watched him turn his back on her and walk out the door. Unable to find the strength to move, she remained there as tears streamed down her face.

She sensed Royce's presence beside her even before he put his arm around her shoulders. Roxie allowed him to pull her into his arms. She lifted her bent knee and rammed it between his legs. With great satisfaction, she watched him drop to the floor like a stone as he cupped his manhood.

"Roxie! I taught you better than that."

She wiped the tears from her cheeks, ignored her mother's admonishing remark, and squatted to where Royce lay. "I'll only say this one time and one time only. I'm not Alicia. I might look like her and have some of her memories, but I'm not her. Beowulf is my mate, not you. I will never accept you as mine. You're my grandfather, nothing more, nothing less. And if you think to try to claim me, you'll have a fight on your hands. I can guarantee you it'll be one battle you'll lose." Straightening to her full height, Roxie said to her mother, "I'm going to stay here for the night in my old room, which is where I'm going to be alone for a while. When I come back down, Royce had better be gone. If he isn't, we'll see just how much power I actually have."

She stepped over Royce's prone figure, then climbed the stairs to her room. Wisely, no one said a word to stop her.

CHAPTER FIFTEEN

Roxie ended up staying with her parents for longer than just the night. She was in a bit of a quandary about where she was going to live. With Gren still a threat, she couldn't very well stay at her own house. That would be the first place he would search. Beowulf's was no longer an option, at least for now. She fully intended to be back in his house, and his bed, before very long. Even though she hated the idea of it, she would have to give him his space, to make him realize he couldn't live without her. Staying at her parents' house for the interim was not an option either. She couldn't take the chance that Gren would somehow track her there. If anything happened to her parents, she would never be able to forgive herself.

Feeling a little lost, she decided to broach the subject with her parents. In times such as this, they'd always helped her make the right decisions.

After their supper, Roxie brought up the matter of her living arrangements with her parents. She listed the reasons she couldn't go back to her house and why she couldn't stay with them. "So until Beowulf comes to his senses, I have to find a place where I'll be safe from Gren."

Belinda got up and started clearing the supper dishes away. "You could stay with Royce."

"No, and no again. That's not an option. I want to get Beowulf back, not alienate him even more."

Her father cleared his throat. "Under the circumstances, I think it's your only option. Your grandfather is more than capable of handling this Gren character. Don't make a rash decision concerning Royce just because he wants to claim you as his mate."

"Oh, so I'm not supposed to hold that over him? Dad, be serious. The man thinks I'm his dead wife, which I'm not. Having your grandfather lusting after you does wonders for the ego."

"Stop being so dramatic, Roxie," her mother said from where she stood looking out the kitchen window. "Come here. I want you to see something."

Roxie went to stand beside her mother and looked out the window. She saw the vague outline of a werewolf in wolf form, sitting in the shadows. The color of the fur marked it as Royce.

"He has been out there every single night." Her mother looked at her. "I'm not saying you have to accept him as your mate, but he is your grandfather and would protect you with his last breath. So he thinks you're Alicia. I agree with you that you aren't, but he has been alone for so long. I think it's mostly wishful thinking on his part. Give him time to realize that. Royce would never do anything to hurt you. Until Beowulf stops acting like an ass, accept Royce's protection. Believe me, he has had lots of practice at scaring away unwanted males. Just ask the boys he ran off before I met your father."

Roxie kind of felt sorry for her poor mother. Having to put up with an overbearing male werewolf through her teenage years would have been pure hell. "I don't know. Yes, I agree with you that Royce would be more than able to protect me, but how it would affect Beowulf is my biggest concern."

"I've been thinking about that. Maybe your moving in with Royce is the kick in the pants Beowulf needs. If the two of you have bonded as he'd said, he won't be able to just stand by and allow it to happen. Dad told me bonded mates can't deal with being apart for very long. How are you feeling, not being able to be with Beowulf, by the way?"

"Let's just say I'm about ready to start climbing the walls. Before I became a werewolf, I could handle it to some degree, but now it's worse. He's never far from my thoughts, and I have an almost overwhelming urge to go to him, but I know that won't help matters."

"Then at least get some satisfaction knowing Beowulf is more than likely going through the same thing. Give him some time. And I really want you to seriously think about what your father and I said about asking Royce for his protection."

Roxie stared out the window at Royce. He never moved, but he stared back at her. Maybe her mother was right. Moving in with Royce could be just what Beowulf needed to make him realize he couldn't live without her.

"Okay, I'll do it. I do have an ulterior motive, though, besides using him to make Beowulf jealous. I have no idea how to use this newfound magic I have. I've only had the one lesson on how to make the change. If I'm to fully embrace my new life, I need to learn everything about it. And Grandpa Royce is going to teach me."

Her mom hugged Roxie. "It'll all work out in the end. You'll see. Thanks."

"For what?"

"Now I can have my father back. When we decided not to tell you anything about your heritage, he felt it was best if he kept his distance. I've missed him."

"Sure, Mom. Make me feel guilty."

"You know what I mean. I'll go out and tell him about your decision."

Not moving from the window, Roxie watched her mother step outside and then walk to Royce. He changed and listened as her mom spoke. Roxie had to fight back tears as Royce opened his arms wide and lovingly hugged her mother. When he kissed the top of her head in a parental show of affection, Roxie turned away. She would have to tread carefully. She didn't want to become the wedge that could drive father and daughter apart.

* * * *

Roxie wasn't surprised to learn Royce lived only a few blocks from her parents. The house was a large two-story that sat on a fair-sized lot. The only thing she knew about the house was that it was the one her mother grew up in. That being the case, Roxie wasn't surprised to see pictures of her mother at varying ages hanging on the walls, but what got her the most was seeing pictures of herself as well. There were pictures of her as a baby all the way up to her photo when she'd graduated from high school.

As she looked at the pictures, Roxie sensed Royce's presence behind her. "It looks as if you know a lot about me, but I don't know much about you."

"Just because I wasn't around when you were growing up doesn't mean I didn't wish to know about you. I held you in the hospital shortly after you were born, and I've been watching you ever since."

Turning to face him, Roxie said, "So you already knew who I was when you came to me at Wulf's Den that night."

"Of course, but it was the first time I actually was able to speak to you. It was then I began to realize how similar you were to Alicia."

Royce tried to pull Roxie into his arms, but she pushed him away. "Enough of that. There's going to be a few ground rules around here, Grandpa. First and foremost, stop thinking I'm Alicia. I'm not."

"The dreams you had said otherwise. Those are Alicia's memories. And don't call me Grandpa."

"I'll call you that every time you try to make a move on me. Yes, they're Alicia's memories, but that's all they are—her memories, not mine. In my dreams, it may have felt as if I were really there. Deep down inside, I know it really wasn't me. It was more like I was an observer looking through Alicia's eyes. Maybe I carry her memories deep inside me because I'm more like her than the others who came after her. Who knows, but the point is you have to stop thinking of me as her. I already have a mate. If I were Alicia, I wouldn't have been able to accept Beowulf as mine, let alone bond with him. I would have known shortly after I met you that you were my mate if you truly were, but that isn't the case. As it stands now, I'm hanging on by a very thin thread since Beowulf has decided to play the martyr and let you have me."

Royce's gaze searched her face. He sighed deeply. "I see you feel strongly about this. I very much wanted you to be Alicia, but you're right. If you were truly my mate, you wouldn't have been able to bond yourself to another. And in my selfishness, I've screwed up your relationship with Beowulf. I made a vow to myself that I would always watch over Nina's descendants, even going so far as to take your mother in and raise her as my own daughter. It would seem I messed up when it came to you. I should never have let your mother convince me that you would be better off not knowing about your werewolf heritage."

"Don't be so hard on yourself, Royce." On tiptoe, Roxie lightly kissed his cheek. "You did what you thought was right. Your intentions were good, but now that you've owned up to your mistakes, you're going to help me fix them."

"What exactly do you have in mind?"

"First of all, you're going to teach me everything I need to know about being a werewolf. Then we'll work on Beowulf. I hope you're up to a little role-playing, because I intend to make Beowulf so jealous he won't be able to put his feelings for me aside."

"I think I'm up to the challenge. As for making Beowulf jealous, that shouldn't be too hard to do. Werewolf males are notorious for not tolerating another male near their mates. All it'll take would be for the two of us to show up at Wulf's Den together and then let nature take its course."

Roxie smiled. Beowulf had been quick to push her into the arms of another man. She was more than willing to show him he'd made a huge mistake. When she was through with him, the poor man wouldn't know what hit him.

* * * *

Wade snorted in disgust as he pushed open Beowulf's bedroom door. The room reeked with the smell of alcohol. Looking at the large bed, he found him stretched out naked on top of the sheets, snoring. An empty scotch bottle lay next to him on one side. A T-shirt that belonged to Roxie was held in his outstretched hand.

Every morning since Beowulf had come home from Roxie's parents' house alone, he could be found looking the worse for wear from drinking most of the night away. Wade decided it was time to snap Beowulf out of his depression. He stalked to the bed, then grabbed him and slung him over his shoulder. Beowulf mumbled something unintelligible as Roxie's shirt floated to the floor.

Once he'd walked into the bathroom, he opened the shower door and stepped inside. He propped Beowulf against the wall. Wade aimed one showerhead in Beowulf's direction and turned the cold water on full blast. Beowulf bellowed with outrage. Wade turned the water off.

"Well, are you back among the living yet?"

Beowulf wiped the water out of his eyes and glared at Wade. "Why the hell did you do that?"

"I've had enough of your sulking. You miss her. I get that. I also think it's time you stopped feeling sorry for yourself and get Roxie back."

"You know I can't do that."

"Wrong answer." Wade blasted Beowulf with the cold water again.

"Cut it out. You're starting to piss me off." Beowulf growled.

"Good. At least I'm making you feel something. I can't stand by and watch you drink yourself into a stupor every night."

"It's the only way I can deal with..." Beowulf's words faded as if he'd found it too painful to say the rest.

"I know it's the only way you feel you can deal with Roxie not being around, but it also means you're still bonded to her. Don't you think she's going through the same thing?"

"No, I don't. She has Royce now."

"Then fight him for her. Make her see she belongs with you and not him."

"I can't. I doubt she would take me back, anyway." Leaning his head against the tile wall, Beowulf closed his eyes.

"And why wouldn't she? I know for a fact she loves you."

"I know. She told me that at her parents' house, but I still gave her to Royce, even though she tried to stop me."

"You gave her to Royce? I thought you were a lot smarter than that, bro." Twisting the tap one final time, Wade hit Beowulf with the cold water before he stomped out of the shower stall and then went into the bedroom.

A few minutes later, Beowulf came out of the bathroom with a thick towel wrapped around his hips. He glared at Wade. "What did you expect me to do? Royce was so sure Roxie was his mate reincarnated. You know what our law states about that. I had no choice."

"Bullshit. Some of our laws are antiquated and have no bearing on modern society, and well you know it. When was the last time a reincarnated mate was claimed? Not in my lifetime."

"It doesn't matter. You know as pack leader, I have to do everything by the book."

"So, you would rather stay pack leader at the cost of finding happiness with Roxie?"

"That's what I told her."

Wade sadly shook his head. "You're pathetic. You wait your whole life for a mate. And what do you do? You throw her away. If and when I'm lucky enough to find my mate, I know there would be nothing anyone could do to make me give her up." He stomped out of the room, then slammed the door behind him.

*

Wincing at the sound of the door slamming, Beowulf rubbed his throbbing temples. Along with his pounding head, his mouth felt like sandpaper. Wade was right to yell at him, but the damage was already done. Still dripping from the earlier dousing, he headed back into the bathroom.

He turned on the shower, and jets of warm water beat on his skin. He could smell the soap Roxie liked to use as the water hit it. Beowulf picked up the bar, held it to his nose, and took a deep breath. Memories of her and what they'd done there in that enclosed space filled his mind.

He rubbed the soap across his chest. God, he missed her. He couldn't think straight when she wasn't around. And now he'd sunk so low he was reduced to using her soap so he could have something of her touching his skin. Beowulf closed his eyes and ran the bar down his body as images of how Roxie looked when he had made love to her played through his head.

He tortured himself, but he couldn't stop his wayward thoughts. His body responded as if she were there in the shower with him. His cock swelled to an aching point. The bar of soap fell as Beowulf wrapped his sudsy hand around his hard length. Groaning, he pumped up and down his shaft.

He placed his other hand on the tiled wall in front of him and quickly brought himself to orgasm. After his body emptied itself, he stood under the spray. The water washed the evidence of his weakness away. Wade was right. He had to get Roxie back somehow. He couldn't live like this. Before he could even try to win her back, he had to deal with the Gren situation. That was one problem that had to be rectified, and was a long time in coming. Beowulf shut off the water. He knew what he had to do.

CHAPTER SIXTEEN

"Try again, Roxie."

Roxie blew her hair out of her face. Who would have guessed that using magic could tire a person out? Royce had her do the change so many times she felt as if she'd been working out at a gym for a couple hours. Her body felt drained, and her head ached from the strain of tapping into the power inside her. She groaned when he looked down at his watch.

"You're going to time me again, aren't you?"

"Yes. I know you're getting tired, but you need to be able to do the change no matter how good or bad you feel. It could save your life. Now try again."

She drew the magic up and out so it engulfed her completely. Roxie's body shimmered into wolf form. She waited for Royce's nod before she changed back. "Was that quick enough for you this time, slave driver?"

"You're definitely getting faster. And no missing articles of clothing either."

Roxie cringed inside. Her first couple of attempts at willing clothes onto herself after making the change had been almost complete failures. The first time she was able to manage only a shirt. The second attempt she ended up wearing only pants. Royce had been good about her nudity problem. He kept his back to her until she told him she was decent. After he turned around, he would remind her again she was only focusing on each piece of clothing instead of on them all as a whole.

"Good. What's next? Is there anything else I should be practicing? You said I took away Beowulf's ability to do the change for a short period of time. Shouldn't I practice that? And is there another wolf form I can change into?"

Royce chuckled. "Don't you think you've had enough for today? We've been at it for hours." When Roxie shook her head, he answered her questions. "To be honest, you've learned from me all I can teach you. Your other powers, I can't help you with. No one can, really. No other werewolf has the same capabilities as you do. You'll have to experiment on your own. Alicia had the ability to stop a werewolf from changing and freezing a person in place, but beyond that, I don't know what she was able to do. She didn't like using her gifts."

"I can understand why she wouldn't want to use them. Okay. I'll have to play around a little on my own, then. What about other wolf forms? In the movies werewolves can change into wolf form or something between a man and a wolf."

"That's only in the movies. The wolf is all we can do."

"That's a bummer. Maybe because this is all new to me, but I find when I'm the wolf, there are a lot of limitations. I can't communicate with anyone, and having paws is a real drawback when you want to open doors."

"True, there are limits, but in that form, you can smell better, see better, and are able to move a lot swifter. It's just something you'll have to get used to. Being born a werewolf, I've never really found my wolf form to be a hindrance."

"Okay. I'll take your word for it." Roxie sat on the couch next to Royce. "Are you all set for tonight?"

"If you're asking me whether I'm prepared to have my ass kicked by Beowulf, I'm as ready as I'll ever be."

"You really think Beowulf will try to fight you?"

"I can almost guarantee it. You're his mate. His first reaction to seeing us together will be to drive me away."

Roxie took her bottom lip between her teeth. "Maybe this wasn't such a good idea, after all. I don't want to see the two of you pound the crap out of each other."

"Relax. Even if Beowulf does come after me, I don't think he would set out to deliberately hurt me. If it will let him save face by smacking me around a little, I'll gladly let him, then slink away with my tail between my legs."

"Whatever you say." Roxie looked at the clock that sat on the mantel above the fireplace, then stood. "Wulf's Den should be opening soon. I should start getting ready."

Roxie headed upstairs, then went to her bedroom. She opened the closet and pulled out the little black outfit she'd worn to the club the first night she'd met Beowulf. Luckily, it had still been at her house and not at Beowulf's. Royce had gone to her place that morning and had picked it up for her. He also had boarded up the window Gren had smashed getting inside the house.

She brushed her hair and prayed her plan for that evening worked. She didn't think she could stand being apart from Beowulf for very much longer. If the stubborn man thought he still had to do the right thing by letting her go, he was going to be in for a nasty surprise. One way or another, she was going home with him tonight whether he liked it or not.

* * * *

Royce helped her out of the car. Roxie took a deep breath to calm her nerves. She didn't know why she felt so nervous, though she worried Beowulf could outright reject her. Throwing back her shoulders with her head held high, she placed her hand in Royce's larger one and let him walk her to the club's entrance.

As they passed Carl, who manned the door, he winked at her and waved them inside. He already knew what she had in store for Beowulf. Candice had let him in on their secret right after Roxie had told her. Surprisingly, Carl hadn't balked at what they wanted to do. He'd laughed so hard Roxie had been able to clearly hear him roaring with laughter in the background while still on the phone with Candice. Once he'd finally gotten himself back under control, he'd only said that Beowulf deserved whatever he got.

The club was crowded, as it was most Friday nights. Roxie clutched Royce's hand and searched the bar for any sign of Beowulf. It was hard to see through the people who lined it, waiting for drinks they'd ordered. Some of the employees gave her and Royce a look that said they weren't exactly pleased to see them. Finally reaching the bar, Royce pushed his way through to one of the empty stools. He took hold of Roxie by the waist, picked her up off her feet, and plunked her onto it.

She craned her neck to look down the length of the bar. Roxie found one of the other bartenders serving drinks. A bit disappointed Beowulf wasn't there already, she turned to Royce. "He's not here yet. I guess we'll have to sit and wait."

"I don't think we'll have to do that for too long. Wade is coming this way."

Sure enough, Wade stepped behind the bar, carrying a case of wine. He seemed distracted as he slammed the bottles onto the counter with more force than was necessary. Roxie called to him. He turned around to see who had, and a look of relief washed over his face. With a wave, he motioned for them to follow him.

Wade took them up to Beowulf's office. Once he'd shut the door behind them, he said, "I've never been so glad to see someone as I am the both of you."

Royce appeared to study the younger man's face. "Where's Beowulf?"

Wade ran his fingers through his hair, making it stick up in places. "The stupid fool decided he had to take care of Gren himself. Beowulf sent Gren a formal challenge."

"And did Gren accept it?"

"Of course he did. He wouldn't pass up a chance like that. I tried to talk Beowulf out of it, but once he has his mind set on something, there's no way you can reason with him."

"I hope he had enough foresight to bring a couple other pack members along with him. You can't count on Gren playing by the rules."

Wade snorted. "No. He went alone, even though he knew Gren would have his men with him."

Royce turned to Roxie. "It looks as if there's a change in plans for tonight. I'll take you home, then go after Beowulf."

Roxie adamantly shook her head. "No. That will take too long. I'm coming with you." Seeing how Royce and Wade were about to argue against her decision, she glared at them until they backed off. "I'm going, and that's final. Now where is this challenge supposed to take place?"

Wade reluctantly answered her question. "At Muir Woods."

"What exactly does Gren find so appealing about Muir Woods?" When Wade and Royce looked at her as if she should know the answer to that question, Roxie glared at them again. "Okay. I get it. Wolves love the forest, and Muir Woods is the closest one to San Francisco. It just seems so stereotypical to me that that had to be the place where two werewolves would challenge each other."

"It's also the least likely spot to draw unwanted attention," Royce added. "Wade, do you want to come with us, or are you needed here at the club?"

"I'm coming with you. I can get one of the others to look after things and close the club up at the end of the night. I'll just have to tell Carl where we're going."

"Fine. Do what you have to do. Roxie and I will wait for you in the parking lot."

Wade quickly left the room. Roxie grabbed Royce by the arm before he could move to follow. "I can tell there's more to this than a simple challenge."

Royce took hold of Roxie by her upper arms and looked into her eyes. "You're right. This is no simple challenge. The grudge Gren has carried for Beowulf is large. He'll use this opportunity to make Beowulf pay for everything he has done to him. This will be more than a simple test of strength between two werewolf males. Gren will make it so it's a fight to the death."

Roxie had just known it had to be something like that, but it didn't make her feel any better. Silently, she followed Royce out of the office and to where he'd left his car in the parking lot. She could only hope they showed up in time to stop Beowulf from making a mistake that could cost him his life.

* * * *

Beowulf followed the Muir Woods main trail until he reached the point where he had to cut a path of his own through the forest. There was a designated spot in the woods that had become the official area where all werewolf challenges took place. He reached the clearing and saw Gren was already there, waiting for him. Beowulf scanned the tree line, searching for clues as to where

Gren's men were hidden. There was no question in his mind that Gren wouldn't have come alone.

He walked farther into the clearing, his gaze boring into his opponent, letting him see how much he loathed him. "I'm glad to see you still have some honor left, Gren, and that you decided to accept my challenge."

"Why would I turn down something I've wanted for so many years? It's a dream come true."

"I'm only doing this so you'll have no choice but to stay away from Roxie."

"How very loyal of you to issue a challenge to protect your former mate. I heard the lone wolf managed to take her away from you. Once I have you out of the way, the lone wolf is next on my list."

Beowulf ground his teeth at the mention of Royce claiming Roxie as his mate. "Roxie is still my mate."

"You claim her as your mate, even though she has let another man get between her legs? You're pathetic."

He knew what Gren was trying to do—make him angry enough to let the fury take away his better judgment and strike without thinking. It still didn't make it any easier for him to let Gren's taunts roll off his back.

"I didn't take you for a gossiping old woman, Gren. Since you've such an interest in my life, maybe you find yours so inadequate, you take great satisfaction in sticking your nose where it doesn't belong. Didn't your mother ever teach you it's rude to spread rumors, especially when they aren't true?"

As Beowulf had expected, Gren snarled with rage and charged him in wolf form. Making the change before Gren reached him, Beowulf met him head-on. Their snarls and growls soon filled the clearing as he engaged the brown wolf in battle.

Gren lunged toward him, trying to get his powerful jaws around Beowulf's throat. He twisted out of range and slammed his shoulder into Gren, knocking him off balance. Gren quickly regained his footing and went after Beowulf with teeth bared. As the fight progressed, it looked as if they were too evenly matched in strength, neither of them able to gain the upper hand against the other. Blood matted fur in places where sharp canine teeth had gouged deep wounds.

Both panting from exertion and feeling the pain of the bites they'd inflicted upon each other, Beowulf gathered his flagging strength and used his body to knock Gren to the ground. Before Gren could get back up, Beowulf pounced on him, taking hold of him by his throat. Gren whimpered.

Having Gren at his mercy, Beowulf was the victor, but the urge to close his jaws and tear Gren's throat out was almost too tempting. With one snap of them, his bad blood against Gren would be over and Roxie would be safe. Gren would no longer be a threat if he were dead. Slowly, he increased the pressure on his jaws.

He realized his mistake a split second before two large male werewolves slammed into him, knocking him away from Gren. Using teeth and claws, they battered him down. Already weakened from having battled Gren, Beowulf had no hope of fighting off the two newcomers. Gren's men subdued him. As one werewolf bit down on the back of his neck, Beowulf knew it was over. Unable to get free, he closed his eyes and waited for the powerful jaws to snap closed and break it.

* * * *

Roxie's ankle twisted for the third time since they'd begun walking along the main trail. She cursed whoever had decided women looked sexy in high heels. Having reached the point where she would rather go barefoot and take her chances with the rocks, she stopped to take off her shoes. She undid the straps, pulled one off, and disgustedly threw it. A second later, Royce grunted in surprise as the shoe hit him in the back of his head. He turned and glared at her as he rubbed the spot where her high heel had made contact.

Roxie removed the second shoe, sheepishly looked at him, and let it drop to the ground next to her. "Sorry. I didn't mean to hit you. I couldn't take walking in these damn high heels anymore."

"So, you had to throw it and my head just happened to be in the way?"

"Don't be such a baby. I'm sure it didn't hurt all that much. You should try walking in heels for an hour, and I bet you would be throwing them away too. Can I help it your big head decided to be in the wrong place at the wrong time?"

Royce shook his head. "If you're done chucking footwear, hurry it along. We're almost there."

Once Royce had turned around, Roxie mimicked him behind his back. Wade fell in beside her. "Nice shot, by the way. That must be a new way to keep your mate in line."

Roxie snorted. "I didn't intend to hit Royce. I've always had crappy aim. And for your information, Royce is not my mate and never will be. The man is my grandfather, for Christ's sake. Thinking of him as my mate is just plain disgusting."

"Royce is your grandfather?"

"He's my great, great, great, etcetera grandfather."

Wade looked between her and Royce. "Beowulf told me one of our kind had mated with a mortal woman long before I was born. It must have been Royce. That explains a lot."

"Well, you can wait to hear the complete story after we rescue Beowulf from his own stupidity."

"You're right." As Wade followed Royce, who'd now left the trail and walked through the bush, his mood grew serious. "Remember what Royce told you, Roxie. Don't get involved, no matter what happens. You'll only end up getting hurt. Plus, we don't need the added worry of trying to protect you from Gren."

"I promise." Roxie's pace slowed as the sound of two wolves in the midst of a fight reached her ears. "It sounds as if we're too late to stop the fight from starting."

Wade ran to catch up with Royce, leaving Roxie to follow them. Both men soon disappeared, but she found she was able to easily pick up their scent trail.

Moving cautiously, she arrived in time to see Wade and Royce change to wolf form on the fly before dragging two werewolves off Beowulf's prone figure. Free of his attackers, Beowulf painfully pulled himself up. Roxie put her fist into her mouth to hold back her gasp. The wounds he had sustained were too numerous to count. She smelled his blood on the slight breeze that blew in her direction.

Roxie scanned the clearing with her keen eyesight and saw Wade and Royce had their hands full with Gren's men. Hearing a low menacing growl, she latched her gaze on to Gren, who stood only a few feet away from Beowulf. His coat was spotted with blood, but he didn't appear to be as badly wounded as Beowulf. Feeling her heart jump into her throat, Roxie watched Gren slowly slink toward Beowulf.

It wouldn't be a smart idea to yell out a warning and alert Gren to her presence, but Roxie decided she couldn't just stand by and let Beowulf become a sitting duck either. Mentally saying screw it to the promises Royce and Wade had gotten out of her, she changed into wolf form and ran toward Beowulf.

She reached him just before Gren did. Standing in front of Beowulf, she took the brunt of the attack. Gren slammed into her, easily knocking her aside. Roxie shook her head to clear it, then got to her feet. By now Gren and Beowulf were locked in combat, sharp teeth and claws tearing into each other. If she didn't do something fast, it would be all over for Beowulf. She closed her eyes and concentrated. She focused on the image she held inside her mind, and the power swelled. She refused to give up and pushed herself beyond what she thought were her capabilities. Once the magic fell away, she opened her eyes and looked down at herself.

Unbelievably, she'd done it. She'd somehow managed to do the impossible. Roxie held out her arm and found it covered in golden fur, as was the rest of her body. She spread her fingers wide. She reached up and found pointed ears sitting on top of her head. She smiled as much as her shortened muzzle would allow her.

Stalking toward Gren in her wolf/human form, Roxie grabbed his smaller wolf's body by the back of his neck and pulled him away from Beowulf. Roxie found her strength had more than doubled while in this new form.

Holding Gren off the ground, she held him by the scruff of his neck and shook him until he stopped struggling. Roxie turned him to face her, then spoke. Her voice was gravelly and harsh-sounding, so unlike her own speaking one.

"You've been a very bad dog. And like the bad dog you are, you can stay in this form until you learn your place."

A rush of power surged through the hand that held Gren and flowed into him. He whimpered and pulled his tail up between his legs. Disgusted, Roxie threw him away. Even in this form, her aim appeared to be off. She cringed as Gren slammed into the nearest tree and slumped to the ground unconscious.

Now that Beowulf was no longer in jeopardy, she turned her attention to the other two werewolves Royce and Wade were still fighting. Grabbing the closest one by his tail, she dragged him off Wade. When he turned, snapping his teeth, Roxie wrapped her hand around his muzzle, holding it shut.

"Bad dog." Balling her other hand into a fist, she slammed it down on top of his head. He dropped like a stone.

By now the others in the clearing had noticed her arrival. The last of Gren's men slowly backed away from her. As he spun around to try to run away, Roxie jumped, easily closing the distance between them. She took hold of him by the scruff of the neck and slammed her fist onto his head as well. Unconscious, he hung limply in her grasp. She opened her hand and let him drop at her feet. With all the bad guys subdued, she turned to find three very stunned men looking at her.

CHAPTER SEVENTEEN

Roxie left the unconscious werewolf where he lay, then slowly walked to the three men. Still in wolf/human form, she was pleased to find she was much taller as well. Where before Beowulf had towered over her, she could now look him in the eyes. She looked from one to the other, finding them still staring at her in shock. "Well, say something. Or are you three going to stand there with your mouths hanging open, catching flies all night?"

Royce was the first to speak. "How did you do it, Roxie?"

"I simply kept the image of it in my mind and sort of willed it to happen."

"Utterly amazing."

Roxie twitched her tail out of the way as Royce walked full circle around her. "Thanks. Now I know I broke my word by getting involved, but I couldn't just stand there and watch the three of you get the crap beat out of you."

"That's a moot point right now, but I will say you have done our bloodline proud this night, granddaughter." Giving her a knowing wink, Royce kissed her furry forehead, then motioned for Wade to help him secure Gren and his men.

Finding herself standing alone with Beowulf, Roxie found Royce's having called her his granddaughter had not been lost on him.

He stared at her with longing in his eyes. "So it's granddaughter and not mate?"

No longer feeling comfortable staying in wolf/human form, Roxie changed to her true self. "It never was mate to begin with. If you hadn't acted like a stubborn fool, you would have realized my feelings for Royce aren't like that. I'll love him as a relative, but not in the way I love you."

Beowulf pulled Roxie to him and held her tight. He flinched when she wrapped her arms around his back. She quickly released him and stepped back. "Sorry. We need to get those bites taken care of."

"There's another part of my body that demands your attention more than my wounds do." Beowulf's voice grew husky with need.

Roxie's pulse raced. Just being near Beowulf, having him look at her as if he wanted to devour her, set her body on fire. "Then I suggest we go someplace that's less crowded."

"I think that can be arranged."

The sound of Wade loudly clearing his throat broke the seductive spell that had been woven around them. Guiltily, Roxie pulled her gaze off Beowulf and looked at Wade and Royce. "Can the two of you finish up here alone? Beowulf really should have his wounds looked at."

Wade chuckled. "Royce and I will clean up this mess. The two of you need to leave before you set these ancient redwoods on fire. It's definitely getting too hot around here."

Beowulf scooped Roxie up into his arms, then bounded through the trees, heading for the parked cars. Even though she protested loudly that he shouldn't be carrying her in his weakened state, he didn't put her down. Once they reached the main trail, he stopped only long enough to pick up her discarded shoes.

Once she was seated in the passenger side of his Mercedes, Beowulf came around to the driver's seat and then slipped in behind the steering wheel. He started the car, but before he drove away, he reached over to Roxie and pulled her toward him.

At the first brush of his lips, her body went up in flames of need. The urge to join her body with her mate's was almost too much to ignore. Threading her fingers through Beowulf's thick black hair, she groaned with wanting. She held him to her and pushed her tongue inside his mouth. Sweeping his with hers, she got her first real taste of him. Being a werewolf had its benefits. She could savor the arousal on his tongue. His scent filled her head until she was almost drunk from it.

Beowulf growled deep in his throat and pulled away. "I'm not going to have you in a car like a desperate teenager. So I suggest you keep your hands to yourself until we get home." After putting the car into gear, he drove out of the park.

Roxie found it almost torture having to sit beside Beowulf and unable to touch him. His kiss had brought her body to fever pitch. No matter what she tried, she couldn't get herself settled down. Her breasts ached along with her pussy. She knew Beowulf could smell her arousal as easily as she could. She peered at him and saw his nostrils flare as he inhaled deeply.

The trip to San Francisco had never seemed to take so long as it did now. With each mile, Roxie became more uncomfortable. Her breath came in pants as she tried to ignore her clamoring body.

Beowulf shot a quick glance in her direction before he focused back on the road. "Hang on. We're almost home. It's the mating bond that's making you feel this way. Now that you're a werewolf, your body will be more demanding when it comes to mating. Being separated from me has brought it on." A smile spread across his face. "This also tells me that you truly are my mate. Only between mates does the urge to reaffirm the bond become so strong."

"Too much talking and not enough driving, Beowulf."

Chuckling, Beowulf rounded a corner at almost full speed as he raced toward the gated drive to his house. He pushed a button on his key ring, and the gates swung open. He sped through them and then brought the car to a screeching halt in front of the large house. After he turned it off, he jumped out. Beyond caring who might see them, Roxie launched herself at Beowulf.

Beowulf picked Roxie up off her feet and held her against his chest as he fumbled with his keys, trying to unlock the front door. Moaning, he finally managed to open it as she scraped her teeth against his throat. He kicked it shut, then lifted her higher and fastened his mouth to hers.

Once up the stairs, he walked them right into the shower. After turning on the water, he let her slide down the length of his body. Roxie took hold of his shirt and ripped it down the middle before she peeled it off Beowulf's body. He hissed as the warm water hit his wounds. She undid his pants, then slid them down his legs. He kicked them aside.

Unable to tear her gaze away from his fully engorged cock, Roxie pulled off her clothes and then threw them into the corner of the shower. She lifted her gaze and found him staring at her body with need written on the hard planes of his face. After picking up the soap, she gently cleaned his wounds.

She laved each bite or claw mark with her tongue after washing it with the soap. Beowulf shuddered under her loving ministration. By the time she finished attending to his many wounds, they were both shaking with need. Roxie turned off the faucet, then took him by the hand and led him out of the shower. She towel dried them both, making sure to give his manhood extra attention.

Seeming unable to wait any longer, Beowulf took the towel from Roxie and put it on the bathroom counter. He picked her up, sat her on it, stepped between her legs, and sheathed his hard cock inside her to the hilt. They groaned with pleasure.

She wrapped her legs around his waist and placed her hands on his shoulders as he rocked into her. The feel of his shaft sliding in and out of her body was almost too much. She looked down, watching Beowulf pump into her slick opening. Roxie tightened her inner muscles around him as her release edged ever closer. Once she reached her peak, she lifted her head and bit the side of his neck. Holding on to her hips, he increased his pace, sending them into an intense orgasm.

Panting, Beowulf kissed her lovingly. "I missed you. And I do love you."

She smiled. "I know you do. Now show me again how much you love me."

"My pleasure."

With their bodies joined, Beowulf took Roxie into the bedroom. His cock was still hard and buried deep within her. She quickly became aroused once more. She rolled him onto his back when he got them onto the bed.

Sitting up, Roxie slowly rode him. She arched her back and

angled her hips so she could rub her clit along his hard shaft. He was in so deep, the head of his cock hit her cervix with each stroke in. Beowulf stared up at her and placed his hands on her full breasts. Using thumb and forefinger, he plucked at her peaked nipples. She moaned, but found it wasn't enough. She leaned forward and offered him her breast. He cupped it in his large hand, then swirled his tongue around her nipple before opening his mouth and sucking it deep inside.

With each pull, Roxie's inner walls clenched. She ground her hips into Beowulf's and increased her pace. His cock swelled even more inside her. She was close, but he stilled her movements by holding on to her hips. He released her nipple, lifted her off him, and flipped her onto her stomach. Knowing what he wanted, she lifted onto her hands and knees.

Beowulf came up behind her and stroked her bottom as he ran his wet tongue down the curve of her spine. She pushed back, trying to impale herself on his hard cock, but he shifted out of reach. "Not yet, Roxie. I want your need to be so great that when I put my cock inside you, you'll be screaming with your release."

Beowulf used his lips and tongue to make a trail from the top of her neck to the base of her spine. Roxie gasped as he explored a particularly sensitive spot. Her body screamed with arousal. She tried to take him inside her dripping pussy. Once again, he moved out of reach. Continuing down her body, he bit each rounded globe of her bottom. He spread her legs wider apart, lifted her slightly, then stroked his tongue between her nether lips. Roxie whimpered.

He gave her no mercy as he pushed his tongue inside, tasting her, alternating between lapping up her juices and swirling his tongue around her swollen clit. Roxie clutched the bedsheets beneath her, almost shredding them. Unable to think beyond wanting him inside her, she growled low in her throat, warning him that she couldn't take too much more.

With a low returned growl, Beowulf shifted his position and impaled Roxie on his cock in one stroke. She screamed as the most intense release she'd ever experienced tore through her. He thrust in and out of her. He rubbed her clit with his fingers, causing her climax to seemingly go on and on. He threw back his head, then groaned loudly as his cock pumped his seed deep inside her.

Collapsing onto the bed, panting, they tried to regain their breath. He rolled to his side, holding her spooned up against him.

Roxie's eyes fluttered shut. Wrapped in Beowulf's arms, she snuggled closer. More content than she'd been in days, she knew he was well and truly hers. And if the stupid man thought for one minute she would let him give her up, even if he thought he was doing it for all the right reasons, she would quickly disabuse him of that notion.

* * * *

Rolling over in bed the next morning, Roxie found the spot next to her empty. She opened her eyes and searched the room for Beowulf. Not finding him anywhere, she rubbed the sleep from them and got out of bed. She needed a shower before she came face to face with anyone else who was in the house. She crossed the room to the bathroom.

Clean and refreshed, Roxie dressed and then headed downstairs in search of Beowulf. She found him with Wade, sitting in the kitchen, eating breakfast. Much to her surprise, Royce was with them.

"Nice of you not to invite me to the party." She slipped onto the chair next to Beowulf, then gave him a quick kiss.

"I thought you could use the rest after what happened last night." Beowulf smiled seductively at her, letting her know he didn't only mean the confrontation in Muir Woods.

"Well, I'm very much recovered. I think I'm game to give it another go, maybe longer this time." Roxie bit the inside of her cheek to stop herself from smiling as Beowulf choked on his coffee.

Royce seemed to take pity on Beowulf and took over the conversation. "You didn't miss too much, Roxie. I got here only a few minutes ago. I had to check on our guests before coming here." He looked at Beowulf and added, "I chained the dog out back. I hope you don't mind. I figured you would rather he stayed out there than come inside."

"That's a perfect place for him."

At first, Roxie didn't know what dog they talked about. She then remembered that was what she'd called Gren the night before. "Oh no, you didn't. Did you?" At Royce's smile she knew he had.

She headed for the doors that led out to the large backyard. She opened the French doors and stepped outside onto the patio. She laughed. Hearing the others come outside as well, she said, "It looks as if he has wrapped his chain around the tree."

Royce had indeed chained Gren to one of the larger trees in the yard. Along with the collar the chain was attached to, he wore a muzzle. He glared at them, but in his present condition, he was harmless.

"We thought it would be best to keep him separate from his men until the spell wore off. Once he understands his bad behavior will no longer be tolerated and will be dealt with by a higher authority, then we'll release him," Royce said where he stood next to her.

Roxie wasn't sure letting Gren go would be the best idea. "Are you sure that'll be enough to stop him from trying something else?"

Beowulf put his arm around her shoulders and walked Roxie back into the kitchen. Once they were all seated again, he took her left wrist and pulled off the band she wore. She looked at him in confusion. "We were talking while you slept. After what we saw you do last night, we feel keeping this a secret is not doing you any favors."

"You want other werewolves to know I'm the one from the prophecy?"

"Yes," Royce said. "Roxie, you're more powerful than any werewolf I know. You're able to do what has been considered impossible. Quite frankly, we've no idea what you're capable of. That being said, to keep anything like last night from happening again, all the packs must know about you. We've already started spreading the word. Soon every werewolf will hear the story of how you defeated Gren and his men basically single-handedly."

"So I'm the one with higher authority, am I?" When all three men nodded, she turned to the one who hadn't said anything yet. "Do you agree with their decision, Wade?"

Wade nodded. "It's the only viable option, Roxie. I know it'll make our lives a little easier." He gestured to Beowulf and Royce as well as himself. "Take pity on the poor males who would feel it's their duty to protect you."

Roxie snorted. "All right, all right. No need to get all noble on me. What do I have to do?"

The sound of the doorbell ringing could be heard. Beowulf got up. "You don't have to do anything. They'll come to you. And if I'm not mistaken, I think the first have arrived."

Watching Beowulf leave the room, Roxie didn't know what to think about all this. He returned accompanied by another werewolf. He introduced himself as the leader of his pack. After seeing the mark around her wrist, he bent his head and offered his throat in submission. Unsure what was expected of her, she looked at Beowulf for guidance. Smiling, he took her hand and placed it on the other man's neck. The ritual now completed, the newcomer left as quickly as he'd arrived.

The rest of the day Roxie spent in much the same manner. Other pack leaders arrived to offer her their submission, which in turn she acknowledged. Beowulf never strayed very far. Smiling at him as he led in the next person who had called, Roxie knew her life had taken a turn for the better. Her hermit days were long over. If it hadn't been for Candice meddling in her life, as was her wont, Roxie would never have met Beowulf at Wulf's Den. Fate, it would seem, had indeed led her to where she needed to be.

The End

WADE AND TARYN

Having inherited her uncle's winery, Taryn Davies goes to Wulf's Den hoping to sell her wines to Beowulf, the owner. While there, she meets Wade, Beowulf's brother. Even though she is instantly attracted to him, her past makes it hard for her to accept his advances.

Catching a whiff of Taryn's lingering scent inside Wulf's Den, Wade is determined to make her his. When their first meeting doesn't go as he would have liked, Wade follows Taryn to her winery, The Pines.

As Wade tries to win Taryn over, he has to find a way to explain that he is a werewolf. Little does he know another of his kind has Taryn in his sights, one who means her no good.

DEDICATION

Special thanks go to Nancy Bialek, Executive Director at Stags' Leap District Winegrowers, and Kevin Morriesy, Winemaker at Stags' Leap Winery, for taking the time to answer all my questions about Stags' Leap and growing wine.

CHAPTER ONE

Down in the cellar at Wulf's Den, Wade took stock of the liquor for the nightclub. He was serving a dual purpose by doing it instead of letting his brother, Beowulf, do it. It kept Wade busy, but it also kept him away from Beowulf and his mate, Roxie.

Wade loved them both but being constantly around a mated werewolf couple and not having a mate of his own was starting to wear on his nerves. He was happy his older brother had finally found his mate after spending many, many years alone. He only wished he could find one of his own. That was something most unmated werewolf males longed for. So far, none of the werewolf females had set off his mating urge, the one true sign that he'd found his mate.

Once he'd completed the task at hand, Wade took a deep breath and prepared to go up to the club. Beowulf and Roxie were there. They'd arrived earlier because Beowulf had scheduled a meeting with the owner of a local winery. Apparently, the woman had inherited the winery from some relative and wanted to expand the business. She was dropping off a sample of her wine for Beowulf to try before he made his final decision to serve it at Wulf's Den.

Wade climbed the cellar stairs and then pushed open the door. The scent slammed into him, causing his wolf side to come to instant attention. He took in big drafts of air, the scent filling his lungs, his very being, until it was imprinted on him forever.

As he headed to Beowulf and Roxie by the bar, the scent grew stronger. He had to fight the urge to snarl at Beowulf just because his brother was near the female whose scent told Wade she was meant for him. Once he reached his destination, he searched the club for the woman, but she was nowhere to be seen.

He brushed past Beowulf and picked up the sheet of paper that sat on top of the bar next to an uncorked bottle of wine. He held the paper to his face and took another deep breath. It was covered with her scent.

Without taking the paper away, Wade asked, "Where is she?"

Roxie spoke. "If you mean the woman from the winery, she just left. And I have to say this is a new one for you, Wade. If you don't stop manhandling that piece of paper, I might just start thinking you have some kind of weird fetish. Let me take it before you make such a mess we won't be able to read it anymore."

As Roxie tried to pull it away, Wade gave a warning growl and pressed the sheet of paper against his chest. "I have to find her."

Roxie smiled broadly. "Oh, now I get it. If the growling didn't give you away, your glowing eyes sure do. So she's your mate, is she? Well, good luck with that one. You're going to need it."

"I don't need luck. She's my mate, and that's all I need to know."

Roxie rolled her eyes. "Typical male werewolf response. I think the rush of testosterone has messed with your brain. Going all caveman will not work on that woman, or any woman, for that matter."

"It worked on you." Beowulf was rewarded for his comment when Roxie's elbow jabbed into his ribs. Before she could jab him again, he wrapped his arms around her and pulled her against his broad chest. He turned his attention to Wade. "What Roxie is so eloquently saying is step carefully. The woman is mortal, and I can guarantee you she has no idea what we are. From our meeting, I got the feeling she won't just fall into your open arms because you feel she is your mate. There's a strength about her as if she's used to taking care of herself."

"I'll keep that in mind. Now if you'll excuse me, I have to hunt down my mate."

Cramming the piece of paper into his jeans front pocket, Wade took off at a run. Once he was outside, he took a deep breath of the early evening air. He caught her scent on the light breeze, then turned into the wind and went in search of his mate.

* * * *

Taryn Davies was pleased with the results of her meeting with Beowulf, the owner of Wulf's Den. She had high hopes he would be placing an order for her white zinfandel wine in the not-too-distant future. If he did, then a lot of her financial problems would be over.

After her uncle had died and left the vineyard for her to run, Taryn had been a little surprised to see how much in debt he'd been. She wasn't strapped for money, but it would be a little tight if she couldn't drum up a few more clients. Wulf's Den had been number one on her list. The night club had been around for years and was one of San Francisco's hot spots in the club scene.

Lost in her own thoughts, Taryn at first didn't notice she was being followed. Hoping it was just someone who happened to be walking in the same direction as she, Taryn quickened her pace as she headed for Wulf's Den's parking lot. The footsteps coming behind her kept pace.

Before she could reach her car, the person called out to her. She turned around and she found herself face-to-face with the most gorgeous man she'd ever seen. Actually, he was the second gorgeous man she'd seen that evening, if she counted Beowulf, who was similar in looks, but this man appealed to her senses more.

As he stood before her, staring at her with stark longing in his ice-blue eyes, Taryn took the opportunity to get a better look at him. He was tall, probably close to six feet seven in her estimation. At five feet eight, she still had to crane her neck to look him in the face. And his was all planes and angles. His chestnut, shoulder-length hair only added to his good looks. She dropped her gaze and couldn't help but notice he was built. Her uncle would have said this guy was built like a brick shithouse. He wore a tight black T-shirt, which showed off his broad, well-muscled chest and arms that bulged in all the right places. Her mouth went dry as her gaze moved down farther still. There was a telltale bulge in his tight-fitting jeans as well.

Taryn jerked her gaze back up to his face and asked, "Can I help you?"

He took a step closer, and her heart beat a little faster. There was something about the way he looked at her that caused her body to stand up and take notice. She was getting more turned-on the longer he stared at her.

"You already have. Come back into the club with me and you'll help me even more."

His voice was deep and seemed to hit a chord inside her. Taryn swallowed. "Ah, okay. Do you work at the club? I didn't see you in there."

She had no idea where he was going with that one. She didn't think he was hitting on her. Guys as good-looking as him didn't usually hit on her. She was passable in the looks department, but there wasn't really anything about her that made her stand out. With her long brown hair, which she mostly kept pulled back in a ponytail, and her brown eyes, she thought of herself as mousy in appearance.

"Yes. My name is Wade. I was down in the cellar when you had your meeting with my brother."

That explained why Wade looked so much like Beowulf. It was obvious good looks ran in the family. Taryn stuck out her hand. "Nice to meet you. I hope your brother and I can do business together."

Wade took it, but instead of shaking it, he pulled her closer. Before she realized his intent, he bent his head and claimed her lips in a searing kiss. And he didn't just kiss her—he devoured her. His tongue pushed past her lips and tangled with hers. Desire slammed into her, causing an ache to build between her legs as her pussy grew wet. Taryn knew she was acting like an idiot for allowing him to kiss her. She usually didn't make it a practice to get this close to a guy she'd only met just seconds before. She hadn't even told him her name, and here she was swapping spit with him. And if that wasn't bad enough, she didn't want him to stop.

That soon changed. He held her tightly as he ground his erection against her. With images of the ugly part of her past flashing through her mind, Taryn whimpered and pushed at his chest. When he didn't release her, she acted on instinct.

Using all the dirty fighting skills her uncle had taught her, Taryn grabbed a fistful of Wade's hair and pulled his mouth off hers. With the flat of her hand, she hit him in the nose. She brought her knee up and kneed him in his most vulnerable spot. He instantly let go of her and dropped to the ground as he cupped his manhood in one hand and his nose in the other.

Taryn quickly raced to her car. As she pulled out of the parking lot, she realized she'd just unmanned the brother of a prospective client. She guessed she wouldn't be hearing back from Beowulf any time soon.

* * * *

Still down on the ground, trying to catch his breath, Wade groaned when a recognizable pair of women's shoes came into view. It would have to be Roxie who found him in this undignified position.

"I told you, you would need luck with that one, Wade. Taryn is one tough cookie. What did you do? Try to overwhelm her with your male werewolf sex appeal? I thought you were the romancer of the family."

"Go away, Roxie," Wade snapped.

He really wasn't mad at his brother's mate. He was just mad at himself for doing the one thing he'd advised Beowulf not to do with Roxie when he'd been trying to win her over.

"Fine. Do you want me to get some ice to put on your…?"

Beowulf, who'd come outside in search of Roxie, said, "You'll not be going anywhere near Wade's crotch. The only one you can touch is mine, and don't forget that."

Roxie stepped into Beowulf's arms. "Don't worry, love. How can I forget what you have in those tight pants of yours? There's more than enough of you to keep me coming back for more."

Wade groaned again. "I think I'm going to be sick. Would the two of you please go somewhere else and let me suffer in peace?"

Beowulf chuckled. "We'll leave you alone. Pull yourself together and come back inside the club. The doors are opening in a few minutes."

Once he was alone, Wade slowly got up on his feet. He rubbed the small trickle of blood from his nose with the back of his hand. Taryn was more than capable of taking care of herself, which was highly regarded in a female in werewolf society, but it meant he wouldn't have it easy trying to win her over. As he brushed off his jeans, he felt the lump of paper inside his front pocket. He took it out and opened it. As he read the information on the page, he had an idea. Stepping through the back door of the club, a plan quickly formed in his mind. One Taryn wouldn't be able to turn down.

CHAPTER TWO

Taryn drove the fifty miles back to Napa Valley, calling herself three kinds of fool. Now that she'd had a chance to settle down, she knew she'd overreacted. Yes, Wade had come on a little strong, but she couldn't deny she was attracted to him. If he hadn't become so dominant, she probably would have been tearing at his clothes, but there was that one part of her that couldn't get over what had happened in her past.

She'd been nineteen when she'd decided she wanted to leave the winery where she lived with her Uncle Colin and move to Los Angeles. Having lived with her bachelor uncle since the age of three after her mother, his older sister, had died, Taryn had thought about nothing else but moving to that big city. Thinking back now, she'd been rebelling against the only father figure she'd ever known. Her real father had left her mother soon after he'd found out she was pregnant. That was the only information her uncle had told her about him.

It'd only taken a few months in Los Angeles for Taryn to realize she'd made a mistake by moving there. Then she'd met Nigel.

One night he'd come to the diner where she waited tables. He'd charmed her, and against her better judgment, she'd agreed to go out on a date with him. He had the whole bad-boy persona going on, trying to break free from his rich parents, who liked to keep him on a tight rein. Taryn had fallen for him, hard, and thoughts of returning home soon came few and far between.

It wasn't until they'd been seeing each other for six months that Taryn saw changes in Nigel. He wanted to know exactly what she did when he wasn't with her, demanding minute details.

Not wanting to end their relationship over the phone, Taryn had invited Nigel to her apartment. He'd flown into a rage. That was when he'd hit her. He didn't stop until he'd pounded her down to the floor. After he'd left, promising to return the next day, Taryn had packed up her belongings and fled back home during the night.

Battered and bruised, she'd arrived at The Pines, her uncle's winery. He'd taken one look at her face and had pulled her close, welcoming her home.

Now at twenty-six, that was long in the past, but it had left her scarred. She could only be with men she could control, who never tried to assert their authority over her. At the first sign of such behavior, she cut them out of her life.

She turned onto The Pines' long drive and pushed the painful memories of her past aside. A feeling of pride swept through her. She loved the winery and felt a sense of accomplishment whenever she returned to it. It wasn't large, by any means, but it was all she needed. She loved it. The sweeping hillside filled with tall pine trees, the large stretches of land planted with grapes, but it was the cave set in the hillside that drew her the most. As a little girl, she'd liked to sit for hours inside it, escaping the heat of the summer. Being a hundred feet underground, it was always cool, no matter what time of year it was.

Arriving at the modest two-story brick house at the end of the drive, Taryn decided to make it an early night. Tomorrow would be busy for her. Harvest was due to begin any day, and there were a lot of things that had to be done in preparation for it. And now that she'd probably blown any prospect of having Wulf's Den as a client, she had the added burden of trying to find some other night club where she could sell her wines. Still feeling as if she needed a kick in the rear end, she walked into the house. Inside her bedroom as she fell asleep, she couldn't stop thinking about Wade and how good it'd felt being kissed by him.

* * * *

It was early morning, two days later, that Wade took the trip to Napa Valley. Shortly after dawn he'd finally given up trying to sleep. Once he had fallen asleep, his dreams had been filled with Taryn naked on his bed, holding him close as he rode her. He'd awakened with a raging hard-on. Now that he knew she was his mate, the dreams would grow more erotic until he claimed her. All male werewolves suffered through this after finding their mates.

As he drove by wineries, Wade smelled the grapes' ripe sweetness. With his acute sense of smell, he could tell they were at their peak, ready for the harvest. Since it was nearing the middle of October, he'd been counting on such an instance.

He entered the Stags Leap District of Napa Valley and picked up the map he'd printed off the Internet that showed how to get to Taryn's vineyard, which was on the Silverado Trail. In a matter of minutes, he pulled onto the large drive of The Pines Winery. He lowered the window on his metallic-gray Infiniti G35, then took a deep breath. He smelled the large pine trees that grew on the property as well as the different kinds of grapes in the vineyard.

He arrived at the house at the end of the drive, then turned off the car. Wade hoped Taryn would be awake, but he thought she would be since she had a vineyard to look after. He took a few deep, calming breaths before he climbed out of his vehicle. He had to take it slow with her or he was liable to end up with a broken nose again. Luckily for him, werewolves healed at a fast rate, and his nose showed no signs of the trauma from a couple days ago.

He climbed the two wooden steps up to the screen door and was about to knock when Taryn pulled open the inner door. Wade realized she hadn't notice his presence as she pushed it, which in turn connected with his nose hard enough to cause it to bleed.

He cursed under his breath and cupped a hand around the abused body part. "What do you have against my nose?"

At the sound of his voice, Taryn jumped. "Oh! Oh God, Wade. I'm so sorry. Here, come inside so I can take a look at it. I didn't see you there."

Wade let Taryn take him by the arm and pull him inside the house. She brought him to the kitchen and forced him onto one of the table chairs. Before he could take a good look around, she'd bent his head back, grabbed a handful of tissues, and held them to his nose as she applied pressure.

"Do you make it a habit of smacking men in the noses? That's twice now you've gotten me."

Wade's gut clenched as Taryn took her bottom lip between her teeth and apologetically looked at him. With her standing this close, and her scent wafting around him, it took all he had not to pull her into his arms.

"Sorry, for both times. Today was a complete accident."

"And two days ago? That was no accident."

"Well, no, it wasn't. You do have to admit you came on a little strong."

His nose stopped bleeding. Wade pulled the tissue away and flashed a smile. "When I see something I like, I tend to go after it."

Taryn scowled. "You can save your charm for another girl. It won't work on me. I know you aren't serious."

"Why wouldn't I be?"

Taryn rolled her eyes. "I do own a mirror, you know."

"And?"

"You're going to make me say it, aren't you? Fine. With my looks and the way I dress, there's no way a man as good-looking as you would be attracted to the likes of me."

"So, you think I'm good-looking?"

Taryn rolled her eyes once again. "Do I have to add conceited to the list?"

Unable to stand having her next to him and not touching her, Wade reached out and pulled Taryn onto his lap. He wrapped his arms loosely around her waist. She stiffened for the briefest of seconds before she relaxed. "For your information, you're exactly what I've been looking for."

"Now *that* I find hard to believe."

"It shouldn't be all that unbelievable. I can prove it as well."

Shifting Taryn on his lap, Wade pressed her bottom against the evidence of his arousal. Her eyes widened slightly, but she made no move to pull away. He took that as a good sign. It was killing him, but he sensed the only way he was going to get anywhere with her was to take it slow and easy.

*

The hard length of Wade's cock nestled against Taryn's bottom. Oddly enough, she couldn't force herself to move away, let alone get off him. Sitting on his lap, she felt protected. She was still finding it hard to believe a guy with his looks was attracted to her, but there was no mistaking the longing in his ice-blue eyes, nor the hardness pressed against her.

She found it no easy task to think straight so she changed the subject. "Why have you come to The Pines?"

"To see if I could get you into bed." She cocked a brow at him, and he chuckled. "Okay. I can see you aren't open to that just yet. I also wanted to discuss business."

"Has Beowulf decided to buy my wine?"

"Not yet, but he'd like to know more about you and your winery. Such as what types of grapes you grow and how your wine is made, that sort of thing. If you're agreeable, I'd like to stay here a few days and get my hands dirty, so to speak. I know it's almost harvest time, and I'd like to help with it. Then when I return to San Francisco, Beowulf will make his decision."

"And if I refuse to have you stay?"

"Then I can't promise you Beowulf will buy your wine."

The idea of having Wade stay at the winery was appealing but made her uneasy at the same time. It sounded a bit like blackmail. She did need the extra pair of hands at harvest time, though, and it would give her a better chance to get to know Wade, but the thought of having him stay at her house, just the two of them, made her a little apprehensive. Not since Nigel had a man slept under the same roof as her, except, of course, for Uncle Colin.

Not wanting to lose out on the business arrangement she could have with Wulf's Den, Taryn ignored her uneasiness and nodded. "All right. You can stay, but there have to be a few ground rules."

"Such as?"

"If you want to help with the harvest, you have to do what I say. I can promise you it'll be no walk in the park. The grapes have to be harvested by hand, which takes many hours."

"I'm up to the task. Now what about us?"

Taryn shook her head. "There isn't any us, Wade. No offense, but you aren't the type of guy I usually date."

"I know you're attracted to me as well. Why not let nature take its course and see what happens?"

"That has no bearing on my decision." She tried to slip off Wade's lap, but he wrapped his arms tighter around her, not allowing her to move. Panic rose inside her. She pushed at his chest and looked at him, hoping what she felt wasn't showing in her eyes, and muttered, "Let me go."

Wade quickly let her off his lap. "I can sense your fear. I would never hurt you."

"It's not you. I'm the problem. If you weren't so dominant, I'd be fine. I have to be the one in charge or I panic."

"What happened?"

"It's nothing."

"I think it's far from nothing. You can trust me. I would never do anything to hurt you."

Taryn sighed. She had no idea why she believed Wade wouldn't do her any harm, but she just knew he wouldn't. "A boyfriend I had when I was younger didn't take rejection too well. When I broke up with him, he didn't…react…too kindly to it."

Wade stood and looked at her. "He hit you, didn't he?"

She heard the anger in his voice. "Yes, but I never gave him the opportunity to do it again. And it was a long time ago."

"He marked you on the inside, not just on the outside. Does he live around here? I'd gladly show him the error of his ways."

Taryn shook her head. "Nigel doesn't live here. I met him when I was living in Los Angeles. I haven't seen him since that day, and I'm sure I'll never see him again. I hadn't told him about my uncle or the winery. Uncle Colin patched me up and made sure I wouldn't find myself in such a predicament again."

"He taught you how to defend yourself."

"Yes. He'd done a stint in the Army for a few years. He left it when his parents died, and took over the winery. Now it's mine through him."

"When did your uncle die?"

"Almost a year ago." Taryn missed her uncle and still found it hard to talk about his passing. "He had cancer. I don't want to talk about it. Just try to understand that this will be a business arrangement only."

"I'm not willing to just let you slip through my fingers. Now that I know about your past, we can work through this together. You were fine with me kissing you the other night when I wasn't holding you to me. How about we try again? I'll keep my hands to myself, and you can stop me if you start feeling panicky."

"I don't think that's a good—"

Wade cut off her protest with his lips and kissed her as if he had all the time in the world. He stayed true to his word and kept his hands behind his back so he couldn't touch her. Taryn's eyes fluttered shut as she enjoyed the feel of his mouth on hers, but soon it wasn't enough. There was something about him that affected her on the basest of levels.

Taryn took the step needed to bring their bodies within touching distance, then placed the flats of her hands on his muscled chest. His heart thundered beneath her palms. Her body reacted to his closeness. Her breasts grew heavy as her nipples tightened into buds. Sighing, she increased the pressure of the kiss.

Wade swept the seam of her lips. She opened for him, allowing him entrance. She fisted her hands in his shirt and clung to him as his tongue twined with hers. Her body liquefied with need as he sucked her tongue into his mouth. Taryn moaned and ground herself against his hard thigh after he put it between her legs.

It was then that his control slipped. One arm snaked around her waist and pulled her hard against his chest. The flames of desire that'd been licking at her body quickly changed to panic. She whimpered. Wade growled in the back of his throat, but he released her before he turned away.

Taryn placed her hand on his back. Wade held himself stiff. "Sorry."

Wade stepped away until she no longer touched him. "Don't. Don't apologize." His voiced sounded strained, almost as if he was on the verge of growling again. "Just give me a minute to get myself back under control."

Without saying a word, Taryn left the kitchen and went outside. She wouldn't blame Wade if he gave up on her. Hell, if she were a man, she would give up on her. No sane member of the opposite sex wanted a head case for a girlfriend. That was part of the reason she'd given up looking for that special someone. She really didn't need a man in her life. She had the winery, and that was all she needed to make herself happy, but she couldn't quite ignore that small part of her that screamed at how unfair it all was. Pulling herself together, she stepped off the porch before she headed for one of the outbuildings. The day was slipping away, and she had work to do.

CHAPTER THREE

Once Taryn was out of the house, Wade let loose the growl of frustration he'd been holding in. It'd been too close. As she had panicked, the wolf inside him had risen, demanding he claim her as his regardless of how she felt. If he hadn't turned his back on her, she would have seen how his eyes had glowed, and that wouldn't have been a good thing.

Now that he knew about her past, it only made things that much more difficult. He'd known his being a werewolf—and Taryn not—would be hard enough to deal with, but with an abusive ex-boyfriend who'd left mental scars? Wade found himself against a rock and a hard place. The more time he spent around her, touching her, tasting her, the harder the mating urge would ride him.

Finally getting a grip, Wade went in search of Taryn. Not seeing her anywhere out at the front of the house, he took a deep breath. He easily picked up her scent trail and followed it to one of the outbuildings.

He stepped inside the larger structure where her scent was the freshest, and was hit with the strong smell of grapes and wine. To a mortal the smells wouldn't have been as powerful, but to a werewolf's sense, it was almost overwhelming. Judging by the machines sitting idle and the empty space, Wade figured this was where the harvested grapes were brought to be processed.

He walked farther inside until he came to a small office. There he found Taryn sitting behind her desk. She scowled at a piece of paper sitting in front of her. "Bad news?"

Taryn looked up. "Not really, more of an inconvenience."

"Anything I can do to help?"

"No. The extra crew I usually hire on to help with the harvest won't be coming this year. Now I have to see if I can find another one to replace them. It'll be cutting it close."

"If you need extra hands for harvesting, and experience is not a necessity, I can manage to get you some help."

In some ways it was nice living in pack society. Other members could be counted on when help was needed, usually with no questions asked. And it helped having an older brother who happened to be the pack leader. If Taryn couldn't find workers, Wade had no qualms about calling Beowulf.

Taryn nodded. "I'll keep that in mind, but I should be okay." Silence fell between them. Once it grew too heavy, she stood. "If you want, I can show you around the vineyard. Or would you rather wait until later?"

"I'm fine. I'd love to be taken on the official tour."

Wade stepped back and let Taryn lead the way. He automatically lowered his gaze to her bottom. The jeans she wore were tight in all the right places.

Distracted, Wade at first didn't realize Taryn was speaking. "Sorry, what was that?"

She stopped walking and turned to look at him. "I said this is the building where we crush the grapes and then put the juice in oak barrels. When the wine is ready for bottling, we do that here as well."

"I smelled them both when I came in."

"Really? I don't smell anything right now. You must have a sensitive nose to have picked up on those smells."

"Yeah, you could say that. Sort of runs in my family."

"I may have to put that nose of yours to work then."

Wade took a step closer, buried his nose in the crook of her neck and took a deep breath. "If it involves smelling you, I'm game."

"Wine. I meant I'd get you to smell some of my wines."

Wade bit back a smile as Taryn swallowed audibly and then

continued with her tour. Once they were outside, she headed for the vineyard where the grapes were growing. He smelled their ripeness even before they came into view.

Seeing all the grapevines growing, row after row, Wade realized harvesting would be no picnic. Doing it all by hand made it seem like a monumental task. Never one to shy away from hard work, he had to give the winery owners their due for doing it year after year. Owning one took a lot of commitment to keep it producing quality grapes. The sense of pride that came with the product of hard work must be enormous. Looking at her, he saw the pride she felt as she looked at the fields.

"What kind of grapes do you grow?"

Taryn's face became animated as she spoke of the vineyard. He could tell this was an occupation she loved doing. "We grow three types—cabernet sauvignon, merlot, and red zinfandel."

"And it's the zinfandel wine you want to sell to Wulf's Den?"

"Yes. Growing the red zinfandel grapes to make white zinfandel wine was my pet project. Uncle Colin kept the family tradition of making cabernet sauvignon, but I wanted to expand. This year will be the third that we'll have enough grapes to make a large amount of white zinfandel wine. They did really well this year."

They were now walking between the planted rows of grapes. Wade looked at the variety Taryn had pointed out as red zinfandel. They were large and grew together in tight bunches. He smelled the juice inside them, which was a lot sweeter than in the other two varieties.

As Taryn continued to speak, Wade looked at the sweeping hillside of tall pine trees. They appealed to the animal side of him. He decided that after she went to sleep tonight, he would go wolf and take a run through the trees. Being around her all day and not being able to claim her would take its toll on him. There was nothing better than shifting into his wolf form and running in the night to work off some excess energy. And he had a feeling he would have a lot of pent-up frustration to work off as well.

* * * *

Taryn settled herself on the loveseat in the living room and looked at Wade who sat in the large plush chair across from her. It'd been a long day, and having him follow her as she went about her chores had made it feel that much longer.

It wasn't that she disliked having him around. The problem was she liked it far too much. She'd caught him staring at her as if he wanted to devour her more than once, and each time, a wave of desire had shot through her.

By the end of the day, she'd felt on edge with thoughts of all the things she would like to do to Wade. The man was total sin, and well he knew it. He'd used every opportunity that presented itself to stand close. So close that at times she felt the heat radiating off him. And as he'd inadvertently brushed against her, she'd gloried in the feel of having his hard body flittingly pressed to hers.

Even now, Taryn felt as if she were on fire. Wade hadn't so much as tried to kiss her after the one they'd shared that morning, but that didn't stop her from being all too aware of him as a man she was attracted to. If he looked at her one more time with longing in his eyes, she would more than likely jump on him and kiss him until they were both breathless. And that would only lead to disaster — again. He was not the type of man to let a woman completely have her way with him. He'd proved that both times he'd kissed her.

Taking a sip from the glass of wine she held, Taryn glanced at Wade. She couldn't help staring at him as if she were a lovesick teenager. With his looks, she was sure he was used to having women drooling over him and fantasizing about what they would do to his hard body if they managed to get him into their beds.

She lifted her gaze and found him staring at her with a look that said he knew exactly what she'd been thinking. She felt her face flush, but she couldn't tear her gaze from Wade.

He drained his glass of wine and then came to her. He knelt on the floor before her, took her wineglass, and placed it along with his on the small table next to the loveseat. Taryn had to look slightly down at him. This way, he wasn't as intimidating as he would have been standing at his full height. Part of her panic stemmed from his large size. In the back of her mind, she knew he could snap her like a twig if he wanted to.

Taryn moved until she sat on the very edge of the loveseat.

Wade shifted forward until he knelt between her legs. He rested his hands on her thighs. He stared up at her, waiting for her to make the first move, looking as if he didn't want to do anything she wasn't ready for.

With a none-too-steady hand, Taryn reached out and ran her fingers through Wade's hair. At her touch, he made a gruff noise that sounded almost a half growl, half moan. For a split second, she swore his ice-blue eyes took on a muted glow before he closed them. When he opened them again, it was gone.

Wade spoke in a low tone. "You can touch me as much as you want, but you're going to kill me if you don't kiss me."

There was longing in Wade's voice. In response, her heart beat faster and her body ached, wanting things she'd long denied it. Unable to keep herself away from him any longer, Taryn placed her hands on his shoulders and lightly brushed her lips against his. Giving herself up to the needs of her body, she kissed him fully.

Wade made no move to pull her to him. He tightened his grip on her thighs as he held himself back. That he tried to let her have control seemed to open a floodgate inside her. With a moan, Taryn wrapped her arms around his neck and pulled him closer until her breasts were against his chest.

Taryn deepened the kiss and slid her hands down Wade's sides until she reached the bottom of his shirt. She slipped her fingers under it and ran them up his back, but it wasn't enough. His shirt was in the way. She broke contact with his mouth, then pulled it up and over his head.

With her hands and gaze, Taryn traced the muscled contours of his chest and well-defined abs. He was a work of art. She could only imagine the number of hours he must spend in a gym to get a chest like he had.

Taryn needed to be even closer, to feel his skin on hers. She quickly pulled her shirt off and then removed her bra. Wade sucked in a loud breath. Not giving him the chance to say anything, she slipped from the loveseat and passionately kissed him. Using her weight, she pressed herself against his chest until he was forced to sit on the floor. Once in that position, she straddled his thighs. He shook beneath her, but he leaned back on his arms, supporting them both.

She seemed to go up in flames. The hard length of his cock came to rest along her pussy. Her inner muscles clenched in response, wanting to have his hard shaft moving in and out of her.

Taryn left a trail of kisses along his firm jaw, then down the side of his neck. Wade's whole body stiffened in anticipation. She gently nipped him on the large vein there. He stiffened even more. She licked her way down until she came to where his shoulder and neck met. As she dragged her teeth across that area of skin, he bucked his hips beneath her. She lifted her head, and he groaned.

She saw the strain on Wade's face. He looked pleadingly up at her. "I have to touch you, Taryn. Just let me. Please."

Slowly, she nodded. Wade sat up so he was no longer leaning on his hands and claimed her lips. As he pushed his way inside her mouth, he reached up and cupped her breasts. With his thumb and forefinger, he tugged on her nipples. Taryn moaned and moved her hips against his erection. Leaving her mouth, he lifted one of her breasts and swirled his tongue around the taut peak. She pressed against him as he sucked her nipple deep inside. She moaned again and threaded her fingers through his hair, holding him to her.

Wade moved to her other breast, then shifted the two of them until he had her once again sitting on the very edge of the loveseat with him kneeling between her legs. With nimble fingers, he undid her jeans and then slowly peeled them down her hips. He sat back on his heels and pulled her pants down the rest of her body. Only in her lace panties, Taryn watched him kiss his way up her inner thigh. Unable to keep the upright position she sat in, Taryn leaned back against the loveseat cushions.

She closed her eyes in anticipation as Wade ran his hands up her inner thighs and pushed them wider apart. The feel of his warm breath through her panties, against her throbbing core, had Taryn lifting her hips. He hooked a finger under the top of her panties and gently pulled them free of her body.

The first flick of his tongue against her clit had Taryn digging her fingernails into the cushions beneath her. Wade spread the lips of her pussy and licked her from bottom to top, lapping at her. Lost in a sea of longing, she arched her hips as she whimpered with need.

Wade showed her no mercy as he continued to tongue her

pussy until it was wet with her juices and his ministrations. When she thought she couldn't take any more, he took her clit into his mouth and sucked. At the same time, he probed her opening with a finger before pushing it inside her wetness. He moved in and out as he continued to suck. A second finger soon joined the first, and an orgasm raced ever nearer to claim her.

Wade alternated between sucking on her clit and swirling his tongue around it. Taryn moaned and clamped down on his fingers with her inner muscles. Her hips jerked under his mouth as her orgasm tore through her.

Once she came back down to earth, she found Wade still kneeling between her spread thighs with his head resting on her belly. He was breathing hard. Knowing he had yet to find his own release, Taryn urged him to look up at her.

"Your turn."

Wade shook his head. "No. This was for you, to show you I can be trusted. That I won't do anything you don't want."

"It wouldn't be fair of me to leave you aching and wanting."

"Having you come for me was enough for now. When I make love to you, I want you no longer afraid. Because when I'm in you so deep you can't tell where I end and you begin, I'm not going to be able to stop myself from having you under me. Not the first time we make love."

Wade's words made Taryn shiver with longing, but he was right. They had to take it one step at a time. As he stood and then picked up his shirt off the floor, she asked, "Where are you going?"

He smiled down at her. "I need to go for a run outside or I won't be able to sleep tonight."

Taryn could tell from the bulge in the front of his jeans that he still had an erection. She held her hand out to him. "Don't go outside. It's dark."

Wade shook his head as he backed away. "You're far too tempting lying there like that. I don't want to mess this up. Besides, I like running outside in the dark. Go to bed. I'll lock up the house after I come back."

Before she could say anything else, Wade quickly left the room. Taryn heard the front door open and then close a few seconds later.

CHAPTER FOUR

Once Wade was far enough away from the house, he went wolf. He willed himself to change as he held out his hand and watched it shimmer, then blur. In a matter of seconds, it was complete. He sniffed the air as a slight breeze ruffled his chestnut-colored fur. Reveling in the freedom the wolf's body gave him, he threw back his head and howled into the night. He bunched his back legs beneath him before he took off at a run. He headed for the tall pine trees.

Now that it was the middle of October, the nights were getting decidedly cooler, not that he felt it through the thick fur that covered his body. After he reached the shelter of the trees, Wade put his nose to the ground. He picked up the scent of a deer, days old. Following it, he found a small animal trail that led through the tall pines. With his excellent night vision, he had no problem keeping to it. He put on a burst of speed, running flat out until he was winded.

The run helped take some of the edge off the mating urge that rode him, but with Taryn's scent still clinging to him, it would only be a temporary fix. It had been pure torture having her naked and willing but unable to claim her. Her climaxing with his mouth on her had heightened his arousal to the point of pain. The wolf had risen, urging him to take her. It'd been a battle he wasn't sure he would win at first. He'd kept the wolf restrained by remembering what he could lose if he succumbed to his desires.

With one last howl, Wade turned and headed back the way he'd come. Now that he'd had his first real taste of Taryn, he didn't like being away from her for very long. The feeling would increase after the first time they made love. For that was when they would be joined completely — body and soul. He only hoped she would feel the same, but with her not being a werewolf, he wasn't sure she would.

Deciding Taryn would be asleep, Wade skirted around the back lawn to the front while still in wolf form. He changed to his human one once he reached the porch. He let himself into the house, then made sure to lock the front door before he headed upstairs. Before moving on to his room, he stood at her bedroom door. All was quiet inside. He gently ran his fingers down the door, silently bidding his mate a good night.

* * * *

The second wolf's howl brought Taryn to her bedroom window. She'd heard the first one soon after Wade had gone outside. With the second howl, she knew no stray dog was capable of such vocalization. A wolf's call was very distinct. It couldn't be mistaken for anything else but what it was.

A little worried that Wade would encounter the wolf while he was out on his run, Taryn pulled opened the curtain and searched the back lawn. At first, she didn't see anything. Then out of the corner of her eye, she saw something moving in the direction of the front of the house. She turned to look at it and gasped. It was a wolf, but it was the biggest one she'd ever seen. It seemed in no hurry as it walked around the edge of the lawn. The outside lights reflected off its shiny chestnut-brown fur. She pressed her face to the glass and watched the wolf until it disappeared.

Taryn tugged the curtain back into place. There was something about seeing the wolf that caused a niggling feeling in the back of her mind. As if there were something she'd forgotten, something that had happened in her past. She shook her head at her own foolishness as she climbed into bed. Why a wolf would set her off so, she had no idea. It wasn't as if she'd ever been up close to a wild one. She'd seen them in the zoo, and those wolves hadn't caused that type of reaction.

Before she closed her eyes, she heard the front door open, and she relaxed. Wade and the wolf had obviously not crossed paths. The last thought she had before sleep claimed her was she hoped she never encountered it when she was outside, working in the vineyard. Even though her fear was unfounded, she would be terrified to come face-to-face with it.

* * * *

She waited for Wade to come closer. She couldn't wait to be in his arms. Once he reached her and roughly pulled her against his hard chest, wrapping his arms tightly around her, Taryn didn't feel the usual panic rise inside her. She knew he would never use his strength to hurt her. In his arms, she felt protected, loved. She felt the rightness of it in her very soul. He was hers, just as she was his.

Taryn threaded her fingers through his chestnut-colored hair, then brought Wade's mouth down to hers. The feel of his lips moving against hers caused an ache to build between her legs. With just one kiss, he set her body aflame. She pressed herself closer, not caring that she pulled his hair as she held him tighter.

Wade growled deep in his throat. The animalistic sound sent a rush of desire surging through her. Moaning, she reached between them and cupped the hard length of his cock.

At the loud, menacing sound coming directly behind her, Taryn pulled away. His lip curled in a snarl as he looked at something over her shoulder. Her heart racing with fear, she slowly turned her head to look behind her.

A cold shiver ran down her back at seeing the large wolf watching them. His silvery-gray fur bristled around his neck as he growled a second time. Frozen with fear, Taryn could only watch as the wolf stepped closer.

Just before he made ready to launch himself at them, Wade pushed her aside. His body shimmered, then blurred as he threw himself at the attacking wolf. Wade was no longer Wade. In his place was the wolf she'd seen outside her bedroom window.

Taryn shook her head, slowly backing away from them as they furiously attacked each other. Their snarls and growls filled her head. She had to get away, especially from the gray wolf. She feared him the most.

* * * *

Taryn gasped for air as she sat up in bed. A whimper of fear escaped her lips before she could hold it back. Her body was covered in sweat, and her heart thundered. Looking about the darkened room, she saw it was still the middle of the night. Not sure if she would be able to go back to sleep, she lay down and pulled the covers up to her chin.

She rarely had dreams that were as vivid as this one had been. She forgot most of them the instant she woke up. This was only the third time in her life she'd had a dream where she remembered it all. The first time had been just before she'd tried to break up with Nigel, and the second was the night before her uncle had told her he was dying of cancer. Both dreams had given her a glimpse of what was to come. She'd ignored the dream she'd had about Nigel turning on her, much to her detriment. The one she'd had of her uncle being ill, she could do nothing about, but it had better prepared her. She'd been strong for her uncle that day, not allowing herself to show the anguish she felt inside when what he had to have been feeling was ten times worse.

This dream, she didn't know what to make of it. If there was a hidden message in it, she didn't know where to look for it. There was no way Wade could turn into a wolf. Werewolves were only real in movies and myths. As for the gray wolf... Taryn shivered just thinking about it. Why she should feel such fear escaped her.

Needing to push away all thoughts of the dream or she would never get back to sleep, Taryn rolled onto her side and hugged the extra pillow on her bed to her chest. She closed her eyes and tried to will herself to sleep.

* * * *

The sound of pots and pans being banged about downstairs in the kitchen, along with the smell of something burning, brought Taryn awake. She groaned when she saw how late it was. It'd taken her over two hours to fall back to sleep, and now she was paying for it.

Another loud bang from downstairs reached her ears, followed by the sound of a plate breaking. Since there was only one other person in the house with her, Taryn decided she'd better get Wade out of her kitchen before he did some major damage. She threw back the covers, quickly pulled on some clothes, and hurriedly went down the stairs.

Taryn walked into the kitchen and had to hold back the laughter that bubbled up inside her. Wade stood at the stove, madly waving a tea towel over a smoking frying pan. The kitchen window was wide open, which she guessed he used to suck the smoke out of the room. She was surprised the smoke detector in the hallway hadn't gone off. There was another frying pan sitting in the sink with something charred beyond recognition still in it. A shattered plate was on the floor by the stove with what looked to be undercooked eggs mixed with the pieces of plate.

Taryn cleared her throat, drawing Wade's attention. "Do I have any plates left or have you broken them all?"

Wade stopped waving the tea towel and gave her a sheepish look. "I had planned on surprising you with some breakfast, but it would seem I can't cook."

"It sounds as if you've never tried to before."

"Well, actually, no, I haven't. We have a cook to make all the meals at home. So I never really had to learn. I just thought since Beowulf cooks for Roxie, I would cook for you as well."

"It's the thought that counts, Wade." Taryn stepped closer to kiss his cheek. "Let me clean up this mess. Then I'll make us some breakfast."

Taryn picked up the pieces of the broken plate, then threw them into the garbage before she set to work cleaning up the egg mess off the floor. Once that was done, she turned her attention to the two frying pans. Holding the pan in the sink, she turned to look at Wade with a raised brow. Whatever the food had been, it now resembled a lump of charcoal.

"That was bacon, and before you ask, in the other frying pan I was trying to make fried eggs."

Taryn didn't think she'd ever seen eggs burned to the point of ash before. DNA testing would have had to be done to determine what it was. She discarded all the burned food, then washed out the two frying pans before placing them onto the stove. She quickly pulled them off when she saw Wade had left the burners on. It was no wonder he'd burned the food he'd been trying to cook. Both burners had been set to high. She turned them off and then put the frying pans on the counter before turning to the fridge to get more eggs and bacon.

Wade sat at the kitchen table as she worked, keeping as much distance as he could from the stove. With the bacon sizzling in one frying pan, Taryn poured them each a cup of coffee. She was glad her coffeemaker had a programmable timer set to automatically start brewing before she got up each morning. There was no telling what his coffee would have tasted like. If his coffee-making skills matched his cooking skills, it would more than likely have turned out to be strong enough to strip wallpaper.

She placed a cup on the table in front of Wade. "If you like your coffee with cream, there's some in the fridge, and the sugar is in the cupboard. At least we don't have to wait for this."

"Hey, I do know how to make coffee, you know."

"Did I say you couldn't?"

"No, but I know that was what you were thinking."

Taryn couldn't quite hold back a smile. "Well, that thought had crossed my mind."

"I'm not completely incompetent. I'm skilled in other areas, ones that count more. I'd be more than willing to show you." Wade suggestively looked at her mouth.

Taryn shook her head and went back to the stove. "Oh no, you won't. There has been enough food burned to a crisp in this kitchen for one day, thank you very much. Play time will have to wait until later. Since I slept in, I'm behind on what I have to do today. And it's time for you earn your keep."

"Are you always such a slave driver?"

"When I have to be." Taryn took the now cooked batch of bacon out of the pan and put it on a paper towel-lined plate. While she placed more bacon into the frying pan to cook, she nonchalantly asked, "Did you happen to see a wolf when you went outside last night for your run?"

"A wolf?"

She looked over her shoulder at Wade and saw he had a funny expression on his face. It quickly disappeared when she caught his gaze. "Yeah, a wolf. I heard one howling last night. When I looked out my bedroom window, I saw this huge wolf in the backyard. I just thought you may have seen it since it would have been at the front of the house when you came back from your run. It'd been heading in that direction when I saw it."

"You sure it wasn't a dog? There shouldn't be any wild wolves around here."

Taryn gave Wade a look that said she wasn't that stupid. "I do know the difference between a dog and a wolf. This was most definitely a wolf."

Wade shook his head. "Nope, I didn't see it. Maybe it got scared and took off."

"I hope so. I know I don't want to run into it when I'm working in the vineyard." Taryn shivered at the thought.

"You know it would probably be more afraid of you than you are of it. Have you always been afraid of wolves?"

Wade leaned forward in his chair as he waited for her to answer. Taryn had the feeling what she said would mean more to him than just a simple answer. "No. I've always thought wolves were beautiful." Taryn shook her head. "I don't know why that one makes me uneasy. Maybe the dream I had last night is feeding my fear of it."

"Want to talk about it? Sometimes it helps to tell somebody."

Finished cooking the bacon and eggs, Taryn dished up two plates and then brought them to the kitchen table. Wade started to eat as soon as she placed one in front of him. She sat in the chair next to him and laughed. "If you want more, help yourself."

"Good. Now what happened in your dream?"

"I don't know. It'll sound silly."

"Come on. I won't make fun of you. I promise."

Taryn would be too embarrassed to tell it if she had to look Wade in the face so she kept her gaze glued to her plate. "All right. The dream starts out fine, better than fine. I'm in your arms, and you're kissing me. Things start to really heat up, but that's when it gets a little disturbing. A large gray wolf appears behind me. The way he growls at us, I know he's going to attack. Before he can, you push me aside and turn into the wolf I saw last night and attack him. That's pretty much around the time I forced myself to wake up." When he remained silent, she looked at him. There was no expression on his face. "I know. It sounds stupid even to me. Forget I said anything."

"It doesn't sound stupid. Have you ever seen this gray wolf before?"

"No. Why?"

"I just wondered."

Since Wade didn't add any more, Taryn let the matter drop. Even though he hadn't said much about her dream, she had to admit it seemed less disturbing now that she'd told him about it. Determined to forget it, she picked up her fork and started to eat. At the rate he shoveled food into his mouth, she thought it would be wise to clean her plate before he ate what was left and then asked for hers.

CHAPTER FIVE

Taryn hung up the phone in her office and sighed. Trying to find a replacement crew to help on the vineyard was not going to be easy. All the crews were either already scheduled to work on another vineyard or had some reason for not being available. This had never happened to her before. If she were a suspicious person, she would think there was a conspiracy against her. That someone didn't want her to get her grapes harvested.

She pushed back her desk chair, left her office, and went outside to see how Wade was managing. She'd sent him out with the permanent workers who worked at the vineyard year-round. Growing grapes needed constant care.

Wade was bent over with his back to her when Taryn arrived at the field. He was busy tying the grapevines to the trellis system where new growth needed to be supported. Taryn slowed and watched him as he worked. She would be quite happy to stand there for hours, watching him. And the longer she watched, the more she felt pulled to him. Even though they hadn't had intercourse the night before, she felt closer to him, as if a connection had been started between them.

The muscles in his arms and back flexed as Wade worked. Her stomach fluttered as she thought about how it had felt to be held in his strong arms. Surprisingly, the idea of him crushing her to him didn't make her feel so panicky. Last night had shown she could possibly trust him. Even though he was twice the size of her, he would never use it against her. At least that was the impression she'd gotten from his touch. He'd handled her with the greatest of care.

Wade straightened to his full height and stretched. Taryn moved her gaze down to his hard ass. His jeans were tight in all the right places. Her mouth went dry, causing her to lick her lips. Feeling eyes on her, she looked up to find him turning around so he could intently stare at her.

Taryn crossed the remaining distance and went to stand in front of Wade. His nostrils flared slightly has he took a deep breath. "I can smell you, as well as the grapes and roses. For a winery, you grow an awful lot of roses." He gestured to the rosebushes growing along the edge of the vineyard.

"Roses serve an important purpose. Both grapes and roses can get a fungus called powdery mildew. Roses tend to get the fungus first. When that happens, we know the grapes have to be sprayed with sulfur to prevent it from spreading to them. The roses warn against other diseases as well." Taryn sniffed the air, but she could only smell the grapes. Wade had one powerful sense of smell.

"And here I thought you were just a rose fanatic."

Taryn chuckled. "Well, I *do* love roses."

Wade came closer until their bodies were almost touching. "Did you have any luck?"

With Wade this near, Taryn smelled his sweat along with his musky, male scent. She dropped her gaze to his mouth. She watched his firm lips form the words he spoke, but she had no idea what he'd said she was so distracted. "What?"

His lips formed into a smile. "I asked if you had any luck finding another crew."

"Oh, no, I didn't." Taryn dragged her gaze back up to Wade's. Her breath quickened as he looked at her with his eyes dilated with arousal. "It looks as if I may have a harder time finding one before the crush starts."

"Crush?"

"The harvest. Crush is what we in Napa Valley call this time of year because we harvest the grapes and then crush them."

"Makes sense." Wade reached up and gently pushed a lock of hair out of her eyes. "How about we talk to Beowulf tonight?"

"How can your brother help me find a crew?"

"It wouldn't be a crew per se. More like a group of guys who would be willing to do the job. Beowulf has a lot of connections, and he probably would be more than happy to help you out. We'll make a night of it. We can go to Wulf's Den and have a few drinks."

"I don't know. I have so much work to do here in the vineyard."

Wade captured her chin with one hand and brushed his lips across hers. "Just one night, Taryn. You work too hard. Once the harvest starts, you'll be even busier. We'll go to Wulf's Den, have a few drinks, maybe dance a bit, and then I'll take you to my house. We can come back to the vineyard in the morning."

The idea of spending an evening out with Wade was tempting. "I don't know. I don't exactly have nightclub wear, you know. I'd stick out like a sore thumb."

"Don't worry about the clothes. The owner is my brother, remember? I can do pretty much what I want at Wulf's Den. And if Roxie, the hermit/computer geek, can manage to feel comfortable at the nightclub, so can you."

Taryn laughed. "Hermit/computer geek? Roxie didn't come across as either of those things when I met her."

"Well, she isn't exactly a hermit anymore. Beowulf fixed that, but she's most definitely a computer geek. She has her own web design business. I think she spends most of the day in front of a computer."

"Okay, I'll go."

She'd barely managed to get those words out before Wade claimed her lips in a searing kiss. He kissed her until she was breathless, and her legs almost gave out. Lifting his head, he grunted with satisfaction and turned her in the direction of the house.

"Get yourself ready, Taryn. I'll give you enough time to shower before I come up to the house. I don't think it would be a good idea right at this moment to be there with you naked. I'm liable to get too distracted and forget about taking you to Wulf's Den."

"And that would be a bad thing?"

"Yes. I plan on showing you a good time before I get you into bed. Don't forget to pack an overnight bag."

Taryn shivered with anticipation. Without looking back, she quickly walked toward the house. Remembering the feel of Wade's mouth on her most intimate spot, she sighed. If the night before was any indication, tonight should end up being very satisfying indeed.

* * * *

Wade took a quick look at Taryn. They were in his Infiniti, heading for San Francisco. She was settled back in the seat, watching the scenery go by. She'd forgone her jeans and T-shirt and now wore a conservative-looking black dress. Even her high-heeled shoes were conservative. She'd made it a point to tell him she never did the sexy look, and that conservative was her middle name. He'd wisely kept his mouth shut on that comment, smiled, and then ushered her out the door.

The next time he looked at Taryn, Wade found her looking back at him with a small smile. "You know, if you don't keep your eyes on the road, you're going to end up hitting someone."

"I can look at you and drive at the same time."

"Stop it anyway. I feel self-conscious enough without you staring at me."

"Why? You look great."

"Not for a nightclub. I look downright dowdy compared to you." Taryn swept her gaze up and down his body. "I still find it hard to believe you would have packed a pair of slacks and a button-down shirt to come work at a vineyard."

"What can I say? I like to be prepared for any eventuality." Wade decided not to tell her he'd packed those clothes knowing he would at some point end up taking her to Wulf's Den.

Taryn shook her head. "I guess." She fell silent for a few seconds before she asked, "Are you sure Beowulf won't mind us asking him for help?"

"Positive. Now no more fretting. We're here."

Wade pulled into the parking lot at Wulf's Den, then parked the car before he came around to the passenger side to help Taryn out. He'd purposely arrived before the club opened. He wanted to have the business part of the evening over as soon as he could manage it. The rest of the night he planned on having Taryn all to himself. He took her by the hand, then led her through the back door.

Voices came from the main part of the club. Wade headed in that direction and was surprised to find Beowulf and Roxie standing at the bar, talking with someone he hadn't seen in years.

With Taryn in tow, Wade walked to them. "Well, look who has decided to show his ugly face. Thought you could fit seeing old friends into your busy schedule, did you?"

At the sound of Wade's voice, the other man turned to face him and smiled. "I thought I'd better drop by and see whether you were still alive and kicking."

Wade turned to Taryn. "Taryn, this is my friend, Braedan."

"Nice to meet you," Taryn said softly.

Wade noted the way Taryn looked at Braedan. Being a werewolf, Braedan was no slouch in the good-looks department. With his wavy blond hair and green eyes, he turned many a female head. Even though Wade knew Taryn had no designs on Braedan, he still didn't like the way she checked his friend out.

Hoping to put a little distance between them, Wade looked at Roxie. "Do you mind keeping Taryn entertained for a few minutes while I talk to Beowulf?"

Roxie smiled. "Of course I can." She linked her arm through Taryn's, then led her to a table a short distance from the bar.

*

Taryn slid into the chair next to Roxie. Roxie groaned with relief as she kicked off her high-heeled shoes. "I see you hate wearing heels as much as I do."

Roxie laughed. "They're the bane of my existence. I'm not the most coordinated person in the world, so the chances of me making an ass out of myself while wearing them are high. They do go with the outfit, though."

Taryn had to agree with that. Roxie was dressed in a short dark gray skirt and a silky black blouse. The strappy black high-heeled shoes she'd kicked under the table gave the outfit an extra bit of sexiness. On Roxie, the whole ensemble looked terrific, but Taryn didn't think she could pull it off.

"Yeah, wearing flats with a short skirt just looks ridiculous."

"Very true. So, what do you think of Wade?"

"I think he's a great guy. Though I still find it hard to believe he's interested in me. Look at them over there. How is it possible that three such utterly gorgeous men could end up being in the same room at the same time? I know Beowulf is your husband, but I have to say he took my breath away the first time I saw him."

Roxie looked at the men. "He did the same thing to me when we met, but I bet you would pick Wade over Beowulf and Braedan. Right?"

Taryn felt herself blush slightly. "Let's just say I'm having a hard time not going to him and dragging him to a dark corner to have my way with him."

Roxie lean in closer and spoke for their ears only. "Then do it." At Taryn's shocked expression, she quickly added, "I don't mean actually drag him to a dark corner here and now and have your way with him. I mean don't fight the attraction you feel for Wade. Go with it. It'll make it a lot easier on the both of you. I know from firsthand experience. I tried to resist Beowulf in the beginning, but it was only a losing battle. We were meant to be together. Just as you and Wade are."

"So, you think it's perfectly normal for me to be obsessing over Wade? That whenever I'm around him, all I can think about is getting him into bed?"

"Perfectly. I'm still that way with Beowulf. He swept into my life and basically changed it for the better."

Taryn smiled. "Wade did say you were a hermit/computer geek before Beowulf broke you of your hermit ways."

"So, Wade thinks I'm a computer geek, does he?"

"Basically."

Roxie smiled sweetly. "Will you excuse me for a minute?"

Taryn nodded. Roxie walked to the bar. She went to Beowulf and stood on tiptoe to whisper something into his ear. He chuckled as he picked up Roxie so she was now level with Wade. She then proceeded to deliver a slap to the back of Wade's head. Taryn laughed as he rubbed the spot and looked at Roxie as if to say what the hell. The sound of Roxie telling Wade to never call her a computer geek again easily reached Taryn's ears.

After returning to the table, Roxie apologetically looked at

Taryn. "Sorry about that. I couldn't let that one slide. Wade needs to be put in his place at times, but learning what you did to him the first time you came to Wulf's Den, I think you're more than capable of keeping him in line."

"Oh, you found out about that, did you?"

"Kind of hard to miss, what with Wade rolling around on the ground outside in the parking lot. You're a woman after my own heart. I have a feeling the two of us will get along just fine."

*

With the club set to open in a few minutes, Beowulf suggested they all go up to his office to talk. Braedan joined them as well.

Wade sat next to Taryn on the couch and squeezed her hand encouragingly before he spoke to Beowulf. "Taryn is in a bit of a jam and wonders if you could help her out."

"If I can, I'd gladly do my best, Taryn. What exactly do you need?"

Taryn shifted beside him. Wade had a feeling this was probably the first time she'd ever had to ask someone for help. She was the type of woman who did everything herself, not wanting to rely on anyone.

"The harvest is about to start, and the regular crew I hire on to help with the extra work was unable to come this year. And I can't seem to find one to replace them for some reason. The problem is I don't have enough people working at the vineyard to get all the grapes harvested in time without the extra hands. Wade seems to think you can find me the workers I'll need."

Beowulf arched his brow at Wade before he turned back to Taryn. "He did, did he? I can see no problem in getting the men you would need. When would you want them at your winery?"

"The day after tomorrow. And you can tell them I'll pay the going rate. It doesn't take much skill to harvest grapes, but it's hard work."

"The wages you would normally pay are fine. And the hard work won't be a deterrent. How many men would you need?"

Taryn shook her head as if she were still having a hard time believing Beowulf could manage to get the number of men needed. "At least eight. I don't mean to be rude, but how is it you can promise me you'll be able to find that many men at such short notice?"

Beowulf chuckled. "Let's say I have a lot of friends and family who would be more than willing to help out just because I'm the one doing the asking."

Braedan, who sat on the corner of Beowulf's desk spoke up. "If you find it agreeable, I wouldn't mind being one of the eight. Working on a winery sounds like something I would enjoy. Besides, it would give me more time to catch up on things with Wade and get to know his ma—" Roxie, who stood beside Beowulf's chair behind the desk, gave Braedan a punch in the ribs and glared at him when he turned to look at her. He quickly recovered his almost slipup. "I mean, it will give me a chance to get to know Taryn better. I take it the two of you are dating?"

Wade was glad it had been Roxie who had stopped Braedan from letting the cat out of the bag. She had been a little more circumspect than he would have been. He didn't need Taryn to know about her being his mate yet. He still had to find a way to somehow convince her he was a werewolf without having her think he was crazy or running from him in terror.

"You could say we're dating," he replied.

"Well, if you want to be really accurate," Taryn chimed in, "this is our first date."

"So, you two just met?"

Roxie laughed and said, "Not really. The first time would have been when Taryn unmanned him in the parking lot."

"Roxie!" Wade glared at his sister-in-law. "Can we just forget about that and move on like adults?"

"Hell no. The thought of you rolling around, cupping yourself, will be one of my fondest memories of you."

Wade turned to Beowulf with an exasperated expression on his face. "Can you not control your wife?"

Holding up his hands, Beowulf shook his head. "Do you think I want to get bashed over the head and then chained out in the backyard like a dog or worse? No thanks."

"Ah, I see your point." At the confused look on Taryn's face, Wade took her hand and pulled her to her feet. "I promised Taryn I would show her a good time, so I won't be working the bar with you tonight, Beowulf." When it looked as if Roxie was going to join them, he said sternly, "I promised I would show her a good time alone, just the two of us. You can spend more time with Taryn tomorrow before we go back to The Pines. We'll be spending the night at the house."

Grabbing Roxie around the waist, Beowulf pulled her onto his lap. "Enjoy yourselves. We'll try not to disturb you when we come in. And I'll get to work getting the men you need, Taryn."

CHAPTER SIX

Sipping from the glass of wine Wade had gotten for her from the bar, Taryn couldn't stop staring at the people around her. Over half the patrons of Wulf's Den were drop-dead gorgeous, men and women alike. She was surprised there weren't any modeling agents around, trying to get them to sign up with their agencies. Hearing Wade clear his throat to get her attention, she smiled crookedly at him. "Sorry. Honestly, what is up with all the good-looking people here? I'm starting to feel a little inadequate. There's no way I can compete with half the women in the room."

"You don't have to. You're perfect the way you are."

Taryn snorted. "I'd like to believe that, but you can't tell me you don't find any of them better looking than I am."

"Enough, Taryn." Wade laced his fingers through hers and brought her hand to his mouth. He brushed a light kiss across her knuckles. "I'm not attracted to any of them. To me, you outshine them all."

Her heart sped up at the feel of his lips against her skin. And the way he looked at her, as if he were slowly stripping off her clothes with his eyes, sent her body into overdrive. The room fell away, leaving only the two of them. The need to have Wade inside her, driving himself deep, caused an ache to build between her legs. Wetness pooled as her breasts grew heavy. Sucking in a deep breath, Taryn could only focus on one thing—the man sitting beside her.

Wade pulled her chair closer until they sat with shoulders and thighs pressed tight. He put his arm around the back of her seat and buried his nose in the crook of her neck, taking a deep breath. Taryn shivered with longing. She had the feeling he could smell her arousal as he made a low growling sound. She had to silence a moan as the growl vibrated against her neck.

She had no idea what was happening to her. She'd never experienced such arousal from having a man innocently kiss the back of her hand. And she was very much afraid if she couldn't act on it very soon, she would do something to embarrass Wade and herself.

Wade pulled his face away from her neck and looked into her eyes. Taryn saw the longing she felt mirrored in their depths. Without saying a word, he pushed her wineglass closer. She quickly picked it up and downed the rest in one gulp.

Wade pulled her to her feet and whispered into her ear. "Try to hold on, Taryn. I'll have us at the house in no time. Then I'm going to lick and kiss every inch of you."

Taryn gasped as another wave of desire hit her. Not caring who saw them, she nodded and wrapped her arm around Wade's waist as he put his around her shoulders, holding her plastered to his side.

In a matter of minutes, Wade had them in his car. He quickly drove down the city streets until he pulled up in front of a gated drive. With a push of a button, the gates swung open and they were driving up the curving driveway. He parked the car and then was at the passenger door, helping her out in no time at all.

After letting them inside the large house, Wade pulled her into his arms and kicked the door closed behind them. He only released her long enough to lock it, and then his lips came down on hers in a searing kiss. Taryn whimpered with need and wrapped her arms around his neck. He lifted her off her feet, then took the stairs two at a time. She didn't care where he took her. All that mattered was he was taking her someplace where they could assuage the raging desire that flared between them.

It barely registered that they were now in a bedroom. Once the door was closed behind them, Wade put her down onto her feet and then stripped her of her black dress. Taryn obligingly kicked off her high-heeled shoes. At his sharp intake of breath, she looked up to find him staring at her body.

"For a woman who thinks conservative is her middle name, your underwear says otherwise."

Taryn grew breathless as Wade stared at the sheer black lace bra and thong she had decided to wear under her conservative dress. It'd been a last-minute decision on her part, but from his reaction, she knew she'd made the right choice.

With none-too-steady hands, Taryn reached for the buttons on Wade's shirt. When she struggled with them, he grabbed the edges and pulled, sending buttons flying. Once he was free of it, he placed her hands on the center of his chest.

"Touch me, Taryn. I need you to touch me."

Having wanted to for what seemed like hours, Taryn eagerly complied. She trailed her fingertips along the hard slabs of muscle across his chest. Before moving lower, she circled each flat nipple. Next, she ran her hands along his washboard abs until she reached the top of his pants.

Taryn cupped the hard ridge of his cock. Wade appeared to be a large man in every way. She took her bottom lip between her teeth as she thought of how good it would feel to have it deep inside her pussy.

She slipped open the button of Wade's pants, unzipped them, and reached inside to take his cock in her hand. He groaned and pushed himself against her. Taryn lifted her face to him and kissed him as she pumped his hard length up and down.

She had a moment of unease when Wade roughly pulled her to him, but as he continued to kiss her, sucking her tongue into his mouth, it quickly went away. Releasing him, she wrapped her arms around his neck and rubbed herself against him.

Wade picked her up and carried her to the king-size bed in the middle of the room. Gently, he laid her in the center and continued to kiss her as he followed her down. The feel of him lying atop her, having the full length of his body against hers, drove her desire to greater heights.

She clutched at Wade's back as he trailed his lips down her jaw to her neck. He dragged his teeth against the large vein there before continuing his downward travels. He reached her breasts, then undid the front clasp of her bra. With them now exposed to his view, he laved each taut nipple. Cupping first one and then the other, he sucked a peak deep inside his mouth.

Taryn threaded her fingers through his thick hair, holding him to her, but it wasn't enough. She wanted all of him. She pulled on the strands and dragged Wade back up her body. She let go of him and impatiently tugged at his pants, trying to push them down past his hips. As he lifted himself enough to strip his slacks and her thong off, she looked him in the eyes. They glowed mutedly. The sight of them caused something to come to life inside her. As if a part of her had clicked into place.

With her body clamoring for Wade to take her, Taryn wrapped one hand around the back of his head and bit his neck where it met his shoulder. She used her other to guide his hard cock inside her. He moaned and sheathed himself to the hilt in one stroke.

As he moved, Taryn squeezed her inner muscles around his shaft. He pumped in and out in slow strokes. She felt something reaching out to Wade, wanting to connect with him. The closer her climax grew near, the more intense the feeling became. She lifted her hips to match his strokes.

Wade rested on his bent arms so he could look down at her. His pace increased as he plunged into her. "Look at me, Taryn. I need you to look at me when you come."

His eyes were still glowing. When her orgasm tore through her, Taryn kept her gaze on him. As her body clutched at his cock, milking him, an inner part of her reached for him. He continued to move in and out of her, as wave after wave of pleasure surged through her. His pace grew faster and his cock swelled inside her. Soon Wade threw back his head and moaned as he climaxed. She gasped as a part of her joined with Wade.

Wade collapsed on top of her. Trying to catch her breath, Taryn realized he was still hard. She held him close and kissed his cheek.

*

Lifting some of his weight off Taryn, Wade brushed featherlight kisses over her face. They were mated now. Their souls had joined. He'd felt it, and was sure she had as well. Still buried deep inside her, he didn't know where he ended and she began. Even though he'd climaxed, he hadn't lost his erection. It was something all male werewolves could do. Being able to keep an erection for hours at a time did have its benefits.

Taryn brushed his hair off his sweaty forehead. "You're still hard. How did you manage that?"

"I'm not done with you yet, Taryn."

"Again?"

"Yes. You're mine now. I'm going to make love to you until you can't think of anything else, except for how it feels to have me buried inside you."

Her inner muscles gripped his cock. He pulled out of her, then lay on his side. He rolled Taryn onto hers with her back pressed against his chest. He brushed her hair away from her neck and licked a path up to her ear. Taking her earlobe between his teeth, he gently tugged on it. He reached around her, cupped her breast, and rolled her taut nipple between his thumb and index finger. She pushed her bottom against his cock. Wade released her nipple, then slid his hand down her side in caressing strokes to her leg.

He took hold of her leg and placed it on top of his, opening her body. Wade placed a steadying hand on Taryn's hip as he entered her from behind. The feel of being sheathed completely in her hot, wet core made him moan with pleasure. She pushed back against him with each of his inward thrusts. The wolf rose inside him so both it and man were joined as they took her as their mate.

With a growl of need, Wade reached around their bodies until he found Taryn's clit. He nipped the back of her neck as he pumped into her body. He caressed her small bundle of nerves, pushing her ever higher, needing to feel her climax around him.

Taryn whimpered as she reached her peak. Wade's cock grew harder as he continued to thrust into her. Before her orgasm finished, he pulled her closer and pumped his hips once as his climax tore through him, filling her with his cum.

Still hard, Wade kept their bodies joined as he pulled the blankets over them. Holding Taryn to him, he kissed her shoulder. She was well and truly his—mated to the man and the werewolf. Her scent was all over his body, as his was on hers. Sighing with contentment, he decided he could let her sleep for a few hours before he made love to her again.

* * * *

Taryn awoke the next morning unable to move, held tightly in a strong male embrace. She briefly panicked, but still in the stage of not quite wakefulness, images of the night before rose in her mind. She felt herself blush, thinking of the things she and Wade had done to each other during the long night. She was a little shocked by her behavior. Normally, it took a lot to get her to that state of arousal. Where all she could think of was having a man take her, and nothing else mattered but him buried inside her.

Now awake, she needed to use the washroom. Hoping to not to wake up Wade, she tried to slide out of the bed. The arm around her chest tightened. Taryn looked over her shoulder to where he lay behind her. He was awake.

"Did I wake you?"

Wade rolled Taryn onto her back and brushed a gentle kiss across her lips. "No. I was just waiting for you to wake up. I like holding you in my arms as you sleep, among other things."

Taryn cringed when she saw the bite mark on Wade's neck. With a finger, she gently touched it. "I'm so sorry. Does it hurt? I don't know what came over me. I can assure you I don't normally go around biting people."

"Relax, Taryn." Wade grabbed her finger and gently nipped the end of it. "You were just marking me as yours. You can bite me like that whenever the urge takes you."

"You want me to bite you?"

"I know you think it's weird, but it actually turns me on."

"Okay, I think."

Wade chuckled. "Don't look at me like that. I'm not into the S and M stuff. How about we forget about your little love bite and get out of bed? I'm starved, and I bet you are too. You can have the shower first, and I'll get us some breakfast."

Wade climbed out of bed and stretched, standing in all his naked glory. The man had a body on him. And she should know since she'd been able to touch and kiss every inch of him during the night. Before her thoughts got too carried away, some of what he had said finally registered.

"Breakfast? You're going to get us some breakfast? I'm not sure that's a good idea."

Crossing his arms over his wide chest, Wade looked at her. "You're not going to let me live that one down, are you? When I said I'd get us breakfast, I didn't mean I was going to be the one cooking it. We usually have a cook here. Even though it's her day off, Beowulf and Roxie are home, and they know how to cook."

Taryn gave him a sheepish grin. "Sorry. I worked up an appetite last night, so burned eggs and bacon won't cut it."

"I can't have you getting weak with hunger," Wade said as he pulled on a pair of jeans. "I have to keep your energy up. Last night was only the start."

Having no idea how to respond to that last comment, Taryn silently watched Wade leave the bedroom. If last night was any indication, she'd be lucky if she could walk in a week's time. The man had the stamina of three men. And his ability to keep an erection after climax just kept him going and going. She got out of bed and then headed for the en suite bathroom. There was soreness in muscles she hadn't even known she had. She'd be lucky if the man didn't kill her, but she had to admit it would be one hell of a way to go.

CHAPTER SEVEN

Taryn took a long, hot shower. The one in Wade's en suite would put any spa to shame. The walls were tiled in slate with a glass surround. More than one showerhead sprayed warm water on her. There was a large one in the middle of the ceiling, but there also were smaller ones set into the walls that she could adjust to any angle. She felt as if she were in heaven. By the end, she decided she would have to look into how much it would cost to get hers back at the winery redone like this one.

She turned off the brass taps, then grabbed one of the fluffy towels piled on a shelf above the toilet, and dried herself off. Just looking at the bathroom, she came to realize how much money Wade's family had. She'd known he had it from the expensive car he drove, but she had a feeling it was a lot more than she had at first thought. The telling would be when she left his bedroom and explored the rest of the house. Last night she had been too impatient to have him to look closely at her surroundings.

After slipping on a well-worn pair of jeans along with a long-sleeve cotton knit top, her usual attire when working in the vineyard, Taryn opened the bedroom door and then headed for the large staircase. Once she reached the bottom of the stairs, the sound of voices coming from a room to her left let her know where to find the other people in the house.

She found Beowulf, Roxie, and Wade all in the large kitchen.

Beowulf stood at the large gas stainless-steel stove, cooking. Roxie and Wade sat at the kitchen table, talking. When they saw her, their conversation ceased. Feeling as if she'd intruded on something she wasn't to know about, Taryn gave everyone a small smile and went to sit beside Wade.

He wrapped an arm around her shoulders. "See? I told you I wouldn't be doing the cooking. So you have nothing to fear."

Roxie looked at Taryn and shuddered dramatically. "Wade tried to cook for you? That would be a traumatic experience. He's the only person I know who is so unskilled in the kitchen he can burn water."

"Don't exaggerate, Roxie. I'm not that bad," Wade shot back.

Taryn and Roxie turned to look at him as if to ask who he was kidding. Taryn patted his hand. "You burned the eggs and bacon beyond recognition, but I won't hold that against you."

"Gee, thanks. See what I get for trying to do something nice?" Wade spoke to Beowulf, who had finished cooking and was now placing plates of food in front of everyone.

"Just be grateful Taryn isn't only attracted to you because of your cooking skills, Wade. I'm sure you made up for your lack in that department in other areas and more than once last night." Beowulf sat beside Roxie, then grunted when she elbowed him in the ribs. He took hold of Roxie's arm and pulled her against his side. "We're all adults here. We all know in whose bed Taryn slept last night. So you can quit elbowing me in the ribs, Rox."

Roxie smiled at him sweetly. "And how do you intend to stop me?"

In one smooth move, Beowulf got out of his chair and had Roxie thrown over his shoulder. As he walked out of the kitchen, he caught Wade's attention. "Tell her. Don't make the same mistake I did with Roxie."

Once they were gone, Taryn questioningly looked at Wade. "Are they normally like this?"

"Yes, sorry to say. Believe me, it hasn't been fun living in the same house as those two while being single." He leaned forward and kissed her cheek. "Now that I have you, I don't mind it as much."

Taryn found it hard to think. Even though Wade hadn't said it outright, she knew what Beowulf and Roxie were doing right now upstairs. The way Wade looked at her said he would like nothing more than to haul her over his shoulder and take her to bed as well.

"What...what did Beowulf mean? What do you have to tell me?"

"It's nothing to worry about, and now is not the time. Let's eat, and then we can head to the winery. Or we can go upstairs." Wade's gaze drifted down to her mouth.

"I have to get back to the winery."

"Are you sure? There's no way I can get you to change your mind?"

It would be all too easy to say the hell with it and let Wade take her back to bed, but her responsibilities won out. She shook her head. "No. I will say, though, the faster I get back to the winery, the sooner I'll get the work done that I have to do. After that, there will be plenty of time for fun and games."

Wade shoved her plate closer. "Then eat up. I'll be ready to go in ten minutes."

Taryn bit back a smile as Wade all but inhaled his food. He hurriedly left the kitchen to collect her things from his bedroom. A few minutes later, she heard him come back down the stairs. When he came to stand in the kitchen doorway, she ate one last forkful of eggs before she pushed her plate away. Judging by how many times he'd looked at the stove clock in the short time he'd stood there, she decided it would be best to forgo the rest of her meal. She had a feeling if she took any longer, Wade would have no qualms about dragging her out to his car.

* * * *

The trip back to The Pines hadn't taken very long at all. It was mostly because Wade had sped most of the way there. When they arrived at the house, Taryn found herself pushed in the direction of the vineyard after she'd unlocked the house. Before shutting the front door behind her, he told her not to take any longer than she needed to. Shaking her head, she headed for her office.

She spent the first hour going through paperwork. Several times she caught herself thinking about Wade. She even had the urge to forget the work that needed to be done and return to the house to see him. It was foolish she knew, but she missed him, which was ridiculous since he was only a short distance away. With grim determination, she ignored the urge and managed to finish the paperwork.

Taryn next went to the vineyard. As the winemaker at The Pines, it was her job to taste the grapes every day once they started to ripen. By doing this, she could tell exactly when they were at their ripest, and when the harvesting should begin.

She tested the red zinfandel grapes first. They were ready for harvesting. She hoped Beowulf could get the eight men he'd promised her. She had to start getting the grapes harvested the next day or run the risk of them being overripe if she waited any longer. It would take at least five or six weeks of hard work just to harvest them all.

As she moved on to test the merlot grapes, Taryn found it hard to concentrate on what she was doing. Thoughts of Wade filled her mind. The urge to be with him, to touch him, grew stronger. She looked at her watch and realized not even two hours had gone by since she'd last seen him. She felt as if she were obsessed with him, and not in a sane way. She hadn't felt like this before. Making love to him had changed something inside her. The separation was not a pleasant feeling.

Beginning to feel desperate now, Taryn hurriedly moved on to test the cabernet sauvignon grapes. A few of her permanent crew who were working in that part of the vineyard shouted a greeting to her. She waved back at them but didn't take the time to go over and talk. She did what she had to do and then quickly headed out of the vineyard. When the house came into sight, she was practically running toward it.

She arrived at the front yard and was brought up short at the sight of Wade pacing up and down the length of the porch. Sensing her there, he stopped and looked at her with desire etched in the hard lines of his face. Her body instantly responded. An ache built between her legs. Turned-on, Taryn closed the distance between them and threw herself into his arms. He hauled her close and picked her up. She wrapped her legs around his waist and took his mouth in a searing kiss as she rubbed herself against him. The feel of his cock, already hard and straining against the zipper of his jeans, caused her pussy to grow wet.

Wade managed to open the door and get them inside the house. He kicked it shut. In between kisses, Taryn somehow was able to tell him what she felt. "I missed you. How can I miss you this much? Am I going crazy?"

Wade headed for the stairs and swirled his tongue around the shell of her ear, making her shiver. "I missed you too. This is normal, Taryn. I have to explain some things to you but not now. God, I want you."

Taryn snaked her fingers through Wade's hair and dragged his mouth back to hers. Only with him did she want to have them tunneled through his thick locks, holding him to her, as she kissed him until he couldn't think straight.

Barely making it to her bedroom, Wade put Taryn down onto her feet before him and then pulled off her clothes. She needed to feel his skin against hers. She tugged at his shirt. Once they stood naked, facing each other, she looked down and found his cock fully engorged. It jerked as she dragged a finger along his full length. She circled the head with her fingertip. He moaned.

Moving closer, Taryn pressed her lips to Wade's chest. She licked and kissed a trail across it. On her way down, she ran her tongue across each nipple and then gently blew on them, causing them to tighten into little nubbins. She continued downward, making a path to his washboard stomach. The muscles there quivered beneath her lips. Now on her knees, she focused her attention on the object of her desire.

Wade's musky, male scent overwhelmed her as she bent forward to drag her tongue along the length of his cock, then circled the large head. His hips jerked in response. She peered up at him and found him staring down at her. His eyes glowed as they had the last time they'd made love. In the back of her mind, Taryn knew she shouldn't be so accepting of it, that she should be more than a little concerned about what it could mean, but his glowing eyes had the opposite effect. They made her want him more.

Taryn looked away, then leaned forward and took as much of his thick cock as she could into her mouth. Wade made a sound that was half growl, half groan as he threaded his fingers through her hair, holding her to him. With a firm hold on the base of his shaft, she alternated between sucking and swirling her tongue around the head. As he grew harder, wetness leaked down the inside of her thighs.

Wade let her pleasure him this way for a few more minutes before he pulled her up onto her feet. With a growl, he frantically kissed her. He wrapped his arms around her waist and walked backward until the back of his legs hit the mattress of her bed. Keeping his hold on her, he fell onto it with her on top of him. He shifted until he had them lying in the middle. The way she ended up sprawled atop him, the head of his cock was nestled between her legs. No longer able to wait to have him inside her, Taryn shifted so the head pushed past the lips of her pussy and touched her hot, slick opening. With a moan, she slid down on him, sheathing his full length deep inside her.

Taryn relished the feel of him filling her, stretching her, and sat up. In this position, his hard shaft pressed against her sensitive clit. She rested her hands on the mattress on either side of Wade's head and slowly rode him. She rocked her hips against him. He was in so deep, the head of his cock hit her cervix with each stroke. With her bottom lip between her teeth, she increased the pace. He lifted his hips, matching her strokes.

All too soon, her orgasm built. She squeezed her inner muscles around him, angling her hips so his cock rubbed her clit with each stroke. He must have sensed she was close to her release. Wade lifted his upper body off the mattress and sucked one of her nipples deep inside his mouth. Taryn closed her eyes and moaned as an intense orgasm tore through her.

Before the last wave of pleasure hit her, Wade took hold of her hips and pushed up, thrusting inside her. Taryn squeezed her inner muscles around him as his cock swelled even more. He groaned and arched his hips into her, almost lifting her off the mattress, when he reached his release. His shaft pulsed as he emptied himself into her. With her heart racing, she collapsed onto his chest. She vaguely noted his cock was still hard as she tried to catch her breath.

After her breathing evened out, Taryn lifted her head to look down at Wade. "How are you able to do it?" To emphasize her words, she squeezed her inner muscles around his still-hard manhood. "I've never been with a man who could keep an erection after ejaculating." She gave his cock another squeeze.

Wade sucked in a breath. "Just another one of my many talents."

Taryn didn't get a chance to respond to that comment before the sound of a wolf howling outside near the house reached them. Wade suddenly stiffened beneath her.

"That must be the wolf I saw the other night," she said.

"I don't know about that." Wade gently disengaged himself from her body and then went to look out the bedroom window. "I can't see anything from here. I'm going to look outside. Stay here."

She was about to remind Wade it was still the middle of the day and that there were people working out in the vineyard, but he walked out of the room before she could say anything.

* * * *

Wade stepped out the back door and quickly changed into wolf form. Keeping to the shaded areas, he stealthily walked past the vineyard and headed for the nearby slope dotted with pine trees. Once he reached them, he stopped and lifted his head to smell the breeze, trying to locate where the wolf call could have come from. Knowing it wasn't the same werewolf Taryn had seen, since that wolf had been him, his hackles rose at the thought of another male werewolf being so close to his mate.

He caught a scent when the wind changed direction and ran through the trees, keeping an eye out for the one he sought. When he glimpsed silver-gray fur directly in front of him, he slowed his pace. Having Wade's scent, the other werewolf stepped out from behind a tree to face him.

Wade didn't recognize the werewolf glaring at him a few feet away. Being the youngest of his pack at three hundred years old, he didn't know many werewolves outside it. Their numbers had decreased over the years, and many packs had broken apart. Feeling this male could be a threat to his mate, he pulled back his upper lip, baring his sharp teeth.

The gray wolf's form shimmered as the werewolf took on his human form. He held his hands out with his palms facing Wade. "Relax. I'm not here to fight. I didn't realize there was another one of our kind in the area."

In a matter of seconds, Wade made the change to his human form. As he did so he willed clothes onto his body. He looked the other male up and down. The man was a stranger to him. He had silver-gray hair that fell to the middle of his neck. Dark brown eyes stared piercingly back at him. He wasn't as tall as Wade, only slightly over six foot. By werewolf standards he would be considered short. Even though he had spoken civilly to him, there was something off about the other male. It made Wade uneasy.

"If you didn't know another werewolf was here, why were you lurking around the property?"

"You could say I have a vested interest in this winery."

"In what way?"

Ignoring the question, the other man instead asked, "What is your name, boy?"

Wade bristled at being called a boy, but he bit his tongue. "Wade Thorsson."

"Thorrson. I do believe I've encountered your brother, Beowulf, a few times. The illustrious leader of your pack. My name is Lars. I'm sure your brother will recognize the name. Since you've asked it of me, I'll do the same. What are you doing here?"

"That is none of your business, but I'm going to ask you to get off the property."

Lars shook his head and chuckled. There was nothing amusing about the sound. "Don't threaten me, boy. Such protectiveness over a lone human female."

Wade snapped his teeth in warning. "The human female is my mate. I protect what is mine."

"She's your mate? My, my. How low werewolf kind has sunk, taking humans for mates." Lars backed away. "I'm sure we'll meet again."

Wade resisted the urge to follow Lars as he once again took wolf form and ran deeper into the trees. Lars's presence didn't bode well. Wade would have to keep a watchful eye on Taryn. He was glad tomorrow eight other werewolves from his pack would be arriving at the winery. He couldn't shake the feeling that Lars would be back all too soon, and it would more than likely spell trouble for Taryn.

CHAPTER EIGHT

When Wade was gone longer than the few minutes she'd expected, Taryn got out of bed and then dressed. She felt foolish, lying in there naked, waiting for him to return. For another thing, she was pretty sure a commotion would erupt out in the vineyard if he decided to look for the wolf there in the nude. He hadn't seemed to care about not wearing any clothes when he'd left.

The minutes ticked by, and still Wade hadn't returned to the house. Taryn went downstairs to see if she could find him. She was halfway to the front door when he opened it and stepped inside. She did a double take at seeing him fully clothed.

"You're dressed? You rushed out of the room so fast I thought you'd gone outside naked."

An emotion she couldn't name quickly flitted across Wade's face. Taryn could have sworn it was a look someone made when they were caught red-handed doing something they didn't want others to know about. She couldn't be sure, though, because it'd only been there for a matter of seconds before he shot her a seductive smile.

He crossed the distance between them and pulled her close. "I managed to grab some clothes from my room before I went outside. And here I thought you would be upstairs naked, waiting for my return."

"You took so long I decided to come looking for you."

Taryn knew Wade wasn't telling the truth about going to his room first. Her house wasn't so large that she wouldn't have been able to hear him moving about in the room across the hall from hers. Why he felt he had to lie about something as trivial as finding clothes to wear, she didn't understand.

"Well, then I'd better make it up to you." Wade cupped her bottom and held her against the hard bulge in his pants. "In a way both of us will enjoy."

Taryn couldn't believe how fast her body became aroused. One touch from Wade was all it took, and it didn't even matter that they'd made love only a few minutes before. She craved his touch. Falling under the seductive spell he wrapped around her, she leaned in to kiss him. Before their lips could make contact, the doorbell rang.

Wade shook his head. "Don't answer it. Maybe if we ignore them, they'll go away."

"I can't. It's more than likely one of the workers from the vineyard. I'm not expecting anyone today." Seeing Wade's look of disappointment, she gave him a quick peck on the lips. "I'll make it up to later. I promise."

"I'll hold you to that."

Taryn opened the front door and was surprised to find Braedan standing on the other side of the screen door. She pushed it open and moved back so he could step inside. "Braedan, what a surprise. I didn't think you were coming until tomorrow when the others showed up."

"I thought I would come and get first dibs on the accommodations." He looked over Taryn's shoulder at Wade and smiled. "I hope I wasn't intruding on anything."

Wade glared at him. "No, of course you didn't."

Taryn couldn't quite hold back a grin. It was obvious Braedan knew exactly what he'd interrupted. And that he was only doing it to get a rise out of Wade, in a good-natured sort of way. "Since you're the first to arrive, you can have the last spare room in the house."

Wade put a proprietary arm around her shoulders, and said, "You mean he can have one of the two spare rooms upstairs. I'll be moving my things into your room."

"I stand corrected." Taryn saw Braedan found Wade's territorial marking amusing. He smiled at her knowingly.

"Whichever room you want to give me, Taryn, will suit me just fine. I'll just grab my suitcase out of the car."

Once the door closed behind Braedan, Taryn turned to look at Wade. She could tell he was far from thrilled that his friend had arrived earlier than planned. "I wasn't going to turn him away, Wade. We'll still have the nights alone in bed together."

"Yes, but I'd hoped to at least have you all to myself for the rest of the day."

"There'll be other days. Starting tomorrow, we'll all be so tired from harvesting, you won't even care Braedan is in the house. All you'll be thinking about is sleeping."

"With you around, I can't see that happening, no matter how tired I am."

Braedan picked that moment to return. Obviously, seeing the heated looks Taryn and Wade gave each other, he said, "Shall I go back outside and give you a few minutes alone?"

Taryn shook her head. "No. Come on upstairs and I'll show you the room you can use. The one Wade was using, one of the others can use."

"If it wouldn't be too much bother, I'd like you to set that one aside for my brother. I spoke to him last night, and he decided he would like to help with the harvest as well."

Wade seemed to perk up at that. "Drake is coming here? He's finally coming out of it?"

Braedan nodded. "Yes. That's part of the reason I was at Wulf's Den the other night. I was letting Beowulf know Drake was ready to take on the world of the living again." For Taryn's benefit, he added, "Drake is my older brother. A few years back, he lost his wife and daughter. He took their deaths rather hard."

"I'm sorry to hear that. He's more than welcome to stay here in the house. I'll put the rest of the men up in the bunkhouse."

With Braedan and Wade in tow, Taryn climbed the stairs to the upper level. She stopped at the room next to the one Wade had been using. Standing aside, she let Braedan walk past her into the room. He gave it a cursory glance and then nodded.

"The room next to this one is where my brother will be staying?"

Taryn nodded. Wade thumped around in that room. She assumed he was gathering up his clothes to move them into hers. "You must be really close to your brother since you look out for him so much."

"Yes, I am. Despite the big age difference, we've always gotten along well. Do you have any siblings?"

"No. Mom just had me. She died when I was three."

"And your father?"

"I have no idea who he was. Mom never married, and she didn't leave any clues as to who he was. Uncle Colin took me in after she died. So he really was the only parent I knew."

Braedan gave her a curious look. "Your uncle's name was Colin?"

"Yes. Why?"

"No reason. The name isn't all that common."

"I guess not." Taryn took a flustered step back as Braedan went to stand before her and seemingly took a whiff of her. "I'll leave you to unpack. You can meet Wade and me downstairs whenever you're ready."

Going to her bedroom, she found Wade there. She softly closed the door behind her. Once he noticed her thoughtful expression, Wade asked, "What's up?"

"Does Braedan have any weird fetishes I should know about?"

"Braedan? No, why?" There was no mistaking the laughter in Wade's voice.

"He just smelled me."

"Are you sure?"

"Yes. He got a good whiff of me."

Wade kissed the tip of Taryn's nose. "Maybe he thinks you smell good. I know I like smelling you."

"I don't mind when you do it. I just found it a little weird when Braedan did."

"If it made you uncomfortable, I'll tell him not to do it again."

Taryn shook her head. "Don't you dare. It's not as if he tried to make a move on me."

"He'd better not or I'll have to tear off his head."

Taryn rolled her eyes. "Whatever. I'm going downstairs to see what I have in the kitchen to whip us up for supper. And before you ask, no, I do not need your help cooking."

Wade held up his hands in surrender. "I wouldn't dream of it. I'll be down in a few minutes. I'm going to see how Braedan is settling in."

"Sounds like a plan. I'll leave the two of you alone to catch up on things."

* * * *

Wade tapped on the open bedroom door before he stepped inside. Braedan turned from the open suitcase that sat on the bed and looked over. "Come to warn me away from Taryn?"

"You heard what Taryn said?"

"How could I not, what with werewolf hearing being what it is."

"You could have done the polite thing and made yourself not listen."

"Don't get your ass in a knot. I know Taryn's your mate. I could smell your scent all over her. That and sex."

Wade glared at Braedan. "I was having a good day until you showed up."

"You know I like to yank your chain," Braedan said, laughing. He grew serious. "How old is Taryn?"

"Actually, I don't know. She has to at least be in her late twenties. Why such interest in Taryn all of a sudden?"

"That puts her at the right age."

"The right age for what? I have no idea where you're going with this."

"You know part of the reason it's taken Drake so long to come out of grieving. The body of his daughter was never found."

"Yes, I know. He thinks there may still be a chance she is alive."

"I may be way off base here, but there's something about Taryn that makes me wonder if Drake wasn't wrong in his thinking."

"Oh, come on, Braedan. Taryn isn't a werewolf. She has no idea our kind truly exists. And besides, Drake's daughter wasn't named Taryn."

"I know she's mortal, but so was Drake's mate."

"Now that I didn't know."

"Drake wanted to keep it a secret. He didn't want it common

knowledge that he'd taken a mortal as his mate. He thought it would help keep her safe."

"Which had the opposite effect."

"Yes," Braedan said softly. "Be that as it may, there are too many things that work out right to completely discount Taryn as Drake's daughter. Her uncle's name was Colin. That was the name of the brother of Drake's mate. I can sort of see some of Drake's features in Taryn, even her scent smells vaguely like his."

Wade shook his head. "Those could just be coincidences. Until you can prove it a hundred percent, I won't have you saying anything about this to Taryn. I still have to find some way to tell her what I actually am. I don't need you stirring things up with your conjectures."

"You have my word. We'll have to see what Drake thinks of Taryn when he arrives with the others tomorrow."

Wade jumped on the chance to change the topic of discussion. "I'll be glad more of us will be around starting tomorrow."

"I thought you wanted Taryn to yourself, without a bunch of other male werewolves roaming the property."

"Oh, I'd love nothing more than to have her all to myself, but there's one male werewolf we have to keep an eye out for."

Braedan stood up straighter. "Who? What happened?"

"Before you arrived, I had to chase him off the property."

"Anyone we know?"

"No. I never met this werewolf before. He wasn't from our pack. He was out in broad daylight, in wolf form around mortals, howling. I went wolf and followed his scent. When I asked him what he was doing on the property, he said he had a vested interest here. I sensed there was something not right about him. Something more than his being a lone male werewolf near my mate."

"Are you going to tell Beowulf? As pack leader, he needs to know. And with Roxie being what she is—"

"I plan on calling him later. We'd better get downstairs before Taryn wonders what's keeping us. Try to remember to keep the werewolf instincts under wraps, at least until I've had the chance to ease her into it."

Braedan nodded. "I promise to keep the wolf buried. Just don't take too long in telling her. I would hate to see what happened to

Drake happen to you because you waited too long to tell Taryn the truth."

"Beowulf already gave me a warning along the same lines. I'll tell her. Soon."

* * * *

Slowly backing away from the open bedroom door, Taryn quietly walked downstairs. The two men would be down any minute. Once again in the kitchen, she picked up a knife and busily chopped vegetables for the stir fry she was making.

She hadn't meant to eavesdrop on Wade and Braedan's conversation. She'd only gone upstairs to ask them if they had any objection to what she was going to cook. Not really knowing them well enough to know what foods they liked, she'd felt it safer to ask. Hearing her name mentioned as she'd reached the upper floor, and then the ensuing conversation, Taryn had found herself frozen to the spot.

She at first thought Braedan was pulling Wade's leg with his comment about Wade wanting her all to himself without other male werewolves being around. When Wade hadn't laughed but went on to tell Braedan about chasing another werewolf off her property, she didn't know what to think. From the conversation, it was apparent both men believed they were werewolves. Taryn wouldn't have thought either man was that delusional. There was no such thing as werewolves. There was something different about Wade, and not just his ability to keep an erection for hours. It was his eyes and how they glowed during sex. She pushed her thoughts aside. She wasn't going there.

By the time Wade and Braedan had joined her in the kitchen a few minutes later, Taryn had her thoughts back under control. In no way did she let on that she'd heard part of what they'd discussed upstairs.

She plastered on a smile and turned to face them. "I hope you guys like pork stir fry. It's about all I have in the fridge. I have to make a run to the grocery store sometime tomorrow."

"That'll be fine," Wade said as he came to see what Taryn was doing. When she raised a brow at him, he slowly backed away. "All right, all right. I'll not go near the stove again."

"As long as it's food, I'll eat it," Braedan informed her.

Taryn nodded and returned to what she had been doing. The men sat at the kitchen table. As she worked, she listened to their conversation with only half an ear. That they were comfortable being around each other was easy to see from all the good-natured ribbing that went on. She was at least happy to note neither one of them said anything more out of the ordinary. She had to wonder if both men had actually known she was outside in the hall, listening, and decided to have some fun with her. To be honest, she wouldn't put it past Braedan. He seemed like the type of person who liked to do things such as that.

Now that she had convinced herself that the whole "werewolf" thing was indeed their way to get even with her for eavesdropping, Taryn felt a small measure of relief. She really didn't want to think the man she was sleeping with was a complete and utter nut job.

Giving the food in the frying pan a stir, Taryn heard the yip of a coyote out in the vineyard. She didn't give it much thought. There were a lot of coyotes living in the Stags Leap District. It wasn't uncommon to hear one at The Pines, but the wolf howl that soon followed the coyote's yip made her instinctively turn to look out the window. Behind her, she heard Wade and Braedan rush to their feet and step closer to the window. She turned as a knowing look passed between them.

"It may be a good idea to make sure all the windows and doors are locked," Wade suggested.

"I agree," Braedan quickly replied. "I'll check the upper floor while you look down here."

The two men left without saying a word to her, intent on the task at hand. Taryn felt a niggling feeling of doubt rise to the surface. One that said maybe the whole werewolf thing hadn't been a joke at her expense, after all.

CHAPTER NINE

The following morning Taryn got up bright and early. She tiptoed around the bedroom, trying not to wake Wade up. Before leaving the room, she gave him one last look. He was stretched out in the middle of the bed. The covers barely concealed his nakedness.

She softly closed the door behind her and then headed for the bathroom. As she brushed her teeth and washed her face, Taryn went through her mental list of things that had to be done that day. The first item was to get what workers she had started with the harvest. The next thing was to go grocery shopping. Having Wade, Braedan, and the seven extra men coming, she figured she would need to stock up. She hoped to accomplish that task before the others arrived later that morning.

Taryn worked in the vineyard with her regular crew for an hour before she returned to the house to see if Wade and Braedan were awake. Stepping into the house, she heard their voices coming from the kitchen. Both men sat at the table, sipping on coffee. She walked to Wade and gave him a quick kiss on the lips.

"I'm glad to see you two finally woke up. The others should be arriving soon, and I need you to keep them occupied until I get back."

"Where are you going?" Wade asked as he pulled Taryn onto his lap.

Giving him a shove, Taryn broke free of his grasp and stood. "None of that now," she scolded. "There's too much to be done today. I have to pick up a truckload of groceries. When I get back, I'm going to need the lot of you out in the vineyard, helping with the harvesting. I was already out there."

"So that's where you disappeared so early this morning. I missed giving you a proper good morning."

Taryn found herself tempted to tell Wade that she would be more than willing to go upstairs with him, to make up for her not being in bed beside him when he'd woken up. Like yesterday, she'd found herself missing him while she'd worked in the vineyard, but it hadn't been as bad. The hard work of harvesting grapes had kept her mind busy, putting a buffer around her longing to be with Wade.

"Get used to it. Until the harvest is complete, there will be no lying around in bed for any of us." Grabbing her purse off the kitchen counter, Taryn waved to the two men and left.

It didn't take her long to arrive at the nearby grocery store. Taking one of the shopping carts at the front of the store, Taryn filled it to capacity. She cringed a bit when the cashier told her what her total grocery bill was, but there was no getting around it. Once again, she felt that uncomfortable feeling of missing Wade, and that something could have happened to him.

Checking that task off her mental list, Taryn loaded all the grocery bags into the trunk of her car before she headed back to the winery. When she arrived, she took note of the extra cars in her driveway.

She parked hers in front of the garage and then opened the trunk. She had her head deep inside it, fishing out grocery bags, when a voice from behind her asked if she needed any help. Caught off guard, Taryn jumped and slammed her head on the inside of the lid. She cursed under her breath and straightened.

"I apologize. I didn't mean to startle you."

Taryn turned around and came face-to-face with another man she would expect to find on the pages of a fashion magazine. He towered over her and was so good-looking no woman would be able to resist staring at him. He wore his dark blond hair on the long side, just past his shoulders. Just like Wade and Braedan, he was powerfully built. His dark brown-eyed gaze looked her up and down. She guessed him to be only a few years older than herself, but his eyes belied that fact. There was something about the way he stared at her that said the years hadn't been kind to him.

"Lisa?"

Taryn shook her head. "That was my mother's name. I'm Taryn."

Thinking it was funny that this stranger would call her by her mother's name, she stuck out her hand. He clasped it in his larger one but didn't shake it. He stared at her for so long she started to feel a bit uncomfortable being under his scrutiny. She tried to pull free, but he didn't let go.

"My name is Drake."

She recognized the name. He was Braedan's older brother. Now that she knew who he was, she noticed the family resemblance, and it also explained the hurt she saw in his eyes. He was supposedly still grieving for his wife and daughter. When he used her hand to pull her closer and inhaled deeply, Taryn figured the two brothers were very much the same in that regard.

"Nice to meet you, Drake. Braedan said you would be coming." She pulled a little harder to free her hand. "I should get these groceries into the house before some of the frozen stuff starts thawing."

Drake looked down at their clasped hands and ran his thumb caressingly across the back of her hand before he released her. "Of course. Let me help you."

Moving a little to the side so Drake would have room to reach into the trunk beside her, Taryn watched him out of the corner of her eye. He grabbed most of the grocery bags and then patiently waited for her to collect the rest. She sensed his interest in her, but she didn't think it was in any way sexual.

After closing the trunk, Taryn led Drake into the house. She casually turned to look into the living room and stopped walking so suddenly Drake ended up ramming into the back of her. Lost for words, she couldn't stop herself from staring at the men congregated there. It looked as if a hunk convention took place. Every single one of them had a face that would turn any woman into an idiot. She had to look like one, standing there, staring with her mouth hanging open. There was so much testosterone in the room she could almost feel it rolling over her in waves.

Wade walked to her and stood directly in front of Taryn, blocking her view. "You're only supposed to look at me like that," he said quietly. Drake, who still stood behind her, chuckled.

Distracted, Taryn stammered, "What? Who?"

"Never mind," Wade ground out as he pushed her in the direction of the kitchen. "I'll help you put the groceries away."

After placing the bags she carried onto the kitchen table, Taryn emptied them. "Those are the men Beowulf sent over?"

Wade just about growled his reply. "Yes."

"All I have to say is, damn. There must be something in the water you guys are drinking. That many good-looking guys in a room would turn any woman into a blithering idiot. I could make a fortune in wine tastings at the winery if I had some of those guys working for me all year long. I'd have women coming from all around just to stare at them."

"Taryn."

"I wonder if I can convince some of them to stay on after the harvest. I'd thought of opening the cave to the public for wine tastings. These guys could be the edge I need to draw more visitors."

"Taryn!" Wade shouted.

Realizing Wade wasn't thrilled to hear her going on about how good-looking she found the others, Taryn sheepishly looked at him. "Sorry. I sometimes tend to get carried away. I don't mean anything by it." She stepped closer to Wade and placed her hand on his chest. "You know I'm only interested in you that way."

"Yes, I know. Sorry if I find it hard to hear you gushing over other men. You're mine, and I'd like to keep it that way."

"I'm not going anywhere."

Drake loudly cleared his throat, drawing Wade's and Taryn's attention. "Would you like for me to leave the two of you alone?"

"No," Taryn quickly reassured him. "We're done. Right, Wade?"

"It would seem so," Wade replied. He turned to look at Drake. "Why don't we leave Taryn alone to finish putting away the groceries? She doesn't like me anywhere near the stove." At Drake's questioning stare, Wade shook his head. "That's a long story. I'll show you the room set aside for you upstairs, and I think Braedan wants to discuss something with you as well."

Before the two men left the kitchen, Taryn spoke up. "Don't take too long upstairs. I'll have these put away in a few minutes, then I want to get everyone outside, working in the vineyard."

Wade closed the space between them once again, tipped Taryn's head back and kissed her until her legs went weak. "That's so you don't forget who you're with."

Not sure if she even remembered her own name after that kiss, Taryn nodded and silently watched Wade and Drake walk out of the room.

* * * *

Wade impatiently waited by the front door for Drake to return with his suitcase, which he'd left outside in his car. Braedan was already waiting for them. Wade didn't want to be upstairs for too long, leaving Taryn alone with the others. He didn't have to worry about any of them making a pass at her. They were part of his pack and knew what she was to him, but seeing her reaction to them earlier did not sit well with him. He wanted her to look only at him that way. Yes, the others would be considered good-looking by most women—werewolves, as a race, were all gifted in the looks department—but he still wanted her to only drool over him.

Once Drake returned, Wade quickly ushered him up the stairs. Inside the bedroom, he closed the door and faced Drake and Braedan. "Since you've just arrived, Drake, let me point out a few things. Taryn is not a werewolf and doesn't know anything about werewolves. She's my mate, and I'll be the one to tell her all about our kind when I deem it's the right time. If either you or Braedan go against my decision, I'll make you wish you hadn't."

"I understand. As her mate, it's your right to protect her in any way you see fit."

"Good. I'll get straight to the point then. Is Taryn your daughter?"

"That, I'm not sure yet," Drake said, thoughtfully. "She greatly resembles my mate. I called her by my mate's name, and Taryn said it belonged to her mother. It seems too much of a coincidence that the mother and uncle were named the same as my mate and her brother. Her scent could mark her as mine, but it's very subtle. It could be because she's a mortal or because your scent is all over her."

Wade groaned. "Would the pair of you quit checking out Taryn's scent? She's already asked if Braedan has some kind of weird fetish because of it."

Braedan chuckled. "I can see that being a bit awkward for you to explain, Wade. The poor girl must think my whole family has some strange tendencies if Drake did the same thing to her."

"Yes, well, refrain from doing it again. So basically, we don't know for sure Taryn is your daughter or not. Besides DNA testing, which isn't an option, where do we go from here?"

"I need to see a picture of Taryn's mother," Drake said, solemnly. "That will tell me one way or the other."

"I'll see what I can do. I haven't noticed any pictures around the house that could possibly have her mother in it. Give me some time." Wade straightened from where he'd been leaning against the closed door. "Now that we have that settled, I suggest we get back downstairs. I know Taryn is anxious to get us out working in the vineyard."

Braedan laughed. "More like you're more worried about what Taryn might be doing downstairs, alone, with the others."

Wade pulled open the door and cocked his head in the direction of the stairs. "You're not too far off the mark with that," he replied distractedly.

Not turning to see if the brothers followed him or not, Wade took the stairs two at a time. With his sensitive werewolf hearing, he'd heard Taryn already in deep conversation with the other members of his pack. The sooner he got them out of the house and working, the better he would feel.

* * * *

Taryn sighed as she sank lower in the bathtub. The warm water felt good on her aching muscles. The first day of the harvest was always the hardest. By the end of it, her body had been shrieking in protest. Her back and shoulders were the sorest spots. Even though she ached, and probably would be sorer come tomorrow, she was well-satisfied with the amount of work that had been accomplished. All the guys had worked hard. This being their first time harvesting, they'd done extremely well. The amount of grapes picked had almost been spot-on to what an experienced crew would have done.

She leaned her head on the back of the tub and closed her eyes, the warm water washing over her. A small smile played on her lips as she thought of how Wade had acted. He'd made sure he worked as near to her as he could manage. When one of the others came too close or showed even the slightest attention to her other than to ask a question about the vineyard, he would come up beside her and throw his arm around her shoulders, holding her against his side. She'd enjoyed the attention, even though it was more for show. Not that he had anything to worry about from her. Yes, she found the others attractive, but Wade was the only one for her.

Almost as if he knew she'd been thinking of him, the bathroom door opened, and Wade stepped inside. He closed and lock it, then stripped out of his clothes.

She sat up in the tub and said, "You can't possibly think you're joining me in my bath."

"I don't think. I know I will." Once completely naked, he stood in front of the bathtub.

"What about Drake and Braedan? What are they going to think?"

Taryn ran her gaze down Wade's form. His cock was fully erect, jutting out from his body. Her pussy clenched at the sight of it. She wasn't usually the kind of person who fantasized about sex, but having him touching her, caressing her bottom or breasts when the others weren't looking while she worked in the vineyard, had her thinking about how she wanted him to take her that night. All his caresses had primed her body for sex.

"Never mind about Drake and Braedan. I told them to get lost for a couple hours."

"Now they're going to know exactly what we're up to."

"Of course they do. I told them we were going to have some hot sex and I didn't want them in the house to hear in case you got embarrassed."

"Wade! You didn't!"

After stepping into the tub at her feet, Wade sat between her legs. The water rose, threatening to spill over. "I did, and I don't care what they think. I've been dying to do this all day."

He took a firm hold of her hips, lifted her lower body out of the water, and licked her pussy from bottom to top. Taryn grabbed the side of the tub as an intense wave of pleasure hit her. She quickly had to press her hand on the tiled wall on her other side when Wade used one hand to spread her nether lips apart and flicked her clit with the tip of his tongue. Unable to move, afraid if she did she'd slip under the water, she held on for dear life as he sucked on that small bundle of nerves and pushed one finger inside her.

"I want you to come, Taryn. I want to taste you as you come for me."

Taryn didn't think that would be a problem. She moaned as a second finger joined the first. Wade circled her clit with his tongue while he stroked his fingers in and out of her. She clenched her inner muscles, her release inching ever closer. Her hips jerked with each lick.

With Taryn almost at her peak, Wade removed his fingers and replaced them with his tongue. Stiffening it, he jabbed it inside her slick opening. It was enough to send her over the edge. As she moaned with pleasure, he continued to lap at her pussy.

When the final spasm subsided, Wade let her hips sink back down into the warm water. He moved to his knees, picked up the soap, and rubbed it in his hands. Once he had a lather built up, he dropped the bar into the water. Unable to look away, Taryn watched him stroke his soapy hands up and down his hard length.

Watching him touch himself that way made her pussy ache to have his cock buried inside her. She shifted, pushed his hands away, and replaced them with her own. Deciding the soap had done its job, Taryn scooped up some water and rinsed it away. She needed to taste him as he had tasted her. She bent her head and swirled her tongue around the tip. At Wade's moan of pleasure, she opened her mouth and took as much of his length inside as she could manage.

He pumped his hips as she sucked. She loved the salty taste of him. She would have continued to pleasure him in this way until he found his release, but Wade wouldn't allow it. After pulling free, he swiftly stood and raised her to her feet. He turned her so she faced the back of the tub. Lifting her right leg, he placed her foot on the edge in the corner where the tiled walls met. Once in that position, he moved behind her and entered her in one stroke, burying his hard length to the hilt.

Taryn shoved her hips back against Wade as he surged in and out of her. Having his hard cock moving inside her pushed her toward another climax. He grew even harder, stretching her. Moaning, she matched his fast pace.

Wade continued to move in her as he slid one hand around her to rub her clit. Taryn ground down on him harder as her climax crested. Her inner walls clenched around his hard shaft, and Wade growled/moaned as he came deep inside her.

Still not completely back to earth, Taryn vaguely felt Wade slide free of her body and then pull the plug out of the tub. Satiated, she allowed him to help her out before he dried her off. She didn't say a word when he placed her into bed and climbed in beside her. The last thing she was aware of before sleep claimed her was Wade holding her close.

CHAPTER TEN

They were now two weeks into the harvest. It would take them a total of six weeks to complete it, but Taryn was sure they'd be able to manage it. All the men Beowulf had sent were hard workers. None of them complained about the back-breaking work.

She'd also come to consider Braedan and Drake close friends. The former sought her out on a friendly type basis more than his brother. Much to her surprise, Wade encouraged her to get to know Drake better. If it'd been any one of the others, Braedan excluded, Wade would have quickly warned them off. Taryn had to think he was fine with her growing friendship, because Drake seemed to pull himself out of his sadness whenever he was around her. She liked him, and if she could help him move on and get over his loss, she was more than willing to spend time with him.

The day was winding to a close when Taryn asked if Drake would like to go with her to the cave. As she expected, he quickly agreed.

As they walked through the vineyard to the cave that had been dug several hundred feet into the hillside, Taryn turned to Drake to find him looking at her. He tended to do that a lot whenever he was alone with her. It didn't bother her, because he wasn't interested in their relationship going any further than friendship.

At the door that barred the entrance to the cave, Taryn unlocked it and pushed it open. Coming there was one of her favorite things to do. They used the cave to age the wines in oak barrels because of its underground location. The temperature and humidity inside stayed consistent throughout the year, making it the ideal place for the wines to reach maturity.

After moving to the first row of barrels, Taryn checked them as she walked by. Drake followed her, peering at the numbers and words stamped on each barrel. "Once the grapes are crushed, the juice is placed in barrels like these and brought here to age before getting bottled. The merlot and cabernet sauvignon are aged for two years before bottling, as most red wines are, and the white zinfandel is aged only a year."

"You enjoy being a winemaker, don't you, Taryn?"

She smiled. "Yes, I do, but I didn't always feel that way. When I was a teenager, I wanted to do something else other than make wine. I learned the hard way I was much better off learning the family business. Now I wouldn't dream of doing anything else."

"What happened to change your mind?"

"It's not something I like to talk about. It's a part of my past I'd like to forget. Suffice it to say, I learned in a very painful way that the world isn't always a nice place."

Drake was about to say something, maybe ask her to explain what she had meant, but he was interrupted by the sound of someone slowly clapping. Taryn looked at the entrance of the cave and saw a man she didn't know watching them. He was slightly over six foot and had silver-gray hair. Even though he was just as good-looking as the men who were around her these days, there was something about him that made a chill run down her spine. He had a cruel look about him. The smile he wore never reached his dark brown eyes.

The man clapped two more times. "Such a heartbreaking story, my dear. I enjoy hearing a sob story now and again." He turned his attention to Drake. "Well, look who has decided to drag himself out of his self-pity."

Taryn jumped as Drake growled at the other man. The sound was so animalistic she inched away from him.

Drake's hand shot out, grabbing her wrist, as he protectively pulled her hard against his side. "What are you doing here, Lars?

You have no business with Taryn." Drake's voice came out as a growl.

"Maybe I do. Maybe I'm interested in buying some of her excellent wine."

"I doubt that. Now leave. The others are back at the house. You're outnumbered."

Lars shook his head. "Such protectiveness for your half-breed whelp." Lars laughed. "I can see from the look on your face that you didn't know Taryn was your daughter. Now that is rich."

Taryn looked between the two men, not knowing what to think. Drake stared at her with his emotions showing in his eyes. She shook her head. "That's not possible. You can't be much older than I am."

Lars's laughter filled the cave. "Oh, this just gets better and better. She doesn't know. I'd thought with nine werewolves practically living under her roof, she would have known what you all were. I guess I was wrong."

"Werewolves?" Taryn shivered. An old memory, one that had been deeply buried inside her, tried to rise to the surface. Not wanting to face it, she ruthlessly pushed it away. "There's no such thing as werewolves."

"There, you are wrong, my dear. You're half werewolf, though you haven't inherited any of our traits. You're nothing but a weak mortal. Your father may appear to be close to you in age, but believe me, he's far from it. Werewolves live a very, very long time."

Taryn pulled away from Drake. "It can't be true. Tell me he's lying."

Drake sadly shook his head. "He's telling the truth, Taryn. We are werewolves, and you are my daughter. I just wasn't sure."

"And Wade?"

"He is as well. All of us are."

"No." Taryn shook her head, not willing to accept that the man she was growing to love was a freak of nature. When Drake tried to pull her back, she slapped his hand away. "Don't touch me." She saw she'd hurt Drake by rejecting him, but she didn't care.

Swinging around to face the other man, Drake growled. His body shimmered, and in a matter of seconds, a large wolf that had the same color fur as his hair stood in his place. The animal snarled and launched himself at the other man. Lars's body went through the same change as he turned to face the cave's entrance. At the sight of the large gray wolf, Taryn whimpered in fear. It was the same one she'd seen in her dream. Both wolves raced outside, leaving her alone. Gasping, not wanting to accept what she'd just seen, she raced out as well and then ran to the house.

Wade's smile of greeting fell away once he got a good look at her face. "What is it, Taryn? Where's Drake?"

He started toward her, but Taryn held up her hands to hold him off. "Don't come near me."

Wade ignored her. "What happened?"

Taryn backed away. "Stay away from me, you freak. When were you going to tell me what you were? After we were married and had a few kids? Or should I say puppies?"

Wade went still. "You know I'm a werewolf?"

Almost at the bottom of the stairs, Taryn reached for the banister. "Hard not to when Drake and some guy named Lars turned into wolves in front of me."

Wade turned to look at Braedan, and Taryn raced up the stairs to her room. She locked the door behind her. She opened her closet, then drew a large box off the top shelf with shaking hands.

Taryn sat on the bed and ripped it open. This was the box her uncle had left for her after he'd died. She'd known nothing about it until the reading of his will. He'd also left instructions that she look at the contents right after his will had been read. She hadn't been able to bring herself to do it. She'd been too upset over losing her uncle to even think about what was inside the box. Now, she had a feeling whatever was in it would hold great meaning to her.

She blindly reached in and pulled out what lay on top. Taryn smiled shakily when she saw it was a picture of her mother when she was a teenager. She hadn't seen any pictures of her mother in years. Uncle Colin had said it was too painful for him to look at them. It had to have been something more than that.

The next picture made her shiver. It was of a man and woman with their baby. Taryn's vision blurred as she stared at it. The woman was her mother, holding Taryn as a baby. The man next to her mother was Drake. He looked at her mother with the love he had for her showing on his face. He hadn't aged a bit since that picture had been taken. Angrily, she swiped the tears from her eyes. She turned the picture over, able to read what had been written on the back. The date handwritten on it was two months after her birth. Her mother's and Drake's name was also listed, along with one that was not her own—Kate.

A vague memory rose to the surface. It was shortly after she'd come to live with her uncle, after her mother had died. He'd told her she had a new name, and that he'd adopted her. That she had to remember her name was Taryn now, not Kate.

Setting the picture aside, Taryn reached back into the box and pulled out what was left inside. It was a stack of journals, written in Uncle Colin's bold hand. She opened the oldest one and began to read.

In the earliest entries, her uncle wrote about how at twenty-two years old her mother had decided to move to San Francisco, and there she'd met Drake. They'd fallen head over heels in love, and she'd written home to tell him they'd been married in a small ceremony a few months after meeting. Her mother had gotten pregnant with her a month later. The rest of the journal was filled with the running of the winery.

The next journal started when Taryn was four months old. Her uncle wrote how Lisa, her mother, had found some of Drake's habits out of the ordinary. How some of the sounds he'd made hadn't sounded human.

Taryn flipped through the next few pages, then stopped at one written when she was a year old. Her mother was alone, having left Drake. Her uncle wrote about a letter he'd received from her mother. Some places he quoted from it word-for-word.

She clutched the journal as she read the one section that seemed to spell it all out. Her mother had written, "Drake is a werewolf. No longer could he hide it from me. At first, I didn't want to believe the man I would love forever could be such a creature, but he proved it to me by changing into a wolf. I knew then I couldn't stay with him. I need to go into hiding. There is one who hunts us. One Drake warned me to stay away from. I'll write when I've found a place that's safe for Kate and I. And if something should happen to me, promise me, Colin, you'll take Kate and keep her safe."

Taryn took a deep, shuddering breath before she reached for the journal dated around the time of her mother's death. She opened it to the page dated the day her mother had died. Her uncle had written, "Lisa is dead. The police assume she was attacked by some wild animal. Her body was ripped to shreds. I now have myself to blame for not believing her when she'd said werewolves were real, and that she'd married one. If I had believed her, maybe I would have been able to prevent her death. But thinking on what I should have done will not bring her back, and now I have Kate to care for. I've started to do what Lisa asked if this situation came about. I've changed Kate's name to Taryn. Tomorrow I'll start the paperwork to adopt her as my daughter. Hopefully, this will help to keep her safe from her father's kind."

Feeling as if she were going to be sick, Taryn slammed the journal shut. She'd never known exactly how her mother had died. Her uncle had only said she'd had an accident, but even as a small child, she had known that wasn't true.

Now that she'd read how her mother had died, the memory she'd pushed aside earlier would no longer be denied. Taryn grabbed a pillow off the bed and clutched it to her chest as the images filled her mind. Once they played to the end, she buried her face in the cushioned softness and sobbed her heart out.

*

Drake placed his hand on the closed bedroom door. Taryn cried on the other side. He didn't know what to do. He'd messed things up with her mother, and he didn't want to do the same thing with his daughter. That she was alive was a miracle to him. All these years he'd mourned, thinking he'd lost them both. His heart felt lighter, knowing a piece of Lisa, his mate, was still alive.

Taking a deep breath, Drake knocked. Taryn ignored him. The need to explain, to make her understand, was too strong for him to allow her to hide from him. He kicked the door in. The sight of her sitting on the bed, with a pillow clutched to her as she looked at him with fear, almost undid him.

He crossed to the bed and slowly sat next to Taryn. She flinched away. "Taryn, we have to talk about this."

She shook her head. "No, we don't." Her voice sounded rough from all the tears she'd shed. "Get out."

"I'm not going anywhere. You are my daughter."

Spying a picture on the bed, Drake picked it up. If he hadn't already known Taryn was his daughter, this would have been all the proof he would have needed to convince him. It was the last picture taken of them as a family. He ran his fingertip along the image of his mate.

"How can you not have aged? That picture was taken twenty-six years ago. You look to be my age," Taryn said, quietly.

"Werewolves don't age the same as mortals. We live very long lives."

"How old are you then? Are you immortal?"

"No, we aren't immortal. We do eventually die, but our lifespan can last thousands of years. I'm eight hundred years old."

Taryn shook her head. "That can't be possible." She fell silent. A wild display of emotions flitted across her face before she spoke once more. "What about Wade? What age is he?"

"He's the youngest of our pack. He's three hundred years old."

"Three hundred is considered young?" Taryn laughed, but there was no humor in it. "What about me? Can I expect to live just as long?"

Drake placed his hand on Taryn's knee, but she pushed him away. "You're only half werewolf. You didn't inherit any of my werewolf genes. You're mortal as your mother was."

"Great. So I'm sleeping with a man who is way too old for me and will outlive me by thousands of years."

"Wade is your mate. He will never leave you, even if you are mortal."

"Like hell he is."

"He *is* your mate, Taryn. If you look deep down inside yourself, you'll know it's true. Your heart, your soul, calls for him. He's a part of you now. When werewolves find their mates, their souls join at their first mating. The bond then becomes strong. They find not being with each other hard to bear."

"Was my mother your mate?"

"Yes. I knew the instant I met her that she was my other half."

"If that is true, how could you have allowed her to leave you?"

Drake sighed. "I told her what I was, and she turned from me. After she left, I thought the separation would show her how much she needed me. Not being with her was the hardest thing I had ever done. I regret letting her go. If I had known..." Knowing he had failed his mate when she'd needed him the most still ate at him.

"Beating yourself up about it doesn't change a thing, especially when the bastard who murdered her is still around."

"What do you mean?" Drake stiffened, having a feeling what Taryn was about to say.

"Seeing you change into a wolf brought back a memory I'd buried of when I was three. Of the day my mother died. I was there. I watched her being murdered. It was Lars. The bastard turned into a wolf and ripped her to shreds."

CHAPTER ELEVEN

After telling Drake who her mother's murderer was, he'd taken hold of her wrist and dragged her downstairs. She hadn't been ready yet to be face-to-face with Wade, but her father had never loosened his hold on her, even when she'd dug in her heels.

Taryn now sat on the sofa in the living room, trying her utmost not to look at Wade. The one time she made eye contact with Braedan, he'd reassuringly smiled at her. It wasn't until that moment she thought about the family connection they shared. Braedan was her uncle. He looked even younger than she did. If this had been a normal situation, with normal individuals involved, finding out she still had family would have been something she would have been ecstatic over. Such wasn't the case now.

Drake, who sat next to her, spoke to the room in general. "We have a situation here, and not just Taryn's reaction to finding out we're all werewolves."

Taryn stiffened at her father's reference to her not accepting them with open arms. Against her will, she glanced at Wade. He stared at her with longing in his eyes. She quickly looked away. She couldn't deal with his feelings right now.

"We figured that much," Braedan said drily. "It's obvious you've had dealings with Lars before, Drake. Your reaction to him was quite violent, to say the least."

"Yes, I've had the misfortune of having to put Lars in his place a few times. He used to be part of one of the packs allied with ours until he went lone wolf. Even before he left their pack, there was something not right with him. He used to enjoy manipulating his pack mates, setting one against another. Some of the fights he caused ended up being quite bloody, but that is nothing compared to what he's done to me."

Wade leaned forward. "What does the bastard want with Taryn?"

"His interest in her only lies with her being my daughter. It all stems from the fact that before Lars went lone wolf, Lisa and I ran into him one night while we were out for dinner. I think Lars would have taken Lisa for his own if I hadn't already claimed her as my mate. It surprised me. Lars thinks a werewolf mating with a mortal is beneath our kind. I should have thought about what his reaction would have been once he found out Lisa had left me."

"He's the one who killed your mate?" There was an underlying growl to Wade's voice.

"Yes. And Taryn was there when he did it."

Taryn felt Wade's gaze on her, but she refused to look at him.

Drake grabbed her hand. Even though she flinched at the contact, he didn't let go. "We need to know what happened the day your mother died, Taryn."

Looking at her father, she could see from his expression it would be just as hard for him to hear what had happened as it would be for her to tell it. "I don't remember all that much. I was only three at the time. It's mostly bits and pieces."

"It doesn't matter. What you have to say will determine what Lars's fate will be."

"What do you mean? Do you have a werewolf court system or something?"

"In a way, we do," Wade answered. "There is one individual who rules over all the packs. She'll have the final say as to what should be done about Lars."

Taryn turned to look at Wade. "She?"

"Yes. It's Roxie, as a matter of fact."

"Roxie? So, she's a werewolf as well? How come she's the werewolf queen?"

"She is now. And she isn't our queen. She's just special. The markings around her left wrist marked her as the one who was foreseen to tie all the packs together."

Taryn was a bit confused. Roxie hadn't always been a werewolf? As for the markings around Roxie's wrist, Taryn had seen the intricate black Celtic design and thought nothing of it. Lots of people had tattoos nowadays.

"So, Roxie is the head honcho and has the final say over anything to do with any rulings within the packs? If she wasn't always a werewolf, does that mean anyone can be turned into one?"

"Yes, she does, and no, they can't. Only Roxie. Let's just say she's unlike any werewolf ever born."

Feeling a major headache coming on from all the information overload she was getting, Taryn turned back to her father. "As to the night my mother died, I only remember a strange man coming into the apartment. Mom had managed to get me out of sight before he forced his way in. She hid me in a closet. Not understanding what was going on, I kept the door open a crack so I could watch. Lars grabbed Mom and forced her to the floor, but she managed to fight him off. He mustn't have liked it that she'd refused him, because he turned into a wolf. I closed my eyes after that, but I could hear her screams." The memory replayed itself in Taryn's mind as she spoke. She swallowed the lump that formed in her throat. "After…after the screams stopped, I opened my eyes and saw the large silver-gray wolf standing just outside the closet door with my mother's blood dripping from his muzzle. He stared at me for a few minutes, shifted, then walked out of the apartment."

Drake growled in the back of his throat. "I have a feeling he left you alive, knowing it would torment me more if I thought both of you had died. I didn't find out about your mother's murder until after it was reported on the news. Obviously, your uncle had already come to claim you and decided to keep your identity a secret."

"I read in his journals that he acted on my mother's wishes to keep me hidden from you."

"I had no idea your mother felt so negative about me being a werewolf. She'd been very upset finding out about it, but I really had thought she would get over it," Drake said sadly. "I'd really hoped she would come back to me, but if what you say is true, I have to face the fact she wouldn't have. She had suspected I wasn't the same as other men. She rarely talked about her brother. Even when we were married, she refused to invite him to the civil ceremony she insisted we have. When your body hadn't been discovered with your mother's, I did try to find you, Taryn. I ran into nothing but brick walls. I finally had to accept that your mother hadn't been truthful with me from the start either. It wasn't until I searched for your uncle that I learned she'd lied about what her maiden name was."

Taryn could easily see how affected Drake had been by learning her mother had gone to such lengths to keep her hidden from him. Now that she'd gotten over the initial shock of learning werewolves truly existed, she was a little irritated that her mother had taken away her choice to learn about her father's kind. She was half werewolf, after all. It was a part of who she was.

"So, what happens now?" Taryn's gaze briefly rested on each of the men. "I don't like the idea of Lars roaming my property."

"We'll have to hunt him down," Wade answered sternly. "He has to pay for what he did to your mother. I think you should keep to the house in the meantime, Taryn. You'll have to be watched at all times."

"Like hell I will." Taryn adamantly shook her head. "It's the middle of the harvest. I can't just stay cooped up in the house being babysat."

"It's for your own good. As your mate, I have the right to see to your protection. Until Lars is found, we have to keep you safe."

Taryn surged to her feet and glared at Wade. "If you want this mate business to work, you had better learn real fast that I don't like being ordered around. I will decide what is best for me, not you. If you can't handle that, then all I have to say is take it or leave it."

In reaction to her challenging words, Wade stood and slung her over his shoulder as if she were nothing more than a sack of potatoes. Taryn lifted herself to peer at her father. Drake shook his head and smiled. Knowing she would receive no help from that quarter, she tried to squirm her way free. She let out a small shriek of outrage when Wade smacked her bottom and then headed for the staircase.

"Stop squirming or I'll end up dropping you on your head," he said as he took the stairs to the upper level two at a time.

Slightly pissed off at his heavy-handedness, Taryn goosed him for smacking her in the ass. Wade stumbled but managed to keep his hold on her. He walked into her bedroom and tried to shut the door behind them. Of course it didn't stay closed. Drake had damaged it by kicking it in earlier. With all the blood rushing to her head, she was a little dizzy as Wade swung her around and muttered about looking for something that would hold the door shut. In the end, he took hold of her dresser with his free hand and pulled it in front of it.

When he finally allowed her to stand on her own two feet, Taryn crossed her arms over her chest and glared at him. "How dare you. Did you bring me up here to punish me because I won't do what you want me to?"

Wade shook his head. "No. I did it because I knew this would be the only way I could get you to be alone with me right now. We have to talk."

They had a lot to discuss, but she didn't think she was in the proper frame of mind right now. She was likely to say something she would regret later. "I agree, but not now. I've been through enough."

"Yes, we have to talk now. It hurts me to see you hurting inside. I know you're mad at me because I wasn't upfront with you from the start. Believe me, I wanted to tell you. I was just afraid if I told you I was a werewolf, you'd turn from me. I didn't want to lose you. Ever since I caught my first smell of your scent at Wulf's Den, I've thought of nothing else but claiming you as my mate."

Some of her anger receded at Wade's words. "Is that why you came after me that night? Because of the way I smelled, you knew I was your mate? I really don't understand this whole werewolf mate business."

Wade stepped closer. "I knew you were my mate at the first whiff. It hit me like a ton of bricks. That's what usually happens when a male werewolf finds the one female who is to be his mate. And until he claims her as his, the mating urge rides him pretty hard."

"Is that so?" Taryn grew breathless as Wade's eyes glowed. "What about after he's claimed her as his?"

"During their first mating, their souls join. They find it hard to be away from each other. If they do have to be apart, the need to be with the other, to reaffirm the bond they share, will be hard to ignore. It can be pretty intense, or so I've heard."

"I see." Taryn had a hard time staying mad at Wade. Maybe it had something to do with them being mates and having their souls joined. No matter how hard she tried to stay angry at him, she couldn't. Now that they were alone, and he was so very near, with his eyes glowing with what she now recognized as need, her body went into overdrive. She leaned closer. "I'm sorry I overreacted earlier when I found out about you being a werewolf. I shouldn't have called you a freak."

Reaching up to place his hand on Taryn's neck just below her ear, Wade closed the remaining distance between them so their bodies brushed against each other. "Are you going to turn away from me because I am one, Taryn? I don't want to lose you. I've waited a long time for you to come into my life."

She wouldn't. Even now, her body craved his. "No," she said softly. "I won't turn away from you. How could I hate the werewolf part of you when it's also a part of me?"

"That's all I needed to hear."

Wade gently pressed his lips against hers. He nipped and sucked them until Taryn couldn't take any more. She grabbed a handful of hair on either side of his head and ground her mouth against his. After all she'd been through, she needed him, quick and hard. Right now, she didn't need him treating her as if she were glass.

Urging him backward, she continued to kiss him until she pushed him back onto her bed. He grunted as she fell on top of him. She released his hair and skimmed her hands down his sides, then pushed them under his T-shirt. The material bunched as she moved them up to the thick padding of muscle on his chest. With her fingertips, she traced the contours of it before moving lower again to outline his well-defined abs.

Taryn pulled free of Wade's lips, then sat up so she could straddle his hips. She set to work on the button and zipper of his jeans. Once she had the front open, she pushed them down past his hips before wrapping her hand around his cock. He watched her stroke up and down. She was more than ready to have him buried inside her. Wetness pooled between her legs. She slid partly off him and then worked off her own jeans. Her panties quickly followed.

With her gaze never leaving Wade's face, Taryn positioned herself above him, then pushed down until the full length of him was deep inside her pussy. Relishing the feel of him filling her, she leaned her hands on his chest and rocked her hips against him.

Wade reached up to cup her breasts. Taking her nipples between his thumbs and forefingers, he tugged at them through her shirt. Taryn increased her pace as the pressure inside her grew. She ground her hips against his pelvic bone and squeezed his shaft as the first flutter of release hit her. A moan escaped her lips as she continued to slide up and down his hard length, pushing herself closer to orgasm. She soon crested as wave after wave of pleasure shot through her.

Before the last surge ended, Wade rose until he sat up on the bed. He took her mouth in a passionate kiss, held on to her hips and arched, thrusting himself into her. He grew harder as he neared his release. With her hands on his shoulders, she squeezed her inner walls around him.

Wade dragged his mouth away from hers and looked at her. "Put your mark on me, Taryn."

Still lost in a haze of desire, Taryn at first didn't understand what Wade wanted. "What?"

"Like you did before. I want you to bite me. I want your mark on me."

To make sure she knew exactly what he wanted her to do, Wade wrapped a hand around the back of her head and pushed her face toward the spot where his neck and shoulder met.

Wade stiffened as if in anticipation. He tightened his fingers in her hair, holding her to him. The thought of biting him, of leaving her mark on his skin, aroused something primitive in her. Continuing to move against him, she licked the spot with her tongue. He pushed her closer and gasped. He dug his fingers into her hip as he urged her to increase her pace. At the feel of another orgasm building, Taryn dragged her teeth against his neck before she bit down on his skin.

Wade groaned as he instantly climaxed. The feel of him coming, pulsing deep inside her core, sent Taryn into her own orgasm. After it was over, she settled against his chest. He was still hard.

Once she caught her breath, she pulled back to look at him, and asked, "Really, how can you stay hard even after you've come? Is it a trick only you have or are all male werewolves able to do it?"

Wade chuckled. "It's something all male werewolves are gifted with."

"Well, from this mortal woman's point of view, it's definitely a gift. It's one I could quite easily find myself craving more of."

Wrapping his arms around her, Wade rolled until he had her pinned to the bed beneath him. "I'm more than ready to satisfy your cravings."

To emphasize his words, he pulled back his hips until only the tip of his cock remained inside her, then inch by slow inch, he sheathed himself in her wet heat.

Taryn's eyes went wide. "Again?"

"Most definitely again. We're just getting started."

* * * *

It wasn't until much later, when they lay cuddled together in her bed, did the subject of werewolves resurface in Taryn's mind. There was a lot she didn't know, and she was sure most of what she did was inaccurate, considering a lot of it she'd learned from movies. It was obvious Hollywood had gotten it wrong when they had their werewolves only able to change when it was a night of a full moon. When Drake and Lars had shifted into wolves, it'd been early evening, and as far as she knew, the full moon was still a week away.

She needed to learn all about werewolf society if she was to find her way in it. Unlike her mother, she would never run from something she didn't understand. Even if Wade had waited until they'd had a child before telling her what he truly was, she wouldn't have run. He was a part of her. She would have been leaving something of her behind and wouldn't have felt whole. It would have been too painful to contemplate being separated from him. It made Taryn wonder if her mother had accepted her father into her soul, as well as her body, as a true mate would have. She had a feeling her mother hadn't. That Drake had grieved for them both for almost thirty years told her he'd loved her mother even after she'd deserted him.

Wade stirred next to her. He gently ran a finger across her brow. "What's going on inside that head of yours? You look a million miles away."

Taryn lifted her head to look into his ice-blue eyes. "I was just thinking about this whole werewolf business. I really don't know what is expected of me, being the daughter of one and a mate to another."

"It's not going to make that much of a difference in your life. You'll still have your winery, only difference is you're going to be stuck with me. I'd never dream of asking you to give up what you love. And I guess I'll have to put up with having Drake around."

"I hoped you would say you'd be happy to move here to be with me, but that isn't what has me worried. What about me being mortal? You're going to stay young for just about forever, whereas I'm going to get old and—"

Wade quickly pressed his lips to Taryn's, stopping her from finishing that last sentence. "Don't say it. I don't want to even think about it."

"There's no getting around it. Unless there is a way to make me almost immortal like you, it's inevitable." Wade's expression turned thoughtful. "What? There *is* a way?"

"I'm not sure, but it may be something worth trying."

Taryn had no idea what Wade referred to. "Okay, you've lost me."

"You know Roxie used to be a mortal like you, but now she's a werewolf." When Taryn nodded, Wade continued. "It was always thought a mortal couldn't be turned into one of our kind. The ability to change is more of a magical gift than a physical one. Unlike the movies, it doesn't hurt us, and I don't have to first rip off all my clothes to do it."

"What a shame," Taryn said with a chuckle.

Wade gave her a mock glare before he spoke again. "Be that as it may, we can will the change to happen at any time because of the magic we have inside us. It's something we're born with.

Because you're half werewolf you may have some of it as well, but it can't be very strong or you wouldn't be a mortal. Roxie was the same way. She had werewolf blood, but there were many generations between her and her grandfather, so it was much weaker than yours. What I'm getting at with all this is — Roxie was changed with a spell that had apparently been tried before and failed."

"Obviously, it worked when tried on Roxie."

"Yes, it did. Roxie thinks it worked because she already had some werewolf blood to start with, that and the fact that she was injected with her grandfather's blood when the spell was done. That the spell worked is something of a miracle, considering who was doing the spell."

"What do you mean?"

"Roxie didn't volunteer to see if the spell would work or not. Gren pretty much didn't give her a choice. At the time, he had taken both Royce, Roxie's grandfather, and Roxie captive. It was just a fluke that Gren had decided to use Royce's blood and not his own."

"I take it Gren is not a member of your pack?"

"You mean our pack. No, Gren isn't. He's from a one that has never gotten along with ours. Beowulf has butted heads with him more than once since he became pack leader."

Taryn nodded. Now it made sense that Beowulf could guarantee her the extra men she needed for the harvest. As pack leader, he could have easily arranged it. Then something else clicked. "Wait a minute here. You said the other guy's name is Gren? Are you saying your brother Beowulf is *the* Beowulf, and Gren is actually Grendel?"

"Correct."

"Holy crap your brother is ancient. That story is fifteen hundred years old. Damn. He looks pretty hot for being a relic."

Wade scowled. "I will try to pretend I didn't hear you call my brother hot. And I won't be telling Beowulf you called him a relic either. I'm sure Roxie would have something to say about that. We're getting off topic here. As I was saying, the spell could have worked because Roxie already had some werewolf blood and from having Royce's blood injected into her system as well. We don't know for sure because no one has attempted to try the spell again. If all it needed for it to work was a mortal who carried werewolf genes and could be injected with the blood of the original werewolf of their bloodline, maybe it would work for you."

Taryn was more than interested in trying that spell. She had a feeling it wouldn't take much convincing on her part to get Drake to consent to give up some of his blood. She was pretty sure he would be more than happy to have her turned into a werewolf. "Okay, I'm game. How do we go about getting our hands on that spell?"

A large smile spread across Wade's face. "I'll talk to Roxie tomorrow. I know she remembers how the spell went."

CHAPTER TWELVE

Wade waited until the others were well occupied with the harvesting before he walked to the end of the vineyard and pulled his cell phone out of his pants pocket. Selecting one of the numbers saved in his phonebook, he pushed Send and waited for Roxie to pick up on the other end.

Roxie sounded distracted. "Uh...hello?"

"Hey, Rox. Can you talk or are you too busy doing your geeky computer stuff?" Wade stifled a laugh when she growled at him.

"Wade, if you don't stop calling me a computer geek, I won't be responsible for what I do to you the next time I see you. Now what do you want? I'm trying to work here, and obviously it's me and not Beowulf you want to talk to since you called me on my cell."

"Such threats, and from my sister-in-law, no less. Fine. I'll make it quick. The spell Gren used to change you into a werewolf, do you remember it?"

Roxie grew silent for a few seconds before she answered him. "Yes, of course I remember it. I'll probably never forget it. Why do you ask?"

"I want to try the spell on Taryn."

"Did she agree to this?"

"Yes. If she hadn't, I wouldn't be calling you."

"There's one thing, though. You know my theory of why the

spell worked on me and not on the others Gren had tried it on. It may not work on Taryn with her not having any werewolf blood."

"It so happens she does. Drake is her father, Roxie."

"Now that sounds like a story I need to hear."

"Well, if you come to the winery, I'd be happy to tell you the whole story. Beowulf is still coming here this evening, right?"

"Yes. He mentioned there was a lone wolf sniffing around Taryn's winery, without going into much detail. The man tries to shield me too much. I planned on coming with him anyway."

"Thanks, Rox. I owe you one. And, Roxie, I wouldn't mention the spell thing to Beowulf."

"What do you take me for?" Roxie asked, laughing. "Beowulf would balk at me coming to the winery if he knew I was going to discuss Gren's spell with you. The overbearing wretch."

"You still love him anyway."

"So true. Now let me get back to work. I'll see you later."

Satisfied with how his conversation had gone with Roxie, Wade returned to the section of the vineyard he'd been working on. As he passed Taryn, he gave her the thumbs-up sign. She gave him a quick nod before focusing back on what she was doing.

* * * *

Beowulf and Roxie arrived shortly after they'd called it quits for the day. Taryn was more than happy to see they had thoughtfully brought enough pizza to feed everyone. She was too worn-out and had been dreading having to cook a meal for such a large group of people after harvesting all day.

Once the men were all preoccupied with seeing how much pizza they could consume, Roxie grabbed a couple of slices and motioned with her head for Taryn to follow her outside. They sat on the porch steps and ate. Taryn waited for Roxie to start the conversation.

"I hear you and Wade want to try the spell."

Taryn nodded as she swallowed her mouthful. "Yes. Now that I know what he is, and that we're mates, I don't want to put him through having to watch me grow old and die."

"I felt the same way when Beowulf finally got around to explaining the whole being-mated business. I'm willing to pass on the spell to you both, but I have to warn you, it still may not work on you, even though you're half werewolf. I'm not your average, everyday werewolf, and apparently, I was born to be different."

"Wade did mention you rule over the packs. At first, I thought it meant you were the werewolf queen."

Roxie chuckled. "Nope, I'm no queen. Though I do like the idea of it, especially for Beowulf. If I were queen, I'd make him get down on his knees and kiss my feet, among other things." She waggled her eyebrows.

Taryn just about choked on her pizza, then laughed. "If you could get Beowulf to do that, I'd have to get you to order Wade to do the same for me."

"Oh, you and I are going to get along famously, Taryn," Roxie said with a laugh. "We're going to have a lot of fun driving the Thorrson brothers crazy. As I was saying, I'm 'special.'" Taking off the wide piece of tooled leather she wore around her left wrist, Roxie showed Taryn the markings there. "I sometimes keep this hidden when I go out. I still feel uncomfortable with the reaction I get when other werewolves see it."

Taryn put down her plate, then held Roxie's wrist for a closer look at the black Celtic knotwork circling her wrist. It was beautiful. Taryn had always thought if she were to get a tattoo, she'd get a Celtic-styled one.

"So, how was it decided you were the one to get the tattoo that would mark you as the special one?"

Roxie snorted. "It didn't work that way. This isn't a tattoo. After Beowulf and I became...intimate...the markings just appeared on my wrist. At first, it was just a rash, and a gross-looking one at that. Once it healed, the Celtic knotwork appeared underneath. It's a mark most werewolves know the meaning of. The prophecy that was told of the one werewolf bearing this mark and ruling over all the packs was originally thought to be just a myth. I proved them wrong there."

"Do you think you were singled out as special because of being turned into a werewolf, something that hadn't been done before?"

"If you talk to Beowulf about it, he seems to think so. I don't really. You see, Royce, who is my grandfather many times removed, took a mortal for a mate. Even though she wasn't a werewolf, she had powers of her own. She could do magic. And I inherited her abilities. Out of all her descendants, I'm the only one to have done so, which is another reason I think I should be the one to say the spell. It may tilt the odds in your favor."

"Thanks." Taryn took a bite of her pizza and chewed it as she thought over how to word the next question she wanted to ask Roxie. "What's it like being a werewolf? Do you ever wish you could go back to the way you once were?"

Roxie shook her head. "No, I would never want to go back. Besides being able to live for thousands of years, all your senses are enhanced. You can see better, especially in the dark, and you can hear more acutely. Your sense of smell will increase too, which would be a bonus for you since you're a winemaker."

"Ah, I get the whole smelling business now." At Roxie's questioning look, Taryn explained what she'd meant with that comment. "Wade has been sniffing me since I first met him. I thought it was because he was attracted to me and it was his way of showing it. When Braedan did it as well, I at first thought he had a weird fetish. Then Drake did it when we first met, so I reasoned it must be something that ran in their family."

Roxie threw back her head and laughed until tears started in her eyes. "A fetish? That's a good one. All I can say is get used to being sniffed a lot. Werewolves can tell who is who just from smelling another's scent. They don't mean anything by it. It's just what they do when they meet someone new."

"I'll have to remember that so I don't haul back and smack the next male werewolf who tries to smell me. What about the whole shifting thing? Can werewolves shift into something else other than into wolf form? The movies always have werewolves shifting into big, ugly half-man and half-wolf forms."

"I can see Wade has told you next to nothing about werewolves. What has he been doing besides helping with the harvest that he couldn't find the time to let you know all this?" Taryn felt the flush covering her face as Roxie smiled. "Ah, I see. That would keep him busy. As for werewolf forms, there usually is only the one—the wolf."

"Usually?"

"I used to think as you do that what the movies portrayed was true. I'm the exception. Being the special girl that I am, I can shift into the half-human and half-wolf form. And I'm not ugly."

"Really? Oh, now you have to show me or I'll die from curiosity."

Roxie put her plate on the porch next to her and then quickly looked around to make sure they were still alone. Satisfied that they were, she went and stood at the bottom of the porch steps.

"I'll do this quick. I tend to make the others nervous when I take on this form."

Taryn's jaw dropped open as Roxie's form shimmered and then blurred as she willed on the change. Once it was complete, Taryn was amazed at the difference in Roxie. She was much, much taller and looked to be about three times stronger in her human/wolf form. Her head was that of a wolf, and her entire body was covered in golden-brown fur. Roxie twitched her tail when Taryn stood to get a better look at her.

"This is amazing. You look as if you could beat the crap out of anyone."

"I can, and have," Roxie said in a huskier-than-normal voice.

"You can talk!"

Roxie nodded. "Yes. It's a little harder to do, but I can manage."

Just then the screen door opened as Beowulf, Wade, Braedan, and Drake walked out onto the porch. Seeing Roxie, Beowulf just shook his head. Taryn had to bite the inside of her cheek to stop from laughing at the way Braedan and Drake stared at Roxie. From their shocked expressions, she figured this was the first time they'd seen Roxie like that, let alone knew she could take on that form.

Braedan was the first one to find his voice. "What...how is this possible?"

Roxie stepped closer to him and pushed his jaw closed with a snap. "If you keep your mouth hanging open like that, you'll end up eating a bug or something."

Braedan jumped back in surprise. "She talked."

Beowulf came to stand in front of Roxie. "Can you please change back to human form now? I'm really not enjoying seeing my mate being stared at as if she were in a freak show."

"Spoilsport," Roxie said under her breath, then willed herself to change back to her human form.

"Thank you. Now if you're done showing off to Taryn, we

came out here to let you both know we're going to see if we can hunt Lars down. Roxie, I want you to stay with Taryn just in case he shows up at the house. I doubt he will. He'd be a fool to do that, knowing how many of our pack is here, but I want to cover all the bases."

"Fine, I'll stay. Where are the others?"

"They went out the back way. We're going to circle around both sides of the winery and meet up at the pine trees. Hopefully, we'll be able to pick up his scent trail and see where the bastard has been coming from."

Roxie kissed Beowulf's cheek. "If you run into trouble, howl and I'll come and kick some werewolf butt. And don't look at me like that. I've already saved your ass once. I can do it again."

Beowulf rolled his eyes at his mate. "I think we should be fine without your assistance. You and Taryn just stay put."

Taryn watched in awe as all four men changed into wolf form and then loped off in a group. She could tell who each wolf was because their fur matched their hair color in human form. Beowulf, who was the black wolf, was out in the front with Wade right behind him. Her father and Braedan ran alongside Wade. She realized this was not the first time she'd seen Wade in wolf form. She recognized him as the wolf from that first night when he had arrived at The Pines. In some ways, it seemed as if that had happened years ago instead of days.

"We might as well head back inside," Roxie said as she watched the men leave. "Since there isn't much to do, except sit around and wait for them to return, how about we crack open one of your excellent bottles of wine. And now that you're family, Wulf's Den will be selling every type of wine you make."

Taryn was a little surprised to hear Roxie call her a member of her family. "I'm family now? Wade and I haven't even discussed the idea of getting married."

Roxie slipped her arm through Taryn's and walked her toward the front door. "There will be no discussion of marriage, I can guarantee you. Werewolves don't usually marry. Once you're mated, you're as good as married in their eyes. And to be honest, it's a heck of a lot more binding. Just the whole missing-your-mate-even-though-it-has-only-been-an-hour thing really shows you how strong the mating bond is."

Allowing Roxie to walk into the house ahead of her, Taryn thought over her words. Roxie was right. Why bother going through a wedding ceremony when being mated meant so much more? It also gave her reason to think her mother had most definitely not been a true mate to her father.

* * * *

The men returned a few hours later. Beowulf, Wade, Braedan, and Drake headed to the house after leaving the rest of the men at the bunkhouse. All four were irritated that they hadn't been able to flush Lars out from hiding. After he'd confronted Drake the evening before, they'd figured he would be back this night as well, considering he'd barely managed to get away from Drake during their last encounter. More worried about how Taryn took the shock of seeing him change into a wolf, Drake had given up on the chase the moment Lars had crossed the road that ran along the back of Taryn's property and entered the trees on the opposite side.

As soon as they entered the house, Wade heard feminine laughter coming from the kitchen. He headed in that direction as the others followed him. Upon entering that room, he was a little surprised to see how animated Taryn was as she spoke to Roxie. It wasn't until he saw the empty wine bottles sitting on the table did he understand why. From the looks of things, Roxie and Taryn had finished off three bottles of wine between them. Being a werewolf, Roxie would hardly feel the effect of the wine she'd drunk. Alcohol didn't affect them the same as it did mortals. It would take a lot more than three bottles of wine to make Roxie drunk, but the same couldn't be said for Taryn. When he came to stand next to Taryn's chair, she looked up at him and gave him a crooked grin.

"Hi...hi there, good-looking." Taryn's words slurred together as she'd spoken.

Drake, who now stood next to Wade, chortled as Taryn reached around and pinched Wade on the ass, causing him to jump. "It looks as if my daughter has been enjoying her own wine a little too much. I have yet to taste it, but after our failure tonight, I could use a glass."

"I'll get another bottle." Taryn tried to stand, but her legs ended up giving out on her and she thumped back down onto her chair. "Hmm, my legs don't seem to work right now. You'll have to get the bottle yourself, Dad. I put another one in the fridge after I opened the last one Roxie and I shared."

Wade turned to look at Drake when the man stiffened beside him. He quickly looked away at the display of emotions running across the male's face. Taryn calling him Dad had not been missed by Drake.

Bending to Taryn's level, Drake placed a fatherly kiss on her forehead. "Not to worry, honey. It's only temporary. I'll get that bottle of wine."

After Drake stepped in the direction of the fridge, Wade turned his attention to Roxie. "Did you decide to get my mate drunk on purpose, or were you not thinking when you let her drink all that wine?"

"Oh, stop being an old fuddy-duddy, Wade. Give the girl a break. She needed to let her hair down, so to speak. She's been through an awful lot the last couple of days. And it's not as if I forced the wine down her throat."

Beowulf pulled out the chair next to Roxie and sat. "Relax, Wade. Just think how much easier it'll be to have your way with her tonight."

Drake thumped the now open bottle of wine onto the table. "Hello, her father is in the room. I haven't had time to adjust to the fact my daughter is old enough to have sex. I don't need you reminding me that she does."

When Taryn reached for the newly opened bottle of wine, Wade slapped her hand away. "I think you've had more than enough. Time for you to go to bed." Shooting Drake a quick glance, he added, "Alone, for now."

He easily picked Taryn up in his arms, then took her upstairs. She laid her head on his shoulder, so by the time he reached her bedroom, she was already asleep. Wade juggled her as he pulled the covers back on the bed. After gently placing her on it, he stripped off her clothes and then tucked her in. He shook his head. Contrary to what Beowulf said, he wouldn't be making love to her in her present condition. He had the feeling she would be out for the rest of the night. Resigned to the fact he would only be sleeping next to her tonight, he quietly walked out of the room and went back downstairs to join the others.

CHAPTER THIRTEEN

Coming awake slowly, Taryn groaned and grabbed her pounding head. She cracked open an eye and quickly shut it again when the bright morning light made the thumping increase in intensity.

Taryn realized how bright the sunlight streaming into her room was and cursed under breath as she quickly sat up. She regretted the movement a split second later. She pressed her hands to her temples and looked at her alarm clock. She cursed again when she saw how late it was. It was then she noticed Wade's side of the bed was empty.

Calling herself a fool for drinking so much wine the night before, Taryn hurriedly pulled on a pair of jeans and a long-sleeved cotton shirt. She only took the time to quickly brush her teeth and splash water onto her face before she headed downstairs.

The house was empty. She wasn't sure if she should be relieved or worried that no one was about. She hadn't checked the bedrooms on the way down to see if the others were already awake or not.

After walking outside, she made a beeline for the vineyard. Much to her relief, all the men were already hard at work. Drake was the first one to see her approaching. He met her halfway and pulled her close into a hug. She stiffened for a few seconds before she reminded herself that he was her father. She found it hard to think of him as such at times, because he really looked no older than she. Taryn returned the hug, thinking of all the hugs she'd missed getting from her father while she was growing up.

After Drake released her, he nodded in Wade's direction. He stood a little away from them. "Someone over there will be happy to see you're up and mobile. He thought you would be a little bit the worse for wear after all the wine you had last night."

Taryn smiled sheepishly. "That assumption wouldn't be too far off the mark. I don't exactly feel real chipper now. I'm happy to see you guys didn't wait for me to get out of bed before getting to work."

"That was Wade's doing. He figured you wouldn't be able to get up that early and suggested we get started without you."

Taryn walked to where Wade stood, waiting, then went on her tiptoes and kissed him soundly. She vaguely heard her father say he would get back to work before leaving them alone. She pressed herself against Wade and wasn't surprised to find he had an erection. If the harvest hadn't been in full swing, she wouldn't have had a second thought about dragging him to the house and having her way with him.

She kissed him for a few seconds longer before she pulled back. "Thanks for getting the men started this morning."

"You're welcome. I would rather you showed me another way how thankful you are, but I guess I'll have to settle for hearing the actual words instead."

Taryn reached between their bodies, making sure her back blocked what she was doing, as she stroked the bulge in Wade's pants. "Then I'll have to make a point to thank you properly later. When we're alone."

Wade bit back a groan as Taryn continued to stroke him. "If you don't stop that, I can't promise you what Drake's reaction will be when I drag you to the ground and make love to you right where we're standing."

"We can't have him getting upset, now can we?" Taryn stepped back, putting some space between them. "How did the hunt go last night? The wine got the better of me before I could find out what happened. I'm surprised Roxie didn't end up in the same condition."

"It takes a lot of alcohol to get a werewolf drunk. Drinking three bottles of wine would have the same effect as two glasses for you."

"Now you tell me." Taryn shook her head. "Great. So only I made an ass of myself by getting stupid drunk."

"Don't beat yourself up about it. Roxie felt you deserved it after all you'd been through, and the others agreed. Once we try the spell, you'll have no problem keeping up with Roxie."

After taking a quick look around to make sure no one was near, Taryn lowered her voice to a whisper. "Roxie and I had a talk about the spell yesterday. She said she would be more than happy to give it to us. She also explained about the mark on her wrist and what it meant. She thinks since she can do magic as her grandmother had done, there will be a better chance the spell will work if she's the one to do it."

Wade looked at her thoughtfully, then nodded. "She may have something there. So that's what the two of you were up to outside last evening. Roxie rarely shifts to her half-human, half-wolf form."

"Then I guess she really must like me. I asked her to show me, so she did. Did she really kick someone's ass while in that form?"

"She mentioned that, did she? Yeah, she did. After Gren turned Roxie, Beowulf challenged him to a fight. Beowulf, being Beowulf, met Gren alone, even though he knew full well Gren wouldn't abide by the rules and would have others with him. To make a long story short, Beowulf was blindsided by two of Gren's men during the fight. We, meaning me, Roxie, and Royce, showed up just in time to see it. When it looked as if Beowulf would lose, that was when Roxie shifted to her human/wolf form and basically beat the crap out of Gren and his men. She also used a spell on Gren to keep him in his werewolf form for a day."

Taryn shook her head. "I can see why you had no worries about leaving only Roxie with me when you went to hunt down Lars. She's a woman who can look after herself."

"Yeah, I wouldn't want to get on the wrong side of Roxie. We still have no idea what the limitations of her powers are. Royce seems to think she's capable of a lot more. His mate had kept a lot of her magic hidden from him. He said she was never very comfortable using it around him."

"I think I like the idea of having a sister-in-law who is 'special.' I can't see life around Roxie ever being boring."

"It never is that. Wait a minute. Did you just call Roxie your sister-in-law?"

"Yes. That was another thing Roxie explained to me yesterday. I understand in your eyes we're as good as married."

"At first, I assumed you would realize that, but Drake told me otherwise. I had meant to explain that to you myself."

Taryn softly brushed her finger along Wade's bottom lip. She sucked in a breath when he opened his mouth and nipped it. "It doesn't matter. Though there is one thing I want from you now that I do know."

"And that would be?" Wade pulled her against him and suggestively rocked his hips into her.

"Get me a damn ring so at least I can feel as if I'm a married woman." Taryn broke out of Wade's embrace before she started walking away. "Now get back to work before I have to resort to getting my whip out."

Wade chuckled. "You never know, I may like it if you took one to me."

"Into the kinky sex, are you? I've never had it before. Maybe we should try it out sometime."

"There's another thing Wade should have told you." Drake's voice drifted over from the other side of the row of grape vines she stood near. "Werewolves have exceptional hearing. I can honestly say hearing my daughter wanting to experiment with kinky sex was something I hoped never to have to hear. So, can the two of you stick to a topic that won't make my protective fatherly instincts kick in and want to rip Wade's head off?"

Taryn felt herself blush. "Sorry, Dad. We'll try to behave."

Blowing Wade a kiss, Taryn left the vineyard determined to get some work done and not think about having hot, sweaty sex with Wade.

* * * *

They were on their final week of the harvest. Thankfully, nothing untoward had happened. The amount of grapes harvested so far had been the best The Pines had seen for years, and the Lars problem had seemingly disappeared on its own. When days and then weeks passed, everyone relaxed their vigilance. The consensus seemed to be that with Lars knowing there were nine other werewolves on the property at all times, he'd been scared off. Far outnumbered, Lars didn't stand a chance of winning against them.

With the grapes just about all harvested, Taryn now had the job of bottling the wines that had sat aging in the cave from previous years' harvests. It was a job she enjoyed. Being able to see the end product bottled and ready to be sold made all the hard work worthwhile.

Taryn left the men to finish picking the last of the grapes, then went to her office to look at the book she used as a log, to record the dates and what type of wine each barrel held inside the cave. Before she started any of the bottling, as the winemaker, she had to taste, smell, and look at a sample of the wine from each barrel that had been aged the required amount of time.

She opened the logbook and soon got caught up in her work. She didn't bother to look up when someone quietly entered her office. Thinking it was Wade, she held up her finger for him to give her one minute as she wrote down some numbers.

"My, my. Aren't you the industrious one?"

Taryn whipped her head up at the sound of the one voice she did not want to hear inside her office. Lars stood before her desk, leering down at her. "What do you want?"

"That's no way to talk to someone visiting your winery. Don't you have wine tastings or something like that?"

"No, I don't. So you can leave if that was all you wanted."

"That's too bad. I really wanted to taste the wines of the winery I plan on making my own."

Taryn balled her hands into fists on top the desk. "I have no intention of selling the winery now or in the future. If you've come to make me an offer, the answer is no."

"I figured you would say that."

Lars lunged at her, moving faster than a normal man ever could. He grabbed her around her upper arms and dragged her across the desk to him. Taryn tried to break free, but it was like trying to escape steel shackles.

Being held against her will and made to stand in front of Lars as he snarled brought all the old memories of her abusive boyfriend raging back. She was now so comfortable around Wade she'd almost forgotten about her fear of men who used their greater strength as a means of control.

Taryn reacted as she would in such a situation. She raised her knee to unman Lars, but he proved to be the quicker. She ended up connecting with his thigh as he moved out of the way at the last second. All that ended up doing was pissing him off. He growled deep in his throat and gave her a good shake until her head snapped back and forth like a rag doll.

"No more tricks." Lars gave her another shake for good measure. "I see you're nothing like your mother. She was weak, not fit to be a werewolf's mate. You, on the other hand, have an inner strength your mother never had. I think I'll have my fun with you until I get tired of you; then I'll put you down for the mongrel you are."

Seeing the fear and disgust Taryn knew must be on her face, Lars laughed. The sound made chills run down her spine. There was something not right with him. He was just as good-looking as the rest of his kind, but there was no mistaking the madness lurking in his eyes.

She couldn't allow him to take her off the property. Her only hope was to somehow alert the men working in the vineyard of Lars's presence. She scrambled to try to come up with a plan to somehow get away before it was too late do to anything.

Lars laughed again as if he knew what she was thinking before slamming his mouth down onto hers. Taryn tried to pull away, which only caused him to increase the pressure of his grip on her arms until she whimpered with pain. Desperate, she took his bottom lip between her teeth and bit down until she tasted blood. He howled with pain and pushed her away and punched her in the side of the head. Seeing stars before her eyes, she dropped to the floor.

He squatted next to her and used the back of his hand to wipe the blood off his mouth. He took her chin in a punishing grip, forcing her to look at him. "Don't ever do that again. The next time, I won't be as gentle. Get up. It's time to go."

Lars let go of her chin and grabbed her arm. Still slightly disoriented, Taryn dragged her feet. Once they stepped outside, she opened her mouth to yell for help, but before she could make a sound, he turned and slapped his other hand across it.

"I can see you're going to cause me no end of trouble. I suggest you keep your trap shut or I'll be forced to shut it for you. It may not be pleasant for you, but I know I would enjoy it. Do I make myself clear?" After Taryn nodded, Lars removed his hand and started walking once more.

Taryn searched the yard, hoping one of the men had returned from the vineyard. It was empty. The area they worked in, none of them would be able to see what was happening near the house.

As Lars pulled her down the driveway to the road, Taryn thought if only she were a werewolf, she would have been able to give him a run for his money. If she'd been able to, she would have shifted into wolf form and sunk her teeth into his ass. The thought of him jumping around in pain as she hung from the seat of his pants made her laugh out loud. She was losing it, but she couldn't stop herself.

Not stopping their forward motion, Lars turned his head to scowl before he looked at her in a way that said he thought there was something wrong with her. That only caused Taryn to laugh harder. He probably thought she was a little nuts. It had to be bad when a raving lunatic thought she was a nut job.

Once they reached the road, Taryn's laughter died. There was a car parked on the other side, a few feet from the entrance of her driveway. Lars dragged her toward it as she dug in her feet, hoping it would slow him down. All it did was make him yank even harder on her arm. At the car, he used his keys to open the trunk. He was about to shove her into it when a yell stopped him.

Lars quickly pulled her to him so her back was against his chest. He wrapped an arm around her neck and his other at the top of her head. Seeing her father standing at the end of the driveway, Taryn wanted to cry out with relief, but instead she whimpered with fear as Lars applied pressure to her head. In this hold he could easily snap her neck.

"I would stay right where you are, Drake, if you want your daughter to live to see another day!" Lars yelled.

"Let her go, Lars. Your argument is with me, not Taryn."

"Why should I? It's so much more enjoyable to watch you suffer. I think I'll be keeping Taryn for a while."

Drake took a step toward them. Lars applied still more pressure, causing Taryn to cry out. Drake instantly stopped moving. A tear trickled down her cheek at the look of pure frustration that crossed his face. She knew he was powerless to do anything. Lars would have no qualms about breaking her neck. Right now, she hoped none of the others showed up. If they did, there was no telling what Lars would do to her.

When Drake made no further moves to come nearer, Lars slowly turned her as he prepared to shove her inside the trunk of the car. Drake yelled to him.

"I challenge you, Lars. I know you were the one who murdered my mate. By rights, I can challenge you to a fight to the death. Let's end this once and for all. Or are you so without honor you would rather take the cowardly way out?"

Lars growled at the insult. "I accept your challenge, but your daughter still comes with me. She'll be my insurance that you won't try to hunt me down before the challenge. Meet me tomorrow at midnight in the woods, and we'll have our fight to the death."

With that said, Lars pushed Taryn into the trunk and then slammed it shut. Enclosed in darkness, she heard Lars start the car before he pulled away, sending gravel from the side of the road flying in his wake. The sound of her father's howls of pain reached her.

CHAPTER FOURTEEN

Wade growled as he slammed his fist through Taryn's living room wall. He didn't feel the pain it caused him. All he felt was his helplessness, his inability to save his mate. Too-clear images of what Lars could be doing to her at this very moment filled his mind. Just the thought of her in pain made him see red. He hauled his arm back again and then punched a second hole in the wall.

Braedan caught Wade's fist before he could put it through it for a third time. "I don't think Taryn would appreciate you punching holes in her living room walls."

Wade pulled his fist free and instead slapped the wall. "I can't do this. I can't just sit here for over twenty-four hours and not try to get Taryn back."

"I know what you're feeling. Taryn is my niece. It's hard, but it's something we have to do. Besides, we have no idea where Lars took her. He's a lone wolf, and he could be anywhere. I have enough to worry about without you losing your head and doing something rash. Drake is not handling this well at all."

Wade looked at the ceiling. After Drake had informed them what had happened to Taryn, he'd gone upstairs to her bedroom and hadn't been seen since. Wade could only guess what was going through the other man's mind. To have found the daughter he'd thought dead, only to have the same person who'd murdered her mother take her hostage, would be a devastating blow to anyone. Allowing himself to give in to his pain wouldn't do Drake any favors. He was the one who would be fighting Lars at Muir Woods, which was the traditional place where werewolf challenges were fought. This wasn't an ordinary challenge of honor. This was to the death. Only the one left alive at the end would be declared the victor.

"All right. I have myself back under control. I'll talk to Drake. While I'm up there, Braedan, could you call Beowulf and let him know what's going on?"

"Consider it done."

After giving Braedan a nod, Wade headed up the stairs to Taryn's room. The door, which had been repaired, was shut. He tapped on it once before he opened it and stepped inside. Drake sat on the bed, slowly flipping through one of Taryn's photo albums. On the floor next to him sat the box Wade knew contained the things Taryn's uncle had left her. Drake didn't look up as he neared.

"Are you going to sit up here all night feeling sorry for yourself?"

Drake's head snapped up. He pulled back his upper lip in a snarl and growled softly. His eyes glowed mutedly. "Watch your mouth, pup."

Wade snarled back. "Back off, Drake. I only came up here because Braedan is worried about you. You have to keep things together if you hope to defeat Lars tomorrow. I don't trust crazy people to do what they're supposed to."

"Lars wasn't always the way he is now. Our fathers were friends when Lars and I were growing up. At one time, I considered Lars one of my good friends, but once we reached adulthood, things changed. He would go into a rage if I did something that could in any way be considered an accomplishment. Eventually, it got to the point he tried to take anything I valued for himself, even the women I showed an interest in. It got so bad I had to cut all ties with him."

"With friends like that, who needs enemies?"

Looking at the bed, Drake picked up the picture of himself with Taryn and her mother. He touched a finger to the image of his mate. "I knew when Lars found out Lisa was my mate that he would want her for his own, regardless that she was a mortal. I blame myself for what happened to her. I should have forced her to come back to me instead of waiting for her to decide on her own that she couldn't live without me." He let out a short laugh that held no humor. "I was an idiot. I may have accepted Lisa as my mate, but she never accepted me as hers. The tie was only one-sided—mine. Even before I told her what I truly was, she couldn't take me into her heart and soul. I didn't want to acknowledge that she didn't love me the same as I did her. So I let her run. If I hadn't, I would have been able to stop Lars. Now I've failed my daughter. I should have been watching her more closely. I knew Lars wasn't going to just go away. He was only biding his time."

"We'll get Taryn back. Losing her to Lars is not an option."

Drake put down the picture, then turned the page of the photo album he'd been looking at when Wade had walked in. It was filled with pictures of Taryn and her uncle at various stages in her life. "I've missed so much. I'm sad but at the same time furious. Lars did this to me out of jealousy. All I can think about is ripping the bastard's throat out."

"Good. Remember what you're feeling now and use it against Lars tomorrow night. Make him pay for all the pain and suffering he has put you through. And know that we'll be there for you during the fight."

Drake scowled up at Wade. "That's against the rules of the challenge. I'm to meet him alone."

"It'll only be me, Braedan, and Beowulf. We'll be well out of sight. Drake, you can't meet Lars alone. The man is crazy. Do you think he'll follow the rules of the challenge?"

"No. To be honest, I have no idea what to expect from him. I'm not going to leave my daughter parentless. All I know is I have to win."

Wade clapped Drake on the shoulder. "You will. Now come downstairs and reassure your brother you haven't sunk so low you won't be able to defend yourself tomorrow."

"I'll come down in a few minutes."

"You'd better. This is where I sleep, and I'd hate to have to throw my father-in-law's ass out into the hall."

Drake gave Wade a half smile. "You can always try, pup."

Giving Drake a nod, Wade left him to go downstairs. He hoped

Braedan had gotten hold of Beowulf. As pack leader, Beowulf needed to be there tomorrow night just in case things got messy.

* * * *

Beowulf arrived at The Pines the following afternoon. Much to Wade's surprise, Roxie was with him. Wade met them in the front yard. He'd been working in the vineyard with the rest of the men. The separation anxiety was getting to him—bad—and the hard work only helped some.

With Taryn absent and to help make the hours go by more quickly, they'd all decided to finish with the harvest. Today was to have been their last day anyway. After working so hard for the last six weeks, none of the men wanted to leave the job incomplete.

Roxie gave him a kiss on the cheek once she reached them. "How are you holding up, Wade? You must be ready to climb the walls by now."

"I've been better. Drake has been the harder hit. What are you doing here, Roxie?"

"She refused to be left behind," Beowulf explained. "Roxie feels it's her right to be there during the challenge, considering she rules over the packs now."

"Well, I do. So the both of you can stop looking at me as if I've done something wrong. Where are all our guys, by the way?"

Wade shook his head, knowing full well Roxie would not change her mind and stay away from Muir Woods. "We're finishing the harvest."

"Beowulf and I will help."

"We will?" Beowulf asked lightly.

"Of course we will. What else do you have to do? If everyone else is out in the vineyard working, we can't very well just sit in the house doing nothing, waiting for them to finish."

"No, of course we couldn't," Beowulf said blandly. He then said under his breath, "Though I can think of another way we can keep ourselves entertained until they call it a day."

"What was that?" Roxie arched a brow at her mate.

"Nothing. Nothing at all."

"Yeah, right. I think you have sex on the brain, Beowulf. Don't you think of anything but that?"

"I do, occasionally. It's just hard to think of anything else when I know you really wouldn't complain if I were to sling you over my shoulder and take you to the house to have my way with you."

Roxie gave Beowulf a heated stare that said he was all too correct. She centered her attention on Wade. "Take us to the vineyard. Now. The faster we get there, the better."

Wade looked over Roxie's head at his brother. Beowulf stared at his mate with affection, and how he felt about her showed in his eyes. Before finding Taryn, Wade had found Roxie and Beowulf's banter sickening at times. He hadn't understood how his brother could go from being the strong-willed leader of their pack one moment, then change into someone who could let his guard down completely around his mate, joking and teasing with her. Now he did. Wade had even acted in very much the same way with Taryn.

Resisting the urge to gnash his teeth at the unfairness of it all, Wade turned on his heel and led Beowulf and Roxie to where the rest of the men worked in the vineyard. As he walked along, he decided after he got Taryn back, he would have Roxie try the spell on Taryn that night. He couldn't help feeling that if Taryn had been a werewolf, she would have been able to get away from Lars. She needed to be able to protect herself. If the spell didn't work, he didn't even want to think about it.

* * * *

Taryn paced the large bedroom Lars had locked her in. It was a beautifully decorated room with a king-size bed and a bathroom en suite, but it was a prison nonetheless. The one window had bars in front of it, which she couldn't have slipped through even if she'd been able to open the window. The bathroom had no windows, so no means of escape there either. It made her wonder who else besides herself had been held captive in that spot. She didn't think Lars had gone to the trouble of making it a prison just for her.

When her pacing brought her back to the bedroom door, Taryn grabbed the handle and pulled. It was still locked from the outside. So far, she hadn't seen Lars or anyone else for that matter since he'd shoved her inside the room and then locked her in. That didn't necessarily mean he lived alone. The quick glimpse of the house she'd had before he'd hauled her inside was enough for her to see that he lived in a mansion. It figured the crazy man was also stinking rich.

Her stomach growled loudly, reminding her she hadn't had anything to eat since yesterday at lunchtime. She figured Lars wasn't going to feed her. At least she had water to drink courtesy of the sink in the bathroom. Her stomach growled a second time. Taryn ground her teeth in frustration. There were too many hours of the day left before it reached midnight. She didn't think she could survive it without going crazy.

It wasn't so much her being held captive as being separated from Wade. Her father and Roxie had explained how she would feel if she ever was away from Wade for a long period of time, but she hadn't realized it would be this bad. All she could think about was getting back to Wade. Nothing else mattered. Not what Lars would do to her or what the outcome of that night's challenge would be. The need to get to him overrode any other thought.

It wasn't that she just needed to see him and she would be fine. No, it was much more than that. Her body wanted him as well. When she was back with him, she'd be lucky if she could restrain herself from stripping naked and throwing herself at him, to connect with him in the most elemental of ways.

At the sound of the bedroom door being unlocked, Taryn spun around to face it. It was Lars who pushed it open. He stepped into the room, carrying a tray of food, which he placed on the dresser closest to the door. He looked at her and nodded, obviously pleased to see her so out of sorts.

"So you truly have become Wade's mate. This has worked out better than I'd thought. Me taking you will have been a blow to Drake, but I have the satisfaction of knowing Wade is suffering from the separation."

Taryn couldn't understand what Lars had against her father. Drake couldn't have done something that atrocious to have caused Lars to go to such lengths to hurt him. "Why are you doing this? Do you hate my father that much?"

Lars dropped his pleasant demeanor. "I despise Drake. It was all his fault."

"What was his fault?"

"Because of him, I never measured up to my father's expectations. Drake was the special one in his eyes. I was never smart enough, never good enough. Every time Drake did something that made his father proud, mine expected me to do the same. When I couldn't, he'd beat me for my failure. In the end, I hated Drake because he was the one who caused my pain and suffering. If he hadn't been so perfect, my father would have left me alone."

"So, you think that justifies everything you've done to my father? Don't think for one minute you killing my mother and holding me captive will make your father respect you any more than he does now, because I doubt it will. All it has done has caused a lot of innocent people to suffer. You should be directing all your anger at your father. He's the one who hurt you."

Lars growled deep in his throat. "I did this for me, not to earn my father's respect. I took care of him years ago. I challenged him to fight to the death and killed him. In the end, I was stronger and faster than he was. That's why I know I'll come out the winner tonight. Drake has wasted the last twenty-six years mourning a woman who never loved him enough to accept him as a true mate. How pathetic. It has made him weak."

"Don't count yourself the victor until you've won. Drake has something to fight for—me. That's just another way you don't measure up. You don't have a child who loves and respects you, and you never will. No woman in her right mind would have a child with you."

Lars crossed the distance between them and raised his fist to strike her. Taryn instinctively raised her arms to protect her face. When the blow didn't come, she slowly lowered them. Even though her heart pounded with fear, she stared at him with disgust.

Chuckling, Lars backed away. "You may put on a brave front, Taryn, but I can hear your heart racing, and I can smell your fear." Once he reached the door, he nudged the tray sitting on the dresser. "Eat. I can't have you passing out from lack of food. I like my women to be high-spirited when I take them to bed, and I have the feeling I'm going to enjoy breaking you."

After Lars closed and then locked the door, Taryn picked up

the tray and took it to the bed. She ate the food he'd given her. It wasn't much—just a couple thick slices of bread with some cheese—but it would do. She didn't eat it because he had told her to. She ate it because it wouldn't do if she passed out from lack of food. She needed to be at her best for tonight. If there indeed was a chance the bastard would win, she wasn't going to give up without a fight.

CHAPTER FIFTEEN

Wade watched the last of the extra members of their pack drive away. Now that the harvesting was complete, they were no longer needed and could go back to their normal everyday lives. They had not been informed about the challenge that was taking place that night. They knew about Taryn's disappearance, but Beowulf had reassured them the situation was being taken care of and that Taryn would pay them after her return for all the work they'd done. Before leaving The Pines, each one of them had told Beowulf to call if they were needed. Beowulf had promised he would do so if it came to that.

It was getting close to the time that they had to leave for Muir Woods. The others had wanted to take one car only, but Wade had said he would be driving his own. Once he had Taryn back, there was no way he was going to hang around for the cleanup. He only hoped he'd be able to get her to his house before he could no longer hold off from having her. Being so long separated from her, anxiety rode him hard. He now understood why Beowulf and Roxie couldn't keep their hands off each other. He'd had a hard-on for most of the day, and it wouldn't go away.

Before returning to the house to see if the others were ready to leave, Wade looked at the night sky. It matched his mood. Thick, heavy storm clouds scudded across the moon, blocking its light and the numerous stars. It was going to be pitch-black during the challenge, but it was no detriment to a werewolf. They had excellent night vision. The only one who wouldn't be able to see much would be Taryn.

Wade stepped inside the house and found Beowulf, Roxie, Braedan, and Drake ready to go. "All set?"

Beowulf nodded. "As we'll ever be. I want you to promise one thing before we go, Wade."

"That would be?"

"Don't do anything foolish. We'll get Taryn back."

"I'll only promise you I won't move against Lars unless he forces me to. If he ends up turning on Taryn, nothing will stop me from taking him down."

"We'll both take him down," Drake added. "One way or the other, Lars won't be leaving the woods without paying for his past actions."

"I thought you were going to fight him to the death."

"I have no intention of killing him. I knew that was the only way I could get Lars to accept the challenge. He thinks no one can defeat him in a fight to the death. He challenged his own father to such and won."

"He must have had a real loving relationship with him," Wade said sarcastically.

"It was far from it. My father suspected Lars's dad mistreated Lars, but he never saw any proof of it."

"That would explain why he's a little messed up in the head. Personally, I'd rather see the bastard out of our lives forever, permanently."

Roxie cleared her throat, drawing the men's attention. "That's where I come in. I fixed Gren, so I'll fix Lars. No killing anyone unless it's in self-defense."

Wade could tell Roxie was serious. She wouldn't allow them to kill Lars outright. It was true; she had fixed Gren. Using her magic against him, and seeing how she was able to shift into her human/wolf form that made her stronger than any male werewolf, had been enough to keep Gren in line, but Lars was an altogether different animal. He had purposely killed Taryn's mother. It had by no means been an accident.

"Fine. No killing Lars. Now let's get going."

The drive from Stags Leap to Muir Woods seemed to take an

intolerable amount of time to Wade, but the closer he came to the woods, the closer he felt he was getting to Taryn. When they arrived, he drove his car to a different parking lot from the one Drake had parked in. They were pretty sure Lars would park in that same lot, since it was the closest one to the challenge area. It was also the reason it'd been decided Drake would use his car. There was a small chance Lars would know which car Drake drove.

Wade jogged back to where the others waited for him. He felt as if his nerves were stretched to the breaking point as all of them set out on the main trail that led to the small clearing serving as the challenge area. He just wanted this over and done with.

Roxie, who had been walking ahead with Beowulf, hung back until he caught up to her. She looped her arm through his and fell into step beside him. "I'm having a bad case of déjà vu."

Wade knew what Roxie referred to. It was not that long ago Beowulf had come to Muir Woods to challenge Gren to a fight. "I know what you mean. Hopefully, this will be the last time we'll have to come here under these circumstances."

Pulling on his arm, Roxie let the other men get farther ahead of them. She spoke in a hushed tone for his ears only. "I'm all prepared to try the spell on Taryn tomorrow."

"I want you to try tonight," Wade replied quietly.

"Wade, I don't think Taryn will be in any mood for it. Plus, I think the two of you will be a little busy making up for lost time, so to speak. I'm sorry, but I'm no voyeur. If the spell does work, it's not really a pleasant experience. Taryn's going to feel a little overwhelmed as well. I know I was. All the extra-sensitive werewolf senses take a little getting used to."

"I guess tomorrow will do."

"Believe me, once you get Taryn into your arms, the spell will be the furthest thing from your mind. I know what you're going through. It was hell when Beowulf decided I was better off with Royce than him. We barely made it to a bed before we were at each other."

"Way too much information, Roxie." Wade pretended to shudder in disgust.

Roxie lightly punched him on the arm. "As long as you get the point I was making, then I won't say any more about how great the sex was that night."

Wade groaned. "What are you trying to do to me, Rox? Now I have to flush my ears out. I so did not need the mental image of you and my brother in bed together."

"Whatever. I won't say a word when I see Taryn and you ripping at each other's clothes. Just try to hold back until you're out of sight of the rest of us; then you can have sex like bunnies."

When they reached the spot where they had to break off the main trail and make their way through the trees to reach the challenge area, Wade kissed Roxie's cheek. "Thanks for distracting me, even though I'll have nightmares tonight after hearing some of the things you told me."

"Any time. We'd better catch up to the others before Beowulf starts to wonder what's taking us so long."

"Too late."

Wade pointed to where Beowulf stood a little away from the main trail, watching them. Roxie hurried to him. Beowulf pulled her close to his side before he walked away with her. Alone, Wade followed them.

* * * *

They had purposely arrived early so they would have enough time to hide their presence from Lars. Only Drake remained out in the open. They'd taken positions downwind and well out of sight from where the two challengers were to meet. Once in position, Wade found the waiting the hardest part of the night. In the back of his mind, he couldn't help wondering if Lars would show up. It would just be their luck if he didn't.

Right at the stroke of midnight, Lars came into view, pulling a bound and gagged Taryn behind him. When he saw Drake standing in the small clearing, waiting for him, Lars shoved her to the ground and then wrapped the length of rope he carried around her ankles. Once he was finished, he turned to face Drake.

"As you can see, your precious daughter is not the worse for wear. I decided I'd have my fun with her after I rid myself of you."

Drake snarled and snapped his teeth. "Release Taryn. Let's keep this between the two of us."

"I think not. She's my prize, and I don't give up my prizes for anyone. Enough talking."

Lars and Drake launched at each other, changing into wolf form on the fly. Wade kept his gaze pinned on Taryn. She whimpered once when the two wolves came a little too close to where she lay.

Wade shifted his feet, thinking maybe he could somehow make his way around the clearing to get to Taryn, but Braedan, who was hidden with him, put out a hand to stop him. He shook his head. Wade ground his teeth in frustration. If Taryn became caught in the middle of the fight, the wolves' claws and teeth could do a lot of damage.

The sounds of the wolves' growls filled the clearing as they tore into each other. Blood splattered their coats as each one wounded the other, neither seeming to have the advantage. Wade had a feeling the fight was not going to be over as quickly as he had at first thought.

*

Taryn watched the two wolves battle. She tried to keep track of which one was her father, but it was so dark she could barely see anything in front of her. Both wolves had light-colored fur so they were a little easier to see, but not by much.

Unable to just lie there and watch, Taryn tried to get her hands free. It was no use. Lars had tied the rope too tight around her wrists. Her fingers were starting to go numb. Craning her neck around, she tried to see if there was a rock or something she could use to try to saw through the ropes, but it was too dark to see anything clearly.

When one of the wolves cried out in pain, Taryn quickly turned her head back in their direction. Her heart lurched in her chest when she saw Lars had Drake pinned to the ground with his jaws clamped around the back of her father's neck. She screamed behind her gag.

Thinking it was just about all over, Taryn struggled with her bonds, hopelessly trying to get free so she could save Drake. Instead of biting down and breaking Drake's neck, Lars pulled back and shifted into his human form. She screamed again in warning as he pulled a large knife out of his coat pocket.

Before he could use it, Beowulf, Braedan, and Wade stepped into the clearing and rushed Lars. Seeing Drake was no longer alone, Lars quickly lurched to his feet and picked up Taryn so she stood in front of him. The knife he held came to rest at the base of her throat.

"You broke the rules, Drake. You were to come alone."

Taryn saw Drake—now in human form—bleeding from many wounds. "You broke the rules by keeping Taryn as a hostage, and then by using a weapon other than teeth and claws. The challenge is over. Let her go and maybe things will go easier for you."

"Like hell I will. I still have the power here as long as I have her."

"Not for much longer you won't," Beowulf said with a snarl. "Roxie, now!"

Something large growled directly behind Lars. Before he could turn to see what it was, a furred arm reached around him and grabbed the wrist of the hand that held the knife and pulled it away from Taryn's throat. The sound of bone snapping was easily heard. Whimpering in pain, Lars dropped his weapon. He looked up in horror as Roxie in her human/wolf form pulled Taryn out of his hold.

Once Taryn was free, Roxie pick Lars off his feet by his throat. "I guess you haven't heard what I do to bad dogs like you," she said with a growl. She held him away in disgust. "And it looks as if you aren't housebroken either."

Taryn jumped as someone came up behind her and worked on the ropes tied around her wrists. "It's only me, Taryn."

At the sound of Wade's voice, Taryn swayed toward him. As he continued to work on the ropes, Braedan came over and removed her gag. Between the two of them they soon had her free of her bonds. She turned to face Wade and threw herself into his arms. She pressed against him as her body shook in aftershock. With her held tightly against his chest, he picked her up and then walked out of the clearing. No one tried to stop them.

Reaching the main trail, Wade briefly let her down on her feet and kissed her for all he was worth. With reluctance, he pulled away. Taryn whimpered at the loss of his mouth on hers. "I know. Just hold on. I'll get us to my house as quickly as I can."

"Why can't I think of anything else but having you inside me? I should be a blubbering idiot right now."

Wade scooped her up into his arms again, then jogged toward the parking lot where she assumed he'd left his car. "It's the separation anxiety. I feel it too."

At his car, Wade quickly helped Taryn into the passenger side before coming around the back end to get into the driver's seat. After starting the car, he backed out of the parking space and then quickly headed for the main road.

Wanting to distract herself from the intense longing that had taken over her, Taryn asked, "What's going to happen to Lars now?"

"It will be up to Roxie to decide what his fate will be. Whatever it is, I'm sure Lars will be punished."

The remainder of the trip to San Francisco sped by in a blur. By the time Wade drove up the winding drive to his large house, Taryn had reached her limit. The second he had the car parked and the ignition switched off, she clambered over to his side and sat on his lap, facing him. She fisted her hands in his hair and claimed his lips in a hard kiss.

Wade blindly reached for his keys, which were still in the car's ignition. He barely managed to murmur against her mouth, "House, Taryn," before she shoved her tongue inside his mouth.

Not letting him come up for air, Taryn pulled the handle and pushed open the door. Wade somehow managed to get them both out of the car. As soon as he stood, she wrapped her legs around his waist and held on for dear life. Once they reached the front door, he fumbled with his keys until he found the right one. She gasped as he shifted her in his arms so her already wet pussy rubbed against the very large bulge in his pants.

He pushed open the door, carried her through it, and kicked it shut with his foot. They hadn't quite made it to the stairs before Wade pressed her back against the wall and reached under her shirt to cup her breast. He stroked her nipple through her bra, then pulled his hands free and ripped her top down the middle. He parted the material and bent his head so he could lick the tops of her breasts.

Taryn moaned with pleasure. "You owe me a new shirt."

"I'll buy you as many as you want." Wade's voice was husky

with desire.

Yanking at Wade's T-shirt, Taryn pulled it out of the waistband of his jeans and then shoved her hands up it. His stomach muscles quivered as she ran her fingers across his skin. "Either take me right here against the wall or get me to a bed. Now."

"A bed it is."

Wade wrapped his arms around her waist, then took the stairs two at a time. Once they were enclosed in his room, he laid Taryn on the bed and quickly rid himself of his clothes. She threw her ripped shirt onto the floor. The rest of her clothing soon followed.

Wade joined Taryn on the bed, falling into her open arms. She clutched his back as he kissed her, stroking his tongue across hers before sucking it inside his mouth. He moved to lie between her legs. His fully erect cock came to rest against her hot, slick opening. She whimpered at the feel of his hard length pressed against her most sensitive spot. More than ready to have him inside her, she took hold of his shaft and led the head of his cock into her dripping pussy.

Wade released her mouth as he pushed himself home and groaned with pleasure. Taryn wrapped her legs around his waist and arched her hips as he pumped his, riding her hard. She panted, loving the feel of him buried deep inside her. He touched her cervix with each powerful stroke in.

The words she'd been meaning to say to him, but hadn't been able to until now, bubbled out of her. "I love you, Wade. I don't want to ever lose you."

Continuing to move inside her, Wade brushed her hair off her forehead. "I love you too, Taryn. I'm not going anywhere."

Taryn reached up and stroked Wade's jaw. She rocked her hips against him, her release charging up to meet her. Closing her eyes, she held on to his powerful arms as her climax tore through her. It seemed to go on forever with wave after wave of pleasure hitting her.

Wade moved faster, pushing himself into her. He lifted one of her legs to her chest, angling himself, going even deeper. Unbelievably, her body exploded in another climax. This time he joined her. With a deep moan, he pushed into her one final time before he climaxed deep inside her, filling her. Out of breath, he collapsed on top of her. Relishing the feel of his heavy weight,

Taryn held him close. With him still hard and buried deep inside her, her eyes drifted shut. She didn't move when he shifted them to their sides and pulled the blankets over them. Tired from her ordeal and satiated, she let sleep claim her.

* * * *

The following morning Taryn and Wade went downstairs to find Roxie and Drake waiting for them in the kitchen. Beowulf and Braedan were nowhere in sight.

Seeing her father appeared not to be seriously injured from the fight the night before, Taryn stepped into his open arms and held him close. Drake kissed the top of her head.

Looking at him, she smiled. "I'm glad to see you're okay."

Drake returned her smile. "I can say the same thing about you."

Stepping away, Taryn turned to Roxie. "Wade said you're willing to try the spell today."

Roxie nodded. "Yes. That's why I have Drake here with me. I figured we could give this a try while Beowulf is still asleep."

"Try what?" Beowulf stepped into the kitchen. "What are you up to now, Roxie?"

"Wade and Taryn want to see if the spell Gren used to change me into a werewolf will work on Taryn."

"Roxie, I can't see it working. I think it was meant for one person and one person only — you."

"Well, I don't agree with that assumption. It's worth a shot. I still think it worked because Gren used Royce's blood and because I'm his descendant. Taryn is half werewolf, and Drake has agreed to give some of his blood to use for the spell. If it doesn't work, then we'll know for sure."

Beowulf stared at Roxie for a few seconds, then shook his head. "Fine. Get on with it then."

Roxie left the kitchen only to return a minute later with a package of syringes, some alcohol wipes, and cotton balls. She opened the package of syringes and pulled one out. Seeing Beowulf eyeing the number she'd bought, she shrugged. "I couldn't very well go to the drugstore and asked for one. I had to buy the package of syringes they sell to diabetics."

Ripping open the alcohol wipe, Roxie turned to Drake. "Can you hold out your arm? Gren took the blood from Royce's neck, but I think he only used that spot because it would hurt Royce more. I'll try to go fast, but I can't promise you I'll be too gentle. I've never done this before."

"If this works, I won't mind having a little pain."

Drake held out his arm. She quickly rubbed the wipe across the inside of his elbow and then jabbed the end of the syringe into his skin. Pulling back on the plunger, she filled it with blood. She removed the needle, then pressed a cotton ball to the spot where it'd been. She turned to Taryn.

"Your turn. I'll inject the blood in the same place I took it from Drake."

Holding out her arm, Taryn asked, "How will we know if the spell worked or not?"

Roxie chuckled. "Believe me, you'll know. It burns like hell."

After wiping Taryn's arm with the alcohol, Roxie took a deep breath and jabbed the needle into her arm, pushing down the plunger. She said the spell.

"The magic of the wolf's blood is now in thee.
A wolf you become to run wild and free.
Where once there were two, now only one we see."

They all held their breath and waited. When a minute went by, and Taryn didn't seem to be feeling anything happening inside her, Roxie shook her head. "Damn. I thought for sure it would work."

"It's all right, Roxie," Taryn said sadly. "I guess it wasn't meant to be. You're the special one. Even though you have more magic inside you, the spell must have been only meant for you."

Roxie's brow furrowed as she got a faraway look in her eyes. A second later, she smiled. "I *am* the special one, aren't I? And you're right, the magic is inside me."

Before the others wondered what she'd meant, Roxie grabbed another syringe, wiped her arm with the alcohol, and jabbed the needle into it. After she filled it with blood, she wiped Taryn's once again and jabbed the needle into her skin. Roxie injected the blood before she quickly repeated the spell.

Unlike the first try, the words resonated inside Taryn. The spot on her arm where Roxie had injected her blood burned. Moving like quicksilver, it sped through her body, making Taryn feel as if she were on fire from the inside out. Gasping at the sensation, she sank to the floor and curled into a ball. When Wade tried to touch her, she shoved him away, unable to stand to have him touching her.

Slowly, the burning sensation let up. Panting, Taryn uncurled her body. She sat up and looked into Wade's concerned face. "I think it worked that time. I feel different."

"In what way?"

She looked around the room. "I can smell each of your scents. They're distinctively different. I can hear insects buzzing outside." It was a bit overwhelming, but she now felt as if she had a closer tie to her mate and father, being the same as them.

"It worked." Wade took Taryn's hand and pulled her up onto her feet. He turned to Roxie and gave her a big hug. "It worked. Roxie, you're amazing."

Roxie pushed him away. "I guess I am. Just something else I can do that I didn't know I could do before."

"And you just gave me something else to worry about," Beowulf said as he pulled Roxie against his side. "We have to keep this between us for now. If other packs find out what you just did here, things could get nasty. They think the spell was written only for Roxie, and they have accepted that."

Wade nodded. "I understand. Roxie's safety has to come first. Now if you'll all excuse us, I'm taking Taryn upstairs so I can teach her how to do the change."

Drake took a step forward to join them. "I'll help, Wade. Maybe with the both of us showing her, Taryn will learn quicker."

Roxie took hold of Drake's arm and held him back. "I don't think that would be a very good idea. If Taryn's first try turns out to be anything like mine, clothes are the last thing she'll be able to get the hang of."

"I see. I'll stay down here then."

Taryn kissed Drake on the cheek. "Once I've figured out how to do the change, I want to go wolf and run with you."

"I'd like that as well."

Turning back to Wade, Taryn grabbed his hand and allowed

him to lead her upstairs to their room. She smiled, letting him see all the love she felt for him in her eyes. Her life was now complete. She had a mate who loved her as much as she loved him, and had the next couple thousand years to show him at every opportunity. What else could she ask for?

The End

ROYCE AND BILLIE

Billie first met Royce at Wulf's Den while there to drag her drunken brother home to his wife. Even though she knows he is attracted to her, Royce refuses to see her again. With four older brothers, and being a personal trainer at her family's gym, Billie is not the type of woman to let a man she wants slip through her fingers.

Royce knows Billie is his mate, but with her being a mortal, he fights the attraction he feels for her. He already lost a mate who wasn't a werewolf and doesn't want to take the chance of getting hurt again.

As Royce's feelings grow for Billie another male werewolf stalks Royce. Thinking Royce's blood is the key to a magic spell, he will do anything to obtain it, even if he has to use Billie to get it.

CHAPTER ONE

Billie York grumbled under her breath as she walked to the Wulf's Den front entrance. It was almost three in the morning. She'd been in a deep sleep when her sister-in-law, Janice, had called, asking Billie to find her husband, Billie's brother, and haul his ass home. Knowing she was the only one who could do it, Billie had assured Janice Hayes would be home soon.

Now there she was in front of a nightclub just before closing time, cursing her brother's existence. Every time he had a fight with his wife, Hayes went to some bar and got stinking drunk. It was always Billie who had to get his drunken ass home since she was the only one who could find him. He tried to hide from her by going to bars and nightclubs he didn't usually frequent, but it never mattered. She had a gift, one only her family knew about — she could find anyone she'd met, no matter how brief their acquaintance. She didn't even need to know their name, just what they looked like. She could bring the image of the person's face in her mind and be able to see exactly where he or she was at that exact moment. She'd been able to do it with ease since she was very young. At first, she'd thought everyone could do it. She soon learned differently once she started school and her friends had laughed at her when she'd told them what she could do. Now, it was something the family kept to themselves.

Since it was almost closing time, there wasn't a line of people waiting to get into Wulf's Den. Billie nodded at the large, bald bouncer before she stepped inside. He waved her through as he eyed the sweatpants and top she wore. She wasn't dressed for a nightclub, but now, she pretty much didn't give a damn. She would be there only long enough to collect Hayes and then she was going back to bed.

It took her eyes a few seconds to adjust to the dimness inside the club. Once she could see, Billie quickly scanned the room for her brother. He wasn't hard to find. The place wasn't filled at this time of night. Focused on where Hayes sat at the bar, talking to one of the waitresses, Billie stomped toward him.

Hayes didn't notice her at first as he continued to tell the waitress in a drunken slur how much he loved his wife, even though she didn't understand him. Billie rolled her eyes in disgust. The waitress, who happened to look as if she'd stepped out of one of the pages of a fashion magazine, gave Billie a small smile before leaving her alone with her brother.

It was then Hayes realized she stood beside him. He scowled. "Shit, Billie. Can't I ever get away from you?"

Billie crossed her arms over her chest and glared at Hayes. "No. Do you think I enjoy being dragged out of my bed to hunt you down? Believe me, I don't. I have other things I would much rather be doing than be my brother's keeper. Such as getting a full night's sleep, for starters."

"Then why do it? It's not as if I asked you to find me." Hayes reached for his drink. Finding the glass empty, he scowled. "Empty. Where's that bartender?" He looked down the length of the bar.

"I think you've had more than enough. Time for you to go home to your wife."

"One more drink for the road; then I promise to go home. I'm perfectly capable of finding my own way, you know."

Billie snorted as Hayes just about fell off the bar stool while he continued to look for the bartender. "I don't think so. Now give me your car keys so we can get the hell out of here."

"Just go home, Billie. I can manage on my own, I told you. How come you only bug me like this and not the others?" The others Hayes referred to were their three older brothers.

"The others don't get stupid drunk every time they take offense to something their wife says to them. Are you going to give me your keys or do I have to take them from you?"

"Go away, Billie. Do you have any idea how humiliating it is to have your baby sister drag you home as if you were a child?"

"Not my problem. Okay. We'll do it the hard way then." Quickly taking hold of Hayes's wrist, Billie bent his arm back behind him and forced it up toward his shoulder blades. Hayes yelped and fell forward onto the bar. For good measure, she dug her thumb into the inside of his wrist, at the base of his palm, to keep him pinned in place. He swore as she rifled through his pants pockets, looking for his car keys.

*

Royce watched the scene taking place at the bar. He sat in the back corner of the club far enough away that neither participant could see him. His lips twitched with amusement.

He'd watched the woman enter the club and then head for the drunken mortal who sat at the bar. She hadn't looked at all thrilled to be there. Normally, he ignored such goings-on, but there was something about the woman that drew his eye. She was pretty in an understated way. Her long black hair fell to the middle of her back. He really couldn't tell what kind of figure she had because of the loose-fitting sweats she wore. He had the feeling she wasn't the type of woman who cared what other people thought of her looks, anyway.

When the conversation seemed to get a little heated, Royce found himself on his feet, then heading toward them. Just as he reached them, the woman pinned the man to the bar before she searched his pockets.

"Do you need any help?"

The woman turned to take a quick look at Royce and shook her head. "Thanks for the offer, but I can manage." With a sound of triumph, she pulled out a set of keys from the man's pocket.

Royce sucked in a sharp breath as he caught his first whiff of her scent. Taking another, he drew it deep into his lungs. The wolf inside him threw back his head and howled with longing. He fought the urge to pull her into his arms, to claim her as his. Her scent said she was his mate, but it was her being a mortal that made him want to resist the mating urge that had risen. He'd lost one mate who was mortal. He couldn't take a second one.

Oblivious to what Royce was going through, she released the man's arm and dangled the keys in front of his face. "Let's go."

Unable to stop himself, Royce stepped nearer to the woman. She wasn't all that tall—the top of her head barely reached the middle of his chest—but there was a toughness about her that made up for her lack of stature. He took another deep breath, knowing her scent would be forever burned into his mind, never forgotten. When she took a step back and rammed into his chest, he bit back a moan of pleasure.

She quickly turned and apologized. "Sorry about that." A look of interest spread across her face as she stared at him.

*

Billie stared, but she couldn't stop herself. The man standing in front of her was breathtaking to the max. Visions of wrapping herself around his well-built body and kissing him until they both couldn't think straight flitted through her mind as she looked into his hazel eyes. She usually didn't find herself instantly attracted to a man. Growing up in a houseful of males, she was much more comfortable around men than she was women so she tended to be treated like one of the guys. She didn't want this guy to think of her in that way. He was someone she wanted to get close and personal with. He had perfect good looks, with his square jaw, chiseled lips, and straight nose. He wore his golden-brown hair long so it fell just past his shoulders. Billie had the strongest urge to run her fingers through its length. And he was tall, which was something she liked in a man. He had to be no less than six feet six.

The silence seemed to stretch between them. Billie could tell the interest she felt was not totally one-sided. He hungrily swept his gaze over her body. Not wanting him to think Hayes was anything more than just her brother, Billie stuck out her hand. "I'm Billie York, and this drunken sot over here is my brother, Hayes."

Reluctantly, he took her hand. When his large one closed over hers, a jolt of awareness zipped through her.

"I'm Royce Larrsson. Billie, is it?"

"It's short for Wilhelmina."

"Nice to meet you, Billie. If you have things under control, I'll leave you to get your brother home."

Not wanting to let him get away that quickly, Billie turned to look at Hayes. He'd gotten off the bar stool and now stood none too steadily on his feet, watching them. He was a big man, just a few inches shorter than Royce and just as muscled. She was strong, but if Hayes took a header while she helped him to the car, there would be nothing she could do to stop him from pulling her down with him.

"Actually, if you don't mind, could you help me get Hayes out to the car? You look as if you're strong enough to sling him over your shoulder if it comes to it."

That way she could keep Royce around for a little while longer. She didn't want him to leave until she tested the waters a little bit more. She wasn't the type of girl to just sit back and let a man come to her. If she met one she liked, and he didn't seem to be moving fast enough for her, Billie had no problem taking matters into her own hands to let him know what she wanted, literally and metaphorically speaking. Sometimes her forwardness paid off, and sometimes it didn't, but she was willing to take that chance with him. The longer he stood beside her, the more her body perked up and took notice.

Hayes snorted. "I'm not being hauled to my car over anybody's shoulder. I'm perfectly capable of walking on my own, thank you very much."

Billie held her breath as Royce looked from her to her brother. He seemed reluctant to agree at first. It wasn't until Hayes tried to walk by her and ended up pushing her into Royce did he give a slight nod in agreement. His arms wrapped around her waist as he steadied her against his larger body. All the air rushed out of her lungs in a whoosh as her hands came to rest on his hard chest. Like quicksilver, desire rushed through her, making her nipples pebble beneath her sweat top. What really had her almost panting was the feel of Royce's fully aroused cock nestled against her stomach.

Feeling as if all the moisture had left her mouth, Billie

swallowed and lifted her head to look at Royce. For a split second, she could have sworn his eyes glowed, but then it was gone before her brain could fully register it had happened.

Royce's nostrils flared slightly as he leaned into her and took a deep breath before he quickly released her. "I'll help you with your brother; then I have to leave."

A scowl settled on Billie's face as Royce took Hayes by the arm and walked away as he headed for the club's entrance. She had to wonder what that was all about. Royce was attracted to her—the hard-on he sported was still slightly noticeable by the bulge in his pants—but now he acted as if she had the plague, and he couldn't get away from her fast enough.

Following Royce out to the parking lot, Billie directed him to where Hayes's car was parked. She unlocked the passenger door and then held it open as Royce shoved Hayes into it. She quickly slammed the door shut on her brother. She ignored Hayes as he yelled at her to watch what she was doing.

Billie had the element of surprise on her side. Before Royce could walk away, she slammed her body into his, backed him up against the side of the car, and kept pushing until he was practically lying on the trunk. With her fingers threaded through his hair, she pulled his mouth to hers and kissed him for all she was worth.

"Not the car, Billie. I just had it washed," Hayes yelled through the closed window.

She waved Hayes's complaint away with a flick of her hand. Not that she was listening to him. She was totally focused on the task at hand. Royce had stiffened at first when her lips had come into contact with his, but now he seemed more agreeable. His arms wrapped around her waist as he deepened the kiss. When he swept his tongue along the seam of her lips, Billie opened for him and sucked it deep inside. She moaned as he explored the inside of her mouth, thoroughly tasting her. That small sound had him going stiff as a board.

He wrenched his mouth from hers and pushed her away. Not expecting it, Billie slid off his body and ended up having to make a grab for the car's trim to hold herself up or she would have been on her butt on the pavement.

Once again back on his feet, Royce held out his hand to keep her from coming any nearer. His breath sawed in and out of his lungs. "That was a mistake."

"I wouldn't go that far." Billie smiled. "I thought it was pretty good."

"I should never have done that."

Billie's smile slowly fell away. "Please don't tell me you're married." That would be all the luck. She'd finally found a man who appealed to her in every way, and to find out he was married would be a real kick in the pants.

"No, it isn't that."

A wave of relief washed over her. "Then relax. We're both adults here. I'm attracted to you, and you're attracted to me. Why not let nature take its course?"

Royce shook his head and slowly backed away. "I think not."

"Can I at least have your phone number in case you change your mind? Or I can give you mine."

"You don't understand."

Royce paused at the edge of the parking lot and gave Billie a stare that was hot and full of longing. A pounding ache of arousal built between her legs. Her pussy grew slick as he stared at her as if he were memorizing everything about her; then he was gone. Biting back the whimper of loss that rose inside her, she swore under her breath and climbed into the driver's side of the car.

Hayes shook his head. "When are you going to learn that most guys don't like a woman to come on so strong, Billie?"

"Shut up, Hayes. I don't want to hear it." After starting the car, she pulled out of the parking lot. Before she turned onto the street, Billie quickly scanned the sidewalk in front of the club. Of course Royce was nowhere in sight.

"You're not going to let him get away." Hayes said it as a statement, not as a question.

"Damn right. I've seen his face, and I know his name. I'll be able to find him anywhere."

"God help the man. If you do intend to hunt him down, try not to be so pushy. A man likes to feel he's seducing the woman, not the other way around."

Billie didn't bother to comment on what Hayes had said. She already knew from Royce's response that coming on strong wouldn't work with him. She had to think of another way to keep him from pulling away. What exactly, she had no idea. Sometime tomorrow she would be paying Royce a visit. She wasn't going to let him go that easily.

CHAPTER TWO

Billie worked as a personal trainer at the gym her father owned. She also taught a self-defense class a couple of times a week. Even though it was the family business, she never felt as if she was expected to work there. In fact, it was her dream job. She loved being at the gym, able to work out whenever she wished. To be around her father and brothers every day was a bonus. They were all the family she had. Her mother had run out on her father shortly after Billie had been born. So her father had the task of raising his only daughter alone. It was no wonder she had turned out to be a tomboy growing up. Her father really had no idea what to do with a little girl. Instead of playing with dolls, she'd followed him around the gym, learning how to run it. When she'd turned fourteen, he'd given Billie her first set of weights, and so began her love of weight training.

Turning back from replacing the set of dumbbells the member she'd been training had been using, Billie found Hayes and her other three brothers circled around her. She ground her teeth, knowing full well what was coming. They did this every time she showed an interest in a guy, especially when it was one they didn't know. She pinned Hayes with a hard stare. He had to have been the one to tell the others about what had happened at Wulf's Den the night before. Not backing down an inch, he crossed his arms over his wide chest and glared back at her.

It was rough being the baby sister to four older brothers, especially when those siblings had enough testosterone between them to choke a horse. All of them lifted weights and were over six feet. They looked like a bunch of linebackers. It was part of the reason Billie had taken up weight lifting and had learned self-defense. She might be shorter than them, but she could give them all a run for their money.

Billie leaned back against the rack of dumbbells that ran along the length of the wall, and looked at each of her brothers. The York siblings all took after their father in looks, or so she had been told since she had no memories of her mother. They all had inherited straight black hair and gray-blue eyes. Keegan, who was the oldest at thirty-five, was ten years older than her and resembled their father the most. And being the oldest, Keegan thought it gave him the right to basically butt into the lives of his siblings. The next in line were Eli and Finn. They were identical twins and were two years younger than Keegan. Then there was Hayes. He was two years younger than the twins. Being only six years older than her, he was the closest in age.

Billie had to admit her brothers were not hard to look at. With their rugged good looks, longish hair, and well-conditioned bodies, they tended to garner a lot of attention from the opposite sex. Only Keegan and Hayes were married. The twins loved women too much to settle for just one, or so they liked to tell everyone.

"All right. Let's get on with it. Start your interrogation so I can have it over with and get on with the rest of my day," Billie said blandly.

Keegan, of course, was the first to start. "So, what is this about you throwing yourself at a guy you just met at a nightclub last night?"

"That is none of your business."

"Like hell it isn't. You're our baby sister. We have to watch over you, especially if you're going to track this guy down."

Billie glared at Hayes again before she turned back to Keegan. "I'm not a little girl anymore. I'm twenty-five years old. I can look after myself. Can you guys give me a break and keep your noses out of my love life? It would be nice not to have the lot of you scaring off a guy I take an interest in."

"From the sounds of it, you managed to do that quite nicely all on your own."

"Yeah, we heard the guy couldn't get away from you fast enough," Eli said with a chuckle.

"After you locked lips with him, he almost pushed you onto your butt so he could get away," Finn added.

Billie scowled at Hayes. "Did you have to tell them everything?"

"Yeah, I did. Maybe that will teach you to stay at home and not come running after me whenever Janice calls."

"I'm so going to tell Janice about the gorgeous waitress you were talking to at the nightclub. You know, the one who looked like a supermodel."

Hayes visibly paled and shook his head. "You wouldn't."

"I'm sure Janice will be thrilled to know you were talking to some hot, skinny woman. And I'm sure it'll make your wife, who is eight months pregnant with your child, feel you don't find her sexy, because she thinks she's as big as a house."

Before Hayes could say anything in return, Eli butted into the conversation. "A hot, skinny supermodel? What's the nightclub called? Finn, we have to check this place out."

Finn nodded enthusiastically. "Most definitely. Was there more than one hot chick there, Hayes?"

Jumping on the chance to divert the topic of discussion away from his wife, Hayes nodded. "The place is called Wulf's Den. You won't believe the number of hot women who were there. It looked as if a supermodel convention took place."

Finn rubbed his hands together. "I know where I'll be going tonight. I have an itch I'm sure one of those ladies won't mind scratching."

Billie pretended to stick her finger down her throat and gag. "And you think I'm bad. Isn't it about time the two of you settled down and started a family of your own like Keegan and Hayes? You aren't getting any younger, you know."

Eli gasped in mock horror. "Not in this lifetime."

"And I second that," Finn quickly added.

"I'll be sure to rub that statement into both your faces when you each find the right woman," Billie said. "The whole playboy persona won't hold up with age, you know. Someday it'll turn a woman's stomach instead of her head. Now if you all are done, I have somewhere to go."

As Billie tried to walk away, Keegan went to stand in front of her, blocking her path. "Oh no, you don't. You're not leaving until you tell us more about the man you met at the nightclub."

Knowing there would be no escape until she told them something, Billie blew a breath out on a sigh. "His name is Royce. He offered to help me with Hayes. Other than he is gorgeous, muscular, and taller than all of you, that's everything I know about him. Now get out of my way before I'm forced to do something painful to you."

Billie bit back a smile as Keegan automatically brought his hands up, protectively cupping his groin as he moved out of her way. She had to give it to her brothers; they were quick learners. None of them took her warnings lightly anymore.

"Tell Dad I'm finished for the day, and I'll see you all tomorrow."

Anxious to be on her way, Billie only took the time to collect her purse before she headed to her car. Once she was behind the steering wheel, she closed her eyes and brought Royce's image up in her mind. Focusing, she honed in on his location. A smile of satisfaction spread across her lips when she found him.

* * * *

With disgust, Royce pushed away the newspaper he'd been trying to read. He'd come into the kitchen to have a coffee and read that day's paper, hoping to distract himself from things better left not thought about. He failed miserably.

Thoughts of Billie haunted him. No matter what he tried, he couldn't get the smell, taste, or feel of her out of his mind. Just thinking about her brought the wolf inside him roaring to life. With the mating urge riding him, he'd had one erotic dream after another about her during the night. He'd woken up with his body hard and aching for her. Even now, he was still semi-aroused.

With a snarl, he tried to rid his mind of the memory of how it'd felt to kiss Billie, have her body pressed to his, but it wouldn't go away. It'd been hundreds of years since he'd held a woman in his arms in that way. After the loss of his mate, he hadn't been interested in having another female in his life. And finding one he wanted to take to his bed for only a night held no appeal.

Now, after the many years that had gone by since Alicia's passing, he'd found another mate. And like Alicia, Billie was not a werewolf. He didn't want to be mated to a mortal again. It had caused him too much pain when Alicia had been taken from him. The only thing that had kept him going had been his baby daughter, Nina. To protect her from the villagers who had killed her mother, and not sure of how his pack would have reacted to his having a daughter who was mortal, he'd stepped down as pack leader and gone lone wolf. He'd taken his daughter away and watched over her as she grew to womanhood, as he had all her descendants.

Royce didn't mind being alone. He still had Roxie and her mother, Belinda, to watch out for. He'd raised Belinda as his own daughter when her parents had died when she was little. She was mortal as all Nina's descendants had been. All of them except Roxie. She had been born a mortal, but through a little-known spell, she was now a werewolf like him. And she was the only one who looked so very much like Alicia. That she had even inherited some of Alicia's memories had caused him at one time to think she was Alicia reincarnated, but she had soon disabused him of that notion. She'd already found her mate in the form of Beowulf, the one he'd chosen to take his place as pack leader. It seemed only fitting that their two families be joined.

After picking up the cup that sat on the table next to the newspaper, Royce took a sip and then grimaced. The coffee was cold. He was about to pour himself another when his doorbell rang. He looked at the clock on the wall. It was just after four in the afternoon. He had to wonder who it could be. He wasn't expecting anyone.

The doorbell rang again. Obviously, whoever was at his door wasn't going to be so easily put off. Royce pushed back the chair he sat on, then got up and headed for the front door before the person could ring the bell for a third time.

All prepared to send whomever it was away, Royce yanked open the door. Seeing who stood on his front porch had the wolf inside him fighting to have control. Ruthlessly, he pushed it back. "Billie, what are you doing here?"

"Nice to see you again as well, Royce," Billie said with a smile. "I thought I'd drop by and see if you'd had a change of heart since last night."

"How did you find out where I lived?"

"The telephone book?"

"I'm not listed in the telephone book."

"Oh, well, I have my ways. Are you going to invite me in or what?"

"I don't think that would be a good idea."

Actually, he *knew* that wouldn't be a good idea. Royce didn't know if he could trust himself to keep his hands off her now that she was there in person. He felt as if he were a bomb ready to go off at any moment. Billie's scent was doing a real number on him. For starters, the semi-erection he'd been sporting for most of the day was now fully erect. Images of pulling her into the house as he dragged her to the floor and sheathed his aching cock inside her moist heat had him clenching his teeth.

"I promise I won't stay long if you're busy. I thought we could get to know each other a little better before you decide you don't want me around."

While Billie spoke, she moved closer. Not wanting their bodies to come into contact, knowing if they did it would have the same reaction as fire being set to tinder, Royce stepped back. She kept crowding him until she had him backed inside the house. He didn't realize what she'd done until she closed the front door behind her.

Hoping to take control of the situation, Royce stood straighter and gave Billie a stern look. "Now that you've managed to get yourself inside my house, I suppose you can stay for a few minutes. I have coffee, if you'd like some." He didn't wait for her reply as he headed back to the kitchen. Billie followed him.

Royce took a clean mug out of the cupboard. After filling it with coffee from the pot he'd made earlier, he placed it on the table where Billie had taken a seat. He sat on the chair across from her and waited to see what she would do next. He had a feeling it would be no easy task to get her out of his house. It didn't appear as if she was going to take no for an answer. If she'd been a werewolf, he would have already had her under him on his bed. To make sure he kept his hands to himself, he crossed his arms over his chest.

Billie took a sip of her coffee. Her gray-blue-eyed gaze never wavered from his face. Once she put the mug on the table, she looked around the room. "Nice place you have here, Royce."

"Thanks. Now what exactly do you want?" he asked in what he hoped was a bored tone.

"Aren't we Mr. Sunshine?" Billie asked sarcastically. "I guess I'll get straight to the point. I find you attractive, and I'd like to pursue that. I know it's not all one-sided either, judging by the way you kissed me last night. So what do you say about us getting to know each other better and see how it goes from there?"

"Last night was a momentary weakness on my part. I think it would be better to leave matters the way they are right now." His gaze fell to the gray T-shirt Billie wore. It had YORK FITNESS stenciled in black across the chest. "Isn't your last name York?"

Billie looked down at her shirt, then back up at him. "You remembered. See? You are interested. York Fitness is the gym my dad owns. I work there as do my brothers."

"I thought you only had one brother."

"No. I have four older brothers."

Royce let out a low whistle. "That must be fun for you, having four brothers watching over you. What do you do at the gym? Do you work in the office?"

"God, no," Billie said with a laugh. "When I first showed signs of wanting to work at the gym, my dad started me off in the office. Let's just say math is not my strong suit, and my phone etiquette sometimes leaves a lot to be desired. I tend to say whatever is on my mind. I'm a personal trainer, and I teach a few self-defense classes."

That explained how Billie had easily subdued her brother the night before, even though Hayes was almost twice her size. Now that she'd mentioned it, Royce could see she had a muscular build. Her shoulders were broad, and there was noticeable muscle tone on her arms. He wondered what her legs looked like under the black yoga pants she wore. He bet they were just as well-toned. He couldn't help picturing how it would feel to have them wrapped around his waist as he drove into her body. Realizing where his thoughts took him, he groaned and closed his eyes. He tried to bring his body back under control.

"Are you okay, Royce?"

He opened his eyes to find Billie staring at him with a look of concern. Fighting the mating urge was turning out to be a losing battle with her in the same room. He had to get away from her, but he couldn't say the words that would make her leave. All he could do was look at her with the longing he felt.

Almost against his will, he ran his gaze lower. He watched her chest rise and fall with each breath Billie took. His fingers itched to reach across the table and cup her surprisingly full breasts. The wolf, too long denied, roared at him to do it. He dragged his gaze back up to her face and found her lips slightly parted as she drew in one rapid breath after another. The scent of her rising desire wafted over him, more potent than the most expensive perfume. Royce clenched his jaw until it ached, stopping the animalistic growl that rose within him. Unable to look away, he fisted his hands on the table in front of him.

CHAPTER THREE

The change that came over Royce happened in a matter of seconds. One minute he was all gruff, acting as if he couldn't get rid of her fast enough, and then the next, he was staring at her with intense longing. In reaction, Billie's heart beat a little faster. When he lowered his gaze to her chest, her body went up in flames. Just that one look sent blood rushing to her core as her pussy ached to have him touch her there. His gaze caressed her breasts. It was so intense it felt almost as if he'd physically touched them. As if he were cupping them in his large hands.

When Royce lifted his head and she saw the stark need in his hazel eyes, she held herself still, waiting for him to make the first move. There was no denying he wanted her — it was written on his face for all to see — but from the way he held himself so stiffly with his hands fisted on the table, Billie knew he fought it. Why, she had no idea. All she knew was she'd never been so turned-on by a man who hadn't even touched her.

The seconds ticked by and still Royce sat silently across from her, not moving a muscle. *Why is he just sitting there?* Unable to take it any longer, Billie launched herself across the table. She landed on him with enough force to send his chair toppling over, taking them along with it. He gave a grunt of surprise as his back hit the floor, and she ended up half sitting, half lying across his chest.

With half an ear, Billie heard the spilled coffee drip over the side of the table and onto the floor. She wondered if she'd really gone too far this time. Royce lay stiff and still beneath her. He stared up at her with no emotion in his eyes. With her hands on his chest, she moved to slide off him. She was about to apologize for her actions, but before she could say a word, he growled low in his throat and hauled her against him.

She had a split second to register the fact his eyes were no longer flat and emotionless before he threaded his fingers through her hair and brought her mouth down to his. Her eyes fluttered shut as his lips moved possessively over hers. Billie sighed. This was what she'd wanted. Clutching his shoulders, she tried to press herself closer. In the position they were in, she couldn't get as near as she wanted to be. She quietly groaned in frustration.

That small sound was enough to have Royce shifting beneath her. He held her close as he somehow managed to get himself off the chair and onto the floor. He quickly rolled Billie onto her back so he was on top.

Billie gloried in the feel of having every inch of Royce's body against the length of hers. The floor was hard, and the puddle of coffee he'd rolled her into soaked through her shirt, but she didn't care. All that mattered was having more of him.

She turned her head to the side as Royce released her mouth and kissed a trail along her jaw to her neck. He nipped the vein that pounded there. He licked the same spot before continuing his downward path. The hard length of his cock pressed against her leg. She squirmed under him, wanting to have that part of him against her core, even if it was only through her clothes.

Royce placed a firm hand on her hip, stilling her movements as he dragged his lips to the hollow of her throat. Billie shivered at the feel of his tongue inching still lower. His fingers left her hip and grabbed for the bottom of her T-shirt. With one tug, he had it pulled up to her chin. The sports bra she wore beneath it soon followed suit, leaving her breasts bared to his view.

Billie sucked in a sharp breath. Royce bent his head and swirled his tongue around her nipple. With the edges of his teeth, he dragged them across the taut peak before sucking it deep inside his mouth. He drew so hard on it she felt her uterus tightening with each pull of his mouth. He moved on to lavish the same attention on her other breast.

While Royce sucked, he trailed his fingers down her side to the top of her yoga pants. A moan escaped Billie's lips as she arched in anticipation. He slipped his hand past the waistband and into her panties. He pressed the heel of his palm against her mound as he pushed one finger inside her slick opening.

Billie pushed against Royce's hand and squeezed her inner muscles around his finger. Her pussy grew wetter as a second joined the first to slide in and out of her. Her arousal built ever higher.

Royce released her breast and shifted until he knelt between her legs. Billie groaned with disappointment when the two digits he'd been working her with pulled out of her. She opened her eyes and looked up at him. She saw that strange glow in his eyes again, but right at that moment, she didn't care about the weirdness of it. He'd taken hold of the waistband of her pants along with her panties and quickly pulled them down her body until he had them off. With a low growl, he knelt between her legs once more and brought his mouth down to her pussy.

At the first swipe of his tongue, Billie's hips bucked beneath him. With his hands, Royce spread her legs farther apart and flicked her clit with the tip of his tongue. She moaned as he laved her before gently sucking on that small bundle of nerves. Hands fisted at her sides, she panted as her climax edged closer.

Royce pushed two fingers deep inside her core as he continued to lick and suck on her clit. Billie clamped her inner muscles around those digits and rode them as the first intense wave of pleasure hit her. Moaning, she grabbed Royce's hair and pushed closer as her climax tore through her.

*

Royce lapped at Billie's pussy until the last wave of her climax receded. Once her body relaxed, he pulled away to lay his head on her thigh. He didn't dare look at her. His eyes would be glowing now that the wolf had risen inside him. He pulled back his upper lip in a snarl as he fought to push that side of him away. With his body hard and aching, the wolf fought him, wanting him to claim her fully as his mate. If he joined his body with hers, he wouldn't be able to stop his soul from reaching out to her. If that happened, they would be fully mated. Neither one of them would be able to stand being separated from the other for very long.

Billie stirred beneath him. "Come here, Royce." She reached down and pulled at his shoulders, urging him up.

He shook his head. "No." An animalistic growl escaped him before he could stop it. Billie stiffened at the sound. "No."

It was hard, especially with her scent and the smell of her release thick in the air around them, but Royce managed to roll away. In one fluid motion he stood with his back toward Billie. She didn't understand the battle that raged inside him, but it had to be this way. He'd thought if he had one taste of her it would be enough. He'd been wrong. Having her come under his mouth had only made the mating urge ride him all the harder. He should have known it would make it worse instead of better.

Billie came to stand behind him. "Royce? Did I do something wrong?" She placed her hand on his back.

"No, you didn't." Unable to stand her touching him when he couldn't claim her as his own, Royce took a step away. "I can't do this, Billie. You don't understand."

"Then help me to. One minute you're cold and pushing me away, and the next you're all over me as if you can't get enough of me."

"I can't."

"Well, it didn't look like that a few minutes ago. You seemed more than up to the job."

"That's not what I meant."

"Then tell me what it is."

"If I were to take you like I want to, you'll get more than you bargained for, believe me. Just go."

"I'm not going anywhere until we work this out."

Royce balled his hands into fists in frustration. If Billie wouldn't leave on her own, he would have to make her. Quickly turning around, he pulled back his upper lip and growled. He snapped his teeth as he took a step toward her, letting her get a good look at his eyes. She quickly stumbled away.

"I said to leave." His voice came out as a half growl.

With no small amount of regret, Royce watched Billie hurriedly pull on her panties and yoga pants. She shot quick glances at him as she did so. Once she was fully clothed, she slowly backed out of the kitchen.

Before she left, she paused long enough to say one final thing to him. "I know you're trying to scare me away, Royce. I don't understand all this." She pointed to his face. "But I'm not the type of woman to be easily scared off. I'm only leaving because you obviously don't want me around for some reason. If you change your mind, you know where to find me. I work just about every day at my dad's gym."

After Billie was gone, Royce slumped onto one of the kitchen chairs. He was in big trouble. She may have been a little bit disturbed by his glowing eyes and the growling, but she hadn't exactly run away, screaming in fear. Damn, if that didn't make him respect her more. A strong female able to stand up to a male werewolf was considered a good mate by his kind. It would seem she was more than up to the task, even though she was a mortal. His head fell back, and he groaned. No matter how hard he fought it, it wouldn't be very long before he went to see her. The big question would be how many days he could keep away.

* * * *

Billie arrived at the gym cranky and out of sorts. It'd been two days since the debacle that had taken place at Royce's house. She had no idea what was wrong with her. She usually didn't become obsessed with a guy, but she seemed to be obsessing over him. He was all she could think about. Much to her shame, she spent most of her work days watching for him to step through the gym doors. When at the end of the day he still hadn't made a showing, she would be a little more than disappointed. She'd really thought he would have come to see her by now. Part of the reason she was so out of sorts stemmed from not being around him, which was pathetic. She could have gone to his place, but she did have her pride.

Then there was the whole glowing eyes thing and growling Royce had done. She didn't think her eyes and ears had played tricks on her. She wasn't the type of person to imagine things such as that, even though it was as far away from normal as anyone could get. It figured. She'd found a guy who she wanted to be around, and he turned out to be a freak.

As she walked past the front desk, one of the girls working behind it called her name. Billie continued walking, but turned to see what she wanted. The girl, who was also on the phone, mouthed that her father wanted to see her. Billie nodded and turned back around.

This was just what she needed. She wasn't in the mood to have a heart-to-heart chat with her father. Her brothers might be overprotective when it came to her, but Tom York was even more so. Billie had lost many a boyfriend when she was growing up because of all the male chest thumping that had gone on in her house. Sometimes it'd really sucked being the only female.

Before going to her father's office, Billie made a quick stop at her desk and locked her purse in one of the desk drawers. On the way she grabbed a cup of coffee. She had a feeling she was going to need a lot of caffeine just to get her through what was turning out to be a bang-up day.

She knocked once on her father's office door, then pushed it open. He sat behind his desk, talking on the phone. Seeing her, he waved for her to come inside. Billie shut the door behind her, then went and sat on the chair in front of him. She sipped her coffee as she silently watched her father. Tom was a large man, a trait all his sons had inherited from him. At almost sixty years of age, his black hair was liberally sprinkled with gray. His body was well-toned, attesting to the number of hours he still spent lifting weights. Even at his age he put some of the younger male members to shame. His gray-blue-eyed gaze flicked to her face as he ended his conversation and then hung up the phone. She braced herself for the barrage of questions that was soon to follow.

Tom sat back in his chair and gave her a hard stare. "What is this I hear about you throwing yourself at a strange man at some nightclub?"

Billie bit back a groan. She was tempted to ask her father which time he referred to, but thought better of it. That would only make matters worse. "So the boys blabbed, did they?"

"They felt it was something I should know."

"Of course they did," Billie said under her breath.

"What was that?"

"Nothing. Look, Dad. I acted on the spur of the moment. As

things stand now, I may not see Royce ever again."

"So that's why you've been so snarky for the last couple days? This Royce turned you down?"

"I prefer not to get into any details with you, if you don't mind. You're my father, and I really don't feel comfortable having my sex life dissected by you."

"So you already had sex with him?"

"No!" When her father's gaze bored into her, Billie sighed in defeat. She'd never been able to keep things from him when he used that look on her. "Okay, sort of. Not that it's any of your damn business."

"Sort of? As in you had oral sex with him?"

"Jesus, Dad, you're starting to make me feel as if I'm a teenager again. I'm old enough to have a sex life if I want one. Can we please move on to something else?"

"You know I worry about you, especially when it comes to the men in your life. I worry that without your mother having been around I haven't raised you the way I should. That I didn't give you enough chance to have more feminine things around you. You've never dated a man more than a couple of months."

Billie put down her cup of coffee and then walked around the desk until she stood at her father's side. She bent down and wrapped her arms around his neck and hugged him. "You did nothing wrong, Dad. I don't think it would have mattered if Mom was around or not. I think I still would have turned out a tomboy. Kind of hard not to with four older brothers. As for my lack of staying power when it comes to men, I just haven't found the right one yet. Let's face it. He would have some big shoes to fill. He'd also have to be able to hold his own against you and the boys."

Her father chuckled as Billie straightened. "Is that so? And do you think this Royce is man enough to face me down?"

Billie nodded. "Most definitely. He's one of the few who you'd have to look up to, and has enough muscle to go head-to-head with any of the boys."

"I see. So, when do I get to meet this paragon of maleness?"

"Didn't you listen before when I told you I may not be seeing Royce again?"

"Yes, but I don't think that will be the case. What man in his right mind would reject you?"

Billie groaned. "One minute you're acting all uptight and fatherly because there is a new man in my life, and then the next you want to meet him. I'll never understand you." She reached over the desk and picked up her coffee cup. "I'm out of here before you drive me insane."

"I only try to drive you insane because I care."

"Whatever you say, Dad."

CHAPTER FOUR

After her last client of the day left the gym floor, Billie decided she wasn't quite ready to go home. It was late in the afternoon, hours until the gym would close that evening. Still feeling out of sorts, she decided an hour of lifting weights was what she needed. In no way was she only staying later in case Royce made an appearance, or so she tried to convince herself.

On her way to the women's locker room, Billie noticed all her brothers were on the gym floor as well. As she walked past each of them, she felt their gazes following her. Billie had the urge to turn around and stick her tongue out but decided it was too childish even for her. Instead, she ignored them and didn't so much as turn her head to look back at them.

It only took a few minutes for her to change into her workout clothes and grab the MP3 player she kept in one of the lockers inside the locker room. One of the perks of being the owner's daughter was being able to claim one as her own without fear of having her lock cut off at closing time. Her father had had to put that rule into effect when too many members left locks on them for days at a time, even after having friendly reminders taped onto them, which had gone ignored. Now, if any locks were found after closing time, they were automatically cut off and the contents put in the large lost and found box at the front desk.

With the music on her MP3 player blaring in her ears, Billie headed back out to the gym floor. Deciding to work on her chest first, she went to one of the flat benches to do some benching. She slapped on the weights onto the long barbell, then lay on the bench under it. She took a firm grasp of the bar, then lifted it off the rack and slowly lowered it to her chest before pushing it back up so her arms were straight once again. She did nine more reps like that before she replaced the bar on the rack. When she sat up, she noticed the commotion near the front desk.

Putting her MP3 player on pause, Billie swore under her breath as she quickly got up. Her brothers had someone cornered at the desk, someone who was quite a bit taller than they were. Billie's heart beat faster at seeing Royce in their midst. He didn't seem overly concerned that Keegan was practically standing toe-to-toe to him, and hearing her brother's raised voice, the conversation wasn't exactly a friendly how-do-you-do.

Not wanting her brothers to drive Royce away after he'd finally come to see her, Billie walked quickly to the front desk. None of her brothers noticed her coming up behind them. She decided Keegan would be the first one she would have to take care of. With the bottom of her foot, she kicked him in the back of one of his legs, just behind his knee, hard enough to knock him to the floor. He quickly looked back to see who had dared to do such a thing with a snarl on his face. When he saw her, he got back onto his feet and wisely moved away from her.

"Can you tell me what you think you're doing, Keegan?"

"Nothing. We're just introducing ourselves to Royce here."

"Is that so? And while you were 'introducing' yourselves, did any of you think that maybe you should get me since Royce is obviously here to see me? I don't think he planned on getting an in-his-face introduction from my dumbass brothers." Billie finally allowed herself to look Royce in the face. He wore a bemused smile. "Sorry I wasn't here when you first arrived, Royce. If I had been, you wouldn't have had to put up with these guys."

"No apology needed, Billie."

Much to Billie's surprise, Royce's look of bemusement changed to one of intense longing. She felt her face flush as his hot gaze raked her from head to toe. She couldn't tear hers off him. Now that she was near him, all she could think of was how good it'd been to be in his arms. How good he was at using his tongue. Her heart pounded as she remembered the intense orgasm he'd given her on his kitchen floor. Not caring about the strange way he'd acted the last time she'd been with him, nor giving a damn that her brothers stood nearby, she took a step closer to Royce. She needed to be in his arms.

Royce met her halfway. He picked her off her feet and easily held her in his strong arms as he claimed her lips in a searing kiss. Billie's world fell away. As he hungrily moved his mouth against hers, she didn't acknowledge her brothers' protests or care that she and Royce put on a show for the gym members. All that mattered was getting closer to him.

"Billie!"

Her father's voice boomed across the room. That too she ignored.

"Wilhelmina!"

The sound of her full name being bellowed across the gym finally snapped Billie out of the sexual haze that had come over her. Breaking contact with Royce's mouth, she turned her head as her father stomped toward them. He didn't look at all pleased at catching his daughter making out with a man she barely knew in front of a bunch of strangers. She shoved at Royce's chest, hoping he would put her down before her father reached them, but he didn't so much as budge.

Much to Billie's horror, Royce kept her pinned to his chest with one arm as he held out his other hand to her father. She figured Royce wouldn't be earning any brownie points from her dad for manhandling her in front of him.

"You must be Billie's father," Royce said calmly, as if it were an ordinary occurrence for him to be holding Billie so close.

Her father accepted Royce's proffered hand and shook it briefly. "And you must be Royce. If you wouldn't mind, put my daughter down."

Royce let Billie slowly slide down the length of his body. She bit her bottom lip to keep the moan inside her from escaping. There was no mistaking the evidence of him not being unaffected by her closeness. It made her wish she and Royce were alone somewhere, able to pursue what they were both feeling.

Once her feet hit the floor, her father turned his attention to her. "Billie, why don't you take a shower before you change your clothes. You must need one after working out. The boys and I will keep Royce company for you."

Yeah, right. There was no way she was going to leave Royce to the sharks for that length of time. "Actually, Dad, I only managed to do one set on the bench press before I noticed the boys had cornered Royce. So I'm good. All I have to do is change my clothes, which I'll do now. Just promise me you won't tear him to pieces before I come out."

"I promise we'll be on our best behavior."

Somehow, Billie didn't think that would last long after she was out of sight. Feeling the need for speed, she almost ran to the women's locker room.

* * * *

Royce's gaze rested on each of the York men. They all looked to be cut from the same cloth. There was no mistaking Billie's brothers as anything other than the offspring of the man who stood in front of him. Her father was the total opposite of his daughter. He was tall, muscular, and seemed to be the type of man who had no qualms about getting in your face if he needed to; same with her four brothers.

He decided to let them try to intimate him with their hard stares. It, of course, wouldn't work. All he could think about was Billie. She'd been all he had been able to think about for the last two days. She was inside him so deep, he didn't think he could ever get her out. The one taste he'd had of her was far from enough. Even though he hated it and had fought it to the bitter end, he could no longer deny what his whole being clamored for him to complete the steps to mating her. He had to fully claim her as his mate or he would suffer the consequences. So he'd finally broken down and come to the gym to see her.

Billie's father was the first one to break the heavy silence that had descended after she'd gone to change. "My daughter didn't think you would be coming to see her, but I told her you would be around eventually."

"Well, I found myself unable to stay away."

"Billie does tend to leave a lasting impression on people."

"That she does."

"Do you mind if I ask you your age? You're a lot older than the others Billie has taken an interest in."

There was no way Royce was going to tell her father his actual age. Being a werewolf, his lifespan was exceedingly longer than what mortals considered normal. His kind wasn't immortal, but they were pretty darn close. The oldest of their kind lived to be around three thousand years old. He had already seen more than fifteen hundred years. To a mortal, he looked no older than thirty-five.

"I can't see what bearing my age has to do with anything."

"It doesn't," Billie said as she approached them. "Now would the five of you back off and leave Royce alone?" She came to stand next to Royce. "I'm going for the day, if you haven't already guessed that. I'll be back in tomorrow. If I'm a little late, don't go forming a search party or anything."

Billie didn't wait around long enough to see if the males in her family had anything more to say. She turned on her heel and headed for the gym's entrance. Royce fell into step beside her. Once they were outside, she led him to the parking lot. At her car, she turned to face him. "I can't help being a bit surprised to see you again, Royce. I'm glad, don't get me wrong, but I was under the impression you didn't want anything to do with me. That kiss you gave me back there says you've changed your mind again. Are you messing with my head or do you really want to pursue this?"

Royce crowded Billie until he had her trapped between him and her car. He put his hands on the car's roof and leaned down to look her in the face. "I'm not messing with your head, Billie. I've concluded that there is no denying what fate holds in store for you. It's just not worth the pain and suffering."

"Okay. You've lost me with the pain and suffering part."

"What I mean is I was too hasty when I decided I didn't want you around. I'd like for us to start over. Get to know each other better. Take things a little slower. I'm not used to having a woman pursue me." As he spoke, Royce took another step closer until their bodies were almost touching. Billie's breath fanned his face as her chest rapidly rose and fell.

"My brothers are forever telling me that I sometimes come on a little too strong." Billie's words came out breathy, her gaze riveted to his mouth as she'd spoken.

"I'm not complaining, Billie, but you do have to give a guy a chance to be the one to take the lead or he might start to question his masculinity." He gently brushed her lips with his. "A man likes to know he can seduce the woman he wants."

"And is that what you're trying to do to me? Are you trying to seduce me?"

"Most definitely."

"Well then, it's working."

"Good." Royce quickly took a step away. "Then how about I take you out this evening?"

"How about we just go to your place and you can show me the inside of your bedroom instead?"

Royce shook his head and chuckled. "Don't you know patience is a virtue? We're going to take things slow and easy."

Billie groaned. "I'm not known for being particularly patient when I want something. For you, I'll try. When do you want me to pick you up?" At Royce's arched brow, she shook her head and rolled her eyes. "Okay, okay. When will you be picking me up?"

"Around seven okay with you?"

"Fine. How should I dress?"

"Something suitable for a nightclub. I want to take you to Wulf's Den. There's someone there I want you to meet."

"All right. I'll see you at seven then."

Billie rattled off her address before she got inside her car. Royce watched her drive away, then crossed to where he'd parked. He was pleased with how things had gone with her. This was a big step for him. After his first mate's death, he'd focused all his attention on raising his infant daughter. Then in time, he had watched over his grandchildren and all those who came after them. During those years, he'd not once become involved with another woman. The loss of his mate had affected him greatly. He hadn't wanted to find another to take her place, and he never had been one for casual sex. Now all that had changed since Billie had come barging into his life. After hundreds of years had passed, he was ready to move on. He only hoped he wasn't making a mistake. If he claimed her as his mate and he ended up losing her as well, he wasn't sure he could survive another loss such as that.

CHAPTER FIVE

Billie stood in front of her closet and panicked. There was absolutely nothing inside it that could remotely be classed as nightclub wear. She would have been fine if the dress code was jeans or yoga pants, because that was all that hung in her closet. There were no skirts, no dresses, or even dress slacks of any kind. She was screwed.

Not wanting to mess things up with Royce before she even managed to make it out on their first date, Billie quickly picked up the cordless phone in her bedroom. She needed help, and she knew of only one person who could do that. After hitting the speed dial button programmed with phone number of Hayes's number, she waited for her sister-in-law to pick up the other end. It rang twice before Janice answered.

"Hello?"

"Hey, Janice. It's me, Billie."

"How are you doing, Billie? Oh, and thanks for bringing Hayes home the other night."

"I'm doing good, thanks. And you're welcome. The reason I'm calling is I need to ask you a really big favor."

"All right. Fire away."

Billie took a deep breath before she continued. "I'm going out on a date tonight, and I have to dress with a little more style than I usually do. I need you to help me find a dress, or a skirt and nice top, to wear for tonight." She heard a noise that suspiciously sounded like the phone being dropped on the other end. "Janice? Janice, are you still there?"

Janice's voice came back on a second later. "Sorry about that. Can you repeat that last part?"

"I need to find a dress or a skirt to wear for tonight."

"I just had to hear you say that a second time so I would know my ears weren't playing tricks on me. Are you serious?"

"Of course I am."

"Who are you, and what have you done with my sister-in-law?"

Billie rolled her eyes. "Are you going to help me or not, Janice? I'm kind of desperate. Royce is picking me up around seven, and I haven't got a goddamn thing to wear."

"Calm down. I'll help. I'll be at your place in ten minutes. We should just have enough time to go to the mall and get you something to wear."

"Are you sure you're up to a shopping trip in your condition?"

"Billie, I'm eight months pregnant. I'm not suffering from a debilitating illness. Besides, I wouldn't miss this for the world."

"I'll see you in a few minutes then."

After she hung up, Billie went into the living room to wait for Janice. Hayes and his wife only lived a few miles away from her apartment, so it wouldn't take long for Janice to arrive. Exactly ten minutes later, Janice buzzed. Billie grabbed her purse and spoke into the intercom to let her know she would be down in a minute.

Stepping off the elevator, Billie found Janice standing outside the apartment building. She had her back to her. From behind, Janice didn't look like she was eight months pregnant, but when she turned around, her baby belly stuck out prominently.

Billie hurried to Janice. "Thanks for coming to my rescue on such short notice."

Janice smiled. "As I said on the phone, I wouldn't have missed this for the world. Now let's get a move on so we can get you back home on time."

After they got into Janice's car, her sister-in-law headed for the nearest mall. As she drove, Janice asked, "So, are you going to keep me in suspense about Royce? I must say I'm very curious to learn more about the man you threw yourself at when you fetched

Hayes the other night."

"Hayes is worse than a gossipy old woman. Is there anyone he hasn't told that story to?"

Janice chuckled. "Probably not. I had to stop him from calling Keegan that late at night. The only way I was able to do that was remind him how drunk he was. You know Keegan has no patience for Hayes when he's drunk."

"And you think I do? If there was someone else who could find him when he takes off, believe me, I would gladly give the job to them."

"Well, is it true? Did you tackle a six-foot-seven guy onto the trunk of Hayes's car and then try to have your way with him in the nightclub's parking lot?"

Billie groaned. "I'm going to kill Hayes. I didn't exactly tackle Royce. It was more like I made sure he knew how I felt about him. And I didn't have my way with him. It was just a kiss."

"I guess with you sprawled on top of him, Royce couldn't mistake your intentions. If you're going out on a date with him tonight, it must have paid off."

"I'm not so sure."

"What do you mean? The way I heard it, the two of you were getting kind of hot and heavy at the gym earlier. And in front of Dad, no less."

"Oh. My. God. Does Hayes have nothing better to do than tell everyone my business? I can just picture him running to get his cell phone the moment Royce and I walked out of the gym."

"He means well, Billie," Janice said with a laugh.

"It would so serve him right the next time I have to chase his ass down to leave him stranded in the middle of nowhere."

"Enough about Hayes. We're here, and I intend to enjoy this girls' shopping trip. I have the feeling once the baby comes, I won't be doing this for a while."

Billie realized Janice was right. The mall loomed ahead. In no time at all, Janice found a parking space and they were headed inside. Billie hoped this would be a quick in-and-out trip, but she soon found out it would be far from it as Janice dragged her from one store to another. At the first, Billie detested all the clothes. She found them to be downright dowdy. In the next, she fared no better. She would have been fine if she liked frilly, flowery concoctions, which she didn't. The third clothing store turned out to be the charm.

The style of clothes looked to be designed not for middle-aged women, as the first store's clothes had been, or for preppy teenagers, as was the second. Billie had already decided whatever she bought would be black and something in a style so if she had to wear a dress to someplace else she could get away with wearing it and not look out of place.

It didn't take her long to find a rack that held a large assortment of black dresses. As she looked through them, Billie noticed Janice had gone to another rack nearby. When Janice made a sound of exclamation, Billie turned to see what had caught her sister-in-law's attention.

As soon as Billie saw which dress Janice had pulled off the rack, she shook her head. "Ugh. No way."

"Ah, come on, Billie. At least try it on. I think you'll look incredible in this."

"Are you kidding me?

"No, seriously, you have to try this on."

Billie eyed the dress. It was a sleeveless sheath made out of a satiny material and was the color of a rich, dark red wine. She'd never worn anything in that color or that style in her life. From the looks of it, she had a feeling it would be formfitting as well. "I don't know, Janice. I want to impress Royce, not make him turn away in disgust."

Janice shoved the dress at her. "Billie, I can guarantee you Royce will not be disgusted. I bet he'll feel the exact opposite. More like he'll be picking his jaw up off the floor as he wipes the drool from his chin."

After taking the dress from Janice, Billie went to the fitting rooms. Once she had the dress on, she could see Janice was right. It looked better with her wearing it than it had on the hanger. It hugged her curves in all the right places. The length of it fell to just above her knees. She gave herself one final look-over in the mirror inside the fitting room before she stepped out to show Janice.

She was immediately blinded by a bright light as Janice used her cell phone to snap a picture of her. Billie blinked away the stars that appeared before her eyes. "Was that really necessary, and what are you doing now?" She suspiciously watched her sister-in-law punch a bunch of numbers on her phone.

"It *was* absolutely necessary. As for what I'm doing, I'm sending the picture to all your brothers."

"You're just as bad as Hayes."

"I think they all need to see you in that dress to remind them how much of a woman you actually are. Your brothers tend to forget the fact you aren't just one of the guys."

"Or you'll have them trying to be even more overprotective than they already are."

"There, it's done," Janice said as she typed in the last number. "Now get back in there and change. We need to get you some shoes to match that sexy dress. Time's a wasting."

* * * *

Billie had just enough time to grab a quick bite to eat since Royce hadn't said anything about taking her out for food as well and have a shower after she got back from shopping with Janice. Normally, she let her hair dry on its own, but that wasn't an option. She dragged out her hardly used hairdryer and quickly blew her hair dry. She left it loose around her shoulders.

Inside her bedroom, she rifled through her underwear drawer. She found she didn't have a bra to wear with the dress. All she had were sports bras, and there was no way she could wear one with her new outfit. That left only one alternative—she would have to go braless. Even though she was far from flat-chested, Billie had built up enough muscle in her upper chest to give her support.

With that settled, she pulled on a pair of panties that could be considered almost sexy. After slipping the dress over her head, Billie smoothed it down her body. She did up the zipper, which was concealed at her right side and ran down the seam. Lastly, she put on the new high heels Janice had convinced her to buy.

The shoes were pretty enough. They were high-heeled sandals that had straps around her ankles. They also matched the color of her dress. Once she had them on her feet, Billie stood and took a few practice steps. The heels were a lot higher than she was used to, but, surprisingly, she found them easy to walk in.

Now dressed, Billie headed for the living room to wait for Royce. At exactly seven o'clock, her buzzer sounded. Pushing the intercom button, she told him to come up as she pushed the button on the console to release the secured front entrance door. A short while later, he knocked on her apartment door.

Billie took a deep breath and opened it. All the air left her lungs in a whoosh. Royce had changed his clothes as well. He now wore a dark charcoal button-down shirt with black slacks. His shirt was open at his throat, revealing some of his chest. Her gaze was drawn to the enticing patch of skin that showed. She had the greatest urge to run her tongue across it.

Royce cleared his throat. "Are you ready to go or are you just going to stand there and stare at me for the rest of the evening?"

Coming back to herself, Billie blinked her eyes a couple times. "Sorry. I'm ready. Just let me get my purse, then we can go."

With purse in hand, Billie closed and then locked her apartment door. Royce threaded his fingers through hers once they waited for the elevator. She turned her head to look at him. His gaze seemed glued to her body.

Feeling a little self-conscious, Billie ran her hand down the length of the dress. "Hopefully the dress isn't too over-the-top, because this is the only one I own. Hayes's wife, Janice, helped me pick this out at the store today. So if you don't like it, it's all her fault."

As she opened her mouth to say more, Royce cut her off with his lips. He pulled her against his body and thoroughly kissed her until her legs were ready to give out.

Ending the kiss, he smiled. "The dress is fine. More than fine, actually. I have to wonder how many males I'll have to scare off before the night is through. They'll take one look at you in that and want to claim you as their own."

"Well, in that case, we don't have to go to Wulf's Den tonight. My apartment is just over there. I'm sure we can think of another way to get to know one another better," Billie said in a coy tone.

"No, we're going. And no throwing yourself at me in the hopes of changing my mind either," Royce replied with a laugh. "I'm going to do this properly. I'm taking you out on a real date and then we'll see about what other ways we can amuse ourselves."

Billie was all set to try one more time when the elevator

arrived. Before she could say another word, Royce led her inside. Luckily for him, there was another couple already on it. As the door slid closed, she admitted defeat and resigned herself to the idea of spending the evening at a nightclub.

*

After helping Billie into the passenger seat of his black BMW sports car, Royce slipped into the driver's side. He couldn't resist taking another look at her. When she'd opened her apartment door and he'd seen her in that dress, he'd felt as if someone had sucker punched him in the stomach. He'd known she had a gorgeous body hidden under the casual clothes she seemed to prefer most of the time, but seeing her wear something that showed off her curves was a nice surprise.

It also made him think of how good it would be to strip Billie out of her tight-fitting dress and explore her body as he licked every inch of her. Just the thought of having her beneath him as he buried his aching cock deep inside her made him wonder if he shouldn't have taken her up on her offer to go back to her apartment. Then he remembered the promise he'd made to himself—to take things a bit slower with her. Spending a couple hours at Wulf's Den with her wouldn't kill him. At least he didn't think it would.

Besides wanting to take her out on a real date, he wanted Roxie to meet Billie. That was the main reason he'd decided they would go to Wulf's Den. He wasn't looking for Roxie's approval. It was more to show her that he'd finally moved on. That she could stop worrying about him being alone. And that he was ready to give up being a lone wolf living on the outskirts of his pack. Those days were long behind him now. With any luck, by the end of the night, he hoped to have found a new lease on life in the form of Billie as his mate.

CHAPTER SIX

Wulf's Den was a lot more crowded than it had been on the night Billie had come to get Hayes. There was quite a lineup of people waiting to get in as well. Seeing how long it was, she groaned. It looked as if she and Royce wouldn't be getting inside the nightclub any time soon.

Much to her surprise, Royce led her past the line of people and up to the front door. She noticed the same bald bouncer stood by the entrance. He was sure to send them to the end of the line to wait like everyone else, but that didn't turn out to be the case. From the way Royce talked to the bouncer, it was obvious they knew each other and were on pretty good terms.

"How are you doing, Carl?"

"Good." Carl's gaze skipped to Billie. "Not alone for a change, I see."

"Not tonight." Royce pulled Billie closer to his side. "This is Billie. Billie, this is Carl."

"Nice to meet you, Carl."

"Nice to meet you too, Billie. And it's nice to see the old man over here out with someone as pretty as you." He turned his attention back to Royce. "Candice is in there with Roxie. You should introduce Billie to them, especially Candice. She won't have to feel as if she's the odd man out anymore with Billie here." For Billie's benefit, he added, "Candice is my ma...my wife."

326

"I already planned on introducing her to Beowulf and Roxie. I'll make it a point to see Candice as well."

Royce pulled open the entrance door to the club and then ushered Billie inside. It took a moment for her eyes to adjust to the dimness. He didn't seem to be affected as she. He kept walking without missing a step. He seemed to know exactly where he was headed. Instead of going to one of the few empty tables, he walked past the bar to a set of stairs that led to a room on the upper floor. At the door, he knocked once, then walked inside.

The five people in the room—Billie saw now that it was an office—stopped talking and turned to look at them. Royce put a possessive arm around her shoulders and brought her to the small group. Three women sat on a couch against one wall, while two men were at the desk that was not too far away from it. Billie had to do a double take when she saw the men. From their similar looks, she had to guess they were brothers. The only real difference between them was the one sitting behind the desk had black hair and the one in a chair in front of it had chestnut-colored hair. It was their looks that made her stare. They were perfect-looking in every sense of the word, just as Royce was. She had to wonder what the chances were of having three such good-looking men in one room. It didn't happen around her very often.

Not wanting to be rude, Billie dragged her gaze off the two men and turned her attention to the three women on the couch. They were pretty, especially the small blonde, but it was the woman sitting next to her who snagged Billie's attention. There was just something about her that stood out to her.

The woman stood and held her hand out to Billie. "Since Royce is standing there, not making any introductions, I'll do it. I'm Roxie."

Billie accepted Roxie's outstretched hand and gave it a shake. "Nice to meet you, Roxie."

Royce turned and gestured to the small blonde. "This is Candice, and sitting next to her is Taryn." Both women said a quick hello before Roxie turned to face the two men. "Over there, sitting behind the desk, is my husband, Beowulf. And that's his brother, Wade, who also happens to be Taryn's husband." They nodded in her direction.

Royce finally spoke up. "I haven't met Taryn before either." He looked the other woman over as a confused scowl formed on his face. He turned to Roxie. "Can I have a word with you outside?" Taking Roxie by the arm, he said to Billie, "This should only take a moment."

* * * *

As soon as the door shut behind them, Royce turned to confront Roxie. "I thought Wade's mate was a mortal. Taryn is a werewolf."

Roxie gave him a broad smile. "Isn't it great?"

"What is great? That Wade found one of our kind for a mate instead of a mortal?"

"No, dumbass." Roxie rolled her eyes. "You aren't getting it. I meant isn't it great that Taryn is a werewolf now."

"What do you mean by 'now'?" Royce pinned Roxie with a hard stare. "How is that possible?"

"It turned out Taryn was half werewolf, something even she didn't know about until recently. To make a long story short, I used the spell on her."

Royce stiffened. "I thought it was only meant to work on you. That it would only change you from a mortal to a werewolf."

"Well, you thought wrong."

"So your theory that the spell only worked originally on you because Gren used my blood, the sire of the werewolf blood in your line, instead of using his own, turned out to be correct?"

"Not exactly." Roxie gave him a sheepish look. "The first time we tried the spell on Taryn, we used her father's blood. It didn't work. So...so I used mine the second time, and it worked like a charm."

"You did what?" he shouted.

"Keep your voice down."

"Are you telling me that spell, combined with your blood, will change anyone into a werewolf?"

"That I'm not sure about yet. The spell could have only worked because Taryn had some werewolf blood already. I'm trying to convince Candice to let me try it on her, but she's afraid she'll get her hopes up and it won't work. Seeing as how Carl is a werewolf, it would be a wonderful gift for Candice and him."

Royce rubbed his forehead. "I think I feel a headache coming on. Do you have any idea what would happen if werewolf society at large learned about this?"

"Do you have any idea how much you sound like Beowulf saying that?" Roxie crossed her arms over her chest and gave him a long look. "You do realize this could be a blessing for you as well?"

"What do you mean?"

"Did you take a stupid pill today or are you being deliberately thick in the head to annoy me? I'm talking about Billie. You've found a new mate, and she happens to be mortal. A mortal who has no werewolves in her family tree, I bet." Roxie took a step closer and placed her hand on Royce's cheek. "Knowing what you went through with your first mate, I have a feeling you're having a hard time dealing with the idea of having another mortal as your mate. I can change that. I could try the spell on Billie and make her like us. Then you wouldn't have to worry about her so much."

Royce took Roxie's hand off his cheek and placed a kiss on her palm before he released it. "I don't know, Roxie. Yes, you're right, I'm worried about Billie being a mortal." He let out a sigh. "I haven't claimed her as mine yet, and she has no idea I'm a werewolf. I'm not sure how she would feel about being turned into one. Give it time. It's too early to be thinking about it right now."

"I understand. Just remember the offer stands. Meanwhile, I'll keep working on Candice. And before you can pull the grandpa thing on me, I know to be careful. You and Beowulf worry too much. Now let's get back in there before Billie wonders what the hell is going on."

* * * *

Billie took a sip from the glass of red wine Royce had ordered for her. They were now downstairs, sitting at one of the tables in the back corner of the room. She watched the people on the dance floor as they moved in time to the music thumping out of the club's sound system. The night wasn't exactly going as she'd thought it would. Ever since she and Royce had left the small group upstairs in the office, he had become a bit withdrawn, lost in his thoughts.

It had to have been something that had been said when he'd taken Roxie into the hall. For when they had returned, Royce had left her with the other women as he went and had a hushed conversation with Beowulf and Wade. Not that she had minded. Billie found Roxie, Taryn, and Candice to be very friendly. When they'd found out her family owned a gym and what she did there, Roxie had been really interested in hearing what she taught in her self-defense classes. Even Taryn had shown an interest. From there the evening had pretty much gone downhill.

Royce was still lost in thought when Billie turned back to face him. Deciding enough was enough, she picked up her wineglass and downed the rest of it in a couple big gulps. She set it down hard, drawing his attention.

"Look, I can see you're really not into this. It was nice that you brought me to meet your friends and all, but sitting here while you stare at your drink isn't exactly what I would call a good time. To be honest, the nightclub thing isn't my cup of tea. It was a great idea to start with, don't get me wrong, but I think maybe it's time I went home. I'll get myself a cab."

Before she had a chance to get up, Royce's hand shot out and clamped around her wrist. His eyes seemed to take on that glow they sometimes had for a split second; then it was gone.

"Don't go, Billie. I'm sorry." He rubbed his thumb back and forth across the inside of her wrist. "I seem to have screwed this up royally. Don't for a second think I'm not into you, because I want you. And seeing you in that dress, all I can think about is stripping you out of it. I want to make love to you until all *you* can think about is having me inside you."

Her body went into overdrive as an ache built between her legs. Her breath sawed in and out of her lungs as images of Royce doing what he'd just said filled her mind. "Then take me the hell out of here. Now. If you haven't already figured it out yet, I'm not the type of girl who needs to be wooed first. I want you, and when it comes to men, I like the direct approach. So get me out of here and take me to bed."

"There is something to be said about a woman who knows exactly what she wants," Royce said with a grin. He pulled Billie to her feet and gave her a hard, thorough kiss. "I'll make this up to you, all night if I have to."

With her hand held firmly in his larger one, Royce quickly led her out of Wulf's Den. Billie had enough time to wave good-bye to Carl and Candice, who had come outside earlier to be with her husband, as they hurriedly walked by. Out of the corner of her eye, Billie saw Candice whisper something into Carl's ear. The big man chuckled and then wished Royce good luck. At that point, she didn't care why Carl figured Royce would need it. All she could think about was the pounding need that was taking over her body. Knowing exactly what was going to happen once they were alone, she couldn't focus on anything else.

The ride in the car went by in a blur for Billie. It wasn't until Royce parked in the driveway in front of his house did she realize where he'd taken them. Not that she really cared where they were. So long as there was a bed and they were alone, that was all that mattered.

Once Royce turned off the ignition, Billie slipped out of the car. She walked to the front end and waited for him to join her. He wrapped his arm around her waist and then led her to the front door. Her skin tingled where his hand rested against her side. A shiver of excitement surged through her.

It only took Royce a moment to unlock the front door. He pushed it open and gestured for her to go ahead of him. Inside the entranceway, she turned around as he closed and locked them in. He leaned back against the door as he ran his gaze up and down her body.

"I think I'll have to call your sister-in-law and thank her for making you buy that dress."

"I'm sure Janice would love to hear she was right. She said the dress would have you slack-jawed and drooling," Billie said softly. The way Royce looked at her was doing wicked things to her body. Wherever his gaze touched, she swore it felt as if he were physically touching her.

Royce chuckled. "Well, she isn't too far off the mark with that comment. What it does do is make me want to slowly strip you out of it, very slowly, and kiss every inch of skin I expose. When I finally have you naked beneath me, you'll be begging me for more."

Billie moaned. Her breasts grew heavy at the mental image Royce had painted with his words. She didn't have to look down to know he could see her pebbled nipples clearly showing beneath her dress. Needing him to touch her, now, she slid her purse off her shoulder and onto the floor at her feet.

"If that's what you want to do, then what are you waiting for? Or are you all talk and no action?"

One minute Royce stood at the door, and the next, he had her in his arms. He'd moved so fast Billie couldn't be sure if she saw him walk to her. He was suddenly just there.

"Oh, I'm definitely not all talk and no action," Royce said in a low tone as he slowly lowered his head until his lips hovered above hers. "I'll prove it to you."

Billie wrapped her arms around Royce's neck as his lips came down on hers, claiming them in a searing kiss. He licked the seam of her mouth. She allowed him entrance as she greedily sucked his tongue inside. He groaned and held her tighter against him. The hard ridge of his cock pressed against her stomach. In reaction, her pussy grew wet, wanting that part of him deep inside her.

Royce continued to kiss her as he picked her up off her feet and then headed for the stairs. She tried to wrap her legs around his waist when he took the steps two at a time, but the dress was too tight to allow it.

Inside his bedroom, Royce let Billie slide down the length of his body until she was standing. She bit back a whimper as he pulled away. She gasped as he lowered his head and dragged his tongue across one of her nipples, wetting the material of her dress. He continued downward until he knelt before her. Taking hold of a foot, he placed it on his hard thigh and gently undid the strap around her ankle. As he worked on the tiny buckle, he kissed her knee. She quickly placed her hands on his shoulders as her legs trembled.

Once he had the first shoe off, he switched to her other foot. When both were removed, Royce stayed on his knees in front of her and ran his hands up along the outside of her legs. He slowly gathered the material at the hem of her dress, lifting it until it was bunched at her waist.

With maddening slowness, he hooked two fingers inside the top of her panties and pulled them down her legs until she could step out of them. He tossed them aside before he placed his hands on her inner thighs and spread her farther apart. The first flick of his tongue across her clit had Billie clutching Royce.

She forgot to breathe. Royce wasn't showing her any quarter as he licked and sucked her clit. Already more than just aroused before he'd even touched her, her climax rushed up to meet her with each swipe of his tongue. With a moan, her head fell forward. He growled deep in his throat. The sound vibrated against her sensitive skin. No longer able to hold still, she arched her hips against his mouth. He opened her even farther, then stiffened his tongue as he alternated between jabbing it into her hot core and flicking it against her clit. With her hands fisted in the material of his shirt, she moaned as her release washed through her. Unable to remain upright, she sank onto her knees in front of him.

She still wanted more. She wanted to have her naked skin pressed against his. As she looked into his glowing eyes, Billie undid the concealed zipper and pulled the dress over her head. She tossed it aside, then reached for the buttons of Royce's shirt. In a matter of seconds, she had them all undone. Pushing the two halves of material open, she leaned forward and ran her tongue across his chest. It was thickly padded with muscle. She trailed her fingers down his washboard abs until she reached the top of his pants. She brushed against the large bulge there as she made short work of pushing open the top button. Once she had the zipper open, she reached inside to wrap her fingers around the hard length of his cock. He moaned as she pumped her hand up and down.

Royce only allowed her to pleasure him in that way for a few moments before he pulled her away. "Enough. I need to be inside you," he said in a gruff voice.

He shrugged out of his shirt and then pulled her against his chest. Billie gasped at the feel of his skin next to hers. She threaded her fingers through his hair and kissed him as he picked her up. He crossed to the bed and gently placed her in the center of it. Without breaking contact with her mouth, Royce quickly shed his pants.

Now as naked as she, he came down on top of her. The head of his cock pressed against her slick opening. She arched her hips and rubbed her pussy against it, wetting it with her juices. When he made no move to enter her, Billie pushed down on him, taking the very tip of his erection inside her. Fully aroused once more, she sucked his bottom lip into her mouth and bit down.

Biting him seemed to open a floodgate. With a growl, Royce placed his hands on her hips as he surged into her, sheathing himself to the hilt. Billie whimpered. She gloried in the feel of his thick cock buried deep inside her, filling her to capacity. She wrapped her legs around his waist and arched her hips against his as she squeezed her inner muscles around his hard shaft. As he moved inside her, a part of her reached out to him. As if her very soul touched his.

Royce kept his hold on her as he slowly pumped his hips between her legs. The long, slow strokes pushed her ever nearer to another climax. She was so close, but he continued his maddening pace, keeping her on the very edge of her release.

Royce swirled his tongue along the shell of her ear and whispered, "I want you to bite me, Billie. I want you to put your mark on me."

At first, she was unsure what he wanted her to do. When she hesitated, Royce wrapped a hand around the back of her neck and lifted her until her mouth was pressed to the side of his throat where his neck and shoulder met. He stiffened, and his hips jerked as she opened her mouth and lightly grazed her teeth along his skin before she gently nipped his neck.

"Harder. I want to feel your teeth on me."

His cock thickened even more as she increased the pressure. Realizing what kind of affect her biting him had on him, Billie bit down even harder. Royce made a sound that was half a moan and half a growl. Pumping his hips faster, he rode up higher on her body. She clutched his back as he pushed her into an intense orgasm. Her inner walls clamped down around his cock, squeezing him. He moved his hands under her bottom and angled her hips so she could take more of him. With a groan, he thrust into her one final time as he too reached his release. His cock pulsed deep inside her as he came. She held him tight as he collapsed on top of her.

CHAPTER SEVEN

Once his breathing returned to normal, Royce held himself up on his elbows and looked down at Billie. Her cheeks were flushed and her lips swollen from his kisses. She was his now. He'd felt her soul join with his, making her his mate. The wolf had risen as they'd made love, thrown back his head, and howled. He was still hard, buried to the hilt inside her. The wolf now demanded he take her again, but this time as a male werewolf dominating his mate.

Billie's eyes fluttered open when he brushed a kiss across her mouth. "You can't sleep now. I'm far from finished with you."

To show her, Royce pulled out of her until only the very tip of his cock remained inside her. He pushed back into her one slow inch at a time. By the time he'd fully seated himself once more, she panted with need.

Royce pulled free of her body and gently pushed Billie onto her stomach. He urged her up onto her hands and knees. Coming to kneel between her spread legs, he ran his hands down the length of her back. She arched under his touch. With a low growl, he held her still as he bent down and gently nipped the back of her neck.

A whimper of need escaped Billie's lips as she tried to impale herself on his erect cock. Royce growled once again. With one hand on her hip to keep her from moving, he used the other to guide his erection into her slick opening. She moaned. In this position he was even deeper than he'd been before. The tip of him hit her cervix as he surged into her.

Needing to possess her, Royce grabbed her hips with both hands and thrust into her again. His pace increased, no longer able to go slow. The wolf wanted her hard and fast. Billie panted and pushed back against him, meeting him stroke for stroke. Her inner muscles clamped down around his shaft. He knew she was close to coming. Wanting to push her over the edge, he reached around her body until he found her clit. Still pumping his hips, he rubbed the nubbin of flesh. She whimpered, and her climax tore through her. As her body squeezed his cock, he threw back his head and howled, filling her with his cum.

When the last wave of his orgasm fell away, Royce shifted so they lay on their sides. Still fully erect, he kept their bodies joined. He pulled Billie close, holding her with her back against his chest. He tugged the covers over them and kissed the back of her neck. In a matter of moments, she relaxed as sleep claimed her.

* * * *

Waking up by slow degrees, Billie reached out to the spot next to her. It was empty. The sheets still held the warmth from Royce's body, so he hadn't gotten out of bed that long ago. Now fully awake, she stretched her arms over her head. Her body ached in all the right places. He was an inventive lover, she had to give him that. He'd taken her in more ways than she'd thought possible. The man did not quit. She'd never slept with a man who could keep an erection for hours even after coming several times. She could more than easily get used to that.

Billie eased up on her elbows and looked around Royce's bedroom. The night before she'd been too distracted to see what it really looked like. All she'd been interested in was seeing where the bed was. Now that lust wasn't clouding her brain, she took the time to look around.

The room had been decorated to a man's taste. The colors were dark and rich. No pastels to be found in this room. The walls had been painted a deep tan to match the thick wall-to-wall carpeting. The furniture was solid-looking and the color of dark oak.

When her gaze rested on the nightstand beside the bed, Billie found a framed photograph sitting on it. She slid across the bed and picked it up to take a closer look. It was a picture of Royce, standing with two women. The younger of the two Billie recognized. It was Roxie. The older lady, who Roxie greatly resembled, Billie assumed must be her mother. The way the three of them stood together in the photograph, she didn't think it would be too much of an assumption to say they were related in some way. It also explained Royce's interest in Roxie. Billie had heard his loud shout of exclamation at the club the night before. That could also explain his quietness after he'd spoken with Roxie. Obviously, he'd been worried about something she had told him.

At that moment, Royce returned to the bedroom. His wet hair was slicked back, and he only wore a towel around his waist. Evidently, he'd been in the shower. Billie swallowed. The man's body was perfection. There wasn't an inch of fat on him anywhere, and she should know, considering she'd explored every part of him during the night. She ran her gaze down his sculpted chest to his washboard stomach. She came level with the towel and her mouth suddenly went dry. It was tented in an interesting place that drew and held her gaze.

"I see you're finally awake." Royce came closer to the bed.

Billie reluctantly dragged her gaze to his face and sat up with the sheet held to her chest. "I see you already had a shower. Why didn't you wake me up? I would have enjoyed washing your back, among other things." She focused on his crotch, then back up again.

Royce chuckled. "I'm sure you would have, but I thought it best to let you sleep."

"Well, you didn't have to get out of bed before I did. You could have slept in with me."

"I would have, except your cell phone has been ringing every fifteen minutes for the last hour."

"It has?"

"Yes. It woke me up. I didn't realize it was your phone until I followed the sound downstairs and heard the noise coming from your purse." Royce stopped talking and cocked his head. "It's ringing again. I'll bring your purse up for you."

Billie shook her head. Royce had to have the most acute hearing of anyone she knew. She couldn't hear a thing. It wasn't until he stepped back into the bedroom with her purse did she hear that indeed it was her cell ringing.

She put the picture on the bed next to her, then quickly took her purse from Royce before she fished out her phone. "Hello?" She wasn't surprised to hear Hayes's voice coming from the other end.

"Finally. I've been trying to get a hold of you all morning."

Billie looked at Royce and rolled her eyes. "Hayes, you'd better be calling me to tell me Janice has gone into labor, because that's about the only thing that would justify you calling me so early in the morning."

"It's ten o'clock, Billie. I'd hardly say it's too early to be calling someone, especially when it's my sister."

"It seems early to me, okay? I just got up."

"What do you mean you just got up, and where were you sleeping? I called your place first and kept getting your answering machine."

"Do the words 'it's none of your business' mean anything at all to you, Hayes?"

"You're our baby sister. You know we'll never stop looking out for you."

"Oh, lucky me," Billie replied sarcastically. "You can tell Dad I'll be at the gym later. You can also tell the rest of the boys you talked to me and that I'm alive and well. One more thing; if you don't stop calling me, I may have to do some head hunting. And I don't mean the one found on top your shoulders."

Billie ended the call. She looked up to find Royce watching her with a bemused expression. "Sorry about that. You don't have to worry. He won't be calling again."

"You do have a way with words. I have to give you that. Just remind me never to get you angry at me."

Billie felt her face flush. "Sorry. I sometimes forget myself. I'm not exactly very ladylike. I grew up with a house full of men with no woman around to teach me the softer things of life."

"Stop apologizing." Royce sat on the edge of the bed, facing Billie. "What about your mother?"

"I never knew her. She left my father shortly after I was born."

"That must have been hard on you growing up, having a bunch of males watching over you."

Billie shook her head and chuckled. "Not really. I learned early on that if I wanted my freedom, I'd have to learn how best to handle my brothers. Believe me, they tried their hardest to make me do what they thought was best for me, but I never let them win. They still do try, much to their detriment."

Royce gently stroked her cheek. "Well, I for one wouldn't change a thing about you. You're perfect just the way you are. Where I come from, a strong woman who can look after herself is thought of highly."

Even though they'd made love for most of the night, Billie ached to have Royce inside her just from having him sitting near her. She had a feeling she would never get enough of him. She felt a closeness to him that hadn't been there before they'd made love. It was almost as if she were now connected to him in some way. She really didn't know what to make of it. It was still too early to be thinking of a happily ever after with him. Considering her track record with men, the chances weren't that good.

She soon lost her train of thought when Royce leaned in and placed his mouth on hers. He nipped her lips before he pushed his tongue between them. She tasted the mint toothpaste he'd used to brush his teeth. Billie let go of the sheet she still held and wrapped her arms around his neck, then inched closer until her nipples brushed against his wide chest. The sound of her cell phone ringing made her pull away.

With one hand still threaded through the hair at the nape of Royce's neck, Billie picked her phone off the bed. She scowled when she saw who called her now. "Damn. Are they going take turns calling until they drive me crazy? Now it's Keegan. If I don't answer this, he'll keep calling until I do."

Royce kissed the tip of her nose. "Then you'd better answer it."

Billie accepted the call and then barked, "Keegan, I told Hayes to leave me alone. I'm fine. I'll be coming to the gym shortly, but if you guys keep calling me, you're only going to make it so I'm really late. I'm hanging up now." The sound of Keegan's raised voice could be heard before she hung up on him.

She put the cell on the bed and her forehead against Royce's. "I think you'd better take me home so I can get to the gym. If I don't,

I can promise you the twins will be calling next. Eli and Finn wouldn't want to be left out of the fun. And if I were to turn off my phone, knowing them, they'd probably come searching for me. It wouldn't surprise me if they already knew where you live. I wouldn't have put it past them to have had one of them following us last night."

"I think you're right. I'd better take you home soon. Do you want some breakfast before we leave?"

"No, it's okay. I'm not a breakfast person, anyway."

"All right. You can use the bathroom. While you do that, I'll get dressed and then take you home."

Giving Royce's half-naked body one last look, Billie sighed with regret as she slipped out of the bed. She felt his gaze on her as she walked about the room, collecting her scattered clothing. Before heading for the bathroom, she turned her head to look over her shoulder. He stared at her with his eyes doing that glowing thing again. Having seen them do that every time they'd made love during the night, she strangely didn't find it so weird anymore. Same with the animalistic growls he made. If anything, they turned her on. Sighing once more, she turned back around and headed for the bathroom.

* * * *

After Royce dropped her off at her apartment, Billie took only enough time to take a shower and change her clothes before she headed to the gym. As she drove through the late-morning traffic, she found herself already starting to miss him, and she couldn't help but feel it made her pretty pathetic. It hadn't even been an hour since she'd last seen him.

Finally arriving at the gym, Billie headed for the entrance. She took a deep breath before she went inside. She knew what she would find. No sooner had she let the door swing closed behind her, she found herself surrounded by all four of her brothers.

"Well, would you look at that? I have my very own welcoming committee waiting for me. Now don't I feel special?"

This time it wasn't Keegan or Hayes who confronted her, it was the twins. "We saw you last night at Wulf's Den, Billie," Finn said while Eli nodded.

"What? Are you guys following me now?"

"No. We just happened to be there. Eli and I have been there a couple of times already. We've decided Wulf's Den is going to be our regular place to go out at night. The girls are definitely hot." Finn stopped speaking when Eli loudly cleared his throat.

"I see. So you just happened to show up at Wulf's Den the same time Royce and I were there because you've now decided the women are better looking there than any place else? If that's the case, then how come I didn't see the both of you?"

Eli snorted. "As if you would have noticed us even if we stood right in front of you. The way you and Royce looked at each other when you left the club, it was easy to see what you two were leaving to do."

"And you and Finn were only at Wulf's Den to find some women to discuss politics with," Billie snapped back. "Look, I have stuff to do before I can leave for the day, and I would very much like to get at it. And before you bring up the topic of my dress, yes, I wore the one in the picture Janice sent to you all. End of story."

"Leave your sister alone, boys."

Peering around her brothers, Billie saw her father standing behind them. After the boys moved off, she went to him. "Thanks, Dad, for getting them to back off. I'm really not in the mood for their protectiveness today."

Billie had no idea what was wrong with her. She was antsy and out of sorts with herself. The more she thought about Royce, the worse it became. She was turning into one of those girls who obsessed over their boyfriends, and she didn't like it one bit.

"I could tell." Her father looked at her for a few seconds before he continued. "This Royce must be something special. In the past, you never let your brothers get to you quite so much."

"I guess you could say he is." Billie sighed. "I hope it's that way. I really don't know."

Her father nodded. "I'll try to put a rein on your brothers then. Just promise me you won't fall too hard or too fast for Royce until you know for sure he's the one. I know from personal experience it doesn't always work out, no matter how hard you try to keep it going."

"I promise."

He referred to her mother. She'd been the love of her father's life, and he'd not been able to forget her, nor get over her leaving him. That was the main reason Tom York had never remarried, let alone dated another woman. Going on tiptoe, Billie kissed her dad's cheek before she left him in the gym's lobby.

CHAPTER EIGHT

She was losing it. That had to be the only logical explanation for what she was going through. It was a little past noon—almost two hours since she'd watched Royce drive away from her apartment—and the need to be with him made her feel as if she wanted to climb the walls in desperation.

The later it got, the more uncomfortable Billie became. She barely managed to stay civil to the gym members she had training sessions with that day. Having sensed her mood from her earlier outburst when she'd first arrived, her brothers had wisely kept their distance.

Though she tortured herself by using her ability to locate people, it didn't stop her from checking every few minutes to see where Royce was. That didn't help matters either. If anything, it increased the need by small increments each time she did it. She just couldn't seem to stop herself.

Another hellish hour went by. After ending her last training session of the day, Billie once again looked to see if Royce was still where he'd been the last time she'd checked. Her eyes snapped open, and she gasped as a wave of need slammed into her. He was no longer at his house. He sat in his car in the visitors' parking at her apartment. The knowledge that he waited for her there was more than she could take. She had to go to him.

In a matter of minutes, Billie had retrieved her purse and

rushed toward the gym exit. In her haste, she just about knocked Janice over, who'd just arrived and was in the lobby. She put out a steadying hand as she quickly apologized. "Sorry. I didn't see you there. Hayes is still on the gym floor." Billie stepped around her sister-in-law.

"What's the hurry? I didn't come to see Hayes. I came to see you. I've been dying to hear how your date went with Royce. I figured it went well since you weren't at your place when Hayes started calling you practically at the crack of dawn."

Billie didn't stop her forward movement. She turned so she could walk backward as she spoke. "I have to see Royce. Yes, it went well, and he says he has to call and thank you for picking out that dress for me to wear. Sorry, but I really have to go. I'll phone you later."

"I told you Royce would love you in it," Janice shouted as Billie slipped out the gym's front doors.

She arrived at her apartment in record time. After she parked her car, she headed for the visitors' parking. Billie was practically running by the time she spotted Royce's black BMW. Just before she reached it, he stepped out. He turned in her direction and swept her up into his arms. Not caring that everyone in her apartment building could see what they were doing, she grabbed a fistful of his hair and pulled his mouth down to hers. At the first touch of his lips, some of the anxiety she'd been feeling slipped away. It was quickly replaced by a raging need like none she'd ever felt before.

It took a surprising amount of self-control on Billie's part not to suggest they get into the backseat of Royce's car and make love like a pair of horny teenagers. Instead, she pulled her mouth away and looked at him. The desire coursing through her still had her in its grip.

"I need you inside me, Royce. I haven't been able to think of anything else but you since you left. There has to be something wrong with me. This can't be normal."

Royce seemed as affected as she. His chest quickly rose and fell with each breath he took. "It's normal." He took her hand and headed for the front entrance to her apartment building. "I suggest we get inside before I do something that could very well get us arrested. I need to be inside you as much as you need me to be there. It has been a very long time since I last went through this. I'd forgotten how bad it could be in the beginning."

Billie quickly used her key to unlock the secured door. They hurried to the elevator. Royce pushed the Up button. "I'm not sure what you mean about forgetting how hard this could be. If you mean this desperate feeling that if I don't make love to you soon, I'm going to go crazy, it's far from normal for me. I'm not the type of woman who becomes so obsessed with the man she's with he takes over her life."

The elevator doors slid open. Once inside, Billie quickly pushed the button for her floor and the one to close the doors. She wasn't in the mood to have anyone else joining them. She kept her hands fisted at her sides and watched the numbers light up at each floor that went by until the elevator stopped at hers.

At her apartment door, Royce yanked her back into his arms. The hard length of his cock nestled against her stomach. Billie sucked in a breath as the ache between her legs intensified and her body grew wet. He ground his hips into her, leaving no doubt that he was as turned-on as she.

"I won't take over your life, Billie. I'm now just a part of you, as you're a part of me. Forever."

Before she could ask what he meant, Royce took her mouth in a kiss that made her legs go weak. Blindly, she fumbled with her keys until she got the right one into the lock. Once the apartment door swung open, he walked her backward inside and then slammed it shut behind them. Now that they were away from prying eyes, Billie let go of the tight rein she held over herself.

With her hands on Royce's chest, she pushed him back against the closed door. She had waited too long to let him take control. It was her turn to do all the things to him that she'd pictured in her mind while they'd been apart. She skimmed her hands down his sides, took hold of the bottom of his T-shirt, and pushed it up to his chest. He continued to kiss her as if he wanted to devour her. His tongue plunged into her mouth, thoroughly tasting her. She moaned. It wasn't enough. She wanted more.

She broke contact and pulled his shirt over his head, then dropped it to the floor. She took a step closer as she dragged her lips down the side of his throat. She swirled her tongue across the small mark she'd left the night before. Royce groaned and bucked his hips against her when she lightly nipped him there.

Billie licked a path across his collarbone and down to his chest. Before moving lower, she circled her tongue around each of his flat nipples. Going down on her knees before him, she made short work of opening his jeans. She watched Royce's face as she slowly inched his pants down past his hips. His eyes glowed mutedly as he looked at her with stark desire.

She focused her attention on what she desired the most, then took Royce's cock firmly in her hand. She pumped up and down until a small bead of moisture appeared at the very tip. Gently, she used a finger to rub it into his skin. With the same digit, she stroked down the length of his shaft before wrapping her hand around the base. He growled deep in his chest as she bent and swirled her tongue around the head.

Billie lifted her gaze to his face once again and parted her lips, taking as much of him as she could manage into her mouth. Royce gasped with pleasure as she greedily sucked. He grew even harder. Unable to keep her gaze on him, she closed her eyes so she could completely focus on what she was doing. With each moan she wrung out of him, her inner walls clenched. Wetness dripped between her legs. She was more than ready to have him deep inside her.

Royce gently pulled her away. He helped her onto her feet, then yanked her yoga pants down until she could kick them off. Her panties quickly followed. Billie removed her shirt and sports bra, leaving her to stand naked before him. His gaze roamed up and down her body as he shed his jeans. She found hers drawn to his cock, which was thick and hard.

She sank to her knees onto the carpeted floor and crocked a finger at Royce to join her. He didn't hesitate. Also on his knees in front of her, he bent his head and sucked one of her nipples deep inside his mouth. Billie moaned. With each pull, she felt it deep inside her core. No longer able to wait to have him, she pushed at his shoulders until he sat on the floor. He leaned back on his hands, supporting his weight.

Billie moved to straddle his hips. She placed her hands on top his shoulders, then slid her wet pussy along his cock, coating him with her juices. With her bottom lip between her teeth, she arched her hips and impaled herself on his hard erection to the hilt.

Slowly, Billie rocked against Royce. She squeezed her inner walls around his shaft as she rode him. The first tremors of her orgasm built in intensity. Leaning forward so the tips of her breasts brushed his chest, she dragged her teeth across his skin where his neck and shoulder met. He stiffened beneath her. As her climax rose to meet her, she bit down hard, which sent him into an instant orgasm.

Spent, Billie collapsed onto his chest. Royce wrapped his arms around her. His cock was still hard, keeping their bodies joined. Once she was able to catch her breath, she kissed his chin before she sat up straighter.

"I can feel you're ready to have another go at it." She gave his cock a squeeze. "You're going to spoil me with that keeping hard trick of yours. How will my future boyfriends ever be able to compete with that?"

With a growl, Royce threaded his fingers through her hair and brought her face closer to his. "There will be no others, Billie. You're mine, and I don't easily give up something that is."

The way he looked at her so intently, Billie couldn't hold back the shiver of longing that shot through her. How she wished she could think as positively as Royce. Out of all the men she'd dated, he was the first one she'd allowed herself to think maybe, just maybe, he could be the one.

"How can you be so sure this will work out?" she asked. "Yes, we're great in bed together, but I haven't exactly had much luck keeping boyfriends around in the past."

Royce brushed a light kiss across her lips. "That's because you were waiting for me to find you."

"Is that so?" Billie's voice came out breathy sounding as she became aroused once more. "I thought it was the other way around. I thought I was the one who found you."

"Either way, you knew the others weren't for you. There's no going back now." Holding her as if she weighed nothing, Royce stood. With his cock still buried deep inside her, he walked in the direction of her bedroom.

* * * *

Royce lay on the bed next to Billie, watching her sleep. They'd made love twice more before she'd drifted off. He could have gone much longer, given the fact a male werewolf could keep an erection for hours at a time even after climaxing, but he'd thought it best to let her rest. He decided he'd made a fine start in proving to his mate that only he could keep her so well-satisfied. He wanted her spoiled for other men.

Billie stirred as her stomach growled loudly. Her eyes fluttered open when it did it again.

"Hungry?" he asked.

She gave him a half smile. "Kind of." Her stomach growled for a third time. "Okay, I'm really hungry. I sort of forgot to eat today. I was a little distracted."

"Well, we can't have that. How about we order some food and have it delivered?"

"Sounds good to me. Do you like Chinese? There's a great place not too far from here. I order from them all the time."

"Chinese is fine with me."

Billie slipped out of bed and then walked naked out of the room. He heard her moving around in the living room. When she returned, she held a takeout menu. Just watching her pad across the bedroom in all her glory caused blood to rush to his cock. He'd forgotten how strong the separation anxiety would be after he'd claimed his mate. It had felt as if he'd been in hell during the hours she'd been at work. The wanting, the longing to be with her, had filled his mind until he hadn't been able to think of anything else but her. That she'd gone through the same thing had shown him they were truly mated. He'd felt her soul reach out to his the first time they'd made love. Being she wasn't a werewolf and didn't know what that had meant, he hadn't known how their separation would affect her.

After plunking onto the bed beside him, Billie opened the menu. "All right. What would you like to have?"

"Whatever you want is fine with me."

"If I were to say octopus and squid were my favorites, would you still be fine with that?"

From Billie's straight face, Royce couldn't be sure if she was joking or not. "You really like those things?"

Billie snorted and smacked him over the head with the menu. "No, they aren't my favorite food. I just said that to show you saying whatever I wanted was fine with you may not necessarily be what you would like. So hurry up and pick something before I get so hungry I have to start eating you."

Royce smiled and flipped back the bedsheet. "Be my guest. As long as you start in the area of my hips, I'm game."

Her gaze landed on his manhood. He all too clearly remembered what it'd felt like to have her mouth on him, pleasuring him until he'd felt as if he were ready to explode. In reaction, his blood surged, sending most of it to his groin. Much to his dismay, Billie gave his now fully erect cock one last look of longing before she pulled the sheet back over his hips.

"Food first. At the rate we're going, I'll be lucky if I can walk tomorrow." She shoved the menu into his hands. "Now pick something already."

After turning his attention to the menu, Royce quickly picked out a couple of items. As Billie phoned in their order, he was shocked by how much he'd come to love her and how badly he wanted her to love him. It scared him a little. It left him too exposed, able to be more easily hurt. If anything happened to her because he'd taken her as his mate, he would never be able to forgive himself. He wasn't yet ready to tell her exactly what he was, but he would have to do it soon. The sooner he eased her into werewolf society, the better. He'd learned with his first mate that keeping Billie on the outskirts could be a fatal mistake. And it was one he didn't want to repeat.

* * * *

Outside in the parking lot of Billie's apartment, Gren sat in his car and watched as a male mortal walked into the building, carrying a large bag of Chinese takeout. From where he sat, Gren easily saw him buzz up to one of the apartments. A few minutes later, a woman came to the door, handed the delivery guy money, and then took the bag. She was the one he'd seen Royce with earlier.

He had started watching Royce the week before. After months of lying low, not wanting to draw attention upon himself, he'd decided now was the time to act. To show the ones who held the most power that he was still a force to be reckoned with. And

Royce was the key.

It'd been the spell he'd spent years trying to find that had turned Roxie into a werewolf. She'd been the first mortal it had worked on. That she'd ended up being the werewolf from an ancient prophecy, he felt had had no bearing on its validity. He attributed it to the fact he'd used Royce's blood and not his own. Royce was Roxie's grandfather, though many times removed. She was special, and as the sire of her bloodline, Royce's blood could have very well been what the spell had needed to work. To test his theory, he would need more of Royce's blood, which the other man wouldn't agree to give him.

So he'd decided he would follow the lone wolf and watch for an opportunity to arise where Royce would have no choice but to comply. He had to find Royce's weakness and use it against him. It'd never occurred to Gren the very thing he sought would present itself so quickly or so easily.

Having seen the passionate kiss Royce and the woman had shared in the parking lot earlier, Gren knew the lone wolf had once again found himself a mate. And he knew what had happened to Royce's first mate. Royce had left his mortal mate unprotected, and in his absence, the local villagers had burned her to death for practicing what they thought was witchcraft. Her death had caused Royce to step down as leader of his pack and go lone wolf, taking his infant daughter with him into hiding.

Now, once again, Royce had a weakness Gren could exploit. He'd seen enough for today. After starting his car, he pulled out of the parking lot. He would return in the morning and see where Royce's mate went during the day.

CHAPTER NINE

Billie placed the bag of Chinese food on the kitchen table. The delicious smells made her mouth water and her stomach rumble. She set two places and then pulled out the hot containers. Impatiently, she tapped on the tabletop. Royce had been in the bathroom when she'd come back upstairs with the Chinese. She hoped he wouldn't be much longer, but men could take forever in the bathroom at times. She couldn't understand why people always said women hogged it more than guys. From her experience living with her father and brothers, it was they who liked to take their time.

Figuring she had waited long enough, Billie filled her plate. "If you don't get out here soon, the food will be cold," she called to Royce.

She looked up when he stepped out of the bathroom. He wore only jeans. His hair was damp in places where he'd obviously used water to fix the spots where she'd tunneled her fingers through it earlier.

He eyed the mound of food she had on her plate. "Are you sure you have enough there?" he asked with a hint of laughter in his voice.

Billie looked at her plate, then back at Royce. She shrugged. "What can I say, I like to eat. I work out enough I can get away with eating whatever I want and as much of it as I want."

"I can attest to that. You're by no means fat, and you aren't one of those stick-thin women who starves themselves either. You're solidly built." Royce blinked when a chicken ball smacked him in the middle of the forehead. "What was that for?"

"Solidly built? Just what every woman wants to hear from the man she's sleeping with."

"Well, you are." A second chicken ball sailed across the table. This time it hit him square in the chest and bounced into his lap. Royce picked it up and put it onto his plate. "I meant it in a good way. There's nothing worse than holding a woman in your arms, having to handle her as if she were glass because you're afraid if you hold her too tightly she'll shatter."

"Okay, I can see your reasoning, but can't you think of better way to describe it? Solidly built makes me think of pickup trucks that are used at construction sites. I know I'm not the most feminine woman on the planet, but I'm not that bad."

Royce made a show of studying her before he said anything else. "All right. How about sleek and strong? Like a leopard or some other large cat."

"Or a wolf." Much to Billie's surprise, all the humor left Royce's face and he went very still. "What? A wolf is strong, and it's built for running. I envy wolves, being able to run wild in the forests. It must be an exhilarating feeling."

"It is exhilarating," Royce said quietly.

He'd spoken so softly Billie wasn't sure she'd heard him correctly. "What did you say?"

"I said yes, it would be." Royce seemed to come out of whatever had come over him. He motioned to her plate. "Eat up or I'm going to think your eyes are bigger than your stomach."

Royce somehow managed to dish up twice the amount of food she had onto his plate. He proceeded to put a remarkable dent into it in a short amount of time. She shook her head. She had a feeling with him around she was going to find it hard to keep food in her apartment. As she picked up her fork and started to eat, she couldn't help but wonder why her bringing up the topic of wolves had caused him to react the way he had.

* * * *

Billie caught herself looking at the clock hanging on a wall in the main gym for the hundredth time in the last half hour. It wasn't nearly as bad as it had been the day before. This time she got smart and didn't use her ability to see where Royce was every few minutes, but it still was annoying that she should feel so attached to him.

Royce was going meet her at the gym when her shift was over. He had at first insisted he would drop her off and then pick her up, but Billie had quickly vetoed that. Even though she was going to his place right after work, she didn't want to put him in the position of having to drive her to her apartment in the morning so she could get her car. It just made more sense for her to follow him to his house.

To help pass the time until Royce was to arrive, Billie kept busy by making sure all the free weights were put back in their proper places. She was in the middle of pulling forty-five-pound plates off the barbell at one of the flat benches when Finn came up to her.

"Billie, do you think you could take a prospective member on a tour of the gym?"

"Isn't there anyone else who can do it?"

Showing people around while trying to sell them a membership wasn't something she enjoyed. Given her state of mind now, she didn't know if she could trust herself to stay in the salesperson mindset that she needed to have to convince someone to buy a gym membership.

"Nope, just you. I would do it, but I have a training session. The others are busy as well, and Dad is out at some meeting."

She slid the last plate onto the rack of weights and nodded. "Fine. I'll do it."

Finn flashed a smile. "Thanks, Billie. I owe you one."

Billie headed for the front desk and took another quick look at the clock. Royce would be arriving in fifteen minutes. If she was quick enough, maybe she could have the tour done and the paperwork finished if this person decided to join the gym before Royce arrived.

At the front desk, Billie saw a man standing by the counter. He was tall, very tall, probably only an inch or two shorter than Royce. He stood with his back to her, but he turned when he heard her approaching. She noticed he was extremely good-looking, and from the way he smiled at her, well, he knew it. The only thing about him that set her on edge was his eyes. They were light brown and had a hint of cruelty to them. The friendliness he tried to portray with his smile didn't seem to reach them.

Billie stuck out her hand. "Hi, I'm Billie. I understand you're interested in joining the gym?"

He took it and gave it a quick shake. Before he released it, he rubbed his thumb back and forth across the back of it. Billie resisted the urge to wipe her hand on her pants.

"I'm Gren. Yes, I'm very interested, especially now that I've met you."

Plastering on what she hoped was a believable smile, Billie motioned for Gren to follow her. "Well then, let's get started on the tour. Once you've seen the gym, we can talk prices."

"By all means. Lead on. So far I definitely like what I'm seeing."

Billie ground her teeth as she led Gren onto the gym floor. His innuendo wasn't lost on her. Ignoring his last comment, she took a deep, calming breath, then started her sales pitch. As she took him around, she felt him watching her every move. A chill of uneasiness ran down her spine. He gave her the creeps, and it didn't want to go away. There was just something about him that had her wanting to get as far away from him as possible. Hoping to get this over with quickly, she picked up the pace.

* * * *

Royce pulled opened the door and stepped into the gym's lobby. He was about to tell the girl behind the front desk that he was there to see Billie when he detected the scent of another werewolf inside the building. And it was one he easily recognized. Curling his lip back in a snarl, he followed the scent trail as he battled to keep the wolf inside him at bay. That Billie's scent was mixed in with the other had the wolf rising, wanting to fight the other who was with his mate.

Not caring that he probably looked pretty threatening to the people he passed, Royce followed the fresh scent to the bottom of the stairs that led to the floor above. He took them two at a time. At the top, he headed for the one door that stood open. He heard

Billie's voice coming from inside the room. The sound of the male voice that answered her had him growling through his clenched teeth.

He stepped inside and barely managed to hold back from going wolf when he saw Gren standing next to Billie. Instead, he growled a warning at the other werewolf. "Get the hell away from her."

Gren ignored it. "Ah, the lone wolf has arrived. Your mate was just showing me around her family's gym. I'm trying to decide whether or not I want to join."

"I won't tell you again, Gren. Get away from her. Now." Royce pulled his upper lip back in a snarl.

"I mean your mate no harm, at least not yet. You have something I want, something I used with a certain spell."

"There's no way I'm giving you any of my blood. And who is to say the spell will work on another."

Gren bared his teeth at him. "I'm sure it *will* work on another. Maybe I'll do you a favor and try it out on your mate here. Wouldn't you like to have her as one of us, able to live for thousands of years? That way you won't have to watch her grow old and die while you remain young looking."

Royce glanced at Billie. He could tell from the confused expression that she had no idea what was going on. Quickly, he turned his gaze back on Gren. "Roxie was special. You know that. It's because of that the spell worked."

A look of hatred came over Gren's face at the mention of Roxie's name. "Ah yes, your precious granddaughter. How can I ever forget what she is? The one from the ancient prophecy chosen to rule over all the packs. If it wasn't for me, she'd still be a weak mortal. And what do I get in return? I get abused."

"You would have killed Beowulf. You deserved what you got."

Gren growled low in his throat. "Watch your step, lone wolf. Remember you have a weakness now. If you don't give me what I want, I won't hesitate to use it against you." He turned and looked pointedly at Billie.

Unable to hold back any longer, Royce howled with rage as he launched himself at Gren. With one leap, he was on the other werewolf and had pushed him back into one of the mirrored walls. The mirror shattered on impact. Holding Gren pinned,

Royce stuck his face into his. "You ever threaten my mate again, you die. I'll gladly do what Roxie should have done in the first place. Dogs who go bad need to be put down."

At the sound of others entering the room behind him, Royce growled menacingly, then roughly shoved Gren away. He kept his gaze on the other werewolf as Gren made a show of brushing himself off. He gave Royce a look that said they would be meeting again before he stepped around the newcomers and left.

Royce fought to keep the wolf inside him leashed. He kept his back to the others. This had not been the way he had wanted to tell Billie about his kind. As with Roxie and Beowulf, Gren had done something to bring it all out into the open. Heedless of the pieces of shattered glass that still hung on the wall, Royce swore and rammed his fist into it, wishing it was Gren's head he hit instead.

*

Unsure of what exactly had just happened, Billie turned to face her brothers. It was no surprise they'd all come rushing to see what was going on. If it wasn't the loud howling and growling that had taken place, she was pretty sure the sound of the mirror shattering had sent them running. Right now, all she could think about was getting rid of them before Royce did anything else that was too animalistic and couldn't be easily overlooked or ignored.

Keegan gazed at the glass on the floor, then back at Royce. "Billie, are you all right?"

She nodded. "I'm fine. It's over now. You can all go back to what you were doing."

Not to be put off, her oldest brother shook his head. "We're not going anywhere until you tell us what happened. It sounded as if a bunch of wild animals were attacking each other up here."

Which Billie had to admit was what had almost happened. Seeing both men's eyes glow as they growled at each other made them appear more animal than human, but what had gotten her the most was when Royce had leaped across the room in one jump. One minute he was at the open door, and the next, he was halfway across the open space, slamming Gren into the wall. It didn't seem humanly possible, which probably was the case.

"It sounded worse than it actually was." Billie took a quick look back at Royce. He was still breathing heavily and appeared to be fighting to bring himself under control. "The prospective member Finn had me show around the gym, Royce knew him. They're not exactly on friendly terms, to put it mildly."

"So, your boyfriend decided to pick a fight with him?" Keegan asked harshly.

"He wasn't the one to pick the fight. It was Gren. He's not the type of person we want at the gym. There's something about him that gives me the creeps. Royce was just warning him off when he showed an interest in me. If it wouldn't be too much to ask, can you guys make sure he left?"

Billie had known that would be more than enough to get all four of her brothers out of the room in a hurry. If Gren happened to still be in the building, he would be lucky if her brothers didn't literally kick his ass out onto the street. She waited until they were alone before she turned to confront Royce.

"Okay, I got rid of them. What was that all about?"

Royce slowly turned to face her. "I never intended for you to find out this way."

"Find out what? I don't understand, Royce. You're going to have to spell it out for me, I'm afraid."

"Not here." Royce ran his fingers through his hair, making sections of it stick up. "Christ, I wasn't ready to tell you about any of this."

Billie crossed her arms over her chest and stared at him. He appeared uncomfortable with the situation. "Tell me what? Is it about this mate business Gren referred to? That will do for starters, but I have questions of my own. Such as, why he called you a lone wolf. Why he referred to you as Roxie's grandfather. Or better yet, what is with the whole glowing eyes and growling the pair of you had going on?"

She didn't know why, but she couldn't help feeling a little pissed off that Royce had kept secrets from her. She was being irrational. It wasn't as if they'd been seeing each other for years. She really hardly knew anything about him. All she knew was she felt more connected to him than she had ever felt to any of the other men she'd gone out with.

Royce closed the distance between them and reached out to

hold her by her upper arms. He bent his head down so he could look her in the face. "Look, I know there must be a million questions running around in your mind. I just can't answer them here. It's too public. I have a feeling you aren't going to believe what I have to say at first. And if that's the case, I'm going to have to give you the proof you will undoubtedly ask for. I'd rather it was at some other place where if you freak out on me, your brothers won't come running to your rescue."

"All right. Then where?"

"I need to make some phone calls first. I'll call you after that, okay?"

"Fine. I'll be at my apartment once I get this mess cleaned up."

Royce leaned in and kissed Billie's forehead. "I promise I'll explain everything to you. You can tell your father I'll pay for the damages as well. I'll see you in a bit."

Royce walked out of the room. She would give him an hour. If she didn't hear from him then, she would find him. As Hayes knew from firsthand experience, there was no hiding from her.

CHAPTER TEN

"So, what exactly are you going to do about the Gren problem?" Royce asked Roxie.

They sat in the living room of her parents' house. Belinda, Roxie's mother, was with them. He'd called Roxie after he'd left Billie at the gym and had asked her to meet him there.

Roxie shook her head. "I don't really know. If we had a werewolf jail or something, I'd be all for locking Gren up and throwing away the key, but we don't."

Before Royce could say anything more, Belinda spoke up. "Roxie, I know you don't want to be the one to make the hard decisions, but you have to. You rule over the packs. That means you're the one responsible for keeping them in line. Maybe it's time to do something to stop Gren, permanently."

"You aren't suggesting what I think you're suggesting?" Roxie asked. "I never knew you were so bloodthirsty, Mom."

Her mother, who was next to her on the couch, patted her hand. "Well, I was raised by a werewolf, my dear." Belinda looked at Royce and smiled before she turned back to her daughter. "Dad may have been a lone wolf, but over the years, he made sure he kept tabs on what happened in werewolf society. When I was growing up, I wasn't sheltered from it as you were."

"I'm seeing a whole different side to you." Roxie looked at Royce. "I guess I have you to thank for raising my mother to be so tough. Way to go, Grandpa."

Royce scowled at Roxie. "I've told you a thousand times not to call me that."

"You are my grandfather, aren't you? And you let my mother call you Dad."

"That's different. I raised your mother as my daughter. I'm the only father she's known. You, on the other hand, only call me that to try to get a rise out of me."

"Whatever." Roxie grew serious. "Leave the Gren problem to me for now. I'll have a talk with Beowulf about it and see what he thinks. All I can say is try to be more careful. Now, what was the other thing you wanted to discuss?"

Royce took a deep breath before he answered. "It's actually a favor I want to ask of you and your mother. It has to do with Billie."

"You haven't told her about you being a werewolf, have you?"

"No. I thought maybe you and Belinda could help explain it to her. She may accept it more if you both were there when I told her."

"Unbelievable," Roxie said. "First Beowulf, then Wade, and now you. What is with you idiot male werewolves claiming mortal women as mates without letting them know what exactly they're getting themselves into?"

"It just happened. You know how strong the mating urge is, Roxie. I admit, I should have said something to Billie before, but it isn't something you can just lay on a mortal and expect them to believe. Look what you did to Beowulf when he went wolf on you. You used your magic to keep him in wolf form for twenty-four hours. I don't call that taking it well."

Roxie flicked his comment away with her hand. "I wasn't exactly thinking straight that night. Sorry if seeing you and Gren go at each other at Wulf's Den upset me. Fine, I'll talk to Billie with Mom. When are you going to bring her around?"

"I was thinking today. Say in the next hour or so."

Roxie narrowed her eyes at him. "Why the big rush all of a sudden?" She swore under her breath. "Billie was there when Gren gave his ultimatum to you. She was a witness to it all. Nice one."

Before Royce could stand up for himself, the doorbell rang.

Belinda stood to answer it. He heard her greet the person who stood at the door. Much to his shock, Billie answered back. He had no idea how she knew where to find him. He hadn't had a chance to call her.

Belinda returned to the room with Billie in tow. Billie nodded at Roxie before she went to stand in front of Royce. "I thought you were going to call me."

"I was going to. I had to discuss something with Roxie and her mother before I did. How did you know where to find me?"

"I have my ways."

"That's what you said when you showed up on my doorstep." Royce had a feeling it couldn't be a coincidence that Billie could seemingly find him so easily. "Seriously, how did you find me?"

Billie rolled her eyes. "Fine. I sort have a little secret as well."

"That would be?"

"I guess you want me to go first. All right. I have an ability that lets me locate people I've come in contact with, no matter how briefly I've associated with them."

"Really?" Roxie asked with interest in her voice. "You can find anyone you want?"

"Yes. So long as I've seen your face I'll be able to find you."

"How does it work? Do you get flashes of images in your mind, or do you get complete addresses?"

"I bring the person's face up in my mind and then I focus on them. I don't really get an address or images. It's like I just know where to go to find them. It's kind of hard to explain."

Royce chuckled. "Now I understand why your brother, Hayes, wasn't thrilled to see you that night at Wulf's Den. He hadn't told you where he was going and still you found him."

"I've lost count the number of times I've had to bring his drunken ass home. Without fail, when Hayes gets into a fight with his wife, he goes somewhere to get sloshed. Then Janice calls me to find him and bring him home. He hasn't been able to get away from me yet, though he does try. You wouldn't believe some of the places he has gone to, hoping I wouldn't be able to find him." Billie shuddered dramatically. "At least the others don't make me hunt them down."

"The others?" Roxie asked.

"My brothers. I have three older brothers besides Hayes."

Roxie gave a low whistle. "Four older brothers? Dating must have been fun for you when you were growing up."

"It was rough at times. Add my father into the mix, and sometimes I was lucky to date at all."

"I can sympathize with you, dear," Belinda said. "I grew up with a father who took great relish in scaring off almost every boy I brought home."

"Hey, I wasn't that bad," Royce said with a laugh.

It wasn't until he felt Billie's gaze boring into him did he realize what he'd said. He turned his on her and saw her looking at Belinda and then back at him. It wasn't hard to see that she was trying to figure out how he could be Belinda's father when he looked much younger than she did. Clearing his throat, Royce motioned for Billie to sit beside him on the loveseat.

After she was seated, Royce took a deep breath before he began. "I guess this is where I say it's my turn now. I can see from your expression that you're finding it hard to believe I'm Belinda's father."

Billie snorted. "You think? There's no way you can be her father. You look to be the same age as Roxie."

"Looks can be deceiving. In actual fact, I'm Belinda's grandfather, not her father. I only raised her as my daughter when her parents died."

"Okay, you're losing me here."

"I don't know of any other way to explain this without just coming out with it. So here it goes. Billie, I'm a werewolf."

Billie laughed. "You're kidding, right? There are no such things as werewolves."

Royce had known she wouldn't believe him, but it still didn't make it any easier for him. "No, I'm not kidding, and werewolves are indeed real."

"No, they aren't." Billie must have realized he was serious, because she stopped laughing. "Royce, you can cut the crap. I'm not that naive to believe werewolves exist. Next you'll be telling me the bogeyman is real too."

Belinda broke into their conversation. "If I might make a small suggestion, Dad, I think maybe you should show Billie or you're not going to get anywhere."

Royce nodded. Belinda was right. He could sit there and argue with Billie until he was blue in the face, and she still wouldn't believe him.

He moved off the love seat and stood so he could look down at Billie. He kept his gaze on her as he drew on the magic inside him and willed the change upon himself. Her eyes grew round as his body shimmered, blurring as it took on his wolf form. Once the change was complete, Royce shoved his muzzle under her limp hand. She fell back in a dead faint.

* * * *

Billie heard someone calling her name as if they were a great distance away. Pushing through the darkness that surrounded her, she blinked open her eyes. Royce, Roxie, and Roxie's mother were all hanging over her.

"What happened?" She tried to sit up, but Royce wouldn't let her.

"Give yourself a minute. You might still feel a bit woozy."

It all came rushing back. Royce had changed into a wolf before her very eyes. One second he was a man, and the next, he was a wolf with fur the exact same color as his hair. She groaned with disgust when she remembered how her world had suddenly gone black as he'd pushed his muzzle into her hand.

"Tell me I didn't faint."

Royce chuckled. "You were out like a light."

"I've never fainted before in my entire life. I can't be one of those women who faint."

"Why not? Is it too much of a woman thing for you?"

"No. It's just something those wimpy women do, and I'm no wimp."

Royce chuckled again. "No one would call you a wimp. I've seen you put all four of your brothers in their place. You're definitely not a wimp."

This time when she tried to sit up, Royce helped her. He sat next to her and took her hand. "Do you believe me now, Billie, that I'm a werewolf?"

How couldn't she believe it? The proof had been enough to make her faint, much to her disgust. "I'd be fooling myself if I didn't. Change again. I promise this time I won't faint."

"Are you sure?"

"Of course I'm sure or I wouldn't have asked you to do it. I didn't get to see much of you in your wolf form."

Not bothering to get off the love seat this time, Royce shifted into wolf form. Billie was surprised by how quickly, and seemingly painlessly, the change took place. Looking into the large wolf's eyes, she knew it was Royce staring back. As a man he was exceedingly handsome, but as a wolf, she could only think of one word to describe him — beautiful.

He edged closer as she reached out and placed her hand on the top of his head. His golden-brown fur was soft to the touch. She stroked down to his back where she dug her fingers into his thick fur. Royce leaned closer and licked her cheek. She gave him a hard stare.

"You can lick my face as long as you don't go around licking your privates while you're a wolf. That's just disgusting."

Royce snorted and shook his large head. Roxie, who stood nearby, laughed, reminding Billie that she and her mother were still in the room. Billie turned to Roxie.

"Okay, Roxie, it's your turn. Gren said you were a werewolf as well. I want to see you as a wolf."

Roxie smiled. "With pleasure. And don't worry, I don't lick myself either, but I do have one nifty trick Royce can't do."

Roxie shifted into her wolf form. She was slightly smaller than Royce, and her fur was just a touch lighter than his. All the air left her lungs in a whoosh as Roxie shifted again. Instead of shifting into her human form, she took on a form that only could be described as half-human and half-wolf. She was much taller, even taller than Royce. Her body was covered in the same colored fur she had as a wolf. Billie also noticed she had a wolf's tail.

"Damn, Roxie. You could kick some serious butt in that form. You're huge."

"Been there, done that," Roxie said in a voice that was gruffer than her normal one.

"Nice. You can talk as well. I'm jealous. I'd love to be able to change like that, even if it were only into a wolf. My brothers would freak."

Something unreadable flickered in Roxie's eyes just before she shifted into human form. Out of the corner of her eye, Billie saw

Royce had changed too and shook his head at Roxie.

Roxie ignored Royce. "Would you really like to be like Royce and me, Billie?"

"Don't even suggest it, Roxie," Royce said in a hard voice. "We don't know for sure it'll work on Billie."

"You're talking about the spell Gren wants Royce's blood for, aren't you?" Billie asked Roxie. When Royce turned to look at her, she said, "Don't look at me like that. I do have more than half a brain, and I was in the same room as the two of you. I can assure you I have perfect hearing."

Roxie bit back a smile. "I can see you're not going to have any problem handling Royce. And yes, I mean that spell. Gren used it to change me into a werewolf. Little did he know his doing so also fulfilled an ancient prophecy."

"Royce told Gren that was the only reason the spell worked on you when it had failed with the others Gren tried it on."

"Well, that isn't exactly true. As far as Gren knows, I'm the only one the spell has changed into a werewolf. He doesn't know I used it on Taryn."

"You used it to change Taryn into a werewolf?" Billie asked with wonder.

"Yes. And contrary to what Gren thinks, Royce's blood isn't the key to making the spell work either. It's mine."

"So, you can make anyone into a werewolf then?"

"That's something we don't know for sure," Royce answered. "Taryn was born half werewolf. Her father is a werewolf, and her mother was a mortal. She already had werewolf genes, just as Roxie had them through me."

"I also thought at first the spell only worked on me because Gren used Royce's blood, the sire of my bloodline, with the spell," Roxie added. "I was proven wrong when we first attempted the spell on Taryn using her father's blood. It was mine that changed her."

"Who is to say it only worked because you both possess werewolf genes to start with? I'm pretty sure Billie won't be having any relatives who happen to be werewolves popping out of the woodwork anytime soon as Taryn did," Royce said.

"That could be true, but what if it had no bearing on the spell's validity? You claimed Billie as your mate; wouldn't you rather take the chance and have the spell work than not and watch her grow old and die as you live on for a great many more years?" At Royce's groan, Roxie cringed. "Sorry. I forgot Billie doesn't yet know about the whole mate thing."

Billie didn't know what to feel. Listening to Royce and Roxie talk brought home to her that there was a lot more going on than the fact they were werewolves. She wasn't particularly thrilled to hear Roxie say Royce had claimed her as his mate. It sounded too caveman-ish for her liking.

Before Royce and Roxie could continue to argue whether or not the spell would work, Billie broke into the conversation. "Let's drop the spell business for a minute. Explain how Royce claimed me as his mate. As far as I knew, we haven't reached that permanent-commitment stage yet."

Roxie gestured for Royce to take over. He turned sideways so he could look at Billie. "When a male werewolf meets a female who is his mate, her scent sets off his mating urge. That alone tells him she is the one for him. It's not something he can ignore. It will ride him hard until he claims her."

"How exactly does he do that?"

"By making love to her."

"Let me get this straight. So when you made love to me for the first time, you knew you would be claiming me as your mate?"

Royce nodded. "Correct. That's when our souls joined. That's also why you started to feel uncomfortable being separated from me for long periods of time. Just as I do when I'm not around you."

Billie grew quiet as she mulled that bit of information over in her mind. She was a bit ticked off to learn all that after the fact, but she kept it to herself. Now wasn't the time to get angry. What was done was done. "Okay, now I know I'm not going crazy. For a while there, I thought I lost it when I started to miss you and it really hadn't been that long since I'd last seen you."

"It will get easier to handle with time."

"Next question. How can you be both Roxie and her mother's grandfather? You don't look that old."

Royce sighed. "Werewolves don't age the same as mortals. Our kind can live up to three thousand years old."

"Three thousand years old," Billie repeated softly. "How old are you, Royce?"

At first, Billie thought he wasn't going to answer when he didn't say anything right away. "I'm a little over fifteen hundred years old."

Billie took a few deep breaths as everything spun. *I'm not going to faint again, I'm not going to faint again.* She repeated that inside her mind like a mantra until the room righted itself once more. She had no idea why now of all times she turned into such a ninny. She was tough and prided herself on it. Stuff like that shouldn't be sending her into an old-fashioned case of the vapors. She was made of sterner stuff than that.

"Okay. All I can say to that is, holy shit, you're too old for me."

"That's what I said to Beowulf when he told me exactly how old he was," Roxie said with a laugh. "Beowulf is close in age to Royce."

Billie shook her head. "Unbelievable." She looked at her hands, which were clasped tightly on her lap. "So I'm mated to a fifteen-hundred-year-old werewolf. I'm only twenty-five, but you'll still outlive me by at least another thousand years. Unless I agree to let Roxie try the spell on me." She looked at Royce.

Royce reached out to take one of her hands. When she didn't unclasp them, he pulled away. "Even if you do let Roxie try the spell, Billie, there's still no guarantee it'll work. You being a mortal doesn't change how I feel about you. My first mate was a mortal as well."

Billie felt jealousy wash over her at Royce saying he'd already had a mate before her. It was an emotion she didn't normally feel. Of course he had to have had another woman who meant something to him, one he had to have had a child with. He couldn't have grandchildren without having a child first. Obviously, this other woman was no longer in his life. At least Billie hoped she wasn't.

"What happened to your first mate?"

A look of pain flashed across Royce's face. "Alicia was different. She could do things no one else in her village could. She had magic of her own. Because of that, the rest of the villagers shunned her, forcing her to live on her own away from them. A boy watched me go wolf one day outside her hut. When the others heard his story, they rose against Alicia. They accused her of witchcraft, dragged her out of her hut, and then burned her. She was able to save our daughter by hiding her inside when she'd heard the villagers approaching. I later found Nina. I was too late to save her mother, but I was able to save her. I stepped down as pack leader and left to raise my daughter where she would be safe. And I've watched over all her descendants since then."

Billie kicked herself for being jealous of a woman who had died hundreds of years before she'd even been born. That Royce had loved Alicia was apparent. The look of pain that had quickly passed over his face said it all. It also made her wonder if she had a chance of filling the empty place in his heart that had been created when Alicia had died. She couldn't help feeling she wouldn't be able to. Now that she knew the story about his first mate, she understood why he'd resisted her. He didn't want another to take Alicia's place. Only with the mating urge riding him, and unable to ignore it, had he claimed her as his own.

Suddenly feeling the need to get away, to try to sort this all out without Royce sitting next to her, Billie stood. "I have to go. I need to think this through before we go any further. It's an awful lot to just dump on my lap."

Royce stood beside her with a look of concern. "Are you going to be all right?"

She nodded. "I think so. I just can't be here right now, with you."

Not wanting to give Royce a chance to try to change her mind about leaving, Billie turned and quickly walked out of the house.

CHAPTER ELEVEN

She drove through the city for what felt like hours. Whenever she got the urge to turn around and go to Royce, Billie ruthlessly pushed it away. In the end, she found herself at a city park that was a couple of blocks away from his house. She sat in her car and watched a Little League baseball game that took place at the diamond.

It was only a matter of time before she sought Royce out. As he'd said, they were connected now. There was no going back even if she wanted to. Strangely enough, she found herself more accepting of the whole mate business, which was better than she'd expected. She'd never been in love before. At one time, she'd thought it was something she would never find, much less wanted. Too many years of having to watch her father be alone, all because he couldn't stop loving the woman who'd walked out on him, had been enough to make her leery of the whole thing. Now that she had time to think, to accept what was between her and Royce, she'd finally found it. The big question was whether Royce could ever love her in return. Even though he'd claimed her as his mate, Billie didn't think being in love had much to do with it. Being mated sounded as if it was more a physical need rather than an emotional one.

Then there was the spell that could change her into a werewolf, if she was willing to try it. It was not something she could easily reject out of hand. If there was even the slightest chance it would work, and if Royce could come to love her, it wouldn't be fair to them if she chose to stay a mortal. She really didn't relish the idea of growing old and feeble while he stayed forever young. He might say it would make no difference to him, but it would for her. It also was something she wasn't ready yet to try. She had her father and brothers to think about as well. They were all so close she couldn't keep something like her being turned into a werewolf from them. The whole not-aging thing would be kind of hard for them not to notice.

With a groan, Billie laid her head back onto the headrest. Her thoughts were still swirling around inside her mind, but at least she now had put some order to them. And one thing never changed — she still wanted Royce. He telling her what he truly was hadn't changed that fact.

Billie sat straighter, then started her car. It only took her a minute to reach Royce's house. She pulled into his driveway and then parked. Before she reached the front door, he opened it and waited for her in the doorway. The way he stood so stiffly with no emotion on his face, she knew he held himself back, waiting to see what her reaction would be.

Sure her face was as free of emotion as his, Billie came to stand in front of him. She lifted her head until she could look Royce in the eyes. "I'm done thinking. I don't care you're a werewolf. I still want you."

Royce growled with pure need as he swept her up into his arms and took her lips in a searing kiss. He carried her inside the house and then slammed the door closed behind them. Moving faster than any mortal man ever could, he had them upstairs and in his bedroom in a matter of seconds. He didn't stop kissing her until he had her on his bed with him stretched out on top of her.

He lifted his head and looked at her. "Are you sure you're okay with this, Billie? I did try to save you from it, but in the end, I couldn't resist you."

Billie swallowed the lump that suddenly formed in her throat. She'd known Royce hadn't wanted a mate, but it still hurt to hear him say it. "Yes. I've come to accept the fact you never wanted this in the first place. It didn't help that I forced myself on you, but what is done is done."

Royce scowled. "Is that what you think? That I didn't want you?" At Billie's nod, he touched his forehead to hers and shook his head. "You've got it wrong. When I saw you that first night at Wulf's Den and I got a good whiff of your scent, I knew you were my mate. All these years of being alone, I'd finally found another to spend my life with. Do you have any idea how many hundreds of years I've waited to find you?"

"Why did you fight it in the beginning? I thought you resisted me because you didn't want another to take Alicia's place?"

"It wasn't because of Alicia. I loved her, and she'll always have a special place in my heart, but I never planned on mourning her for the rest of my life. I know she wouldn't have wanted that. I just never found the right woman until now. It was you being a mortal that made me hold back. I'd already lost one mate who was one. I don't think I can handle it if something happened to you as well. Werewolf society can be pretty primal at times."

Billie snorted. "I can look after myself. Nothing is going to happen to me."

Royce kissed the tip of her nose. "I know that now, but as long as you're a mortal, I'm still going to worry. I do know this—I don't regret that I claimed you as my mate. I want you and only you. I only have to think about you and I get a hard-on. And I've done nothing but think about you since you left Belinda's house. I need to be inside you."

Billie moaned with need when Royce rocked his hips into hers. The hard length of his cock pressed against her through his jeans. The time for words was over. The need to have him buried inside her overrode everything else. She wrapped her hand around the back of his neck and brought his mouth down to hers. He hadn't pledged his undying love for her, but she hadn't wanted that, at least not today. After everything that had been said, it wouldn't have rung true for her. That he wanted her, needed her, was good enough for now.

She slanted her mouth across his and kissed him with all the desire that was coursing through her body. She sucked his bottom lip and bit down gently before she pushed her tongue inside. Royce wrapped his arms around her and rolled until they lay on their sides, facing each other. He pushed one hand under her shirt until he cupped her breast. Billie groaned as he pinched her nipple between his thumb and forefinger, rolling it between them.

She pulled back, breaking contact with his mouth. Royce's eyes glowed. She now knew what that meant. They were glowing with desire. The sight of them made her want him even more.

Billie nipped Royce's chin. "I'm going to make you howl before I'm through with you."

"Are you now? And how exactly are you going to do that?" Royce asked with a voice husky with desire.

"Oh, I can think of a few things." Billie pushed herself against him until he rolled onto his back. She rose and straddled his lap. "First, let's get rid of your clothes."

It didn't take her long to take off Royce's garments. Once they lay scattered on the floor, she made short work of removing her own. Leaning forward, she dragged her tongue across the spot where his neck and shoulder met. He stiffened and groaned.

"You like it when I bite you here." She licked the spot again. "Is that a werewolf thing?"

"Yes," Royce answered with a groan. "Female werewolves mark their mates with a bite in that place. It warns other females away."

"I see." She gently nipped him. "I'll have to remember that."

When she moved away without biting him, Royce groaned again. "Don't be a tease, Billie."

"I have no intentions of teasing you. Be patient."

She inched down his body. She pressed featherlight kisses to his chest and stomach. Once she reached his hard cock, she kissed the very tip. It jumped at the brush of her lips. Taking a firm hold of him, Billie licked him from base to tip before she swirled her tongue around the head. She repeated the process until Royce clutched at the bedsheets.

She decided she'd tortured him enough and opened her mouth and took as much of him as she could inside. As she sucked, she moved her hand up and down his thick shaft. His cock grew even harder. Wetness dripped down the inside of her thighs as Royce moaned and growled at the same time.

After taking her mouth off him, she moved back up his body. With her hands braced on either side of his head, she pushed her breasts forward, offering them to Royce. Greedily, he cupped one and sucked the nipple deep inside. It was Billie's turn to moan with pleasure. As he continued to suck, she rubbed her wet pussy up and down his cock until he was slick with her juices.

Completely aroused, Billie arched her hips until she could take the very tip inside her. She slowly rode it, teasing them. When Royce lifted his hips, trying to force her to take more of him, she pushed down until he was buried to the hilt. With him inside her so deeply the head of his cock touched her cervix, she rode him. She slid up and down, angling her hips with each stroke.

As her climax built, she squeezed her inner walls around his cock. She moved faster, inching ever closer to her release. At her peak, with her inner muscles clutching him, Billie leaned forward and bit Royce where he'd wanted her to bite him before. Applying enough pressure to break his skin caused his hips to buck beneath her as his orgasm tore through him. He howled, as she'd promised she would make him do, and he emptied himself deep inside her.

Satiated, Billie collapsed onto Royce's broad chest. With their bodies joined, he was still hard. She smiled against his skin. Without even asking, she knew that had to be another werewolf trait, and it wasn't one she was going to complain about.

* * * *

The next morning Billie decided she was going to take the day off. She wanted to spend it with Royce. They really hadn't taken much time to really get to know each other. So far, they'd spent a lot of it in bed rather than talking; not that she didn't expect to spend a great part of the day in bed making love. She didn't think she could ever get enough of him. Now that she knew what was behind her obsessive behavior, her very real need to be with him, she didn't feel quite so bad about it.

While Royce was in the shower, Billie called the gym and asked to talk to her father. He didn't keep her waiting on hold for very long. "Hey, Dad, I'm just calling to let you know I won't be coming into the gym today."

"Are you with Royce?"

"Yes. Why?"

"Your brothers told me what happened yesterday. That Royce attacked a prospective member you were showing around the gym."

"He was no prospective member. Royce knew Gren, the guy I was showing around. Royce wasn't so much attacking as warning Gren off."

"That was a warning? Slamming him into the wall with enough force to shatter the mirror? I'd say that was more of an attack."

"Royce had his reasons for the way he acted. He also said to tell you he would pay for the damages."

"I'm not worried about that. I'm more worried about you. Who is to say Royce won't turn on you one day."

Billie ground her teeth together to stop herself from saying something she would regret later. "Royce isn't like that. I know for a fact he would never do anything to hurt me." When she was met with silence on the other end, she forged on. "Not that it's any of your business, but Gren was showing too much interest in me. Royce told him to back off, and when he didn't, that's when he slammed Gren into the wall. Gren is the bad guy here, not Royce."

Her father sighed. "I'm sorry. I didn't mean to give you the third degree about what happened. I know you are a good judge of character, and if Royce was in any way abusive, you wouldn't be seeing him. I just worry about you sometimes."

There was a touch of sadness in his voice. Every once in a while, he would go into a bout of depression. It never lasted long, and he was usually able to pull himself out of it, but this time it seemed to be hitting him harder.

"What's going on, Dad? Are you feeling okay?"

"Never mind me. Enjoy your day off, and I'll see you tomorrow."

"I will. I have my cell phone with me. If you need anything, just call."

"I'll be fine. I'll tell your brothers you won't be in."

"Thanks, Dad."

Royce walked into the room, wearing nothing but a towel as he rubbed his wet hair with a second one just as Billie ended her call. He asked, "Everything okay? Your dad didn't mind you taking the day off work?"

"No, he didn't."

"Was he upset about the broken mirror?"

"Not really. He was more concerned about how you handled Gren. He was afraid you could turn on me like that one day."

"I hope you reassured him that I wouldn't do anything of the kind."

Billie smiled. "Of course. I can't have my family thinking badly of you, now can I? You are my mate, after all." She shifted over on the bed so Royce could sit beside her. "Speaking of mates, I've been meaning to ask you this. Does this mean we're engaged?"

Royce reached up and tucked a strand of her hair behind her ear. "No, Billie, it's much more than that. It's closer to being married. The only difference is the bond is stronger, more permanent."

"That's sort of what I figured. I guess I'd better have a talk with my father tomorrow and explain everything to him." She looked Royce in the eyes. "I mean *everything*."

"Do you want me to come along with you?"

"No. I think it would be best if I did this alone." Billie let out a chuckle when she thought of what her father's reaction would be to her explaining she was married to a werewolf. "I have a feeling Dad won't believe me, but I should be the one to break the news to him first. If I can't convince him that I'm not insane, then you can see him and go wolf. It worked for me; it'll work for him."

CHAPTER TWELVE

They ended up doing a lot of talking. Billie still found it hard to believe Royce was over a thousand years old, but when he talked about his past and how far back it went, it really brought it home for her. Listening to him tell stories of things he'd seen and done was like taking a walk through history, only he had firsthand knowledge of it.

One of the other things they discussed was their living arrangements. Now that Billie knew what being mated meant, Royce suggested she move into his house. She'd felt a momentary wave of panic. She'd tried to quickly hide it, but from his reaction he had to have seen the look of it that must have showed on her face, no matter how briefly it'd been there.

They were in the kitchen, trying to figure out what to make for lunch out of the things they could find in Royce's fridge. He put the food onto the counter and pulled her into his arms. "Am I moving too fast for you?"

She smiled sheepishly. "Maybe a little. I've never lived with a guy before, with the exception of my father and brothers, of course. To be honest, I never wanted to live with any of the guys I dated before you."

"Maybe I am going a little fast, but with Gren on the prowl again, I think it would be wise that you move in with me. The sooner, the better."

"You think he would actually follow me home and try something?"

"I know for a fact that if it suited his purposes, he would. How do you think he got hold of Roxie to try the spell on her? Beowulf was working at Wulf's Den that night. Roxie was alone at her place when Gren and two of his men broke in and took her."

"Gren is starting to sound like a real piece of work. Okay, I see your point."

"Grendel isn't known for his sparkling personality. He's been a thorn in Beowulf's side for many years."

Billie shook her head with wonder now that she knew Gren's name was actually Grendel. In high school she'd been required to read *Beowulf and Grendel* so she knew that old story very well. "Beowulf and Grendel. You do realize I'm not going to be able to look at Beowulf and not think about that story. Gren is obviously no troll."

"No, he's not. He's just a werewolf gone bad."

"All right. Let's do this then." Billie stepped out of Royce's arms. She gathered the food and then started to put it back into the fridge.

"Let's do what?" Royce watched as she put each item away with regret showing on his face. "I thought we were going to have something to eat."

"You're just as bad as my brothers. All you can think about is filling your stomach. We can pick something up on the way to my apartment. If you want me to move in, I'll move in. Today. Well, just my clothes today. We can move the rest of the stuff later."

"Are you sure you want to do that right now? I thought you'd want to at least tell your landlord that you would be moving out first."

Billie waved his concern away with a flick of her hand. "Don't worry about him. My dad is my landlord. He wanted to make sure when I moved out that I lived in a half-decent neighborhood. So he bought the apartment and let me rent it from him."

Royce gave her a double take. "Did I hear you correctly? Did Miss I-can-take-care-of-myself just say she let her father buy an apartment for her to live in?"

"Ha ha. Very funny." Billie threw one of the cheese slices she still held at Royce's head. She grumbled under her breath when he caught it in midair.

"Werewolf reflexes are quicker and better than a mortal's, my love." To prove it he caught the second slice of cheese with his other hand.

"Is that so? I guess I'd better give up since I'm so inferior to you."

She turned as if she were going to finish putting the food away. Once she heard Royce step closer, she quickly spun around and threw the tomato she held. Not expecting it, he didn't even try to catch it. She cringed as it splattered across his face. The tomato had been a little too ripe. Seeds and juice ran down his cheeks and dripped onto his shirt.

"So much for werewolf reflexes, huh?"

Royce wiped the remains of the tomato off his face. "You do have a penchant for throwing food, don't you?"

She valiantly tried to hold back her laughter, but in the end, she couldn't stop herself. The look of shock that had come over Royce's face when the tomato had hit had been priceless. As she laughed, he crossed his arms across his chest and stared at her. "I'm sorry. If only you could have seen your face."

"You think it's funny, do you? If I were you, instead of laughing, I'd be wondering right about now what I'm going to do to get you back."

Billie's laughter died. "What are you going to do?" She slowly inched around Royce as she headed for the kitchen doorway.

Like the wolf he was, he slowly stalked her. "I'm not sure yet, but I'll think of something."

As Royce lunged for her, Billie turned and ran out of the room. She only got as far as the living room before he caught up with her. Much to her dismay, he had her thrown over his shoulder before she realized his intention.

"I think I've lost count of the number of times I've seen Beowulf sling Roxie over his shoulder like this," Royce said. "I'm beginning to see the advantages of carrying one's mate in this position. One, it's a good way to keep you subdued, and two, I have a wonderful view of your gorgeous bottom." Keeping a firm hold of her legs, he turned his head and bit her nearest butt cheek.

Billie shrieked with indignation. "That isn't fair."

"All is fair in love and war," Royce said with a chuckle.

"I'll give you fair." She hung farther down on his back until she could grab hold of the waistband of his jeans. She tugged on it.

"What exactly do you think you're doing back there?"

"I'm trying to give you a wedgie," Billie replied as she yanked harder on Royce's pants.

"You can pull as hard as you like, but it isn't going to work. I'd have to be wearing underwear to get a wedgie, which I don't have on now."

Sure enough, Billie shoved her hand down inside the back of his jeans and all she encountered was the skin of his hard, muscled ass. Taking advantage of the situation, she gave it a good fondle. It flexed under her hand as Royce walked toward the stairs. It didn't dawn on her until after he'd thrown her onto the bed and loomed over her that he'd called her "my love" downstairs in the kitchen.

* * * *

It wasn't until much later that they finally went to Billie's apartment. She was now busily stuffing the clothes she couldn't fit into the two large suitcases she owned into black garbage bags when Royce's cell phone rang. Quiet she was not, so she didn't blame him for going to her living room to take the call.

She'd just closed the top of the last garbage bag when he returned. "What's up?"

"That was Belinda. She's invited us over for supper, along with Beowulf, Roxie, Wade, and Taryn. It's supposed to be a welcome-to-the-family kind of meal for you."

Billie took hold of one of the suitcases. "That was good timing. I'm all finished. It may take a couple trips to get everything downstairs, though." Along with the two suitcases, she'd filled three garbage bags.

Royce grabbed the other suitcase as well as one of the garbage bags and then followed her to the apartment door. "I must say your taste in luggage leaves much to be desired."

"It isn't as if I can damage anything. And if they get a little wrinkled, I'll just throw them into the dryer for a quick spin, and they'll be as good as new."

Before she could pull open the door, Royce leaned in and

kissed her passionately. He straightened and smiled. "Whatever you do, Billie, don't ever change. I love you just the way you are."

Billie forgot to breathe for a few seconds. That was the second time Royce had used the *L* word about her. As he proceeded to walk into the hallway as if he hadn't just professed his love for her, she quickly pulled herself back together and followed.

"What did you just say, Royce?"

He casually pushed the down button for the elevator. "I said don't ever change."

"Not that. What did you say after that?"

He turned to look at her. "That I love you the way you are."

"You love me?" Billie asked quietly.

"Of course I do." Royce shook his head and chuckled. "I can see you're surprised by this."

The elevator dinged, and the doors slid open. There was a woman already inside. Royce told her they would catch another one as he pulled Billie off to the side. He waited until the elevator door was closed before he spoke again. "I sometimes forget you don't know all that much about werewolves. I couldn't have truly mated with you if I didn't love you."

"How could you have known you loved me? You only knew me for a few days. I figured being mated was more a physical bond."

"It is when two mates are first drawn to each other, but once they complete the mating, being in love is generally the outcome. How could you not love the person you've forged such a strong bond with? Only on rare instances, and I mean really rare, does a mating end up being one-sided where only one of the mates bonds their soul to the other and it isn't returned."

Billie threw herself into Royce's arms with enough force to make him stagger. Unfortunately, one of the garbage bags was behind him. Unable to catch himself, he fell over backward. She ended up sprawled on top of him.

She quickly sat up. "I'm so sorry, Royce. Are you okay?"

"I'm fine. I just wasn't expecting it."

"Good." Billie cupped his face and gave Royce a hard kiss. "I love you too."

Royce smiled. "Now that we've both told each other how we feel, I think it would be a good idea if we got off the floor. I'm sure your neighbors wouldn't be exactly thrilled to see us in this position."

"I don't mind at all, young man."

Billie looked up to find her neighbor, Mrs. Taylor, standing in her open doorway, which she and Royce happened to be in front of, watching them with a twinkle in her eye. Mrs. Taylor was eighty, if she were a day. Billie felt her face flush at being caught in such a predicament by her elderly neighbor. She hurriedly slid off him and stood.

"Sorry, Mrs. Taylor. I forgot myself there for a moment."

The older lady laughed. "No need to apologize, my girl." She turned to gaze at Royce as he came to stand next to Billie. "If I were fifty years younger, I might have done the same thing. He's quite a looker." She looked back at Billie. "You'd better hold on to this one. He's definitely a keeper."

"I intend to," Billie assured her.

After Mrs. Taylor closed her apartment door, Billie pushed the elevator button. As she waited for one to arrive, she found herself unable to stop the large grin that formed on her lips. Royce loved her. That left one thing still up in the air — whether she should try the spell or not. It was a decision she couldn't make lightly. In a way, it'd worked out to her advantage that she would be seeing Roxie and Taryn later. She could get the lowdown on exactly what to expect if she went through with it. Talking to them and then going to have a talk with her father the next day, she figured she'd be more than ready to make her decision.

* * * *

After making room in his closet and emptying out a couple of dresser drawers for Billie to use until they moved her furniture from her apartment, Royce lay propped up on the bed as she put away her clothes. He was content, something he hadn't felt in a very long time. Billie filled a void inside him, one that'd been created when Alicia had died. Raising Belinda as his daughter had filled some of it, but not all. Then she'd grown up, gotten married, and had a family of her own, leaving him to live alone once again. Now he had Billie.

Even though he was happy and felt as if his life was back on track, there was still one niggling question that wouldn't go away. Yes, he had Billie as his mate, but for how long? A mortal's lifespan was so much shorter than a werewolf's. He wanted her with him for the thousand or so more years he was sure to have left. The spell was the only thing that could give them that, if it would work on her. The decision would have to be hers, though. He would never push her into to it if it wasn't something she wanted, but it would make things better for them. It would also give her a fighting chance if Gren, or any other werewolf of his ilk, ever decided to go through her to get to him. As a mortal, she wouldn't stand a chance.

Lost in thought, Royce at first didn't notice Billie had finished and now stood by the bed, looking down at him. "What had you off in la-la land?"

"Nothing."

"It must have been important enough you didn't hear me ask you what time we had to be at Belinda's. You were so deep in thought I bet I could have taken off all my clothes and done a dance and you wouldn't have noticed."

Royce wrapped an arm around her waist and pulled her onto the bed with him. "I think I would have noticed that. You definitely would have gotten my attention."

"I should hope so. I don't dance naked for just anyone, you know."

"The only person you'll be dancing naked for from now on will be me." He buried his face into the crook of Billie's neck and growled as he held her closer. "Maybe you'd like to do a little naked dancing right now."

Billie arched her neck to give him better access to it as he dragged his tongue along her skin. "What time do we have to be at Belinda's?"

He moved down her body and pressed wet kisses against the hollow of her throat. "We have to be there by six." She shifted against him as she turned her head to look at the bedside clock.

"If that's the case, we're going to be late if we don't get a move on. It's almost six now. So no, there's no time for hanky-panky."

"Not even for a quickie?" Royce pinched her nipple through her shirt.

She slapped his hand away. "No. You can't be that desperate.

We did spend most of the morning making love and most of the night as well."

"So? I'm sure Belinda won't mind if we show up a little late."

Billie shoved at his chest. "Behave, Royce. You said it was a meal to welcome me into the family, and it would be rude on my part to show up late."

Royce knew there was no point in pushing the issue. Once Billie made up her mind, she stuck to it. "You win." He let go of her. She got off the bed with hooded eyes. "That means you owe me a naked dance."

"You might come to regret that. I can't dance worth a crap."

"As long as you're naked and moving, I couldn't care less."

Billie rolled her eyes and shook her head. "Whatever. I'm just going to clean up a bit; then I'll be ready to leave."

Once she left the room, Royce tugged at the front of his pants, trying to make room for the hard-on he now sported. He hoped Belinda hadn't decided to do a large, elaborate meal. If she had, it was going to be a very long evening for him.

CHAPTER THIRTEEN

It was exactly six o'clock when Royce and Billie arrived at Belinda's house. Her husband, Lucas, greeted them at the door. Opening it wide, he ushered them inside. "Nice to see you again, Royce. And this must be Billie. I'm Lucas, Belinda's husband."

Billie shook the hand Lucas offered her. "Yes, I'm Billie. Nice to meet you."

Lucas had to be in his fifties, but like her father, he took good care of himself. His dark brown hair was graying at the sides. His gray eyes looked warm and friendly. Billie took an instant liking to him.

"You are the first to arrive," Lucas said as he led them to the living room. "Belinda will be pleased to see at least two of our guests showed up on time."

"See," Royce whispered into her ear, "we would have been all right showing up a bit late. We could have had our quickie and probably still would have beaten the others here."

Billie casually took a step back and stomped on Royce's instep. He made a satisfying yelp as he picked up his foot and rubbed the offended area. When Lucas turned to see what the matter was, she smiled. "Never mind Royce. He sometimes doesn't watch where he's stepping."

Lucas gave her a knowing smile. "It wouldn't be the first time

Royce has had a woman in the family make sure he stopped stepping where he shouldn't have. Roxie just did it in a more vulnerable spot on his anatomy."

"Well, then I'll have to tell Roxie that she doesn't have to worry about Royce anymore. I'm more than capable of keeping him on the straight and narrow."

"I just love it when people talk about me as if I'm not even in the room," Royce said mildly. "And thanks for sticking up for your fellow male, Lucas."

The other man chuckled. "You're welcome. You two can make yourselves comfortable while I tell Belinda you're here."

Royce and Billie had only just sat when the front door opened. They heard Roxie call out to her parents just before she walked into the living room. Beowulf, Wade, and Taryn were with her.

Seeing the two of them on the couch, Roxie said, "It looks as if the gang is all here. Mom will be pleased that she won't have to keep the supper waiting."

"Yes, I'm happy to see you all are here." Belinda gave Roxie a kiss on the cheek. "The food is ready, so if everyone would like to come into the dining room, we can eat."

There was enough space at the large dining room table to seat everyone comfortably. As the smell of perfectly cooked roast beef hit her, Billie's stomach growled. Sitting next to Royce, she eyed the large amount of food on the table. There were mashed potatoes, peas, corn, and gravy to go along with not one but two roasts of beef. At first, she thought Belinda had cooked two of them because the men were big eaters, but it wasn't until Beowulf carved one roast while Lucas carved the other did she see the one Beowulf worked on was practically raw on the inside. Billie liked her roast beef on the pink side, but she didn't think she would be able to stomach meat quite that undercooked.

Roxie was quick to assure her. "I can see you eyeing the roast Beowulf is carving, Billie. Don't worry, it isn't for us. That one is for Beowulf, Wade, and Royce to eat. Werewolves like their meat to barely touch a pan before eating it."

"You're a werewolf now. Don't you like your meat that way as well?"

"Good God, no. That's disgusting." Roxie shuddered. "I think you have to be born a werewolf to be able to eat something that raw and enjoy it."

"Same here," Taryn added. "I like my meat cooked the way it's supposed to be."

Billie filed that bit of information away. She was glad she wouldn't have to worry that she would start craving raw meat if she became a werewolf as well.

Once everyone had food on their plates, Taryn opened four bottles of wine that came from her winery. Billie thought maybe that was a lot for the number of people there. As the meal progressed, and the werewolves of the company seemed able to drink it as if it were water and have the wine not go to their heads, she realized the four bottles weren't going to last long.

She turned to look at Royce as he drained his fourth glass of wine. So far, she'd only had one. "Am I going to have to drag your drunken ass home like I do Hayes's?"

Royce reached for the nearest bottle and then refilled their glasses. "I'm fine, Billie. Alcohol doesn't affect us the same as it does mortals. I would have to drink a vast amount to come anywhere near to being drunk."

From the amount of wine Roxie and Taryn had consumed, Billie figured alcohol didn't affect them either now they were werewolves. "Good to know. I've had more than my share of dragging drunken men home to last me a lifetime."

At the end of the meal, Belinda cleared her throat to get everyone's attention. When all eyes were on her, she spoke. "I want to say how pleased I am that Billie is part of our family. She has been a long time in coming. Not only has my father found his mate, but I now have a stepmother."

Billie had just taken a big sip of wine when Belinda started speaking. She ended up spraying it across the table when she heard the word stepmother come out of Belinda's mouth.

Hastily grabbing her napkin, Billie wiped the wine off her chin. "Stepmother?" Her voice came out in a croak.

"Of course you're my stepmother, dear. Royce, after all, is my father, the only father I've ever known."

"I guess that makes you my grandmother, Billie," Roxie cheerfully added. At Royce's hard stare, she was quick to say, "Which I will never call you. I'll just save the grandparent name calling for Royce."

Billie took some deep, calming breaths. She'd known about the family connection between Roxie's family and Royce, but she hadn't put herself into that equation. She should have realized that being Royce's mate meant she was now a stepmother and a grandmother. Taking hold of her wineglass, she drained the rest of it in one big gulp.

Royce worriedly looked at her. "Are you okay, Billie?"

She nodded. "Yes. I hadn't thought this all through."

"Here. Have another glass of wine, but this time sip it."

As Royce filled her glass once more, Billie could only guess what her father was going to say when he learned she was not only "married," but also had a stepdaughter and a stepgranddaughter.

* * * *

After the table was cleared, Belinda suggested Roxie take Billie and Taryn outside to sit in the backyard while she did the dishes. The men were already talking among themselves. Billie readily agreed, thinking this would be the perfect time to find out more about the spell.

Once they were seated at the patio table, Taryn poured them each another glass of wine from the full bottle she'd brought outside with her. Billie was already feeling a bit on the tipsy side but figured one more glass wouldn't put her under. Taking a sip, she looked at the sky. It was a beautiful night. There wasn't a cloud to be seen.

"So, Billie, how are you handling being mated to a werewolf?" Roxie asked. "I know we've dumped a lot on you the last couple of days. It can be a bit overwhelming."

Billie turned to look at the other two women. "You could say that." Her voice held a trace of humor. "I never expected to be a grandmother at twenty-five."

"I guess not. Though I must say you handled finding out about Royce being a werewolf remarkably well. I wish I could say all I did was get a little lightheaded when Beowulf finally told me."

"You didn't take the news well?"

Roxie laughed. "Hardly. I had Beowulf go wolf to prove he told the truth when he finally revealed he was a werewolf. At the time, I hadn't known I had inherited Alicia's magic. Having no idea what I was doing, I accidentally used it on Beowulf."

"What did you do to him?"

"I made it so he was stuck in his wolf form for twenty-four hours, which wasn't a pleasant experience for him. Luckily for Beowulf, Royce realized what I'd done and reassured him it was only temporary. I guess Alicia had done the same thing to him at one time."

"What about you, Taryn?" Billie asked the other woman. "Did you take the news well?"

"Not really, I'm afraid. I called Wade a freak of nature and locked myself in my bedroom."

"I can see what you mean about me taking the news rather well." Billie took another sip of wine. "I guess I should direct this next question to Taryn since you, Roxie, didn't have a choice in the matter. When you found out about the spell, did you hesitate or were you able to quickly decide that you wanted to try it?"

Taryn shook her head. "I didn't even need to think about it. As soon as Wade told me about it, I wanted Roxie to try it on me."

"I see. I guess I'm different in that respect. I still haven't made up my mind. I know there's a huge advantage to trying it. I wouldn't have to worry about growing old and dying while Royce stays young, but there is one thing that is holding me back—my family. I have no idea how they'll react."

"That is something you have to consider," Taryn said. "See for me, I didn't have to take that into consideration. My mother died when I was three, and my uncle who raised me, died a year before I met Wade. And there's also the fact my father was a werewolf, who doesn't look any older than I do, I might add. It was a no-brainer. I wanted to be just like Wade and my father."

"You know Royce would never force you to try the spell if it really wasn't what you wanted, Billie," Roxie quickly added.

"I know he wouldn't, but I can't help feeling that if I don't try it, I would be cheating him out of something. That I would be holding back something he really wants. I know me being mortal has him worried I won't be able to protect myself if anything should happen, which is completely understandable, considering what happened to Alicia."

Roxie nodded, then said, "Now I'm not trying to sway

whatever decision you make, but I can see where Royce is coming from. To be frank, a mortal is no match for a werewolf. Compared to other mortal women, you are strong. As a werewolf, you would be twice as strong. And there are some big advantages besides being stronger. Your hearing will be a lot better; same with your eyesight and sense of smell. And being able to go wolf, able to run free, is like nothing you've ever experienced before."

Billie smiled at Roxie. "I guess being able to shift into a half-human, half-wolf form would definitely have its advantages for you as well. Royce mentioned something about you ruling over the packs too."

Roxie was quick to agree. "Being able to take on that form does give me the upper hand, but there are times when ruling over the packs isn't much fun. For instance, now I have Gren to contend with once again. I wish he could have just stayed in his hole and left everyone alone, but I guess that was asking too much."

"What are you going to do?"

Roxie shrugged. "There's not much I can do now. He really hasn't done anything. Right now, all we can do is watch him. If he does move against Royce, then something will have to be done to put him in his place."

Billie didn't ask what exactly would be done to Gren that would "put him in his place." Given the way Royce had reacted to Gren at the gym, she had a feeling werewolf laws were a little less civilized than mortal ones.

A little while later, the men and Belinda joined them. Billie didn't miss how Beowulf and Wade sat next to their mates, holding Roxie and Taryn protectively under their arms. Nor did she miss the fact Royce did the same to her. It felt good. To know that as long as she was next to him, he would do everything in his power to make sure no harm came to her. Some women would have taken it as an insult, that in this day and age a woman didn't need to have a man to look after her, but for Billie, it was a nice change. She was perfectly capable of looking out for herself. With the amount of self-defense she'd learned, she could bring down most men twice her size. The whole aspect of not having to use it if she didn't want to and that she could rely on Royce if such a situation ever arose made her feel cherished. And it made her love him even more because of it.

* * * *

Gren hauled the unconscious body of the man he'd chosen to be his next guinea pig over his shoulder and then shoved him into the backseat of his car. After getting into the front, he headed for the place he'd acquired to perform his little tests. It'd been relatively easy to lure the mortal. The man had fallen for the female werewolf Gren had sent to entice the man outside. Not that the mortal knew what she was. All he'd cared about was that she was beautiful and seemed willing to spend the night with him.

Instead of taking him to her place, the woman had led the mortal to the back alley behind the club where Gren had been waiting. A quick bash to the back of the head, and the mortal was his. The woman, who had been a part of his pack before their numbers had dwindled to almost nothing, had accepted the money he'd offered and then left him with his prize.

Now all that was left to do was to get some of Royce's blood. He wouldn't hand it over of his own free will, but that wasn't going to deter Gren. There were ways to get the blood other than asking.

CHAPTER FOURTEEN

Royce waved at Billie as she pulled away from the house, then waited until her car was out of sight before he stepped inside. She was on her way to her family's gym to meet with her father. Before she'd left, he'd suggested he go with her in case her dad didn't believe what she had to tell him, but she had said no. She thought it would be better if she talked to him alone first. At least she wasn't going to say anything about his being a werewolf to her brothers yet. He could imagine what their reactions would be. He had a feeling just learning that their baby sister was "married" was going to be hard enough for them to handle.

Royce headed for the stairs. Since Billie would be moving her furniture in soon, he decided there was no time like the present to make some room for it. He was going to start upstairs in their bedroom. It would also help keep him distracted while she was away.

He was about to start up the stairs when he caught the scent of another in the room. Curling his upper lip in a snarl, he turned to face the intruder. "Get out of my house, Gren."

The other werewolf leaped at him. Royce caught him in midair and grappled him to the floor. Gren went down hard, but he somehow managed to take Royce down with him. Royce rolled into a crouched position. An evil smile played on the other man's face a split second before Gren charged him once again. This time something entered his side as Gren slammed into him.

Gren pushed Royce away and got to his feet. "You made it too easy for me, lone wolf. You really shouldn't leave your back door unlocked. There's no telling who might just walk in and decide to take whatever they want."

The room tilted at an alarming angle as Royce fell to his knees. Looking down, he pulled out the syringe that was still in his side. The plunger had been pushed in all the way. It fell from his fingers as his world started to fade. Fighting to stay conscious, he shook his head.

"Don't worry, I didn't poison you. You're just going to sleep for a while." Gren came to stand over him. "You left me no other choice."

Unable to fight whatever drug Gren had injected into his system, Royce slumped onto his side. His last thought before everything went black was that Billie was safe. That was all that mattered.

* * * *

The gym was quiet when Billie arrived. There were only a dozen or so members working out on the gym floor. Three of her brothers were already there. Eli met up with her as she headed for her desk. "How was your day off, Billie? Did you spend all of it with Royce?"

"It was good, and yes, I did. Is Dad in?"

"Yeah, he's in his office. Why?"

"I just need to talk to him."

"About what?"

Billie put her purse into her desk drawer and then slammed it shut with more force than was necessary. "Don't start, Eli. Where's Finn, by the way?"

Eli chuckled. "Finn got lucky last night at Wulf's Den. He managed to hook up with this really hot chick. So I don't imagine he'll be in until later. He's probably still recovering from a hot night of sex."

Billie rolled her eyes and walked around Eli, then headed for their father's office. "I really didn't need to know all that. I was just curious where Finn was since you two seem practically joined at the hip."

"We aren't that bad."

"Eli, you two live together. You couldn't even move out of the house and get separate places of your own."

"Hey, we only did that to save money. It's not as if we plan to live together for the rest of our lives," Eli said defensively.

Billie stopped and kissed Eli on the cheek. "See, not much fun to have a sibling put you through the third degree, is it? I know you and Finn have the whole twin thing going on."

Eli scowled. "Fine. You made your point. I'll back off. After what happened with Royce the other day, we're all a little worried about you."

"Don't be. Now get out of here and leave me alone so I can talk to Dad."

"You're still not going to tell me what you want to talk to him about, are you?" When she narrowed her gaze, Eli held up his hands and slowly backed away. "I'm going, I'm going."

After a quick knock on the door, Billie walked into her father's office. He'd been sitting slumped in his chair, staring off into space, but when he saw her, he sat up and gave her a half smile. She noticed the dark circles under his eyes and how haggard he looked. Whatever was going on with him obviously kept him up at night.

Billie sat in the chair in front of his desk. "Have to say, Dad, you look like crap. What's going on?"

"That's my girl, always to the point. I'm just not sleeping well these days." He quickly changed the subject. "What can I do for you?"

Now that she was there, Billie didn't know where to start. She wondered if maybe she should have taken Royce up on his offer to come along, but it was too late for second thoughts. With a deep breath, she jumped in feet first.

"Okay, first of all, I'm moving out of my apartment. So as my landlord, you've just received your notice. I'm moving in with Royce." When her father opened his mouth to interrupt, Billie shook her head. "Please, Dad, let me finish first; then you can say whatever it is you want." Once he leaned back in his chair and nodded for her to continue, she pushed on. "I know you think this is all very sudden, but it really was meant to be. Now here is where you're going to think I've lost all my marbles, but I really haven't. Royce is different. I mean really different. He's a werewolf, Dad. Not the scary werewolf from horror movies, though. He can only change into a wolf and his eyes glow and he can make all the sounds a wolf does. I'm getting off track with all that, but Royce knew I was his mate the first time we met and he smelled my scent. To make a long story short, he claimed me as his mate, and our souls have joined, which means I don't like being away from him, and he doesn't like being away from me. That's why I've been so out of sorts for the last couple of days when I've been here working. And since I am his mate, that means we're basically married. So you have a new son-in-law."

As she'd spoken her father's face had lost all emotion. Once she stopped talking, he just continued to stare at her, not reacting to anything she'd said. Billie worried that maybe it hadn't been such a good idea to just dump it all on him like that.

"Dad? Are you going to say anything at all?"

"Royce is a werewolf?" His voice held no emotion either.

"Yes. I know it's hard to believe. I didn't believe him at first when he told me, but seeing him go wolf was more than enough to convince me he wasn't crazy. He's willing to show you if you don't think I'm telling the truth."

Her father slowly shook his head. "That won't be necessary. I believe you."

Billie hadn't expected him to be so accepting, nor had she expected him to look so sad about it either. He seemed to withdraw into himself. "Dad, you're scaring me here. This is not at all how I pictured you would react."

He sighed deeply. "I guess it's time you knew. I wanted to keep this from you, but after hearing you tell me Royce is a werewolf, you should know."

"Know about what?" A chill ran down her spine. She couldn't help but feel that what her father was going to tell her next would have a profound effect on her life as she knew it.

"It has to do with your mother, Billie."

"What about her? She took off when I was a baby, and that was the last you heard or saw of her."

"That's only what I told you when you were old enough to start asking about your mother."

"You mean that isn't what happened?"

"No. I'm afraid it's much worse than just your mother abandoning you as a baby. You see, your mom has her own gift as you do, except with her, she can see things before they actually happen. Unlike you, she isn't a strong person. She always hated her ability to see into the future. It affected her. It didn't come to her very often, but when it did, sometimes it wasn't something she wanted to see. Once you kids started coming, her gift seemed to go away. She was happy that she no longer had it, but it really hadn't disappeared. When you were about a month old, she had a vision. I don't know exactly everything she saw, but it caused something to snap inside her." Her father's voice cracked with the emotion. Once he brought himself back together, he continued. "I came home from the gym one day to find all hell had broken loose. Your brothers were screaming, yelling at your mother to stop. I found Keegan desperately trying to pull your mother off you. She had a pillow over your face, Billie. She tried to smother you. If I hadn't have come home when I had, you would have died that day."

Billie gripped the arms of her chair until her knuckles turned white. "Why did she do it? What did she see?"

"After I pulled her off you, she kept repeating over and over again that she couldn't allow her baby to turn into a wolf."

Billie's face had to have turned white. She was in shock. Her mother had seen her as a werewolf? "Where is she now, Dad?"

"She's in a place where she can be looked after properly. She never came back mentally, and there was no way I could leave her alone with you ever again."

"She's in a mental institution?"

"No. It's more like a home for people who have mental conditions. She's well taken care of."

"She's been there all these years, and you never said a word to me about it?"

"I wanted to protect you from this. And if it wasn't for what you just told me, I probably would have taken it to my grave. Even your brothers swore they would never tell you the truth. Your mother took a turn for the worst a couple of days ago. They've had to heavily sedate her almost around the clock. She keeps screaming about her baby being turned into a wolf. That the wolf will kill, and she doesn't want her baby to be a killer."

Billie sucked in a sharp breath. "The spell. She must have seen something about the spell."

"What spell?"

"There's an ancient spell that can turn a mortal into a werewolf. It has only worked twice before, but it has been offered to me so I can be like Royce. If Mom saw me change into a wolf, then the spell will work on me."

"Are you saying you would willingly want to become a werewolf?"

"You have to understand something. Werewolves live very long lives. Royce is over fifteen hundred years old, and he can live to be three thousand. Without the spell, I'll die long before he does. I can't let him mourn me for the next thousand or so years when there's a chance I can be with him until the end."

"You love Royce that much?"

"Yes. I came here to get your blessing, if you want to call it that."

Her father got up and came around the desk until he stood in front of her chair. He took her hand and helped her onto her feet. He pulled her into a hug. Billie closed her eyes and leaned into him.

"You have my blessing. I don't really understand all of it, but I'm sure you'll explain it better after it's all done. Just know I love you and want you to be happy."

"I promise I will."

"I hope you don't think any less of me because I didn't tell you the truth about your mother."

Billie looked at her father. "Never. I know you did it to protect me, but I'm a big girl now. It was a shock to hear what she'd tried to do, but I can handle it. I have a feeling it affected the boys more than it will me."

"It did, sorry to say. After that day, all four of them became fiercely protective of you. They haven't grown out of it, I'm afraid."

"I'm used to it, and now I can understand their motives."

Stepping back, her father let her go. "Get out of here and go be with your husband. I can't believe I said that."

"Believe me, Dad, it took a lot of getting used to for me as well."

After giving her father a kiss, Billie left his office. There was no point in trying to work. Now that she'd made up her mind about the spell she needed to tell Royce. There was no way she would be able to concentrate on anything until she did.

* * * *

Billie pushed open the front door and called out to Royce. "Royce, I'm home."

When she didn't get an answer, she walked to the bottom of the stairs and called up to him. He still didn't answer. Thinking maybe he was outside in the backyard, she headed to the kitchen. The door that led to the backyard stood wide open. Billie walked onto the deck and looked around. She couldn't see any sign of Royce anywhere. She wondered where he could be. He had to be home. His car was still in the driveway, and the front door had been unlocked. As she walked back into the kitchen, she took her cell phone out of her purse and dialed his. After the first couple of rings, she heard it ringing somewhere inside the house. Following the sound, she found it sitting on the dining room table along with his keys.

A feeling of something not being right crept over her as she ended the call. It was when she walked back into the front entrance hallway that her foot kicked something that had been lying on the floor. Billie bent down and picked it up. It was an empty syringe, the type diabetics used. She knew it wasn't Royce's. He'd told her werewolves rarely, if ever, got sick, and they didn't suffer from the diseases mortals did. So the big question was, how had the syringe ended up in the house in the first place?

As her uneasiness grew, Billie did a thorough search of the house. Nothing looked out of place. It almost appeared as if Royce had just walked out of it, but finding the syringe said otherwise. Once again on the lower level, she took a deep breath to stop herself from panicking. It wasn't as if she couldn't find him no matter where he was. She closed her eyes and concentrated on his face, focusing on it. A second later, she gasped. She'd seen exactly where he was, and he wasn't alone. Gren had not only taken

Royce; he'd also taken her brother Finn.

CHAPTER FIFTEEN

Royce tried to lift his head off the floor, but it felt as if it were a lead weight. Groaning, he let it fall back down. Whatever drug Gren had used, it was doing a number on him. His mouth was dry as sandpaper, and when he cracked open his eyes, he had a hard time focusing on anything. He tried to move his arms and found he couldn't. They were tightly bound behind his back. He didn't have to look at the rope to know there would be silver threads mixed in with the fiber. Silver didn't harm werewolves as the horror movies so often portrayed, but it did hamper a werewolf's ability to go wolf and hold that form. Basically, he was trussed up like a Thanksgiving turkey, and there wasn't a damn thing he could do about it.

He strained against his bonds and tried to sit up. The movement caused his head to spin. He closed his eyes until the wave of dizziness subsided. He opened them again when he heard a shuffling noise behind him. He lifted his head and looked in the direction it had come from. He swore under his breath once he was finally able to focus on the only other occupant in the room. Billie's brother Finn was bound hand and foot. There was also a gag over his mouth.

Finn shuffled forward on his backside across the floor until he was able to get to where Royce lay. He mumbled something through the gag that Royce didn't understand. When he didn't respond, Finn jerked his head in an upward motion a couple of times. *That* Royce understood. He tried once again to get into an upright position. This time, Finn inched closer and used his shoulder to help prop him up. Royce leaned against him, panting as the room spun.

After a few minutes, the dizziness faded again. Royce turned his head toward Finn. "Now don't think I'm going to try to kiss you, because I'm not. I'm going to see if I can pull the gag off." He took hold of it at the side of Finn's face with his teeth, then tugged. It didn't take long for him to pull it away from the other man's mouth, leaving the gag to hang around his neck.

Finn swallowed and cleared his throat a couple times before he tried to speak. "We need to get the hell out of here."

Royce quickly scanned the area. From what he could see, they appeared to be locked in some kind of storage room. There were a few boxes piled in the far corner, and there weren't any windows. The only light came from the florescent lighting on the ceiling.

"How long have I been out?"

"An hour, maybe more. Where's Billie? That asshole better not have taken her as well."

"Billie's safe. She'd already left for the gym when Gren arrived. How long have you been here?"

"Since last night. He bashed me over the head out back at Wulf's Den. He had some woman lure me out there. What the hell does he want with me? I can understand Gren taking you since you two don't exactly get along, but I haven't done anything to warrant this."

"I assume Gren filled you in on some of our bad history. I think I have a pretty good guess as to why he took you. You're to be his lab rat."

"What?"

Royce didn't get a chance to answer Finn. He heard the sound of the lock being turned on the other side of the door before it was pushed open. Gren walked into the room. He nodded when he saw Royce was awake.

"I'm happy to see I didn't kill you with that tranquilizer, lone wolf. One never knows how much to use."

"I'd have to take your word for it since I've never resorted to using such a cowardly way to subdue an opponent," Royce said blandly.

Gren snarled and snapped his teeth at him. "Watch your mouth. You're not exactly in a position to be taunting me."

"We both know perfectly well you won't do anything to me. At least not until you try the spell again."

"That might be true, but if your blood turns out not to be the key, I see no reason to keep you around. It would be to my advantage to do away with one who has been a thorn in my side more than once, but the spell will have to wait. I can see you're still feeling the effects of the drug. I'll wait until it's completely out of your system. I don't want to take the chance that it would in some way affect the outcome of my little experiment." Gren walked forward and grabbed a handful of Finn's hair. He pulled his head back as he looked down at him. "Especially when I have such a fine specimen here to try it on. This one will make an excellent werewolf."

"Werewolf?" Finn asked with a harsh laugh. "Now I really know you're nuts. Werewolves don't exist, and you sure as hell can't change me into one."

"You mortals are all the same." Gren let go of Finn's hair. "If something is beyond what you consider the realm of possibility, you think it doesn't exist. In this case, you're wrong."

Royce growled loudly in warning as Gren went wolf and lunged for Finn's throat. Gren's sharp teeth missed the other man's jugular by mere inches. Finn didn't move a muscle. The widening of his eyes was the only sign that gave away his uncertainty.

"Back off, Gren."

Gren shifted to his human form. "What do you think you're going to do, lone wolf? As long as you're bound in those ropes, you can't go wolf, and you know it." He chuckled as Finn looked at Royce with shock on his face. "It looks as if I've given you both something to talk about after I leave. How about I make it even more interesting?" He waited until he had Finn's full attention. "Royce has claimed your sister as his mate. That means she has bound herself to a werewolf. How do you feel about your sister letting one of my kind between her legs every night?" Gren left the room, once more locking the door behind him.

Finn roughly shoved Royce away. Royce just barely managed

to catch himself before he lost what balance he had. Finn's gaze raked his face. "He's telling the truth, isn't he? You're both werewolves. Christ, your eyes are glowing just as his did before he changed into a wolf. You're an animal like Gren."

Royce shook his head. "Yes, I'm a werewolf, but don't compare me to Gren. He's just a bad example of one. Just like you mortals, we have good and bad werewolves."

"Does Billie know what you are? Or have you been keeping it a secret from her?"

"Billie knows now what I am. She has accepted me as her mate."

"Bullshit. Billie wouldn't sleep with an animal."

Having reached his limit of how many insults he could take from Billie's brother, Royce growled threateningly. "I've had just about enough of you calling me an animal, boy. I love your sister, and she feels the same way about me. Get used to it."

"If what you say is true, then we have an even bigger problem than trying to get ourselves free. I assume you know about my sister's ability to find anyone?"

A chill ran down Royce's spine. "Yes."

"Well then, you know once Billie finds out both of us are missing, she's going to 'look' for us. And she'll know exactly where we are."

Finn was right. Unless they could somehow manage to get away from Gren, Billie was bound to show up looking for them. And when she did, she would come face-to-face with Gren.

* * * *

Billie rolled down her car window and pushed the button on the panel that buzzed up to the large house at the end of the gated drive. Once the gate swung open to allow her entry, she quickly drove through it. Any other time she would have been impressed by the landscaped grounds and large mansion, but she was too focused on what she needed to do.

The front door opened before she could knock. Beowulf took one look at her face and ushered her inside. "What's wrong, Billie?"

"I need Roxie. I know she's here."

Beowulf grinned. "Roxie told me about that gift of yours. It must come in handy." He grew serious when she didn't elaborate on her ability. "Billie, where is Royce?"

"I really need to talk to Roxie first; then I'll tell you the rest."

"I'll get her for you."

"That won't be necessary." Roxie stood at the bottom of the large staircase. "I heard Billie's voice and came down to see what was going on. How about we go into the kitchen for our talk? There should be a fresh pot of coffee on."

Billie nodded. She followed Roxie into the kitchen and then took a seat at the table. Beowulf went to pour the coffee as Roxie sat in the chair next to her. She didn't wait for the coffee. Instead, Billie got straight to the point. Time ticked away for Royce and her brother.

"I want you to try the spell on me. Now."

Roxie met Beowulf's gaze across the room before she turned back to Billie. "Why the rush? Wouldn't you like to wait until Royce can be here?"

Beowulf placed three cups of coffee on the table and then sat next to Roxie. "I think that's why Billie doesn't want to wait. Royce can't be here. Right, Billie?"

With her hands fisted on the tabletop, Billie nodded. "I need the spell to save them. I'm no match for a werewolf as a mortal."

Beowulf grew still. "Them?"

"Gren has Royce and my brother, Finn. I have to get them back."

"Are you sure about this?"

"Yes. When I came home from the gym, Royce wasn't there, but the front door was unlocked and his car was in the driveway. I found an empty syringe lying on the floor in the entrance hallway. I knew something was wrong. So I used my gift to find him. Gren is holding him and my brother in some abandoned warehouse."

Roxie turned to Beowulf. Billie saw the look of concern that passed between them before Roxie spoke. "Billie, you don't have to do this alone. The spell can wait. Beowulf will handle this. It will only take him a few minutes to call some other members of our pack to go with him."

"No. You don't understand. It has to be me. My father told me the truth about my mother. She has the gift of sight. When I was a baby, she saw that I would turn into a wolf. And a few days ago, she saw it again."

"That doesn't necessarily mean you have to be the one to take on Gren. It might just mean you're meant to try the spell."

"I know it has to be me." Billie kept the part of her mother seeing the wolf as a killer to herself. Beowulf and Roxie didn't need to know about that. To Billie it was all the proof she needed to know she had to be the one to save Royce and Finn. "Please, Roxie. They're safe for now, but I don't know for how much longer." When Roxie didn't quickly agree, she tried one more tactic. "What would you do if you were in my place and it was Beowulf who Gren had? I know you wouldn't stay behind and wait. You're like me. You protect what's yours."

Roxie gave her a small smile. "You're right, Billie. I didn't stay home when Beowulf decided he had to be the man and take care of Gren when we had our problems with him. Even though Beowulf won't admit it, I saved his butt that day. I cleaned Gren's clock and the two thugs he had with him."

"Then you'll do it?"

"Yes, she will," Beowulf said as he stood. "You won't be going alone, Billie. Let me make a couple of phone calls; then Roxie can try the spell on you."

Her nerves stretched almost to the breaking point as Billie sat alone in the kitchen, waiting for Beowulf and Roxie to return. Roxie had gone to get the supplies she needed to do the spell. Billie could only guess at what they were. Beowulf had left the room as well to make his phone calls.

Needing to do something, Billie closed her eyes and focused her thoughts inward. She concentrated on Royce until a picture of his face filled her mind. Last time she had looked he had been unconscious, but now he was awake. He and Finn were bound hand and foot, but they appeared to be unharmed. The need to go to him was getting harder for her to ignore. She ground her teeth in frustration.

"Are they still all right?"

Billie opened her eyes and nodded at Roxie. "So far, yes." She eyed the syringe and alcohol wipes Roxie put on the table in front of her. "Those aren't exactly what I pictured you would need to use for a magic spell."

"They're only part of it. I need to inject you with some of my blood. We might as well do it as hygienically as possible. Once the blood is in your system, I'll recite the spell."

At that moment, Beowulf walked into the room. "They're on their way. I suggest we hurry and get the spell over with. I don't want them to know about it." For Billie's benefit, he added, "We don't want it to become common knowledge that Roxie can change a mortal into a werewolf, more so if it works on you. It could put her in a lot of danger from those who would like to use the spell for their own purposes."

"As Gren thinks he's doing by taking Royce. I still can't figure out why he took Finn."

"He hopes to turn your brother with the spell. Gren will not be thrilled when it doesn't work."

Determined to do what needed to be done, Billie put her arms on the table. "Then I suggest we get a move on."

Roxie gave her a quick nod. She opened one of the alcohol wipes and ran it across the inside of her elbow. With the same efficiency, she jabbed the needle into her arm and then filled the syringe with blood. She used a wipe on Billie's arm. Before she pierced Billie's skin with the needle, Roxie waited, giving Billie the chance to change her mind.

"Do it."

She nodded and pushed the needle home. Once she injected the blood, Roxie pulled it out and recited the spell.

"The magic of the wolf's blood is now in thee.
A wolf you become to run wild and free.
Where once there were two, now only one we see."

The words seemed to resonate deep inside her. Billie gasped as the spot on her arm where the blood had been injected burned. With lightning speed, the sensation spread throughout her entire body until she felt as if she were on fire from the inside out. She panted as she tried to breathe through the pain. She squeezed her hands into tight fists, causing the muscles in her arms to stand out. When she thought she couldn't take any more, the burning slowly ebbed. Once it was gone, her body felt as if it'd been through a hard workout.

She lifted her gaze to Beowulf and Roxie. "I don't think I want to do that again anytime soon."

Beowulf shook his head and smiled. "I'll be damned. You are one tough lady, Billie. Roxie and Taryn have said how painful it was to go through the change. You barely flinched."

Ignoring Beowulf's comment, Roxie asked, "Do you feel any different, Billie?"

She *did* feel different. All her senses were stronger. She smelled Beowulf's and Roxie's scents. She heard the sound of insects buzzing outside, even though the window inside the kitchen was shut. It was a bit overwhelming at first, to be able to hear, see, and smell so much better than she had before.

Wanting to see if her gift was stronger as well, she focused her thoughts inward. It was stronger, and she noticed something else—power. There was a spark of it that she hadn't had before the spell. She reached for it. At her first tentative touch, it grew until it surrounded her. Even before she looked down at herself, she realized she had somehow managed to go wolf. She had felt the magic surge through her as she'd shifted. She threw back her head and howled.

It was Roxie's turn to be impressed. "Are you sure you've never done this before, Billie?" she asked with a laugh. "Try to change back. Call the magic inside you, just as you did when you went wolf, but this time, picture yourself in your human form. And don't forget about clothes either. Hold on. Let me cover Beowulf's eyes before you try it. Just in case you can't manage the clothes part. I ended up naked the first time I shifted back to human form." Roxie clapped a hand over Beowulf's eyes and waved her other in front of his face to make sure he couldn't see anything. "Okay. Go for it."

Billie reached for the new power inside her. She did as Roxie said. She concentrated on what she looked like in human form. The magic surrounded her once again. When the change was complete, she looked at her body and smiled. She wore the clothes she'd arrived in.

Roxie picked up Billie's left arm and flipped it back and forth. "Are you sure you don't have any new markings you'd like to tell me about?"

"No. Why?"

Holding out her own arm, Roxie showed Billie the Celtic-designed markings that encircled her wrist. "This appeared shortly after I started seeing Beowulf. It's the mark of the one who would rule over the packs. I just wanted to make sure you weren't sporting any new tattoo-like markings. You seem to have adjusted rather well. Neither Taryn nor I could make the change as easily as you've done. I guess you're a natural."

The doorbell rang. Beowulf went to answer the door while Roxie cleared away the used syringe and wipes. Billie flexed her muscles a few times. Along with the extra-sensitive senses, she found she was even stronger than she had been. She smiled to herself. She was pretty sure she would be able to give Gren a run for his money now.

CHAPTER SIXTEEN

It'd taken another hour for the rest of the tranquilizer to completely leave Royce's system. During that time, Finn had done a pretty good job of ignoring him. Royce had been quite happy to leave the other man alone. After managing to get himself seated with his back against a wall, Royce dozed off and on until he felt back to normal.

Now that he was fully awake, he decided Finn had had enough time to stew over matters. "You know you can't ignore me indefinitely, Finn. We have to try to get out of these ropes before Gren comes back."

Finn gave him a hard stare. "Can't you turn into a wolf? Your ropes would slip off once you do."

Royce shook his head. "Didn't you hear what Gren said? As long as I'm bound by this rope, I can't get free. The one he used to bind me has silver threads in it. Silver inhibits my ability to shift into a wolf. I can't make the change fully."

"What do you want me to do?"

"Let's sit back-to-back and see if either one of us can work the knots free."

Royce pushed away from the wall, then inched to where Finn sat. Once they were in position, he pushed his bound hands against Finn's. "See if you can get my ropes untied first. I'll be able to handle Gren better than you will."

"What makes you think I wouldn't be able to handle him?"

"You're not a werewolf. Plain and simple."

"So werewolves are so much more superior than mortals, is that it? If the bastard hadn't blindsided me, I'm sure I would have wiped the floor with him."

Royce snorted. "That wouldn't have happened. Regardless of how big you are, Gren would still have been able to take you. We aren't so much superior as stronger than you mortals are. Now if you're done thumping your chest, could you try to get this rope untied?" He leaned slightly forward and pushed up his hands until he brushed against Finn's bound ones.

Finn shifted closer. He tried to work the rope with his fingers for a few minutes, then cursed. "He's bound my hands too tightly. I can't feel my fingers. There's no way I'll be able to work those knots loose."

"All right. Let me see if I can get you free instead." Royce straightened and moved his hands until he felt the rope around Finn's wrists. Gren obviously hadn't tied his as tightly. He still had feeling in his fingers. Gren must have counted on the silver being enough of a safeguard so he wouldn't have to worry about Royce being able to free himself.

Once Royce set to work on the knots, Finn asked, "Just how many of you are there?"

"You'd be surprised. Our numbers have slowly declined over the years, but there are still quite a few of us werewolves around."

"I find that hard to believe."

"You've been to Wulf's Den, I believe?"

"Yeah." Finn sounded leery.

"I'm sure you noticed all the very good-looking people that either work there or come for a few drinks. Let's put it to you this way. My kind is known to be better looking than the average person." Royce bit back a smile as Finn stiffened behind him.

"Are you telling me I've been trying to pick up werewolves every time I've gone to Wulf's Den?"

"It would seem so. Beowulf, the owner of Wulf's Den, is my pack leader."

"Damn. I never would have guessed."

"Of course you wouldn't have. It isn't as if we want all mortal kind to know of our existence. That could cause innumerable problems for us. Those of you who would fear what we are would take great joy in annihilating our kind." Royce felt the rope around Finn's wrists loosen.

"And Billie is fine with you being different?"

"Yes." Having managed to untie the final knot, Royce dropped the ends of the rope. "I got it. You should be able to get the rope off now."

Finn hissed with pain. No longer bound, the blood would be rushing back into his hands. "Give me a few seconds to get my feet free; then I'll get you untied."

Royce heard the lock being turned on the door a split second before Finn did. He shook his head when the other man got up and went to stand beside the door. Finn ignored him. Once Gren was in the room, Finn stepped out from behind it and grabbed him by the shoulder. He spun Gren around and slammed his fist into his face. Gren barely moved. As Finn gathered himself for another strike, Gren lunged. With his hand wrapped around Finn's throat, Gren lifted him off his feet until he dangled in the air. His face turned red as Gren cut off his windpipe.

"I see I shouldn't have left the two of you alone together. I'll let this one slide, mortal, only because I want you in one piece when I try the spell. If you do that again, you won't get off so easily."

Gren threw Finn across the room. He landed in a heap against the wall. Finn pushed himself into a sitting position and coughed as he tried to draw deep breaths into his lungs. Royce snarled at Gren.

"Your time of reckoning has come, lone wolf. Let's put your blood to the test."

Gren stalked to Royce and grabbed a handful of his hair. He painfully wrenched his head to the side, exposing the large vein in Royce's neck. Holding him in place, Gren pulled an empty syringe out of his pants pocket and then pulled the plastic guard off the needle with his teeth. After spitting it out, Gren jabbed the needle into the side of Royce's neck. Royce gritted his teeth as it penetrated his skin. As Gren filled the syringe with blood, Royce vowed he would make Gren pay before the day was over.

* * * *

"Are you sure this is the place, Billie?" Beowulf asked as she got out of the car to stand next to him.

"Positive. I'm never wrong."

Using her gift, Billie had instructed Beowulf to drive to an older industrial area in the city. In the car that followed behind them were four other men from his pack. Each one of them looked as if they could tear a brick wall apart with their bare hands.

Billie scanned the empty warehouse that was in front of them. She knew Royce was inside there with Finn. If she'd had her way, she would already be in the building, looking for them, but Beowulf had warned her not to be too hasty. He didn't want to take any chances. It was killing her, but she managed to hold herself back.

She wasn't handling being forcibly separated from Royce well. The need to be with him was almost impossible to ignore. And now that she was a werewolf, it hit her that much harder. It also made the need for him to take her stronger than she'd felt before. It made her edgy and downright bitchy. All she could think about was tearing Gren apart for taking Royce away from her.

Beowulf signaled for his men to take a quick search around the outside of the warehouse. Once they were gone, Billie grew impatient. She fisted her hands at her sides and growled low in her throat.

"Easy, Billie," Beowulf warned. "Don't let the wolf rule you. Wait until the others come back. We don't want to walk into a trap."

A minute ticked by and then another. As she waited, the muscles in her legs tightened with the strain of keeping herself reined back. She closed her eyes and looked for Royce. She quickly snapped them open. She growled and bared her teeth.

"Billie." Beowulf reached out to stop her, but she shook him off.

"We have to go now, Beowulf. I can't wait for them to get back. Gren is making his move."

She took hold of the locked doorknob and wrenched it until the lock broke. Billie pushed the door open and then rushed inside with Beowulf close on her heels. Her nose zoned in on Royce's scent. Without missing a step, she crossed the large, open space to the back of the building. There, she found the storage room. The door stood wide open.

Billie reached for the magic inside her and went wolf as she launched herself through the opening. She didn't stop her forward motion until she rammed into Gren, who stood over Royce. She hit him with enough force to push him away. Landing on her feet, she ended up next to Royce and growled.

Gren easily regained his balance. "What do we have here? It would seem someone has been using my spell."

Billie felt Royce's gaze on her, but she knew better than to take hers off Gren. She edged closer to Royce until her side was pressed up against his shoulder. She bared her teeth and gathered her muscles under her, ready to strike if Gren so much as moved.

From across the room, Finn asked, "Billie, is that really you?"

Beowulf, who'd slipped into the room, went to stand over Finn. "There will be more than enough time for questions later."

Gren snarled with rage. "Have you come to take me to your bitch, Beowulf? It would seem she's taken something of mine."

"The spell was never yours to take, Gren," Beowulf snarled back. "You've gone too far this time. Roxie will decide what needs to be done about you. And I can guarantee you it won't be as simple as chaining you outside in my backyard for a day either."

That seemed to incite Gren even more. Turning away from Billie, he leaped across the room and grabbed Finn. Before Beowulf could stop him, he jabbed the syringe he held into Finn's neck with what Billie assumed was Royce's blood.

"Now we'll see if Roxie is the only who can change an ordinary mortal into a werewolf."

Gren let Finn go and stepped back. He recited the words to the spell Roxie had used earlier on her. Billie knew it wasn't going to work. Roxie's blood was the key, not Royce's. Moving lower to the ground, she stalked closer to Gren.

When Finn showed no reaction, Gren threw back his head and howled with rage. Then everything seemed to happen at once. The men Beowulf had brought rushed into the room just as Billie leaped at Gren. This time she didn't have the element of surprise, and he proved to be just as quick as any of his kind. Sensing her coming, he spun around and caught her in midair. With a grim smile, he squeezed her ribs until she stopped struggling.

"You may be a werewolf now, girl, but you're still no match for me."

Billie quickly shifted into human form, which caused Gren's hold on her to shift. "We'll see about that."

Using the same strikes she taught in her self-defense classes, Billie stomped on the inside of Gren's foot hard enough to cause him to release her. Next she brought her knee up into his crotch. As he sank to the floor, she slammed her linked hands down onto the back of his head. He fell like a stone where he lay stunned and moaning in pain.

Panting from exertion, Billie looked around the room. She met the stunned expressions of the other men. While she'd been battling Gren, someone had freed Royce of his bonds. He took a step toward her. As he grew nearer, his look of surprise left his face to be replaced with a look of pride. She smiled back, but it soon fell away when Royce's expression changed into one of shock as his gaze focused on something behind her.

Not taking the time to even think of what she was doing, Billie went wolf as she spun around. She bunched her back legs under her and jumped as Gren dived for her brother with a knife in his hand. She caught Gren's throat in her powerful jaws and took him to the floor.

A rage like no other she'd ever felt before overtook her. Her hackles rose around her neck and she growled as she thought of what this male could do to her family, to Royce, if he was ever allowed to go free. The wolf inside her pushed to the fore. It took her over and did what needed to be done. Her strong jaws snap shut, breaking Gren's neck.

With the taste of Gren's blood in her mouth, Billie let him go. Beowulf pushed her aside as he bent over Gren. Still in wolf form, she looked up at Finn, who stood where Gren had dropped him. He eyed her with unease, as if he expected her to attack him next. She took a step toward him only to be brought up short when he backed away.

A large hand landed on the back of her neck. Billie looked up to find Royce next to her. "It's over, Billie. Let the wolf go."

Back in human form, she shook as she realized what she'd done. She still tasted Gren's blood, and she could smell it on her skin. Royce quickly gathered her up into his arms and held her tight against him. She closed her eyes as she breathed in his scent.

"It's all right, Billie. I'm going to take you out of here." Royce rubbed her back. He called Beowulf's name. "I have to get her out of here."

Beowulf pulled his car keys out of his pocket and then tossed them to Royce. "Take my car. We'll take care of everything."

With Royce's arm held protectively around her, Billie kept her face pressed to his chest as he led her outside to Beowulf's car. She was numb inside. She'd just taken a life. Her mother's prediction had come true. The wolf *was* a killer.

CHAPTER SEVENTEEN

Royce worriedly glanced at Billie in the passenger seat. She'd withdrawn into herself. She sat huddled at the door with her forehead pressed against the window.

"You did what you had to back there, Billie. By our laws, you acted within your rights. Gren attacked members of your family, of your pack."

"Finn is not part of the pack." Billie spoke in a low emotionless tone.

"By you becoming my mate, your family will be considered part of our pack even if they aren't werewolves."

Billie continued to look out the window. She was silent for so long Royce thought she wasn't going to say anything more. Then she said in a voice so quiet he almost didn't hear her, "I think Finn is afraid of me."

"I don't think he's afraid of you. You're his sister."

"Then why did he back away when I was in wolf form? I only did what I had to do to save his life."

"He's probably a little confused right now. That's all. I know I was surprised when I realized it was you when you first charged Gren."

When a streak of black had rushed Gren, Royce had at first thought it was Beowulf, but after getting a good look, he'd noticed it was smaller than his pack leader, and that it was a female. By her scent he had immediately known it was Billie.

Billie fell silent again. It wasn't until he pulled into the driveway of the house that she spoke. "I feel so cold. I need you to make me warm. I know I should be a mess emotionally, but all I can think about is having you. I need you inside me to make me feel whole again."

She turned to look at him. Royce sucked in a breath. Her eyes glowed with desire. He quickly turned off the car's engine and then came around to get her. She clung to him as he walked her to the front door. Once he had them inside, he took her straight upstairs to the bathroom and turned on the shower. As it warmed up, he stripped Billie of her bloody clothes. He scooped her up into his arms, then stepped in under the spray with her, not caring that his clothes were getting wet.

He washed her hair and body as he would have a child. Even though the need to take her was strong, he resisted. Billie needed Gren's blood cleaned away first. Once he was finished, he turned off the water before he lifted her out of the shower. He toweled her dry. Before leaving the bathroom, he stripped off his soaking wet clothes and left them in a pile on the floor.

Inside the bedroom, he pulled back the covers on the bed and put Billie under them. He climbed in next to her and held her close. Pressed skin-to-skin, she snuggled against him. Royce resisted the urge to grind his fully erect cock against her. She needed to make the first move.

At the first brush of Billie's lips against his chest, his heart pounded, but when she reached down and wrapped her hand around his aching cock, he couldn't hold back the growl of need that slipped past his lips. He needed to be inside her as much as she needed him to be there. Seeing his mate able to take down a male werewolf almost twice her size had laid all his fears to rest. Never again would he have to worry that she would be taken from him as Alicia had been. Billie was one of the strongest females he'd ever known. He wasn't even sure if Roxie would have been able to take out Gren in just her wolf form.

Billie pumped her hand up and down his hard length. He didn't want to rush her, but he felt as if he were ready to explode. When she growled against his skin, Royce rolled her onto her back. Holding his weight on his elbows, he looked down at her.

She grabbed a handful of his hair and brought his mouth down hard onto hers.

That was all Royce needed. With a moan, he kissed her thoroughly. He swept his tongue along the seam of her mouth, then pushed his tongue inside. As he kissed her, he rocked his hips against her. His cock brushed along her pussy. He groaned deep in his throat at how wet she was for him. He could have taken her fast and hard. He knew she was more than ready for him, but he wanted to give her pleasure first.

Easing down her body, he kissed a trail along the slender column of her throat to her chest. He swirled his tongue around one puckered nipple. Billie moaned as he dragged his teeth against it before he sucked it deep inside his mouth. Her hips bucked beneath him as he drew hard on it. He did the same to her other one until he had her panting with need.

He inched ever downward, placing kisses across her ribs and stomach. At her belly button, he swirled his tongue inside it. Moving so he lay between her legs, Royce licked her pussy from bottom to top. Billie made a sound that was half-growl, half-moan. His cock grew even harder.

With the tip of his tongue, he flicked it against her clit before he sucked on the little nubbin of flesh. Billie shoved her fingers through his hair, holding him to her, as she rocked her hips against his mouth. He continued to lick and suck as he pushed one finger inside her core. Her inner walls squeezed down around it as he moved it in and out of her slick opening. Royce growled as the scent of her desire filled his nose, and as he tasted it.

He continued to work her clit as he pushed a second finger inside. He knew she was close to her release. Working her faster, he felt her fall over the edge. As she climaxed, she pressed herself closer and moaned. Before the final spasm ended, Royce rose above her and sheathed his cock inside her core with one stroke.

No longer able to hold back, he surged into her again and again. Billie clung to his back, matching his strokes. The feeling of her inner muscles clamped around his hard shaft was almost too much to bear. He wanted her to come again before he found his release, but he didn't know if he could hold out that long. He was too close.

Billie brought his lips to hers and sucked his bottom lip into her mouth. She nipped it before she let it go. "Come for me, Royce. Don't hold back."

Her words broke the hold he had over himself. With his hands on her hips, he surged into her. Each thrust in his cock butted against her cervix. He increased his pace until his orgasm overtook him. He pulsed deep inside Billie, filling her with his cum. He moaned as her inner walls clutched his shaft, milking him dry, as she reached her own orgasm.

Royce collapsed on top of Billie. He rolled them to their sides and pulled her leg high up on his hip, keeping their bodies joined. Once his heart stopped racing, he softly brushed his lips against her mouth. She blinked open her eyes.

"How do you feel now?"

"Better." She seemed to get lost in her thoughts.

"Don't go back there, Billie. Stay with me."

There was a sadness in her eyes that hadn't been there a second before. "Did I do the right thing, Royce? I took a man's life."

Royce wrapped his hand around the back of her neck. "You did what you had to do to protect your brother. No one will question your motives."

Billie pressed her lips to his and kissed him until they were breathless. Once she pulled away, she looked into his eyes. "At least Roxie doesn't have to worry about the spell being in the wrong hands now."

"No, she doesn't. And what about you? Are you sure being a werewolf was what you really wanted?"

She nodded. "After my talk with my father, I knew it was something I had to do."

"No regrets even after what happened today?"

"None. I wanted to be your mate in all ways."

His cock was still hard inside her. Royce thrust his hips against hers. "That you are. Now I get to look forward to making love to you for the next thousand years or so. I couldn't ask for more."

Billie took her bottom lip between her teeth and moaned. "I can say the same thing about you. Now shut up and make love to me."

"With pleasure."

Royce ran his hand along her hip and down to her bottom, then slowly pumped between her legs. He would never be able to get enough of her. Billie lifted her leg higher and angled her hips so his shaft rubbed her clit as he moved deep inside her.

Teasing them both, Royce pulled back until only the tip of his cock was inside Billie's hot core and then he slowly pushed his length back inside. He looked down between their bodies and watched as his shaft slid in and out of her. The sight of their bodies joined made his blood surge.

He kept the pace slow, thrusting hard, until they came once again. Gathering Billie close, he watched her slip into a deep sleep. With a kiss to her brow, Royce closed his eyes as sleep claimed him.

* * * *

The following day Billie and Royce went to the gym. She had arranged to meet her father and brothers there before it opened for the day.

Once they were all gathered inside the aerobics room on the upper level, she touched her gaze on each of the men in her family. They all met hers, except for Finn. He didn't appear to be the worst for wear from his run-in with Gren, but he didn't seem to be his usual self either. Since she'd arrived, he'd done his best to avoid her.

"I know you're wondering why I asked to talk to you all today. I thought it would be easier to have this conversation here instead of going to see each of you and explain. Something has happened. Something I hope you'll all be able to accept."

Not leaving anything out, she told her brothers and father everything that had been going on in her life. When she got to the part about Royce being a werewolf, and that through a spell she'd been turned into one as well, she went wolf so there wouldn't be any question that she wasn't telling the truth.

Amazingly enough there was no freaking out done by any of them. The only one who held back was Finn. When the others welcomed Royce into the family, Billie silently watched Finn slip out of the room. Saddened that he couldn't bring himself to be near her or Royce, she figured he just needed time. Turning back to Royce, she smiled. She'd found her mate, and now had more than a lifetime to share with him.

* * * *

Finn pounded down the stairs to the main floor of the gym. Needing some air, he kept going until he was outside. As the slight breeze hit his face, he drew in great draughts of it. He started walking as a myriad number of scents bombarded him.

He was no longer the same. The spell might not have worked to change him into a werewolf, but Royce's blood had done something to him. Besides being able to smell better than he had before, he had somehow gained a new sense.

He'd woken up in the middle of the night with images filling his mind. They'd continued to flash before his eyes even after he was awake. The blood had given him a gift he did not want. His mother had such a gift, and it'd destroyed her. He did not want to end up the same way.

With no destination in mind, Finn kept walking. If only it could be so easy to escape what he'd turned into as it was to get away from Billie and Royce. He was changed forever, for better or worse.

The End

FINN AND JOCELYN

Finn York had a bad experience with werewolves. Marked emotionally and physically from the experience, his aversion causes him to fight the attraction he feels for the female werewolf he meets at Wulf's Den. Yet her scent draws him with the irresistible power of a werewolf's mating instinct.

Jocelyn works as a waitress at Wulf's Den. She'd noticed Finn months before but the sudden changes in him confuse her. When she serves him drinks one night he growls and sniffs the air as if he can smell her arousal and Jocelyn's confusion escalates. But her interest in Finn heightens and she plots a way to force him to overlook his disgust to claim her as his mate.

CHAPTER ONE

Finn York sat in a dark corner at Wulf's Den and watched the people around him. He quickly downed the shot of whiskey he held, disgusted with the number of werewolves he could pick out in the crowd. He slammed down the empty glass and then reached for the full bottle of beer on the table in front of him. He didn't know why he couldn't stop himself from coming to the nightclub when he disliked being around the employees and patrons who mostly were werewolves. They stood out in the crowd with their cover-model good looks, well-shaped bodies, and above-average height. At one time, he'd loved coming to Wulf's Den with his twin brother, Eli, in the hopes of picking up gorgeous women. Now that he truly knew what they were, all that had changed. He found himself drawn to the place at least three nights a week to watch werewolves — his new sick obsession.

At least Eli had stayed home tonight instead of following him to Wulf's Den. His twin worried about him, but Eli's show of concern grated on Finn's nerves. As did Keegan's, his older brother, and Hayes', his younger brother. Billie's displays bothered him the most. As the baby of the family and the only girl out of four siblings, he and his brothers had always watched out for her. Now that she had taken an over fifteen-hundred-year-old werewolf for her mate and been turned into one herself, she no longer needed her brothers to protect her. She and the rest of his family focused their caring attention on him because of what had happened to him three months earlier. If they ever found out about the changes that had taken place inside him, they would be more than just a little concerned about his behavior.

Finn gritted his teeth as a fresh wave of mingled scents washed over him. They battered his senses and gave him a wealth of information about the people who sat close to his table. He hated it. He hadn't asked for this "gift" or the gift of sight he now possessed. Being injected with Billie's werewolf mate's blood had wrought these changes. Royce's blood had had a permanent effect on him.

He took a long swig from his beer when he spotted Beowulf and Roxie at the bar. Beowulf owned Wulf's Den and was the leader of his pack. Finn tried to avoid him as much as he could, mostly because Roxie never seemed to be too far from her mate. She, Finn wanted to avoid at all costs. Descended from Royce and the first mortal to be turned into a werewolf, Roxie had been the one responsible for turning Billie. He couldn't look her in the face, knowing what she'd done to his sister. It was the same spell Roxie had used on his sister that a rival male werewolf had tried to use on him three months before. Gren, thinking Royce's blood had been the key to turning Roxie into a werewolf, had taken him and Royce captive so he could try to turn Finn. The spell hadn't worked the way Gren had intended, but Royce's blood had left its mark on Finn anyway.

With another long pull on his beer, Finn caught the eye of the nearest waitress. He intended to sit there until he got shit-faced drunk. Only then would he go home, fall into his bed, and not have to worry about the visions that invariably invaded his dreams.

*

Jocelyn kept half an eye on the mortal who sat alone in the dark corner of the room while she brought drinks to other tables. She had noticed him the very first time he'd come to Wulf's Den with his identical twin brother. He'd been a lot more carefree and happier then. Now, he appeared to be a different man entirely. No longer did he flash appreciative looks at the women as they walked by, nor did he laugh and joke with his brother when they came to the nightclub together. Something had happened three months ago to change him, and not for the better. More and more, she caught him giving the werewolves inside the club looks of disgust, as though their mere presence angered him. If that was the case, she couldn't understand why he continued to come to Wulf's Den week after week.

As she delivered drinks to a table close to the mortal's, Jocelyn glanced at him. Her heart beat a little faster when his gray-blue eyes caught her gaze and he waved her to his table. She gave him a nod as she served the last drink on her tray.

Unable to stop herself, Jocelyn settled her hungry gaze on the mortal. She wanted him. Before the changes in him, she'd been working up her nerve to talk to him, to test the waters, but with the hatred of her kind he seemingly felt, she'd decided to keep her distance. It hadn't stopped her body's reaction whenever he came to the nightclub, though. Just one sight of him and she became aroused. Even now her nipples tightened into buds beneath her blouse and her pussy ached to be filled as she drew nearer to him.

At his table, she smiled at him, thankful he wasn't a werewolf. A male of her kind would easily smell her arousal. "What can I get you?"

He spoke through gritted teeth. "Give me another shot of whiskey and a beer." His nostrils flared as he drew in deep breaths.

Jocelyn drew her brows together in confusion as he appeared to inhale her scent. His hands fisted on the table while his hot gaze raked the length of her body and back up to her face. The muscle in his jaw jumped as he made a quiet, animalist growl of need. Her pussy clenched at the sound. If she didn't know better, he showed all the signs of a male werewolf who had just found his mate. She pulled the smell of him into her lungs. He smelled mortal, but she detected something else—the underlying scent of a werewolf. It was minute compared to the mortal one, but she picked it up nonetheless. And he was aroused. The musky, male scent of arousal washed over her, growing stronger the longer she stood in front of him.

Unsure of what to make of it, Jocelyn nodded. "I'll be back in a few minutes with your drinks."

She felt his gaze follow her as she turned and headed to the bar. Jocelyn placed her drink order, then found Beowulf and Roxie giving her curious looks. She stared back at them. Beowulf stood with his arm around Roxie's shoulders while she sat on one of the barstools. Rarely did you see one without the other. Jocelyn found Beowulf a little more protective of his mate than males usually were, for which she couldn't blame him. Roxie was special. The Celtic-like design around her left wrist marked her as the one foretold in an ancient prophecy to rule over all the werewolf packs.

When Beowulf and Roxie continued to stare at her, Jocelyn cocked a brow in their direction. "What?"

Roxie gave her a knowing smile before she looked at the mortal's table and then back at her. "You like Finn, don't you?" Jocelyn gave her a confused look. Roxie added, "The mortal whose table you came from. His name is Finn. I can tell you like him."

Jocelyn turned back to put the opened bottle of beer and shot glass of whiskey on her tray. She felt her cheeks grow warm, knowing exactly how Roxie knew she found Finn attractive. "Maybe I do."

Roxie chuckled. "I'd say it's much more than a maybe. I think you're just what Finn needs."

"Rox," Beowulf warned. "I *don't* think it would be a good idea to play matchmaker where Finn is concerned."

"I think it would be a perfect way to get him out of his snit."

"I would hardly call Finn's behavior a snit. It's a little stronger than that, and I don't think his attitude is going to change that easily."

Roxie rolled her eyes. "Never mind Beowulf, Jocelyn. That's just his opinion. I'm only going to say one last thing, and then you can make your own decision."

Beowulf gasped in feigned shock. "Only one? When did you learn such restraint?" He grunted when Roxie jabbed him in the ribs with her elbow.

"As I stated before I was rudely interrupted," Roxie said to Jocelyn, "I'll say one last thing. Finn learned about our kind in a way no mortal should. It has given us a bad name in his eyes. If you showed him all werewolves aren't as evil as he thinks, you might be able to get him to see us in a better light. It would do him and his family a favor. Just something to think about."

Jocelyn nodded. Roxie had explained some of the reasons Finn had changed, though she didn't go into much detail. Now that she thought about it, his behavior had become different around the same time the pack learned Gren — Beowulf's one-time nemesis — had been killed. Could Finn have been involved?

She picked up her tray. "I'll think about it. I better give Finn his drinks. I can feel him staring daggers into my back."

Roxie smiled. "Oh, I wouldn't describe that look quite in that way. I would say it's very much the opposite."

Jocelyn shifted her gaze in Finn's direction and sucked in a sharp breath. He gazed hungrily at her. It was so hot she was surprised she hadn't melted into a puddle on the floor. When he realized she'd caught him staring at her, the hunger left his face to be replaced with the oh-so-familiar look of disgust.

With a sigh, Jocelyn carried the tray to his table. She placed each drink in front of him and then collected the empty beer bottle and shot glass. "Can I get you anything else?"

She focused her gaze on his longish, straight black hair, high cheekbones, and sculpted lips. Finn made the same animalistic growl as he had made earlier when her gaze locked on his mouth, and she licked her suddenly dry lips.

"No. Just keep the drinks coming," he said with another growl.

Jocelyn forced herself to walk away. She would make sure she didn't stray too far from him. She had a feeling that by the end of the night he would be lucky if he could stand on his own two feet.

* * * *

Finn slowly pushed back his chair as the room spun around him. He'd reached the stage of shit-faced drunk and then some. He blamed it on *her*. Every time she brought him drinks, her scent slammed into him, causing his cock to harden with need. He couldn't stop himself from drawing the smell of her arousal deep inside until it would be forever engraved in his brain. Even now — so drunk he had doubts he could manage to walk outside to catch a cab, let alone stumble out of Wulf's Den — he sported a raging hard-on. He fought the urge to adjust himself inside his jeans that felt too tight in the crotch.

With his hands flat on the table, Finn tried to lever himself up. He leaned for a few seconds as the room seemed to spin faster. Once the pace slowed, he forced himself to stand straighter. So far so good. Now he had to manage the task of walking across the room to the entrance. At that point, it seemed almost too great of a distance for him to manage. Determined to walk out of the nightclub without falling on his face, he took an unsteady step away from the table.

He didn't rush as he walked across the almost-deserted Wulf's Den. The nightclub's doors had closed for the night a few minutes before. About halfway to the door, Finn ran into trouble. The alcohol he'd consumed rushed to his head. He stumbled as he listed to one side. Before he completely lost his balance, an arm came around his waist and his settled around a feminine set of shoulders. He bit back a groan as he looked and saw who helped to keep him upright.

Finn's gaze collided with his waitress's incredible light green eyes as she stared back at him. Unable to stop himself, he took in her long, straight auburn hair before he peered down her slim body. She had all the right curves in all the right places that seemed to be a perfect fit against his side. Like all her kind, she was taller than most mortal women. At six feet three, he towered over a lot of the opposite sex but not this one. She had to be at least six feet tall.

He tried to take his arm back, but she tenaciously held on to him. "I can walk on my own." His voice sounded slurred even to him.

She gave him a snort of disbelief as she walked them toward the entrance. "I doubt that. I'm Jocelyn Swen, in case you're interested."

The side of Jocelyn's breast brushed against Finn with each step they took. His stiff cock throbbed inside his jeans. It didn't care she was a werewolf. It just wanted to be buried to the hilt inside her wet pussy. He gritted his teeth against the intense arousal.

"Since you won't let me go, and I'm in no condition to fight you, you can just put me into a taxi," he said.

"I don't think so. I'll drive you home. You would probably pass out in the cab, and then where would you be?"

Much to his disgust, when they reached the door, Jocelyn easily managed to hold him against her side with one arm as she used her other hand to push it open. Even though he weighed more than she did, and he had a lot of muscle that made him quite heavy, she had no problem maneuvering him about. Being a werewolf, she probably could wipe the floor with him, if she wanted to.

It didn't take Jocelyn long to get them to the parking lot behind Wulf's Den. She walked him to the black Ferrari that sat at the very back. *Do all werewolves drive expensive cars?* Finn didn't have more time to dwell on that question once she got him propped along the car while she fished her keys out of her purse. Without her support, his legs slowly gave out on him, and he slipped downward. Jocelyn caught him around the waist so he leaned against her before he could hit the ground.

Her breasts pressed against his chest as she held him close became too much for him. The need to taste her overrode everything else he felt. The same animalistic growl he hadn't been able to control back in the nightclub rose inside him as he threaded his fingers through her hair. Finn held her in place and took her mouth in a hard kiss. He moved his lips across hers, pushing his tongue between them. He twined his with hers. The taste of her had him thrusting his erection against her lower stomach. She tasted sweeter than the headiest wine. He couldn't get enough of her. When she whimpered with need, he brought his hands down to her ass and hauled her closer while he ground his cock against her.

Lost in a haze of sexual arousal, Finn lifted a hand to the buttons of Jocelyn's blouse. He tried to work one free so he could slip a hand inside to cup her breast, but she jerked away, breaking the contact of their lips. He noticed hers were puffy from his kisses. The need to pull her into the car, lift her tight skirt, and bury his aching cock inside her beat at him. He almost couldn't ignore it. Before he could try to take her lips once again, she unlocked the passenger side door and held it open for him.

She shook her head when he would have pulled her to him again. "No, Finn. First of all, I'm not going to have sex with you in a car in a parking lot. I'm not that desperate. And secondly, I'm not sure this is something you really want to do. You're not able to think straight now. I have no intention of sleeping with you and then having you regret what you did the next morning. Now into the car with you."

The world spun again. He had no idea how Jocelyn knew his name. He hadn't told her, but now, he didn't much care how she'd found it out. She shoved him inside the car and then put the seatbelt on him before she shut the door. He watched two Jocelyns walk around the front of the car and then get into the driver's side. Finn's eyes grew heavy as he settled into the corner of the seat. He gave up the battle to stay awake as she started the engine.

CHAPTER TWO•

Finn cracked an eye open but quickly shut it with a groan against the pain in his head. It felt as if someone had driven a spike through it. He threw an arm over his eyes. Another couple of hours of sleep and he would be able to face the world. After that, he would have a hot shower and find something to take for his killer headache.

On the verge of going back to sleep, Finn felt the bed move as someone shifted next to him. He lowered his arm and turned to look at the woman who lay beside him. Her scent—one he would never forget—swirled around him. Jocelyn. Finn stiffened as it dawned on him that the bed he slept in wasn't his own, nor did he recognize the bedroom. How the hell had he ended up there?

The sheets rustled as the woman next to him rolled onto her side so she faced him. He plastered a scowl on his face as she looked at him while a small smile played across her lips.

"How's the head?"

"Fine. What am I doing here?"

"Liar. I heard you groan a minute ago. As for you being in my bed, you really didn't leave me much choice. You passed out in my car before you told me where you live. So I brought you to my place. After I put you to bed, I searched your jeans for your wallet, but I only found the cash you had in your pocket and nothing else."

Finn quickly lifted the sheets to find he didn't have a stitch of clothing on. He also noticed his cock had taken an interest in the woman next to him. It lengthened and grew hard. He let the sheet drop back over him.

"Why am I naked?"

Jocelyn chuckled. "Well, I thought only to take off your shirt and jeans so you could sleep more comfortably. What a surprise I got when I found out you go commando under your jeans. By that time I'd already gotten an eyeful, so I took your pants off anyway."

Finn's cock jerked at the thought of Jocelyn stripping him naked while he slept. "So it didn't bother you to sleep beside a naked man you barely know?"

"No, not really. You weren't exactly in any condition to ravish me or anything. Plus, I don't make it a practice to sleep with men who won't remember we had sex. Now that you're sober, I wouldn't mind starting where we left off last night."

The kiss they had shared in the parking lot came back in a rush. Finn remembered the feel of her in his arms as he tasted her mouth. His heart beat faster as it sent more blood to his already engorged dick. He reminded himself that Jocelyn was a werewolf. That he had made a pact with himself he wouldn't ever sleep with one. That he disliked them all for what had happened to him. It didn't work. Instead, erotic images of her under him as he rode her until they both couldn't move filled his mind.

He moved to the very edge of the bed. "I think not. I have to leave now."

Jocelyn shook her head. "For someone who supposedly dislikes werewolves so much, you sure aren't acting like it. If anything, that erection there tells me you would be more than happy to kiss me and then some."

Finn glanced down his body and saw his cock had tented the sheet over him. "I can take care of that on my own."

Moving faster than any mortal could, Jocelyn jumped on top of him and straddled his hips as she hovered over him. She took each of his wrists and pressed them onto the mattress on either side of his head. Luckily for him, she wore baby-blue boxer-style pajama shorts and a matching T-shirt.

"Why take care of that little problem by yourself while I would be more than happy to do it for you? I know we would enjoy that more," she said with a sultry smile.

With a groan, Finn tried to lift his hands, but Jocelyn easily kept them pinned to the bed. "Oh God, you would have to be like Billie when it comes to men."

"Who is Billie?" Jocelyn dragged her tongue across his lips.

It took a few seconds for Finn to work out what she'd asked him. "Billie is my sister."

Jocelyn kissed a path along his jaw to his ear. "And what does your sister do to men?"

"She has always felt that if a woman really wants a man, she shouldn't have to wait for him to make the first move." With Jocelyn's scent filling his head, Finn found it decidedly harder to concentrate. His cock throbbed painfully.

"I see. I think I'd like to meet your sister. It sounds as if she and I would get along. She's a girl after my own heart."

"Why? Because you jump unsuspecting men as well?"

"I'm all for that. I just have never tried it before. I guess you could say I'm a bit on the shy side."

Finn couldn't stop the small animalistic growl that slipped past his lips as Jocelyn gently bit his earlobe. "I find that hard to believe."

"It's true. You're the first man I've ever jumped without him having jumped me first."

He could no longer think straight. He hadn't ever found himself this attracted to a woman before. Arousal burned through his body. The disgust he usually felt toward a female werewolf who showed interest in him didn't happen with Jocelyn. He found her scent addicting and brought something he didn't recognize in himself to the surface. Something that wanted to take her, claim her as his mate.

He didn't want to face those feelings, but when Jocelyn bent to take his lips in a languid kiss and her nipples brushed against his chest through her shirt, he was lost. With a moan, he pushed his tongue inside her mouth. This time, when he tried to free his hands, he didn't do it to push her away. The need to touch her made him growl low in his throat. As if she understood what it meant, she released him and lowered her hips until her pussy made contact with his cock. The feel of her moist heat through her boxer shorts had him wrapping his arms around her waist as he rolled her onto her back.

Finn settled between her legs as he took over the kiss. He sucked her tongue into his mouth. Jocelyn whimpered as she gripped his shoulders. He lifted the hem of her shirt and dragged it over her head. Cupping one of her breasts, he tugged at the taut peak as he left her lips and kissed a path down her neck to her chest. He flicked her nipple with the tip of his tongue before he sucked it deep inside. He took hold of the waistband of her boxer shorts and pulled them down past her hips. She kicked them the rest of the way off.

Now pressed skin-to-skin, Finn fought the urge to bury his cock inside her. The smell of her arousal made him crave the taste of her pussy. He released her nipple, then moved down her body. Once he lay with his shoulders between her spread thighs, he dragged his tongue along the swollen folds of her pussy. The smell and taste of her caused another growl to emerge from his throat.

Jocelyn's hips rose off the mattress as he spread her folds and dipped his tongue inside her core. He continued to lap at her sex until he made her moan with need. Slowly, he pushed a finger into her pussy. Her inner walls clamped down on it as he moved it in and out. As he slipped a second finger inside her, Finn swirled his tongue around her clit. She threaded her fingers through his hair and held him to her as he sucked on the small nubbin of flesh. Her hips jerked as she rode his fingers. When her inner walls spasmed around his digits, he sucked harder. She moaned while she climaxed against his mouth.

Finn rose between her legs. He rested his weight on his elbows as the head of his cock pushed against the wet heat of Jocelyn's pussy. He was about to push himself home when images slammed into his head. He gasped as they flashed before his eyes. As if from a distance, he heard her ask what was wrong, but he couldn't answer. By the time the pictures faded, he had broken out in a cold sweat and lost his erection.

Breathing heavily, he threw himself away Jocelyn and sat on the edge of the bed as he tried to sort through what he'd just seen. The feel of her hand on his back caused him to flinch. He had to leave her. Through the disjointed images that had played inside his mind, there had been one that he'd seen with great clarity: Jocelyn lying dead in a pool of her own blood. From that he'd sensed he had been the cause of her death. His gift of sight—a legacy from his mother that had driven her mad—had been awakened after he'd been injected with Royce's blood. He hated it more than he hated the other side effects.

Jocelyn kneeled behind him. "Are you all right?"

Finn quickly stood. Seeing his clothes neatly folded on the end of Jocelyn's dresser, he went to it and then started to dress. "I have to get out of here." He kept his back to her so she couldn't see how deeply he'd been affected by what he'd seen.

"I'll give you my cell phone number before you go."

"No."

Jocelyn come to stand behind him. "What do you mean 'no'? I want to see you again."

Now dressed, Finn turned to face Jocelyn. He had to fist his hands at his sides to prevent himself from pulling her into his arms. She stood gloriously naked with her lips still swollen from his kisses.

"I don't want to see you again. I'm going to go call myself a taxi."

Finn walked around her and then out the bedroom door. He took the stairs down to the main level of the house two at a time. Before he could find the phone, Jocelyn joined him. She'd pulled on a bathrobe, thank goodness. He didn't know how much longer he would have been able to hold on to his control with her naked.

"Where's the phone?" he asked.

"You don't need to call for a taxi. I can drive you home."

"I don't think that would be a good idea."

"I think we need to talk about this, Finn."

"There isn't anything to discuss."

Jocelyn crossed her arms over her chest. "I beg to differ. The way you acted last night and the way you acted up in my bedroom are definite signs."

"Definite signs of what?"

"You're showing the signs a male werewolf displays when he's found his mate."

Finn stiffened. "Get this straight, Jocelyn, I'm not a werewolf." His upper lip curled in disgust when he said the word werewolf.

"I know you aren't, but your scent confuses me. You smell mortal, but there is an underlying scent that says you could be werewolf as well."

"Because of the way I smell and have acted you think I want to claim you as my mate?"

"Yes."

"I hate to break it to you, babe, but I'm not looking for a mate, and especially not one who is a werewolf. I know what happens when werewolves mate. The real need to be with each other, how the souls of the mates reach out for each other and join. I don't want anyone to have that kind of hold over me."

Jocelyn's brows snapped together as she frowned. "You may not be looking, Finn, but it has already started. I, at least, can feel the closeness forming between us, the hunger for each other. It isn't as if you'll have much say in the matter, either. A male's mating urge starts to ride him, and hard, when he finds the female meant for him. You'll be drawn to me, unable to keep away. Until we make love, you're going to be a bomb waiting to go off. Your dreams will be filled with all the ways you want to take me, which will push the mating urge even higher. Whether you want this to happen or not, it will."

Through gritted teeth, Finn said, "I'm not a goddamn werewolf, so stop comparing me to one. Now where the hell is your phone?"

She gave him a sad look. "Keep telling yourself that, Finn. Just keep telling yourself that and maybe you'll start to believe it. The phone is in the kitchen down the hall."

Finn forced his feet to move as he walked past Jocelyn and headed for the kitchen. Once he was away from her, he would okay. The arousal that boiled in his blood would dissipate as soon as he couldn't see her or smell her alluring scent. He'd be back to normal and wouldn't think of her again.

*

Jocelyn stood in the open doorway as Finn climbed into the back of a taxi and then slammed the door shut. He didn't even look back when it pulled out of the driveway before it drove away. She shook her head as she stepped back, then shut the front door. The man would find out the hard way.

Contrary to what he told himself, Finn wouldn't be able to ignore what his body demanded. Yes, he was mortal, but he still showed all the signs of wanting to claim her as his mate. If the growls he'd made hadn't been enough, the way he'd kissed her and touched her despite his dislike of werewolves gave him away. There had only been one missing piece—his eyes had not glowed.

As for her, the first time his lips had touched hers in Wulf's Den's parking lot, she'd wanted him. Even though Finn had made her come, Jocelyn's body still throbbed with arousal. She wanted to have his muscular body wrapped around hers as he took her. While he'd slept last night, she'd been able to look over every inch of him. He might not be as tall as a male werewolf, but he had the build of one. His body rippled with muscle, which meant he had to have spent hours at a gym to get it that way. She'd also been pleased to see he could be described as large when it came to all aspects of his body. Even drunk and passed out his cock had stayed hard and thick.

Jocelyn bit back a groan as she thought of how close she'd come to having that big cock of his inside her. She had no idea what had happened in her bedroom. One minute the tip of him was pressed against the opening of her body, and the next, he was gone. Whatever had happened was enough to make him run from her. She would let him go for now, but she wouldn't let him walk out of her life. She would be damned if she let the one man meant for her go free without a fight.

CHAPTER THREE

Finn arrived home to an empty apartment, which pleased him. He hadn't wanted to look at his twin and find Eli staring at him with pity in his eyes. Bad enough he got that look from the rest of his family, but to have his identical twin look at him like that bothered him the most. He and Eli were close. So close, in fact, they had even moved out of their father's house together to share apartment. They liked the same things, enjoyed the same pursuits. They had been like two peas in a pod, but no longer. Finn couldn't bring himself to tell Eli about the changes in him, and that caused tension between them. Before, they'd almost been inseparable. Now Finn kept mostly to himself.

After a quick shower, he dressed in a pair of gray fleece pants and a black T-shirt that had YORK FITNESS printed across the chest in white letters. York Fitness was his family's gym, and where he worked as a personal trainer along with his three brothers and sister.

He grabbed a piece of toast before he'd left to go to the gym. If he hadn't already had clients booked for training sessions today, Finn would have stayed home. He didn't feel like himself, and the vision he'd had unsettled him more than he would have liked. Hopefully, after he finished up with his last client, he would have a chance to work out. Maybe if he slugged the weights around long enough, he could make himself numb to the emotions that battered him.

It didn't take Finn long to drive to the gym and then park his red Mustang at the back of the building. Pocketing his car keys, he walked to the entrance doors. He managed to almost make it past the gym floor before his sister, Billie, came to confront him. Just what Finn did not need this morning.

"What do you want, Billie? I just got here, and I have a training session with a client in about fifteen minutes."

Billie gave him a crooked smile. "So? What's her name and what's she like?"

Finn glared at Billie. He didn't like the glint he saw in her gray-blue eyes, so very much a match for his own. All the York siblings had ended up with their father's eyes and black hair.

"She who?"

"You know who I mean." Billie took a quick look around before she said, "The female werewolf whose place you slept over at last night after you passed out."

"Damn it, Billie. Can't you keep your nose out of where it doesn't belong?" His sister had the ability to find anyone she came in contact with. Even if she only met the person for a few seconds and didn't know their name, she could find them. "I thought you only pulled that crap on Hayes."

Billie blocked his path when he tried to step around her. "You're not getting off that easily. You know Hayes smartened his act up after Janice gave birth. Since little Tiffany's arrival, he hasn't gone to a bar to get stinking drunk. Wish I could say the same about you, Finn. So until you do, get used to me 'looking' for you. Eli got worried last night when you didn't come home, so he called and asked me to 'see' where you were. Imagine my surprise when I 'found' you passed out in a female werewolf's bed."

"It didn't mean anything. I drank more than I should have at Wulf's Den last night. She works there as a waitress. She saw the condition I was in and took me to her place to sleep it off. Nothing else happened."

Billie reached out and put her hand on his arm. Finn jerked away. Since she'd been turned into a werewolf, he couldn't stand her touching him. She slowly let her hand fall back down to her side and looked at him with hurt in her eyes.

"I thought you being there meant you had a change of heart about what I've become. I guess I thought wrong."

"Let it be, Billie." Finn stepped around her, but she called his name before he got very far. He turned back to look at her. "What?"

"I just wanted to say you look like shit more than you usually do. Are you sure you're okay?"

"Gee, thanks. I'm fine."

He couldn't stop the low rumbling growl that left his throat when he'd said the last part. Billie's eyes narrowed at the sound. Before she could say anything more, he spun around and headed for his desk. He counted himself lucky that she didn't follow him and start giving him the third degree.

Finn's first two training sessions went well. By the time the third one had almost finished, he started to get distracted. Thoughts of Jocelyn seemed to take over his mind. And they weren't just thoughts of her as a person. No, they were more erotic than anything else. The more he thought of what she'd smelled and tasted like, the more aroused and tighter his body became. Finally, he had to cut the training session short and hide in the men's change room to get his wayward body back under control. He couldn't exactly hide the raging hard-on he had going on in his fleece pants. Nor the fact he'd gone commando. His father would have had a shit fit if he'd seen him on the gym floor with his cock tenting the front of his pants. In the end, when no one else was around, he stripped and took an ice-cold shower. The cold water did the trick, but he had a feeling the effect wouldn't last long.

Once he left the change room to work out, Finn's steps faltered when he noticed Royce standing just inside the gym floor, talking with Billie. He swore under his breath when his brother-in-law's head swung in his direction and he gave him an assessing look. It didn't take much guessing on Finn's part to conclude Billie must have told Royce about their conversation earlier that day.

Finn ignored Billie and Royce as he walked by them and headed for the leg press machine in the back corner. He turned on his MP3 player and loaded up four forty-five-pound weights on either side of the machine. He sat in the chair and then placed his feet on the machine. While he did his first set, he watched out of the corner of his eye as Royce came to stand beside the machine. Once he finished his reps, he got up and put another forty-five-pound weight on each side. He pointedly ignored Royce's presence.

Royce took him by the arm and stopped Finn before he could sit back down. "You can ignore me all you want, Finn, but I'm not going away."

Finn hated that he had to look slightly up at his sister's mate. Royce stood three inches taller at six feet six. Finn pulled out one of his earphones. "Let go of me." He jerked his arm from Royce's grasp. "I'm trying to work out here. Either leave me alone or hurry up and say what you want to say."

Royce's hazel-eyed gaze searched his face as he took a step closer and sniffed the air around Finn. His brows drew together when he stepped back again. "Is there something you should tell Billie and I?"

"Besides the fact I hate that you both are werewolves? No."

"I would watch what you say about Billie around me, Finn. You might be her brother, but that won't stop me from pounding you to the ground if you continue to insult her."

"Back off, wolf," Finn said with a snarl. "Don't threaten me." He growled low in his throat.

Royce quickly grabbed Finn by the back of the neck and forced him to walk with him. Unable to break his hold, Finn growled once again. "Finn, I suggest you calm down before you make a scene."

As Royce walked them up the stairs to the aerobics room on the upper level, Finn snapped, "You would be the one who made the scene, not me."

Once they reached their destination, Royce shoved him inside. Finn turned around to see Billie had also joined them. She closed the door behind her. Royce grabbed Finn by both his arms and pushed him against the wall. His nostrils flared as he took a deep breath.

"I think your bad attitude has gone on long enough. We're going to have it out here and now. And from the way your scent smells, it's not a moment too soon. Now talk," Royce said.

Billie came to stand next to Royce. "We're all worried about you."

Finn clenched his jaw against another growl that built in his throat. *Where did this newfound ability to growl come from?* "I told you before to leave it be, Billie. I'm fine."

"Bullshit," Royce shot back. "I think you've been hiding something from us. And, for some reason, today I can pick up the smell of a werewolf in your scent."

"I'm not a fucking werewolf," Finn said with a snarl. "It doesn't matter what I smell like."

Royce's gaze settled on Finn's face. "I'm not the first person, or should I say werewolf, to tell you that you have the scent of a werewolf, am I? The female you spent the night with last night told you, didn't she? Maybe I should pay her a little visit. Billie can find her."

Finn's full-throated growl filled the room as he snarled at Royce. "You won't go near Jocelyn, wolf, if you know what's good for you." Just the thought of Royce going anywhere near her made him want to take the other man down.

"Holy shit. The mating urge has its claws in you."

Billie turned to look at Royce. "What? Male mortals do not get werewolf mating urges."

"No, but I have a feeling Finn here isn't exactly a hundred percent mortal anymore. Are you, Finn? That spell may not have worked, but my blood did something to you. Jocelyn is your mate, and for some reason, you have the mating urge riding you until you claim her as such."

"Is what he said the truth, Finn?" They all turned to look at Eli who stood in the now open doorway. He shut the door and then crossed to where they stood. "I've known something has been wrong for the last couple of months. And I know it doesn't entirely have to do with you having been taken captive by that crazy werewolf Billie took down, either. Tell us what's wrong. You and I used to be a team. Now you push me away every chance you get."

Finn tried to put some space between him and his twin, but Royce kept him pinned to the wall. Eli was the one person he couldn't lie to. He had avoided him so a situation like this wouldn't happen. As his gaze rested on Eli's face, an exact match of his own, Finn decided he wouldn't tell him all of it. The family didn't need to know about his visions.

"You really want to know? Fine. Royce is right. The spell didn't work, but his blood marked me, changed me. I now can smell three times better than I did before. Everything has a scent, and I can read it. I can't walk down the street without inhaling someone's. It's as if I can smell whatever they're feeling. Their pain, if they're aroused, whatever."

"The ability to growl?" Royce asked. "Did that start at the same time?"

"No. That didn't start until last night when I met Jocelyn. Not until I got my first sniff of her scent."

Royce released Finn. "You may not like it, Finn, but you are going through what every male werewolf does when they first meet their mates."

"Jocelyn is not my mate, and I have no intention of seeing her again."

"That may be what you want, but you will go to her eventually. There is no way to deny the mating urge. I learned that with Billie."

Billie snorted. "You were a stubborn ass. It's a good thing I'm a take-charge sort of woman. I wonder if we should take Finn to see Roxie."

"No!" Finn snapped.

"Why not?" Billie scowled at him. "You're stuck in the middle here, Finn. You're not quite werewolf, but you're also not fully mortal, either. It's not as bad as you think it is to be a werewolf."

"*Really* now?" Finn asked in a sarcastic tone. "Look what it did for you, Billie. It turned you into an animal capable of taking a man's life. Can you honestly tell me you enjoyed going wolf so you could snap Gren's neck with your jaws?"

Billie moved so fast Finn had no time to defend himself. She grabbed him by the arm and flipped him onto his back on the floor. She kneeled on his chest while she held his arms to the carpet. Her eyes glowed as she looked down at him and snapped her teeth.

"You know I only did what had to be done to keep you and Royce safe. Gren would have come after you both again if we allowed him to walk away. So don't judge me," she said with a snarl.

Royce pulled Billie off him. "Settle down, love." He tugged her against his side before he turned to Finn, who had pulled himself off the floor. "I'm not going to warn you again. Next time you hurt Billie like that I'm going to show you how much stronger a werewolf is compared to a mortal."

Finn headed for the door. It wasn't Royce's threat that made him walk away without another word. It was the look of disappointment Eli had given him. It hurt him more than Royce ever could with his fists.

* * * *

When the hours ticked by and Finn didn't make an appearance at Wulf's Den, Jocelyn finally had to face the fact he wouldn't be coming to see her after all. She had hoped by nighttime he would have been more than happy to be around her again, that the mating urge she knew had to be riding him would have forced him to seek her out. She'd guessed wrong on that one it would seem. Either she'd mistakenly read the signs or Finn had more willpower than she'd thought he had.

Disappointed, Jocelyn tried to stay focused on her job rather than worrying about Finn, which turned out to be hard to do. She'd done nothing but think about him all day. She wanted to be with him, to touch him, have him hold her, to have hot, sweaty, mind-blowing sex with him. Never had she become so obsessed with a man, or wanted one as badly as she wanted Finn. She just chalked that up as another sure sign he was her mate.

After Wulf's Den closed for the night, Beowulf came to talk to her while she collected empty glasses from one of the tables. "Can you stick around for a little while longer, Jocelyn?"

She nodded. "Yes. What do you need me to do?"

Beowulf smiled. "It's not extra work I have for you. I just need to talk to you. When you're finished here, come up to my office. I promise I won't take much of your time."

He walked away. *Why did he single me out?* It hadn't been a year since she first started working at Wulf's Den. She didn't think Beowulf wanted to let her go. She'd never heard of him letting go any of his employees. She had wanted to work at the nightclub for over a year but had to wait for the opportunity to apply for the job when one of the other waitresses left when she'd become pregnant.

Curious as to what Beowulf wanted to talk to her about, Jocelyn quickly finished clearing the table and then took the dirty glasses to the bar. She headed up the stairs to his office. At the door, she took a deep breath before she knocked on it. Beowulf opened it and motioned her inside. Much to her surprise, Roxie and two others were there as well. She recognized Royce, but the woman who sat next to him she didn't know. The woman's features seemed familiar to her, though.

Beowulf motioned for Jocelyn to sit on the chair in front of his desk that had been turned to face the others, who sat on the only couch in the office. "Have a seat, Jocelyn. I'm sure you know Royce, and sitting next to him is his mate, Billie."

"Billie?" Jocelyn studied Royce's mate. Now she knew why she seemed so familiar to her. The black hair and gray-blue eyes reminded Jocelyn of Finn. And hadn't he told her he had a sister named Billie? But this Billie couldn't be his sister. The woman sitting next to Royce was pure werewolf. "Your name is Billie?"

"Yes." Billie smiled. "I can see my name rings a bell with you. I guess Finn must have mentioned me to you when he slept over at your place."

Jocelyn gave Billie a confused look. "I don't understand. If you're Finn's sister, how come you're a full-blooded werewolf and he is mortal?"

Roxie spoke before Billie could answer. "I think it best I answer that particular question. You can't tell anyone what I'm about to say you. You understand?" She waited until Jocelyn nodded before she continued to speak. "You know I used to be mortal."

"Yes, of course. Everyone knows you're the one foretold who would rule over all the packs. And that a spell turned you from a mortal into a werewolf. The spell is said to have been made just for you."

"That last part you said," Roxie said with a smile, "isn't really correct. It's what we want the main population of werewolves to believe. You see, the spell didn't just work on me. It has turned two others as well."

"You mean anyone can use the spell to turn a mortal into a werewolf?" Jocelyn couldn't keep her shock out of her voice.

"Not exactly. It only works when I use it. I guess I'm special enough to make it work."

Royce laughed. "I'll say you're special, Roxie, in more ways than one."

Roxie turned to Royce and wagged a finger at him. "I'd watch it, Grandpa. You may be my grandfather, but that won't stop me from getting Billie to kick your ass. You know she can do it too." When Royce held up his hands in surrender, Roxie continued, "Anyway, when Royce claimed Billie as his mate, she decided to become a werewolf."

"Finn? Did you try the spell on him? His scent has the underlying scent of a werewolf."

Roxie's face grew serious. "Finn is the reason I had Beowulf ask you up here, Jocelyn. We know you're his mate, and that he hasn't claimed you as his yet. That being the case, Billie and I both decided it would be best if we let you know what's going on with him. I think Billie should explain the rest since he's her brother."

Jocelyn turned to look at Billie. "So you know I'm Finn's mate? Did he tell you about me?"

Billie gave her a half smile. "Yes, I know. Kind of hard not to notice the way he has been acting since he spent the night at your place. Let's just say he has been hell on wheels all day today."

"Do tell." Jocelyn couldn't stop the smile of pleasure that formed on her lips. It did her heart good to hear Finn hadn't been unaffected while not with her.

Billie laughed. "I can see you're pleased by that. Good. That means you aren't prepared to let Finn go."

"I told him that much when he walked out of my house."

"I think my brother's bachelor days are numbered. That being the case, you need to understand what happened three months ago. It'll help you when it comes to dealing with Finn." Billie sighed. "To make a long story short, Gren took Royce and Finn captive. He thought Royce's blood was the key to making the spell work, and he decided to use Finn as his guinea pig. It didn't work in the end, but since that day, Finn has withdrawn into himself and has taken a dislike to anyone who is a werewolf. Even me."

Jocelyn could easily see the hurt Billie felt in her eyes. "Given what happened, I can understand where he's coming from. I'm sure he just needs time to get over it."

"That's what we thought as well, but it's much more than his having been captured by Gren. Royce's blood somehow altered Finn. He can now smell scents like a werewolf, and as you said, his own has the smell of one too. Since he met you, his behavior is more of a male werewolf's than a mortal's. He feels the mating urge, even though he fights it. If you want Finn as your mate, you're going to have to be the one to hunt him down and claim him as your own."

Jocelyn smiled. "That won't be a problem. Just give me an address where to find him and he's as good as mine."

CHAPTER FOUR

The next day, Jocelyn prepared herself to go on her manhunt. She showered, put on her favorite jeans that fit tight in the right places and a nice blouse. She decided not to wear any perfume. Masking her scent wouldn't do her any favors when it came to getting Finn as her own. She counted on it being one weapon he would be unable to fight against.

Thanks to Billie, Jocelyn had a list of ways to contact or find Finn. She had his cell phone and home number along with the phone number to their family's gym where she now knew he worked. Billie had also given her the address where he lived with his twin and the address to the gym. Jocelyn checked the time before she left her house. According to Billie, Finn would be at the gym at this time of day. Her first plan of action was to corner him there where he couldn't make much of a scene.

The closer she came to her destination, the faster her heart beat with excitement. Just the thought of seeing Finn again made her body go up in flames. After she parked her car, Jocelyn went into the gym. She stopped just inside the lobby and took a deep breath. It didn't take her long to filter out his scent from the others. It smelled fresh and strong, which meant he could be found somewhere in there. With a smile she headed for the reception desk.

Just as she reached it, Finn's twin brother, Eli, intercepted her.

Even though Finn and Eli were identical, Jocelyn could easily tell them apart. Each man's scent had subtle differences, one being that Eli didn't have the scent of a werewolf as Finn did.

Eli held his hand out to her. "You must be Jocelyn."

"Yes, I am."

"Billie told me to keep an eye out for you."

"Did she now?" Jocelyn placed her hand in his.

"She did." Eli didn't shake it as expected. He pulled her closer and said in a conspiratorial tone of voice, "She also said for me to play things up a bit with you as well. Billie thinks if I were to act as if I'm interested in you, Finn won't be able to stop himself from making sure I keep my hands to myself." He leaned in even closer. "You see I've made a name for myself as being a bit of a lady's man. So did Finn until recently."

Playing along, Jocelyn put her other hand on Eli's chest. "Really? I never would have guessed that. It isn't as if I've watched the pair of you hit on anything in a skirt at Wulf's Den."

Eli chuckled. "I guess it's a good thing I never tried to pick you up. If you had accepted my offer, it would make things a trifle uncomfortable now."

"Never would have happened. Sorry, I only had eyes for Finn."

"Even then, huh? Finn's a lucky bastard."

Jocelyn looked over Eli's shoulder. "Well, Billie's plan seems to have worked. Don't look now, but Finn is headed this way. Let's see how far I can push him before he cracks."

She threaded her fingers through the back of Eli's hair and lifted her face to his as she slowly moved in to close the distance between them. With a growl, Finn roughly shoved them apart. He snarled at his twin before he clamped his hand around her wrist and dragged her away. Jocelyn had to bite back a smile of triumph as Finn pulled her through the gym and then shoved her inside one of the offices. He slammed the door behind them and then locked it.

"What the hell do you think you were about back there with Eli?" Finn stalked across the room until he stood in front of her.

"Nice to see you again as well, Finn." Her pussy clenched as his hot gaze raked her from head to toe and back up again. His wide chest rose and fell rapidly as he drew in great drafts of air. "Why do you care if I talked to Eli? It's not as if you want me for yourself. Eli is your identical twin so, why wouldn't I find myself attracted to him too?"

"So you would settle for the other twin?" Finn asked as he took her by the upper arms and forced her to walk backward until she hit the closed door. "Then why, when Eli touched you, couldn't I smell your arousal, but now that I do, it's so strong I feel as if it's drugging me?"

Jocelyn shivered at his words. The ache between her legs intensified as wetness leaked into her panties. Her nipples pebbled beneath her blouse. Billie's plan had worked like a charm. The heat that came off Finn's body hit her in waves. The scent of his arousal mixed with hers. Her body clamored for his. She was so turned-on, she had to fight the urge to demand he take her right now, against the door, regardless of who could hear what they would be doing, but she wouldn't do that. She couldn't let him. Even though her body screamed for her to touch him, take his lips that hovered so very near hers in a demanding kiss, she clamped down on her desire. She had to push him to his very limits, to make him so hot for her he wouldn't be able to resist her.

She licked her lips. Finn's gaze latched on her mouth. "I never said I still didn't want you. I prefer you over Eli, but if you won't accept me for what I am, I'll gladly take him to my bed instead."

"I don't want you anywhere near my twin, or any other man for that matter." Finn took a step closer so their bodies came in contact.

Jocelyn groaned to herself. This would torture not just Finn but herself also. His hard length brushed against her stomach. "You can't have it both ways, Finn. Either you claim me as your mate or I *will* go to other men."

Finn growled as he pushed away. "I can't. I'm not the one for you."

"Then prove it. If you aren't meant for me, you'll be able to resist the offer I'm about to make. I have the night off tonight. I'm going to sit at home and wait for you. If you show up, that means you'll have me as your mate, and there will be no going back for you. If you don't show up, I'll take that to mean I'm free to find another man to take your place in my bed. The decision is yours to make."

He stood a little away as he held himself so stiffly the muscles in his arms bulged. She wanted nothing more than to rip the T-shirt off his body and run her tongue across all that bared flesh. Instead, Jocelyn unlocked the door and left him to think over what she'd said. She hoped to God he came to her tonight and put them both out of their misery.

* * * *

Finn was in absolute hell. He felt as if he were in a perpetual state of arousal. It became so bad he had to leave the gym early. He couldn't think straight. And his brain played tricks on him. Images of Eli and Jocelyn in bed together, their naked bodies straining as they made love, played over and over inside his mind until he thought he would go crazy. He still couldn't stop picturing them.

He paced his apartment as he fought not to go to Jocelyn's place, but his body slowly wore down his willpower as it demanded he be with her. He couldn't eat, and he sure as hell couldn't sleep. As soon as he closed his eyes, the erotic dreams of Jocelyn he'd had last night would start up again. His aching cock couldn't take too many more of those.

Each time he paced he came closer to the apartment door. For the thousandth time, Finn reminded himself Jocelyn was a werewolf, that he shouldn't be attracted to one of her kind. He also reminded himself about the vision he'd had of her lying dead in a pool of her own blood. He didn't want to be responsible for her death. The rein he held over himself slipped once again as he thought of how good she'd looked and smelled when she'd come to the gym.

He'd cornered Eli after Jocelyn had left and told his twin that under no uncertain terms was he to touch her again. Eli had been quick to explain he'd done that for Finn's benefit, and that it had been Billie's idea. That didn't surprise Finn at all. It explained how Jocelyn had known where to find him. His baby sister had probably given Jocelyn phone numbers as well as addresses where he could be.

Finn paced the length of the apartment twice more before his resolve to stay away from Jocelyn disappeared in a puff of smoke. He snatched up his car keys on the way out, then headed down to the parking garage. His Mustang roared to life as he quickly started it before he drove to the street.

The drive to Jocelyn's house seemed to take forever, and it didn't help that he hit just about every red light. By the time he pulled into her driveway, Finn's control had reached breaking point. After he slammed his car door shut, he wasted no time knocking on her front door. Once Jocelyn opened it, he wrapped his arms around her waist and claimed her lips in a fiery kiss.

As he walked her back inside the house, Finn kicked the door shut behind them. He slanted his lips over hers as he pushed his tongue inside her mouth. He growled/groaned against her lips when Jocelyn wrapped hers around his. The smell of her arousal made him so hard it was almost a physical pain. He desperately needed to be inside her, but he didn't want their first time together to be on the hard floor.

He backed her toward the stairs that led to the upper level. Jocelyn broke their kiss only long enough to say, "Not the bedroom. I want you. Now."

Finn lifted his head. "I won't take you on the floor."

Jocelyn nipped his chin. "Then the couch in the living room. It's closer."

The couch sounded perfect to Finn. Somehow, he managed to get them into the living room. He kicked off his running shoes before he lowered Jocelyn onto the large black leather couch. Settling on top of her, he shoved his hand up her shirt and cupped her breast. He rubbed his thumb across her bra-covered taut nipple as he kissed a path down the side of her neck. She yanked on the bottom of his T-shirt and pulled it over his head. She shoved him off her so they lay on their sides and faced each other.

Finn made quick work of removing her shirt and bra. He cupped her ass and held her to him as he ground his erection against the crotch of her pants. Her pebbled nipples brushed against his chest as she nipped her way along his jaw and down the side of his throat. He stiffened and moaned with anticipation when she dragged her teeth across where his shoulder and neck met. The feel of them against his skin made his cock jerk inside his jeans.

Jocelyn's hand dropped to the top of his pants as she shifted lower on the couch. She ran her tongue across his chest while she

worked the button free and then pulled down his zipper. His hips
bucked as she reached inside his jeans and wrapped her fingers
around his straining erection. She squeezed him tightly as she
pumped up and down. The feel of her hand as it worked him
while she inched her way still lower on his body caused Finn to
growl deep in his chest.

As her lips and tongue made a wet trail down his abs, he
sucked in a breath. The air left his lungs with a moan when
Jocelyn tightly gripped his cock and swirled her tongue around
the head. She licked him from base to tip before she opened her
mouth and took as much of his length inside as she could. Finn
had to stop himself from coming when she sucked. It felt almost
too good to have her pleasure him this way, but he didn't want to
come like that. He wanted to be buried to the hilt in her wet pussy
when he did.

He soon pulled away and brought her back up so he could
claim her lips once more. With one hand, he undid her pants. No
longer able to be patient, Finn pushed them and her panties down
her legs. He dipped his hand between Jocelyn's legs and growled
in satisfaction when his fingers came away coated with her juices.
He quickly worked his jeans off. Once he was free of them, he
placed her leg over his hip and sheathed his cock inside her with
one hard thrust.

Jocelyn's strong inner muscles gripped his shaft as he
withdrew, then surged back inside. Finn looked down at their
bodies and watched her pussy take the full length of his cock as he
pumped his hips between her spread thighs. Still on his side, he
rode her slowly as she moaned. He wouldn't last long. His climax
built inside him.

Finn pushed Jocelyn onto her back. He pumped his hips faster
as he angled his hard shaft so it rubbed against her clit with each
thrust. She wrapped her legs around his waist. She moaned and
lifted her hips, matching his strokes. As her core spasmed with the
first flutter of her climax, he rode her harder until he pushed her
over the edge to release. Her inner walls clenched around his cock
in a tight fist. His own orgasm came to the point of no return. He
slammed into her, then gasped as a part of her reached out for
him. Unable to stop himself, that part of him caught and wrapped
itself around that part of her. They moaned as the two halves

joined and became whole.

Jocelyn arched up and bit Finn where his shoulder and neck met, sinking her teeth deep enough to break the skin. The effect was enough to send him into the most intense orgasm he'd ever felt. His cock pulsed deep inside her pussy as he filled her with his cum.

With his weight resting on his elbows, Finn gently kissed Jocelyn. He knew what had just happened between them. He'd once heard Billie describe it to Eli. He and Jocelyn were now mates. Their souls had joined, become one. They wouldn't be able to stand being separated from each other for very long. What had he done?

Jocelyn reached up and brushed his hair off his sweaty brow. "No regrets, Finn. There's no going back. We're mates now. You belong to me as much as I belong to you."

"The question is will you come to regret tying yourself to a mortal? You barely know me. I have a real aversion to werewolves, except when it comes to you, it would seem. I don't want you to end up hurt because of me."

"I don't care that you're mortal. All that matters to me is you're mine. We can work out the rest as we go along."

Much to Finn's pleasure, he hardened once again inside Jocelyn. Not with any other woman had he recovered after an orgasm so quickly. "I want you again, Jocelyn. This mating urge, or whatever the hell it is, still rides me. I feel as if another part of me wants to stake its claim on you as well."

He had a hard time even describing what he felt to himself. It was as if a wilder, animalistic part of him had risen to join him. It wanted to take Jocelyn as its mate as well, but in a dominating way.

Jocelyn wiggled out from under him. She got down on the floor on her hands and knees so her bottom faced him. She turned her head to look at him. Her eyes glowed as she gazed at him.

"I *know* what you want, Finn. You may not be a werewolf, but there *is* a wolf somewhere inside you. It wants me as his mate as well. Come. Take me as a male werewolf would."

Finn didn't hesitate to slip off the couch to the floor. The sight of Jocelyn's wet pussy as she lifted her bottom in offering made his cock harden even more. He moved behind her and settled to his knees. With a hand on either side of her hips, he rubbed the head of his cock back and forth against her pussy. She moaned as she backed against him and tried to impale herself on his hard shaft. He stilled her movements. He continued to tease them until she whimpered with need. Tightening his grip on her hips, he placed the tip of him at her core. He flexed his hips so only that part of him entered her. As her inner muscles clamped down on the head, he surged forward until he buried himself to the hilt.

He gritted his teeth against the intense wave of pleasure that washed over him. In this position, Jocelyn took more of him. When he pulled back only to slam into her, the head of his cock hit her cervix. This time he couldn't take things slowly. With a very wolflike growl, he slammed into her over and over again. He kept his hands on her hips and didn't allow her to move. He held her still for his invasion. From the moans she made, he knew she wouldn't complain later about the way he took her now.

The sound of his groans filled the room as Finn quickened his pace. Wanting Jocelyn to come before he did, he reached around her body until he found her clit. As he thrust into her, he stroked it. Her pussy clenched. She moaned as her core flexed around his shaft while she climaxed. He pushed into her harder, faster, until he climaxed as well. He stroked into her one final time and threw back his head on what sounded damn close to a wolf's howl while he spilled deep inside her.

Finn leaned forward and kissed the back of Jocelyn's neck as he wrapped his arms around her waist. She was now his. He only hoped his taking her as his mate hadn't signed her death warrant.

CHAPTER FIVE

Jocelyn watched Finn sleep. They'd moved upstairs to her bedroom now that the desperate need to have each other had eased a bit. It wouldn't totally go away. All it would take to set if off again would be for them to be apart, especially for a long length of time. As mates, they would crave each other's touch, and when they were apart, the need would have their minds playing tricks on them. They would miss each other as if they had been separated for weeks rather than hours. It would only intensify as time went on, and could become quite unpleasant. Not that Jocelyn had firsthand experience since she'd never had a mate before.

Using the tip of her finger, Jocelyn ran it across the stubble on Finn's cheek. His eyes fluttered open. He captured the digit and kissed the tip of it. "If you want to make love again, you're going to have to give me a little more time to get my strength back. Unlike the males of your kind, I can't keep an erection for hours at a time after I've had an orgasm."

She chuckled. "You know about that ability they have, huh?"

Finn snorted. "Not like I asked or anything. Let's just say Billie can be very frank when the moment takes her."

"I got the impression when I met her that Billie speaks her mind."

"So I was right. Billie helped you find me."

"Among other things, yes."

Finn's brows drew together. "What does that mean?"

"She and Roxie explained what happened to you three months ago. About what happened when Gren took you and Royce captive."

As Finn tried to sit up, Jocelyn pushed him back down. Being stronger than him had its advantages. "Relax, Finn. They felt it would help me to understand where you were coming from. And I can understand why you don't like my kind very much. I'd probably feel the same way."

"Did Roxie explain about the spell as well?"

"Yes. That Gren's attempt to use it on you failed, and that Royce's blood ended up having an effect on you."

"Did Billie also tell you that she wants Roxie to try the spell on me again?" When Jocelyn didn't say anything, Finn cursed under his breath. "I won't, Jocelyn. I can't. Not for you, not for Billie."

Jocelyn sighed. "I would never force you to do it. Even though it will kill me to have to watch you grow old and die, I wouldn't make you do anything you didn't want to do."

Finn placed her hand on his chest over his heart. "How old are you, Jocelyn?"

"Are you *sure* you really want to know?"

"Yes."

"I'm five hundred years old."

"Which means you could live for another two and a half thousand years," Finn said in a flat voice.

"Yes." Jocelyn didn't know how she would be able to live if Finn chose to stay a mortal and she would have to watch him die while she had many years ahead of her, but it would be his decision to make. He already had a hard enough time dealing with the whole idea that werewolves did exist, that they weren't a thing of legends only. "How old are you?"

"I'm thirty-three. Makes me a baby compared to you."

Jocelyn smiled and snuggled closer. "I don't know about that. I can say from firsthand experience that you can in no way be described as a baby. You're most definitely a man in every way."

Finn gave her a half smile. "Give me a couple of hours and I'll show you again how much of a man I am. Right now, I feel as if I could sleep for a year. I haven't been able to the last few nights.

Thanks to you, I might add."

"I'll make it up to you. I suggest you go to sleep, my mate. I'm starting to get hungry for you again," Jocelyn softly growled into his ear.

"You think I'll be able to sleep now after you told me that?" Finn rolled her onto her back and came down on top of her. "It would seem I have enough energy for one more time before I rest."

Jocelyn lifted her hips to met Finn as he slowly entered her. She held him tight while he made love to her. If she would only get a mortal's lifetime with him, she would make every minute of it count. She would need the memories to last her the long, lonely years after he left her.

* * * *

The next morning Jocelyn made a big breakfast for herself and Finn. She prepared an omelet for each of them, home fried potatoes, and bacon. It pleased her to see how much food he could eat. Males of her kind usually ate a lot of food, which they needed, given how tall and muscular they were. Finn would have no problems keeping up with any of them.

Jocelyn smiled as Finn cleaned his plate and looked at the stove. "Would you like another helping? There's more home fries and bacon. If you want, I can make you another omelet."

Finn shook his head as he swallowed a mouthful. "Home fries and bacon are fine."

She took his plate and went to the stove to get the food. After she put the plate back in front of him and sat, she said, "I'm glad to see you're enjoying the meal."

"You're a good cook, Jocelyn."

"Thanks. I enjoy cooking. I learned how from the chefs my uncle has hired over the years."

"Your uncle didn't mind you going to his house to bug his hired chef?"

"Actually, my uncle raised me after my parents died."

"I guess I put my foot in my mouth with that comment. I'm sorry to hear you lost your parents."

Jocelyn waved Finn's apology away with a flick of her hand.

"It's okay. I was young when I lost them, so it isn't as if it just happened. I've had years to accept they're gone." Even though she'd gotten over the pain of losing her parents, she didn't like to remember how they'd died. "What about you, Finn? Are your parents alive?"

"Yes. My dad runs the gym. I think he still works out more than I do."

"And your mom? Does she work at the gym too?"

Finn's face went blank. "No, she doesn't. She hasn't lived with us since Billie was a baby."

"Did you see her much after your parents divorced?"

"They aren't divorced." Finn locked his gaze with hers. "My mom lives in a special-needs home for people who have mental conditions. She tried to kill Billie when she was a small baby because of the visions she had."

Jocelyn had the feeling Finn watched her to judge how she would react to what he'd told her about his mother. By how guarded his expression had become, she got the distinct impression what she said next would have an effect on him.

"What did she see?"

"She saw Billie would turn into a wolf and kill. My mother had visions before, but this one drove her over the edge."

Jocelyn sucked in a breath, but she thought it best not to comment on what Finn's mother had seen in her vision. "Did she pass on her ability to have visions to any of you?"

Finn stiffened, then looked at his plate. "No. She didn't pass on her ability to have visions to any of her children."

"So none of you inherited any kind of ability from her?" Jocelyn couldn't shake the feeling that Finn had just lied to her. Why else would he seem so touchy about the subject?

"If you count Billie's ability to find anyone she comes in contact with, anywhere, anytime, then I would say yes."

"I'm sure she finds that a handy."

"Too much, if you ask me." Finn looked at the clock on the wall. "I have a training session scheduled in an hour. I should swing home first before I go to the gym."

Finn was trying to put some distance between them again. She guessed she must have touched on a sore spot when she brought up the subject of his mother. "I'll come to the gym later to be with you."

"That's not necessary." Finn stood and came around the table to give her a quick kiss. "I have training sessions booked for most of the day. I won't have much time to spend with you. I'll come back when I'm finished and take you out to dinner."

After Jocelyn heard the front door close behind Finn, she got up and cleared the breakfast dishes. She shook her head. If he thought he could stay away from her that long and not feel the separation, he would be in for a big surprise.

* * * *

Since he really didn't have that much time before he had his first client of the day, Finn decided to drive straight to the gym instead of returning to his apartment to change. At the gym he had a spare set of clean clothes in his locker. He would shower there.

Once he arrived at the gym, Finn headed straight for the men's change room. He put the clothes he wore in the bottom of his locker and then went to the showers. While he washed his hair, he found his thoughts strayed to Jocelyn. He'd only left her place fifteen minutes ago, but he already missed her a little. Even though he knew it was part of being mated to a werewolf, he told himself to get a grip. He could stand not having her with him. They worked at different times. He didn't expect her to come to the gym with him every day when she had to work at night at Wulf's Den, even though he would go to the nightclub with her. He didn't like the idea of her around other men, especially other single male werewolves.

Finn rinsed his hair and opened his eyes to see Eli at the edge of the tiled shower area. His twin stood with his arms crossed as he watched him. "Are you getting your jollies watching me shower?"

Eli snorted. "Not really, no. I saw you duck in here pretty quick. I thought I'd come and see how your night went last night."

"Good enough." Finn grabbed his bar of soap and washed his body.

"When you didn't come home last night, I figured you must

have gone to be with Jocelyn. So, do I have a new sister-in-law?"

Finn stood under the water and rinsed. He turned off the shower, then grabbed his towel. As he dried, he said, "If you mean did I claim her as my mate, then I guess you do."

Eli shook his head and smiled. "Well, damn. Now I'm the only one not married. And here I thought the pair of us would never settle down."

"It isn't as if I planned on this, Eli." Finn jerked the towel around his hips and brushed past his twin as he went to his locker. Eli followed.

"No, I guess you didn't. I don't have a client for the next couple of hours. Do you want me to keep Jocelyn entertained while you work with yours?"

Finn barely managed to keep a growl from coming out. "That won't be necessary. I told Jocelyn I'd see her later."

With incredulity in his voice, Eli asked, "So, she isn't coming to the gym?"

"That's right." Finn pulled his shirt over his head before he gave his twin a curious stare. "Why do you find that hard to believe?"

"You've heard Billie talk about what it's like to be mated to a werewolf. You know it drives her and Royce crazy to be apart from one another. Why do you think Royce is here whenever Billie is? I think you're asking for problems, brother of mine."

Finn slammed his locker door shut and then put on his lock. "I'll be fine," he snapped. "It's not as if I won't see her later."

Eli snickered. "Keep telling yourself that. I think you already have started to feel the separation, if you ask me. What has it been, a half hour since you left Jocelyn? And already you're in a mood."

"I didn't ask you. I can handle it."

"Maybe you can, but what about Jocelyn? Remember this goes *both* ways. She'll be just as affected as you. At least think about what she'll be going through before you test your limits too far."

"Your concern has been noted. Now if you'll excuse me, I have a client to get ready for." Finn headed out of the change room.

Eli called to him before he reached the door. "Just to let you know, most of my day is pretty empty. If you end up having to leave early, I can take on the rest of your clients for today."

With a shake of his head, Finn walked out of the change room. He wasn't that pathetic. He could handle the separation just fine.

* * * *

Jocelyn tried to keep herself busy while Finn worked at the gym. She decided she would bake something sweet for her mate. At first, she thought only to make brownies, but they didn't take too long to mix together and put into the oven to bake. Already she found her thoughts drawn to him. She had to remind herself more than a few times that nothing bad had happened to him and that he would be coming back to her. Once the urge to call him on his cell phone took her, she knew she would be in trouble if she didn't find something else to distract her wayward thoughts. That's when she made the decision to continue to bake.

While the brownies were in the oven, Jocelyn made pastry for an apple pie. After she had that assembled and in the oven with the brownies, she moved on to making cookies. By that time, her kitchen had filled with the delicious scent of baked goods, and she'd managed to make it through two hours without Finn. Her thoughts constantly wandered as the need to be with him ate at her, but she did her best to stay focused as much as she could.

With the cookies on a rack to cool, Jocelyn seriously considered baking a cake from scratch, but she looked at all the dessert things she'd already made and thought better of it. She really didn't know if Finn even liked to eat sweets, and she'd already made more than one man would want to consume. She would help him eat it, but still, there was more than enough for two people. The four dozen cookies she'd made put things over the top.

Now that she didn't have anything else to distract herself with, Jocelyn felt as if she could climb the walls. Her need to be with Finn rose to an almost unbearable level. She paced the length of the kitchen, ready to curse him for making her go through this. It was all his fault. He had to have known this would happen to them when he'd left. His sister had taken a werewolf for a mate. Jocelyn felt sure Billie would have told her family what the separation would do to her and Royce.

The telephone rang. Jocelyn rushed to it and looked at the call display. She frowned when she saw it wasn't Finn who called.

From the number, she knew her uncle would be on the other end if she answered it. Not exactly in the mood to make chitchat, she let her answering machine take the call. Her uncle called at least four times a week just to check up on her, or at least that was what he told her.

Jocelyn had a feeling he did it for other reasons. Her uncle hadn't been at all thrilled when she'd gotten the job at Wulf's Den and then announced she would be moving out of his house. Uncle Grant, at nine hundred years old, still held on to the antiquated belief that women needed to live with a male member of their family until they married, or in their kind's case, found her mate. He'd also pushed her in the face of every eligible single male werewolf he thought came from a good bloodline. At one time, her uncle had aspirations of her being mated to Beowulf since he was the leader of their pack. Luckily for Jocelyn, Roxie's arrival in Beowulf's life had put an end to that. She had felt smothered in her uncle's house, which had prompted her to get a job and a house of her own.

After the phone stopped ringing, Jocelyn looked at the clock. She would give Finn a half hour more. If he didn't have his ass back at her place by then, she would go to him. She hoped he suffered as much as she did.

CHAPTER SIX

He was a pathetic mess. Finn glanced at the clock on the wall in the main gym. He had only five more minutes to go with the client he now worked with. He could make it. Five minutes passed quickly, at least it did when he didn't feel as if he'd lost his mind.

Two hours had gone by since he'd arrived at the gym. Finn found his ability to concentrate had reached an all-time low. One thought filled his mind—getting back to Jocelyn and having sex. Sex with her in her bed, on the kitchen table, the big leather couch in the living room, even up against a wall. He could barely manage to keep the perpetual hard-on he sported hidden. The clipboard he carried while training clients helped to keep his condition out of sight. He spent more time with it held in front of his crotch than he did writing anything on it.

When he finished with his client, Finn had to admit defeat. He couldn't stay at the gym any longer. He had to get back to Jocelyn. He'd thought he could control the need to be with her, but he'd only fooled himself. Now he knew why Royce made the choice to hang around the gym while Billie worked when he didn't have to. The longing and other emotions that raged inside him showed him how connected he'd become to Jocelyn. Only one night with her, and he couldn't function without her nearby.

After Finn booked the client's next appointment, he went in

search of Eli. His twin would say "I told you so," but right now he didn't much care. Eli sat on the edge of Billie's desk as he spoke to her and Royce.

His twin took one look at his face and stood. "I guess my day got busier. When is your next client expected?"

"In fifteen minutes." Billie and Royce watched him closely as he'd spoken to Eli.

"Okay. I'll go now and look over what workout routine you've been using."

After Eli left, Finn would have left as well, but Billie stopped him. "Finn, wait. You look rather…uncomfortable."

He clenched his hands at his sides at the unwanted delay. "Just say what you have on your mind, Billie, so I can get the hell out of here."

Billie smiled. "Congratulations on your mating, Finn. It's about damn time. You know you'll have to bring Jocelyn around to meet the rest of the family. Dad will want to meet his new daughter-in-law."

"I plan to do that soon."

"Good. Now you can go. Just make sure you both make it inside the house before you start banging your mate."

Royce shook his head. "You do have a way with words, Billie. Take pity on your poor brother and let him leave to be with his mate."

Billie stepped closer to Royce and drew lazy circles on his chest while she gave him a heated look. "I only thought to give him fair warning. I know more than once we've almost never made it past the front door before the urge to bang me overtook you."

Any other time Finn would have been disgusted to hear anything about his baby sister's sex life, but right now it just reminded him of how badly he needed to have Jocelyn under him.

"I'm out of here. Tell Dad where I went." He didn't wait around to hear Billie's response.

* * * *

At the sound of a car pulling into her driveway, Jocelyn rushed to the front door and then looked out the small side window. Her heart beat faster when she saw Finn get out of his Mustang before he slammed the door shut. She pulled open the house door for him as soon as his feet hit her porch.

With stark lust blazing in his gray-blue eyes, Finn swept her into his arms and kicked the front door closed. Jocelyn knew they wouldn't make it to her bedroom again when he took her lips in a hard kiss.

Once he kissed her sufficiently enough to make her legs go weak, Finn lifted his head and sniffed the air. "Something smells really good. It smells almost as good as the scent of your arousal."

It took Jocelyn a couple of seconds to get her brain to function enough to respond after that comment. "I did some baking when you were gone. I think I may have overdone it, though."

Finn kept his arms around her and walked her backward toward the kitchen as he nibbled on the side of her neck. "Let's see what you baked."

Inside the kitchen, Finn moved away from her neck and took in all the baked goods she'd placed on one end of the kitchen table. He gazed at her. "I think I know why you did all this. I'm sorry, Jocelyn. I really didn't think it would get this bad, but I'll make it up to you."

She shuddered as he bent his head and dragged his tongue down the side of her neck. "You better. And you better not be that stubborn again. We could have avoided this if you'd just let me go to the gym with you."

He shoved his hands up her shirt and cupped her breasts while he nibbled the corner of her mouth. "I learned my lesson."

Jocelyn opened to allow Finn entrance when he took her lips in a full kiss. Their tongues twined as he pinched her taut nipples through her bra. Her body went into overdrive. The need to have him deep inside her made her moan. Her pussy ached in reaction to having his fully engorged cock nestled against her stomach. She would never get enough of him.

Finn let go of her breasts, then pushed up her shirt. He dipped his tongue between her breasts before he pulled her top over her head. The bra came off seconds later. As he trailed kisses across her collarbones, he worked her jeans down her legs and off. He picked her up and sat her on the edge of the table on the opposite end of the baked goods. He came to stand between her spread legs. He swirled his tongue around one of her nipples before he took it deep into his mouth. Jocelyn leaned back on her hands as he sucked.

Finn lavished the same attention to her other tight peak before he made his way lower on her body. His wicked tongue tasted every inch of her skin as he continued his downward travel. Once he reached the top of her panties, Jocelyn thought he would remove them. She prayed he would remove them. Instead, he sank to his knees on the floor, and with a hand on each of her thighs, he spread her legs farther apart. He dragged his tongue along her pussy through the lace of her panties. She moaned as he continued to lap at her, teasing her. The thin barrier of her underwear was enough to keep her from really feeling him tonguing her. He didn't stop until they were soaked from her juices and the wetness of his tongue.

After he pulled away and once again stood between her legs, Jocelyn groaned. Finn leaned over and reached for the pan of brownies she'd made. He placed it next to her.

"I bet these will taste even better if I eat them off your delectable body."

Before Jocelyn could say anything, Finn grabbed a handful of the brownie and rubbed it across her chest. She gasped as he licked the sweet confection off her skin. Once he ate it all, he scooped up another handful, smeared it between her breasts and down her stomach. He meticulously licked her clean until once again he'd reached the top of her panties. With his clean hand, he hooked the waistband with a finger and dragged them down her legs.

Finn looked at her pussy and then at his brownie-covered fingers. He brought his hand to his mouth and licked it clean. Jocelyn couldn't believe how hot it made her to watch him use his tongue on each finger, then his palm. By the time he finished, she panted with need.

She locked gazes with him as he slowly sank to his knees once again. He gave his hand one last lick. "You taste sweet enough on your own."

Jocelyn moaned as Finn licked her pussy from bottom to top. He swirled his tongue around her clit before he flicked it with the tip of it. She rocked her hips against his mouth as he sucked on the small bundle of nerves before he spread her nether lips and jabbed his stiffened tongue into her core. When he replaced his tongue with two of his fingers, she matched his strokes as he moved them in and out of her slick opening. She whimpered and gasped while she rode the digits. He latched on to her clit and sucked, pushing her ever closer to her release.

Then she was there. Her head fell back as she moaned loudly. Wave after wave of pleasure surged through her. After the last spasm eased, Jocelyn lifted her head. Finn climbed to his feet. He quickly worked the button and zipper on his jeans. He pushed them down just past his ass. Her core clenched at the sight of his thick, hard cock standing out from his body. A bead of precum sat on the very tip.

Finn lifted one of her hands and led it to his cock. He wrapped her fingers around it. "Put me where you want me, Jocelyn."

She pumped her hand up and down his shaft a couple of times before she moved closer to the edge of the table. In that position, she put her legs around Finn's waist, then slowly led him to her pussy. Without letting go of his shaft, she brushed the head of it against her core, then rubbed it against her clit. He grabbed her bottom and dug his fingers into the soft globes of flesh while she continued to stimulate herself with his erection. Once she couldn't take any more, Jocelyn brought the head of his shaft to her slick opening and pushed down on it. With a jerk of his hips, he pushed himself home.

The pace Finn set was hard and fast. Jocelyn held on to his shoulders as he surged into her. She squeezed down on his shaft as he impaled her over and over again. Taking hold of the collar of his T-shirt, she pulled it away from his neck. She licked the bite mark she'd made earlier. He shuddered as she dragged her teeth over it. She couldn't ignore the instinct to mark him as her own. With a low growl, she bit him on the same spot where his shoulder and neck met. His cock hardened even more.

Finn growled/groaned. He pumped his hips faster as she held on to him with her teeth. The sounds he made as he thrust into her made another climax inch closer. She released his neck, then arched her back. He bent his head and sucked a nipple into his mouth while he rode her harder. That was enough to send her flying over the edge. Her strong inner walls gripped his cock as her orgasm tore through her. As her body milked his shaft, he pushed into her once, twice, before he groaned loudly. Hot spurts of his cum filled her as he came.

Panting, Jocelyn rested her forehead on Finn's shoulder. Once she could breathe at a normal pace once again, she lifted her head and lightly brushed her lips against his. "I don't think I'm going to be able to bake brownies without thinking about what you did with them."

Finn chuckled. "I was right, though. They tasted a lot better licked off your skin."

Jocelyn groaned. "You're killing me here."

"In a good way." Finn reached up and touched the bite mark she left on his neck. "You bit me again."

She pulled his hand away and dragged her tongue across it. Finn shuddered against her. "That means you're mine. If another single female werewolf sees that mark, she'll know you're off limits. It's also a turn-on for a male werewolf to be bitten."

"Well, it would seem it's one of mine too. You can sink your teeth into me anytime you want." His softening cock jerked inside her. "Actually, it makes me horny just thinking about it."

"I'll have to bite you more often then."

"And since it's a mark to keep other female werewolves away from me, I guess I'd better wear a shirt that'll show it off when I go to Wulf's Den with you tonight. The only werewolf I want lusting after me is you."

Jocelyn wrapped her arms around the back of Finn's neck. "So you're going to come to work with me tonight?"

"I told you before that I'd learned my lesson. I'm not going through that again tonight. I'm going with you to Wulf's Den tonight, and every night you have to work." Finn picked her up into his arms. Jocelyn kept her legs around his waist and locked her ankles at his back. Before he carried her out of the kitchen, he picked up the pan of the remaining brownies. "I think there will be enough time."

She gave him a questioning look. "Enough time for what?"

He headed for the stairs. "I think there'll be enough time to enjoy more of your brownies before you have to get ready for work."

Jocelyn groaned. "I think you're right. Besides, I haven't had a chance to taste them yet, either. I wonder if they'll taste just as good licked off your body as well." She held tighter to Finn as he took the stairs two at a time.

Much later, after they had consumed half a pan of brownies off each other's body, Jocelyn suggested they take a shower together. Of course that ended up in another bout of lovemaking. After that, she got dressed in a black skirt—one of her longer ones that Finn had picked out for her to wear—and a dark pink silk blouse, which didn't have a very low neckline. Then they left to go to Finn's apartment so he could get dressed for the night.

Eli had already made it there before they'd arrived. He'd been sitting on the couch in the living room while he watched television, but when they walked through the apartment door, he got up to greet them.

He gave Jocelyn a hug and kissed her cheek. "Welcome to the York family, Jocelyn. Though I have to say you've left me in an awkward position."

"How so?"

"Now that you have become Finn's mate, I'm the only York sibling who is still single. I have a feeling Billie will do her best to match me up."

Finn pulled Jocelyn closer to his side. "It's not as bad as we thought it would be. I like the idea of being a one-woman man now."

Eli made an overexaggerated cringe. "Still not for me." He quickly changed the subject. "So when can I expect you to move out, Finn?"

Jocelyn tried to glance casually at Finn to see what his reaction had been to his twin's question. His brows drew together as if he hadn't understood what he'd been asked. Then slowly, he looked at her before he answered.

"I'm not sure. I haven't thought that far ahead," Finn mumbled.

"Oops. I thought now that you two were mated you would..." Eli's words fell away when Finn scowled at him.

She quickly jumped into the conversation. "That's okay, Eli. Things have happened so fast we haven't had a chance to discuss our living arrangements yet." Jocelyn made a show of looking at the clock. "I suggest you hurry up and change, Finn. I have to be at the nightclub before it opens."

Finn nodded, then left to go to his bedroom. Eli gave her a sheepish look. "I'm sorry. I didn't think that one out."

"It's all right, really."

Eli placed a hand on her chin and made her look at him when she stared in the direction Finn had gone. "If it's any consolation it doesn't have anything to do with you being Finn's mate that has him acting a bit reluctant. It's a twin thing. We've never lived apart—ever. Back at my dad's place, we always shared a room, and when we decided to move out, we got this apartment together. The only reason it isn't bothering me as much as him is I thought about him having to move out first. I've had a little time to come to grips with it. Not that it won't seem strange not to have him around all the time."

Jocelyn smiled and kissed Eli's cheek. "I'm not stealing Finn from you. You're welcome to come to my house any time you like. Plus, you'll still see him every day at the gym."

"That's true." Right then, Finn came out of his bedroom dressed in charcoal slacks and a black button-down shirt. He headed to them. Eli said, "You two have a good night. I guess I'll see you tomorrow morning at the gym."

Finn clapped Eli on the shoulder. "You could always come to Wulf's Den with us."

"No. Maybe some other time."

Jocelyn took the hand Finn offered her as they left the apartment. She made a mental note to herself. Billie wouldn't be the only one trying to match Eli up. Maybe the two of them could find a nice female werewolf for him to take as his mate.

CHAPTER SEVEN

Once Jocelyn and Finn arrived at Wulf's Den, Roxie greeted Jocelyn with a hug. Finn reluctantly let her kiss his cheek. "I hear congratulations are in order. I couldn't be happier for the both of you."

"Thanks," Jocelyn said.

Roxie went to stand between Jocelyn and Finn and looped an arm through each of theirs. She walked toward the bar where Beowulf waited. "To celebrate, a good bottle of champagne is in order." She added in a mock whisper, "I finagled Beowulf into opening one of his expensive bottles."

As they reached the bar, Beowulf, who stood behind it, filled the four champagne glasses he'd set out in front of him. "I heard that, Rox. Just so the two of you know, she didn't finagle so much as order me to open it."

"Because you knew if you didn't, I wouldn't be happy. If I'm not happy, I'm capable of doing something to you that you don't like." Roxie barked like a dog twice.

Beowulf handed the full glasses to each of them. "Now, Roxie, you know if you used that ability of yours to keep me locked in my werewolf form, you'd have a very lonely night. If you know what I mean."

Roxie made no further comment and held up her glass and said, "To Jocelyn and Finn."

They clinked glasses together in a toast, then downed their champagne, except for Finn, who sipped his. Being werewolves, Jocelyn, Roxie, and Beowulf could drink three times the amount of alcohol Finn could without feeling its effect. At least this night Jocelyn wouldn't have to drag him drunk out of Wulf's Den.

A short time later, the club's doors opened for the night. Jocelyn suggested Finn sit at the bar while she waited tables, but he declined. Instead, he went and sat at the very back of the room. Even though he seemed more comfortable around her and hadn't acted too distant to Roxie and Beowulf, she had a feeling he still didn't much like being around others of her kind. She didn't argue with him when he went to sit at the table with a beer in hand.

In between waiting on tables, she spent as much time as she could with Finn. They mostly talked about inconsequential things. To help him adjust to the fact he would now be considered part of her pack since he was her mate, Jocelyn pointed out other members to him. When one came by, she'd introduce them to Finn. It made him uncomfortable, but it didn't stop her from doing it.

Halfway through the night, Jocelyn heard an all-too-familiar voice say her name as she chatted with Finn. She plastered on a smile before she turned to face her uncle, Grant. Her gaze flicked briefly to her cousin, Ben, who stood next to his father.

"What a nice surprise, Uncle Grant, to come and see me at work." Her uncle gazed over her shoulder at Finn. "And I see you brought Ben with you as well."

Grant dragged his gaze from Finn and gave her a smile before he kissed her cheeks. "When you didn't answer your phone when I called earlier today, and then didn't return my message, I thought I'd come by to see if everything was all right. Ben decided he wanted to tag along."

"As you can see I'm fine. I saw you had called, but I got a little sidetracked and forgot to call you back before I came into work."

"What could have been so important that you couldn't call me back? As the head of our family, it's my responsibility to watch over you. I can't do that very well if you don't return my phone calls."

Jocelyn bit the inside of her cheek to stop herself from telling her uncle she was perfectly capable of looking after herself. She hated when he talked to her like that. It felt so demeaning. Once she had herself back under control, she opened her mouth to respond but didn't get the chance. Finn stood from the table and came around to her. He put his arm around her shoulders and pulled her against his side. Grant's eyes narrowed at the proprietary way Finn held her.

Finn stuck out his hand to shake her uncle's. "You can put the blame for Jocelyn not calling you back on me."

Her uncle reluctantly shook Finn's hand. "And you would be?" Grant's upper lip lifted infinitesimally in a sneer as he looked down his aquiline nose at Finn.

"Finn York."

"I see." Grant leveled his gaze on Jocelyn. "You didn't tell me you'd met...somebody new, my dear."

Jocelyn took a deep breath. She hadn't planned on telling her uncle about Finn in quite this way, but no time like the present. "Finn is more than just an acquaintance, Uncle Grant. He's my mate."

Her uncle's face grew hard. "When did this happen?"

"Last night."

"So you allowed this mortal to claim you as his mate without my permission?"

Her uncle said the word mortal as someone would a dirty word. Jocelyn didn't like that one bit. "I'm an adult now, Uncle Grant. I don't need your permission to take a mate. It isn't as if we had much control over the matter. What's done is done. Why don't you sit and have a drink while you and Ben are here? I'll be happy to get you whatever you want, on me."

Grant sent an icy glare in Finn's direction before he leveled a stern gaze on her. "We'll take the drink, but we'll sit at another table."

Jocelyn felt like giving her uncle a smack as he turned his back on them and then sat at a table a good distance away from the one Finn had chosen. Her cousin gave her a look of disgust before he joined his father. Actually, both of them needed a good smack, preferable to the backs of their heads.

She turned to Finn. "I'm sorry about that. I had no idea my uncle and cousin would show up here. And I didn't expect that kind of reaction from them when they learned you were my mate."

"Don't worry about it, Jocelyn. Let's just say the feeling is mutual. I hope you don't expect me to play buddy-buddy with them, because it isn't going to happen."

"No, I don't. I have a hard time dealing with them myself. My uncle has outdated ideas. He thinks females are weak and must be told what to do." She gave Finn a quick kiss on the lips, done mostly for her uncle and cousin's benefit. "I'll get them their drinks, then I'll be back."

Finn pulled her to him before she could walk away and kissed her thoroughly. "If you're going to yank their chains, Jocelyn, at least do it right."

Jocelyn shook her head and laughed. "You're worse than I am."

She headed for the bar. On the way, she glanced at her uncle's table. His eyes practically shot daggers in Finn's direction. Finn had succeeded in yanking Grant's chain.

*

Grant watched his niece and the mortal she had allowed to claim her as his mate. The thought of a mortal being part of his family repulsed him. They were beneath werewolves. That Jocelyn would lower herself to bind herself to one made him more than a bit angry. God forbid if they produced a child. The pure bloodlines of his family didn't need the taint of a mortal added to it.

His son growled quietly enough not to be overheard. "Look at them, Father. They can't keep their hands off each other. It's disgusting. How could have Jocelyn done that?"

"I've asked myself that very question, Ben. Obviously, I have been too lax in my vigilance over her. I should never have allowed her to take this job or move to her own place. If she were still living under my roof, this never would have happened."

Grant waved away the waitress who came to their table to see if they wanted another drink. He didn't miss the appreciative look she sent in his direction before she walked away. At nine hundred years old, he was in his prime. His dark hair, dark eyes, and good looks garnered him a lot of attention from women, werewolf and mortal alike. Not that he'd ever dirty himself by taking a mortal to bed. When he and his son, who took after him in looks, went out together, women noticed them.

Ben took a sip of his wine. "Then what are you going to do about it?"

"I think a talk with Jocelyn is in order, one that won't include the mortal. It's time she learned her place."

*

Finn let himself relax when Jocelyn's uncle and cousin finally got up and left Wulf's Den. The pair of them had done nothing but shoot disgusted glances his way. Now he knew what it must have felt like for the other werewolves at the nightclub when he used to look at them with the same expression. Being on the receiving end had been a bit of an eye opener. He just hoped he hadn't come across as high and mighty as her uncle and cousin had.

Jocelyn served one of her tables their drinks. She laughed at something one of the women had said. With the music blaring out of the nightclub's sound system, he couldn't hear what they'd spoken, and he didn't much care. He only cared about Jocelyn. Even the werewolves who sat around him didn't bother him as much as it had before he'd taken her as his mate. And the memory of what had taken place three months before didn't seem to bother him to the extreme it had in the past. He now understood why Billie had done what she'd done. If he'd been in her place and Gren had had Jocelyn as his captive, Finn probably would have put the werewolf down to make sure he never touched her again too.

The thought of having Jocelyn taken from him almost made him feel physically ill. Bound together as they were, he couldn't imagine being able to go on if anything happened to her. With those thoughts, what he'd seen in his vision that had showed Jocelyn dead came to the forefront of his mind. He hadn't seen what had caused her death, just that he'd somehow been responsible for it. At that moment, she looked at him. Her brows drew together as she stared at him with an expression of worry.

Obviously, she'd seen the anxiety on his face that he felt every time he thought of that vision. He pushed those thoughts away and gave her a smile. She walked from the table and headed to where he sat.

"Is everything okay, Finn? I see my uncle and cousin left. Did they say anything to you before they did?"

He wrapped his arm around her waist and pulled her so she stood next to his chair. Finn looked up at her and shook his head. "Everything is fine. No, they didn't say anything." He flashed a sexy grin. "How about you talk to Beowulf and see if he'll let you off a bit early? All I can think about it getting you to your place and into bed."

Jocelyn smiled. "I think that can be arranged since we're newly mated. I'll be right back."

She walked to the bar, which Beowulf stood behind serving drinks. She leaned over it to speak to him. Beowulf looked around her at him. Finn nodded in acknowledgment. Beowulf chuckled and nodded. Jocelyn returned a short while later with her purse.

Since he'd had more than a couple of drinks, Finn let Jocelyn drive his Mustang to her place. As soon as they were inside the house, he pulled her to him and be brought his lips down to devour her mouth. This time they managed to make it to her bedroom before their clothes came off.

* * * *

Jocelyn snuggled sleepily against Finn's side. By his even breaths, she knew he'd fallen asleep. It wasn't any wonder. Their lovemaking had been intense. It had been as if he couldn't get enough of her. Not that she complained or anything. So what if she couldn't walk the next morning? It would be well worth it, considering how she'd ended up in that condition in the first place.

She'd just started to drift off to sleep when Finn twitched. When he called out her name in an agonized voice and thrashed about, Jocelyn propped herself up on her elbow and shook his shoulder. "Finn, wake up." As he continued to dream, she shook him harder. "Wake up, Finn. It's only a bad dream."

He came awake with a start. His chest rapidly rose and fell as he looked at her. Whatever he'd dreamed about couldn't have been pleasant. His eyes were dilated, and a thin film of sweat dampened his forehead.

She gently brushed it away. "Okay now?"

His reaction made Jocelyn gasp in surprise. Finn pushed her back onto the bed as he rolled on top of her. The feel of his hardening cock as the head probed her still-wet pussy made her gasp again for a different reason. She caressed his cheek as he slid the full length of his shaft inside her and lay still. His body shook as he stared at her with fear in his eyes.

"Don't ever leave me, Jocelyn." Finn's voice shook with emotion. "You're so much a part of me now. I don't want to ever lose you. I love you."

Jocelyn cupped his stubble-roughened cheek. "I'm not going anywhere, Finn. I love you too. We never would have been able to become mates if we hadn't fallen in love at first sight. It's the way it works."

With a low growl, Finn moved inside her as he took her lips in a fierce kiss. He set his pace slow, pulling back until his cock almost left her body only to slide back into her. Jocelyn moaned against his mouth. The sound caused him to thrust into her harder. Then, as if a dam had broken, he threaded his fingers through her hair as his mouth became more demanding. She lifted her hips off the mattress to meet each of his strokes. He rode her faster, harder, until her pussy clutched his hard shaft. A keening moan left her as her inner muscles contracted around his cock as she came. He lifted his upper body onto his hands. The muscles in his chest bunched as he pumped his hips faster. Once he reached his peak, he threw back his head on a loud groan. His cock pulsed as he filled her with his cum.

Finn collapsed on top of her and wrapped his arms around her. Keeping their bodies joined, he rolled them to their sides. He positioned her leg over his hip, then pulled the covers over them. When he finished, he tucked her head under his chin and held her against his chest.

Jocelyn stroked Finn's back. He clung to her, almost as if he were afraid to let her go, that she would leave him if he relaxed his hold. Even after he'd drifted off to sleep, he still held her tightly. She continued to stroke his back until she too fell into a deep sleep.

CHAPTER EIGHT

The next morning Finn was subdued, lost in his thoughts. Not that he ignored Jocelyn. He might not have been too talkative, but he made sure he touched her in some way. And his gaze seemed to follow her wherever she went.

After she dished up breakfast and went to sit at the kitchen table next to Finn, Jocelyn asked, "So, what are your plans for the day?"

Finn inched his chair closer so their thighs touched before he answered. "I have to go to the gym. I have a few training sessions to do today."

Jocelyn nodded. "Okay. How about I meet you there then?"

"You don't want to leave when I do?"

"I have to make a quick trip to the grocery store. You're eating me out of house and home." Seeing Finn's look of concern, Jocelyn added, "It won't take me long. I promise I'll be at the gym to be with you before the separation gets to be too much."

"Why don't you wait to do the shopping until I'm finished work, then we can go together?"

"No. You can go to the gym on your own. I want to cook you a nice meal tonight, and I want it to be a surprise. So, no, you aren't coming with me."

"Don't you have to work at Wulf's Den tonight?"

Jocelyn smiled. "Nope. Beowulf told me I could have it off to spend with you when I asked if I could leave early last night."

Finn seemed to perk up a bit at that. "That gives me something to look forward to, then. Fine. Do the shopping by yourself. Just don't take any longer than you must. I don't want to go through Jocelyn withdrawal like I did yesterday."

"Hmm, I like that sound of that. Jocelyn withdrawal. I never thought to have a man addicted to me before."

He leaned toward her, buried his nose into the side of her neck, and took a deep breath. Jocelyn shuddered in response. "Babe, you're one addiction I don't ever want to break." Finn sat straighter. "Hurry up and eat. The faster you do the shopping, the faster you can meet me at the gym."

Jocelyn picked up the slice of toast on her plate and took a big bite. As Finn ate his breakfast, she thought of the fear that had lurked in his eyes after he'd had the bad dream. Did his not wanting to be away from her for very long have to do with their being mated, or did it stem more from whatever he'd dreamed about? She didn't know, but if he wanted her close, she didn't have a problem with it.

Once they'd finished eating, Finn left for the gym. Jocelyn watched his Mustang pull out of the driveway before she went upstairs to her room to get her purse. On the way back down, she was surprised to hear the front door open. Thinking he had come back for some reason, she hurried to the main floor. She stopped short on the bottom step when she saw her uncle standing in her front hall.

"Uncle Grant? What are you doing here?"

"I don't think I need a reason to visit my niece."

"I was just headed out. I have to run to the grocery store."

"That can wait. I have something I need to discuss with you. I need you to come with me to the house."

"Can't it wait?"

Grant shook his head as he came to stand in front of her. "I'm afraid not."

"At the very least, can't you talk to me here about it instead of me having to go to the house with you?" A small skitter of unease ran down her back when Grant took her by the upper arm and pulled her off the step.

"No, Jocelyn, I can't."

He tightened his grip as he pulled her out of the house. Jocelyn tried to wrench free, but her uncle refused to let go. Once they were outside, she dug in her heels. Grant easily dragged her behind him to his Mercedes-Benz sedan that sat parked in her driveway. After he yanked open the back door and then shoved her into the arms of her cousin who sat there, she felt real fear.

The Mercedes' locks clicked into place after her uncle slid into the driver's side. Jocelyn elbowed Ben in the ribs as she tried to get out of his arms that he'd tightly wrapped around her. He only shook his head.

In a panicked voice, Jocelyn asked, "Uncle Grant, why are you doing this? You can't just abduct me out of my own home."

Her uncle didn't answer until he'd backed out of her driveway and then drove down her street. "Oh, but I can, Jocelyn. As the head of our family, I can do whatever I deem necessary to safeguard you."

"I'm not in any danger."

"No, but it's obvious to me you're incapable of making the right decisions in your life."

"What?" Jocelyn shouted. "I don't understand."

"Really? Then let me spell it out for you. You let a mortal claim you as a mate. It's bad enough you allowed one to touch you, but to take one of them inside your body is more than I can tolerate."

"You can't tell me who I can take as my mate. Finn *is* my mate. The bond has been forged. Even you can't break that."

"Maybe not, but that doesn't mean I'll allow you to live with a mortal as your mate. Until you've come to your senses, I'll keep you away from him."

Knowing there wasn't anything she could do while trapped in her uncle's car, Jocelyn turned her head and looked out the window. She'd had no idea his hatred of mortals ran so deep. She'd known he thought they were beneath werewolves, but she'd never guessed he would do something this extreme because of his hatred toward them. In the case of Finn not liking werewolves, he'd had a legitimate reason. Not so with her uncle. As far as she knew, he went out of his way to make sure he didn't have to deal with mortals.

Once the privacy gates in the front of her uncle's house loomed ahead, Jocelyn thought maybe she would have a chance to get away after they took her out of the car, but Ben soon disabused her of that notion.

He whispered into her ear, "Try to run from me, Jocelyn, and I'll make you wish you hadn't. There's more than one way to put a woman in her place."

Her uncle parked the car inside the large three-car garage. Once the door closed behind them, he got out before he opened the back-driver's side door. He reached in and took hold of her arm. Ben shifted his grip so he could hold her by her other one. They managed to get her out of the car, then with her between them, her uncle and cousin walked her into the house.

Jocelyn had thought her uncle intended to lock her in her old bedroom upstairs, but she soon realized he had something else in mind when the two men forced her down the steps to the lowest level. The basement was as lavishly decorated as the rest of the house. Her uncle wanted nothing but the best around him. She looked around the large open space. The only door that had a lock on it down there was the bathroom, and even then it locked on the inside. Where did her uncle intend to put her?

She soon found out the answer when he led her to the wall at the back of the room. He pressed a spot on the wainscoting, and a section swung open to reveal a smaller room. Jocelyn had lived in her uncle's home for years and had had no idea that even existed. Grant flipped on the light switch. Jocelyn took in the only items the room held—a single bed and the television that sat on a small table across from it. They threw her onto the bed.

With his arms crossed over his chest, her uncle glared down at her. "This will be your new home until you decide to give up the mortal. And just so you don't waste your breath, the room is soundproofed."

Jocelyn tried not to really panic as she continued to look about her. "What is this room?"

Her uncle chuckled. There was no humor in the sound. "It's the room females are kept when they don't do as they've been told. Your aunt forced me to build this for her. Like you, she didn't accept my authority over her."

Jocelyn gasped in shock. "She was your mate. How could you do that to the woman you joined your soul with?"

Grant snorted. "I never joined my soul with hers. I chose her, but not because my body demanded I claim her. I chose her because of her bloodline." Her uncle snatched her purse off her arm before Jocelyn could stop him. "I'll take this." He reached inside it and then pulled out her cell phone. "Not that you would get a signal in here. It's always better to be safe than sorry." He dropped it back into her purse and turned to walk out of the room with Ben in tow.

Beyond stunned, Jocelyn silently watched the wall close shut. Her aunt's suicide now made sense. No wonder the poor woman had taken the one option out her uncle wouldn't have any control over.

Jocelyn pulled her legs up onto the bed and rested her chin on her knees. With no way to call for help, Finn wouldn't know what had happened to her. He would go crazy with worry. Already feeling the separation, she sat there and waited to see what her uncle would do to her next.

* * * *

Where the hell was Jocelyn? It'd been over an hour since he'd left her at her place. Finn thought for sure she would have made it to the gym. How many groceries did she have to buy?

Every five minutes, his gaze drifted to the clock while he put his client through his workout routine. The separation from Jocelyn was slowly getting to him. He'd tried calling her on her cell phone, but she hadn't picked up. That worried Finn just a little bit and made him wonder if something could be wrong. It could be her cell phone lost its signal while she was in the store or she just hadn't heard it ring, but that last one he couldn't see happening. Werewolves could hear a pin drop almost a block away.

After he finished with his client, Finn left the gym floor and went to his desk. He sat behind it and once again dialed Jocelyn's cell phone number. It rang and rang. Just when he thought it would go to her voicemail again, someone picked up.

He drew his brows together when he didn't hear Jocelyn's voice say hello right away. "Jocelyn, are you there?"

Another couple of seconds went by before he heard a deep, male voice answer him. "No, it isn't Jocelyn, Finn."

Finn stiffened. He knew that voice. It was Jocelyn's uncle. "Where's Jocelyn?"

"She's in a safe place where you won't be able to reach her."

A growl emerged from Finn's throat before he could hold it back. "What have you done with her?"

"Well, well, what do you know? The mortal can mimic one of his betters. Is that how you attracted my niece to you? Did you pretend to be a werewolf? How crass is that?"

"Where is Jocelyn?" Finn demanded.

Grant sighed deeply. "I see you aren't going to listen to reason so I'll just come out with it. I've taken Jocelyn away from you. I won't allow my niece to mate and breed with one of your kind. Mortals are weak and far below any werewolf. Even a male werewolf who goes lone wolf is better than a mortal. I intend to teach Jocelyn the mistake she has made when she took you as her mate. Once she accepts that, I'll find a proper mate for her."

Finn growled again before he shouted, "You have no right to keep us apart. Either you let her go or else."

Grant laughed. "Or else what?"

"I'll hunt you down and make you sorry you ever came between Jocelyn and me."

"Don't threaten me, mortal," Grant snapped. "Fine. We'll do this by werewolf law. I challenge you to a fight. We'll see who has the right to Jocelyn then. Meet me tonight at midnight at Muir Woods. Don't be late. I'm really going to enjoy showing her just how weak your kind is."

Finn slammed down the phone when Grant hung up on him. He looked up to find his entire family — Billie and Royce, his twin, his other two brothers, Keegan and Hayes, along with their father — standing in front of his desk, looking at him with concern.

"Is everything okay, Finn?" Billie asked.

He shook his head. "It's Jocelyn."

About to explain further, a vision slammed into him. He gasped as the images flashed inside his mind. He put his hands on his head and groaned while his brain tried to process what he saw. This vision was almost the same as the first one he'd had of Jocelyn, but this new one gave more details. The images showed exactly what would be the cause of her death. As the vision faded, Finn knew what he had to do to save her.

Able to once again function, Finn looked back up at his family. Their expressions ranged from shock to concern. He grimaced when Billie came around his desk and went to stand next to his chair.

She turned him to face her, then leaned down and put her hands on each of the armrests. "What just happened to you, Finn?"

Before he could answer, his father spoke. "He had a vision. I watched your mother go through many of them. I recognize the signs when one hits."

Billie leaned closer. "Is this what you've been hiding from us? That you now have visions?"

Finn glanced at Royce before he answered Billie. "Yes. Royce's blood did more than give me a great sense of smell and the ability to growl like a werewolf. It also gave me the ability to have visions." He took hold of Billie's arms and gently pushed her away so he could stand. He turned to face Royce. "I want you to call Roxie and tell her to get over here—now. Tell her to bring whatever she needs to do the spell."

"Are you sure, Finn?" Royce asked as he pulled his cell phone out of his pants pocket.

"Yes. Jocelyn's uncle has just challenged me to a fight for her. In my vision I saw what would happen if I'm not a werewolf when I meet him at Muir Woods tonight. If I don't do it, it will be the deaths of Jocelyn and me. Her uncle will kill me, and Jocelyn will take her own life after I'm gone."

Royce gave him a curt nod even as he dialed his cell. "I'll tell Roxie to hurry."

After Royce moved off to make his call, Billie squeezed his hand. "Don't worry, Finn. You won't have to face this alone. It's not that bad being a werewolf. As for that fight you'll have to face, you'll have Beowulf, Roxie, Royce, and me to back you up. We'll get Jocelyn returned to you."

For the first time in three months, Finn pulled Billie into his arms and held her close.

* * * *

Roxie and Beowulf arrived at the gym a half hour later. Roxie carried a brown paper bag with her. They all piled into the upstairs aerobics room. Keegan, who'd entered last, locked the door behind him. With his brothers, father, Billie, Royce, and Beowulf standing close by, Roxie had Finn sit on the floor. She went on her knees beside him and pulled two alcohol wipe packages and a brand-new syringe out of the paper bag she'd brought with her. Knowing what had to be done with the needle, Finn turned his head so she could have better access to his neck.

Roxie tsk-tsked and turned his head back so he faced her. "It doesn't have to be done that way, Finn. Gren only chose the neck to make sure it hurt more. Your arm will do just fine."

He gave a nod and stuck out his right arm so the inside of his elbow faced up. "Good to know. I didn't look forward to a needle being jammed into my neck again."

"I suppose you didn't," Roxie said with a laugh. "Though I must warn you, if this does work, it's still going to hurt like hell. So no screaming."

Finn gave her a crooked smile. "Can I still swear?"

She nodded and smiled. "Swearing is permitted. Whatever gets you through this, go for it."

Roxie picked up one of the alcohol wipe packages and ripped it open. She ran the white square along the inside of her elbow, then took the plastic cover off the end of the syringe before she stuck the needle into her arm. It filled with blood as she pulled back on the plunger. Once it was filled completely, she passed it to Beowulf to hold while she ran an alcohol wipe along the inside of Finn's arm. He took a deep breath to prepare himself for what came next. Roxie took the syringe from Beowulf, jabbed it into Finn's arm, and pushed the plunger home. She recited the spell.

"The magic of the wolf's blood is now in thee.
A wolf you become to run wild and free.
Where once there were two, now only one we see."

Finn immediately noticed the difference from when Gren had tried the spell on him. The words resonated deep inside as Roxie spoke them. Where she had injected him with her blood, the pinprick mark burned. Like quicksilver, the sensation whipped through his body as if it was on fire from the inside out. That was when he began to swear.

"Holy shit. Motherfucker, this hurts. Fuck. Fuck." He fisted his hands on his lap.

He panted while he wondered how much more he could take. Then by slow degrees, the burning sensation faded. Finn slowly uncurled his hands and stood. He saw everyone looked at him with expectant expressions.

Billie went to stand next to Roxie. "Well, from the swearing you did, I would assume the spell worked. Do you feel any different, Finn?"

He did feel different. He felt stronger, his senses now more acute. He heard the sounds coming from the main gym floor below as if he stood in that room instead of being above it. His eyesight seemed better. The sense of smell stayed the same, since he'd already had that increased before. He nodded. "Yes. I feel...stronger."

Billie smiled. "I told you you'd like it. Now let's see if you can go wolf. Look deep inside you to find the new spark of magic you have. Tap into it and picture yourself as a wolf."

The others stepped back to give him room. Finn did as Billie had said. Sure enough, he soon found what could only be described as a spark of magic. When he lightly touched it, power surged through him. Taking a firm hold of it, he pictured himself as a wolf. It happened very quickly. One minute he stood as a man, and the next a wolf. He caught his reflection in one of the mirrors on the wall. A black male wolf stared back at him. A sense of wild freedom like he'd never felt before washed over him. He bunched his back legs under him and ran around the room, wishing he was outside.

Billie grabbed him by the scruff of his neck once he'd made a full circuit of the room. "Okay, hot shot, enough of that. There will be plenty of time to run later. Now let's see if you can shift back to human form just as easily. And, Finn, don't forget to picture yourself with clothes on. I know I don't need to see your bare ass, among other things."

Finn reached for the spark of magic once again and pictured himself in human form. In seconds, he stood before Billie and Roxie clothed, looking like himself once again.

Roxie *humphed.* "Show-off. Do you know how many times it

took me before I could manage the change with clothes? Billie was able to do it the first try as you did. Are you sure there aren't any werewolves in your family tree?"

"Not until Billie and Finn," his father said with a chuckle.

Roxie rolled her eyes. "Figures." She grew serious. "I'm sure Billie already told you, Beowulf, Royce, Billie, and I will come to Muir Woods with you tonight, Finn." She glanced at his brothers and father. "Sorry, no mortals. Beowulf doesn't know Jocelyn's uncle very well, so I don't trust him."

"What is the big deal about this fight?" Finn asked.

Beowulf was the one to answer him. "It's more like a test of strength, really. It isn't supposed to be to the death. It's usually a challenge that takes place between two males over a female, be it between two males who want her as a mate, or in this case, a head of a family who doesn't agree with the female's choice of mate. Whoever can bring his opponent down first with his jaws around the back of his opponent's neck wins and is proven to be the better male. The loser must give up his pursuit of the female. If you beat Jocelyn's uncle, he can't keep her away from you. It's law."

"And if he thinks to break that law," Roxie chimed in, "I'll be there to set him straight."

Finn nodded. He would defeat Jocelyn's uncle. He didn't have any choice.

CHAPTER NINE

Jocelyn sat up on the bed when the wall swung open. She'd been lying there, staring at the ceiling. She had no idea what time it was. Hours had gone by, she knew that much. Being separated from Finn so long had her tied in knots. If she didn't get to be with him soon, she didn't know what she would do. This felt close to being tortured.

Her uncle stepped into the room and shook his head when he looked at her. "Pining after your mortal I see. Well, get used to it, because after tonight you'll never see him again."

"What do you mean?"

"I challenged him to a fight. He accepted. Now you'll see what you tied yourself to. Get up."

Jocelyn slipped her shoes on and then stood. Her uncle grabbed her by the arm and led her out of the basement to the garage. This time her cousin sat behind the steering wheel of her uncle's car. Her uncle sat with her in the backseat. As they drove to Muir Woods, she sat in silence with her mind in turmoil. No way could Finn ever defeat her uncle. He might have had a chance if they were both mortal, but his not being a werewolf gave her uncle a big advantage. Fights weren't supposed to end with the death of the loser, but she couldn't shake the feeling her uncle would not only beat Finn, he would also take his life. As long as Finn remained alive, she would do anything she could to be with him. Her uncle had to know that.

Once they arrived at the darkened woods, Jocelyn allowed her uncle and cousin to lead her to the clearing in Muir Woods where all werewolf challenges took place. As they stepped past the tree line, she hoped Finn would be smart enough to tell Billie and that she and Royce would come with him.

* * * *

Finn sped down the highway as he followed Beowulf's car to Muir Woods. Billie and Royce sat in the backseat of his car. Both gave him tips on how best to fight in wolf form during the trip. The one thing they both stressed—he had to let his wolf, the savage part of his nature, have free rein. If he allowed himself to think like a human, he would lose.

After they arrived at the woods, Billie directed him to park his car in a lot that was a distance from the main entrance. Beowulf and Roxie continued without them.

Finn turned off his car and then turned to look at Billie. "Now, why did you want me to park here?"

Billie gave him a knowing smile. "It's to give you and Jocelyn a bit of privacy after you get her back."

"Why would we need that?"

Billie rolled her eyes. "Why the hell do you think? You've been separated from Jocelyn too long. Your blood will be up, along with other parts of you, after the fight is over. You'll be feeling a bit desperate, if you catch my drift."

Finn shook his head and looked at Royce. "Does she always have sex on the brain?"

Royce chuckled. "I'm afraid so. Not that I'm complaining."

He held up his hand. "I don't want to hear any more. Let's just meet up with Beowulf and Roxie."

They climbed out of the car, and all three of them went wolf. Finn ran beside Billie while Royce remained on her other side. They streaked along the road until they reached the main parking lot where Beowulf and Roxie waited. They too went wolf as they approached, adding another black male wolf and a female whose golden-brown fur was a shade lighter than the other brown wolf's. The five of them plunged into the trees and headed to the clearing.

Finn burst into it first. He was just past the tree line and snarled at Jocelyn's uncle and cousin who stood with Jocelyn between them. Grant stepped forward when the other wolves arrived. His gaze swept the small group.

"Where is the mortal? If he isn't here, he forfeits."

Finn stepped away from the others until he stood in front of Grant. He growled low in his throat. Jocelyn's uncle gazed down at him and shook his head. "Do you think I'm a fool? This male is a werewolf. He can't be Finn."

Jocelyn tried to break free from her cousin as she called out to him, "Finn? Is that really you?"

Grant's brows lowered. "That is impossible. A mortal can't be turned into a werewolf."

Finn took a step back, then willed the change. Grant's face grew thunderous as he watched Finn shift.

"It is possible," Finn growled back. "Now let's get this over with."

He and Grant shifted to wolf form as they launched themselves at each other. Their snarls and growls filled the clearing as they fought. Knowing what he would lose if Grant defeated him, Finn let his wolf loose. He ignored the pain of the bites and scratches Grant inflicted on him, but in the end, Finn turned out to be the stronger of the two. He fought Grant down until he was able to take the back of Grant's neck in his powerful jaws. Jocelyn's uncle lay still and whimpered in defeat.

Finn released him and stalked to Jocelyn's cousin, who still held her. He curled his upper lip at Ben and snarled. Ben quickly let Jocelyn go. Finn shifted to human form and then gathered her close. Before he could kiss her, he heard a menacing snarl behind him. He spun around and held her close as he confronted her uncle, who had stood behind him.

Grant shifted to human form. "This isn't over. I can't allow Jocelyn to go with you."

"Finn won fair and square. Jocelyn is his." Roxie, in her half-wolf/half-human form, grabbed Grant by his shoulder and turned him to face her. She lifted him until his feet left the ground, then gave him a shake. "Back off," she said in her raspy voice. "We all witnessed your defeat to Finn. He is the better male. Accept your loss." She pulled him closer until they were nose to nose. "And it won't just be me you'll have to deal with if you try to interfere with Finn's and Jocelyn's lives again. You see the black female wolf over there? That's Billie, Finn's sister. She's the one who took out Gren, not Beowulf as the rumor says. So if you don't want her gunning for you, I'd accept things as they are."

Grant fell to the ground when Roxie opened her hand and let him drop. She turned to Finn and Jocelyn. "You two get out of here. We can clean up the rest of this mess."

Finn took Jocelyn's hand and pulled her out of the clearing. He now knew why Billie had suggested he park so far away. The need to have her, to hear her cry as he took her, just about overpowered him. Once they reached the main path, they went wolf. He ran beside her as he herded her toward the parking lot. He brushed up against her auburn-colored furred side as they ran.

In no time they reached his car. Finn shifted to human form, then swept Jocelyn into his arms as she shifted as well. He savagely took her mouth as he opened the passenger side door and then flipped the seat forward. Somehow, he managed to get them onto the backseat before he shut the door behind them. Jocelyn moaned and sucked his tongue into her mouth as she tugged at the front of his fleece pants. He tore open her jeans. With quick movements, he pulled them down her legs. He shoved his hand between her thighs and groaned. She was wet and ready for him.

Moving to kiss the side of her neck, Finn held Jocelyn around the waist as he shifted on the seat. He sat up and pulled her so she straddled his lap. Her hands came down on the tops of his shoulders for support. He wrapped his hand around the base of his throbbing cock and held it as she took the head into her pussy and pushed down. He let go of his shaft as she took him deep. She rose to her knees, then lowered herself onto him again. As she rode him, he cupped her breasts through her shirt and bit down on a taut nipple. Her head fell back, and she moaned.

The feel of Jocelyn's inner muscles gripping him almost made him come. With gritted teeth, he fought to hold back until she'd reached her peak. He brought one hand between them and rubbed her clit as she bounced up and down on his cock. That was all she needed to push her over the edge. She dug her fingers into his shoulders as she cried out in pleasure. Her pussy gripped his hard shaft in a tight fist. Finn thrust up into her once, then found his own release.

The sound of their heavy breathing filled the car. Finn cupped the back of Jocelyn's neck and gently kissed her. "Are you okay?"

Jocelyn smiled against his lips. "Never better. How about you? You let Roxie use the spell on you."

"I had to. If I hadn't, I would have lost you forever."

"How do you know that?"

"I have visions, Jocelyn," he said with thick emotion lacing his voice. "Just like my mother. That first morning at your place, I had one about you. I saw you dead, lying in a pool of your own blood. I didn't know how you died, only that I was somehow responsible. It wasn't until your uncle took you that I saw everything. He would have killed me, and you would have taken your own life afterward. As a werewolf, I could stop it."

Jocelyn kissed his forehead. "I probably wouldn't have been able to go on without you. Especially if I had to endure being under my uncle's control. I'm glad you had Roxie use the spell. Now I don't ever have to lose you. And now that you're a werewolf, it does have some added benefits, I see." Jocelyn squeezed her inner muscles around his still hard cock.

Finn chuckled. "It would seem so. Shall we see if we can fog up all the windows in my car like a couple of horny teenagers?"

Jocelyn smiled. "Most definitely."

As Jocelyn moved on top of him once again, Finn threw back his head and howled.

The End

ELI AND SASKIA

Eli vowed he would never tie himself to one woman. But when he sees a lone werewolf female at Wulf's Den with six large male werewolves at her back, he finds himself instantly attracted to her.

Saskia and her brothers-in-arms have come to Wulf's Den in search of the foretold one, the one they have trained most of their long lives to protect. What she didn't expect was to have one of her visions while there. Or to see that she and the male mortal who looks at her with hunger in his eyes would eventually end up in bed together.

As Eli and Saskia try to sort through the feelings of an unexpected mating, a new enemy rises to threaten Roxie in her position as the foretold one. An enemy who could end their mating prematurely.

CHAPTER ONE

"How about that one? She looks pretty hot."

Eli York looked at the woman his sister, Billie, had pointed out inside Wulf's Den. Yes, he found her more than pretty, but that would be a given since the woman was a werewolf. The species were known for their exceptional good looks.

He shook his head. "No. Not interested."

Billie narrowed her eyes. "Why do I get the impression you're just saying that to blow me off? You've said no to every woman Jocelyn and I have pointed out, werewolf and mortal alike."

Finn, who sat next to Eli, chuckled. "That's because he *is* trying to blow you off, Billie. Eli is still holding strong to his decision not to be tied to any one woman."

"Traitor," Eli said to Finn. "I thought you of all people would at least back me up."

Seeing as how Finn and he were identical twins, they were extremely close. They were mirror images of each other, with their matching gray-blue eyes, longish, straight black hair, and muscular build. Personality wise, they were the same as well. The only difference between them now was Finn had chosen to become a werewolf after he had taken Jocelyn as his mate.

"You know I'll back you up anytime you need me to, but in this case, I have to side with Billie and Jocelyn. It's about time you settled down." Finn leaned back in his chair and wrapped his arm around Jocelyn's shoulders. "Being mated does have its benefits, if you know what I mean."

From the heated look Finn gave Jocelyn, Eli knew exactly what his twin meant. The sex was frequent and mind-blowing, or so Finn had told him more than once.

Eli turned to look at Royce, Billie's mate. "What about you, Royce? Do you think I should shackle myself to one woman?"

Royce smiled. "All I can say is nothing compares to being mated. To find that someone who makes you feel whole, complete. Your sister does that for me. I can't begrudge her that if she wants the same for you."

Eli shook his head. "Man, I have to stop hanging around you guys. If I don't watch it, I'll spout that romantic crap as well. Ow!" He reached down to rub the shin Billie's foot had connected with under the table.

Billie glared at him. "Watch it, buster. There's nothing wrong with a man being able to express how he feels." She turned to Royce and brought his head down for a quick kiss. "It makes me hot when Royce talks like that."

Eli pretended to heave. "I think I just threw up in my mouth. Can you please keep comments like that to yourself? I really don't need to know what turns my baby sister on." Billie flipped him off. "Nice."

As she stood, Jocelyn shook her head and laughed. "Poor Eli. They do like to pick on you. Break time is over. I'd better get back to work."

Finn kissed her soundly before she left to take an order from one of the tables she'd served drinks to earlier. Eli had to wonder how much longer Finn would want Jocelyn serving tables at Wulf's Den. It drove his twin nuts just thinking about his mate being around all the single male werewolves who frequented the nightclub.

Eli sometimes found it hard being around the two mated werewolf couples. The hot looks they at times gave each other made him feel as if he bordered on voyeurism. Thankfully, he didn't live with any of them. Finn had moved out of the apartment they'd shared shortly after he'd taken Jocelyn as his mate. Eli could easily live without listening to Finn have hot monkey sex—or in his twin's case, hot wolf sex—all night long.

He picked up his beer and took a swig from the bottle, then just about choked on it two seconds later when he spotted the small group near the bar. "Holy shit."

"What?" Billie asked.

"Over by the bar. Those guys have to be werewolves. They're huge."

Billie gave him a knowing smile after she glanced at the newcomers. "I don't think it's just the men who have snagged your attention, Eli. I think the woman with them has made a part of you stand up and take notice. Your scent just gave you away."

Damn werewolves and their damn sense of smell. He could no longer hide how he felt from Finn and Billie. Of course Billie would have to be the one to point out he'd gotten an instant hard-on the moment his gaze had landed on the woman who stood with the six very large, very muscular men.

Unable to tear his gaze away, Eli took in the woman's long, straight, almost white-blonde hair and slim build. Even though she was tall—she had to be around five feet eleven—the men dwarfed her. He sucked in a sharp breath as she turned and looked directly at him. His cock jerked as their gazes locked. The rest of the world seemed to disappear.

The sound of Finn loudly clearing his throat brought Eli back to his surroundings. "Hmm, don't look now, but I think they're headed this way."

Royce sat straighter. "Where the hell is Beowulf? I have no idea who they are. They're not from any packs I know."

Eli ignored the others and Royce as his brother-in-law craned his neck around to search the nightclub. With eyes only for the female werewolf who walked closer, his heart beat faster in anticipation.

* * * *

Saskia paused near the bar as she did a quick scan of Wulf's Den. She didn't see the one she sought. The men stood stiffly at her back. Most of them weren't comfortable in a setting such as this. Generally, they made it a practice not to have any interactions with mortals if possible. Having to come to a place where mortals and werewolves rubbed elbows made most of them edgy.

Dirk nudged her. "Are you sure this is the place?"

Saskia nodded. "Yes. She's here."

Jager snorted. "The big question is *where*, exactly."

"This place is jam-packed," Kye said in a disgusted tone. "How are we supposed to find her in this crowd when we don't even know her name?"

"And it's not as if I want to spend the rest of the night here looking for her," Skylar added.

Leif, the only one of them who didn't mind being this close to mortals, chuckled. "Quit your complaining. Look at it as an opportunity. With all these females around, I'm sure one of you can find a woman to make the night more enjoyable."

"Unlike you," said Jager, "we don't use our dicks to do most of our thinking."

Saskia rolled her eyes. Usually, she could take their good-natured ribbing of one another, but they were there for a purpose. "Knock it off. Focus."

She looked around the crowded nightclub. As her gaze swept the occupied tables, she found it drawn to one table where a couple and two identical-looking men sat. When one of the twins looked in her direction, Saskia stiffened as a vision slammed into her. She gasped as images of the two of them naked in bed as he rode her filled her mind.

Pulled to him because of her vision, Saskia slowly walked to the man's table. Her men followed. As she wound her way around the other tables, she kept her gaze on the man. She liked what she saw. His gray-blue gaze followed her, sweeping up and down her body. As it landed on her breasts, her nipples pebbled beneath her long-sleeved T-shirt. He wanted her. She could see the look of longing in his eyes even from that distance.

Just before she reached his table, Saskia took a deep breath. The smell of aroused male filled her nostrils with each breath she took. Her pussy clenched in response. An ache built as wetness pooled between her legs. She took another deep breath. Her brows drew together in confusion.

Now that she'd reached the man's table, his scent was stronger. Feeling even more confused, Saskia looked from the man who would be her lover to the one who sat next to him. They were identical twins, but their scents didn't match. The man from her vision smelled like a mortal while his twin smelled like a werewolf. *How was that possible?* It also made her question her vision, something she rarely did. She'd never taken a mortal as a lover before. Not that she didn't like them. She just preferred to sleep with the males of her species.

Saskia looked at the others who sat at the table as her men went to either side of her. The male werewolf who was next to the only female werewolf at the table stood. This was no young male but a man in his prime.

"We're looking for a woman." As she spoke, Saskia watched the mortal out of the corner of her eye. He still gazed at her with longing as his scent washed over her—a heady mix of man and desire. She had to lick her suddenly dry lips.

"You'll have to be a little more specific than that. As you can see, there's quite a few here." The male's gaze flicked over her men before he looked back at her. "I'm Royce. You would be?"

She could tell her men made Royce uneasy as he stepped to stand closer to his mate. Six unmated male werewolves tended to make any mated male leery. "I'm Saskia," she pointed to her men, "and these are my brothers."

Royce's mate chuckled. "And here I thought I had it bad having to grow up with four older brothers. I feel for you. I'm Billie, by the way. And these two over here are my brothers. Just so you can tell them apart, Finn is sitting next to me and next to him is Eli."

Saskia's gaze settled on Eli before she focused back on Billie. She could see the family resemblance between the three siblings. She still found it confusing that two of them were werewolves and one wasn't.

"Actually, they aren't my real brothers. They're my brothers-in-arms—Dirk, Leif, Kye, Roan, Skylar, and Jager." Each man nodded when she said his name.

"Now that we have the introductions over," Royce broke in, "why don't you tell us who you're looking for?"

"We don't know her name. We just know she's the foretold one. The one who rules over all the packs. Do you know her?"

Royce went on the defensive as his upper lip pulled back and he growled low in his throat. "What do you want with my granddaughter?"

Saskia held up her hand to keep her men back as they crowded closer. She looked around the nightclub. Their exchange had started to draw the stares of the others there. "I must speak with her. Away from prying eyes."

*

Eli looked from Saskia to Royce and back to her again. The tension in the air was thick enough to cut with a knife. He still had a lot to learn about werewolf society, but it didn't take much guessing on his part to realize Saskia asking to talk to Roxie privately with six large male werewolves at her back would raise some hackles. Christ, he wouldn't want to be the focus of attention of any of those guys. They each stood an inch or two taller than Royce, who already stood more than a few inches taller than Eli.

He studied each of Saskia's brothers-in-arms as they and Royce sized each other up. Dirk, who stood on Saskia's right, had dark brown hair with blond highlights running through it and fell past his shoulders. His dark green gaze was locked on Royce. Leif had short auburn hair and blue eyes that flicked back and forth between Royce and the women around him. Kye, who stood on Saskia's other side, had dark blond hair that just touched the tops of his shoulders. His brown eyes didn't seem to miss anything as his gaze settled on each of them. Roan, Skylar, and Jager looked similar enough to be brothers. They each had light brown hair and light blue eyes that verged on the color of turquoise. Roan wore his hair shoulder-length whereas Skylar and Jager had their long hair pulled back into ponytails. Their overall impression left Eli with one thought: you sure as hell didn't want to get on their bad side. Surprisingly, even though she was much smaller than them, Saskia was able to keep them in line with just a flick of her hand.

Royce shook his head. "If you want to talk to Roxie, you'll have to clear it with her mate, Beowulf, first. He's our pack leader and is very protective of her."

"Which is to be expected. We're not here to do her harm. We're here to look out for her safety as well."

"I'll see what Beowulf says."

Royce grabbed Billie's arm and pulled her to stand next to him. Billie gave Saskia an apologetic look, then glared daggers at Royce as he forced her to leave with him. Finn shot to his feet and without a word left the table to stand near his mate. *Well, aren't I the special one?* Eli wouldn't have minded being left alone if he just had Saskia to worry about. Obviously, the others thought his being mortal would somehow keep him under the radar of the six male werewolves who had now zeroed in on him. Just what he didn't want.

Deciding to ignore the men, Eli focused his attention on Saskia. He pulled out the chair next to his. "Why don't you take a seat until Beowulf comes?"

He sucked in a sharp breath as Saskia turned her violet-eyed gaze his way. The tip of her tongue came out to wet her lips. Eli resisted the urge to reach down and adjust the front of his pants to make room for his erection. As if she knew what it did to him, she licked her lips once more. He bit back a moan as he thought of how it would feel to have her use her tongue on the part of him that throbbed, begging for attention. Before she could answer, Beowulf arrived.

"Royce tells me you wish to see Roxie."

Saskia turned to face Beowulf. "Yes."

"Well, this isn't the time nor place. We like to keep pack business out of the nightclub."

"Then where can we meet?"

Beowulf handed Saskia a piece of paper. "Here's my cell phone number. Call tomorrow afternoon, and we'll arrange a time for you to talk to Roxie."

Saskia nodded. "Fine."

Beowulf walked away while Saskia and her brothers-in-arms headed for the nightclub's exit. He wasn't ready to let her leave. He wanted a chance to get to know her better, but with the six men at her back, he didn't know if they would let him anywhere near her. Deciding he would be an idiot to just let her walk away, he got up and rushed after her.

Outside, he spotted her walking down the sidewalk toward the nightclub's parking lot. He called out to her. "Saskia, wait."

She stopped and signaled for her men to go on without her. Eli quickened his pace. Her gaze swept down his body, lingering on the bulge in his pants before she looked him in the eyes. "Do you want something?"

Oh, he wanted something all right. He wanted her naked beneath him as he sank his aching cock into her wet pussy, which was something he had thought he wouldn't crave, considering what she was. He wanted to taste and stroke every inch of her. "I was wondering, if you had some free time, if you'd like to go out for dinner sometime."

Saskia gave him a half smile. "Are you asking me out on a date?"

"Yes. Isn't that how it's usually done when a man wants to get to know a woman better?"

"Not where I come from. No offense, but I don't usually go out on dates with male mortals."

"Why not?"

"Because I just don't."

Eli took a step closer. Her eyes dilated as she drew in a deep breath. "What kind of answer is that? You must have some reason. We're really no different from a male werewolf." He shifted even closer so they stood toe-to-toe. Saskia's eyes glowed softly, telling him that she could be more than a little interested in him.

Saskia swallowed. "I find I'm not attracted to mortals."

"Well, maybe you just haven't met the right one."

"Let me guess. You think you're the mortal to help change my mind?"

"Of course." Eli focused on her lips. Her tongue came out to wet them. His cock jerked at the sight. With a groan, he said, "The hell with it."

Taking a page out of Billie's book, Eli pulled Saskia to him as he took her lips in a kiss. He threaded his fingers through the hair at the back of her head and angled his mouth against hers. Much to his pleasure, she didn't push him away. Instead, she opened and sucked his tongue inside. He moaned as he dragged her closer and ground his erection against her hip. A second later, he gasped as she threaded her fingers through his hair and pushed him until he slammed up against a brick wall. She kissed him for all she was worth. Lost in a sexual haze, he forgot where they were until a deep voice called her name. Reluctantly they pulled apart.

Jager stood a foot away with his arms crossed over his broad chest. He shook his head. "Saskia, if you're done checking the mortal's tonsils, we'd like to leave."

Stepping out of Eli's embrace, Saskia nodded. "I'm coming."

Jager snorted. "Yeah, I could see you were well on your way."

Saskia glared at him before she turned back to Eli. "I have to go."

As she went to walk away, Eli stopped her. "When can I see you again?"

"I don't know."

"Can I at least have your phone number?" When she hesitated, he said, "Okay, I won't push, but if you change your mind, you can find me most days at my family's gym, York Fitness."

"See you around, Eli." With that, Saskia disappeared around the corner.

Eli blew out a deep breath. That had gone well. Not. He'd sounded like a desperate teenager, begging the girl he liked to go out with him. He usually didn't make such an ass of himself around women. He pulled the ends of his button-down shirt out of his slacks to try to hide the raging hard-on he sported, then turned to go back inside Wulf's Den. He needed a couple more drinks before the night was through if he planned on getting any sleep. With the taste of Saskia still in his mouth, he doubted he'd be able to without her filling his dreams.

CHAPTER TWO•

Eli arrived at the gym the next morning grumpy and feeling out of sorts from lack of sleep. For most of the night he'd dreamed about Saskia. Some of the dreams had been so erotic he'd woken up on the verge of coming all over himself. Since meeting her last night, he seemed to be in a perpetual state of arousal. The cold shower he'd taken before coming to work had helped some with that problem but not by much.

After throwing himself onto the chair behind his desk, Eli opened his schedule book. He had a few clients listed for training sessions that day. With an hour to kill before his first client showed up, he decided a cup of coffee was in order.

Hayes, his younger brother, and Keegan, the eldest York sibling, stood by the coffeemaker, waiting for a fresh pot. They looked at him as he went to grab one of the clean mugs off the counter. Eli covered his mouth with his hand and yawned.

"Another sleepless night?" Hayes asked with a snicker. "Let me guess. It was a brunette who kept you awake."

"No."

"A redhead?"

"No."

"A blonde then?"

Eli shouldered Hayes out of the way as the last of the coffee dripped through the coffeemaker. He picked up the pot and filled his mug. "Shut up, Hayes."

Keegan elbowed Hayes. "I think you hit it with that one. It must have been a blonde."

Eli scowled at his brothers. "Would the two of you get a life already? Don't you have anything better to do than to speculate about my sex life?"

Hayes shook his head. "No, not really. This one must have been special. It has never bothered you before when we've asked who your babe *du jour* is."

"Who said it was a woman who kept me awake all night? Maybe I just had a hard time falling asleep."

Keegan snorted. "Yeah, right. We know you went with Finn and Billie to Wulf's Den last night. You can't tell us you didn't try to pick up a woman. And it's not as if the women ever turn you down." As Eli scowled even more, Keegan laughed. "Well, what do you know? The great lady's man got shot down for once."

Not in the mood for his brothers' ribbing, Eli walked to his desk. Of course Keegan and Hayes followed.

"Come on, Eli," Hayes said as he sat on the edge of Eli's desk. "You can tell us. Did she shoot you down right away? Or did she play you along for a bit, then shoot you down?"

Hoping if he ignored his brothers they would just go away and leave him alone, Eli sipped his coffee. Considering he hadn't been able to get Saskia's phone number or even a promise for her to see him at the gym, Hayes had hit on a sore spot.

"Was she pretty?" Hayes asked. He lowered his voice. "Was she a werewolf? She must have been drop-dead gorgeous."

Before Eli could tell Hayes to shut the hell up, Billie came over to his desk. She pegged Keegan and Hayes with a hard look. "What are the two of you bugging Eli about now?"

Hayes stood. "We think a blonde turned him down last night at Wulf's Den, but Eli isn't talking."

Billie looked down at Eli. "So that's where you went last night. You went outside to hit on Saskia after she left the nightclub. I knew you were interested in her."

"Now we're getting somewhere," Keegan said. "So her name was Saskia."

Billie crossed her arms over her chest and shook her head. "You two are pathetic. For your information, I'm surprised Eli managed to even talk to her alone without her men being around."

"What men?"

"Saskia's brothers-in-arms." Billie smiled. "I think Saskia is one tough female werewolf. She had those six huge male werewolves under her control. She must be their leader or something. And the men seemed to respect her."

"Brothers-in-arms?" Hayes asked. "Do you mean as brothers who carry swords and fight by her side type thing?"

Billie nodded. "Even though Saskia never said exactly, Royce seems to think that's what they are. And for some reason, they wanted to see Roxie."

Eli sat back on his chair and listened with half an ear as Billie told Keegan and Hayes about Saskia and her men's visit to Wulf's Den the night before. He felt as if he were in hell. Just the mention of Saskia's name had him remembering all the hot, sweaty sex dreams he'd had of her during the night. He still remembered what she'd tasted like, and he ached to taste her again. Thinking of how good it would be to have her in his arms, her body pressed to his, made his blood flow to his groin. He gritted his teeth as his cock lengthened and hardened. *What the hell is wrong with me?* Eli never obsessed over women, but there he was obsessing over the one woman he probably would never see again. How sad was that?

When Finn and Jocelyn arrived, and Royce a few minutes later, the topic of Saskia and her men didn't end. Eli decided he'd had enough. He stood and stepped around the others.

Billie stopped him before he got very far. "Eli, where are you going?"

He turned to face her, but kept walking backward. "I promised Dad I'd check and see what supplies we need to order for the gym. I have some time to kill before my first client shows up, so I might as well get started."

Not wanting to give anyone else a chance to stop him, Eli turned back around and hurried away. He pulled his keys out the pocket of his sweat pants, then unlocked the supply room door. As he shut it behind him, he leaned against it and took a deep breath. It was going to be a long day.

* * * *

Saskia looked up at the large sign that hung above the glass doors of the building she stood in front of it. The sign read YORK FITNESS in big, bold letters. She didn't know why she'd come there. Actually, that wasn't true. She did know. She just didn't know why she couldn't stay away.

She'd told herself more than once after she'd left Wulf's Den last night that she would not seek out Eli. It didn't matter that in her vision she'd seen them together making love. It couldn't be. He was a mortal, and she was a werewolf. A werewolf who had more important things to do with her time than finding the man she desperately wanted to have sex with.

She told herself to walk away. To get back on her motorcycle and leave before she did something stupid like molest the man while he worked, but of course, her body didn't listen. Just the thought of Eli being somewhere on the other side of the glass doors made her heart beat faster. Her pussy clenched as she remembered the kiss they'd shared the night before. The man sure knew how to kiss. And that he'd just grabbed her and pulled her to him had only made her want him more.

Saskia had no tolerance for timid men. She liked the opposite sex to be assertive, able to show her exactly what they wanted. Not surprising, considering she'd spent most of her adult life around six men who had enough testosterone between them to choke out everything else in a room.

There was no point in fighting it. She grabbed the handle of one glass door, then yanked it open before she stepped inside the gym. She took a deep breath as she walked to the front desk. She easily filtered out Eli's scent from the many that hung in the air. Her nose also picked up the presence of the four werewolves in Eli's family. She stopped next to the front desk and waited for the girl who stood behind it to get off the phone.

"Well, this is a nice surprise."

Saskia turned to find Billie heading toward her. "Hey, Billie. Is Eli around?"

Billie smiled as she looked behind Saskia. "No brothers today?"

She shook her head. "No. I left them at home."

"You left without telling them where you were going, didn't

you?"

"I may have neglected to say exactly where I would be."

Billie laughed. "I've been known a time or two to do the same thing to my brothers." She motioned for Saskia to follow her. "I'll take you to Eli. I think you may have just made his day."

Following Billie, Saskia took a quick look around. In the large open space to her left, a number of mortals worked out on the various weight machines and free weights. From the outside she hadn't thought the gym so large. She stopped walking when Billie pointed to a door that had a sign with the word SUPPLIES painted on it.

"Eli is in there. I'll make sure no one bothers the two of you." Billie gave her a wink before she walked away.

Saskia slowly opened the supply room door. Her gaze latched on to Eli, who stood in the back seemingly counting items on one of the metal shelves that lined the wall. After stepping inside, she quietly closed herself in.

Saskia watched Eli. Today he wore a pair of black sweat pants with a gray T-shirt that stretched nicely across his wide back. She ran her gaze lower to his muscled ass. The sweats were tight enough to give her a good view of it. She bet he'd look good in a pair of fitted jeans.

On silent feet, Saskia crossed the short distance between them. Her nipples grew taut as she drew Eli's scent into her lungs. She fought to keep back the growl of need that rose inside her. The smell of his arousal caused an ache to throb between her legs as wetness pooled. Obviously, he hadn't been unaffected by their encounter from the night before. At least she hoped the hard-on he had was for her. Coming up behind him, she pressed her front to his back and wrapped her arms around his waist. He jumped as she skimmed her lips along the side of his neck.

He turned his head to look over his shoulder. "Saskia? I thought you..." Eli's words fell away as she trailed one hand down his lower stomach to the impressive bulge in his pants. He moaned as she stroked his cock through his sweats.

She nudged his longish black hair aside and kissed the back of his neck. "Never mind what I said. Right now, all I can think about is touching you. I haven't been able to get you out of my mind, even though I know I should forget about you."

Eli groaned as she gave his hard cock a squeeze. "Do you know how many times I dreamed of you touching me like this last night?" He jerked his hips against her hand. "This may not be such a good idea."

Saskia rubbed herself against his ass as she let go of him and then shoved her hand down the front of his sweats. She smiled when she found Eli had gone commando. She wrapped her fingers around his shaft and slowly pumped up and down his full length. "I think this is a very good idea."

A loud moan escaped Eli as he grabbed the metal shelf with both hands. "Oh, this is a very, very bad idea. If you keep this up, I'm going to come."

"That's the whole point. Enough talking."

She nipped and licked a trail down the side of his neck to where it met his shoulder. With a firm grasped on his thick erection, she continued to work him. Saskia growled low in her throat as his cock grew even harder. Feeling how big and hard Eli was, she ached to have him buried deep inside her pussy but not right now. For now, she'd settle for this. Later, preferably in a bed, she'd take him inside her body.

The smell of their arousal filled the small room. Saskia squeezed his cock harder as she pumped her hand faster. Eli bucked his hips, and his head fell forward onto his chest as his breaths came in rapid pants. The muscles in his arms bulged as he gripped the shelf harder.

"Saskia, I'm going to come," Eli gasped.

"I know. Come for me, Eli."

She dragged her teeth against the spot where his neck and shoulder met once, twice, before she bit him and held on. Eli let out a long moan as he fell over the edge into an orgasm. His cock pulsed as he came. She didn't stop working his shaft until the last spasm ended.

Eli pulled her hand out of his sweats before he spun around and pulled her to him. "Your turn."

Taking her mouth in a heated kiss, he backed her against the closed door. He increased the pressure of his lips as his tongue came out and swept the seam of hers. Opening for him, Saskia sucked it deep inside. The taste of him heightened her arousal. She wrapped her arms around Eli's neck and ground her pussy against the hard thigh between her legs. She growled softly with need. It'd been too long since she'd last slept with a man.

Eli cupped one of her breasts. Using his thumb and forefinger, he rolled her taut nipple between them. She arched her back and pressed closer. Needing more, Saskia took hold of his hand and shoved it under her short-sleeved top. He kneaded her before he yanked her top to her chin. With a flick of his wrist, he undid the front clasp of her bra. She moaned as he released her lips and moved to draw a nipple inside his mouth. He circled his tongue around her nipple before he sucked on the taut peak.

Unable to stop herself, Saskia rode Eli's thigh. The friction felt good, but it wasn't good enough. Sensing what she needed, he quickly undid the button and zipper of her jeans. She held on to his shoulders for support as he cupped her sex through her soaked panties. He lifted his head and claimed her lips once again.

As he kissed her, he slipped his hand inside her underwear and ran a finger down the crease of her sex. Saskia groaned into Eli's mouth as one digit and then a second pushed inside her wet pussy. She clamped her inner walls around them as he pumped in and out of her. His thumb brushed her clit, pushing her even higher toward her release.

Eli lifted his head and kissed a trail along her jaw to her ear. "God, you're so wet. You're making me hard again."

Saskia plunged her hands into his hair as she rode his fingers. The feel of his hardening cock pressed against her increased the pleasure building inside her. Eli stroked her faster, angling the digits so they rubbed against her clit. She soon broke apart as her climax claimed her. Her inner walls clamped down around his fingers as she came.

Gasping for breath, she held on to Eli for support as her legs shook. The sound of their heavy breathing filled the room. Before either one of them could say anything, someone pounded on the door. He quickly turned the lock, something they'd neglected to do earlier.

"What?" Eli barked through the door.

"You'd better get out of there before Dad catches you," a man said from the other side. "And don't you have a client soon?"

"Go away, Hayes. I'll be out in a few minutes." Eli groaned and pressed his forehead to hers. "I guess playtime is over. Sorry."

"There'll be more time to play later. And we won't have to hide away in a supply room to do it either."

"So there is going to be a later?"

She cupped his face and kissed him lightly. "I'm not ready to let you go just yet."

Pulling back, Eli smiled. "Good, because even though this was nice, I want more. Much more."

Saskia pushed him away. "I think we'd better put some space between us or we'll never get out of here." She quickly did up her pants, then fixed her bra and top.

Eli grimaced as he pulled at the front of his sweats. "I'd better change." He reached around her and unlocked the door.

After they stepped out of the supply room, Saskia noticed Billie and Royce stood nearby. Eli stood in front of her so he blocked her from their sight with his back toward them.

"I'll see you later this evening," she told him.

Eli nodded. "Do you want me to pick you up?"

"No. I think it would be better if I picked you up here." She thought it best to keep Eli away from her brothers for now.

"Okay. I get off at six. Is that all right?"

"I'll be here."

After a quick, hard kiss, Eli left. Saskia sighed as she watched him walk away. She took a deep breath, knowing there would be no getting past the two werewolves who stood watching her every move.

CHAPTER THREE

Billie gave Saskia a knowing smile. "I guess we'll be seeing more of you around here?"

"Maybe."

"I don't think I've ever seen Eli this hung up on a woman before. I can't see him letting you go that easily."

"Time will tell," Saskia said. She glanced at Royce. It wasn't too hard to guess he wanted to talk to her, and not about what she and Eli had been doing in the supply room either. "You have something on your mind, Royce?"

"Actually, I do. Have you called Beowulf?"

"Not yet. I planned to do that shortly."

"Do you mind calling now? I'd like to hear what the outcome of your call will be."

"Roxie is your granddaughter?"

"Yes. She's descended from the daughter I had with my first mate many, many years ago. I raised Roxie's mother from the time she was small, so I'm very close to her and Roxie. I don't want anything bad to happen to my granddaughter, if you understand my meaning."

Saskia bit back a smile. Royce's warning wasn't lost on her. He obviously felt very protective of Roxie, which she couldn't fault him for. It was something she'd counted on. Being the foretold one, Roxie needed to be protected at all costs. "I can make the call now."

"Let's go to my father's office," Billie said. "He won't mind if we use his phone. It has a speakerphone as well."

Following Billie and Royce back through the gym, Saskia caught sight of Eli as he came out of the men's change room. He now wore a pair of black warm-up pants. She gave him an appreciative look as they walked by. The man was all muscle, and she couldn't wait to explore his body in detail.

Eli caught up to them. "Where are you guys going?"

Billie answered. "Saskia is going to use Dad's phone to call Beowulf."

"I'll come with you."

"No, you won't. I looked at your schedule when you were fooling around in the supply room with Saskia. You have a client in five minutes."

Eli glanced at his watch. "Well, damn." He looked undecided as he continued to walk beside Saskia. "All right, I'll go, but I'm warning you, Billie. Don't bother Saskia."

Billie rolled her eyes at her brother. "Eli, honestly. What would I do to her, anyway? Saskia is the first woman I've ever seen you go nutso over. I'm not going to scare her away for anything. I don't want to miss seeing my who-wants-to-stay-single brother finally fall for a woman. I'm going to enjoy watching this."

"Don't listen to anything she says, Saskia," Eli quickly warned her before he turned and headed to the main gym floor.

Interesting, Saskia thought. So Eli wasn't a big fan of permanent relationships. That suited her just fine. She wasn't looking for a mate, not that she thought Eli could be hers. Given his being mortal, he wouldn't show signs of what a male werewolf goes through when he finds his mate. This put things in a whole new light. If they could keep their relationship casual, they could have their fun and at some point, end it amicably. Neither one of them would have expectations that the other didn't want.

Once they reached a closed office door, Billie knocked, then pushed it open. "Hey, Dad. Can we borrow your office and phone for a few minutes?"

The older man, sitting behind the desk looked up and smiled at Billie. Saskia could see who the York siblings had taken after in looks. They all had their father's black hair and gray-blue eyes.

"I take it this is..." Billie's father let his words trail off as he glanced meaningfully at Saskia.

Billie nodded. "Yes, this has to do with werewolf business." She motioned to Saskia. "Saskia is a werewolf too. And Eli likes her — a lot."

The elder York stuck out his hand to Saskia. "Nice to meet you, Saskia. Eli has great taste in women I see."

Billie cleared her throat. "She's a werewolf, Dad. Of course she's drop-dead gorgeous. Just give us a few minutes and then you can have your office back."

Billie's father laughed. "Okay, I can take the hint. Maybe I'll see Eli for a bit until you're done here."

After the eldest York left the office and closed the door behind him, Royce shook his head at Billie. "Eli isn't going to thank you for that. It's bad enough you guys harass him about not finding a mate. When he finally takes a real interest in a woman, you sic your father on him."

Billie stuck out her tongue at her mate. She pulled the phone across the desk. After hitting a button to put it on speakerphone, she motioned for Saskia to proceed.

Saskia took out the piece of paper that had Beowulf's cell phone number on it from her front jeans pocket and then punched in the numbers. The sound of the phone ringing through on the other side filled the office. After the third ring, Beowulf picked up.

"Hi, Beowulf. This is Saskia."

"Hi, Saskia. I guess I'll get right to the point. Why do you and your men need to see Roxie?"

Saskia chuckled at Beowulf's straightforwardness. "Okay. I'll get right to the point as well. It's the duty of my men and me to be Roxie's protectors. We've trained for this for hundreds of years, waiting for the day the foretold one would be found."

A long silence stretched before Beowulf responded. "You want to watch over Roxie?"

"Yes."

"Then why have you waited until now to come forward? The leaders from the other packs pledged themselves to Roxie months ago. Wasn't your leader one of them?"

"My men and I don't belong to any pack. If there was a leader, it would be me. We just recently heard of the foretold one being found or we would have been in contact with you sooner."

"I don't understand how you can't belong to a pack. No offense, but how is it you, a female, are the leader of six large werewolf males who have obviously gone lone wolf?" Beowulf then said, "Ow! Rox, what did you hit me for now?"

A muffled sound came across the phone before a woman spoke. "Hi, this is Roxie. I have to apologize for Beowulf. Sometimes he doesn't think before he speaks. I *think* it's great that you're the leader of your men."

"Roxie, it would be best if you put Beowulf back on," Royce said.

"Royce, is that you? What are you doing with Saskia?"

"Saskia is at the gym."

"What is she doing there?"

Billie answered before Royce did. "Saskia came to see Eli. They like each other."

"Is that so?"

Royce groaned. "Roxie, can we focus on the topic at hand and not on Eli for the moment?"

"Cool it, Grandpa. No need to get your undies in a bunch. I think it's great Eli has taken a liking to Saskia. Matching him up as been a pet project for Billie, Jocelyn, and me."

In the background, Saskia heard Beowulf say, "I pity the poor bugger." Then. "Ow. Would you quick smacking me, Rox?"

"Then stop saying things you know will get you smacked," Roxie told him. "Saskia?"

Saskia found the banter between Roxie and the males of her family very amusing. It also showed her Roxie didn't take any guff from them either. "Yes."

"We need to meet face-to-face to discuss this business of you and your men being my protectors. How about you bring them to my house tonight for supper?"

Before Saskia could answer, Billie said, "Eli and Saskia planned to go out tonight after he got off work."

"Okay. Bring him along with you, Billie. I know Royce will want to be here. Right, Grandpa?"

"Yes," Royce growled. "Stop calling me Grandpa."

Roxie ignored Royce's last comment. "Is that all right with you,

Saskia? You come with your men to my place for supper, we'll have our talk, then you and Eli can go do whatever you had planned."

"I don't have any problem with it," Saskia said.

"Good. Royce and Billie can give you my address. I look forward to seeing you all later tonight. Bye."

Billie hung up the phone. "That went well. You're going to love Roxie, Saskia. We hit it off right away when I first met her."

Saskia nodded. "I must say I like the way she handles her mate."

Royce grunted. "Great, another assertive woman. What happened to the time when a male could expect his mate to actually do what he says?"

Billie crossed her arms over her chest and glared at Royce. "That kind of attitude died out with the Dark Ages. You're showing your age, mate of mine."

"Well, I did live through the Dark Ages. What do you expect?"

Billie rolled her eyes. She grabbed a piece of paper from her father's desk and quickly wrote down an address before she handed it to Saskia. "This is Beowulf and Roxie's address. Since Eli is more than likely still with his client, I can tell him about the change in plans for you. I'm sure you want to get home to tell your men."

"Thanks. I guess I'll see you later this evening."

Saskia left the office and then headed for the gym's entrance. On the way past the main gym floor, she scanned the large open room. Her gaze immediately latched on to Eli, who was spotting another man on one of the weight machines. Their gazes collided as he looked up. She gave him a small wave before she continued on her way. She'd be lucky if she kept her hands to herself while they were at Beowulf and Roxie's. Hopefully she and Eli would be able to leave there sooner rather than later.

* * * *

When six o'clock finally rolled around, Eli left the gym and hurried to his apartment. He had an hour to get home, take a shower, and get ready for his evening out. After arriving at his apartment, he stripped out of his clothes even before he reached his bedroom.

He resisted the urge to turn the tap on the shower all the way to cold as he stepped under the spray. After Saskia's visit to the gym, he'd spent most of the day half-aroused. He didn't think he ever would be able to go into the supply room again without thinking of what they'd done inside there. His cock twitched just thinking of how she had sounded as she'd come. He wanted her to make those sounds again as he pumped his cock in and out of her. Becoming more aroused, Eli groaned and stuck his face under the showerhead.

After a quick wash, he got out and then dried himself. With the towel wrapped around his hips, he went to his bedroom to get dressed. He decided not to wear anything fancy. The meal at Beowulf and Roxie's would be casual, so he opted for a pair of blue jeans and a black, long-sleeved tee. Once dressed, he returned to the bathroom and quickly blew dry his hair.

He ran his hand across his cheek and grimaced. He'd have to shave again. Not that he liked to shave twice a day, but he didn't want to give Saskia whisker burn. And considering what he wanted to do to her that night, she would have whisker burn if he didn't get rid of the bristles. He pulled his shirt off and then quickly lathered his face with shaving cream.

Eli had just about finished shaving when his apartment door slammed open and Billie called out his name. He winced as he nicked himself. "I'm in the bathroom. And have you ever heard of knocking first?"

Billie came and stood at the open bathroom door. "I thought you'd be ready by now." She peered closer at him. "You cut yourself."

He turned on the water and rinsed the rest of the shaving cream away, then patted his face dry. "Hmm, I wonder how I managed to do that. Maybe because someone startled me by barreling into my apartment as she yelled my name."

As Eli put on his shirt, Billie nodded. "Very nice. You look good. You'll be lucky if Saskia doesn't jump you the moment she sees you."

"Yeah, right. Not with her big, hulking brothers around she won't. With them there, I'll be lucky if I can get Saskia to myself later tonight."

"Don't worry about them. We'll manage to get the two of you away. I have lots of experience in getting out from under my four older brothers' watchful eyes, don't you know."

Eli shook his head and chuckled as he turned off the bathroom light. He headed to the living room with Billie at his side. "Yeah, you were good at that. I'm glad you're Royce's problem now."

Billie smacked his arm. "I am not a problem. And speaking of Royce, hurry up. He's outside waiting in the car for us."

Slipping on his running shoes, Eli said, "I thought I'd follow instead of catching a ride with you and Royce. If Saskia isn't driving herself, it would be kind of hard for us to get away if neither one of us has a car."

"Fine. I'll go down and tell Royce. We'll be waiting in the visitors' parking lot."

Once Billie left, Eli gave the apartment a quick look-over just in case he and Saskia came back to his place. He wasn't a slob, so it wasn't too messy. Spotting a dirty shirt he'd thrown onto the couch, he snatched it up and put it in the laundry basket in his bedroom closet. Satisfied he wouldn't be embarrassed to bring her there, he picked up his keys and left.

Down in the parking garage, Eli got into his dark gray Accord. Not as fancy as some cars out there, but it still got him from A to B. Spotting Royce's black BMW sports car in the visitors' parking, he pulled up close to him and waited for Royce to back out.

Eli followed his sister and Royce. As they reached the richer part of San Francisco, he let out a low whistle. He knew Beowulf was loaded, same with Royce, but he hadn't known Beowulf had *that* much money. Waiting behind the BMW, he watched the large gate open in the front of the drive. As they drove up the curving driveway, he looked at the grounds and the large house that loomed ahead. Beowulf wasn't just rich; he was stinking rich.

Eli parked his car next to Royce's and then got out. There didn't appear to be any other cars near the house. Either Saskia and her brothers hadn't arrived yet or they'd parked somewhere else. He hoped it was the latter. On the drive there, he couldn't stop thinking about her, and that he would see her soon. Their encounter earlier that day had left him hungry for more.

Roxie pulled open the front door after Royce knocked. She greeted them with a smile and waved them inside. "You guys are the first to arrive." As Eli walked past her, she looked him up and down. "You're looking good this evening, Eli."

"Thanks."

She closed the door behind them. "I'll make sure Saskia gets to sit beside you during dinner."

"Good to know."

Beowulf greeted them after they followed Roxie to the large living room. Billie and Royce sat on one loveseat, while Eli took the armchair nearest it. Beowulf and Roxie claimed the loveseat across from Billie and Royce. That left the sectional couch and the only other armchair for Saskia and her men to sit on. Eli eyed the couch. He didn't think it was big enough to fit all of them. He would have no problem asking Saskia to sit on his lap if that turned out to be the case.

"So, Eli," Roxie said. "Are you going to follow in your twin's footsteps and take a female werewolf for your mate?"

Eli cleared his throat. He hadn't expected to be hit with that question so early on in the game. "Um, it's a little too soon for that, don't you think? I just met Saskia. We really haven't had much time to get to know each other really."

Billie snorted. "With the time the two of you spent making out in the supply room at the gym, I would think you guys got to know each other quite well."

Roxie gave Eli a knowing smile. "The supply room, huh? Sounds interesting."

Eli leveled a hard stare at Billie. "And who told Saskia she would find me in there? I know she wouldn't have known unless someone had showed her."

"I don't hear you complaining," Billie replied. "The fact you had to change your pants after you left the supply room wasn't totally lost on me, you know."

Eli looked at Royce. "Would you mind too much if I killed her now?"

Royce chuckled. "As a matter a fact, I would."

The sound of a buzzer interrupted the conversation. Beowulf got up. "That must be the rest of our guests. I'll go open the gate for them." He left the living room.

Now that Saskia was about to arrive, Eli decided he'd better set some ground rules for Billie. "Before Saskia gets here, Billie, I want you to promise you won't go out of your way to embarrass me, especially in front of her men. And for God's sake, don't bring up the subject of the supply room again. I really don't want Saskia's men to decide they want to use me as a punching bag. I doubt I would survive it."

"What do you take me for? I would never say anything like that in front of them. I'm on your side, remember?"

"Sometimes it's hard to tell."

A booming knock on the front door reached his ears. Eli shifted in the armchair as he watched the entrance to the living room. It didn't take long for Beowulf to appear with Saskia and her men.

Much to Eli's surprise, Saskia walked to him, sat on his lap, and kissed him until he couldn't remember his own name. Once she finally lifted her head, he glanced at her men. Oh, he was so screwed.

CHAPTER FOUR

Settling more comfortably on Eli's lap, Saskia followed his line of sight. She wrapped her arm around his shoulders and focused a hard stare on her scowling brothers. "Would the six of you sit down and stop trying to be so intimidating?"

Jager crossed his arms over his chest. "We'll sit after you get off the mortal's lap."

Saskia sighed. She'd known this would be her brothers' reaction to her staking her claim on Eli, but she'd thought it best to get it out in the open right from the start. They hadn't been too impressed when she'd come home with Eli's scent all over her. Not that she cared what they thought. It wasn't as if she ever questioned any of them when they came home stinking of sex and females.

"I'm quite happy where I am," she said. "Now behave yourselves and sit down. We haven't even been here five minutes and already you're all being rude." When they remained on their feet, Saskia pointed to the unoccupied sectional couch. "Sit. Down."

With a curl of his lip, Jager reluctantly sat. The others, just as reluctantly, followed suit. Once they'd all taken a seat, Saskia looked at Beowulf, who had gone to sit next to the woman she assumed had to be Roxie.

"I hope you don't mind if I sit with Eli. It just makes things easier." She looked meaningfully at her brothers, then said, "I guess I'll be the one to do the introductions. I'm Saskia. And the grumps over there are my brothers-in-arms—Jager, Dirk, Kye, Roan, Skylar, and Leif."

Roxie smiled. "I completely understand," she said with a chuckle. Roxie's gaze settled on her brothers. "It's nice to meet you. All I can say is, wow."

"Rox," Beowulf warned.

"What? I'm not dead, Beowulf. I'm mated to you, but it doesn't mean I can't admire from a distance."

Saskia couldn't hide the smile that formed on her lips. Her brothers appeared to suddenly not know where to look. Taking pity on them, she directed Roxie's attention back to her. "Do we have time to discuss why we sought you out before we eat?"

Roxie nodded. "We do. I must say I've been curious."

She shifted on Eli's lap, then bit back a moan. The hard length of his cock pressed against her bottom. Swallowing, Saskia did her best to ignore it. "As I told you on the phone, we've trained for hundreds of years to be the protectors of the foretold one. It's our duty to keep you safe, Roxie."

"If I don't want to accept you and your men as my protectors, what then?"

"We won't go away that easily. You must be protected."

"I'm flattered that I would have you around to look out for me, but it really isn't necessary. I can take care of myself."

Saskia looked Roxie up and down. With her long, gold-brown hair and slim body, Roxie didn't look as if she had the strength to stand against a male werewolf. "Don't take this the wrong way, but you wouldn't last ten seconds against one of my brothers, let alone all of them at once."

Beowulf laughed, something Saskia hadn't expected. "Saskia, you're wrong with that assumption. Roxie is more special than the prophecy said."

"I don't understand."

"I think it best you show them, Rox." Beowulf moved to sit on the arm of the loveseat.

Roxie stood and stepped to the middle of the room where all of them could easily see her. Something was up. Saskia noticed Royce and Billie grinning knowingly. She looked at Eli and found he wore the same grin as his sister and her mate.

"Watch," Eli told her.

Saskia turned back to Roxie as the other woman shifted forms. Expecting her to shift into her wolf form, Saskia's mouth dropped open as Roxie turned into a half-wolf/half-human creature. She glanced at her brothers. They too stared at Roxie with an expression of incredulity. This was supposed to be impossible for any werewolf to do. Roxie now stood taller than she did in human form, and she looked much, much stronger. Her body was covered in light, golden-brown fur, not quite the same color as her hair. She had a wolf's muzzle and pointed ears on the top of her head. Instead of paws, she had human hands and feet but covered with fur. She also had a wolf's tail. Then Roxie shocked the crap out of Saskia by being able to talk as well.

"See, I told you I could look after myself. Plus, there's more."

Roxie's voice sounded gruffer than it normally did. Saskia couldn't tear her gaze off her. "More?"

"Yes. I have a bit more magic than your average werewolf." Roxie went to stand in front of Skylar. She placed her hand briefly on top of his head. "Now try to get up."

Skylar tried to move, but nothing happened. He gasped in shock as he tried again and again. He appeared as if couldn't get off the couch even if his life had depended on it.

He looked up in awe at Roxie. "I can't."

Roxie laughed a raspy laugh. "Of course you can't. Now that I've touched you, you won't be able to move until I let you. Try now."

This time Skylar shot to his feet and would have fallen on his face if Roxie hadn't been there to catch him. Saskia also noticed she handled Skylar as if he weighed next to nothing.

"How is this possible?" Saskia breathed.

Royce answered as Roxie shifted back to her human form, then sat next to Beowulf. "We're really not sure, but we have come to one plausible reason. My first mate, the great, great, great, etc. grandmother of Roxie, was a mortal. She also had magic of her own. Alicia had abilities. To what degree they extended, I don't know. She didn't like to use them or talk about them. All I know is out of all her descendants, Roxie is the one who resembles Alicia the most. So it stands to reason Roxie also inherited her abilities as well."

Leif looked at Saskia before he spoke. "Did you see any of this in your recent visions about the foretold one?"

Saskia shook her head. "No."

"You have visions?" Eli asked.

"Yes."

Beowulf's head snapped in her direction. "Hold on. Recent visions of the foretold one? You can't be the female werewolf who prophesied Roxie's coming."

"I'm not, but I'm from her bloodline. Kara was my grandmother. She is the one who brought my brothers-in-arms and me together to be Roxie's protectors. She picked the strongest and biggest lone wolves. Kara trained us to work together, to fight for one purpose. My grandmother saw the trouble that is to come now that Roxie has been found."

"Why did she pick six lone wolves? Why didn't she choose males from her own pack?" Beowulf asked.

Saskia looked at her brothers. She loved them all as if they were indeed her true brothers by birth. "By this time, the numbers in our pack had diminished to almost nothing. It was no more, and ours wasn't the only one. So my grandmother chose males who no longer had packs. Dirk, Leif, and Kye come from three different packs. Skylar, Roan, and Jager are true brothers and come from a fourth pack. I used to have a seventh brother."

"What happened to him?" Roxie asked.

Saskia turned to stare seriously at Roxie. "He left us. Miles once trained to protect you, but now he's the one we must watch out for. He'll fight to take you as his own. Mated or not, he will claim you as his if he can. Then with you tied to him, he'll use you as a figurehead while he rules the packs in your stead."

* * * *

Eli pulled out the chair next to Saskia's at the large dining room table. He sat and tried to ignore the six identical warning stares her brothers shot his way. He hoped once they all had food on their plates they would concentrate on that rather than him.

After Saskia's statement about her seventh brother, the room had grown so silent you could have heard a pin drop. And right about that time, Beowulf's cook had stepped into the living room to let them know dinner was ready to be served. Saskia had gotten off his lap as everyone else stood and then followed Beowulf and Roxie to the dining room.

Now with everyone seated, the food started to make its way around the table. Eli loaded his plate with the garlic roasted potatoes and steamed mixed vegetables. When Saskia passed him a serving platter filled with thick steaks that had barely touched a grill, he quickly passed it on to Beowulf, who sat at the end of the table next to him. He liked his steaks medium rare with some pink showing, but those were so rare, they looked as if they would get up and walk away at any time. Those who had been born werewolves ate the almost-raw meat with gusto.

Roxie spoke to him from the other end of the table. "Billie has the platter with the steaks that have been cooked properly."

"Good. I was a little worried there," Eli replied.

She laughed. "I could tell. If I had to eat meat that raw, I would never get it down."

Kye looked at her. "You're a werewolf, Roxie. I find it strange that you don't like your meat practically raw like the rest of us."

Roxie shrugged. "Maybe because I wasn't born a werewolf I still like my meat the way I did when I was a mortal."

"What about you, Billie?" Saskia asked. "You took your steak from the same platter Roxie and Eli did."

Billie shuddered. "You won't catch me dead eating meat that undercooked. That's just disgusting. I have to agree with Roxie; it has to be a byproduct of having once been mortal." When Kye's fork dropped to his plate in a loud clatter, Billie grimaced. "Oh, crap. I said too much, didn't I? Sorry, Rox."

Saskia stiffened. If Eli been sitting next to Billie, he would have given her a kick under the table for not taking the time to think before she'd spoken. Roxie, and most especially Beowulf and Royce, didn't want the rest of the werewolf population to know she could turn mortals into werewolves with a magic spell after they'd been injected with a small amount of her blood. Billie had put her foot in it this time.

Saskia slowly lowered her knife and fork to her plate. "Was Billie once mortal, Roxie?"

Eli held himself perfectly still and prepared for the shit to hit the fan. Taking quick glances at Beowulf and Royce, he noticed they looked ready to jump out of their chairs if the other six male werewolves so much as made a move toward Roxie. Eli hoped if the fur began to fly, which it could quite literally in this case, he wouldn't get stuck in the middle of it.

Roxie smiled. "Yes, Billie used to be mortal."

"I don't understand," Saskia said.

"I guess you might have heard about the spell that turned me into a werewolf."

"Yes, my brothers and I learned about it a few years ago, but until you, we thought it wouldn't work."

"Well, the spell has worked on a few others as well. And before you can ask, it only works if my blood is used and if I'm the one performing the spell."

Pandemonium broke loose as Saskia's brothers all talked at once. To say they found the news disturbing put it mildly. Jager let loose with a string of swear words, some of which Eli hadn't even heard before. Skylar and Roan were doing their best not to be outdone by their sibling. Kye rubbed his temples as if he'd gotten a sudden headache and bellowed that they were so screwed. Leif and Dirk argued over what they thought would need to be done to keep the knowledge of Roxie being able to turn mortals into werewolves from the rest of their kind. Their shouting didn't last long, though. Roxie put two fingers into her mouth and whistled loud and shrill.

She gave the six males a hard stare. "You will behave yourselves right now or I'll be forced to do something really nasty. Something I did to another male werewolf who really pissed me off. How would you guys like to be stuck in your wolf forms for twenty-four hours while I keep you chained up in my backyard like dogs?" When none of Saskia's brothers said anything more, she nodded. "Smart boys."

Saskia turned to look at Eli. "Roxie turned your twin as well, didn't she? That's why he's a werewolf and you aren't."

Eli nodded. "Yes. After Finn and Jocelyn mated, he made the choice to become a werewolf. Well, actually, he came to the decision to do it to save Jocelyn's life, but that's another story." By now everyone had focused their attention on him and Saskia.

"How many mortals and werewolves have become mates?"

Saskia asked in a shocked voice.

Beowulf must have taken pity on him, because he answered Saskia's question. "It hasn't happened very often, but it does happen more than you think. My brother, Wade, mated with his mate, Taryn, while she was still mortal. As did I with Roxie before she became a werewolf. Royce's first mate was a mortal as well, remember?"

Saskia shook her head. "I never thought it possible that that many werewolves and mortals had become mates. The mating bond, the joining of the mates' souls, is forged through the magic inside us. A mortal doesn't have that kind of magic."

"There you're wrong," Beowulf said. "Maybe not all mortals have the magic, or ability, as we do, but some do have abilities of their own. For instance, Roxie was born able to do all the things her great-grandmother could. She just never knew she could. Taryn is half werewolf. Her father, Drake, took a mortal woman as his mate. Taryn has dreams that sometimes come true. Billie has the ability to find anyone she meets. Finn has visions as you do, Saskia."

Saskia grew thoughtful. Eli could almost see the wheels turning in her head. "And these are all the mortals who have been turned by the spell. I wonder if these abilities they were born with determined whether the spell worked or not."

"That is something we've considered as well," Roxie said from her end of the table. "I've never tried the spell on a mortal who hasn't shown some kind of ability, so there's no way to tell for sure right now."

"I'm going to suggest you don't use the spell to find out the answer to that."

Roxie laughed at Saskia. "Don't worry. I have no intentions of doing that. Beowulf has made himself perfectly clear on how he feels about that idea."

"Let's just say I almost had an aneurism the first time Rox tried the spell herself and it worked," Beowulf added. "I don't want this to become general knowledge any more than you do."

Roxie cleared her throat. "Enough talk about the spell. The food is getting cold. Besides, I'm sure Eli and Saskia would like to leave soon to go out on their date."

"Date?" Roan asked in a loud voice.

"Yes, date. You boys" — Roxie gave each of Saskia's men a hard look — "will let her go or else I'll have to dig up some more chains for the backyard."

That threat seemed to do the trick. None of the six male werewolves seated across from Eli said another word. They all kept their gazes on their plates as they ate. Eli mouthed a silent *thank you* to Roxie, who in return smiled at him.

As the meal progressed, Eli found himself checking his watch every few minutes for the time. With Saskia beside him, her leg pressed against his thigh, his unruly body refused to settle down. It didn't help that he couldn't seem to stop thinking of what he wanted to do to her that night. He had originally thought to take Saskia out for a nice meal, then invite her back to his place for a drink, but after Roxie had invited them for dinner, it had messed up his plans.

Hopefully, Saskia wouldn't be too offended if, after they finished eating, he just asked her back to his place. He didn't think he could last another couple of hours sitting at some bar as he made small talk with her. The need to touch her, to taste her, became harder to ignore as time went by.

In the end, Saskia took matters into her own hands. As soon as she finished eating, she looked at Eli. "Are you finished?"

"Yes."

"All right then."

She took his hand and stood before she pulled him to his feet. Saskia quickly thanked Roxie and Beowulf for the enjoyable meal. Before she led him out of the dining room, she told them she would be in touch.

Once they were out of sight of the others, she pulled Eli to a halt and took his mouth in a hard kiss. After a few seconds, she pulled away. "Take me to your place. All I can think about is having you buried deep inside me."

Panting as if he'd just run a marathon, Eli grabbed Saskia's hand. Before he led her out of the house, he said, "What the lady wants, the lady shall have."

In no time flat, he had them in his car as he raced down the large driveway. He prayed there wouldn't be any cops around as he sped to his apartment.

CHAPTER FIVE

Given how fast Eli drove, he was just as anxious as she to finally be alone together. The smell of his arousal also gave him away.

In no time Eli pulled his car into the underground parking garage at his apartment building. After he parked, he came around to her side to meet her. With her hand in his, he led her to the elevators, then they were on their way up to his floor. Saskia debated whether or not to throw herself into his arms as soon as the elevator door slid shut, but in the end, she decided against it for a couple of reasons. The first, even though she couldn't see a camera, that didn't mean there wasn't one somewhere inside the elevator. The other big reason she didn't do it provided the most restraint—once she started kissing him, she didn't think she would be able to stop. Having sex in an elevator where other people could chance upon them didn't happen to be high on her list of things to do.

After the elevator dinged at Eli's floor and the door opened, he hurried with her down the hallway to his apartment door. It swung open after he unlocked it; then they were inside. Once it shut behind them, he locked it before he went to turn on the lights. Saskia would have told him not to bother because she could see just as well in the dark as she did in the day, but that wouldn't be the case for him.

He turned on enough lights before he came back to stand in front of her. "Would you like something to drink?"

"No. I just want you."

With a groan, Eli wrapped his arms around her waist and hauled her against his broad chest. His mouth slammed down onto hers. Saskia tunneled her fingers through his hair as she kissed him back. At the feel of his tongue running along the seam of her lips, she opened to give him access.

Saskia moaned into his mouth. The feel of the hard length of his cock pressed against her belly made her pussy clench. She grew wet as she rubbed herself along his erection. Eli lowered his hands to her bottom and pulled her closer. He pumped his hips. The ache between her legs intensified.

After Eli lifted her off her feet, Saskia wrapped her legs around his waist as she rubbed her pussy along the hard ridge of his cock through his jeans. He swung around, then walked down the short hallway before he pushed open the door to his bedroom. This time he didn't bother turning on the lights. He continued to kiss her as he walked the short distance to his bed. He climbed onto it and lowered her to the mattress. They moaned as he came to lie on top of her between her legs.

Eli released her lips and kissed a trail along her jaw to the side of her neck. He tugged her blouse out of her jeans and shoved his hand inside to cup her breast. Saskia shivered as he swirled his tongue into her ear before he took her lobe between his teeth with a small tug. She panted and took hold of the bottom of his shirt and lifted it so she could run her hands along the smooth skin of his back.

Eli released her breast, then swiftly undid the buttons on her blouse. He parted the material and ran the flat of his tongue across her tight nipple through her bra. With nimble fingers, he undid the front clasp. He brushed the straps over her shoulders and down her arms until she was free of it, taking her top with it.

Saskia arched off the bed as Eli swirled his tongue around one taut nipple before he greedily sucked it deep inside his mouth. With each pull, there was a corresponding one in her pussy. Wetness leaked into her panties. Needing to feel his naked skin pressed to hers, she yanked his shirt over his head and then threw it to the floor. As he sucked her other breast, she rocked her hips against the large bulge in his jeans. After he shifted so he laid half on top of her, she reached down and undid his pants. She shoved her hand inside, then wrapped her fingers around his thick shaft and squeezed.

Eli moaned but gently pried her hand off his erection. "If you keep that up, you'll make me come. I want to taste you first."

He shifted down her body before he undid the button and zipper of her jeans. Saskia gasped as he licked and kissed every inch of skin he exposed as he pulled her pants down past her hips. She kicked them the rest of the way off, leaving her only in her thong.

Eli positioned himself between her spread thighs, then dipped his head and dragged his tongue along the crotch of her thong. He hooked the material that covered her pussy and pulled it aside with his finger. Saskia lifted her hips off the bed as he licked her naked flesh. A low growl left her lips as he continued to lick her from bottom to top before he circled her clit with his tongue. She held him to her and rocked her hips against his mouth. He pushed first one, then a second finger, inside her pussy as he sucked on her clit. She clamped her inner muscles around the digits as he pumped them in and out.

She wanted to wait until he was inside her when she came, but Eli wouldn't allow it. "Come for me, Saskia," he breathed against her. "I want to taste you while you come against my mouth."

Eli removed his fingers and jabbed his stiffened tongue inside her core as he rubbed her sensitive clit. It was enough to send Saskia over the edge. With a keening moan, she pressed her head back against the bed as her release tore through her. He continued to lap at her sex until the last ripple of pleasure faded.

It had felt good, but it had only whetted her appetite. She wanted the hard length of his cock as it filled her wet pussy. As he rose on his knees, she yanked his jeans down. His stiff cock sprang free as soon as she had the material past his hips. Before he could stop her, Saskia moved to sit up. She wrapped her hand around his thick shaft and licked him from base to tip. He moaned. She looked up to find his heated gaze on her as she continued to lick his shaft. She returned her attention back to his member, holding him tight as she circled the broad head with her tongue. He jerked his hips as she took the tip into her mouth and sucked.

Eli's moans filled the room once she opened wider and took as much of his cock as she could handle inside. As she sucked, he hardened even more. She would have continued to pleasure him this way until he came, but he had other plans. He pulled away and pushed her down onto her back. He kicked off his jeans before he grabbed her thong and yanked to remove it. Saskia spread her legs as he came down on top of her.

The head of his cock brushed against her wet core. Eli took her lips in a hard kiss as he surged forward, fully seating himself deep inside her. Saskia sucked his tongue into her mouth and moaned. As he pulled back and then pushed inside, another orgasm slowly built.

While he pumped his hips between her legs, Saskia gripped Eli's cock with her inner muscles. The slow pace he'd set increased. He released her mouth as he lifted his upper body off her, supporting his weight on his hands. She wrapped her legs around his waist as he thrust into her. Her orgasm crept ever closer.

Eli pumped his hips faster. He groaned as he angled them so his thick shaft rubbed her clit. The friction caused her body to coil even tighter. She was so close. Lifting her hips, Saskia met his strokes as she squeezed down on him harder.

A vision slammed into her. She saw Eli and herself as they were now, making love. What made her gasp was what happened once they both reached their climax—their souls joined, mating them together as one.

Unaware of what she'd seen, Eli rode her harder, faster, pushing her climax to the point of almost no return. Saskia dug her fingernails into his arms. "Eli, stop."

Eli lowered himself on top of her and cupped her bottom as he angled her hips in just the right angle to send her flying. "Too late," he moaned.

He moaned again as her inner walls fisted his cock in a tight grip. Saskia whimpered as intense waves of pleasure ripped through her. Eli's cock pulsed deep inside her core as he came. While he climaxed, she felt his soul reach out to hers. Unable to stop herself, hers reached out to him and wrapped around his. They gasped as they joined.

Out of breath, Eli panted, "Was that what I think it was?" He pulled her close and nuzzled the side of her neck.

Saskia stared at the ceiling. She'd gone cold inside. This couldn't be happening. She couldn't be mated. Long ago, she'd made the decision to never take a mate. She had her duty to protect the foretold one. There wouldn't be room in her life for a mate, especially for a mortal one. Feeling as if she suffocated, she pushed Eli off her. She curled her upper lip and growled when he tried to pull her closer.

A look of confusion flashed across his face. "Talk to me, Saskia. Something happened between us. I felt it. It felt like what Finn described when he and Jocelyn became mates."

"I have to get out of here." Saskia searched the bedroom floor for her clothes. She slid off the bed to gather them up.

Eli sat up. "We're mates now, aren't we?"

She jerkily pulled on her clothes. "Yes."

"Then where are you going?" Eli got off the bed and came to stand gloriously naked beside her. "I know this is a bit unexpected, but I'm not unhappy about it, surprisingly enough. We can make this work. I can feel you inside me. You're a part of me now."

And she felt a part of him inside her as well, but that didn't stop her from snapping her teeth at him when he tried to reach for her again. "Don't touch me."

Eli took a step back. "Look, we have to discuss this."

Saskia yanked on her blouse. "There's nothing to discuss. I'm leaving."

"I don't understand what has you so pissed off with me. It isn't as if I forced this on you. Christ, I didn't know anymore than you did that this would happen. I'm not a male werewolf who recognizes his mate from the first whiff of her scent."

"Exactly." Now dressed, Saskia scowled. Feeling trapped, she said the first things that popped into her mind. She didn't care what her words would do to him. "You aren't a werewolf. I never wanted a mate. Not ever. What makes this even worse is that you're a mortal. I thought we would have our fun, then go our separate ways." The look of hurt he gave her almost made her stop, but her emotions were too jumbled for her to rein herself back. "I thought I would have an enjoyable night of sex. Instead, I now find myself tied to a mortal."

"I can understand you being a little out of sorts about being mated when you never wanted to be. I wasn't exactly looking for that kind of connection, believe me, but what's done is done. We can't go back. You need to calm down, Saskia."

"No. I need to leave."

Saskia turned to go, but Eli grabbed her arm to stop her. "You can't. We need to be near each other or it'll mess with our minds. I've seen my brother and sister go through it when they were too long apart from their mates. It isn't pretty."

She pulled her arm free with a rough yank. "I guess we'll see how bad it actually gets because I'm still leaving, and there's nothing you can do to stop me."

Moving at a speed Eli couldn't match, Saskia hurried to the apartment door and flung it open. After she slammed it shut, she rushed to the elevators. Luckily for her, the door to one slid open as soon as she pushed the button. As it closed, she took a deep breath. She closed her eyes and thought of all the hurtful things she'd said to Eli. What was the matter with her? A part of her wanted to go back up to his apartment and tell him how sorry she was, but she didn't. The thought of going back to him, to her mate, made her gasp for breath. Until she got her head screwed on straight, she would have to stay away from him. She'd already hurt him enough. He didn't need her to make things any worse than they already were.

*

Feeling as if someone had just sucker punched him in the gut, Eli sat on the bed as his apartment door slammed shut. He made no move to go after Saskia. The things she'd said and the way she'd acted told him she wouldn't listen to him even if he did manage to catch up to her. His mate had not reacted well to their mating. He snorted. That could only be described as an understatement.

His mate. He shook his head. He never thought to have that one word—mate—connected to him in any way. Finn must have been right, after all. He'd told Eli once he found the right woman there wouldn't be any others for him. That was how Eli felt about Saskia. Even though she didn't like the fact, she had turned out to be the one for him. Making love to her had been beyond anything he'd experienced with any other woman. His cock stirred just thinking about how good it'd felt to be inside her. He wanted her again. One time hadn't been enough.

"Damn."

Eli punched the mattress with the flat of his hand. Already he felt Saskia's absence. Right now, he could handle it, but he had no idea what he would be like hours from now. With no way to contact Saskia, he had to hope when it got bad for her, she would seek him out. If she didn't, he would be a walking mess.

CHAPTER SIX

He was living in hell. Eli couldn't describe it any other way than that. Hours had gone by since Saskia had run out on him. The need to be with her, to touch her, seemed almost too great to bear at times. He felt empty and out of sorts. *How the hell had Finn and Billie survived this?* Being separated from one's mate could only be described as excruciating.

Unable to fall asleep, let alone relax, at five in the morning, Eli decided he couldn't stay in the apartment any longer. He needed something to distract himself. Knowing the gym wouldn't be open for at least a few hours, he made the decision to go there. A couple of hours of lifting weights should help, or so he hoped.

He threw on a pair of old sweats and a T-shirt with the sleeves cut off. Before he left, he put a clean, dark blue T-shirt that had YORK FITNESS in white across the front and a pair of gray warm-up pants in a backpack. After grabbing his keys, he headed down to the parking garage.

The birds chirped to the new day when he arrived at the gym. Eli parked his car in the lot and then headed for the front entrance. He unlocked the door and made sure to lock it behind him after he stepped inside. Once he had the security alarm disabled, he flipped on the lights in the darkened space.

Eli put his backpack inside his locker in the men's change room before he headed for the main gym floor. First thing he did was turn on the sound system. Grateful the gym didn't sit next to any homes, he turned up the music louder than they normally played it. The deep bass of the rock song that blared out of the speakers thumped through him.

Eli crossed the gym floor to the rack of dumbbells that ran along the mirrored wall and grabbed two forty-pound dumbbells and went to one of the benches that set in a row in front of the mirrors. He sat, fixed his grip on them, then stood. Holding them perpendicular to his body in front of his waist, he swung them up in a fly. He did two more sets of flies before he moved on to the shoulder-press machine.

The weightlifting took the edge off his need for Saskia, but only enough so he didn't feel as if he would climb the walls. He worked out for an hour before the music that blared out of the speakers suddenly cut off. Eli looked up to find his older brother Keegan headed his way. Eli's chest rapidly rose and fell with each breath he took. Soaked in sweat with his hair plastered to his forehead, Eli nodded.

Keegan looked him up and down. "Don't you look like shit. What the hell brought you to the gym so early? You look as if you're trying to work out until you drop."

Eli wiped the sweat from his forehead. "You could say that. So far, it isn't working."

"It still doesn't explain what you're doing here so early. I thought you had a date with Saskia last night."

He gritted his teeth at the sound of his mate's name. "Just stop talking, Keegan. I really need you not to talk about Saskia right now. Okay?" He took off one of the plates from the barbell he'd been using.

Keegan shook his head. "Holy shit. You mated with her. You're acting like Billie and Finn do when they're separated too long from Royce or Jocelyn. How did that happen?"

Eli brushed past his brother and headed for another machine. "I don't know. It just happened."

"Where's Saskia?"

"I don't know."

"What do you mean you don't know? If you're this bad, she can't be any better."

"Keegan, please. I'm not in the mood for this right now."

"Who isn't in the mood for what?" Billie asked as she and Royce came to join them.

Eli swore under his breath. "Can all of you just please leave me the hell alone?"

Of course that only caused Billie to get right up in his face. "I don't believe this. The confirmed bachelor became mated."

"What do I need to do to get you to go away?" Eli snapped.

Billie backed off. "Sorry. You're in rough shape there. Where's Saskia?"

"I don't know. She ran out on me before I got a chance to ask for her cell phone number and address."

"What?"

"You heard me. She's gone."

"What do you mean she's gone? You're mates now. She knows what the separation does to mated couples."

Eli sat at the machine and scrubbed his face with his hand. "I don't think she cares. Let's just say she wasn't pleased to have me for her mate. I guess she never wanted a mate, and she sure as hell didn't want one who also happens to be a mortal. Does that answer your question?"

"Why didn't you call Billie earlier?" Royce asked. "She could have found Saskia for you."

"Yeah, why didn't you call me? I can look for her now if you want."

Eli sighed. "I don't think that'll be a good idea. You didn't see how she looked once our souls joined. She couldn't get away from me fast enough. She even growled and snapped her teeth at me when I tried to touch her. I don't think she'd take too kindly to me just showing up."

Billie's brows drew together in confusion. "So you would rather sit here slowly going insane from missing Saskia rather than track her down and end the anguish you both are going through?"

"Yes."

"Are you nuts? What happens if she doesn't ever come back? It'll only get worse."

"I'll take things as they come." Eli stood. "Since you've interrupted my workout, I might as well take a shower."

Once inside the men's change room, Eli stripped out of his

sweat-soaked clothes and then threw them onto the bottom of his locker. He would have to take them home at the end of the day to wash. After he grabbed his shampoo, conditioner, and the bar of soap from the top shelf, he headed for the showers.

Standing under the spray, he let the water pound on his back for a few minutes before he washed his hair. Eli had just started to soap his body when he felt another pair of hands run down his back. He spun around to find Saskia standing naked behind him. She took the bar of soap from him and ran it across his chest. His cock instantly became rock hard. He had to bite back a moan as he fought the urge to pull her to him and devour her mouth with his own. Instead, he looked around to make sure no one else had come in.

"Saskia? What are you doing?" He groaned as her soapy hand pumped up and down his shaft.

"I'm putting us both out of our misery."

As Saskia fondled him, Eli found it hard to think straight. "I thought you didn't want a mate. Plus, I don't think this is a good idea. It isn't as if there are any doors in here."

In retrospect, Eli didn't really care so much if someone walked in on them. He wanted to be inside Saskia so bad he shook with intense need. He didn't think he could ignore the longing another minute.

Saskia dropped the bar of soap and moved him under the spray to rinse the suds off his body. "I have to apologize for the way I acted earlier. I shouldn't have said what I did about not wanting you because you're mortal. I intend to make it up to you, but this will have to tide us over until we can be alone together. Your older brother said he would give us ten minutes, so I think we'd better spend what time we have left doing other things besides talking."

Eli didn't need to be told twice. He lifted Saskia off her feet, turned, and walked her back against the tiled shower wall. She wrapped her legs around his waist and clutched his shoulders. He took her mouth in a hard kiss as he reached between her legs. He moaned at the slick moisture he found there. Gripping his hard cock in one hand, he led it to the entrance of her body. They both moaned as he stroked her pussy with the head before he pushed his full length into her core. Seated to the hilt, he tipped his hips back, then surged into her again. As he drove into her again and again, he felt as if his world had suddenly righted itself once more.

Saskia locked her ankles at his back as she matched his strokes as best she could. She pulled away from his mouth and leaned forward to bite him where his shoulder and neck met. Eli's deep-throated moan filled the room as he rode her harder and faster. The inner muscles of her core squeezed down on his cock. His orgasm edged nearer.

"I don't think I can hold back anymore," Eli panted.

Saskia lifted her head. "I'm almost there. Don't stop. Take me harder."

Eli cupped her bottom with both hands, angling her higher on his shaft as he pumped his hips faster. As his orgasm tore through him, his moans mixed with Saskia's as she came with him. Her inner walls clutched his length, milking him, as his cock pulsed deep inside her.

They both were breathing hard as Eli buried his face in the crook of Saskia's neck. She wrapped her arms around his shoulders and held him tight. Once their breathing returned to normal, he slowly let her down on her feet. He brought them under the warm spray of water to rinse the sweat from their bodies. Their time almost up, he left her to get two white towels from the stack that sat in the corner near the showers.

He passed her a towel, then used the other to dry himself. With them wrapped around their bodies, Eli led Saskia to his locker. He looked around for her clothes and spotted them on a bench close to where they stood. She went to them and dressed as he pulled the fresh clothes he'd brought from home out of his locker.

Turning back to face her, Eli found Saskia had come up behind him as he'd dressed. She pulled his head down for a gentle kiss. "Let's get out of here. I think we should have that talk you wanted to have last night now that we'll be able to think straight."

Eli put his hands on either side of her waist. "Your place or mine?"

"Yours."

"Okay. Come on then." He took her hand and led her out of the men's change room. "I just have to let the others know I'm leaving."

He found Billie, Keegan, and Royce sipping on coffee in the office area. All conversation stopped as he and Saskia walked to them. "I don't have many clients today. Do you think you guys can manage to cover them between you? I'm sure Finn will help. He owes me one."

"Just go," Billie said. "We've got you covered." She stepped closer and stood on tiptoe to whisper into his ear. "Make sure you screw her brains out; then she won't have enough energy to run away again."

Eli cringed. Given how there were two other werewolves nearby, Saskia being one of them, he felt pretty sure Billie's whisper hadn't been quiet enough for them not to hear what she'd said. Royce tried to cover a laugh with a cough. Glancing at Saskia, Eli found her trying to keep a straight face.

"Ah, thanks, Billie. I'll try to do that." He leaned in closer and whispered, "If you don't stop making comments like that, I may be forced to put a muzzle on you."

That statement made Royce chuckle. Not so with Billie. She pushed him away before she slapped him on the chest. "Just try it, buddy."

Eli took Saskia's hand again. "Time to go before Billie gets nasty. I'll see you all tomorrow."

He quickly led Saskia outside to the parking lot. Seeing the black Triumph Sprint ST motorcycle parked next to his Accord, he looked at Saskia. "The Triumph is yours?"

She nodded. "Yes. Give me a fast motorcycle over a car any day."

Eli smiled. "A woman after my own heart. You're going to have to give me a ride on that sometime."

"You can have a ride anytime you want."

He somehow had the feeling Saskia meant more than just the motorcycle, given the hot look she gave him. "Okay, I think we'd better hurry up and get to my place before I do something that'll get us arrested for indecent exposure. You can follow me if you want."

Saskia let go of his hand and walked to her motorcycle. She unclipped the helmet from the side of it. Before she put it on, she said, "I'm ready whenever you are."

He quickly unlocked his car and then got in. The engine came to life as he turned the key in the ignition. A second later, Eli heard the roar of Saskia's motorcycle.

Eli kept his eye on Saskia through his rearview mirror as they drove the short distance to his apartment. Once they reached it, he stuck his arm out the window and motioned for her to follow him into the underground parking garage. He pulled into his spot and parked with the front of his car as close to the wall as he could get it. After turning off the ignition, he got out. Saskia parked her motorcycle sideways behind it.

He didn't give her a chance to take off her helmet as he grabbed her hand and walked her to the elevators. When one came, they stepped inside. Saskia pulled off her helmet, and he pushed the button to his floor. Once he let her inside her apartment, Eli closed and locked the door behind him. He stepped back and leaned against it as his gaze lingered longingly on her.

"So you want to talk," he said.

"Among other things."

"Then I suggest if you want to we'd better sit on the couch in the living room. If I get you anywhere near my bedroom, I won't be able to concentrate. At least on the couch, fully clothed, we should be able to say the things that need to be said before I jump you."

Saskia smiled. "All right."

They sat on the couch and shifted so they faced each other. Unable to be this close and not touch her, Eli laced his fingers through hers. "Why did you run from me, Saskia? Did the idea of me as your mate disgust you that much?"

She reached out and cupped his cheek. "It didn't so much as disgust me as scare me. It was the truth when I said I'd never planned to take a mate."

"Why? Because of your brothers?"

"No." Saskia shook her head. "It's not because of them. It's just something I decided. I've trained for so long, for hundreds of years, with one purpose in mind—to be one of the protectors to the foretold one. I didn't know if there would be room for a mate in my life."

Eli placed his hand over top hers. "I would never ask you to give that up. It's something you've trained for long before I was ever born. I'm not that selfish."

Saskia took her hand from his cheek and moved closer. "How old are you, Eli?"

"I'm thirty-three."

"I'm a thousand years old."

Eli blew out a breath. "Wow. I can't picture living for so long." He swallowed. "Does it really bother you that I'm mortal?"

"It does." Eli felt his face fall, but Saskia quickly added, "Not in the way you think. It bothers me to think I could lose you one day. I would feel the loss greatly." She paused before she spoke again. "Would you be willing to let Roxie use the spell on you to turn you into a werewolf?"

"Are you sure that's what you want? You'd be stuck with me then for a very, very long time."

"You're my mate. Of course I want to be stuck with you."

"I'm willing to try, but..." Eli let his words trail off.

"But what?"

"I'm not sure it'll work on me. I don't have any special abilities. I'm just a plain old ordinary mortal."

Saskia's brows drew together. "Why wouldn't it work on you? It worked on your identical twin brother."

"Yes, but he has visions, and I don't."

"I would have thought both of you would possess that ability."

"Finn couldn't always have them. It wasn't until he'd been injected with Royce's blood that they started."

"I thought he had to be injected with Roxie's blood for the spell to work?"

"He was, but Finn had been injected with Royce's before he was turned. He and Royce had been captured by another male werewolf, the one who originally used the spell on Roxie to turn her. He thought Royce's blood would be the key to make the spell work on another mortal since he'd used it on Roxie. It didn't work on Finn, but it changed him nonetheless. One of the changes ended up being his ability to have visions like our mother."

Saskia crowded closer as she forced him to sit back against the couch. She straddled his lap, facing him. "I guess if the spell doesn't work the first time Roxie tries it, we could always inject you with Royce's blood, then try it again."

Eli looked at Saskia. He tucked her long hair behind her ear. "I guess we could. I don't think Royce would mind donating some."

"Good." She leaned down and nipped his chin. "I don't know about you, but I think we can continue this conversation later. Much later."

CHAPTER SEVEN

Saskia shifted on Eli's lap so her pussy settled against his erection through their pants. She rubbed along him as she kissed him. She slanted her lips across his and pushed her tongue inside his mouth. She sighed when his met hers.

The hours of being separated from Eli had been the most unpleasant thing Saskia had ever gone through. It had felt as if she'd left behind a piece of herself when she'd run from him. She never wanted to go through that again. It made her come to terms with the fact he *was* her mate, and that denying it would not make it disappear because she wanted it to.

She kissed him, lifted his T-shirt, and ran her hands across his washboard abs. His cock jerked inside his pants as she pulled his shirt higher. Saskia stopped kissing Eli only long enough to pull it off the rest of the way.

Becoming more aroused, she left his mouth and trailed kisses across his jaw to his neck. She licked and kissed her way down to where she'd left her mark on his skin. She swirled her tongue across it before she lightly nipped him there. She continued her downward trail as she pressed kisses along the thick slabs of muscle in his chest. She loved Eli's body and doubted she would ever get enough of it.

Saskia kneeled between Eli's spread thighs and kissed a path across his abs. She ran her hands down his sides until they reached the top of his warm-up pants. With a tight hold, she tugged them down past his hips. His thick cock sprang free. Now that she had the object of her desire in front of her, she focused her attention on the part of him that felt so good inside her.

She licked her lips, reached out with a finger, and gently rubbed the single drop of precum that had leaked from the tip of his cock. A deep moan left Eli when Saskia wrapped her hand around his shaft and pumped it up and down his length. Wetness pooled between her legs as his erection grew even harder. She continued to pump him until another bead of moisture appeared on the tip. This time she bent forward and licked it off. The taste of him made her want to take him inside her mouth. Instead, she lapped at him, swirling her tongue around the head as she worked her hand up and down.

Eli threaded his fingers through her hair to hold her to him. He gasped. "You're killing me."

"You'll survive," she said against his sensitive flesh.

With a firm grip on his shaft, Saskia sucked the very tip into her mouth. Eli fisted his hand tighter in her hair. He lifted his hips off the couch, wanting her to take more of him. She slowly sucked more of his length inside inch by inch until she couldn't handle any more. He bucked his hips and moaned and panted. She sucked harder. The combination of the sounds he made as she sucked him, and the feel of his hard cock in his mouth, pushed her arousal even higher.

Unable to wait any longer to have him inside her, Saskia released him and stood. She quickly pulled off her clothes until she was naked before him. His heated gaze followed her movements as she cupped her breasts and lifted them. Eli pushed his pants the rest of the way off. He sat back on the couch and watched her. His hard cock stood straight from his body. She took her bottom lip between her teeth as his erection jerked. Moisture leaked from her pussy, coating the inside of her thighs.

She climbed back onto the couch and straddled his thighs. Eli tried to sheath himself inside her, but Saskia held herself away. She took hold of the back of the cushion on either side of his head as she pressed a nipple against his lips. He flicked the taut peak with his tongue. He sucked it deep, and she rubbed her slick opening along the length of his shaft.

Once his cock slid between her moist folds, Saskia angled her hips and pushed down until she'd impaled herself on his hard length. Eli's hardness filled her to capacity. She moaned at the feel of being stretched as her body accustomed itself to his thickness. She slowly rose onto her knees and then sank once again on his shaft. She set a slow pace as she rode him. In this position, he was in deep enough to hit her cervix with each stroke in.

Eli leaned his head against the back of the couch. He held on to her hips and lifted his own to match her strokes. Saskia squeezed her inner walls around him and increased her pace. Her climax inched closer. She sank harder and faster on his cock and growled low in her throat as he reached between them. With his fingers, he rubbed her clit. It was enough to send her over the edge. She moaned and growled and climaxed around his shaft. He held on to her hips and thrust into her until he came too.

After the last wave of pleasure receded, Saskia fell forward onto Eli's chest. He wrapped his arms around her. His now-soft cock slipped free of her body.

He kissed her forehead. "Sorry. I can't keep an erection for hours like male werewolves can. You'll have to give me a few minutes to recover; then I'll be good to go again."

Saskia sat up and kissed him softly on the mouth. The more they made love the stronger their bond became. She already felt intense feelings for him. "Do you hear me complaining? It doesn't matter to me. You're doing a pretty fine job of it without being able to do that."

Eli chuckled. "Well, thank you. I do try."

Gathering Saskia close, Eli managed to get off the couch with her in his arms. She wrapped hers around his shoulders. "Where are you taking me?"

He walked toward his bedroom. "I'm taking you to bed. I intend to take Billie's advice. I'm going to make love to you until neither one of us can move. I figure that should use up the rest of the day and most of the night."

Saskia growled with pleasure. "I can handle that. It should be more than enough time for me to do all the things I want to do to you." She whispered into Eli's ear everything she wanted to do. With a groan, he practically ran with her to his bedroom.

* * * *

Eli looked at Saskia where she slept next to him on the bed. His alarm clock had gone off a couple of minutes before, but she hadn't reacted to the sound. He smiled. He'd done his best to tire her out. It looked as if he'd succeeded.

He rolled onto his side and ran his gaze over her sleeping form. Life without Saskia was something he didn't want to imagine. His bachelor days were far behind him now. He smiled to himself and shook his head. *Who would have thunk it?* Eli sure as hell hadn't seen it coming, considering only a couple of days before he'd found the whole idea of being tied to one woman for the rest of his life abhorrent. Now, especially after the many hours they'd spent together, he had fallen for her. Not just that he liked her but had tumbled head over heels for her. He'd never felt this way about any woman before.

Saskia groaned and rolled onto her side toward him and then snuggled closer. She pressed a kiss to his bare chest. "I can feel you staring at me. Go back to sleep."

Eli chuckled. "Wish I could, but I can't. Since I played hooky from work yesterday, I have to go to the gym today."

She groaned again. "I don't want to get up yet. Call them and tell them you'll be late."

"This might be a guess, but I'm thinking you aren't much of a morning person."

"I'm not, especially when I don't get to sleep in late after I've spent most of the night making love to my mate."

"Come on, sleepyhead. I really need to go to work on time. I feel bad enough that I dumped all my clients onto my family yesterday with next to no warning. I'll make you a deal. You get up, and I'll see if I can find a place for you to take a nap. I'll make sure we can leave early."

Saskia snuggled closer. "What time is it?"

"It's just after nine." Eli gave her a smack on the bottom. "Let's get a move on."

"All right already. I'm moving. I'll get out of bed on one condition—we take a shower together."

"You really do want to make me late."

She titled her head back and gave him a saucy smile. "Not if we have a quickie."

His cock rose to the occasion. "You're insatiable."

"You wouldn't have it any other way."

He smiled. "God, no." Knowing if he didn't get her into the shower soon, they would end up spending even longer in bed than he really should, Eli flipped the covers off them. "Shower. Now. Before we never get out of here."

In the end, they washed each other, which inevitably led to them making love in the shower. After, as they dressed, their stomachs growled loudly. Considering they'd hardly come up for air the day before to eat, Eli didn't think it odd that he and Saskia were starved.

"We should have just enough time to go pick up something for breakfast and take it to the gym to eat. That is if you don't mind take-out."

Saskia pulled his comb through her damp, light blonde hair. "That's fine with me. Just so long as I get fed. Why don't you leave your car here today? You can ride on my bike with me."

"I'd love to, but what about the food? I don't think I would be able to hold on to it and you and not drop it. Or better yet, fall off the bike entirely."

"Fine. Take your car. It would be a shame to have you drop the food." Eli cocked a brow at her. "And, of course, I wouldn't want you to fall off my motorcycle."

Eli rushed them out the door to the underground parking garage. As Saskia pulled on her helmet, then took the motorcycle off the kickstand, he said, "There's a great diner a couple of blocks from the gym that serves all-day breakfast. If you want, you can meet me at the gym while I pick up the food. Is there anything you want in particular?"

"Okay. I'll see you there. Get me whatever you're having."

Eli flipped up the visor on Saskia's helmet and gave her a thorough kiss before he pushed it back into place. He waited until she'd left the garage before he got into his car. The trip to the diner didn't take long, but having to stand around as he waited for his food order seemed to take longer than it should. He already missed Saskia. This would be something he would have to get used to—the separation anxiety he would invariably feel whenever they were apart.

With food in hand, Eli left the diner and then headed for his car. As he crossed the parking lot, he couldn't shake the feeling that someone watched him. The sensation persisted even after he reached his car. Unlocking it, he looked around the crowded parking lot. He couldn't see anyone who seemed to stare at him from a distance. He slipped into his vehicle and then headed for the gym.

Eli found Saskia leaning against her motorcycle in the parking lot. He parked next to her, got out of the car, and waved the bags of take-out food in front of her. "I got their breakfast special. I hope you're really hungry, because there is a ton of food."

Saskia briefly closed her eyes and took a deep breath. "It smells delicious. I'm starved."

With his fingers laced through hers, Eli walked her into the gym. He kept walking until he reached his desk. After he shoved a few things that sat on top of it aside, he took the food out of the bags. Saskia grabbed the chair that sat on the other side of his desk and placed it next to his. They then sat and ate.

Billie walked to his desk as she sniffed. She shook her head when she saw what they ate. "That's a good meal to bring to a gym, Eli. Fried eggs, bacon, sausage, hash browns, and toast. We're supposed to promote a healthier way of living, not one where the person will keel over with a heart attack from all the grease."

Eli used his toast to mop up some of his yolk. "Stuff it, Billie. We're starved."

Billie laughed. "I guess you took my advice. You both seem to be practically inhaling your food."

Eli slapped Billie's hand when she reached to take one of his sausages. "Get your own."

Saskia pushed her Styrofoam container closer to Billie. "Here, you can have one of mine."

"Thanks, Saskia." Billie took one, then turned back to Eli. "At least someone was nice enough to share."

When Billie didn't show any signs of leaving, Eli asked, "Is there something you wanted? Other than trying to finagle us out of food, that is."

Billie didn't answer until she'd eaten her sausage. She picked up one of the napkins that sat on his desk and wiped her fingers.

"There is one thing. Since the two of you seem to have worked this whole being mated business out, I thought to ask when you would like to see Roxie."

Saskia answered for him. "If you mean about getting her to use the spell on Eli, we already discussed it."

"And?"

"Eli is willing to try it, even though he isn't a hundred percent sure it will work on him."

"Of course it will work on him. It worked on Finn, it will work on you."

Eli swallowed a mouthful of food. "Yes, but that was after he'd been injected with Royce's blood."

"Don't get hung up on that theory about mortals needing to have a special ability to make the spell work. Even if that ended up being true, we know how to fix it so it will work. Royce will be more than willing to get jabbed for the cause."

"Depends on what I get jabbed with," Royce said as he walked to them. He swiped one of Eli's sausages before he could stop him.

Eli gave an exasperated sigh. "Can the pair of you keep your paws off our food?"

Billie ignored him. "I was just telling Eli and Saskia if the spell doesn't work the first time on Eli because he doesn't have visions like Finn that you wouldn't mind getting a needle jabbed into you for your blood."

Royce nodded. "If it comes down to that, I won't say no. Just keep the needle away from my neck. Anywhere but the neck is acceptable."

"Anywhere?" Billie asked with a sly smile.

Royce's hands automatically covered his crotch. "That's off-limits too."

Eli groaned. "Hello, I'm trying to eat here. Can we talk about something other than Royce's dick?"

"I could talk about it all day long," Billie said as she suggestively looked Royce up and down.

"You want to see me throw up on my desk?" Eli asked. "Keep it up and I will."

Billie rolled her eyes. "Whatever. So when do you want to meet with Roxie?"

"Whenever it's good for her." Eli turned to find Saskia smiling. "Once I'm turned, we can work out the rest."

Saskia's smile slowly slipped away as she turned her attention on a spot near the front desk. Eli stiffened when he saw Roan standing with his arms crossed over his large chest as he stared at them. When he saw he'd caught their attention, Roan came to his desk. Eli noticed the girl at the front desk was too busy ogling Roan to ask if he had a membership card.

Once Roan reached them, his gaze swept over Eli and Saskia. "So you decided to keep him as your mate after all I see," he said to Saskia.

Saskia glared up at him. "I hope you didn't come all this way just to discuss my mating."

Roan shook his head. "No, I didn't."

"Then why are you here?"

"I need to talk to you. Alone. I wasn't sure you would answer your cell phone since you've had it turned off since yesterday morning. Something has come up."

Saskia pushed back her chair and stood. She looked down at Eli. "I'll be back in a minute."

Eli closed the lid on her food. "I'll make sure the vultures don't take your food while you're gone."

Saskia nodded, then followed Roan back to the front entrance.

CHAPTER EIGHT

"All right, what's so important you had to chase me down here?" Saskia asked as soon as they were out of hearing range.

"Miles is on the move. He's learned about Roxie and is making plans to claim her as his own."

Saskia let out a disgusted breath. "Are you sure? We've heard rumors of him gathering other lone wolves before and they were all false."

Roan shook his head. "Not this time. Leif heard one of Miles's flunkies bragging to another lone wolf about how he was going to be a part of something big. And that he had the job of finding new recruits for the bastard."

"And where exactly did Leif hear all this?"

"At a mortal bar. It's a place where the women and booze are plentiful, just the way Leif likes them. It's also a place where lone wolves sometimes like to go."

"Great." Saskia sighed. "Did Leif learn anything more besides Miles recruiting lone wolves?"

Roan gave her a half-smile. "You could say that. Since neither of the lone wolves knew him, Leif went to their table and led them to believe he wanted in on a piece of the action they discussed. By the end of the night, he had Miles's flunky believing he was his new best friend. Leif knows how to lay it on thick when he needs to."

Saskia snorted. "You don't have to tell me. So what did his new best friend tell him?"

"They're holed up in an abandoned factory near the outskirts of the city. I guess Miles has been a busy boy the last couple of months. Supposedly, he has twenty lone wolves under him. Most, if not all, were kicked out of their packs for bad behavior. It seems the nastier the lone wolf the more Miles wants him."

Saskia grew thoughtful. "We need to check out this abandoned factory ourselves to make sure Miles is using it as his headquarters."

"That's what we thought you would want to do. We're ready to go whenever you are."

She looked at Eli, who still sat at his desk while he talked to Billie and Royce. "Shit. Eli isn't going to like this. I know I won't look forward to the separation."

Roan chuckled. "Yeah, you mated does throw a wrench in the works, doesn't it? You can't get up and leave whenever you want now."

"Shut up, Roan. You aren't helping. It wouldn't be safe for Eli. At least not right now. Later it won't be so bad."

"You talked him into letting Roxie turn him?"

"Yes. He's my mate. I would rather not lose him to a mortal death."

"I never thought I would see the day that you would take a mate. Or see you fall so hard for a man."

"That doesn't mean I still can't beat your ass in sword practice."

Roan held up his hands. "I know you can. Remember I ended up on the receiving end of your sword after you came running home the other night as if the hounds of hell chased you. I'm just glad it was in practice only and you weren't set on killing me. I would have been in trouble then."

"Don't you forget it. Where are we supposed to meet with the others?"

"They're in the parking lot."

Saskia's brows rose. "You *all* came here? How come only you came in to look for me?"

"I lost the vote to stay behind. The others figured you would be less likely to bite my head off if I was the one to tell you the news."

Her brothers knew her so well. Roan had been the perfect choice to send in after her. The others would have been bossier about it, and would have demanded she leave without giving her any details.

"I guess I'd better explain to Eli why I have to go when I said I would spend the day with him."

"I'll tell the others you'll be on your way shortly. Don't keep us waiting too long. Jager is getting antsy."

Roan left the gym before she went back to Eli. He came around his desk when she stood in front of it instead of going to sit next to him. He gave her a questioning look.

"Sorry, but I have to change our plans for the day. I have to leave."

"Where are you going? I can go with you."

"Not this time you can't."

"Are you sure it isn't something your men can take care of without you?"

Saskia shook her head. "No." She placed a finger against Eli's lips as he opened his mouth to say something else. "Remember how you told me you wouldn't ask me to give up what I've trained for most of my life? Well, this is something I must do as one of Roxie's protectors."

Eli sighed as he pulled her finger away and then kissed the tip of it. "Just try not to be too long, okay? I don't think I can handle being away from you so long again."

"I promise."

Before she could walk away, Royce stopped her. "Is Roxie in some kind of danger? Because if she is, I should let Beowulf know."

"No, she's not in danger, at least not yet. My brothers and I are just going to check something out. If it turns out to be a threat to Roxie, you and Beowulf will be the first ones we call."

Reassured, Royce nodded. Saskia gave Eli a hard kiss. Making a vow to herself, she promised to return sooner rather than later to share more than just a kiss with him. She turned and walked out of the gym before she talked herself out of leaving.

* * * *

Saskia followed the black Cadillac Escalade SUV her brothers rode in on her motorcycle. They had suggested she ride with them at first, but she'd quickly vetoed that. She wanted to be able to get back to Eli as soon as possible. Waiting around for them to drive her would only delay her.

They parked the SUV and motorcycle half a block away from the abandoned factory after they did a drive-by. Saskia met up with her brothers at the SUV. "Now, no rushing in there blind." She gave Jager a pointed look. He tended to run into the action without thinking first.

"Hey, don't look at me like that," Jager said.

"I just wanted to remind you that we're here only to observe. If this does turn out to be the place where Miles is holed up, I don't want to tip him off that we know about it until we're ready. That means we leave the swords behind so there isn't any temptation."

Jager swore under his breath as he placed his hand on the hilt of the sword he wore strapped to his waist under a black duster. "Ah, come on, Saskia. You take the fun out of everything."

She crossed her arms and waited for him to do as she'd asked. Jager rarely went anywhere without his sword. It'd been a struggle for her to convince him to leave it behind when they'd gone to Wulf's Den and Roxie and Beowulf's house.

Grumbling under his breath that he would feel naked without his sword, Jager unbuckled his sword belt and placed it on the floor of the SUV before he slammed the door shut. "Happy now?"

Saskia smiled. "Yes. Let's check out the factory."

They walked down the street at a brisk pace until the abandoned factory came in sight. Knowing there very likely would be more than one werewolf inside, Saskia and her brothers made sure they stayed upwind. They didn't need their scents to give them away. She signaled for them to split up. Roan, Skylar, and Jager went one way while Saskia, Kye, Leif, and Dirk went the other.

Sticking to the shade as much as possible, Saskia took a deep breath. There definitely were werewolves somewhere inside. She smelled their scents, and most were fresh. Her brothers must have detected them as well, because the three of them had curled their upper lips in a silent snarl.

Not until they'd gone halfway around the outside of the factory did they find a pair of windows they could easily look into. They spread out with Kye and Leif at one window while Saskia and Dirk took the other. Saskia stood at the side of one and slowly turned her head until she could look inside. What she saw made her bite back a string of curses.

Inside the partially sunken open room were at least ten male werewolves. They appeared to be taking part in various forms of training. Some trained with swords, while others were in their wolf forms, practicing with their teeth and claws. For a bunch of lone wolves, they seemed more disciplined than she would have thought. No real fights broke out, and none of them seemed to be drawing blood from their sparring partners.

As she watched them closer, warning bells went off in her mind. She recognized some of the training exercises the lone wolves used. They were the same ones she and her brothers had been trained in. If nothing else, it spoke of Miles's involvement. He'd learned the same tactics while he'd been with them. Saskia stepped away from the window and motioned for them to continue. Now she really needed to know if Miles could be inside.

Once they were well away from the windows, Dirk asked in a quiet voice, "Did you see what I saw?"

Kye's lips thinned and he nodded. "Yeah. The bastards are using our moves."

"It looks as if the sack of crap I talked to at the bar hadn't lied, after all. This has Miles written all over it," Leif said grimly.

"Let's see if Roan, Skylar, and Jager found anything interesting," Saskia said.

They were about to round the corner at the back of the building when Saskia spotted three male werewolves in front of an open door. She and her men quickly drew to a halt. She peeked around the corner. Luck must have been on their side, because the three didn't seem to realize they were no longer alone.

"Where are the others?" Leif asked Saskia in a whisper.

"I don't know. I can't see them." She caught sight of a dark head peeking around the other corner of the building. "No. Wait. I see one of them. They're in the same position as us but on the other side."

Dirk leaned against her back as he took a quick look around the corner. "What now?"

Saskia shoved him away. "It looks as if that door could be our way in. We'll just wait for them to head inside." She took a closer look. "We should be able to catch it before it shuts completely. It looks as if it has one of those closer thingies on it."

Kye snorted. "Closer thingy?"

"You know what I mean."

"Sadly, yes, I do."

After a minute went by and then another, Saskia wondered if the three who stood outside would ever go inside the factory. Another five minutes ticked by before they turned and headed through the open door. Once the last one disappeared, Saskia and her men ran to catch it before it swung shut behind them. Roan, Jager, and Skylar rushed over just as Leif managed to grab hold of it.

They waited a few seconds, then slowly slipped inside. Saskia heard the three male werewolves as they talked somewhere up ahead. Following the sound, she and her men stealthily walked farther into the building.

The stretch of corridor they walked down was gloomy at best. Most of the lights set in the ceiling either had missing light bulbs or they'd burned out. Not that any of them really needed the light to see where they went.

As they neared a closed office door, Saskia's steps slowed. Two voices sounded from the other side. One she found very familiar—Miles's voice. Her brothers had stopped when she did and now stood around her as they listened to the conversation going on inside the office.

"So, is it true?" Miles asked whoever was with him in a demanding tone.

"It's true. I've been following them the last couple of days. Not that they left his apartment much. It seems the mortal has been showing her a good time."

"I don't give a shit about that. I just wanted to know if they're mates."

"The way they left the place where he works yesterday morning, I'd say that's a big yes. They practically couldn't keep their hands off each other. They also stank of sex."

Miles chuckled. "This is working out better than I'd thought. So the bitch Saskia has finally found a mate, and a mortal one at that."

Saskia stiffened at the sound of her name. That she and Eli were the topic of conversation made a chill run down her spine.

Miles talked once again. "Did you leave a message for the bitch to find before you returned?"

The other man laughed, but there wasn't any humor in it. "I did better than that. I had one of the other men give the message to her mate for her to find later. Mortals can be so vulnerable, don't you think? They can die so easily."

Miles laughed. "I would love to see Saskia's face when she finds her mortal is no more."

Saskia felt the blood drain out of her face. She looked at each of her men. Fear for Eli had her almost gasping for air. Her brothers moved into action. Roan pulled the small spray bottle of vinegar he carried in his pocket and sprayed it in the hallway as they slowly headed for the door. It would cover the scent trail they left behind better than anything. It would also burn the inside of a werewolf's sensitive nose if breathed too deeply.

Once they reached the outside, Saskia took off at a run, not caring if they ended up being spotted or not. All she could think about was getting to Eli before it became too late.

* * * *

Eli couldn't take being stuck inside the gym another minute. Saskia had been gone for just over an hour, and already he wanted to climb the walls. He wanted to touch her, to have her in his arms so badly he practically ached with the need that coursed through him. Even though he understood why she hadn't let him go with her, his still being mortal and all, it didn't make what he went through any less hard to bear.

Thinking a walk would help clear his head, Eli headed down the sidewalk toward the parking lot at the side of the gym. As he reached it, he heard a cat meow pitifully. He shook his head as he changed course and cut through the parking lot to the alley that ran behind the building. The gym's Dumpster sat out there, and occasionally a stray cat ended up stuck inside it. Either they jumped in and couldn't get back out again or the lid of the Dumpster shut, which closed them inside. The cat's meows grew louder the closer he came to the alley.

Sure enough, the Dumpster's lid was closed, and the meows seemed to come from inside it. Since this wouldn't be the first time, Eli decided he would have to talk to his father about doing something to keep the cats away. He grinned to himself as he thought of one solution. Maybe he could get Royce and Finn to do a little territory marking in their wolf forms. Cats didn't like dogs so it stood to reason they wouldn't like werewolves either.

Eli lifted the lid to the Dumpster and peered inside. A small tabby cat hissed up at him. "Didn't your mother ever teach you not to jump into Dumpsters?" He reached in to grab the cat, but quickly had to pull away as it tried to take a swipe at his hand with its front claws. "Take it easy. I'm only trying to help." Moving faster, he grabbed the feline by the scruff of the neck and pulled it out.

He quickly put it down before it tried to sink its claws into him again. Instead of taking off as Eli expected it to do, the cat hissed and spit at something as all the fur along its back stood on end. It arched its back like a Halloween cat.

Eli turned to see what had the little thing acting as if it'd suddenly become possessed. A man stood a foot away. Now used to being around werewolves so much, he instantly recognized one when he saw one. So it came as no surprise to find one now standing nearby. If not for his height and extreme good looks, the loud menacing growl he made gave him away. The cat hissed one last time before it ran.

The werewolf stepped closer. "How cute. The mortal saved the little kitty cat."

"What do you want?" Eli shifted on his feet as he took up a better stance. This werewolf looked far from friendly. He didn't know if he could beat him in a fight, but Eli wouldn't just stand there and take it.

The werewolf smiled, one that didn't reach his eyes. "I have a message for your mate."

"What message?"

"A message from an old friend. I was told to personally deliver it to you."

The werewolf leapt into the air and went wolf at the same time. Eli didn't have time to move away as the large animal slammed into his chest. He went down hard with the wolf on top him. It snarled and snapped his sharp teeth in front of his face. Eli grunted with pain as the wolf clawed him across the chest.

The werewolf's form blurred as he shifted back into human form. Moving faster than Eli could have blocked him, the werewolf sank a long-bladed dagger into his stomach. He stabbed him a second time before he stood. Gasping in pain and shock, Eli clutched his belly.

"I was told I had to make sure the wounds would leave you alive long enough for your mate to find you. Let's hope she doesn't take too long to come looking for you." The werewolf reached inside his pants pocket and threw a piece of paper onto Eli's chest. "I suggest you hold on to that, mortal, just in case you croak here all alone." With a cruel laugh, he walked out of the alley.

Eli struggled to breathe around the pain as he tried to sit up. Blood gushed from his wounds, spilling over his hand. With his other, he grabbed the piece of paper. Even though help was just a short distance away, he would never make it inside the gym. He was losing too much blood too quickly. Already he spots formed before his eyes.

His only hope was for someone to come looking for him— soon. Eli managed to drag himself across the alley to sit propped against the wall. He leaned his head back against it and concentrated on not passing out.

CHAPTER NINE

After roaring up in front of the gym, Saskia parked her motorcycle on the street. The SUV squealed to a stop behind her bike a second later. She didn't wait for her brothers as she ran inside the building. With her heart in her throat, she searched the main gym floor for Eli but couldn't see him anywhere. She raced to his desk, praying he would be there. Her heart fell when she saw he wasn't there either.

By this time her brothers had caught up to her. They drew more than one stare from the people around them, but Saskia barely noticed. She frantically searched for one of Eli's siblings. Surely they would know where he'd gone.

Billie came out of her father's office and stopped dead in her tracks when she saw Saskia and her brothers. "Saskia? You look white as a ghost. Are you okay?"

Saskia rushed to her "Where's Eli?"

"I think he went out for a walk. The separation was getting to be too much for him."

"How long ago did he leave?"

Billie's brows drew together as she studied her face. "A few minutes ago I think. You're really scaring me here."

Saskia spun on her heel, then took off at a run. Her brothers ran behind her. Before she made it to the front entrance, Billie yelled for Royce. Saskia pushed open the door and burst outside. Kye just about ran into her as she drew to a sudden stop when she reached the sidewalk and sniffed the air for Eli's scent.

It took some doing to filter his scent from the many the wind carried, but Saskia soon latched on to his and jogged toward the parking lot at the side of the building. She put on another burst of speed as the metallic scent of fresh-spilled blood filled her nose. Praying it wasn't Eli's she smelled, she followed the scent to the back alley behind the gym. She cried out when she spotted him slumped against the alley's wall.

Saskia knelt beside him. "Eli!" His head had fallen forward onto his chest. Her heart skipped a beat when she saw blood over his hands and stomach. She pushed his head back. "Eli! Open your eyes."

He slowly lifted his eyelids. "Saskia?" Eli asked weakly.

"Yes, it's me. You have to tell me what happened."

Saskia jumped when Skylar came down next her. She blinked up to find the rest of her brothers standing around them. Billie cried out in anguish when she and Royce caught up with them.

"Saskia, let me look at his wounds," Skylar said gently.

Saskia sat next to Eli, then wrapped her arm around his shoulders and shifted him so he leaned against her with his head supported against her. Eli gasped in pain when Skylar moved his arm away and lifted his shirt to expose his wounds. She held him tighter. "Hang in there."

Eli swallowed audibly. "He left a message for you."

Saskia stiffened. "The one who did this to you?"

"Yes." Eli placed a crumpled, blood-stained piece of paper on her lap.

Feeling anger unlike anything she'd felt before, Saskia grabbed it and shoved it into her jeans pocket. "Don't worry about the message. Okay? Right now, we have to concentrate on you."

Eli grimaced as Skylar probed his wounds. "Sorry."

"What are you sorry for?"

"If I'd been a werewolf, this wouldn't have happened. I would have been on equal footing then," Eli said in a weak voice.

"You have nothing to be sorry about."

"I should have gotten Roxie to try the spell earlier. None of this would have happened then. Now it's too late."

"Stop it, Eli. There will be plenty of time to try the spell once you heal. We'll call an ambulance." Saskia looked up at her brothers. They all wore the same grim expression. "Would one of you get on the goddamn phone and call an ambulance?"

Skylar shook his head. "It's too late for that, Saskia. He's lost too much blood."

Saskia growled deep in her throat. "I won't accept that. I won't just sit here and do nothing while my mate dies. Do something. Now!"

"They won't be able to save him even if we manage to get him to the hospital. The knife hit some major organs."

"There is another way," Royce said. He held Billie close as she sobbed in his arms. "The spell."

Skylar sighed. "Maybe, but we don't even know if it will work on Eli. Plus, Roxie would have to get here within the next minute or two."

"I'll call her. We have to try."

Once Royce pulled his cell phone out of his pants pocket, Saskia focused inward as a vision played inside her head. "You don't have to call Roxie, Royce. She'll be here in less than a minute. Finn and Jocelyn are with her. Finn saw what happened to Eli in a vision." She shook her head as her vision receded. She noticed how limp Eli had become as he leaned against her. "Eli? Wake up. Do you hear me? Wake up." He groaned as she gave him a shake, but he didn't open his eyes.

"Eli!" Finn shouted as he, Jocelyn and Roxie ran into the alley. He squatted next to his twin as he took in Eli's wounds. "We have to do the spell now."

"We can't do it out here in the alley," Billie said.

"You move him too far and he *will* die," Skylar said as he stood. "I wouldn't even recommend trying to get him inside the gym. For one thing there are too many mortals in there who would ask too many questions."

Roan backed away. "The SUV. I can bring it into the alley. It has enough room inside. The tinted windows should stop anyone from seeing what we're doing if they happen to come back here." At Saskia's nod, he turned and took off at a run.

In a matter of seconds, Roan had the SUV inside the alley. Jager and Kye carefully lifted Eli as Saskia clambered into the back of it. She helped them get Eli into the very back seat so he lay stretched out with his head on her lap.

Roxie climbed in next. She knelt on the floor as she pulled a syringe out of her purse. "Usually, I'm a little more hygienic than this when I use the spell, but I think time is of the essence right now."

As she spoke, Roxie pulled the plastic end off the needle of the syringe and stuck it into her arm. Once the syringe was full, she took Eli's and jabbed the needle into it. Just as the last of her blood left the syringe, she spoke the words of the spell.

"The magic of the wolf's blood is now in thee.
A wolf you become to run wild and free.
Where once there were two, now only one we see."

Roxie sat back on her legs. "It's done."

"How will we know if it worked," Saskia asked.

"If it did, right about now he should feel as if his insides have caught on fire."

Saskia looked down at Eli. He'd slipped into unconsciousness even before they'd managed to get him inside the SUV. *Would he even feel it?* She soon had her answer as his eyes moved rapidly beneath his closed eyelids. He stiffened and groaned.

"I think it's working," Roxie said with a smile.

Saskia bent and kissed Eli's forehead. As her lips touched his skin, he suddenly relaxed. "Eli?"

When he didn't stir, she pressed her fingers to the major vein in the side of his neck. She breathed a sigh of relief when she felt a strong pulse. She took hold of the collar of his T-shirt and ripped it down the center. The deep claw mark across his chest healed before her eyes. The two stab wounds had stopped bleeding, but given the severity of them, it would take a couple days for them to heal over completely.

Skylar pushed his way into the SUV and put his hand over Eli's heart. "Nice and strong. He seems to be out of danger. Let him sleep. Right now, it's the best thing for him."

With the crisis over, and while the others were distracted, Saskia took out the message Eli had given her. Short and to the point, it made her snarl with anger. In Miles's handwriting a single sentence had been scrawled across the paper. *She will be mine.*

"We should take Eli to his place," Finn said where he stood crowded near the SUV's open door.

Saskia shook her head. "No. They know where he lives. Eli and I were followed. It won't be safe for him there."

"Then where? And who are they?"

"He'll be safer at my brothers' and my place."

She decided not to answer Finn's last question. It was more important that they brought Eli to some place safe where he could recover. She would feel better about leaving him there when she went after the bastard who had done this to him.

"We'll follow you then," Billie said.

"No. Just in case they're still watching us, we don't want to draw their attention to a big group of us leaving at the same time. I'll give you our address in Marin County. Give us a half-hour head start."

It didn't take them long to get Eli settled comfortably into one of the seats with the seatbelt around him. Skylar sat beside him to make sure Eli didn't get bounced too much during the trip. The rest of her brothers piled into the SUV. Saskia gave Eli's family their address before she raced to the street to collect her motorcycle. As the SUV drove by, she fell in behind it. She searched the nearby area. If the bastards were watching and decided to follow them, she would take great joy in making them wish they'd never been born.

* * * *

Eli came awake slowly. His eyelids were heavy, but he forced them open a crack. He would have liked nothing more than to roll over and go back to sleep, but something tugged at his memory. Something bad had happened. To him. Stretching, his brows drew together as he felt an unfamiliar pain in his stomach. It all came back to him in a rush—the alley, the werewolf, and being stabbed not once but twice. He came fully awake as he pushed down the sheets that covered him and looked at his stomach. He found two pads of gauze taped to his skin. He went to take off one of the gauze pads, but a voice stopped him.

"Leave it alone."

He turned his head to find his twin sitting in a chair next to the bed. Eli also noticed two things—he was in a strange bedroom, and that all his senses seemed to be three times stronger than before. He heard voices from a level below the bedroom he lay in as if they were in the same room. Scents he had no idea had even existed washed over him, giving him more information with one inhalation of air than he thought possible.

Eli sat up. He felt as if he'd been bombarded with too much information. "What happened?"

Finn smiled. "You gave us quite a scare there. What do you remember?"

"Other than being stabbed by a sadistic werewolf, not too much. The last thing I remember was Saskia and her brothers finding me in the alley." Eli put a hand on his stomach. "I don't understand. I thought for sure I'd be a goner."

"You probably would have been if I hadn't happened to be with Roxie when I had a vision. I saw you lying bloody in the alley. We arrived just in time for Roxie to save you. If we'd been a few minutes later..." Finn let his words trail off.

"Roxie? Roxie saved me?"

"Well, actually the spell saved you."

Now Eli understood why he smelled and heard things so much better. "She turned me."

"Yes. Now we're back to being identical in every way."

Eli gave Finn a broad smile before it quickly fell away. "Where's Saskia?"

Finn shook his head. "I don't know. Her brothers were trying to talk some sense into her, but I don't think she listened. I heard her slam out of the house fifteen minutes or so ago."

A chill ran down Eli's spine. "She's going after the one who stabbed me?"

"Yes."

Eli swung his legs over the side of the bed, then slowly stood. Much to his surprise, he didn't feel nearly as weak as he should have, considering the amount of blood he must have lost. Being a werewolf did have its benefits.

Finn went to stand beside him. "Where are you going? You're not fully recovered yet."

He walked to the closed door and opened it. "I'm fine. I have to talk to Saskia's brothers."

He walked out of the room and then headed for the stairs, and Eli caught the scent of dried blood. He looked down to find he still wore his blood-stained warm-up pants. He had no idea where his T-shirt had gone.

Taking the stairs two at a time, he followed the sound of voices once he reached the bottom. As he walked through the house, Eli took in the large rooms and luxurious setting. He turned to Finn who walked at his side. "Whose house is this?"

"This is where Saskia and her brothers live."

Eli wouldn't have thought in a million years that Saskia's six hulking warrior brothers would ever live in a house such as this. It seemed too refined for their taste. He went down one large hallway and stepped into a big living room. He stopped just inside the doorway as he took in the occupants. His gaze landed on his father and two other brothers. Billie and Royce sat with Jocelyn close by them. His family seemed more than relieved to see him. Saskia's brothers, on the other hand, appeared distracted, to say the least. They stood together at one side of the room as they argued over who should go after Saskia.

With his voice raised so they could hear him, Eli said, "I'll go after Saskia."

They all turned in his direction. Skylar spoke first. "I don't think that would be a good idea. You haven't recovered your strength yet."

He fisted his hands at his sides. "I'm not mortal anymore so stop coddling me as if I were. I won't let Saskia face the bastard who stabbed me alone. I'm her mate. It's my right to protect her."

Jager snorted. "You better not say that in front of Saskia. She prides herself on her ability to take care of herself. She thinks she doesn't need anyone to watch her back."

Eli ground his teeth together. "That won't stop me from going after her. Will you help me or not?"

Leif nodded. "We'll help you, but first you need to learn how to go wolf before we go anywhere. Saskia will have our balls if you get hurt again."

"Then I suggest we hurry up and get the lesson over with."

Just as his other two siblings, Eli managed to make the change from man to wolf and back again as if he'd been born to it. After he changed into the clothes Finn had thoughtfully brought for him, he felt ready to kick some werewolf butt. The wolf inside him howled, anxious to be reunited with his mate.

CHAPTER TEN

The trip to the city took too long as far as Eli was concerned. Sitting in the SUV with Saskia's brothers, he listened as they gave him pointers on how to fight while in wolf form. They also made him give them his word he would not provoke a fight if they happened to run into any of the bad guys. At first, he thought they wanted it that way because he'd only been newly turned, but he soon learned there was more to it than that. These werewolves would most likely fight with swords rather than in wolf form.

"Why with swords?" Eli asked Dirk.

"Because it's Miles's weapon of choice, as it is ours. It stands to reason Miles will train his recruits to fight that way. A sword can do more damage than anything we can inflict in wolf form."

"Where are you guys from? The Dark Ages or something?"

Dirk smiled. "Well, yes, we are."

"Royce and Beowulf are older than all of you, but I don't see either of them swinging swords now. I know they did at one time, especially Beowulf."

"That's because most werewolves our age try to keep up with the times. We, on the other hand, knew we had to keep in practice if we were to protect the foretold one properly."

"Okay, I get that, but why not use guns instead? They're a lot deadlier than swords."

Jager scowled at Eli. "There is no honor in taking down your enemy from a distance when you can look him in the eye when you take his life."

"Okay," Eli said. "Remind me never to piss you off, Jager."

The others laughed. In the driver's seat, Roan slowly pulled the SUV over to the side of the road. Eli looked out the window. They were in an older industrial area of the city. From what Saskia's brothers had told him, Miles had set up a kind of headquarters inside one of the abandoned factories nearby. It was the only place Saskia would have gone in search of Miles.

They all got out of the SUV. Eli followed the other men as they walked down the road to a building that stood a little away from where they had parked. The tension inside him coiled tighter. The separation and need he felt to be with Saskia hit him harder than it had as a mortal.

As they reached the abandoned factory, Eli looked around. The place looked deserted, but that didn't mean anything. They walked to the back of the building. Once they rounded the corner, Saskia's brothers came to an abrupt halt. Eli tried to look past them to see what had made them stop, but they kept him behind them, shielding him from whatever was up ahead.

Leif slightly turned his head, then said to Eli, "Go wolf. Now. Miles is here. He knows you were mortal. We don't need him to find out you have been turned. In wolf form, neither he nor the two lackeys he has with him will recognize you."

Eli quickly went wolf. From his earlier attempts at shifting, he knew he took on the form of a black wolf. Poking his wolf's head between Jager and Kye, he spotted Miles and his men, who stood a short distance away. What made his hackles rise was the sight of Saskia standing a foot away from Miles with her sword drawn. Eli looked from Miles to Saskia. They both had the same light, almost white, blond hair. Even from this distance he could see the similarities in their features as well. He made a grumbling noise in the back of his throat. *Could Miles and Saskia be related?*

As if he'd read his mind, Dirk said for his benefit, "They're brother and sister. Miles is younger than Saskia by four years. Miles couldn't stand the fact Saskia had been chosen by their grandmother to be our leader over him. He's resented her since that day. It hurt Saskia far more than the rest of us when he turned on us and walked away."

Walking as a group, they headed closer to Saskia until they stood at her back. Miles's gaze skimmed over Eli in his wolf form before he focused on the other men.

"I see your faithful lapdogs have arrived, sister. I'm not surprised."

Eli growled and pulled back his upper lip when he saw the werewolf who had attacked him stood on Miles's left. He and the werewolf locked gazes. Eli would have launched himself at him if Roan hadn't reached back and taken hold of him by the scruff of his neck.

Miles chuckled. "I see you've added a new member to your group. Is he shy or do you like him to stay in wolf form so he can be your mascot?"

"Shut up, Miles," Saskia said with a snarl. "This is your final warning. You'll stay the hell away from the foretold one. We won't let you anywhere near her."

"We shall see. This conversation is starting to bore me."

"I'm not done saying what I came here to say."

"Ah, let me guess. It has to do with your dead mate? Was he still alive when you found him?" Miles pointed to the werewolf who stood on his left side. "My friend here said he bled like a stuck pig."

Saskia struck the werewolf responsible. With a swing of her sword, his head went one way as his body collapsed onto the ground. She pointed the bloodstained sword at Miles.

He shook his finger as he backed away. "Now that wasn't very nice." He reached inside his jacket pocket and pulled out a small device that resembled a garage door opener. "As I said before, I've grown bored with this conversation. I hate to run, but time is of the essence." With a smile, he pushed the single button on the device he held. "Things are going to get pretty hot around here in about sixty seconds."

Miles and his man turned and went wolf as they took off at a run. Saskia and her brothers did the same as Eli ran at Saskia's side, his black wolf to her white. They just managed to clear the abandon factory's property when an explosion went off inside. The building instantly became engulfed in flames.

Once they reached the SUV, they all shifted to their human

forms. Saskia quickly cut off her brothers before any of them could speak. "Go back to our place. Eli and I will be there shortly."

Saskia grabbed his hand, then led him down another side street to where her motorcycle sat parked. Eli pulled her into his arms and hungrily kissed her. The need to be inside her right that instant just about took him over. If she hadn't pulled away when she had, he would have pushed her to the ground and taken her right there.

Saskia held her palm to his cheek. "Hold on. I need you too."

"I don't think I can make it back to your place. Let's go to my apartment."

Saskia nodded. "It should be safe now. Miles thinks you're dead."

Eli urged Saskia to get onto the bike as he climbed on behind her. "Right now, Miles is the furthest thing from my mind."

Saskia revved the motorcycle's engine, and Eli wrapped his arms around her waist. Holding her tight, he shifted so her backside nestled against the hard bulge in his jeans. He barely paid attention to where they went as she put the motorcycle into gear and then pulled away from the curb. He had to concentrate on not coming as her bottom pressed harder against him with each bump the bike hit. By the time they reached the underground parking garage at his apartment, his cock threatened to burst the zipper of his jeans.

Once he had Saskia safely inside his apartment, Eli kicked the door shut behind them before he locked the door. His lips came down on hers and he pulled her against him. He backed her toward the living room as he tore at her clothes until he had her completely naked. She moaned against his lips and sucked his tongue into her mouth. She undid his jeans before she wrapped her hand around his erect cock. He let her go only long enough to shuck his pants. When he couldn't take any more, he pulled her hand off his shaft and then yanked his shirt over his head. He would have taken her on the floor on her back, but Saskia turned and rubbed her bottom against him.

"I want the wolf to take me, Eli," she said as she leaned her head against his shoulder.

A growl slipped past his lips as he skimmed his hand along her breasts to her waist. Holding her to him, he sank to his knees onto the floor. He trailed his hand lower until he reached her pussy. He moaned at how wet and ready she was for him. Eli positioned Saskia on her hands and knees before him, then went to kneel between her spread thighs. With a firm grip on her hips, he sheathed himself with one stroke.

Unable to take things slow, Eli reared back and plunged into her. He rode her fast and hard. Saskia's moans of pleasure made his cock harden even more as her strong inner walls squeezed down around it. He couldn't hold back his release as he pumped in and out of her. With a howl, he came deep inside her.

Even though he'd climaxed, Eli found he hadn't lost his erection. He pulled out of Saskia, then urged her onto her back as he came over her. She smiled up at him as she took hold of his still-hard cock and led it back to the opening of her body.

"I guess the spell has given you all the attributes a male werewolf has."

Eli sank into her and hooked one of Saskia's legs over his arm. "It would seem. Now let's see how many times I can make you come."

Pistoning his hips, Eli rocked into her. He didn't stop until he pushed them over the edge. The sounds of their groans as they climaxed filled the apartment. He propped himself up on his elbows as he brushed Saskia's lips with his.

Their bodies still joined, he said, "I love you."

She reached up and pushed his hair off his sweat-dampened forehead. "I love you too."

"I guess we're stuck with each other now."

Saskia smiled. "I guess so, but I wouldn't want to be stuck with anyone else."

"Good, because it could be for a very, very long time."

Eli pulled out of her and then scooped her into his arms. He headed for the bedroom. He intended to show his mate just how much of a male werewolf he'd become.

The End

ABOUT THE AUTHOR

Marisa Chenery was always a lover of books, but after reading her first historical romance novel she found herself hooked. Having inherited a love for the written word, she soon started writing her own novels.

She now writes young adult books and erotic romances.

Marisa lives in Ontario, Canada, with her boyfriend, Steve, four children, four grandchildren (she's a young grandma in her fifties) and rabbit and dog.

www.marisachenery.com

www.ingramcontent.com/pod-product-compliance
Lightning Source LLC
Chambersburg PA
CBHW030742030726
47497CB00001B/89